Needing Moore

The Complete Series

Julie A. Richman

A Julie A. Richman Book / published by arrangement with the author.

Needing Moore: The Complete Series

Front Cover Photo: Lawrence Spark

Cover Model: Jason Caselton

Back Cover Photo: Cleida Roy/Sally A. Bowditch

Designed by: Jena Brignola of Bibliophile Productions

Proofing by: Elena Pizzarello

Table of Contents

Searching For Moore ---------------------------- 1

Moore To Lose ---------------------------------- 277

Moore Than Forever ----------------------------- 519

Sneak Peek at Moore Than a Feeling -------------- 743

For Max …
Everything I am in 1000 pages.
But most of all, I was blessed with you.

Searching For Moore

Julie A. Richman

Table of Contents

Part One Schooner 5
Chapter One 7
Chapter Two 11
Chapter Three 13
Chapter Four 16
Chapter Five 18
Chapter Six 22
Chapter Seven 24
Chapter Eight 27
Chapter Nine 31
Chapter Ten 35
Chapter Eleven 37
Chapter Twelve 40
Chapter Thirteen 43
Chapter Fourteen 45
Chapter Fifteen 49
Chapter Sixteen 52
Chapter Seventeen 53
Chapter Eighteen 57
Chapter Nineteen 60
Chapter Twenty 63
Chapter Twenty-One 66
Chapter Twenty-Two 70
Chapter Twenty-Three 74
Chapter Twenty-Four 76
Chapter Twenty-Five 78
Chapter Twenty-Six 83
Chapter Twenty-Seven 88
Chapter Twenty-Eight 93
Chapter Twenty-Nine 96
Chapter Thirty 98
Chapter Thirty-One 103
Chapter Thirty-Two 105
Chapter Thirty-Three 108
Chapter Thirty-Four 113
Chapter Thirty-Five 116
Chapter Thirty-Six 117

Part Two Mia 121
Chapter One 123
Chapter Two 126
Chapter Three 131
Chapter Four 135
Chapter Five 136
Chapter Six 142
Chapter Seven 145
Chapter Eight 148
Chapter Nine 152
Chapter Ten 157
Chapter Eleven 161
Chapter Twelve 163
Chapter Thirteen 165
Chapter Fourteen 170
Chapter Fifteen 174
Chapter Sixteen 178
Chapter Seventeen 187
Chapter Eighteen 193
Chapter Nineteen 197
Chapter Twenty 201
Chapter Twenty-One 203
Chapter Twenty-Two 206
Chapter Twenty-Three 209
Chapter Twenty-Four 212
Chapter Twenty-Five 216
Chapter Twenty-Six 219
Chapter Twenty-Seven 225
Chapter Twenty-Eight 229
Chapter Twenty-Nine 232
Chapter Thirty 241
Chapter Thirty-One 246
Chapter Thirty-Two 249
Chapter Thirty-Three 254
Chapter Thirty-Four 257
Chapter Thirty-Five 260
Chapter Thirty-Six 263
Chapter Thirty-Seven 269
Bonus Chapter 272

Part One
Schooner

Chapter One

Now...

Schooner Moore did not like turning forty-three—not at all. It didn't sound as old as say fifty, but it wasn't as cool and sexy sounding as thirty-five or even thirty-seven had been. *Forty-three—was that even still hot*, he wondered. If he judged by the way women continued to come on to him, clamored to get his attention, overtly tried to pick him up—then yes, it was still hot. It just sounded so damn old and that was what was really pissing him off.

Leaning over the railing of a surprisingly empty deck at Newport Beach hot spot, *The Dock*, Schooner stood alone breathing in the humid sea air, listening to the boats clanking in the marina. Behind him, echoes of laughter pealed from inside the packed restaurant—a restaurant that his wife, CJ, had rented out in its entirety on a Saturday night for this little birthday soirée. He shuddered to think of what this had just cost him.

CJ meant well, but Schooner knew this shindig really had very little to do with him and everything to do with her coveted social standing aspirations. And a party for turning forty-three? Seriously, who does that? Forty, he could understand. Forty-five, he could understand. But forty-three? This party wasn't about him. And he knew it.

He heard the creaking of worn planks rather than footsteps and felt the familiar slap on his shoulder.

"Hiding, eh?" Beau Gordon leaned on the railing beside him. Beau was a dead ringer for Pee Wee Herman, and with a few drinks in him and the right audience, was significantly funnier.

Schooner laughed, "I can't get far enough away."

"Ahhh, it's not that bad." Beau breathed the dank harbor air in deeply.

"No, I guess it isn't," Schooner acquiesced, with an All-American boy smile, a smile that even at forty-three could stop women—from ages eight to eighty—dead in their tracks.

"There are some really hot babes in there."

Schooner let out a wry chuckle, "Watch out or you'll be picking up an extra mortgage by morning. Don't let those sweet, Botoxed looks fool you. That is a shark tank in there, my man, and you are shark chum!" he ended, dramatically.

Beau leaned back on the railing and surveyed the crowd on the other side of the glass wall. "Yeah, I had a few store-bought racks' of the soon-to-be-divorced, rubbed on me tonight. Not that I'm complaining, but those women were definitely not happy about having to be changing zip codes."

"Still have your wallet?" Schooner chided.

Beau patted his pockets, pulling something out. He sauntered over into the shadows, as Schooner squinted into the darkened corner of the deck to see where his old college roommate was going. Schooner smelled it before even hearing Beau's first loud exhale.

"You did *not* just light up a dube, Bro!" Schooner quickly scanned the deck, after a paranoid jolt to both his stomach and sphincter.

Beau sat down on a chair and put his feet up on the railing. He slowly inhaled a long drag of the joint, held it and let out a thin stream of white smoke that curled into the night air in paisley patterns. Taking the seat next to Beau, Schooner lifted his boat-shoe clad feet to the rail, stretching his long, athletic legs. Beau silently handed his buddy the joint, and Schooner took it from him in a ritual that seemed nearly as old as they were. Gingerly dragging on the glowing joint, Schooner tried to remember the last time he had gotten high. A decade before, maybe—but he really wasn't sure.

Almost immediately, Schooner felt the relaxation spread through his body, feeling the tension roll away from his too tight neck and shoulders. *And there it goes. It's moving out with the tide*, he silently thought.

"Man, I need to hang out with you more often." Schooner coughed slightly.

Beau just smiled. They were in different worlds. Beau had never married, traveled extensively for work, and spent most of his free time vetting the world's great scuba spots, while unsuccessfully trying to pick up women. Schooner, on the other hand, had married CJ almost immediately upon graduation, after dating her for almost all four years of college. His photogenic, California-boy good looks, as well as his sharp business acumen, entrepreneurial spirit, and a hefty bankroll from a childhood modeling career had made Schooner a very rich man by the time he was twenty-eight. Everyone who was anyone, from Malibu to the OC, worked out in one of Schooner's clubs. State-of-the-art equipment, coupled with a concierge based staff and entertainment amenities, catered to the elite under one roof.

Schooner and CJ. Like Ken and Barbie come to life. They were the epitome of every out-of-stater's fantasy of what the quintessential California boy and California girl looked like. Schooner and CJ. They were beautiful and they looked like they belonged together. Everyone said so, and they knew it the first time they had laid eyes on one another. They were like two sides of the same golden coin.

Handing Schooner back the joint, Beau let out a stream of smoke before asking, "Do you remember the first time we got high together?"

Schooner thought for a second and a slow smile spread across his handsome face, his clear sky-blue eyes crinkling at the corners. With a warm glow spreading throughout his chest, Schooner also oddly felt the sting of tears behind his eyes. "Yeah, it was at that freshman retreat in the mountains."

"What was that chick's name, that friend of yours that we got high with?" Beau turned to Schooner, a questioning look on his face, trying hard to grab hold of a memory just out of his reach.

"Mia Silver." Her name tumbled out like a waterfall. Just verbalizing it, after all this time, put a smile in Schooner's heart.

"That was Mia Silver?" Beau broke Schooner's pleasant moment.

"Yeah, why?"

"The chick with the glasses? Seriously, dude? That was Mia Silver?"

"Yeah, that was Mia." Schooner sat up straight in his chair, wondering what his buddy was about to tell him.

"I'll be damned." Beau shook his head. "I just got into one hell of a fight with her on Scott Morgan's Facebook page. She always was a freaking liberal bitch." He shook his head again, "She grew up nice though. She is smokin' hot now. I would not have recognized her, not in a million years."

I would have, something deep inside of Schooner screamed, feeling like his heart was being mashed up in someone's hands, as if dough were being kneaded roughly without regard to being torn.

The humid air was no longer making its way deep into his lungs. *WTF?* He shook his head. Not after all these years, to have such a visceral reaction. Must be the effects of getting stoned or maybe this turning forty-three bullshit.

Even after a few deep breaths, he was trying to process what Beau had said… He'd had contact with Mia. *He'd had contact with Mia. Holy shit.*

Suddenly feeling like he was ready to jump out of his own skin, Schooner wanted to be anywhere but there. He wanted to be away from Beau. Away from the party. Away from all their supposed friends—a room filled with *The Real Housewives of Orange County* clones. He knew he needed to take another deep breath and calm himself, because he wasn't going to be going anywhere anytime soon.

Chef Jonathan walked out onto the deck where Schooner and Beau sat. Beau silently went to hand him the joint, but Jonathan waved him off.

Looking out over the night harbor, he announced "Hey, it's cake time. You'd better go back in there, Birthday Boy".

"Lucky me," Schooner muttered.

Taking his last deep breath of harbor air, he silently said to himself, "Showtime," and bravely headed into the packed restaurant to face the gaggle of his wife's friends, acquaintances and other assorted hangers on.

Chapter Two

Schooner politely made small talk, a plate of expensive, fondant-wrapped cake in hand. He could not remember if the woman he was talking to was on *The Real Housewives of Orange County* or wanted to be on it, or if she was from Beverly Hills. Maybe she was one of those Housewives. He couldn't remember her story and didn't care enough to ask. They all seemed to run together.

As he surveyed the crowd, he made an observation. All these women wanted to look exactly like CJ and had spent a lot of money to try and achieve her look. He wondered why they didn't realize that what their doctors were doing to them stopped way short of the natural beauty his wife possessed. What was being done to them didn't look natural. Not the long blonde hair, not the full lips, nor the perfect profiles. They all wanted to look like CJ, but they didn't. No one wanted to look different. No one wanted to be different. *Typical Orange County*, he thought.

The Real Housewife was touching him. Gently stroking his arm and standing too close as she spoke. Someone tried to push past in the crowd behind her and she had to step closer to Schooner. Dropping her hand, she let her fingers graze his crotch, her long manicured nails searching out his cock, which thankfully was uncharacteristically non-responsive. Schooner choked on the piece of cake he had just put in his mouth and politely excused himself, in search of a much-needed single malt scotch. *If I'm paying for it*, he mused, *I might as well drink what I like.* And he needed a drink. Badly.

As he approached the bar, he spied Holly standing alone, surveying the crowd as if they were one big sociology experiment. Coming up behind her, he casually, and gently, slung an arm over his daughter's shoulder and kissed her temple as he pulled her close. Having her home from school for this abbreviated trip made enduring being the guest of honor slightly more palatable.

"How's my gorgeous girl?" Schooner asked his flaxen-haired beauty.

"Better now that I've got the most handsome man in the room all to myself."

He smiled at their banter. "Can we leave now?"

She laughed, "And endure the wrath of Mom? I think not."

Holly was so unlike her mother. She had CJ's cheerleader good looks, but they sat differently on Holly. A sophomore at Brown University in Providence, Rhode Island, Holly was not going to be a trophy, she was going to collect them. He missed her terribly and wished she'd stayed closer to home, wished she'd chosen a school in Southern California. But Holly wanted to go east and she wanted to go Ivy. A Biological Sciences major, his daughter was the antithesis of Orange County and he was secretly thrilled that she'd escaped. He was also thrilled that she had flown in for the weekend for his party. Schooner missed his son Zac too, but Zac's prep school semester abroad landed him in Zaragoza, Spain—too far to journey home for a *forty-third* birthday party.

Holly's phone buzzed and she looked at the screen, laughed and started typing rapidly with both thumbs.

Schooner looked at her quizzically and she shrugged and offered "Facebook," as her explanation.

As if that explains it, he thought and tried to look over her shoulder at what she was typing.

"Dad!"

"Okay, okay." Schooner held up his hands in surrender, smiled and continued on his journey for that single malt scotch.

Leaning up against the bar, he let the burn slide down his throat. *Damn, that's better than sex*, he thought.

As he let the amber liquid warm his insides and calm his rapidly fraying nerves, Schooner thought to himself, *I really need to join Facebook.*

Chapter Three

Then...

Walking along The Quad, map in hand, Schooner tried to find Brewster Hall. The next part of orientation had the freshmen reuniting with their parents and he knew that is where his would be waiting for him.

The tree-lined Quad sat like a large rectangular park at the center of campus. Lined along its length were old Spanish Mission style buildings that were built in the early 1920's and capped with red barrel tile roofs. At the far end, like a patriarch at the head of the table, was the University Chapel, with its bell tower standing out in relief against a mountain range partially obscured by Inland Empire smog.

She was standing on the sidewalk talking to her parents, white linen dress gently billowing in the breeze. He had noticed her in the last session. How could he not? She looked like an angel—long silky blonde hair flowing down her back, wide cornflower blue eyes and a pouty pink glossed mouth. Tall, slim, and athletic, Schooner was betting she had been the prom queen at her high school. She was perfect. *We look like we belong together,* Schooner thought. She was the female version of him.

As he walked by, she stole a glance and smiled.

Oh yeah, she had noticed him and from the look in her eyes, she liked what she saw. Schooner flashed his All-American boy smile, a smile that began gracing catalogue covers when he was only four years old. Watching her eyes widen, he knew she'd be finding a way to sit near him in the rest of the orientation sessions. He smiled to himself... *oh yeah, college was going to be great.*

As he approached, his parents were talking with another couple outside a door to what he assumed was Brewster Hall. Immediately catching his eye, his mom waved him over. "Schooner. Over here."

Schooner Moore had inherited the best from both of his parents. Had they had a checklist of physical attributes, he was the embodiment of all the checks in all the right places. From his mother, her fine bone structure and square jaw, high cheekbones, straight nose and full lips. From his dad, clear blue eyes and thick, fair hair with just a slight wave, making the ends flip out. Both parents were tall, and he was blessed with his mother's easy grace and his dad's wide shoulders and narrow hips.

As he approached his parents and the other couple, his dad took over the introductions, "Schooner, meet Mr. and Mrs. Silver. Their daughter Mia is also a freshman."

Schooner shook Mr. Silver's hand, noting the man had that east coast intellectual look about him, with slightly long wavy gray hair and gray-blue eyes. Turning to Mrs. Silver, he politely offered his hand. Her forthright manner was immediately evident, as her warm brown eyes instantly captured him. She sized him up. He could feel it and couldn't control his smile, a real smile.

"You are adorable," she said, treating him to her strong New York accent.

Used to women—of all ages—fawning over him, Schooner never blushed, yet now, he could feel the heat in his cheeks. There was something in Mrs. Silver's gaze that cut through all that external California bullshit, and he could feel that she was really seeing him, and she still thought he was adorable.

In that moment, Schooner felt more special than he'd ever felt. Inexplicably, he wanted her approval and was so happy to have it.

"There's Mia," Mr. Silver's voice cut into Schooner's thoughts, jolting him, and he dropped Mrs. Silver's hand.

Schooner turned. Coming down the path to Brewster Hall was Mia Silver. Cocking his head to the side, trying to take her all in, he could feel the small smile on his face. Mia didn't look like any of the girls he knew.

Bounding up the walk, quirky lopsided smile taking over her cute face, Mia had a mane of long dark curls bouncing behind her. She was wearing funky Lisa Loeb glasses, and as she got closer, he could see that the irises of her big eyes were an ombre green that grew lighter as they moved in toward her pupil. The pupil itself was surrounded by rich caramel colored flames. Not only was there sharp intelligence in her beautiful eyes, but Schooner thought they looked like a devilish invitation, like they were beckoning to him, "Let's be bad together. Let's have some fun."

Schooner felt his chest tighten.

Not more than 5'2", clad in faded Levi's, a tee-shirt and clogs, he wondered if she realized that she was probably the only girl in the entire freshman class not wearing a dress. And he surmised, she probably wouldn't even care. *What was she doing on this campus?* he wondered. She did not fit in.

"Hey." She smiled at him, confidently, her freckled nose scrunching up.

"Hey," he returned, captured by her energy. At barely five feet nothing, he was sure she made an entrance everywhere she went. This girl had presence. And she was different. She was clearly not a California girl. He wasn't quite sure what to make of her.

"Honey, meet Mr. and Mrs. Moore and Schooner," Mrs. Silver offered.

Mia beamed at the Moores, offering a firm handshake and immediately engaging Mr. and Mrs. Moore in conversation, while Schooner became acquainted with the Silvers.

As they entered Brewster Hall, he could see Mrs. Silver giving Mia a little nudge and instinctively he knew it was about him. Mothers loved him. Mia rolled her eyes at her mom. He loved that.

Over the next two days, the Moores and the Silvers spent the majority of their time together, while Schooner and Mia attended the different freshman sessions. As expected, the prom queen found a way to be seated near Schooner, separated by one of her friends who struck up a conversation with him, then quickly included the prom queen.

While Schooner started gravitating toward the prom queen, her equally pageant-girl-like friends and other jock guys from his dorm, Mia's growing entourage seemed to be a group from her dorm of Out-of-Staters, über-intellectual potheads and a few gays and lesbians. They were clearly migrating toward their comfort zones, which were as far apart as opposing football teams' goal lines.

On the last night of orientation, the Moores and the Silvers dined together off-campus. When they parted at the end of the evening, Mr. Moore pulled Schooner aside to where he and Mr. Silver were standing. "Keep an eye out for her, son," motioning toward Mia. "She's only sixteen. Make sure you're there for her."

Only sixteen? This little ball of fire who clearly already had her own following on campus was only sixteen. *Wow—she has the confidence of a twenty-five-year old*, he thought. *Only sixteen?*

"I will, sir," promised Schooner, trying not to act stunned at the revelation.

He'd be turning nineteen in just a few months and little Mia was, well, in fact, little Mia. She certainly didn't seem to need any looking after. In fact, he felt pretty certain Mia Silver could take very good care of herself.

Chapter Four

Getting settled in the first few weeks of college turned out to be more of a juggling act than Schooner had anticipated. Classes. Studying. Tennis practice (he was determined to make first string his freshman year). Learning to live with a roommate (Beau Gordon was a trip, he could not sleep without the radio on all night and hated the way headphones felt). And CJ. Schooner had already started dating the prom queen, who had been, yes, in fact, the prom queen at her high school.

CJ MacAllister was well-schooled in getting precisely what she wanted, and from that very first day of freshman orientation, Schooner Moore was everything she wanted. Incredibly handsome, smart, athletic, from a well-to-do California family. Schooner Moore was the bomb. And she was going to get him. And never let go. Their children would be magnificent. And CJ MacAllister was going to be the mother of Schooner Moore's children.

CJ started to show up at the tennis courts to watch Schooner practice. She always brought a friend or two (*Bitches*, Schooner thought, laughing to himself, *travel in packs*.). He wasn't past putting on a show for the girls, taking his shirt off at the end of practice and letting them watch the sweat run down his impressive golden pecs toward his six-pack abs. Her friends would suddenly disappear when it was time for Schooner to get off the courts, leaving CJ waiting alone for him.

After a few days of walking CJ back to her dorm, she invited Schooner up to her room. Acting coy and coquettish (acting, being the operative word… and he was aware of that, but let her act), they had a hot make out session.

Schooner backed CJ up to her bed with its Victorian Rose pattern spread and gently pushed her down onto it. Propped up on her elbows, looking up at him innocently through long lashes, Schooner quickly recognized that CJ knew just how to get to him. This was clearly not her first rodeo, although she wanted him to believe that it was. He also knew, two could play this game and it would be so much fun to make sure he controlled it. Controlled a girl who always got what she wanted—*no problem*, he thought. Schooner was the master.

Sliding on top of her, he kissed her deeply, her tongue meeting his perfectly in its dance. As his hands slid up the back of her thighs, he pressed in gently until she wrapped her long legs around his waist. The bulge in his tennis shorts was straining against his zipper and all he wanted to do was take it out and give it to her, hard. Cupping his hands on her perfectly rounded ass, he pressed his hard package against her moist underwear and she moaned.

"Feels good?" he asked.

"Mmm-hmm," was all she could muster, as he relentlessly ground himself and rammed against her underwear.

Locking eyes, he ran his thumb and forefinger over the front of her pink cotton blouse until he could feel her nipple harden to his touch, never letting up on the intensity and the motion until her nipple felt like a stone. It was only then that his thumb relented, as he dipped his head and sucked it through her shirt, biting it and pulling it with his front teeth.

Her sounds were telling him that she was coming undone fast.

Grabbing her ass again, he pulled her into him, pressing the bulge in his tennis shorts tighter against her.

CJ strained against him, desperately trying to rub herself against his hardness and get herself off on the friction.

And without removing a single piece of her clothes or his, Schooner Moore gave CJ MacAllister one mind blowing orgasm.

He dropped her back on the bed, looking dazed and still quaking, as he adjusted the raging hard on in his now too tight, uncomfortable shorts.

"Thanks for coming to see me practice today." Leaning forward, he gave her a rough kiss on her already bruised lips, grabbed his tennis racquets and turned to leave CJ's dorm room. Stopping at the door long enough to turn to her, he graced her with a full-blown killer smile and reveled in how utterly stupefied she looked.

Carrying his racquets in front of him, to hide the sizable erection he was sporting, Schooner left the all-girls dorm with a smug smile on his face. Tables turned, Prom Queen! She'd be giving it all to him in no time flat, without having to wait for her to play the virgin game, deciding if she should "let him be the one." He'd met enough cock-teasing prom queens in his life. This was college now, and if CJ MacAllister wanted him, then she was going to play by his rules.

Four days later they became lovers.

Chapter Five

The following Saturday morning, The Quad was lined with buses for the entire freshman class to take them up into the mountains for Freshman Retreat.

Freshman Retreat was mandatory. Schooner, Beau and assorted tennis, basketball and football players from their dorm headed to the buses together. He knew CJ would be looking for him and secretly hoped that she wouldn't find him (6'2" blonde god was hard to miss). Today he wanted to establish relationships with the other guys in his dorm, without being part of a couple and without the ribbing—which was already beginning.

The ride up to the retreat center in the San Bernardino National Forest seemed to take forever as the convoy of buses slowly meandered up the highway's steep incline and hairpin turns. One of the dorm RA's announced on the bus loudspeaker that a BBQ lunch was being served in the main lodge, class elections would take place immediately following lunch and the rest of the afternoon was free for hiking, swimming or the leisure activity of their choice.

Beau grabbed Schooner's arm as they got off the bus and motioned to a trailhead. "I brought a dube," he whispered.

"You are the man!" Schooner acknowledged, heading down the trail.

About a quarter of a mile down the path, away from anyone with curious eyes, they looked for some boulders to park their butts on when Schooner saw Mia's telltale long dark curls in front of them. Without even thinking, he called out to her and she turned, meeting him with a big grin.

As she walked up to the guys, Schooner realized his smile matched hers. "How have you been doing?"

She just shrugged her shoulders, "I am so not into the group thing. I hate all this kumbayah shit."

Schooner laughed out loud, "You into smoking some shit?"

Mia's eyes lit up and that little devil, partner-in-crime look he had seen on the day they first met, reemerged.

The three found a path off the main trail and hiked to an area where they wouldn't easily be found. It was hard for Mia to keep up with the two long-legged tennis players. Lounging on some large rocks, Beau reached into the pocket of his shorts, pulled out a joint and lit it up. Schooner could tell that Beau was not comfortable with Mia. He doubted that he'd ever met anyone quite like her and didn't know how to take her.

Schooner, on the other hand, thought she was a blast. He'd never had many girls who were just friends, not flirting their asses off to try and get his attention, and Mia was so comfortable to just hang out with—kind of like hanging out with the boys, but there was something so cute about her and damn, she had great tits. He had to remind himself that she was only sixteen.

Beau held up the joint to her, "I hope you're not a virgin."

Schooner saw the blush flare in her face and knew that while his little sixteen-year old friend might not be a virgin to getting high, sexually she was really innocent. Her urbane New York exterior masked just how innocent she really was and Schooner felt this strong need bursting to protect her. Protect her like a little sister, he told himself.

They smoked the rest of the joint while Beau pointedly ignored Mia, just talking directly to Schooner, as if she were not even present. It was uncomfortable and Schooner wondered what the hell was Beau's problem. He thought maybe Beau was just used to pining over the California Barbies who shot him down, but whatever it was, Mia took off immediately upon finishing the joint.

"See you guys up at the lodge. Thanks for the smoke." And she quickly retreated up the trail.

Schooner wondered where her entourage was and why she seemed to be in loner mode today. But being stoned, that thought quickly evaporated and was replaced by something else, as was the fleeting thought that maybe he should not let her be wandering in the woods alone.

By the time Schooner and Beau made it up to the lodge, freshman class elections were well underway. They leaned against the wall near the door and Schooner surveyed the crowd. In the second row, paying rapt attention, were CJ and her soon-to-be group of sorority sisters. Continuing to scan the room, he finally saw Mia sitting on a chair in the back.

The look on her face was one of pure fright. Crouched down and clutching the back of her chair was Tim Vandergrift, freshman class President-elect and the class equivalent of douche bag Greg Marmalard from the movie *Animal House* (he looked like him, too!). From his bent over position, he appeared to be sniffing Mia.

Schooner and Mia made eye contact and he could see she was paranoid as all hell that Mr. Brownie Points was going to turn her in to some school authority for reeking of pot, and that she was going to get sent home for getting high at the Freshman Retreat (which, of course, was held at a Christian retreat center).

Schooner could see Mia's eyes pleading with him for help as she mouthed the word, "Fuck!"

The noise of the room seemed to evaporate and all Schooner could hear were his father's words, telling him to look out for Mia.

From her omniscient perch in row two, CJ noticed Schooner leaning against the wall and followed his line of sight back to Mia. It was evident that Mia's gaze was locked in on her boyfriend.

The loud crash, as a pitcher of ice water smashed onto the Mexican tile floor, turned all heads to see the source of the crash.

Schooner had *inadvertently* knocked a pitcher off the table. The crash had brought Tim out of his crouched position to his full standing height of 6'4" and his attention to the left wall of the room. Using the diversion as an escape mechanism, Mia popped out of her chair, quickly heading out of the lodge's main room through a door on the right.

Watching her seize the moment, Schooner silently gave himself a pat on the back.

Mia was standing out at the driveway in front of the lodge waiting for one of the earlier buses back to campus, when CJ noticed her there. CJ had been in search of Schooner, but quickly changed her mind, deciding, *let him have his boys' time. I've got something more important to take care of.* Grabbing her roommate and some girls from her dorm, she convinced them it was time to leave.

Positioned directly behind Mia on the bus, CJ became very animated as she reveled her followers with tales of her prom court and of what a wonderful kisser her new boyfriend, Schooner, was (still playing the virgin act, she was not going to let any of her virginal friends/soon-to-be sorority sisters know that Schooner liked to pull her hair when she blew him or that he liked it rough… and that she was learning to like it that way, too). She even went so far as to make the prediction that he was *the one*. Her followers giggled with delight.

Mia sunk deeper into the green faux-leather seat, wishing she'd had her Walkman and some headphones with her, so she didn't have to listen to a show she somehow instinctively knew was being put on for her benefit. She couldn't understand why though. CJ was gorgeous and had clearly already captured Schooner's attention, and from the sounds of it, his heart. So why the big show? Why did she have to make sure Mia knew he was hers?

Discreetly, Mia wiped a tear that began to roll down her right cheek and buried her face against the cold metal inside of the bus so that no one could see the wet trail that had begun to stream down her face.

She couldn't help but think of the lyrics of one of her favorite *Blondie* songs, where the singer is warned to stay away from a certain guy by his girlfriend. Today's warning had been loud and clear.

Mia Silver had never felt so alone or so very far away from home.

Chapter Six

He had been sitting with his mother in a coffee shop, eating a grilled cheese sandwich, when the man approached their booth.

Four-year old Schooner was not very interested in what they were talking about, because the grilled cheese had bacon that tasted really good and the French fries had bumps (his mother had called them crinkle fries). She was also letting him drink Coke that day instead of milk with his lunch, which never happened at home. So, everything on his plate, and in his glass, were much more interesting than anything this man had to say.

But Schooner knew they were talking about him.

"Photographs so well…All-American Boy…Pay for his education…"

The man handed Mrs. Moore his card and two weeks later, Schooner was in a photographer's studio having his headshots and portfolio done. First, the photographer dressed him in a baseball uniform and posed him with a bat. Then, a bathing suit and they had him stand next to a giant flowered surfboard, in front of a large mural of the beach. The stylist finished up with school clothes and oversized glasses, with Schooner pretending to read a book.

"A natural…The camera loves him…Big career in front of him…"

Schooner learned early the importance of his good looks and what those looks could do for him. From the age of four until fourteen, his photo graced the covers and pages of every major catalogue in the US (and internationally, too). All the while, a trust account in his name became sizable (a trust account that would one day help him to become a very successful businessman, at a very young age).

Hitting adolescence, Schooner worried when he peered in the mirror and noted that his face had started changing. With skin prone to breakouts, he stressed out that he wasn't perfect anymore and that would mean letting people down—especially his mother, who managed his career very tightly and whom he wanted to please more than anyone.

Sometimes during those extended sessions of studying his face in the mirror, Schooner would think about "the mask" he was looking at. The mask that had perfected the heart-stopping smile. And he would wonder, *what does my real smile look like?* and *who am I really beneath the mask?* And it frustrated him that he did not know the answers to those questions.

And so, Schooner truly became the ultimate actor—acting out the role he thought would make his parents happy. He was the All-American Boy. Handsome, polite, top student, great athlete, buddy, boyfriend, son, soon-to-be frat brother. He kept everyone happy.

Schooner Moore had no fucking idea who he really was.

Chapter Seven

CJ and Schooner sat on the big stone steps outside her dorm studying for a Biology exam. It was a perfect fall day to be outdoors, the air was clear, free of smog, puffy white cumulus clouds with towering tops floated by on the breeze, and the mountains appeared as if they were the campus' hand painted backdrop.

"But I'm still confused," CJ's pretty brows were knit together, "which one is oxidation and which one is reduction?"

"Oxidation is the loss of electrons or increase in oxidation state, while reduction is the gain of electrons or a decrease in oxidation state," Schooner explained, again.

"But if it's a reduction, how is it gaining?" CJ was getting frustrated trying to grasp the concept.

"Okay, just remember OIL RIG for the test. Oil is the acronym for oxidation is loss and Rig is for reduction is gain. Write down Oil Rig when you sit down to take the test."

She sighed.

"The best thing you can do is to keep drawing the Citric Acid Cycle and the Electron Transport Chain over and over until you memorize it," he offered and pulled out a piece of paper from his notebook and handed it to her.

Sticking her tongue out at Schooner, CJ snatched the paper from his hand and dug into her backpack for colored pencils to start her drawing.

Schooner lounged back on the steps, enjoying the warm sun and the breeze on his face. He squinted in the bright sunlight under the visor of his tennis team cap and started checking out the people hanging out on The Quad. Frisbee players, people studying on blankets, a few footballs being tossed and a group of about six kids in a circle doing something weird.

He started watching the circle people and tried to figure out what they were doing. At first it looked as if they were doing the wave, but then one popped up and jumped in place, spinning around. And they each followed.

"Does this look right?" CJ asked, startling him.

Taking the paper, he looked at her diagram. "Don't forget to show the loss of CO2 and the NADH+H2 reactions."

As soon as she went back to her drawing, he started to watch the circle people again. They were all facing outward now, holding hands and doing an odd kick dance. He could tell they were laughing and having fun. They began a new formation of a line snaking around the trees on The Quad, and that is when he noticed who was leading the pack. Mia Silver.

Dressed in a white flouncy gáuze peasant shirt and jeans, Mia's hair was flying wildly with each of the group's movements. He didn't even realize he was smiling watching her and her friends until CJ asked him what was so amusing.

"I'm just watching that group, I have no idea what it is they're doing, but whatever it is, they're having a blast. It looks like some kind of improv thing."

Mia now had the group in a kick line and after a few attempted high kicks, they were soon all bent over in fits of laughter.

Schooner was laughing just watching them. Coordination was clearly not their strong suit.

"Ick, aren't they all from that stoner dorm?" CJ's lip was up in a sneer, "That place is like the 'Island of Misfit Toys'."

Schooner laughed, "Yeah, it really is an odd assortment of people there, isn't it?" He handed CJ another piece of paper. "Okay, give me the one you just drew, close your book and now draw it from memory."

Her eyes widened with panic.

"C'mon CJ, this is the one thing we know will be on the test for sure and it's the only way you're going to learn it. You have to know cellular respiration or the rest of the semester is just not going to make sense."

Grabbing the paper from him, she gave him a dirty look.

"You are a brat!" he laughed.

As CJ attempted the diagram from memory, Schooner continued to watch Mia and her friends. They were now lying on their backs and pointing up at the clouds. They must be finding shapes in the clouds, he thought. He hadn't done that since he was a little boy. The memory of lying on his front lawn with the kids from his neighborhood made him smile.

He felt CJ's eyes on him. "You finished it?" he asked.

"Let's finish this upstairs." She stood and put out her hand to him.

Taking it, he followed her into her dorm.

"I'm going to give you a biology lesson now." She undid the button and zipper on his tennis shorts. "And I don't need a diagram for this."

She sunk to her knees and took him deep in her mouth.

"Oh yeah," was all he could say as he held her head in place and drove deep into her mouth. It felt so damn good. He was lost in his rhythm pounding into her mouth. “Just like that.”

With eyes closed, he let go to the sensation of the tightness of her lips around him and she sucked him to the back of her throat. Not wanting to come and needing to make it last longer, he kept one hand on the top of her head to hold her in place as he thrust. When he had her position and the rhythm just right, he opened his eyes, continuing to drive relentlessly into CJ’s wanting mouth.

Outside the window, movement below on The Quad caught his eye. It was Mia and her friends and they were now doing a crazy, abandoned dance. Her arms were outstretched wide and her long hair was flinging with her head, her hips thrusting rhythmically. It was so much fun to watch her being so free, and he realized he was thrusting into CJ’s mouth to the rhythm of Mia’s wild abandoned dance. The realization of being mesmerized by one woman’s motion while being sucked off by another, made his balls tighten and the pressure begin to rise. This, he could no longer control.

When he left CJ’s dorm, Mia and her friends were still out on The Quad, sitting in the grass, hanging out talking. Catching Mia’s eye as he walked past, he greeted her with a head nod and smile. Mia did the same in return. Suddenly, Schooner felt shy and hoped she didn’t notice that he was actually blushing. Why did he feel like he had just taken advantage of her?

Chapter Eight

The remainder of first semester flew by alarmingly fast. Schooner made first string on the tennis team, an unusual feat for a freshman, and represented the team in the fall regional tournaments with a string of wins. Come spring semester and the aggressive team schedule, he would be juggling studies and travel—including trips to many of the small Ivy's on the east coast. He looked forward to the travel matches and exploring campuses he had only seen in pictures.

The month of January was known as Interim. For four weeks, students took only one intensive class for four credits. Some classes were on campus, others were travel oriented—European capitals, Theatre in NY, Outdoor Adventure: Australia/New Zealand, Spanish Immersion in Ecuador and dozens of other equally interesting classes.

For those who stayed on campus, the course catalogue offered intensive seminars on a wide array of subjects, including in-depth study on specific authors, film genres, American popular culture, music (from intensive instrument instruction to analysis of Beatles lyrics). While there would be papers to write and tests to take, Interim allowed students to actually enjoy studying and really delve into a topic of interest that wasn't a part of their normal core curriculum.

Schooner spent the time between Christmas and New Year's with CJ's family. Parents loved him. Moms for the obvious reason, dads because he was an athlete and could be a man's man.

When CJ's mother, Barbara, had Schooner pose with the family on a staircase photo (they were each lined up on consecutive steps, leaning on the banister and all wearing red sweaters—CJ's Christmas gift to him), Schooner realized that CJ and her mother had this whole thing mapped out. Barbara MacAllister was clearly already naming her little blonde haired, blue eyed grandchildren and their last name would be Moore. It got worse when they took a few shots of just CJ and Schooner on the staircase, the banister decorated in garland and red bows, CJ and Schooner in matching red sweaters.

Feeling used and manipulated, as if they were sucking away his freewill with a very well-orchestrated masterplan, Schooner could feel the anger and resentment set in. He didn't like being used and manipulated or having life-altering decisions being made for him. His girlfriend's thinly veiled scheme was making him exceedingly unhappy.

That night when everyone was asleep, an angry and frustrated Schooner snuck into CJ's room. Her pink satin robe hung over the back of a chair. Schooner silently pulled the sash tie from the loops of the robe and approached CJ's bed. He sat down on the edge and the movement from his weight woke her.

"Shhhh," he whispered. "Keep quiet."

He took her hands and pulled them above her head tying them tightly with the satin sash to the post of her canopy bed.

"Do *not* make a sound," his voice was gruff and commanding. CJ laid there wide-eyed and nodded her head.

"Your parents think you're a good girl, don't they?"

CJ nodded.

"They think you're a virgin." Schooner went on, "but we know better than that, don't we?"

CJ nodded again.

"We know what a hot little slut you are," a moan escaped CJ's throat. "I told you to be quiet," his tone harsh. "You are such a slut that every day you suck my sweaty cock and balls when I get off the tennis courts. I don't even shower and I fuck you."

CJ started writhing, clearly turned on by Schooner's monologue.

"Stay still," he hissed and she stilled. "Tonight, your mother lined us up on the stairs. Her sweet little virginal daughter and her hot boyfriend. Show me off to all her friends. Brag to them. Well, if she only knew how much you love to suck my dick, do you think she'd still be bragging? And now I am going to fuck her little *virgin* in her pretty little girly bed." And with that, Schooner got between CJ's thighs and rammed his cock deep into her dripping wet pussy. "And you won't make a sound."

Schooner rode CJ hard, ramming into her. Angry at her manipulation. At her mother's manipulation. When he was done, he untied the sash and silently got up and left the room feeling slightly more in control than he did posing on the staircase.

As had been previously planned for New Year's, CJ was a guest at the Moore's home and there was no way she was not going to be present at his family's annual New Year's Eve party, no matter how cold their son had been for the past few days. CJ had one chance to make a first impression and the

Moores were going to love her.

By New Year's Eve, Schooner could not wait for winter break to be over. He yearned to be back on the courts, practicing like a motherfucker for a full month before the spring semester tennis schedule began. More than anything, he was secretly very happy that CJ would be off for the month exploring European capitals.

When she had first signed up for the class, he was not ecstatic about her being away for four weeks. But with intensive pre-season tennis practice, his own class and the feeling like a noose was being tightened around his neck, as his future was being decided for him, he was ready to tell CJ to, "Have a great trip. See you in February."

Dee Moore was famous for her parties. The consummate hostess, with a natural knack for putting people together and launching conversations, she would get the group started and quietly move on to the next guests needing her help. Dee liked to think of herself as the sand in the oyster—she'd get it all underway and then her job was done.

As she surveyed the room that night, she noticed Schooner's girlfriend, CJ, was part of her husband's conversation group, which was made up of all men. CJ hung onto Gavin Moore's every word and laughed brightly. While the girl had been nothing but pleasant and solicitous, Dee's motherly red flags were up. CJ was showing the Moores what she thought they wanted to see and Dee instinctively knew they had yet to see the real CJ.

Dee exited the great room wondering where her son might be. Gavin's home office was empty and Schooner was not with the crowd in the kitchen. Dee made her way to the family room and still there was no sign of Schooner. She saw a slight movement through the French doors and found her son out on the deck, alone.

Schooner was such a social young man, that finding him alone, instead of socializing with family friends he had known his whole life, told Dee that all was not right in her son's world.

"Getting some fresh air?" she asked, intruding on his silence.

"Hi Mom." He leaned down and kissed her on the cheek.

"CJ is very lovely, Schooner."

"Yes, she is. We look like we belong together, don't we." It was more of a statement than a question.

"No doubt about it, you two make a very striking couple. Whether you belong together is another story. While it's nice to see you in a committed relationship and caring for someone, you are both very young. First love can sometimes be overwhelming." Dee rubbed Schooner's back, reassuringly.

Schooner remained silent.

"Are you feeling overwhelmed?"

He closed his eyes and sighed, "Mom, I'm really glad she's going away for the month. Is that a bad thing? Is that telling me something I should be listening to?" Schooner turned to his mother, a pained look on his face. Her heart ached at his confusion.

"No Sweetheart, it's not a bad thing. It is what it is and those are your feelings. Whether it's telling you something or not, only time will tell. Maybe it is, maybe it isn't. And the time you spend apart may give you a lot of answers. The two of you have just gone through several very intense months learning to live on your own, coming into your own. Take a breath and just give yourself credit for successfully embracing all the change in your life and doing a really great job with it."

Schooner hugged his mother tight. He just wanted to be the man she wanted him to be, yet always had something gnawing deep in his gut that if she really knew what was going on, hidden in his psyche, that he would disappoint her.

"Let's get inside." She led him toward the door. "It's almost the new year."

At the stroke of midnight, in a room filled with revelers, Schooner kissed CJ deeply. "I'm going to miss you," she said, lower lip out in a full pretty pink pout.

"I'm going to miss you, too," he whispered softly in her ear, not being able to voice it out loud. And in that moment, Schooner hated himself just a little bit more for telling her what she wanted to hear.

Chapter Nine

January was historically a cold and rainy month and it looked like history was going to repeat itself. Half of the student population was abroad or doing domestic travel classes, leaving only about 1200 students on the entire campus. It kind of had a ghost town feel to it and Schooner thought it felt damn good.

No roommate. Beau was in Ecuador.

No girlfriend. CJ was going to be in London, Paris, Rome, Vienna and Prague.

Practice at the new indoor tennis center, which had just been completed over the holiday break, and an American Popular Culture class on the History of American music from blues to modern day, would be his life for one month. Sweet.

After a great two hours of returning serves from a relentless machine from 6:00 A.M.—8:00 A.M., Schooner headed to the dining hall for some breakfast. He thought this would be his January schedule. Early morning time on the court, breakfast, then class from 9:00 to 12:30, Monday through Thursday. Coach had practice from 2:00—4:00 daily and then the evening was his, open for studying, projects and hanging out. He liked this new plan and couldn't wait to get into the groove.

Refusing to carry an umbrella, Schooner pulled up the hood of his windbreaker and made his way across The Quad to Clawson Hall. The class was in one of the theatre-style lecture halls and Schooner did a quick scan of the crowd when he walked in, looking for people he knew and hopefully an empty seat.

She looked up just as he scanned the section in which she was seated and broke into a huge smile as their eyes met. *A real smile*, he thought. Smiling back (a real smile), he started up the stairs, two at a time until he reached her level. She was at the center of the row and he had to climb over a few people to get to the empty seat next to her.

"Hey, how was your holiday?" He was really happy no one else had been sitting on her right.

"Great, and yours?"

"It was good. My dad was asking about you. He said to say hello if I saw you."

"Please tell him and your mom hello from me." She gestured to her friends sitting on the other side of her, "Do you know Henry and Rosalie?" And she turned to them. "Guys, do you know Schooner?"

Schooner recognized Mia's two friends from her *entourage,* but had never actually

spoken to either of them before. He was pretty sure that both Henry and Rosalie were gay. Where he lived, in the jock dorm, if anyone was gay, they certainly were not out. Mia, Henry and Rosalie lived in a dorm whose motto could have been, "Anything Goes."

"Do you know anything about this professor?" Schooner asked.

Mia's face lit up and she became very animated, "I had him last semester and he is the coolest prof on campus. He grades really tough though. He truly makes you think and expects a lot from your papers. I hate his freaking red pen."

"Oh crap. Writing is not my strongest skill," Schooner admitted.

"Rut roh," Mia did a Scooby Doo imitation. "It *is* my strongest skill and he still beat the crap out of me. But he's a great lecturer and he just makes everything really fun. He's also like the best guy to talk to."

Dr. Richard Stevens took the podium in the front of the room. He was dressed in faded jeans and a worn blue work shirt and looked every inch the *cool* professor. He was very articulate and there was just a hint of a British accent.

Schooner noticed that Mia was looking at him like he was hot. She definitely had a Prof Crush.

"Welcome to Interim," he began. "One class. Just one class. For those of you who are freshman and this is your first Interim, you are thinking that you just got an extra month of vacation. You're thinking you'll be keeping the ole' bong fired up." Chuckles and murmurs coursed throughout the room. "You're thinking marathons of Hearts and Spades. You're thinking you're going to be shitfaced for a month." He paused, "Well, you're wrong. For the next month, you will be learning about the American soundtrack. You will be learning how music is the universal connector from generation to generation. It is the mirror that reflects society and its mores. You will be sitting in your dorm rooms, quite possibly with a bong in hand." More chuckles from the lecture hall. "And will hear the music you are playing, differently than you've ever heard it before. You'll want to write about it, dissect it, discuss it, argue about it and get lost in it. Listening to music will never be the same."

Mia smiled at Schooner, her eyes alight.

She was right, he thought, this guy is dynamic. *This is going to be amazing.*

"Four weeks. Three individual papers, the first one due this week." He paused, "Yes, you heard me right. I said this week. There will be one group project. No tests." A small cheer from the lecture hall at the mention of no tests. Professor Stevens continued, "Your group project will make up 40% of your grade, each paper is worth 20%. So, as you can see, there is no room to screw up. There are twenty-eight of you in this class and you will break into seven groups of four for your group project."

Mia looked left at Rosalie and Henry and right to Schooner, "Us four?" And they all agreed.

Professor Stevens turned to the board and began writing.

> Our culture finds its tension and its life within the borders of the glimmer and the dying away, in attempts to come to terms with the betrayal without giving up on the promise" ~ Greil Marcus[1]

He turned back to the class and pointed to the board, "If you haven't already begun to write down this quote, I would suggest you start immediately, because this is what we will be discussing for the next four weeks. This is what all your papers will be about and this is what your final project will be about. Learn that quote, digest it, process it and start applying it to your thinking."

He turned back to the board and started to write again.

Harmonica Frank
Robert Johnson
Blind Lemon Jefferson
Muddy Waters
John Lee Hooker
The Band
Bob Dylan
Laura Nyro
The Grateful Dead
Creedence Clearwater Revival
Sly Stone
Allman Brothers
Elvis Presley
Bruce Springsteen
Chrissie Hynde
CSNY
Dr. John

Beach Boys

"This list goes on and on. It's dynamic and it's intertwined. Where does one influence end and another begin? Can they be separated?" Professor Stevens hit a button, static crackled through the room.

Schooner and Mia both looked at one another in the same moment, wide eyed and wide smiled as the first strains of Robert Johnson's blues classic "*Come on in My Kitchen*" began to play.

Interim had officially begun.

[1] Greil Marcus, Mystery Train: Images of America in Rock 'n Roll Music (New York: Penguin Group, 1975), 35.

Chapter Ten

Three and a half hours flew by as they listened to music and talked about its meaning, its cultural significance and the topics they would delve into daily—What is the American birthright? What are the promises? What are the betrayals? How, as a people, do we come to terms with the chasm between promise and betrayal, and how is that portrayed in music?

It was fascinating, and being exposed to music they'd never heard before, had the foursome pumped up. By the time they got out of class and walked across The Quad to the dining hall for lunch, their excitement was palpable, thoughts and theories beginning to formulate and flow out of them. As they walked through the food line, they tossed around topics for their project, which they didn't even have the guidelines for yet, but that's how psyched up they were.

Schooner found Henry and Rosalie to be down to earth, fun and really funny. He loved the way they busted on one another and the easy camaraderie in this group. They were just accepting him and taking him in. Making him one of their own. No questions asked. No judgments. No need for any particular status. He was okay with Mia, so he was okay with them. *Ironic*, he thought, as it was absolutely the antithesis of how Beau had treated Mia.

When they all had their trays, they made their way to a table and it appeared to Schooner that the three had just assumed he would say goodbye and head over to sit with some of his jock friends or tennis teammates, but he didn't do that. Following them to their table, he sat down next to Mia.

The surprise immediately registered on Mia's face and he liked it. He'd had more fun with them in the past few hours than he'd had in his entire first semester with his dorm mates and the tennis team.

"So, *Little Miss Writing is my Strong Point,* are you going to help me with my papers so I don't end up being totally annihilated by the famous red slash of death?" Schooner gave Mia his best megawatt smile.

Mia sneered back at him, "You're going to have to do better than that, Pretty Boy." And then she smiled, her freckle smattered nose, crinkling.

Catching him off-guard, she made Schooner's heart smile—a feeling he didn't easily recognize, but was surely enjoying.

He just looked at her, loving that she had called him on his shit. "Seriously, can you at least look them over before I turn them in?"

Nodding her head, she agreed. "Yeah, of course. No problem. I'm not going to let my team mate look like a stupid jock," she teased. "That would make us all look bad." Motioning to Henry and Rosie, they didn't skip a beat joining in on the "Bust on Schooner Session."

It was in that instant, that Schooner knew, *this* is what he had been missing out on so far in his college experience. Thinking back to his New Year's Eve conversation with his mom, where he was so out of sorts, he was aware something wasn't quite right in his life (besides feeling railroaded into a predetermined future), something was missing. *This* was what was missing.

"Are you guys going to start reading and studying tonight? I've got tennis practice from 2-4 every afternoon, but I can meet after that."

Henry turned to Mia and Rosalie, "What time do you guys want to eat dinner?"

"5:30?" Rosalie offered. Mia nodding her assent.

"Cool," smiled Schooner. "That gives me time to get back from the Tennis Center, shower, change and grab my books. I'll meet you guys for dinner and then we can go back to your dorm to work."

And that was how it began and a new group of friends formed. Schooner was amazed at his immediate comfort level with this group. They were funny, smart and not afraid to bust on him. They were fun. And he didn't need to pretend with them; he could be Schooner and they actually liked him. It wasn't work to fit in with his new friends.

When Schooner hit the courts that afternoon and Coach Boland started putting them through their paces, he felt a confidence that surpassed his usual bravado. This confidence was coming from a new place. A place with which Schooner was not familiar, but really liked.

Chapter Eleven

The nightly ritual had begun. Meet for dinner and then head over to one of the study rooms in Mia, Henry and Rosie's dorm. They would spend a few hours working in the study room, scanning the reference books, listening to tapes of the music, working on papers, batting around ideas. Their conversations were lively, punctuated by Rosie's sarcasm and Mia's quick wit. Often, they'd have to draw themselves back from off-topic tangents that would lead into fits of laughter. Schooner had never remembered laughing so hard in his life. His face would hurt, his gut muscles would ache. He and Henry often played the straight men (no pun intended) to the girls and their antics. One of the greatest surprises for Schooner was how at ease he was with his burgeoning friendship with Henry. Henry was just another guy—and that really came as a revelation to Schooner. He would forget about the gay thing and just enjoy his banter and discourse with Henry. And if he were to really think about it, Schooner was more at ease with Henry than he was with any of his teammates.

After a few hours in the study room, they would leave the protected enclave and move the discussion to Mia's room. Mia's roommate, Caroline, was also on the European capitals trip. The three friends would break out the bong (which Professor Stevens had predicted) and Schooner would just stick to beer. With training four hours a day, he knew getting high would be detrimental to peak performance, and he did not want to lose his hard earned, highly-coveted, first string spot.

The group would listen to music and the conversation would just flow. Sometimes it centered on what they were learning and how they applied it to themselves and their worlds. Other times they played marathon poker tournaments. And most of the time they just opened -up and shared with each other.

Henry's first experience with another man happened when he was only nine. His mom's younger cousin from Ohio was living with them in exchange for babysitting Henry and his little sister when their mother was at work. One of the cousin's boyfriends had molested Henry and did so nightly under the pretense of helping him with his homework and putting him to sleep, while the cousin tended to Henry's little sister. The others sat horrified, listening to the details of what happened to the 4th grader. Henry just looked at the friends he had shocked into silence.

"It's okay," he said. "I liked it."

"But you were just a child. He took advantage of you," Mia countered, horrified. "That was wrong."

Henry casually blew it off with a shrug of his shoulders. "If it wasn't him, it would've been someone else. At least he didn't hurt me."

Schooner wondered if the girls were thinking the same thing that he was—that this man had hurt Henry immeasurably. Henry actually thought he deserved it. Deserved to be abused and violated. Feeling deep sorrow for his new friend, the brute jock in him wanted to pull this guy's nuts off and hit them around the court with his racquet. It was in that moment, that night in Mia's room, that Schooner realized how protective he felt of Henry and this crew. They were his people.

Rosie broke the tension with a snorting laugh. The other three just looked at her questioningly.

"I was just thinking about one of my "early" sexual experiences," she said, making quotation marks with her fingers at the word early. She continued to laugh, shaking her head, before she was able to gain control of herself enough to share the memory.

"Okay, so when I was little, I used to defy my mother all the time. I know that's hard to imagine," she laughed and was met with a chorus of "Oh yeah, really hard to imagine." She continued, "So, my mother used to put me up in my room to 'think about what I had done' and told me that I could come out when I was 'ready to apologize'." She stopped and laughed, "I'm actually surprised I'm out of the room now."

Another round of laughter ensued.

"So, I would go up, sit on my bed and stew. I usually had no idea what I had done wrong or why my mother had put me up there. Maybe she needed a break. I don't know," she paused and loaded herself a bong hit, lit it and inhaled.

With the smoke still in her lungs, she continued, "So, I must've been about five years old." She blew out the smoke and started to laugh. "And my mother had put me up in my room one day and I got really bored and started checking out my toys. I had this magic wand. It was a wooden stick with a purple plastic star on one end filled with like water and glitter and a picture of a unicorn on it. I think it came with a My Little Pony."

Schooner sat up abruptly from the big overstuffed throw pillow he was lounging against and grabbed Mia's arm, practically spitting out his swig of beer. "Oh no, where is she going with this?"

They all started to laugh again.

"You are a bright, bright boy." Rosie pointed at Schooner and continued, "So one day, I took off my frilly little pink and white panties. Do you believe she dressed *me* in frilly stuff? Lord knows why I'm so fucked up! Okay, back to the story. So, I took my panties off and started to masturbate with this magic wand. I remember masturbating with it and singing…La La La La La…"

Schooner, Henry and Mia were literally rolling on the floor laughing, all making hand motions and singing, "LaLaLaLaLa."

Mia was pounding on the floor with her fists, her face planted in the carpeting and Schooner had his face buried in the back of her head, nuzzled into her hair, cracking up.

When they sat up, he turned to Mia and said, "When is her birthday?" Motioning to Rosalie—which set off another round of laughter. "You're going to be an easy one to shop for this year."

When they all regained control over their laughter, Rosie continued, "Okay, so picture this…"

"We are!" Henry interrupted and the laughter started again.

Through her laughter, Rosie continued, "So, I had no clue what I was doing, but I knew it felt good so I started getting in trouble on purpose, just so I could get sent to my room and do this thing that felt so great. I guess I had gotten away with it for a few weeks when my mother walked in during the middle of one of my sessions, saw the magic wand in me, freaked out and grabbed it." Rosie pouted out her lower lip, "She took my magic wand away," she sniffed.

"I got your magic wand right here for you, Baby." Henry motioned to his crotch.

Rosie scoffed. "You might have a magic wand for him," she motioned to Schooner, "but not for me."

"Umm, I can have fun with my own wand," Schooner choked, blushing.

"I'll bet you can!" Rosie teased and they all broke into another fit of laughter.

Chapter Twelve

The general consensus on campus was that no new food had been delivered to the dining hall for Interim and that the staff there was just recycling old food and using leftovers. The already questionable food quality seemed to degrade by the day—making dining during the regular semester seem like a Wolfgang Puck-inspired meal (which it clearly was not).

Everyone was pissed off and grumbling about how much their parents were paying for this high priced private college education and that they should at least get some decent food. How many days in a row were they going to be expected to eat 'Chicken Surprise'?

Sitting at the next table from Schooner, Mia, Rosie and Henry, were some of the football jocks from Schooner's dorm. They were complaining loudly about the food and the one complaining the loudest was an offensive tackle known as Beast. Schooner realized he didn't even know Beast's real name, although he had lived in the same dorm with him since late August.

Fall semester, Beast had been rushing one of the jock fraternities. As part of his hazing, he spent one month, day and night, in a pink leotard and a pink lace tutu. During that month, he was not allowed to shower—or wash the leotard. Now while the leotard and tutu were a bit strange for Beast, not showering for extended periods of time was more the norm than the exception. A few days into the hazing, Beast was odiferous. By the end of the month, it was hard to walk past him without gagging. Tables in the dining hall cleared, classroom desks were rearranged to one side of the room and his roommate, Vince, took up residence on a couch in the dorm's lounge.

Beast was huge, 6'4" and 300 lbs. He had a head full of unkempt hair and a straggly beard. Not known for his eloquence or intellect, the joke around campus was that he would probably scare off small children and possibly farm animals.

"This food fucking sucks!" he proclaimed, loudly.

"Tell us something we don't know." Rosalie muttered and the four chuckled.

"We don't have to take this!" his bellowing continued.

Beast then stood suddenly, pushing back the bench he was sitting on and causing everyone down the entire length of the bench to be jostled.

"I'm revolting!" he yelled on the top of his lungs.

"Actually, you're disgusting," Mia countered in a loud voice and the whole dining hall broke into laughter.

Beasts eyes enlarged and his nostrils flared, creating the visage of an insane escapee. "Bitch!" he bellowed, as he dove toward Mia.

Schooner instinctively threw his body at Beast pushing him out of the way before he assaulted Mia full on. They both fell to the floor with a sickening thud. Rosie grabbed the food off her tray and threw it at Beast and Henry followed. The rest of the jocks cleared off the benches to join in the mêlée and were met with hordes of flying food. Beast and Schooner were wrestling around on the food slick floor.

Mia started to kick Beast, "Get the fuck off him, you gross pig!" She wailed away on him, stabbing him hard in the lower back with her clogs.

The Campus Police arrived almost immediately and grabbed Beast off Schooner, cuffing his hands behind his back. A second officer cuffed Schooner.

"Officer," Mia pleaded, "he was just coming to my defense when that guy tried to jump me."

The officer looked Mia up and down (stopping momentarily on her very attractive rack), all 5'2" of her, and then looked at Beast.

"He tried to jump you?" he asked, incredulously.

"Yes, he tried to attack me."

"Did you provoke him?"

"I told him he was disgusting." Mia's chin was stuck up high in the air.

"Maybe you should come with us, too."

Mia smiled sweetly at the Campus Police Officer and said, "Will you cuff me as well?"

He choked out a "no" and Mia pouted at him, causing the officer to stammer and blush.

Schooner watched her with amusement and remembered his first impression of her in front of Brewster Hall, that devilish look that said, "Let's be bad kids together." *Well, the devil is out in full force tonight,* he thought.

She smiled at him and put her lips close to his ear. "You look really hot in cuffs."

Feeling the heat rise in his face and in his jeans, he stared at her and leaned close to her ear, where he hissed, "Now is *not* the time to give me a raging hard on, Mia."

Backing away, an astonished smirk on her face, she looked him square in the eyes, suddenly serious. Not saying a word, she silently leaned forward and kissed his cheek, softly. “Thank you for defending me tonight, Schooner.”

He sighed, feeling his heart melt. What was she doing to him?

An entourage of about twenty-five students trekked to the Campus Police station following Schooner, Mia and Beast. The statements from everyone were consistent. Beast went to physically attack Mia and Schooner jumped in to thwart the attack. The Campus Police were alarmed that a student the size of Beast had a hair trigger temper that did not preclude violence toward women. The guy was bad press waiting to happen.

Beast was not seen again until spring semester.

Chapter Thirteen

It was late by the time all the paperwork was filled out and Mia and Schooner walked back together toward their dorms.

Mia left the officer with a wink, "I'm still bummed you didn't have cuffs for me."

Schooner thought Mia's dorm would be seeing some extra patrol these next few weeks.

"Let's go, Mia, before you start another riot." Schooner ushered her out of the campus police building.

She smiled, his remark clearly pleasing her devil.

"Are you okay?" Mia asked, genuinely concerned. Schooner had a nasty cut on his cheek and some other scrapes. "I'm fine." He made light of it.

"I would tell you that I'd come back to your dorm and help you clean out those cuts, but I have a feeling I'm persona non-grata there."

"Yeah, probably not safe," he agreed. "Might not even be safe for me!"

"Oh fuck," her hand flew to her mouth. "I didn't even think of that. I am so sorry."

"It'll be fine. Everyone knows what an ass Beast is. These guys can be jerks, but I'd bet most of them have real issues seeing a girl being attacked. You notice no one came up to the Campus Police station in his defense."

"Hmm, that's true."

They walked along in the cool, dank late-night air in silence. Schooner put his arm around Mia's shoulder and pulled her into him as they continued to walk. Not fighting the gesture, she seemed to find her place right under his arm.

She is so tiny, he thought and smiled. *A tiny, uncontrollable fireball.* "So, you like the way I look in cuffs, huh?" It was time to give her some of her own medicine.

"Mmm-hmm, you looked hot." She didn't miss a beat.

Laughing, he pulled her tighter into him. This time her arm went around the back of his waist, and without thinking, he kissed her on the top of her head. She was really getting under his skin and he didn't know whether to be excited or scared.

They reached her dorm and Schooner stopped.

"You want to come in and I can take a look at your cuts?" Mia asked.

"I want to," Schooner whispered, "but it's after 1 A.M. and I've got to be on the courts at six. Not sure how good I'm going to be feeling in the morning or what flak I'll be taking from the coach when he gets a load of me."

Mia nodded her head. "Schooner," she paused, clearly grappling with word choice, "what you did tonight… well, it was amazing. That crazy son-of-a-bitch was going to tackle me. He could've really hurt me. And you went against one of the guys you live with. That's huge."

Schooner quickly closed the space between him and Mia and wrapped his arms around her tightly. He smiled as her arms circled his back. With his chin resting on the top of her head, softly he said, "I would never have let him hurt you, Baby Girl."

He was as surprised by the term of endearment as she was, and if he could have seen her face at that moment, she was smiling into his chest.

Gently, he pushed her away by the shoulders and kissed her forehead. "Get some sleep," he ordered and she giggled at his stern tone.

And with that, he quickly turned on his heel, heading in the direction of his dorm, leaving her standing there, as confused as he was, by the tremendous onslaught of feelings.

Chapter Fourteen

On Saturday, the gang decided to take their studying someplace conducive to opening up their minds to understanding how American culture is reflected in music, and that meant being anywhere, other than stuck on campus. Schooner borrowed a teammate's car and pulled up in front of the dorm to pick up the gang.

"Nice wheels," Henry commented, easing his thin, lithe frame into the front passenger seat of the silver Camaro. The girls piled in the back, giddy with the prospect of getting off campus.

The week-long rain had finally ended and the low clouds lifted revealing the raw beauty of the San Bernardino National Forest. The mountains appeared majestic against a pristine clear blue sky (that ironically matched Schooner's eyes), with their snow-capped peaks.

Down vests and hiking boots and gloves were broken out for the trip as well as cassette players, lots of cassette music, extra batteries and notebooks to work. In the backseat, Mia pulled a black knit cap out of her backpack and leaned forward and pulled it down over Schooner's head, "My gift to you from New York."

Schooner pulled down the visor to look in the mirror. "I like it," he smiled. "Can I keep it?"

"Sure, consider it a gift."

Schooner thought, *she has no idea how much I will treasure this.*

They headed up Hwy. 38 into the town of Mentone. "Hey, pull in here." Henry said to Schooner and jumped out of the car.

He ducked into a donut shop and the girls squealed in the back. The winter sun glinted off Henry's copper-tinged waves as he rushed back to the car. "Get 'em while they're hot," he announced and flung open the heavenly smelling box of apple fritters.

Hands grabbed and sounds of "mmm" and "oh my god" filled the car.

"How'd you guys find this place?" Schooner asked.

"You forget we're stoners," Rosie offered, stuffing the last bite of an apple fritter into her mouth and slowly licking off her sticky fingers. Rosie had full-curvy deep pink lips that always looked like she was wearing lipstick, and later in life, people would wonder if she'd had "work done" on them. "We are not beyond traveling for munchies."

Once through Mentone, the highway started taking on sharp curves and a steep incline, as it became known as the Rim of the World Highway, sporting views of snowcapped saw backs and pine dotted ridges. The clear skies made the view seem as if it went on forever, creating the feeling that anything was possible.

Schooner looked back and laughingly said to Mia, "Hey, I remember the last time I was in the mountains with you."

She slapped him on the shoulder. "Oh crap, don't remind me!"

"Remind you of what?" Rosie asked and Henry turned to Mia to hear the story.

Mia and Schooner filled Rosie and Henry in on the event that took place during the freshman retreat and Mia's encounter of getting sniffed by Tim Vandergrift.

"He sniffed you?" Rosie appeared grossed out.

Before Mia could respond, a laughing Schooner chimed in, "Sniffed her is an understatement. He was nose raping her. The only thing that would've made him happier would've been if she'd handed him her panties to sniff."

"Eww! Stop that!" Mia started slapping Schooner on the shoulder, while the others hooted.

"Seriously, he sniffed you?" Henry asked through his laughing tears.

"He did," Mia laughed. "I thought he was narc'ing me out for stinking of weed. He was seriously hanging on my chair and sniffing me. It was freaky. I thought for sure I was going to get kicked out of school in my first two weeks and that my parents would kill me and give me the 'We knew you were too young to go away and be on your own' bullshit."

They were still laughing as Schooner pulled the car into a National Forest recreation area parking lot.

"But this guy saved the day." Mia patted Schooner's shoulder. "He caused a diversion and I escaped the evil sniffer."

"You know who that Tim guy reminds me of, that character Greg Marmalard from the movie *Animal House*. You know the straight-laced preppie guy who led the brigade against Otter, Boon, Bluto and the gang," Henry said.

"Exactly," Schooner chimed in. "Total dick. You should've seen the look on Mia's face." He laughed, "It was like get me the hell out of here. Now!"

They parked the car and grabbed their gear and began down the Big Falls Trailhead. About a half mile in, a clearing opened to a heart stopping, unobstructed view of Forest Falls. They all stood there silently enjoying the majesty of the unspoiled falls and listening to the rush of water as it flowed over ancient rock.

Crossing a creek bed, they cautiously stepping from boulder to slippery boulder until they reached the other side, where they followed the trail alongside the creek bed. When they came upon a huge sign, *These Falls Have Claimed Many Lives*, they turned off on a trail through the woods, packing down snow as they hiked for about another twenty minutes until reaching their destination, a large snow filled meadow that had yet to be disturbed by anything other than deer tracks.

As they walked out into the opening, they were greeted by a different clear vista of the falls. Laying their backpacks on some large boulders, the four walked toward the ridge to view the sublime waterfall. Standing there silently for a few minutes, they were all overwhelmed by the perfection of nature.

Mia pulled out her Nikon SLR and started to take pictures of the falls. She used a low broken branch of a pine to set her camera on and act as a tripod. As she pulled several lenses out of her bag, Schooner realized that he had seen her shooting around campus.

"That's a nice camera," he commented.

"Thanks. It was my birthday present to myself," she offered proudly.

"What do you like to shoot most?" Schooner was enjoying learning what made her tick.

"This." She gestured to the scenery around them. "I love landscape photography. If anything comes out good from today, I'll make you a print."

"You make your own prints?"

"Yeah, we've got a great dark room on campus. So, I roll my own—umm, film, that is," she chuckled, "and then develop it and print it. Right now, I'm shooting black and white."

"Are you going to teach me how to shoot one of these days?" Henry nudged her.

"Any time you want," she responded, clearly too focused on the falls to continue the conversation.

"Just make sure she's behind the lens," Henry clued Schooner in. "She hates having her picture taken."

How odd, she's comfortable behind the lens and I've spent my life in front of it, Schooner thought. He wondered how she would see him through her lens, what she would see? Would she see him or just his well-crafted disguise?

After a few minutes more of shooting scenery, Mia turned the camera to her compadres capturing them playing in the snow, rolling in the snow, making lewd snowmen with giant erections and pretending to throw one another off the mountain ridge.

Mia turned and walked away from the group to go put her camera back in her backpack, where it would be safe.

A moment later, Schooner heard her call his name and turned as a snowball whooshed past his head, missing him by mere inches.

"Oh, so that's how you want to play." He gathered up snow in his hands and packed a snowball quickly and winged it at her.

"Ouch," she screamed, getting nabbed in the arm. "Son of a bitch!"

"You started it," he laughed.

Henry and Rosie joined in the fun with Henry chasing Rosie down and stuffing snow down the back of her jacket.

"I hate you!" she screamed at him and smushed snow in his copper hair.

Flinging snowballs like he was serving tennis balls, Schooner bombarded Mia, until he finally decided she'd been pelted enough. Slowly, he walked toward her with one last surprise. Smiling brightly at her, he launched his sneak attack, smushing a glove full of snow in her face.

"Oh man, you play dirty. I give up." She held her hands up in defeat and he beamed at his victory.

Putting his arms around her, Schooner pulled Mia into his chest. "Body heat," he whispered in her ear.

She looked up at him and he pulled her cap down over her face playfully.

This was the first time either Henry or Rosie had seen him be physical with Mia. He wanted to kiss her in this light, perfect, fun-filled moment on a mountain alongside a waterfall. But they weren't alone and he didn't want to cause anyone any embarrassment. And he wanted that moment to be just theirs alone, shared with no one, when the time was right.

They went back to the rocks where their backpacks were and sat down. Pulling out their cassette players and notebooks, they started listening to music and discussing how tracks would either fit in or not fit in with their group project.

After about thirty minutes, their butts and fingers and toes were so cold and so wet from their snowball fight, that they decided to bail on studying in the mountains and finish studying in a nice warm dorm room.

Chapter Fifteen

The dorm room didn't feel much warmer than the mountaintop and the gang all changed into dry, warm oversized sweats and thick socks and lounged on throw pillows on the floor of Mia's room.

"Okay, clearly we need to address Bob Dylan's work, Crosby Stills Nash, the Buffalo Springfield stuff," Henry said, as he made notes.

Schooner flipped through some books, "I don't want to ignore Woody Guthrie and Pete Seeger and we need to bring in the ties to Steinbeck's work. Honestly though, I feel like Phil Ochs gets totally overlooked and I really want to focus on him, but at the same time, I think we really have to be careful of it becoming too derivative."

"Yeah, that's my concern, too," Rosie chimed in, making a face. "Whoever thought we'd hear a jock use the term derivative."

Schooner tossed a pillow at her, which she arranged under her head, smiling at him.

"I think they all help build a linear foundation for groups like the Pretenders, for Leonard Cohen, for REM and for Springsteen," Mia said, without looking up from her notes.

"Oh no, here comes the New Yorker with Springsteen." Henry teased and Mia threw a pillow at him, still not looking up from her notes.

"Hey, if anyone's music focuses on the promise, the betrayal, coming to terms with everything on both a cultural level and a personal level—it's Bruce's. I've kind of been cataloguing it to look at what is more cultural than personal—if you can even separate it—and I think we can clearly make strong cases with: *Thunder Road*—the ultimate redemption song, *The Promised Land*—totally about coming to terms with the betrayal, *Badlands*—taking the power back, feeling the birthright, *Born to Run*." Mia continued, "Basically, a good portion of *The River* album can be tied back into Marcus' premise. Even some of the covers Bruce has chosen, Jimmy Cliff's *Trapped*." She looked around for her notes, "Oh, and trying to pull it down to the individual level—that of personal betrayal and questioning of the promise. Check this out, listen to this song."

Grabbing her cassette recorder, she played with the forward and reverse for a few minutes, stabbing at the buttons, until the tape was at the right point. The quiet guitar strains of a bare, haunting tune began.

Mia laid back on her throw pillow, eyes closed, quietly singing harmony as the others listened intently to the lyrics of the starkly beautiful song.

"Play that again." Henry requested and Mia obliged, rewinding the tape to the song's opening notes.

Listening closely again, Schooner was slightly distracted by Mia's proximity on the next throw pillow.

Hearing the lyrics to *One Step Up* a second time, cut deeply. They were words of self-doubt and self-disappointment. And for Schooner, they hit too close to home.

Schooner Moore was concerned that maybe he wasn't the man he hoped he could be.

Lively discussion ensued and after a few more hours, they'd worked out how they were going to divide the work amongst the group and then bridge it together into a seamless project. The rest of the evening they focused on putting together their opening statement and then began to plow through the exhaustive material for each of their individual sections.

It was past midnight when Rosie got to her feet. "I'm toast," she announced. "All that fresh air today knocked me out."

"Ditto," agreed Henry. "I need to peel these lenses out of my eyes."

Rosie pulled him to his feet.

"We got a lot done tonight, guys." Schooner was pleased.

"Yeah, I feel good about it." Rosie looked beat, "Have we lost you, Mia?"

Mia pulled the throw pillow off her face and smiled. "Still here… barely," she giggled.

"Don't wake me for breakfast," Henry yelled back as he and Rosie closed the door.

Mia rolled on her side and looked at Schooner. He reached out and took a long curl in between his fingers, playing with it.

Here it was, finally the moment they were alone. "C'mere," he said, pulling her head down on his chest as he continued to play with her curls.

Snuggling her face into his chest, she pulled off her glasses, placing them out of the way. Mia looked up at Schooner and he smiled at her beautiful ombre green eyes, making her blush. Slowly, he rubbed her arm up and down in an attempt to reassure her.

This little devil, so outgoing and fearless, was actually so shy when it came to guys. *Wild and innocent*, Schooner thought. He wanted her to be his. And just the thought of that shot feelings of guilt through him. He was CJ's. Or so she thought. But what he was feeling toward Mia was something he'd never felt in his life. His heart felt like it was overflowing with emotion, a longing so deep it was physical.

He wanted to be with her every moment, needed to know everything about her, ached for her to be in his arms all the time, by his side. Looking up, smiling at him. Wanting him. He didn't know he could feel these feelings for someone else.

Wrapping both arms around her, he hugged her tightly to him—so overcome with feelings. With a content sigh, he kissed the top of her head and she looked up at him, a combination of yearning and fear of the unknown in her eyes. He smiled at her and rubbed his nose against hers, which elicited a little giggle. This made him laugh and he kissed the tip of her nose.

"I think you've figured it out already," he smiled down at her.

"Figured out what?" she asked.

"That I'm crazy about you."

She blushed and buried her face in his chest, too shy to look into his eyes.

God, she's adorable, he thought to himself.

"Mia, look at me."

Tentatively, she looked up.

He smiled at her and ran his thumb along her high cheekbone, then pushed a mass of curls away from her face. Bringing his lips close to hers, he whispered, "Really, really, crazy about you, Mia. I want to be with you all the time. I never want to leave you at the end of the day."

"Then don't," she whispered.

He smiled, his lips up against hers and he could feel her returning the smile. Taking her face in his hands, he kissed her lips softly. Mia's reaction was a soft *mmmm* sound which he felt immediately between his legs. Kissing her lips harder, she responded perfectly, opening her mouth. Letting his tongue slip in to find hers, Mia's tongue met his, cautiously at first and then a little bolder in its exploration. As her fingers raked through his thick luxurious hair, she pulled him deeper into her mouth. The urgency of their kisses increased until they were both breathless.

Schooner pulled away and reached up to Mia's bed, pulling down her blanket and draping it over them. She leaned back on his chest and he kissed the top of her head again.

"Oh, Baby Girl," he sighed, "you have no idea of what you do to me."

"It's smoochal."

They both laughed.

She snuggled deeper into his chest as he wrapped his arms around her tighter and within minutes they both drifted off to sleep.

Chapter Sixteen

It was still dark out when Schooner woke up with stiff joints the next morning from sleeping on the throw pillows on the floor. He didn't want to wake Mia, but she was draped on him and he needed to get up for tennis practice. Maneuvering into a seated position with one arm behind Mia's shoulders and the other under her knees, he struggled to his feet and carried her to her bed. Gently, he laid her down and tucked the blanket around her. Taking a moment to sit on the edge of the bed, he just looked at her and gently moved her curls from her face.

She stirred, eyes opening a little, a smile overtaking her face.

He bent down and kissed her softly. "Hey you…" he whispered.

"What time is it?"

"It's really early. Go back to sleep. I've got to head over to the tennis center."

"Mmmm." She stretched the sleep from her body and just watching her made him hard.

If I don't leave now… he thought. "I'll bring you coffee and a bagel."

She smiled, "My keys are on the desk."

Before heading for the door, he stole a final soft kiss. "I'll see you soon, Baby Girl."

She was already curled up and back to sleep by the time he closed the door.

With her keys in hand (her keychain had a little silver camera charm hanging from it), he exited her dorm. First, he needed to go back to his dorm, change clothes and grab his racquets.

He wasn't two steps out of Mia's dorm, when two of his teammates jogged by, racquets in hand, "Slumming, Moore?"

He heard their cackles and "Freaking crazy, son of a bitch. If he doesn't want his girlfriend anymore, I'll take her off his hands."

Reality was ramming its way into his bubble and he felt both sadness and anger start to surround him. He clenched Mia's keychain tighter in his hand.

Chapter Seventeen

She was in the same position, had not moved an inch, when he returned several hours later. He put the coffee and bagels down on her desk and sat down on the desk chair across from her bed where he watched her for a few moments. Feeling his heart start to do that brim and overflow thing it had been doing lately, he said a silent *thank you* to her for showing him who he really was, allowing that person to just be and exist. And amazingly, she seemed to really like that person.

Silently, he pulled off his tennis shoes and socks, then stood and pulled off his pale blue Izod shirt and white tennis shorts. Standing there in blue plaid boxers, he made his way over to her bed, lifted the covers and crawled in next to her. Spooning up against her tightly, he pulled her snugly against his chest.

"Mmm," she moaned, fitting herself against him securely.

He smiled into her hair thinking, *sorry about the morning surprise*. But he wasn't sorry at all—he'd had a raging hard on for days just at the thought of her.

Pressing his hard cock against the back of her sweatpants, Schooner was surprised to feel her grinding back against him. He wasn't even sure if she was awake.

"You're killing me," he moved her curls back and whispered in her ear. Softly, he began running his lips down her neck before burying his face in the nook.

He slipped his hand underneath her sweatshirt, quickly discovering she wasn't wearing a bra. He cupped her right breast. The skin was so soft and he pressed it in his hand.

She moaned into her pillow and he took that as an invitation to continue.

Slinging a leg over hers, he used his long limbs to pull her tighter against his hard cock and found her nipple with his thumb and forefinger. Gently, he rolled her nipple, which responded immediately, and then added a little more pressure, until it was a hard peak.

He continued to nuzzle into her neck and she moaned, "That feels good."

Pinching her nipple tightly, "And this?"

"Mmm, really good."

Next, he pressed his hips into her, "And this?"

"Really, really good." She ground her ass against his hard cock.

He grazed her neck with his teeth, gently biting her smooth, flawless skin. "And this?"

"Too good."

"Too good? Should I stop?" he teased.

"Nooooo," she protested, continuing her slow grind against his cock.

"You are trouble, Baby Girl."

She chuckled, "Certainly, you're not just figuring that out now."

He pinched her nipple harder and she groaned. "I knew you were trouble the minute I laid eyes on you." He paused, "serious trouble."

Mia rolled over and turned to him, initiating a kiss. This was the first kiss that she had initiated and he smiled. Running her hands over his chest, which still had some of its golden tan from summer, she picked at the smattering of golden blonde hairs.

"What are you smiling at?" he asked.

"You're so big." She marveled at his chest and arm muscles, running her hands lightly over them.

He laughed and pulled her against his hard cock. "Mmm, yes, I am."

Her eyes widened and she blushed, "Sch..Schooner," she stuttered. "I, uh, don't know if I'm doing things right."

Her innocence and honesty were just adorable causing him to throw back his head in laughter.

She looked hurt.

"No, no, no, Baby Girl—don't look like that. Feel that." He ground himself against her.

Her eyes opened wide.

"That means you are doing everything very right." He kissed her softly. She was so sweet.

"Oh please," she rolled her eyes. "Guys get hard at anything."

"Baby Girl," he raked her curls from her face, "you can't even imagine what I want to do to you."

"But you haven't," she whispered.

Schooner sighed. "No, I haven't." He inhaled deeply and blew it out slowly. Her eyes were intent upon him and he spent a very long moment pushing his fingers through her curls. "There's a big Pink Elephant in this room. Pink being the operative word," he muttered, picturing CJ's pink robe, pink sweaters, pink frilly blouses. "No secret that I've got a girlfriend."

Two big tears popped from Mia's green eyes and started their journey down her freckled cheeks. Schooner brushed them away with his thumb. "Don't cry."

Mia looked at Schooner with a dubious glance, silently asking, *how can I not?*

"Mia, I don't feel for her what I feel for you." He let that sink in, but she just continued looking at him sad-eyed, not breathing. She was clearly waiting for the other shoe to drop. "I have never felt for anyone what I feel for you. This is the first time in my life I have felt that I can really be me in a relationship. And you still like me. And that amazes me."

"Still like you? Of course, I like you. Schooner, you are smart, funny, sweet, giving, so much fun to be with. You are a really good person. Why would I not like you?"

He leaned forward and kissed her lips lightly. She had just listed for him what she thought his greatest attributes were and not one of them had to do with his looks.

"I have spent my life acting, Mia. I'm good at playing a lot of roles. I'm just not really good at being me."

She cocked her head to the side, taking in what he was saying, but not really understanding it.

"And then you came along. And I could be me. I have never felt so connected to another person or so happy."

She smiled, more tears springing from her eyes.

"You are so sweet and innocent and I want to make this really special for you. You mean that much to me, Mia." He reached out, running his fingers down her cheek. "I'm going to end it with CJ. But she's not here, so I can't do that and I'm not going to call her and ruin the rest of her trip. I owe it to her to do it in person." He closed his eyes and exhaled slowly, "I want your first time to be amazing, Mia. Your first time *is* going to be amazing."

She leaned forward and kissed him.

"It would be really wrong not to end it with CJ first though." He continued, "And then when we are together there is nothing hanging over our heads."

"And you wonder why I like you, Schooner?"

A huge weight lifted as he listened to her speak those words. Soon he'd be able to tell CJ and then he would be Mia's first lover. Something very possessive inside of him knew that he wanted to be her first lover and her last lover. He pulled her to him, placing her body under his. With hands on either side of her head, he kissed her deeply. Letting his hard cock grind into her, she would absolutely have no doubt just how much he wanted her.

The next day he showed up in Mia's dorm room with a large travel duffle bag filled with clothes, toiletries, and other personal items. He also brought his racquets. With the exception of the time he had to spend on the courts, Schooner would be spending the rest of January with Mia, not wanting to be away from her for even a second. There was not a time that he could not remember feeling so happy or so free. Never had he imagined being himself could actually be so easy.

Chapter Eighteen

The days leading up to the group presentation were the happiest days Schooner could remember. Their presentation was coming along and was going to be kick-ass, they just knew it. Professor Stevens had invited the whole class back to a party at his home after the presentations were over and they were all really looking forward to that.

Schooner and Mia poured over the tennis schedule. Two to three weekends per month he'd be playing in matches and about half of them would require travel, taking him away for a few days.

"I miss you already," Mia told him, sitting on his lap at her desk.

He pulled her face in for a kiss. "I'm going to really miss this," he tightened his arms around her waist, "when Caroline gets back and I've got to move back into my dorm".

"Ugh, it's going to suck." she pouted. "I like waking up with you."

He leaned down and bit her pouty lower lip. "Grrrrr. I love waking up with you."

"I didn't know I could feel so addicted to someone," she admitted, a surprised look fleeting past her eyes. "I didn't know I'd ever want to," she paused, thinking. "It scares me. Yet, I don't want to lose this."

Schooner pulled her head against his chest and rested his chin on top of her head. "We won't lose this. I promise."

She looked up at him, searching his eyes, silently begging him to keep his promise, he thought. And for him, in that moment, the floodgates broke.

Taking her face in his hands, he kissed her eyes, her cheeks, the tip of her nose and then softly her lips. "Baby Girl," he sighed, "I love you."

Mia's eyes widened, registering her surprise.

He was nodding his head, "I love you. I really do. And I've never said that to anyone. I don't want to freak you out, Mia, and I'm sorry if I am, but I could see us together forever. Can't you?"

Breaking into a huge smile, fat tears coursed down her cheeks and she just nodded her head. Schooner took her face in his hands and started out softly kissing her lips, intensifying as she weaved her fingers into his hair, gently pulling. He heard a growl sound rumbling from the base of his throat and picked Mia up as he stood. Her legs were wrapped around his waist as he walked to the bed, their kiss never breaking.

Laying her down on her back, he got in beside her, facing her. With a smile, he pushed her irreverent mass of dark curls from her face, taking the opportunity to kiss her softly.

He leaned down next to her ear and whispered, "I want to make you happy."

Mia put her hand to his face, brushing her thumb across his cheek and smiling into his beautiful, clear blue eyes. "You make me very happy."

Schooner reached down and unbuttoned the top button on her Levi's. Sliding the zipper down, he eased his hand into her underwear, his eyes never leaving hers. The smile on his face was real. as he dipped a finger into her, eliciting a moan.

"I love how wet you are." He pulled his wet finger out and rubbed it on her clit. Her eyes grew large with surprise and he laughed. "Did I get the right spot."

All she could do was nod vigorously.

"Feels good, huh?"

She continued to nod, her smile matching his.

He pulled her jeans and underwear down together and she kicked them off her feet.

"Much better," he acknowledged. Dipping two fingers into her, he moved them to a spot on the front wall that made her gasp. His smile took on a devilish lilt—he knew he had her now.

Pulling his fingers out of her, he slipped his forefinger into his mouth, sucking it slowly. "You taste good," he ran his middle finger, which had just been inside of her, along her lips.

She reached for his hand and sucked his middle finger into her mouth, tasting herself. Licking his finger from base to tip, she then sucked it back in her mouth.

"You are killing me," he growled.

She smiled. "Good."

And he laughed. Bending down, he nipped her playfully on her hipbone and kept nipping in a line to the top of her thighs. "Now we'll see who is going to kill who." And with that he buried his face in her, taking the tip of his tongue and licking slowly from back to front. When he reached her clit, he stopped and pulled his tongue away.

"Noooooo," she moaned.

He smiled and without lifting his head said, "No? As in no more? Okay, if that's what you want."

"Motherfucker," she growled.

He smiled at her *Inner New Yorker* surfacing and the shy girl getting lost somewhere in the heat of the moment.

In the nanosecond since he had stopped, he felt her hands in his hair, pressing his face back toward her pussy.

"Are you trying to tell me you want more?" He was most amused. "I'm not quite understanding what you are telling me, Mia."

"Son of a bitch!" She yelled, laughing at the same time.

"Umm, hate to break it to you, but those are not the magic words to get you what you want."

She sprang up in one move and knocked him on his back, surprising him. "Then, I'll just take what I want."

"What is it you want, Baby Girl?" He was breathless.

"You," she stared intently into his eyes. Suddenly very serious. "You."

"Why is that?"

"Because," she searched his face, "because I love you."

And there they were, the words he had shared with her earlier. And she was now saying them back to him. He hadn't scared her away. He smiled at his sweet little freckle-faced Baby Girl, flipped her back over onto her back and made his way down between her thighs again. "Excuse me," he said, "but I was rudely interrupted."

Chapter Nineteen

The four were all jumping with nervous energy as they got ready to give the oral part of their group presentation. They had a thirty-page supporting document that would also be a part of determining their grade, but the presentation was what would kick it off and if they could nail it, they would be halfway home.

The *baby* of the group was taking the lead, because she was clearly the most fearless. She was also a great communicator, especially on subjects about which she was passionate. Schooner ran his hands up and down her arms as she took deep breaths.

"You okay?" he asked.

"Yeah, yeah. I'll be fine once I'm up there. This is the hardest part, it's like being a horse at the gate. Just let me run and I'm fine."

And that she was. They got up in front of the lecture hall and Mia kicked it off. Slides, music, analysis—they had it all. It flowed, it was logical, it was passionate, it was interesting and at points, even pushed the envelope.

Schooner watched Professor Stevens' composed face as they presented, thinking *I bet he's a great poker player*. But even great poker players have their tell and his was at the corners of his eyes. His pride in watching Mia was evident. She was clearly what made teaching at the collegiate level satisfying for him. Schooner was so proud of her and a tinge jealous at the same time of another man being entranced by her, even if it was just intellectually. They each took turns presenting and ended with a breathtaking and emotional slideshow to music portraying the dichotomy of the promise and the betrayal.

The class cheered when they finished. Professor Stevens joined the four at the front of the lecture hall, casually slinging an arm around Mia's shoulder.

"Wow!" he exclaimed. "I am actually speechless. What we all just witnessed was a Master class in American Popular Culture. I am really proud of all of you. You took on some of the voices that others would have overlooked." He looked directly at Schooner, "Phil Ochs—what a joy to see him getting his due. Well done."

Schooner beamed.

"Okay, everyone, let's take a fifteen-minute break while the next group sets up."

The four gathered their materials and headed out into the hall for a group hug and high fives. It was an amazing culmination of a month long high. Friendship, love, learning, success, growth—the four were flying high.

Together they walked to the Stevens' house that evening. Rick's wife, Wendy, a former student fifteen years prior, was welcoming and clearly up to date on all that had happened throughout Interim. She was as excited for the groups as they were, knowing the focus of each of their presentations.

Schooner stood behind Mia, his arms over her shoulders, as she leaned against him. They were "out" in public as a couple and he loved how it felt. He just wanted to say to everyone there, "You saw her today. That is *my* Baby Girl!"

Finding himself alone talking to Wendy, Schooner was surprised and impressed to find out she knew that he had made first string on the tennis team—the only freshman to do so. She clearly followed all the university's sports teams and regaled him with stories of team's past and some of his coach's minor indiscretions. Rosie joined them, and Wendy had them laughing with stories of what the school had been like when she was a student.

Mia was engaged in a serious conversation with Rick, and Schooner consciously had to tell himself to chill out, that there was no reason to be jealous. Not used to feeling jealous of other men, it was sitting oddly in his gut.

Wendy noticed Schooner's gaze. "Rick was so glad when she signed up for his Interim seminar," she began. "He came home after class one day last semester and said, 'I've got one that is really thinking' and so I asked him where she was from, figuring it couldn't be California," she laughed. "And Rick said, by the sound of her accent, I think she's a New Yorker. He wants her to TA for him next year. It's going to be a stretch getting approval on a sophomore—but he thinks if she's interested, he can get it done."

Schooner looked over at them and smiled. He was so damn proud of her.

"So, you think she'll be interested?" Wendy asked, hoping to get advance scoop.

"Well, I can't answer for her, but..." he paused, for effect, "I'd be really shocked if she wasn't interested." Wendy looked satisfied.

"So, Phil Ochs?" she said to him, "That's really freaking impressive.

Rick's been teaching this seminar for five Interims and you are the first person to cover Phil Ochs. We've been waiting for someone to do it. He called me right after class today to tell me."

Schooner nodded proudly.

She looked at him slyly out of the corner of her eye, "So, at the beginning of the month, Rick and I made bets on how many Springsteen songs Mia would incorporate over the month into her papers and the final project." Schooner nearly spit his beer on the floor, he started to laugh so hard. Wendy had a hand on his arm, steadying herself while she laughed, heartily. Mia looked over toward them with an inquisitive look on her face. He winked at her, turned back to Wendy and continued their laughing.

"That is freaking hysterical. You'll have to let me know who wins." He looked at his sweet Baby Girl talking to her Prof, who clearly saw how special she was, and thought how much richer his college experience had become now that she was a part of it.

Chapter Twenty

They were still riding their high when they got back to Mia's dorm room. Entering the room was the first dampening of their moods.

Schooner's stuff was all over and he knew he was going to have to pack it up and move back to his dorm. He didn't want to go. He didn't want to leave Mia's room. He didn't want to leave Mia's bed. He didn't want to leave Mia. He didn't want to leave Rosalie down the hall and Henry downstairs. He didn't want to leave the other people in the dorm who had been so accepting of him over the past few weeks. People who were so different than the people he typically knew. People who didn't fit in with the campus norm—and didn't try to fit in. They pursued what made them happy. They didn't fit in, so they expanded out. He had come to love and respect that about them and the thought of going back to an all-male jock dorm made him feel lonely and alone. He was going to miss the quirky camaraderie of the "freak" dorm.

He had never felt more at home.

Schooner started to shove things into his duffle bag, while Mia sat cross-legged on her bed, watching him with a perplexed look on her face.

"Are you staying tonight?" she asked, tentatively.

"Do you want me to?"

Looking at Schooner as if he had two heads, Mia was shocked that they were even having this conversation. "Are you kidding? Of course, I want you to stay. It's my last night without a roommate. I can't believe you are thinking about leaving."

The air in the room was starting to become tense.

Schooner stood in the middle of the floor, belongings in hand, but did not speak. It was impossible not to see the sadness in Mia's eyes and he thought fear, also.

Tomorrow they would all be back.

Tomorrow, this idyllic little bubble they'd just spent the month in would cease to exist.

The thought made his stomach start to ache and he felt a burning at the back of his throat.

Mia smiled at him and jumped off the bed. "Hey, I have something for you."

"You do?" He was glad she had saved the moment.

"Mmm-hmm." She nodded her head and her devilish smile was back. "Sit," she ordered, pointing to her bed. He sat down.

Going over to her desk, she pulled out a large manila envelope, then sat down next to him on the bed. "This is for you." She beamed, her little freckled nose wrinkling.

"Should I open it?" He was intrigued.

She nodded, smile still bright on her face as he opened the envelope. He slid out a couple of thin pieces of cardboard that were taped together. Setting the envelope aside on the bed, he began to open the tape. Intently, she watched him, both smiling and biting her lower lip.

Schooner smiled back at her, a real smile. *What had she done for him?*

Inside the cardboard was a stack of B&W prints. Looking up at her, he smiled. "When did you do this? We're together all the time."

She shrugged and smiled. "I've been logging in some darkroom time when you're on the courts."

Looking back at the stack, the first photo was of the falls. The landscape was perfect for a B&W rendition with white clouds in stark contrast with what appeared to be an almost black sky. "How did you do that?" he asked.

"Red filter." She seemed proud.

He went to the next photo in the stack. It was a picture of him and Henry pretending to throw Rosie off the edge of the mountain. They both laughed looking at it and he bent over to give Mia a soft kiss. She certainly knew how to make him feel better when he was starting to tank. The third photo in the stack was of their lewd snowman with the giant erection. In this shot, he and Henry each had a hand on the snowman's penis and Rosie was kneeling before the snowman. They couldn't help but break into hysterics upon seeing the picture.

"Oh my God, that is too good." Schooner hooted. "Holy crap."

Both wiping tears from their eyes, they laughed at the funny memory, so perfectly, *and lewdly*, captured for all posterity.

Schooner moved to the next photo and wondered if his gasp was audible. Mia had shot a photo of him in a moment when he was not aware the camera was on him. It was an introspective photo as he was reveling in the pristine beauty of nature. He thought that he'd never seen such a perfect photo of himself. It was really him. "Would you mind if I gave this to my mother? I would really like her to have this."

Mia's smile was brilliant. "I love that idea." She clapped her hands.

There was one photo left and when he lifted the portrait off of it, he felt the stab in his chest. It was a photo Mia had shot of their feet. They were facing each other, his hands were on Mia's shoulders as she pointed the camera down and shot the photo of their sneaker clad feet, toes touching each other. Mia had hand painted the B&W photo, the bottom of her blue jeans, her red and white Converse sneakers, his white sneakers with blue laces and tennis socks with a navy blue border at the ankle.

It was the only picture of Schooner and Mia together that existed.

He stared at the last photo for a while—it wasn't lost on him that this photo was it, the only thing documenting their relationship. Mia had taken a simple B&W photo, painstakingly hand colored it, and brought to life their sweet, quirky love.

Schooner picked up the envelope and photos and put them on the desk so that they would not get ruined. Sitting back down on the bed, he took her face in his hands and kissed her roughly. He was overcome by a myriad of emotions. Her unexpected gift had been so personal and touched him very deeply. He didn't think there was another soul on Earth who got him quite the way she did.

She reached over and started to unbutton his white Ralph Lauren shirt. He just watched her, smiling. A month ago, she would have been way too shy to do this to him. When she had it unbuttoned, she pushed it off his shoulders and got up on her knees on the bed and leaned forward, gently kissing his shoulders and working her way to his neck, where she let her teeth graze his skin.

"Oh Baby Girl, the things I want to do to you."

"Can't wait," she whispered in his ear.

He woke her in the morning before he left for the tennis center. He had his packed duffle bag and was holding the oversized envelope of photos and his racquets. On his head was the black knit cap she had given him. It was pulled down almost to his eyes.

Sitting on the edge of the bed, he brushed her curls from her face and looked at her intently. Not saying anything, he just leaned forward and placed a soft kiss on her lips.

Had he looked closer in the darkened room, he would've seen the two plump tears that had escaped the outer corners of her eyes and rolled into the curls he had just brushed off her face.

But he was already out the door.

Chapter Twenty-One

He had put it off all day. First, he spent time hanging with Beau, hearing all about his month abroad and the hot Ecuatoriana babes (not that he got any). Then, he stretched an extra hour of practice time on the courts hitting balls. From the Psych class he had taken first semester, he knew that this was classic "Escape-Avoidance" behavior. When there was something really unpleasant to do, he wanted to escape confrontation at all costs, and was working himself up to do it, but in the meantime, finding every way he could to avoid it.

He began feeling bad for CJ and he really didn't want to embarrass her or make her feel like she'd been cheated on while she was away. But that is exactly what happened. He fell in love with someone else and while technically he and Mia had not had sex (he was amazed at his own self-control and that Mia was still a virgin), they were lovers in every other sense of the word.

Schooner wondered how much CJ might have heard already about what his Interim had been like. Her roommate, her dorm mates had all seen him with Mia, Rosalie and Henry every day for a month, so this might not come as a huge shock to her. He'd successfully missed every one of her phone calls but one, and was thankful for the poor connection.

Why does this all have to be so difficult? he asked himself. *Why can't I just be with the girl I love?* Schooner's deep-seated fear of disappointing people was raging in full throttle. He just wanted to get it over with and get back to Mia. Wearing the black knit cap pulled almost down to his eyes, he felt like he was taking a little piece of Mia with him that would give him strength.

He walked up the stone steps of the old dorm building and entered the lobby, ignoring everyone that was sitting on the couches. Heading directly to the staircase, he bounded up two at a time. *Let's get this over with,* he thought.

Rapping on her door with his knuckles, he heard her turning the knob. CJ stood before him, looking perfect, wearing her pink satin robe. Before he could even utter a greeting, CJ had flung herself against him, her barely tied robe opening. With her arms snaked around his neck, she pulled him down to her lips. Schooner stumbled through the threshold, not wanting this scene to play out in the hallway.

When she peeled herself off him, she emphatically led him by his hand toward her bed which was covered with beautifully wrapped gifts and gift bags from Europe's finest shops. Although European Capitals had been a course offered through the Political Science Department, it appeared CJ had taken it through the Economics Department, supporting the economies of several European nations.

CJ went into monologue mode and Schooner feared that she knew he was coming to end it with her and was not going to let him speak. He wondered if she was operating under the premise, *if he can't speak, he can't break up with me*.

"I have missed you so much. Everywhere we went, all I could think about was sharing the experience with you. Being away from you made me realize how much I love you and I never want to be apart from you, ever again. Wait until you see all the presents I bought you. You are just going to love the leather racquet covers I got for you in Italy and the silk boxers from France and the blue silk bow tie from England that matches your eyes perfectly …" and she went on and on, not coming up for air.

"CJ," his voice came out harsher than intended, but he had to get her attention and he had to get her to stop talking. "We need to talk."

"Oh baby, we will," she got up off the bed and stood before him allowing her baby pink satin robe to puddle at her ankles.

"CJ, I'm serious." He stood up, not wanting to be on her bed.

"Schooner, I am too." One hand was on his crotch, rubbing his cock through his jeans. The other hand was unbuttoning and unzipping his jeans. She squeezed his cock. Squeezed it in a way he had taught her how to, because it immediately got him rock hard.

"CJ, please stop." He wasn't quite sure what to do. If she was a guy, he would have just shoved her away from him. But she was a girl and shoving her was not appropriate behavior.

"Don't you like the gifts I bought you, Baby?" Her hands were inside his pants and he was beginning to panic.

"We can't…" he sputtered, not finishing the sentence because in a heartbeat she had dropped to her knees and deep-throated him.

"CJ, no…" And he put his hands on her head to push her away. She reached around and grabbed him by the ass and pressed him deeper into her mouth. CJ was using the moves he had taught her against him.

He had never in his life not wanted to be somewhere more than he did not want to be in her room with his cock rammed down her throat. And as if a cruel joke of the universe, the guy who could control himself and make the pleasure last until he was ready, came in about 15 seconds flat. He was mortified and distraught that he had just come in her mouth.

CJ pulled away smiling, a dribble of Schooner's cum at the corner of her pink lips. She slowly cleaned it with a lick from the tip of her tongue.

"By how quickly you came, it's clear that you missed me, too," she purred.

Schooner didn't know how to decipher the onslaught of emotions flooding in and drowning him. Anger (*at her or himself?*), disgust (*definitely at himself*), disappointment (*overwhelmingly at himself*), confusion (*how the hell did that just happen*) and death of a dream (*he could feel the pain already seeping in)*.

As the walls were closing around him and sound began to muffle, Schooner felt like he was tumbling down the rabbit hole. He would learn, much later in life, that this was a panic attack.

CJ picked up her robe and eased back into it, letting it hang open.

He looked at her blankly and said, "I've got to go." Practically running from the room. He could not escape fast enough.

As he closed the door, he heard her scream after him, "I hate that hat."

Making it only as far as the stairwell, Schooner leaned his head against the cold stone wall. It felt good against his face. A few deep breaths later and he knew he had to get out of there. Rushing through the lobby, head down, he ignored the multiple greetings from all the girls who knew him as "CJ's boyfriend."

Outside the night air offered a welcome caress to his hot cheeks. He descended the stone stairs, less than a mere ten minutes after having ascended them.

Without a destination, he started to walk. He couldn't go to Mia's dorm. His own dorm room would be intensely claustrophobic, especially now with Beau in there. "Where to? Where to? I need to think," he muttered aloud.

With lights glowing against the night sky, the track beckoned and he began to run.

What the fuck did I just let happen? I didn't break up with her. She fucking sucked my cock and I freaking came in her mouth. What do I tell Mia? She grabbed me and before I knew it my cock was in her mouth and I didn't want to come, but I did—really fucking fast. I love you, Baby Girl and I was just in someone else's mouth, but I didn't fuck her (great consolation).

Holy crap, I can't go to Mia's room now. How can I tell her the truth?

And if I did, she would probably throw me out. She's going to hate me. Fuck, I hate me. Could I disappoint more people? Could I be a bigger fucking disappointment? How the hell did I fuck this up so royally? What the fuck am I going to do? How do I make this better? How do I fix this? Fuck. Fuck. Fuck.

Over an hour later, Schooner stepped off the track. He had no answers. There was no way he could go to Mia tonight and tell her what had happened. He couldn't bear to see the hurt, the disappointment. But if he no-showed her tonight, she'd think they were over, that he'd gone back to CJ. And although they probably were over, because of what he had let happen, he couldn't even consider being back with CJ.

With what seemed like no plausible options, he finally went back to his dorm, thankfully finding a jetlagged Beau was already crashed out. Schooner went to his desk and took the oversized envelope out of the drawer. He pulled out the picture Mia had shot of their feet and just stared at it.

"I am so sorry, Baby Girl," he whispered to the picture. "I love you so much and I know I don't deserve you. I don't know how to fix this." He slid the picture back into its envelope and placed it back in the desk drawer.

He lay in bed staring at the darkened ceiling for what felt like hours, knowing that he had just ruined everything. He ached, realizing the pain it was going to cause Mia, and knowing that five minutes of his life had robbed him of everything he had ever wanted and dreamed. Laying on top of his blankets, fully clothed, he pulled his black cap over his eyes, and at that moment felt close to the character in Springsteen's "*The River,*" whose loss of dreams felt more devastating than lies.

How ironic, he thought as he finally drifted off into an uneasy sleep, *even he was now thinking about Springsteen songs and yet he'd never know if Rick or Wendy won the bet.*

Chapter Twenty-Two

Schooner went into a deep funk, avoiding everyone and everything, with the exception of the tennis courts. He'd never experienced anything like it before. Getting out of bed every day took everything he had, his concentration was shit, he had to force food down his throat to keep his strength up to make it through tennis practice.

Every night after he finished his reading and homework assignments, he went to the track and ran. Running was the only time he could get into his head and process his misery. The lone workout helped ease the pain which felt like it was oozing out of him in waves.

His weight was dropping and his boyish face became more angular. The black cap took its place as a new permanent feature, except he was on the courts where it was against regulations. Pulled down to his eyes, the gift Mia once gave him, became a part of his dark, haunted look. Now, instead of appearing like a gorgeous All-American boy, Schooner had the look of a handsome, bad boy model.

He was aware of Mia's schedule and made sure he avoided all the routes she would be taking to her classes. The dining hall was no exception and he avoided times when he thought that either she or CJ might be there. When he wasn't in class, Schooner was on the courts or in his room studying.

When the first travel weekend came, he was glad to get off campus and away from everything that added to his misery. He couldn't look anywhere on campus without something reminding him of their time together. It wasn't difficult, he found, to loathe himself for destroying the best thing he'd ever had and for hurting the only girl he'd ever loved.

On Valentine's Day, CJ showed up at his dorm room. Beau happily let her in. She flirted with him a little and then he quickly cleared the room to give Schooner and CJ some privacy.

With wide, sad eyes, she handed Schooner a package wrapped in red.

"I don't have anything for you," he said.

She nodded and said, "Please open it."

Carefully, he tore the paper from the package and opened the box. Inside was a black photo frame holding an 8 x 10 of Schooner and CJ in their matching red sweaters on the stairs in her parent's home.

Can this get worse? he thought, but smiled politely and thanked her. He even went so far as to tell her she looked very beautiful in the photo.

"Schooner," she began, "I'm offering an olive branch here and I hope you'll take it. I want you to know that I forgive you."

"You forgive me?" he tried to keep his tone even, but was thinking, *What the hell are you talking about?*

"Yes, Schooner," she said through very tight teeth. "I forgive you." She paused for a moment, took a deep breath and straightened her back. "This is a small school. Not a lot happens that people don't find out about."

Schooner just looked at her. He was feeling so dead inside. He thought if he'd had a pair of sunglasses sitting on his desk, he would've slipped them on, even though it was nighttime and he was indoors.

When he didn't answer, she continued. "I want to put Interim behind us. I want you back, Schooner."

"Why?" he asked, totally stupefied.

"Because I love you."

Sighing, he sat down on his bed. "CJ, you love the idea of me. You do not love me, because frankly, you have no clue who I am."

"How can you even say that?" she protested, her beautiful alabaster skin starting to turn red, as the tension increased.

"Because it's true. You love that we look great together, and I'm not going to lie to you, that was part of the initial attraction for me, too. We look like we belong together. But I'm not me around you, CJ. I'm someone you want me to be. And I don't want to be that person anymore."

She sat down on his bed next to him and took his hands in hers. "Please don't give up on us. I know I can make you happy."

He was shaking his head no. Only one person in the world could make him happy and he'd never have the chance to show her just how happy she made him. He didn't deserve her.

"I can. I can," she insisted. "Please let me."

And so, he let her. This time he didn't come so quickly (*another tragic joke from the universe,* he thought, wryly) and decided that maybe this was what he deserved.

After she left that night, Schooner picked up the picture frame and looked at the toothpaste commercial photograph inside the frame. Turning the frame over, he opened it up and slipped out the picture of him and CJ. Opening the desk drawer, he pulled out the oversized envelope and extracted the feet picture, put it into the frame and closed the back. Turning the frame over, he studied the hand painted B&W photo.

Setting the frame down on the desk next to his bed, he faced the feet image so that he could view it.

"I am so sorry, Mia. I am so sorry."

It was a few days later, when he was walking on The Quad that Mia and Rosie were walking toward him. It was the first time he had seen her since he'd left her in her bed that last morning. He felt his heart stop at just the sight of her. As they approached, he said, "Hi," searching her face for something, anything. She stuck her chin up in the air and did not make eye contact with him. As he passed them, he heard Rosie say, "You should get your fucking hat back from him." Schooner turned around and Rosie was turned around sneering at him. Mia never turned around.

Closing his eyes, Schooner let out a deep exhale, trying to lessen the force squeezing his heart and not letting up. Consciously, he breathed in deeply through his nose and blew it out slowly through his mouth until the pain in his chest subsided. Telepathically, he tried to send her a message, *I'm wearing your hat, Baby Girl—doesn't that tell you something?*

The next two times he passed them on The Quad, the exact same thing happened. He said, "Hi" to them and Mia's chin went up in the air. The first time Rosie muttered, "Douche," and the second time he thought he heard her say, "God, he really looks gaunt."

He looked in the mirror that afternoon, doing an examination like he had not done in a long time and realized Rosie was right. The tennis, the running, the appetite loss—he did look gaunt. *Crap, I look like shit,* he realized.

And for the first time in his life, he felt his inner vision matched his outer visage.

A week later, he saw them again walking toward him on The Quad. Maybe someday I'll get a hello back, he hoped. As they approached, he said, "Hi." There was still no verbal response, but Mia looked at him for the first time. Her eyes seemed flat and he hoped his eyes said to her, "I am so, so sorry, Baby Girl."

It was an evening in early March when he saw Mia, Rosie and Henry in the dining hall for the first time and he ached to go sit with his old friends. Knowing that wasn't possible, he went and joined his dorm mates at the next table. Sitting on the bench facing the opposite direction of Mia so that he could look at her, all he wanted was to steal a few glances, even though every one ignited a stabbing pain through his chest.

Schooner pretended to listen to the guys and made a few attempts to laugh at some of their jokes. When he caught her looking at him, he tried to smile at her, but a cold veil dropped back down over her face and she looked away. He knew he had made it worse by never going to talk to her. Hours had stretched into days, which slowly became weeks, and now over a month had gone by. It was too late to try and rectify the damage.

Over a glass of milk, he was willing her, *Mia look at me, just look at me* and she did. He put the glass of milk down and was just beginning to mouth to her, "I …." when he saw her eyes, first questioning, and then widening, as CJ and her roommate sat down next to him, and momentarily blocked his view, before he finished what he was trying to say to Mia. He felt the panic rise. He didn't finish telling her. She saw CJ sit down next to him. *Shit. Shit. Shit.*

CJ was talking to him, but he couldn't hear her, he was trying to look past her to make eye contact with Mia again, but her seat was empty. Looking toward the exit in time to see her mane of curls pass through the door. His first thought was, "I need to stop her."

CJ put a hand on his forearm, dragging him back into reality. He looked at her, not focused as she asked sweetly, "Will you please pass the salt?"

He passed it to her and then sat silently while she chatted with her roommate.

I cannot catch a break, he thought.

Chapter Twenty-Three

As he passed by the Coach's office at the end of practice, Schooner heard the coach call to him.

"How are you doing, Schooner?" he asked.

"Great, Coach. I think having the indoor tennis center and extra practice time has made a huge difference in my game. I feel good."

Coach's glance was intense. "I'm concerned about you, son. Why don't you have a seat."

Oh shit, thought Schooner. *This is not just a casual conversation.*

"Sir?"

"The intensity you have brought to the court these last few months, well—it can be good and bad. The good is, we've been clocking your first serves at 111 MPH and you're only a freshman. If I have you on the team for a few more years, we'll be kicking everyone in the division's butts and you'll be at the top of the NCAA rankings. But after watching you these last few weeks, I'm not so sure this intensity is borne out of a good thing. You are angry, Schooner."

Schooner sat silently for a moment and then took a deep breath. "Yes, Coach. I am angry".

"Who or what has made you so very angry?" pressed the coach.

Looking Coach directly in the eyes, Schooner admitted, "I'm mad at myself, sir."

Coach nodded and didn't say anything for a while. "Son, I see you as leading this team. I think with another year under your belt, you will make a fine team captain."

Schooner was shocked by the coach's statement and sure that the surprise was registering all over his face. "Wow. Thank you, sir. That is a tremendous compliment. I really appreciate your faith in me."

"I'd like to see you have that same faith in yourself, son. I don't know what the circumstances are that you are continuing to punish yourself for, but what I see is a young man filled with remorse. Whatever it is, you need to let it go. You can't keep up this penance, Schooner. It's not healthy and you need to work on getting healthy."

It was a few moments before Schooner looked up at the coach. "I didn't realize it was that obvious."

"You need to look in a mirror more often, son. Your weight loss has been pretty dramatic and you look haunted."

"I've been running," Schooner offered.

The coach made a *hmm* sound. "You certainly have been running. It's time to stop. You need to figure out a healthier way to work through your issues."

Schooner sat silently for a few moments, then looked Coach in the eyes. "Thank you. I appreciate this talk."

Coach nodded. He was done talking.

Schooner left his office. The talk had been like a splash of cold water on Schooner's face. It was time to take control again. He'd been spiraling downward for so long, it was hard to figure out how to put the brakes on, but the coach was right and he needed to figure out how to pull himself out of this.

Some habits die hard, he mused. For the only thing he really wanted to do that day was tell Mia that the coach felt he could be the team captain. Team captain of one of the top ranked tennis programs in the country. He still wanted her to be proud of him.

Chapter Twenty-Four

CJ showed up at Schooner's room with yet another package in hand.

"What's this?" he asked.

"It's part one," she responded. The box was from Hugo Boss. "I bought this for you in London." Inside was a blue raw silk bow tie.

"It's really nice," he looked up at her, questioningly.

"Well, when I was in Hugo Boss, I bought something for myself, too." she smiled and shrugged.

"I'm thinking that maybe there's a dress in this color somewhere in this story."

CJ laughed, "You know me well." She then took a deep breath. "Will you take me to the Spring Fling?"

The Spring Fling was the annual spring formal dance and the tradition was that the girls invited the guys and then took them to dinner before the dance. The dance was usually held in the ballroom of a hotel facility and this year's was at The Huntington Sheraton in Pasadena.

CJ immediately picked up on Schooner's hesitation and forged right on. "I have not asked much of you and this really means a lot to me, Schooner." CJ had made a ritual of showing up at Schooner's room several times a week. Sexual activity was limited to CJ blowing Schooner. He knew that her hope was if she waited it out, all would go back to "normal."

"Okay, sure."

"Really!" she squealed and threw her arms around his neck, planting kisses all over his face. "We are going to have the best time."

"Sounds great," he offered, trying to feign enthusiasm. He had taken the coach's talk to heart and knew it was time to start living again. His misery had been spiraling down for so long that he knew taking little steps, like saying yes to CJ for this dance she wanted to go to, would help stop the descending momentum.

Baby steps, he thought, but at the same time wondered if Mia was going to be there. Maybe she'd take Henry or maybe there was someone special in one of her classes this semester. He didn't know. He didn't know anything about her world anymore.

And from that, a fantasy was born about the Spring Fling. He would see Mia there, come up behind her and her date as they danced and cut in.

Mia would be in his arms before she had the time to protest and somehow, he would find the words to make it all right. She'd see how much he loved her. And this time, he would not let her go. Not now. Not ever.

He knew chances were, *Miss I'm Not into the Group Kumbayah Thing*, would probably not be there, but if she was… There would be at least one dance in his arms. He would not take no for an answer.

Chapter Twenty-Five

The Huntington Sheraton had been built just after the turn of the century and was one of the architectural gems of Pasadena. The hotel harkened back to a time past of refinement and luxury. CJ, her roommate and another friend had rented a limo to take them all to the hotel, where they had arranged dinner for the guys before the dance.

CJ looked breathtaking that evening in her Hugo Boss dress of sky blue raw silk that matched Schooner's eyes. Her long blonde hair was styled in an elaborate up do with soft tendrils falling around her face. In his black suit with the matching bow tie that CJ had given him, Schooner and CJ were red carpet worthy. A photographer could have come along and shot a Vogue spread of them that evening.

Tucking her hand inside of Schooner's in the limo, CJ smiled at her handsome date. He surprised her when he gave her hand a squeeze and did not pull away. The vow he had made to himself for the evening was to make the best of the situation and be on his best behavior, which meant no sulking.

There were photographers set up at the entrance to the hotel, capturing photos of the arriving couples, that would later be available for purchase. Schooner and CJ posed in the grand entranceway and Schooner, no stranger to the camera, was able to give CJ the photo he knew she so very much wanted.

Heads turned as the golden couple walked through the lobby of the hotel. And it wasn't just a few people—every head turned. Hotel guests assumed they were some young Hollywood stars. A leading man and his beautiful starlet lady. They had people that they did not know literally walk up to them to tell them how beautiful they looked. CJ was in her glory. Schooner was mildly distracted, but mostly embarrassed. And it dawned on him, he had really changed. Somewhere along the way, the superficial California boy had been left behind.

He was thrilled that the girls had dinner set up in a small wine cellar so that there were not a million sets of eyes on him, watching as they ate. Dining with them was one of his dorm mates, Dane. Schooner knew Dane only casually, and was pleasantly surprised when Dane turned out to be an amusing conversationalist, keeping the dinner talk going and regaling them all with stories of growing up abroad. As a State Department brat, he'd lived throughout Southeast Asia from the time he was six, until he came back to the states for college. Fluent in multiple languages, his plans were to join the Foreign Service upon graduation.

From dinner, they headed upstairs to the Georgian Ballroom, one of two ballrooms retained throughout many remodeling's of the grand hotel. An arched ceiling, dotted with crystal chandeliers and intricate gilt work, canopied the ballroom and transported its occupants more to a Baroque era than a Georgian one, Schooner observed.

The ballroom was crowded, dark and smoky. Tables were set up along the perimeter of the room with the dance floor located center. It was very loud, making it impossible to hear what anyone was saying. Schooner found himself smiling and nodding at people, not having a clue as to what was being said to him. *Nod every so often and laugh at intervals and you'll be good*, he decided.

He danced much of the evening with CJ, her roommate and several of her friends, hung out with some of his tennis teammates and dorm mates and spent a lot of time people watching. CJ was truly in her glory and he could envision her in the future throwing lavish events and holding court—clearly the most beautiful woman in the room.

The evening was not nearly as painful as he had anticipated. It was actually good to be amongst the living again, even though his fantasy dance with Mia did not come to pass. Although he'd hoped, he hadn't really expected her to be there.

As they were descending the hotel steps toward their limo, CJ noted, "Wasn't so bad, was it?"

"I had a really good time tonight. Thank you." And he meant it.

The limo dropped them off and Schooner walked CJ up to her room, secretly thrilled that her roommate was right there. He stayed in the hall to say goodnight to her.

She put her hands on both of his arms and looked up at him. "Tonight meant a lot to me, Schooner."

He smiled at her, "I know."

"Thank you," she mouthed the words. Then asked, "Can you promise me something?"

"Depends."

"Promise me you'll try."

"CJ, why do you want to settle for this?"

She looked at him wide-eyed, "Because I know how good we can be together. Please try," she pleaded. "Please."

"I'm not trying to be difficult, CJ, but neither of us should have to be trying. It should just be natural. This shouldn't be work."

A hurt look eclipsed her beautiful face. "I'm work?"

"I didn't mean it that way. Look, I had a great time tonight. I really did. Thank you for asking me. Thank you for a great dinner. And thank you for this." He fingered the beautiful, classic silk bow tie which was now hanging untied around his collar.

"Can we call tonight a start?" she asked.

He smiled and nodded his head. "I can live with that."

"Okay, me too." She smiled.

He gave her a hug and a quick kiss on the lips. "You looked beautiful tonight." And with that, he was off down the hall. Bounding down the steps of the dorm, he turned onto the sidewalk of The Quad, thankful for to be alone and breathe in the night air.

Hands in his suit pockets and head down, Schooner started toward his dorm. He was glad he'd made it through the night, and fairly painlessly at that, until the end, and he wondered if tonight was actually one step forward and two steps back. He knew that as much as he'd had to push himself, the socializing was good for him and he really had enjoyed it after months of self-imposed exile. Schooner knew he needed to rejoin the world. *Tonight was a start at trying to have a life again—but was it also a step backwards,* he wondered, thinking about his conversation with CJ. *Was it a start or merely a restart?*

Along with knowing he needed to learn from his mistakes and that falling back into old patterns would be anything but a new start, came the realization that he was no longer the same person he had been when school first started in the fall. He so desperately wanted to be happy again. It was as that thought crossed his consciousness that he saw her walking up ahead on the empty quad. The telltale mane of dark curls bounced behind her.

"Mia," he yelled. He hadn't planned to. It was a gut reaction, as was taking off in a fast jog to catch up to her. "Mia. Mia, stop."

She kept walking, quickening her pace (which was a moot point based on the difference in their leg lengths).

"Mia." Schooner caught up to her and was walking beside her. "Mia, talk to me," he pleaded.

She remained silent, walking as fast as she could, head down.

"C'mon Mia."

"Schooner. Leave. Me. Alone."

"Sorry, but you are not getting that lucky tonight." He was now a foot in front of her walking backwards and talking to the top of her head, because she wouldn't look up at him. "Mia, I know I fucked up. I fucked up because I didn't come and talk to you. What you assumed happened, didn't happen. Actually, it's never happened. But something did happen and I felt so awful and I just didn't know how to come to you because I thought you'd just tell me to go fuck myself, and I didn't know what to do and clearly doing nothing was the worst thing I could've done. I am so, so sorry, Mia."

"Schooner, go fuck yourself. Okay, you happy now? Self-fulfilling prophecy. Now leave me the fuck alone," her voice was rising dangerously loud and high.

He stopped walking backwards and she either had to stop or bump into him. She stopped and immediately put his hands on her shoulders to stop her.

Mia stepped back to get away from him, recoiling from his touch, which landed like a sharp blow to Schooner's gut. She had physically cringed when he touched her and the devastation rushed over him in a wave, dragging him under. As she stepped back to avoid his touch, the light from the streetlamp captured her in its glow. It took Schooner a moment to process that something did not look quite right. Mia's shirt was ripped open, exposing part of her right breast and it looked like there was blood on her shirt.

"Oh my God, Mia, what happened to you? Who did this to you?" Alarms were going off inside of him exploding like a string of Roman candles on July 4th.

She tried to sidestep him. "Schooner, get the fuck out of my way. *Now*."

"Not a chance." He blocked her with his body. "Mia, look at me."

"Schooner, please let me go," her voice cracked and he felt his own throat close. The irony of those words were not lost on him.

Reaching out, he gently lifted her chin so that he could see her face. She winced and he realized that he was hurting her. The bile began to crest in his throat as the streetlamp revealed her bruised jaw and bloody lip—which from the looks of it was still bleeding as fresh, wet blood glistened in the light over the already caked, dried blood.

Enveloping her in his arms, he protectively crushed her to his chest. She immediately stiffened like a steel rod. "Oh my God, Baby Girl."

"You have *no* right to call me that," she hissed and it felt as if her body were shrinking in his arms, as if she were imploding upon herself, trying to somehow become smaller and smaller, so that she could actually disconnect totally from his touch, and disappear.

In that moment, he was glad she was as stiff as steel, because his knees were starting to buckle and although she didn't realize it, she was the one holding him up. Feeling the pain and fear radiating off her, intuitively he knew, beyond a shadow of a doubt, that this was not just a mugging.

His Baby Girl had been raped.

Chapter Twenty-Six

Schooner stood there with his arms around Mia, swaying back and forth, for what seemed to be a long while, but he guessed that maybe it was only a few short moments. She let him hold her. And he needed to hold her. He needed to give her his strength, his protection, hoping that he could transfer his energy to her by just holding her tight.

I'm going to kill the motherfucker who did this to her. Kill with my fucking bare hands. Calm down, need to protect, don't scare her, keep a level head, I'm going to kill whoever did this, we need to go to the police, I need to get her to the ER, I should've been with her tonight.

With thoughts all over the place, he fought to streamline them into a coherent plan of action. He needed to take care of her and he needed to do it now and that needed to happen by him taking control. She needed him to think for them both.

Still holding her, he gently kissed the top of her head. "Mia, we need to go to the police."

She panicked and began to thrash in his arms, "No. I can't go to the police. I'll get sent home. They'll make me go home." She was in full panic mode, her eyes wide with fear.

"Okay. Okay. Okay." Still rocking back and forth as he held her tight, Schooner gently stroked her hair attempting to soothe her, or maybe to calm himself—he wasn't really sure. "No police." He understood what she was thinking.

Mia was still a minor. Her parents would come and pull her out of college. But it made him sick to think this animal would be out there, would get away with this. His anger soared just knowing this creep could do this to someone else. Consciously, he pushed his rising fury away. We'll deal with that later, he thought. Take care of Mia now.

With a shrug, he slipped out of his suit jacket and draped it over Mia. Putting his arm around her shoulders, he turned her around and started walking her toward the entrance of campus. She went along willingly, sobs racking her body every few minutes.

"Shhh, it's going to be okay, Baby Girl." But he wasn't sure that it would ever be okay again.

They walked for several blocks in silence before she seemed to realize that they were no longer on campus. "Where are we going?" she asked, through her tears.

"To the ER," he said softly. Then added, "Is that okay?"

She nodded and he pulled her closer into him, again kissing the top of her head. *I am never going to let her out of my sight again*, he thought. *Ever*.

As they walked through the silent streets of the city, he felt closer to the animal kingdom than he'd ever felt before (he would feel this way a few more times in his life, when each of his children were born). Animals protect and kill. He got it.

There was so much he wanted to say to her, to promise her, but it all was going to have to wait. What he wanted didn't matter right now. The only thing that mattered was getting Mia immediate medical attention and then helping get her through the aftermath. If she'd let him.

The hospital was finally in view, just a few blocks more to go. "Are you doing okay?" he asked.

She nodded her head.

"Good girl." He rubbed her arm.

They entered the bright, unfriendly glare of the emergency room, eyes adjusting to coming in from the dark. There were only a few people in the waiting room. A Hispanic couple with a small infant, a guy who had his arm in ice and his friend who was with him and a middle-aged couple. The large waiting room was nearly empty and there was plenty of room, so they would not have to sit near anyone else.

"Sit here." Schooner led her to a bank of chairs in a section where no one was seated. "I'll go see about getting you checked in, okay."

As Schooner approached the reception desk, the nurse looked up and smiled, appreciatively. It was then he realized he was still in his white dress shirt and suit pants with his sky-blue bow tie hanging open.

"Hi," he began. "I'm here with a friend of mine and she's been attacked tonight and I think she's probably been raped."

"You're not sure if she's been raped?"

Schooner shook his head, "No. But I think it's highly likely."

She handed him a clipboard to fill out some basic information and he went back to where Mia was sitting.

"You hanging in there?" he asked. She looked like a little kid playing in her parent's closet in his suit jacket. He was glad that she was wrapped up in it and the telltale evidence of her ripped shirt out of view.

"Barely."

"You're doing great," he reassured her. "Help me with this, okay." He wanted to distract her and motioned to the clipboard.

"Birthday?" He realized he didn't even know when her birthday was.

"July 12th."

"Ahhh, a summer baby. You never had to be in school for your birthday," he commented, as he wrote down her birth day, pausing at the year, before writing down the year of his birth, instead of hers. She was right, the fact that she was still a minor would cause a whole host of issues. He wanted to spare her anything she didn't think she could deal with or need to deal with.

Mia saw what Schooner wrote and whispered, "Thank you." He looked at her and winked, conspiratorially. She smiled for the first time and he could see how much it hurt her lip to smile.

"Insurance?" he asked.

"I'm covered under my parent's plan, but I don't want..." He could see the tears welling up and the panic grabbing her like a riptide, and immediately, he cut her off.

"No worries." He pulled out his wallet and filled in his credit card information on the form.

She started to cry.

"Hey," he said to her, pointedly.

"Sorry." She sniffed and he smiled at her.

Schooner brought the completed form back to reception and waited with Mia until they called her in to Triage.

He walked her to the door. "I'll be waiting out here. If you want me with you at any point, send someone out to get me, okay?"

She nodded, a sob escaping.

He hugged her tightly once more and kissed the top of her head. "I'll be right here."

And she disappeared behind the door.

Schooner went and sat back down. He wanted to be there on the other side of the door with her. *This has got to be so scary for her,* he thought. *Or was it? Compared to what she'd already endured that evening.* He was on overload, just muddling through and could not even begin to imagine what Mia was going through.

"Mr. Moore?" A hand on his shoulder drew him out of his reverie. How long had he been sitting there?

"Is she okay? Is everything alright?" he asked the young emergency room doctor. He was glad for Mia's sake that the doctor was a woman.

"She's doing okay, considering the circumstances," she paused. "Do you know much of what happened to her tonight?"

"No." He shook his head. "I saw her walking. It didn't take long to realize there was a problem and I got her to come here."

The doctor smiled and put a hand on Schooner's forearm. "You're a good friend."

Not quite, he thought.

The doctor continued, "She told me that it was alright to fill you in on some of the details. Sometimes it's easier to have a third party deliver the information." She paused again, "Mia was raped by two men tonight."

Sound immediately began to fade away. He could see the doctor's lips still moving for a brief moment before the room began to spin. Schooner hurtled head first, tumbling down a tunnel. He heard his own voice say, from somewhere, "bathroom" and the doctor led him by the arm to a bathroom fortuitously located only a few feet away. He made it as far as the sink before vomiting. Endless waves and waves wrenched his gut muscles. *Two men, oh my God. One must've held her, while the other…* and the retching began again.

When the dry heaves finally ended, the doctor was waiting with a cup of water. She led him out to the chairs again and they sat down.

"Are you okay?" she asked and he nodded.

"Mia doesn't want to bring in the authorities."

"I know. I wanted her to go to the police, but she refused."

"Do you think you can change her mind? I wouldn't pressure her about it tonight, but maybe over the next few days. These animals need to be off the street."

"I agree, Doctor." He felt his anger rising again and consciously told himself to check it.

"She's got some pretty significant bruising, but x-rays didn't show any fractures. I'm going to be giving her some high dosage hormones that we typically use in rape cases. They basically make the uterus an inhospitable environment for egg implantation and we can help mitigate the odds of pregnancy."

Schooner felt the warm rush of tears coursing down his cheeks. This was a fucking nightmare.

The doctor continued, "The biggest side effect we see with this type of treatment is nausea and vomiting, so don't be alarmed if that happens. If it appears she's dehydrating, I want you to call me. I'm also going to prescribe pain killers and some anti-anxiety medication that will help her sleep." She handed Schooner her card. "I'm going to sew up her lip now and she asked if you'd come back and be with her while I do it."

He followed the doctor back into the authorized area past small curtain partitioned rooms, until they got to Mia's.

"Hey you…" He smiled at her. Knowing he had to keep it together for her, consciously he collected himself as they walked through the ER to her room. "So, you want me back here for the gory stuff, huh."

"Stitches seemed like a guy thing."

He was so happy to hear her banter.

The doctor was loading a syringe of Lidocaine to numb the area. "I think I can do this in about four stitches, Mia, and I'm going to make them as small as I can so that you won't have any significant scarring."

Maybe not of her lip, Schooner thought and was hoping Mia was not thinking the same thing.

"Okay, I'm going to numb the area now and we'll let it sit for a few minutes to take full effect."

Mia grabbed Schooner's hand, squeezing tightly, as the doctor injected the numbing agent around her mouth.

He rubbed her knuckles with his thumb to calm her down. "You're doing great, Baby Girl," he encouraged, squeezing her hand back.

"I'll be back in a few minutes." The doctor left Mia's room to attend to one of the other patients.

Siting on the side of the bed facing Mia, Schooner continued to hold her hand. "You are so brave," he whispered. "I have always been in awe of you."

Two fat tears rolled slowly down her cheeks. "I wanted you to be my first," her voice broke.

He felt hot tears splashing down his face and leaned his forehead against hers. "I will be, Baby Girl. When you are ready, I will be the first guy to make love to you. I'll be your first." Schooner didn't know if his face was wet from his tears or hers, but cheek to cheek they sat and cried together. Cried for the loss of a dream that had been savagely ripped from them.

Your first and your last, Baby Girl, Schooner vowed to himself. *Your first and your last.*

Chapter Twenty-Seven

Mia fell asleep lying in the back seat of the cab with her head in Schooner's lap.

"Baby Girl, we're here." Gently waking her as they pulled up in front of the dorm, he paid the cab driver and they walked up the front steps. Schooner took Mia's keys from her and opened the door. Feeling the dangling little silver camera made him smile. It was past 4 A.M. and the lobby was dark and empty. They walked down the hall and up the staircase, Schooner with his arm around Mia who was still wearing his suit jacket.

Unlocking the door to her room, he flipped the light on, immediately thankful that her roommate Caroline was staying at the Sheraton in Pasadena with her boyfriend, Dennis. Tossing the keys onto Mia's desk, he turned to her.

Mia looked drained as she gazed up at him and sighed, "What a fucking night."

Cocking his head to the side with a sad look that matched hers, he held out his open arms to her. Without hesitation, she went to him, wrapping her arms around his waist as he held her tight.

"You got really skinny," she observed, looking up at him with a wry smile.

He wanted to tell her that it was called "The Misery Diet," but he didn't want to say anything that would make her feel bad or upset her.

"Let's get you in bed, Mia. You need to rest." He opened their mini-fridge and pulled out a bottle of water and poured her a cup. Taking the prescription bottles out of his suit pants pocket, he got Mia the pills she needed.

She had changed into an oversized tee-shirt while his back was turned and he suspected there were probably some bruises she didn't want him to see. She sat down cross-legged in the center of her bed and he sat on the edge and handed her the water and medication.

"You'll tell Rosie and Henry?" she asked, eyes filling with tears again.

Schooner nodded and reached out to stroke her cheek.

She leaned her face into his hand, closing her eyes.

"Okay, under the covers, Baby Girl." She slid underneath her bedspread and he tucked her in, smiling down at her.

Mia reached for Schooner's hand and brought it up to her lips, kissing his palm and then held his hand in both of hers. "Thank you for everything tonight."

"Shhhh," he stroked her hair gently.

After a few minutes, she drifted off to sleep, a combination of exhaustion, pain meds and anti-anxiety pills taking effect.

He waited several minutes to make sure she was in a deep sleep, leaned down and softly kissed her forehead.

Grabbing her keys, Schooner headed down the hall to Rosie's room. Aware that it was now after 4:30 A.M., he knew this was not going to be a pleasant greeting when he knocked on her door.

Rosie opened the door, looked at Schooner and sneered. "What the fuck?"

"Good morning to you, too. Throw on a robe Rosie, we need to go grab Henry and talk."

"What are you, high?"

"I wish I was. Get your robe on." And he leveled her a "do what I say now" glance. He was beyond taking her shit tonight.

Schooner was three steps in front of Rosie when she started following him down the hall, into the stairwell and downstairs to Henry's room.

Again, he began the process. Although, at least, Henry was a little more civil. "Hey, sorry to wake you. Throw on your robe. We need to talk."

Henry emerged from his room and Rosie just shrugged her shoulders at him as Schooner started walking toward the study lounge, the room where they had spent many hours together laughing and creating their masterpiece. They just followed him silently.

Flipping on the lights, they entered the room and Schooner motioned for them to sit, before closing the door.

"Nice outfit," Rosie snarked. His blue bow tie was still hanging open around his neck, but now the top few buttons of his shirt were open.

"Yeah, well it's been a long night," he ignored the snark. "Mia is upstairs in her room and she's asleep. She's okay, she's safe in bed, but she wanted me to talk to you guys." He could see the immediate alarm on Henry's face. Rosie was too pissed off to register any emotion other than, well, pissed off.

"I ran into Mia a few hours ago walking on The Quad and she had been attacked."

They both screamed, "What?" and "Oh my God!"

"What do you mean attacked?" Rosie was yelling and Henry put a hand on her shoulder to calm her.

Schooner sighed. "She was roughed up pretty bad. And she was raped."

Rosie burst into tears, her tough resolve evaporating at the mention of the word rape, "No. No. No," she moaned.

Henry put his arms around her and Schooner could see the anguish in his eyes and the pulsing tension in his strong jaw.

"I took her to the hospital and she received medical attention. She needed a few stitches because they busted her lip."

"They?" Henry's eyes flew open wide.

Schooner just nodded, the sick feeling rising again, as tears sprung from his eyes. Taking the heels of his palms, he openly wiped away his tears. When he was able to get control of his voice, he continued. "There were two," his voice cracked, despite his best efforts to hold it together. "The doctor gave her some hormones to help mitigate the chances of pregnancy," his voice broke on the word pregnancy, "and pain killers and anti-anxiety medicine." He sat down and put his head in his hands.

"She doesn't want to bring in the authorities, because she's afraid she'll get sent home. She was adamant about that. And I understand her not wanting to go through all that shit, but those fucking animals are out there." His anger was flaring. "And I just want to kill them."

"What can we do to help her?" Henry asked, softly.

"She doesn't want anyone to know about this." They nodded and agreed. "If you can bring her meals to the dorm and get class assignments and stuff. I don't think she's going to want anyone to see her just yet."

"Are you going to stay with her?" Henry asked.

Schooner nodded, yes.

Rosie flashed him a look filled with venom. "And what are you? The fucking white knight? You blow in playing big man savior and then you break her heart to pieces again. Don't you fuck with my girl." She was out of her chair and wagging a finger in Schooner's face.

He surprised her by taking her finger and kissing it, causing confusion in her big brown eyes.

Schooner began softly, "I know I'm not your favorite person, Rosie. As a matter of fact, I haven't been my favorite person either. Something happened, and it's not what you think happened, but I didn't want to hurt Mia and I didn't want her to tell me goodbye, and I fucked everything up. I just fucked up." Looking up at the ceiling, in an attempt to stop a torrent of tears, he finally was able to look Rosie straight in the eyes. "But I never stopped loving her for a single second. I don't think I'll ever stop loving her."

And the tears he tried so hard to stop fell freely from his beautiful eyes.

"We're going to need to tell Caroline when she gets back." Schooner was thinking out loud.

"Caroline can stay with me, if she wants to, so that you can stay with Mia." Rosie offered, softening from her previous stance and Schooner nodded.

"Schooner," Rosie began, "you look like shit."

He knew she was referring to his new *haunted* look.

"I think he looks hot!" Henry countered, putting his arms around Schooner and giving him a much-needed hug, which Schooner gladly accepted.

They walked Schooner up to Mia's room. "We'll bring you guys breakfast."

Schooner quietly opened the door knowing they wanted to come in and see their friend to make sure she was really okay. Mia was on her back snoring loudly and that gave them all a relaxing chuckle. Seeing her pretty little face bruised up was heartbreaking.

Rosie took Schooner's hand on the way out of the room and gave it a squeeze. No words were needed.

Sitting down on the desk chair across from her bed, Schooner stretched out his long legs and tried to start processing everything, but his mind was just too jumbled. He knew he needed sleep and maybe things would be clearer after a few hours of rest, but he just wanted to look at her for a few minutes more. Watch her sleep. Know that she was safe.

Finally, he took off his dress shoes and socks. They had been on his feet way too long. Hanging his shirt (with the bow tie still dangling from the collar) and suit pants over the back of the chair, Schooner crawled into Caroline's bed in his boxers. He hoped she didn't mind.

Lying there, listening to Mia breathe for a while, he drifted into a fitful sleep, dreaming of the hospital and the Sheraton, searching hallways for Mia where hotel rooms had hospital beds with green curtains on tracks. He felt her climb into bed next to him, but wasn't sure if it was a dream, until she rested her head on his chest and he pulled her close into him.

"You okay?" he asked, nuzzling his face into her curls.

"Mmm-hmm," her arm tightened around him.

"It's going to be okay, Baby Girl." He kissed her forehead. He just had to believe it would be alright. There was no other option. They would get through this together. He would help her. He'd be her strength, her guide back from Hell. Her love. And when she was ready, her lover.

"Don't let me go, Schooner."

"I won't, Mia."

She nuzzled into his chest. "Promise?"

"I promise." He tightened his hug around her and the irony did not elude him as to how easy this promise was to make.

"They really hurt me tonight. I wanted to die."

His heart ached. It ached for her, it ached for him and it ached for everything he'd never be able to change.

"I'm so sorry, Baby Girl. I am so sorry this happened to you. I wish I could change it for you."

"Me too. It was horrible."

"I'm here for you, Mia." He threaded his fingers through hers and brought her hand to his lips. She was silent, so he went on. "I never stopped loving you, Baby Girl. Not for a minute."

"Don't make me smile, Schooner, it hurts."

He laughed. "Okay. Sleep." And she nuzzled back into his chest and fell back to sleep, while he gently stroked her hair.

As he held her tight, he knew that he would get her through this. He would get them both through this—together. This was the start. And this time, he was ready for it. She was his and he would do whatever he needed to protect her and to help her heal. He would always take care of what was his and that would start now.

He wondered if maybe he had been wrong earlier that evening. Maybe a restart could be a good thing after all.

Chapter Twenty-Eight

Feeling her stir in his arms, he looked at his watch. 8:45 A.M. His head ached from lack of sleep and tension. Closing his eyes, he tightened his muscular arms around her.

"Schooner?"

"Yeah, Baby Girl?" He looked down at her on his chest, looking so sweet and so young.

"Nothing. I just felt like saying your name."

Schooner smiled and kissed her forehead. "How are you feeling?"

She looked up at him, as he pushed her hair from her face, and his heart brimmed at the sight of her ombre green eyes.

"I feel like I got hit by a Mack truck." Mia moved off his chest and up to the pillow, looking into his eyes, which were now a mere few inches away. "I dreamed you told me that you never stopped loving me. Not even for a minute."

He gently ran a finger down her swollen, bruised cheek. "It wasn't a dream, Baby Girl."

A tear squeezed from her eye, "I thought you'd stopped. Then, I just thought that maybe you never really did."

He wiped her tear away with his thumb. Shaking his head, he whispered, "Never stopped. Never will."

"Me neither." She tried to smile, but the pain and the swelling stopped her.

"Awww, poor baby." Kissing the tip of her nose, he could see the smile forming in her eyes.

"Mia, I want to talk to you about something." He paused to stare into her beautiful eyes for a moment. "I don't want to upset you, but I also don't want to fuck up. And more than anything, I don't want to lose you. Ever." He sighed and looked up at the ceiling. "I will do this any way you want to, my only concern is you, keeping you safe and making sure that you don't have to deal with any shit."

Schooner could tell by the confusion on her face that she wasn't following. "I'm not leaving your side Mia, from now until the end of the semester. And maybe not even then." He smiled and ran his thumb down her cheek. "So, I know I am going to get some flak and I want to make sure

I handle it in a way that there isn't fallout for you."

"You're talking about CJ," she whispered.

He nodded. "I don't want her or any of her bitchy little friends bothering you. She still wants a relationship and…"

"… and you were at the Spring Fling with her last night." Mia interrupted, her eyes starting to fill up.

"Yes, I was."

She thought for a moment. "So, it will be a shock to her for everything to just be different."

"I could tell her I love you and she just needs to deal with it. I just want to do what's best for you. And I want to protect you from any nastiness that you don't need to deal with."

"You could tell her we're friends and you're helping me deal with something. That's not a lie." His brows furrowed and she continued, "And then maybe that way she'll feel less threatened and won't act out. I'm okay with that. As long as she doesn't know what happened to me."

"She'll never know. It's not her or anyone else's business."

There was a knock on the door and Schooner got up to answer it. Rosie and Henry had trays of food.

"Nice outfit," Rosie reprised her remark of the night before, gesturing at Schooner's plaid boxers.

"Very nice outfit," Henry concurred, taking in Schooner's bare broad chest and tennis player arm muscles.

Henry bit his lower lip and made a hand motion fanning himself to Mia, who attempted to smile. "Don't make me laugh, it hurts," she scolded.

"Oh Girlfriend, you are rocking some poufy lips." Henry kissed her cheek, softly.

"You just watch, they're going to come into vogue. You know what a trendsetter I am," Mia countered. "It's a New York thing."

Schooner looked through the food offerings. "Good job, guys. Mia, there's a bunch of things that are soft. Scrambled eggs, grits, oatmeal, applesauce."

"Okay."

"Okay to all?" Schooner was surprised and thrilled as Mia nodded yes. Her resilience and spirit were just a marvel to him. *A good appetite is a good sign*, he thought and as soon as he got food into her, he would make sure she took her meds.

Schooner was sitting in the middle of Caroline's bed with his back up against the wall and after eating her entire breakfast and taking her meds (at Schooner's insistence), Mia came and sat down between his legs, leaning back against him. His arms were around her and she was holding onto his hands. It was then, in the safety of Schooner's arms, that Mia began to open up about some of the details of what had happened to her. Schooner was learning along with Rosie and Henry of her ordeal.

They sat silently listening, not a breath taken between them.

She had been working late in the darkroom, which had been virtually empty all evening with many people off-campus for the Spring Fling. As the last person to leave, she locked up the darkroom for the night and left to come back to the dorm. Shortly after exiting the Fine Arts Building, she was jumped by two guys and dragged to the park across from campus. When they were done, they left her there on the ground, casually walking out of the park as if nothing had happened.

Mia was choking on her tears as she finished recounting the details.

All Schooner could do was hold her tighter to him. She felt very small and defeated in his arms.

Feeling his intense anger building, Schooner knew that Rosie and Henry were seeing it on his face and in his eyes. He was glad Mia's back was to him and that she could not see his rage. It scared him to realize of what he might be capable.

He felt very close to the Animal Kingdom.

Chapter Twenty-Nine

This is really not going well, Schooner thought. He hoped she would be cool about it, but there was nothing cool in her demeanor at the moment. CJ MacAllister was spitting mad.

"I don't understand why you are going to be spending time with her and not with me."

He tried to stay calm and appeal to reason. "CJ, if there was some shit going down in your life, wouldn't you want the people you consider your friends to be there to support you? Mia is my friend. I know you don't get that, but she is a really sweet kid and she needs my friendship right now."

"And you're not going to tell me why?" Her hands were now firmly planted on her hips.

"Would you want me sharing your shit with other people?" He just shook his head.

She didn't answer, so he continued, "No, you wouldn't. And I wouldn't share your personal business with other people."

Then he had a stroke of brilliance. "This is really important to my dad, CJ."

"Your dad? What does your dad have to do with this?"

He had her listening now. CJ labored overtime at Christmas working her magic in an attempt to ensure Gavin Moore liked her. She wanted Gavin as her father-in-law and now her curiosity was piqued.

"My dad and Mia's dad became friendly. And my dad asked me to take care of this. I don't want to let him down, CJ." Okay, it was a stretch on the truth, but it was based in reality and it seemed to be doing the trick.

She sighed, "Oh, I didn't realize that."

"Look, there's only a few weeks left of school here, just let me do the right thing."

She nodded her head okay, but it looked to Schooner as if her wheels were still spinning.

"And I'm telling you now, CJ—Mia gets no shit from you or any of your friends. Is that clear?"

"We would never," she began her protest, and he cut her off.

"I am dead serious, if anyone fucks with Mia in any way, shape or form, I will be so fucking pissed. Clear?"

"Clear," her wide-eyed, tight-lipped response belied her words. CJ was not happy.

What he really wanted to tell CJ was that there was not a shot in Hell that they were ever getting back together again. Truth be told, he wanted to tell her that Mia was the love of his life and that all he cared about was Mia's happiness and well-being.

But he knew if he did that, CJ and her evil minion would do something heinous to hurt Mia and all he really wanted to do was keep them all away from her through the end of the semester.

As he left CJ's dorm, he thought, crisis averted for now, and by the time fall semester comes, he and Mia would be old news and CJ would be moving on.

Protecting Mia was his utmost concern.

Chapter Thirty

Schooner was lying in bed holding Mia in his arms. "So, tell me about New York beaches."

"They are wonderful." It had only been several weeks, but Mia's smile was back to its adorable state, now that her stitches were out.

Schooner made a face at her. "I'm from Newport Beach, California—it's going to take a lot to impress me."

"Okay, well we have different kinds of beaches." He loved seeing how excited she would get talking about home. "Up on the North Shore we have rocky beaches. That's on the Long Island Sound and there are great harbors and little 300-year-old whaling towns, and the sailing is really amazing up there. And on the South Shore we have ocean beaches, so it's just miles of dunes and sand and good waves. The east end is really nice with Montauk and the Hamptons."

"That's where the Hamptons are?" Schooner asked and Mia nodded. "I've heard my dad talk about ancestors that were in Southampton, Long Island in the 1600's. Does that sound right? 1600's? Could that be possible?"

"Yes, absolutely. That is when those towns were first settled. We could research your family. Maybe find some old family graves. And maybe some living relatives, too. Wouldn't that be amazing? I can't believe your family was in America in the 1600's. That is so cool."

"That would be a fun thing to do." He kissed her lips, softly. With her stitches now gone and the gash healed, he was loving finally being able to kiss her lips again and was treating them as if they were made of porcelain. "What are you thinking?" He was looking at her dreamy face.

"I was thinking about after a day on the beach, when the sun goes down and it gets chilly and you're even colder because you're all sunburned, so you throw on a sweatshirt with your shorts. And I was thinking about us doing that and going to one of the lobster places on the water and picking out our lobsters from the tank and getting steamers and corn and just sitting out at a picnic table by the water, having the perfect night, after having the perfect day."

Schooner just smiled at Mia who was painting a picture for him of memories with her that they were yet to create, but that he could see vividly. He could see the late afternoon sun on her sunburned, freckled cheeks, smell the salt on the breeze, hear the tide lapping against the shore, feel the salt water dried in her curls.

"I love you, Mia and I really don't want to be away from you this summer. I will find a job there. I can teach tennis, lifeguard, bus tables—I don't care. If your parents are cool with me staying, I really want to spend the summer with you in New York."

"My parents loved you, Schooner—and they have plenty of room, so I don't think it's going to be a problem."

He pulled her close to kiss her some more.

"Mmm, I feel that."

Mia was referring to his hard-on that he was trying desperately not to press into her.

Inching the lower half of his body away from her, the last thing he wanted to do was make her fearful or uncomfortable.

"Mmm-mmm," she shook her head "no" while continuing to kiss him and slung a leg over him and used it to pull him closer to her, his cock now pressed up hard against her.

Schooner pulled away from their kiss to search her face.

With a smile, Mia touched his cheek. "It feels good," she whispered and he moaned just hearing her say that.

"Tell me what you want, Baby Girl. You have to call the shots here."

She gave him a shy smile and cast her eyes down for a moment before returning his intense gaze. "I'm ready, Schooner. I really am. I don't think I can wait another day. I don't want to wait another day."

"You sure?" He tried to read her eyes, knowing that he would forever hate himself if he pushed her into anything too soon.

And she nodded.

His deep kiss was soft as he said against her lips, "I love you so much, Baby Girl, but I'm so afraid I'm going to hurt you."

Mia pulled back to look at Schooner, pushing fallen blonde locks from his forehead and smiled. "Hurt me? Schooner, you have been my protector, you watch out for me, take care of me. You keep me safe. I know you're not going to hurt me."

"You know we're the real deal, Mia." He watched the smile from her lips reach her eyes.

She nodded.

Pulling her underneath him, with arms on both sides of her head, he kissed her lips softly, exploring her mouth, pulling back to look at her and smile and then kiss her some more. Used to being turned on and feeling the heady rush of sex, he was not used to feeling his heart brim and overflow. He wasn't used to caring or wanting the experience to be amazing for his partner. He had never really thought about what it was like for the other person.

In the past, it had been about his own physical release and need for control. It had been about the hunt and the victor, but as he looked down at Mia's sweet face, he realized the only thing he cared about was that this was wonderful for her, that she knew how much he loved her, that this was the ultimate expression of his love for her.

Pulling his shirt off over his head, he bared his tan chest and her hands went to his shoulders, gently moving down his arms, reverently. It was an amazing and unexpected treat to watch her face as she explored him, and he loved that she was enjoying his body. Schooner tugged her tee-shirt and pulled it over her head, swinging it like a lasso before tossing it off into the room. They both laughed. His eyes were smoldering like pale sapphires. He had never felt so turned on. Pushing the shoulder straps from her bra down, he lifted her gorgeous tits out of her bra. He rimmed one nipple with his tongue and she moaned. He grazed it in his teeth, before saying, "You absolutely have the most gorgeous tits on campus."

"Oh, do I?"

"Without a doubt." And between sucks, "The day we met, I noticed your gorgeous eyes and smile and this damn fine rack."

She giggled and he bit down on her nipple, causing a yelp.

"My damn fine rack. Mine." He staked ownership.

Her fingers threaded through his thick blonde locks as his sucking and pinching drove her wild. She wrapped her legs around him, moaning.

"You have such sensitive nipples. I love that." He marveled, as he moved back up to her mouth, kissing her deeply.

When she pulled at his hair, he lost it and ravaged her mouth without restraint. Her hand reached for him and he curled into her so that she could grasp him, gasping into her mouth, when her little hand encircled his throbbing cock.

Gently, her fingernails skimmed over his balls and he shivered. "Feel good?" she asked.

"Oh yeah." He breathed into her neck.

"And this?" She gently kneaded his balls in her hand. He knew his cock felt like steel. It was so hard, it hurt.

"Feels damn good." He looked at her face to see her satisfied little smile.

"I love getting you hard." She smiled at him.

"You have quite the knack for it," he was gasping. He gave her a hard kiss and her arms went around his neck. "Are you ready for this?"

Mia nodded her consent and Schooner got off the bed, rustled through his duffle bag and came up with a condom packet. He sat down on the edge of the bed. She looked at him wide-eyed. "I don't want you to feel like we have to do this."

Shaking her head, Mia was certain. "I want to do this. I want to do this with you."

The look in her eyes was pleading and he realized that she needed this to wipe away the nightmare and replace it with something wonderful. That while he stressed this might be too soon, Mia, in actuality was telling him that this was part of her healing process, that she needed him to help her heal. What he really wanted was to wipe a night out of her life and he felt impotent that he didn't have the power to do that. What he did have the ability to control, was to ensure that Mia could now equate the physical act with love. He could give her that. Leaning forward, he kissed her, not a deep passionate kiss, but one that let her know they were together in this. Schooner was honored to help make wonderful memories with her.

"Want to help me with his?" he asked, opening the condom packet. Holding the condom, he took her hands in his and hand over hand had her roll it down over him. He wanted to make it *th*eir experience. And what she didn't realize was that everything that was happening was new ground, with new emotions for him, too. The touch of her rolling the condom onto him and smoothing it out, with such care was blowing his mind.

She looked pleased at her *handiwork*.

Pulling her beneath him, he kissed her as the head of his cock starting to sink into her. "You ready?" He searched her eyes, ready to swipe away any demon.

She nodded her assent and with his eyes locked onto hers, he mouthed, "I love you".

"I love you" was the response she mouthed back, and with a quick thrust, he was inside of her.

She gasped, but was still smiling. He realized he was smiling too and just took a moment to enjoy how tight she was around him before he began driving into her. Bending down to kiss her, he thrust into her deeper, quicker, harder. Mia returned his kiss passionately and he lost himself in the sensation… she was so tight around his cock, she felt so damn good.

He pulled his face back to look at her. Her eyes were closed and he could tell she was coming undone.

"Mia," his voice was hoarse, "look at me."

Mia opened her eyes.

He wanted to watch her as she came, but he also wanted to make sure she was okay and didn't go anyplace dark. "You are so beautiful."

She smiled at him and he rammed into her hard. "So, so beautiful." Harder. "You. Are. My. Baby Girl." Harder and faster. "Come. For. Me. Baby Girl." And those were the magic words.

Her eyes widened and her muscles clamped down and spasmed around him, milking his cock.

He could hear both their moans in his ears and "Oh God, Schooner," which totally pushed him over the edge.

Collapsing on top of her, forehead to forehead, both panting, he pushed her curls from her face and smiled down at her. It took a moment as she regained her breath, but when she smiled back at him, his heart relaxed. She was okay.

"Wow," she was rendered speechless.

"Wow is right," Schooner laughed.

"Is that what it is always like?"

He shook his head no. "I have never experienced anything like that before." And he wasn't lying.

There was a self-satisfied smirk on Mia's face. Schooner kissed her softly. He had still not pulled out of her and started to gently grind into her.

Her eyes grew wide and he laughed. "Figured that would wipe that self-satisfied smirk off your face."

"Oh, did you now?" She squeezed his cock hard with her muscles and his eyes flew open. "Two can play that game."

"Yes, two can… and two is going to need to help me with another condom if she keeps this up." He ground into her clockwise.

They kissed and laughed and made love again and all of Schooner's protective instincts were satisfied for one night.

He had made good on his promise. He promised her that he would be the first person to make love to her. And he was. Seeing the way she responded to their lovemaking and her happiness in the aftermath was a heady, powerful feeling for him. He had given this to her. And she had given herself to him. She was his.

Chapter Thirty-One

Finals and packing and goodbyes and the last tennis matches, the days were winding down quickly and if Schooner had an extra second to just stand still and feel, he would have recognized his mounting ambivalence. He was ready for the semester to end and for finals to be over, but the last month with Mia was a moment in time that he forever wanted to hold onto.

Schooner shoved the last of his belongings into his duffle bag as Mia and Caroline continued to pack and tape their boxes.

Their dorm RA, Dawn, poked her head into the room to remind the girls that all cartons being shipped needed to be packed, sealed, addressed and out in the hall by 9 P.M.

"I'll walk you out." Mia grabbed her keys.

"Have a great summer, Caroline." Schooner gave Mia's very accommodating roommate a hug goodbye.

They stopped by Rosie's room. She was just about finished packing. "Eight A.M. final and I am outta here!"

One more stop for Schooner to say goodbye to Henry, but he was nowhere to be found.

Mia and Schooner walked out of the dorm and stood on the front steps.

"Stop pouting," he said to her. "You're killing me."

"I'm not used to spending the night without you. I miss you already."

"C'mere, Baby Girl." He sat down on the stone balustrade railing and pulled her between his legs. Her arms immediately went around his neck and they got lost in a kiss. "I'll be by right after my final. We'll have at least an hour before the limo comes for you," he promised.

She continued to pout.

"You'd better put that lip away or I'm going to bite it," Schooner threatened with a non-threatening smile.

They stayed that way for a long while, with Mia standing between Schooner's legs, arms wrapped around his neck, foreheads together.

"Tell me again, what's the place we have to get to by boat?"

"That's Fire Island. We'll take the ferry over and there's no cars. Just little red wagons to cart groceries with and bicycles. No streets, just boardwalks. Ocean on one side, the Great South Bay on the other side."

Smiling, he kissed her, "And that's where you want to spend your birthday?"

She nodded, smiling.

"Okay, your birthday on Fire Island. I just can't wait to see these places you talk about. They just sound so idyllic."

"That, they are!"

"Do you want me to bring you anything from here when I come?"

"Certainly not pizza and bagels," she laughed. "Just bring you, that's all I need."

Saying goodbye, even for the night, was killing him. Taking her face in his hands, he knew that he was just dragging out the inevitable and pulled her in for one more deep kiss to send him off. "I'd better go study. Flunking out of school will not go over well with my parents. I'm thinking I should probably finish my test between 11:30 and 12:00 and I'll come right over, okay."

He squeezed her hand and they held hands until he was down the steps and their fingertips finally broke contact.

Schooner turned around. "Hey," he yelled, "those pizzas and bagels better be as good as you've been bragging about."

Mia just stood on the steps smiling at him, watching him go.

It was dusk when he reached his dorm on the other side of campus. As he crossed the lobby, he got a lot of ribbing from the guys hanging out.

"Hey, do we know this guy?" "I remember him… vaguely."

"Ah, the Prodigal Son returns."

Beau was in their room studying for a Chemistry final. He looked up when Schooner walked in. "Oh hey, did you see CJ?"

"No, why?" Schooner pulled his books out of his duffle bag to study.

"She left just a few minutes ago. She was looking for you." He punched some numbers into his calculator.

"Did she say what she wanted?"

Beau just shook his head. "No. I just assumed it was to say goodbye. She hung out for a little bit waiting for you and then finally left."

Chapter Thirty-Two

Schooner filled in the last of his answers and took a run back through the test to see if he'd missed anything. There were four questions he'd flagged with checkmarks, indicating he should go back and relook at them. Glancing at his watch, it was 11:25 A.M. He was still in good shape to finish up and have some time to spend alone with Mia before she left. Taking a deep breath, he went back to concentrating on his final. At 11:38, Schooner handed his test booklet into the professor and wished him a good summer.

Crossing The Quad, heading toward Mia's dorm, Schooner felt that joy of freedom moment that hits once every spring when school is over and summer officially begins. What a year! So much had happened. As he walked past Brewster Hall, he smiled thinking about the first time he'd laid eyes on her. His first impression was that she didn't belong here. He also thought that he fit in perfectly. Laughing to himself, Schooner realized he was wrong on both counts.

Walking into Mia's dorm, it was already starting to resemble a ghost town. Doors to dorm rooms were open and the rooms were bare, just institutional mattresses on frames, dressers, desks and chairs still in the rooms. All the posters were off the walls, books were gone, green plants taken home for the summer, all cartons for shipping had been removed from the hall. Schooner headed up the stairwell and down the hall toward Mia's room.

The door was ajar, so he walked in. He didn't immediately process that the room was completely empty. Nothing was in the room. No one was in the room. No Mia. No luggage. He looked at his watch. It was 11:55 A.M. Mia wasn't supposed to be picked up until 1 P.M.

"Mia," he called out. He ran down the hall to Rosie's room. It was empty, too.

Maybe she's waiting in Henry's room, he thought and ran down the stairwell. He could feel panic beginning to rise. Something was not right. What the hell was going on? He knocked on Henry's door. His roommate answered. Henry had left hours ago. And no, he hadn't seen Mia.

He ran down the hall checking rooms, maybe someone knew where she was. He checked the lobby again. She wasn't anywhere. He went back up to her room. That's where she would look for him. She knew approximately what time he was going to be there. She'd meet him at the room. Maybe she was just saying goodbye to someone.

He got back up to her room. Still no Mia. No luggage. Nothing. He paced around her room. 12:15. 12:20. 12:25. What the fuck happened? Maybe the limo came early. Maybe she left a note. He searched her desk. Nothing. All the drawers. Nothing. Her dresser. Nothing. Under her pillow. Nothing. He got on his knees and looked under the bed, under the desk, under the dresser. Nothing. Nothing. Nothing. He checked her closet. Nothing.

Hearing the click of a key in a door lock down the hall, he went running from the room. It was Dawn, the RA.

"Dawn."

"Hey Schooner," she looked surprised to see him.

"Have you seen Mia?" He searched her face.

She looked confused. "Schooner, Mia left hours ago."

"Hours ago?" he repeated, emptily. "Mia left hours ago?"

She nodded. A look on her face saying "sorry"—like she was sorry to deliver bad news and he also saw something more on her face, something that said sorry this is happening to you. And then she locked her door and headed down the hall to leave for the summer.

He turned and started to walk down the hall. What the fuck? Why had she left like this? Was she okay? Was everything okay? Surely, she would have left him a note or had someone get a message to him. And that's when it dawned on him that he didn't even have her number. He was going to get all that info before she left and give her his. And now she was gone. Just gone. And he had no way to find her. No way to find out what had happened. No way to find out why she had left him. When they said goodbye last night, everything was fine. They were going to spend her birthday on Fire Island… together. And now she was gone, without a trace.

As his brimming heart rapidly deflated, the pain felt like he was being knifed with a shredding blade. His handsome face was contorted with anguish as he yelled out in the empty hallway, "Why Mia? Why did you leave me?" and took the side of his closed fist and slammed it into the institutional green cinder-block cement wall. The sound of bones breaking was deafening, but he neither heard the sound nor felt the pain radiating up his arm because the pain in his heart eclipsed anything he felt physically.

One week earlier, after the last match of the season, Coach Boland had predicted to his staff that Schooner Moore would lead their highly-regarded tennis program to a National Championship and be the top ranked NCAA player in the United States within two years.

Three surgeries. Six months in a cast.

Schooner Moore's promising tennis career came to a shattering conclusion in a dormitory hallway on the last day of his freshman year.

Chapter Thirty-Three

Dr. Malcolm Faulkes was a golf buddy of Gavin Moore's. An orthopedic surgeon who specialized in Sports Medicine, he had a client roster that was a Who's Who of LA sports teams. Over the years, he had seen Schooner play tennis many times and had been following his impressive first college season.

When Gavin called to say that Schooner's right hand suffered an injury, Dr. Faulkes met them at his office after hours. The x-rays showed multiple fractures and Faulkes performed the first of what would be three surgeries that very evening after admitting Schooner to the hospital, where he stayed for three days heavily drugged with his hand immobilized.

A week later, Schooner was back at Dr. Faulkes office. Malcolm asked Dee to stay out in the waiting room while he spoke to his patient alone.

His office was warm and inviting, with dark cherry wood wainscoted walls proudly displaying his love for everything golf. Schooner sat down in one of the Hunter Green leather and wood chairs across from the doctor's desk.

"On a scale of 1-10 where is your pain level?"

"About a six," a subdued Schooner replied.

"The surgery I performed was a first, Schooner. From what I can tell, you're going to probably need at least two more within the next three months."

Schooner winced at his words and nodded as the doctor continued, "I'm not going to kid you, that hand is held together by pins right now. You did extensive damage to the bones."

"Guess I won't be team captain next year." Schooner looked up at the ceiling.

"Son, I'd like to be optimistic, but after your surgeries, there is going to be an extensive rehab period. The good news is, you're young and you're strong. Will you ever regain the strength in that hand to grip a racquet tight enough to knock out those 110 plus MPH serves again?" he paused. "Schooner, I don't know if that is going to be in your future."

Schooner continued to look at the ceiling, trying his hardest not to let the tears burning at the back of his eyes have their way.

"The reason I wanted your mother to wait outside today was so that you and I could talk. I've known you most of your life, Schooner. You're a good kid. You've always been happy, level-headed. Clearly, there's something going on here." Malcolm's voice showed honest concern and Schooner could feel that.

"Dr. F., I just got dumped. And it came as a shock and I just wasn't thinking and slammed my fist into a wall. Not the brightest thing I've ever done. I wasn't thinking. I just reacted."

"Heartbreak will do that to you." Malcolm sat back in his chair.

"I got blindsided," Schooner began. "She left without a word. I was supposed to spend the summer with her in New York. I don't even have a number to find her. Everything was fine the night before and then she was gone. I don't even know why she left me." Schooner's eyes told the doctor everything he needed to know.

"Can't you get her number from Directory Assistance?"

"Her last name is Silver and she lives in New York."

Dr. Faulkes actually laughed out loud and Schooner laughed with him at the absurdity of it. "That would be like finding a Smith in most areas of the country, I suppose." He sat back in his big leather chair, tapping his finger against his lip. He looked at Schooner and smiled, "So, let me see if I've got this right—you're heartbroken and now you have no plans for the summer—except for a few dates with me for surgeries."

"Pretty much sums it up, Doc."

Faulkes smiled at Schooner, a gleam in his eye. "So, that pretty much frees you up for an adventure."

Schooner cocked his head, narrowing his eyes at the doctor, wondering what he was getting at.

"You know Schooner, in my experience, two things can help you get over a broken heart. The first is—fall in love with someone else, the second is a change of scenery. Since my daughter is only nine, I can't offer you the first, but I can help you with the second. I'm going to be spending four weeks in Zambia this summer, helping to set up a hospital in a rural area of their Southern Province. There's a lot of work to be done and we can always use an extra set of hands. Or in your case, hand." He smiled at his own joke.

Zambia? I don't even know where the fuck Zambia is, Schooner thought. *Somewhere in Africa. Zambia. Helping people. Getting a hospital set up. Zambia.*

And in that moment, Schooner felt alive again. He had a purpose. He was going to Zambia.

And with the quintessential Schooner Moore smile on his face, he asked Dr. Malcolm Faulkes, "Where do I sign up?"

After a day and a half of travel, they arrived in the capital of Lusaka, a vibrant modern city with wide avenues lined with Jacaranda trees. The friendly natives predominantly spoke English, and Schooner made quite the splash with children at the Lumumba Market, who wanted to follow around the tall, blonde haired, blue eyed young man. Before heading out on their five-hour Jeep ride to Macha, they visited the Moore Pottery Factory and Schooner bought his mom a tea set decorated with a local native motif from this namesake gallery/factory.

They drove over rough, rutted dirt roads through the savannah, not coming upon villages for hours at a time. Schooner documented the journey with his new Nikon camera, from the vast plains to the small grass roofed huts in the villages. As they passed through, the children would wave and run after them until they reached the edge of the village.

Their travel brought them into Macha late in the day and Schooner was captivated by its stark beauty and simplicity. They began to unload the supplies and equipment that had been shipped in containers from the U.S. Local children looked on, smiles covering their faces. The news of the American specialty doctors' arrival had spread quickly. Soon villagers were welcoming them, bringing local specialties such as Chikanda, a vegetarian sausage made from orchids, Samp, a dish of cooked hominy and dried beans and other assorted delicacies made from boiled leaves. The offering took on the feel of a street festival and Schooner felt proud to be a part of the doctors' important work.

Their accommodations were simple. Cots had been set up for them in the schoolhouse. Schooner was struck by how little the people had and how little they needed. There wasn't much in the way of industry, one coffee house/ gathering spot in town (mostly for ex-pats) and a general-type store, several places of worship, a school and the new hospital, which would serve a large area in the southern region of the country. That was all they had and they didn't appear to need more. The villagers seemed content and happy, greeting all with warm smiles. It struck him that their happiness was not contingent upon having a lot. It was just about being.

The first few days had Schooner busy unpacking supplies and helping the medical staff set up. The word was out of their arrival and natives from near and far began to arrive. There were so many orthopedic issues ranging from small crippled children to the arthritic elderly. The doctors saw as many patients as they physically could in a day. The ophthalmologists, dentists and prosthetic specialists with them were equally stretched with their caseloads.

After a few days, Schooner approached Malcolm. "Dr. F., I've been thinking about how I could be of most help here and what I've noticed is that people are coming long distances for care and they are bringing their children with them, who then have to wait for hours with their parents. Maybe I could take the kids and do a sports camp with them to keep them busy while their parents are getting medical attention. I could teach them how to play soccer—I don't need my hands for that." Schooner held up his casted hand.

Malcolm clapped Schooner on the back, "That is brilliant and will make things so much easier for the families. I love it. Do it!" As an afterthought, he asked, "Do you have a soccer ball?"

And the doctor didn't appear totally surprised when his young American patient sheepishly admitted, "It was one of the last things I stuffed in my duffel bag."

The first day, Schooner had four kids in his Sports Camp. He started the kids in the morning with stretching, mat exercises and running. Then they started working on the basics of soccer. Within a few days, Schooner's camp not only encompassed kids whose families were seeking medical treatment, but local village children were waiting every morning for the big blonde instructor they called "Coach." There were nine local children, six boys and three girls, who became the core of Schooner's camp. There before everyone arrived in the morning, they set up the exercise mats and the makeshift soccer goals and were the last to leave at night, after they broke down camp.

This core group would go to the hospital every day and find the children that were waiting with their parents and escort them to camp. They also became expert recruiters within their village, and soon Schooner had enough participants to form teams. With the help of hospital staff, he also taught the children about lifesaving techniques such as oral-rehydration therapy and CPR.

At night, he would fall onto his cot, exhausted, but his mind would race a million miles an hour. He wondered where she was, what she was doing, was she thinking about him, did she miss him, did she hurt as much as he did, was her heart missing a huge chunk too and did she still love him? And the same question always plagued him—why? Why did she leave without a word? What had happened? What changed everything?

He wanted to remember every detail of this trip so that he could share it with her. She would have loved the village and the people, especially the children. He imagined her finding photographic images in all that surrounded her.

And every night before sleep finally saved him from the demons that haunted his heart, he would try and send her a message, "Come back to me. Just be there in August. We'll make it right. Baby Girl, come back to me."

On their last night in the village, Schooner held the "Macha Grand Soccer Tournament and all the local families joined to cheer on their children from the sidelines.

The kind and grateful people of Macha brought food to share with the doctors and staff to thank them for their work. It was Macha's first sports event/tailgate party. One of the village elders, Levi Mambwe, sat down next to Schooner. "You seem to have found your calling."

"Maybe so," Schooner agreed.

"You have a passion for this. You are a born leader, Coach Schooner. You have made a lasting impact on the children of Macha, teaching them the importance of exercise on health, and you have made learning fun for them. It is a gift. Follow your passion and share your gift."

The next morning, they left Macha for the last time. The children followed them to the edge of the village waving after them. Schooner was surprised at how sad he was to leave the simple village. He thought about Levi's words from the night before and thought that they had given him as much, if not more, than he had given to them.

The last leg of the journey was to Livingstone to see Victoria Falls—the largest waterfall in the world. They drove to the Zimbabwe border and followed the Zambezi River to the falls. Hiking down paths through the rainforest, every so often they captured glimpses of the magnificent falls whose mighty roar filled the air with its growling magic and misted rainbows. When they came to the Knife Edge Bridge, they were afforded a full view of nature's majesty and force.

Schooner stood there in awe trying to mentally etch the image into his mind and then parked his Nikon on the railing, using it as a makeshift tripod, a trick he had learned at another waterfall. White clouds stood in relief against an azure blue sky. Schooner screwed a red filter to the end of his lens so that the clouds would pop out against the dark sky. He shot short exposures and long exposures knowing that the effects would be very different. *I did listen, Baby Girl, when you tried to teach me this stuff,* he thought.

Before they hiked back to the Jeep, he had Malcolm shoot a picture of him with the falls in the background.

He thought that shot might make a great gift.

Chapter Thirty-Four

Schooner dropped his bags off in his dorm room and headed out to The Quad. He was amazed at how many people he knew as he walked toward Mia's dorm. Everyone wanted to stop and say hello, ask about his summer and find out why his hand was in a cast. All he wanted to do was get across campus. He had waited for this day since May. Today he would get his answers.

Reaching her dorm, he took a deep breath as he walked through the front door. In the lobby were several people he knew (since he had basically been a resident there Spring Semester). Everyone wanted to know about his hand and several new freshman girls were checking him out, trying to catch his eye.

He finally made it through the lobby and up the stairwell. And there he was standing outside her door. Reminding himself to breathe, his hands were shaking as he knocked on the door with his good hand.

The door opened and Caroline stood there, "Schooner!" She gave him a big hug.

"Hey Caroline! How was your summer?"

It was then he noticed the girl with the short blonde hair putting her stuff out on Mia's desk.

She stopped when she saw Schooner and gave him a bright smile, "Hi, I'm Alison."

"Hi. Schooner."

He turned to Caroline, "Where's Mia?"

"I don't know. I was hoping you would tell me. We were supposed to room together." She looked concerned.

"Did you hear from her at all this summer?" *Please say yes*, a voice inside him begged.

"Not a word. Didn't you spend the summer with her?" Her confusion was apparent.

He shook his head. "She bailed before I had a chance to say goodbye to her that last day."

"What? No fucking way." She ran her hands through her hair as if she were thinking something and then just shook her head. "What did you do to your hand?"

"These walls are made of cement."

Her hand flew to her mouth, "You didn't."

He nodded his head, "Yeah, I did."

He could see the pain on her face as she realized something went very wrong for two people who seemed hopelessly in love with one another. He gave her shoulder a squeeze and left the room.

He checked both Rosie and Henry's rooms, but neither of them were there.

Beau was still not in their room when he got back and he was glad. He was not up for answering any more questions about his hand.

Opening his backpack, he grabbed an oversized envelope. Inside were photos of his soccer team, village huts, Victoria Falls and the photo Dr. F. had taken of him in front of the falls. He'd had them made for Mia. He wanted to tell her of his journey and show her his photography, a now common passion that he looked forward to sharing with her.

With the envelope in hand, he headed for the Dining Hall. Maybe there he'd finally get the answers he wanted.

He stood at the entrance surveying the crowd. Where were they? And then he saw Henry waving to get his attention, a huge smile on his face and Schooner felt relief. He maneuvered through the crowd to get to Henry's table.

"Hey man!" They hugged.

Rosie stood and her arms went around Schooner, surprising him, "Schooner." He gave her a tight hug.

Before they could ask about his hand, he blurted out, "Where's Mia?"

"She's not back." Henry shrugged.

"What do you mean she's not back? What is going on?"

"When she wasn't in her room and Caroline didn't know where she was, we asked the dorm director and he said she wasn't on the list of returning students." Rosie was as clearly in the dark as he was.

His heart began to crumble for a second time as he realized that Mia had not returned for their sophomore year. Overwhelmed at the finality, he had not anticipated that this moment was going to hurt as much as finding her gone at the end of the semester had, for he had not let his heart believe this moment would come to pass.

"What the fuck? What the fuck happened to her?" Schooner was confused and angry. This was the nightmare that he prayed every night would not come to pass, convincing himself it wouldn't happen to them. *What the fuck, Baby Girl*, he thought.

"Didn't you guys spend the summer together in New York?"

"No." Schooner sat down on the bench, because he knew his knees would buckle if he kept standing. "I never even said goodbye to her. I got out of my last final, went to her room to go hang out with her and she was gone. She didn't even leave me a note."

Rosie put her forehead into her hands and shook her head. "That doesn't even make sense."

"Why'd she leave me?" He looked from Rosie to Henry, then back.

His friends had no answers.

Chapter Thirty-Five

It was the night before Christmas Break that a candle ceremony took place in an all-girls dorm across campus. All the dorm's residents, as well as selected friends from other dorms, were invited to participate.

The girls gathered in a circle as the dorm director lit a candle and handed it to one of the girls. The girls would pass the candle around the circle from one girl to the next. When the candle stopped, everyone in the circle would know that the girl holding the candle was the one who had just become engaged.

That night, the candle stopped on a beaming CJ MacAllister.

CJ and Schooner were engaged.

Chapter Thirty-Six

Now …

"Don't poke the bear!" Yolanda Perez came into Schooner Moore's office carrying very tall lattes.

Schooner laughed and motioned her in.

"So, rumor has it you've ripped a few new assholes this morning." She made a face at him saying, *is that true?*

He loved Yoli. She was the only person in his world who always told it like it was. No bullshit. No pretense. And that was why he could trust her. They'd been together for twenty years—she'd been with him since the beginning. Earlier in the year, on her twentieth anniversary with the company, he gave her a percentage ownership of the business. CJ went ballistic when she learned about it. She totally did not get Schooner's relationship with Yoli.

He laughed, "None that didn't deserve to be ripped."

"So, how was the big party?"

"If you miss another one of my birthday parties, I am firing your ass." He pointed his finger at her.

"You're going to have to buy me out, buddy." She laughed at his threat.

"The big party was a *Real Housewives* Reunion Bash masquerading as my birthday party." Schooner rolled his eyes and shook his head.

"I would've so fit in."

Schooner almost spit out his coffee laughing at Yoli's snark. Yoli was a cargo pants and tee shirt lesbian with short, awful colored red hair.

"Bet you could've gotten some action," he teased and this time she almost spit out her coffee.

"Oh yeah, *Real Housewives* in search of a taste of the other side. Think I'll pass! How's my sweet girl Holly doing?" Holly and Yoli had a kindred spirits relationship from the time Holly was a toddler.

"Awesome and she said to send you and Debbie her love. She was bummed you two weren't there. At one point, I looked over at her and the look on her face was classic, like she was taking in data on a roomful of aliens."

"With the amount of chemicals those women have had injected into themselves, they might not be classified as human anymore."

Yoli was the one person who instantly put him in a great mood. He knew why—he could be himself with her. And that reminded him of someone else, the person responsible for teaching him to be himself.

"So, are you on Facebook?" Schooner abruptly changed the subject.

"Umm, yes. Why do you ask?" Yoli looked at Schooner with a *where did that come from* look.

"I guess everyone is on it, but me. How does it work? Can everyone see what you say on there or can you talk to someone privately?" It was time to get schooled.

"Okay, well you set up your profile and your own page, known as your wall and then you friend people. If you write something as your "status," it goes on your wall and all the people you friend can see it. Same thing if you write on their wall. But if you just want one person to see your conversation, you can private message them and then the conversation is only between the two of you."

"Okay, good." He nodded.

"So, you want to go on Facebook?" Yoli was surprised.

"I'm thinking about it," Schooner tried to keep pokerfaced.

"No. No. No. No. No. Don't you play that game with me, Schooner. All of a sudden you want to go on Facebook and you want to know about sending private messages. Spill it!"

He sat back in his chair and tapped his forefingers against his lips, wondering how to start this conversation. Or if he even should. But it was the only thing he could think about since Beau had brought her up on Saturday night. He couldn't get her out of his head—not even for a second. And Yoli was truly the only person he could trust enough to confide in.

"When I was in college, there was this girl. Her name was Mia." He smiled. "You guys would have been best friends. You would have loved each other. Anyway, I was crazy in love with her and I thought she was in love with me, too. We were supposed to spend the summer together and then she just disappeared. I mean. literally, disappeared. I went back to her room after my last final. We were supposed to hang out together that day until she left for the airport and when I got there she was gone. No note. Nothing. And we had been like living together up until that point. And she just freaking disappeared and never came back to school. Gone. Without a trace."

"I thought you were with CJ all through college?" Yoli looked puzzled.

"Well, except when I was with Mia. I left CJ for Mia. Oh man, did CJ hate Mia."

"Maybe CJ killed her." Yoli's eyebrows shot up in mock horror.

Schooner laughed. "Don't think that hadn't crossed my mind." He took a sip of his latte and shook his head. "So anyway, at the party Saturday night, my old college roommate Beau Gordon …"

"Pee Wee Herman?" Yoli interrupted.

"Yes, Pee Wee Herman." Schooner laughed. "So, Beau and I started talking about this thing that happened freshman year and he asks me who the girl was that was with us and I tell him it was Mia and then he tells me that he just had a fight with Mia on Scott Morgan's Facebook page."

"Scott Morgan, the advertising guy?"

"Yeah, he went to our school. I didn't even know Mia knew him. I mean he's really kind of a random person to be in touch with."

Yoli's palms were up in the air. "So, have you looked her up on Facebook yet?"

"No. I don't even know how."

Coming around to his side of the desk, she laughed as she shoved him slightly out of the way. "You are so useless. What would you do without me?"

Schooner leaned his head into her arm. "I'd be lost."

"That's for shit sure! Okay, let's see if we can look at Scott Morgan's page and his friend list without you being on Facebook yet. It's going to depend on what he's got his privacy settings on. Let's Google him first because there are probably a lot of Scott Morgans." She continued to punch away on his keyboard. "Okay, bingo, here he is. Let's hope he doesn't have his info set to private."

Schooner could feel his stomach knot. He was so close to finding Mia—after all this time. Yoli might just be a few keystrokes away. He could feel his hands shaking. Just knowing he was so close to finding her still had such a profound physical effect on him.

"Thank you, Scott! Okay, here is his Facebook page. He's got 319 friends and we are looking for Mia who?"

"Mia Silver."

"Okay, let's put that in search. Bingo. Is that your Mia?" She turned to him.

He sat back in his chair and let out a long, slow exhale. He nodded his head, because he couldn't speak and when his voice finally came out, it was choked and cracking, "Yeah. That's my Mia."

Yoli punched him in the arm, "Shit, she's cute. I'd do her."

He laughed, but was still unable to speak, overcome by emotion that had gnawed at him for over twenty years.

Mia, all grown up. She looked the same, just older, more mature. Still so pretty. No glasses now and the wild curls were now soft shoulder-length waves with long dark bangs hanging in her eyes. He wanted to reach into the picture and push them from her eyes. It was a long moment before he realized he was sitting there smiling at her picture and Yoli was standing there smiling at him.

"Talk about the antithesis of OC women," Yoli observed. "So, are you going to just sit there and stare at her picture all day long?"

"Yeah, I just might."

"Okay, shove over. Let's get you on Facebook." She began tapping away again. "We need a picture of you." Going around to the other side of the desk, Yoli picked up her cell phone. "Smile. No. No. No. Don't give me that bullshit male model smile. Think of Holly looking at the *Housewives* like they were aliens." And she snapped the picture. "Perfection! If I do say so myself. Okay, I am emailing this to you and then we are going to attach it to your profile. Done." She came back around the desk. Tap. Tap. Tap. "You are now officially on Facebook. Ready to send her a friend invite?"

"What if she doesn't answer or doesn't accept it?" Yoli was shocked to see the ancient serpent of rejection rearing its ugly head in a man she knew to be in control and extremely confident in all he did, especially in his dealings with women.

"Well she definitely won't answer if you don't send it." Yoli's hands were on her hips. "You don't ask, you don't get."

Schooner just stared at the screen. What if she didn't want him to find her? He was looking at her. He was looking at Mia. There she was. There she *was*. He couldn't pull his eyes away from the beautiful ombre green eyes on his computer screen.

"You really loved her," Yoli said, softly.

Schooner nodded his head. "I really loved her."

And with that admission spoken aloud, he pushed the Send Friend Request button.

Part Two
Mia

Chapter One

"Could today get any freaking worse?" Mia rhetorically asked her associate, Seth Shapiro. She raked her hand through her hair, while staring at her computer screen. "I can understand losing a client because we didn't do a good job, because we didn't deliver. But because his daughter got engaged to some guy who works for a competitor? Do we need to start pimping out our staff? Because I am not above pimping out our staff." Mia was on a tear. "Fuck!"

"Kami thinks you're going to fire her." Seth looked a little scared of Mia at the moment.

"That's ridiculous. She's done everything to keep these assholes happy. This is not the way she deserves to lose this account." Mia pulled up a spreadsheet on her computer. "This really hurts our cash flow."

Seth had been Mia's right hand since before she started the agency—there was no aspect of the business that she didn't confide details with him, which is why they made such a great team.

"Do not make me give up my massages." Seth glared at Mia in the way only an over the top queen can.

"Don't worry, Princess, we won't be eating cat food for another few months yet." She sneered back at him, "Do you have the latest weekly sales pipeline?"

Seth handed Mia the report, she tapped the page a few times with her index finger and then dialed an extension, putting the call on speakerphone.

"Hey Boss," the voice came through the phone.

"Hey Dave, so how far away are we from automating that new work from American Express? Give me worst case scenario." She and Seth looked at each other dubiously, holding their breath.

"Well, you know what they're like with the endless conference calls and doing everything by committee, but their IT guy and I have been kind of doing our own thing. So, I'd say worst case is live traffic in six weeks." Mia fist pumped the air and mouthed a silent *YES* to Seth. "Excellent, Dave. You made my day!"

He laughed on the other end, "I thought that might make you happy and I'll step it up even more to see if we can be live in four to five weeks. I know what a hole we've now got after today's bullshit."

"Yeah, bullshit is right," Mia agreed. "I'm going to start pimping out the staff. It's the only answer," she kidded.

"Count me in, Boss. Pimp me anytime."

Mia laughed, "That's why I love this staff, Seth."

"Ho!" Seth yelled at Dave.

"Damn right, I get the job done," he kidded back.

They disconnected the call and Mia looked at Seth, "Okay, let's plan on two months of it being tight. I don't want to stop the sales team from selling, but expenses need to be kept down until we have the additional cash flow from AmEx."

"Memo or staff meeting?" Seth asked.

"Staff meeting—let's do this face-to-face and get Kami in here first. I need to talk to her before she slits her wrists and bleeds out all over her office." Mia smiled at Seth, "Mondays suck!"

Two hours later, a drained Mia and Seth sat in her office alone again.

"I'm glad we did the meeting, Mia. They were all freaking about losing their jobs."

"The last thing I want to do is lay off people. We have never had to lay off anyone. I will give up my salary if we need to make payroll."

Seth loved working with Mia. She had built a small ad agency that was more like a wonderful dysfunctional family than a place of business, and Mia saying she would give up her salary not to lay off people was not just empty words and he knew it. That was the ethos of the organization and precisely why Mia's staff would run through walls for her.

Looking at her watch, she smiled, "I bet the turkeys are out of the oven at the deli." She went to get her purse out of her drawer and Seth stopped her.

"Sit down. Let me run down and get you a sandwich. I am sure this morning put you way behind schedule. Turkey on rye with Russian dressing and an Iced Tea?"

"Yes, thank you. Put your lunch on my card, too." She handed him her Gold Card.

"Shall I close your door?"

Mia nodded, as he headed out.

Thank God for Seth, she thought. If anyone could keep her life in order and keep her on track, it was Seth. Anal, persnickety, bitchy as all hell, incredibly loyal and very competent. He was her rock as well as her personal fashion police, making sure that her somewhat BoHo style was always trendy and chic.

Mia took a swig from a bottle of water on her desk and thought, today has sucked and it's only lunchtime on Monday. Please don't get any worse, I've had enough already.

Waking up her sleeping computer screen, she clicked the email icon and started to scan her inbox. Geez—in just a few hours fifty-seven unread new emails—Junk, junk, junk, deal with later, delete, delete, delete, Business Journal, NY Times alert, junk, Advertising Age, Facebook friend request from Schooner Moore …

Facebook friend request from Schooner Moore.

She just stared at the email subject line, her blood stopping, halting in her veins, followed by her heart racing, as the air in the room disappeared. *Breathe, Mia, breathe*, she consciously told herself. Facebook friend request from Schooner Moore. Ho-ly Shit!

She opened the email.

Trying to regain her breath, Mia stared at the little block with the confirm button. Schooner had sent this. This day was getting stranger by the minute. *Schooner had sent this*. He had sent this to her. Ho-ly shit!

Covered in goosebumps, Mia closed her eyes and took a deep breath. She tried to still her thoughts, but every cell in her body was in overdrive, and each and every one of those cells, including the ones in both her head and her heart (which rarely agreed), were in perfect harmony.

Mia hit confirm.

Chapter Two

Holy shit. Schooner just friended me. Mia was astounded.

Quickly logging onto Facebook, she immediately went to her friends list. There he was, she clicked his name and went to his page. He had one friend. She was his first and only friend. *Holy shit.*

Moving her cursor to his picture, she clicked on it so that it came up full-sized, filling her screen. She was shocked when she heard herself gasp.

She was looking at Schooner. And he was smiling at her. His real smile.

He was a grown man now. A forty-something year old man. Still so handsome. So, so handsome. The crinkles in the corners of his eyes made her smile. They were new. Oh, those eyes. Those beautiful clear eyes. She realized that not only was she smiling at her computer screen, but that there were also tears in her eyes and her throat had tightened.

In her mind, he had always remained nineteen. Not this man she was looking at. But this was Schooner. This stranger, who was not quite a stranger, was Schooner.

She heard the ding and the message screen popped up.

Schooner: Mia, are you there?
Mia: Yes
Schooner: What's your phone #?

She just stared at the screen. Her hands were shaking. Literally shaking.

Schooner: Mia, what is your phone #?

Wow. He was forceful.

She typed in her cell number, with badly trembling hands and hit send. A nanosecond later, her cell phone rang, the display portraying a number with a 949-area code. Mia realized she was somehow still expecting a 714-area code. Their old area code. Times had changed.

"Hi," she tried to keep her voice even, but it came out breathy.

"Hi," it was his voice. A little more mature sounding. But it was

Schooner.

She knew it was her turn to speak next, social graces would dictate a "How are you?" but she had paused for a moment and he jumped right in, this time his voice hoarse and tight, "Why did you leave me?"

Wham to the solar plexus. She literally was thrown back in her chair. The air momentarily knocked out of her.

"You told her what happened to me." They both knew to whom she was referring.

"No. I never told her. Mia, I never told her anything," his tone was adamant. "Did she tell you I told her?"

The tension crackling off his voice was unmistakable.

"Schooner, it was a long time ago." Immediately, Mia felt the pain as if it were yesterday, and she didn't want to revisit it.

"Mia, I didn't tell her. I never would have betrayed you that way. All I ever wanted to do was protect you. And I didn't know why you left me. I never knew why you left me. But I swear, I never, ever told her."

They were both silent, clearly equally reeling from one another's revelations.

He was the first to speak again. "If she told you that she knew, then she was bluffing and she played you." Mia let out an involuntary sob and he paused and then sighed, "Holy fuck," as if he'd come to some huge realization.

Mia thought she was going to be sick.

"Please believe me, Mia. You know all I wanted to do was protect you."

And with those words, it all came flooding back. Now with twenty-four years of hindsight, Mia finally realized that she had been played, and CJ had gotten the knee jerk reaction out of her that she had intended. Mia had played right into her hands and the now enormity of her own actions and how it had drastically changed her life and how she had hurt Schooner came down on her with a weight so heavy she thought her chest was going to cave in.

The emotional onslaught overwhelmed her, making it impossible not to cry, "Oh my God, Schooner, I am so sorry. I am so, so sorry. Oh my God."

"Do you believe me?" his voice was soft.

"Yes," she managed between sobs. "I do."

Hearing him sigh brought on another round of tears.

"Schooner, how do I begin to apologize for being an immature sixteen-year-old, for not trusting you, for believing what she said? I am so, so sorry

I hurt you."

"Shhh don't, Baby Girl. You were a victim in this, too. What she did was malicious with the intent to hurt you and to put an end to us. And my whole freaking life has been based on a lie."

Hearing the anger in his voice, it was then Mia realized that Schooner had married CJ, sending a torrent of fresh tears down her cheeks. She won. She fucking won. She played a dirty game and won.

There was a soft knock on her door and Seth peeked in. Mia motioned for him to come in and he looked at her questioningly as he put the lunch bag on her desk. Seth's eyes telegraphed alarm at coming in and seeing her so distraught.

"Schooner, my associate just came in and I've got to prep for a 2 o'clock meeting."

"Schooner?" Seth mouthed. "Schooner?" Then muttered, "Are you talking to a boat?"

"What time are you up until at night?"

"I'm kind of a night owl, usually between midnight and one."

"Mia, are you going to answer the phone when you see my number come up?" his voice was very soft.

"Yeah."

"Say it, Mia," his tone was now more forceful.

"I will answer your calls, Schooner."

Seth was looking at her, brows knit in a *what's going on here* look.

"You promise?"

She smiled. "Yes. I promise."

"Okay, I will call you later."

"Okay."

"Mia," he paused, "It's really good to hear your voice."

And that caused another sob to escape. "It's really good to hear your voice too, Schooner," she replied, softly.

"I'll talk to you later, Baby Girl."

A cascade of tears flowed from her eyes at his final two words. Those two final words. "Okay. Bye." And she hung up her phone.

Seth sat there looking at her, completely speechless.

"Am sure I look lovely." She smiled at Seth, wiping her running nose on a napkin from her lunch bag.

"Schooner?"

"Schooner."

"First off, who names their kid Schooner? Is this some WASP thing?"

"Might be," Mia laughed, tears still running down her face.

"Was he totally teased for being named Schooner?" Seth was obsessing over Schooner's name.

"No. Not at all. It totally fit him. I'm sure there's a generation of little Schooners out there born to women who were crushing on him."

"So, who is he and why were you crying hysterically?" He unwrapped her turkey sandwich for her and put the straw in her Iced Tea and slid them across the desk to her.

"Schooner was my college boyfriend freshman year. He was my first love."

"Go on."

She clearly was not going to get away with the abridged version with Seth.

"Do you remember I told you about being raped in college?"

Seth nodded.

"Well, Schooner was the one who found me that night and took me to the hospital. And then he didn't leave my side the rest of the semester. The last night of school he went back to his dorm to study for his last final and his ex, this bitch CJ—who I think he probably married, showed up and said a bunch of stuff that led me to believe he told her what had happened to me and I freaked. I thought he betrayed me and I cut out early the next morning and got an earlier flight home. I just left and never said goodbye or spoke to him ever again, until, well, you just heard it."

"Oh my God." Seth's hand flew to his mouth, "What did he say?"

"He asked, 'Why did you leave me?'." A small sob escaped, accompanied by another fresh burst of tears. "And I told him that he betrayed my confidence with her. He was adamant that he never told her and that she was probably bluffing and that she had played me and that I fell for it."

"Holy shit, Mia. Do you believe him?"

She nodded, "I do. He was clearly very angry. That fucking bitch played me."

"And so, he never knew why you left him. Until now. Oh God, this is so tragic. You loved him?"

Mia nodded, "I loved him so much, Seth. No one has ever come close, not even..." Mia's bottom lip trembled at memories only she held.

"Mia, he came and found you."

More tears.

Seth flipped open his iPad case. "What's his last name."

"Moore."

He began typing. "Schooner James Moore of Newport Beach, California. Is that him?"

Mia nodded.

"Okay, there's a Wiki here on him. Schooner James Moore, American Entrepreneur, age 43, his birthday was just two days ago, wow, it was Saturday. Holy crap, Mia, he owns Level 9. Totally famous health clubs in LA. The *Real Housewives* work out there. Oh yeah, he married her, Colleen Janice (CJ) Moore, two kids, Holly, 19 and Zac, 17. Let's Google Image him."

Seth looked up at Mia, mouth hanging wide open. "*You* are the Queen BBC!" he yelled. "The Queen. The Ultimate!" His jaw was still slack as he continued to point a finger at her.

BBC was their acronym for "Bitch Be Crazy"—women who acted crazy or did wacko things or were just plain loopy, were known as BBC's.

"Why?" laughed Mia.

"You walked out on this man? Bitch, you *are* crazy." He looked up from his iPad. "I love him."

"Let me see." Mia grabbed at Seth's iPad.

He pulled it out of her reach. "No. No. No. You are not taking Schooner away from me, Bitch."

Mia laughed and got up and walked around to the other side of the desk. She looked over Seth's shoulder. "It's so weird to see him as an adult. He was so gorgeous when he was young."

Seth shot her a BBC look. "He's still gorgeous. Robert Redford wished he looked like this in his best days. Mia, this is your Schooner?" He flipped through the pictures.

She nodded and more tears sprung from her eyes. "That's my Schooner."

Chapter Three

Mia paced around her apartment. Her cell phone had not rung and it was 12:10 A.M. *I'm waiting for his call like a teenager*, she sighed. Maybe he'd reconsidered after their brief talk earlier in the day. He now had the answer to his question and after all, CJ was his wife. They had kids together. They had built a family. They were a family. Mia looked around her beautiful apartment, a place that usually provided her solace, but tonight she felt both alone and lonely. No kids, no family, no current significant other.

Thanks, Schooner, she thought, you really needed to find me so that I can dwell on being forty and alone.

Finally, at 12:30, Mia crawled into bed and turned off the lights. Today has been so emotionally draining, she thought. Lost and found. Today was lost and found. And she realized that now she was scared it would be lost, found and lost again. How crazy is that, she thought.

She was in that quasi-sleep state, having odd dreams of Schooner, when her cell phone rang. Reaching for it, the display read that 949-area code. It was 2:47 A.M.

"Hi," she tried not to sound sleepy.

"Hi," his voice sounded like silk and she curled up deeper into her blanket. "I'm sorry it's so late. No, go ahead and put those bags over there," he said to someone else. "Sorry, I'm just getting settled," he sighed. "I moved out tonight. I'm at the Ritz in Laguna Niguel."

"Oh my God. I'm so sorry, Schooner."

"This was a long time coming. I just didn't know how long until today. What she did to you. What she did to us. There's just no coming back from that," he sounded absolute.

"Are you okay?" her voice was sweet and soft. She wanted to comfort him.

"There's a yes and no to that, Mia. Today has been a lot to process."

Mia was nodding her head on her end of the call, as if he could see her. "If I could change things, Schooner," she let out a long sigh. "I should've come to you. I'm so sorry."

"I know. I wish you had. Everything would have been different," he too sighed. "Mia, I went to pieces when you left. I was so blindsided. I really thought we were going to spend our whole lives together."

She was silent and he asked, "You still there?"

"Yeah, I'm just lost in thought and I'm listening to your voice. I never thought I'd hear your voice again."

"Well, talk to me so that I can hear your voice, too." She could hear him settling in on the other end of the phone. "After I left California, I just sort of emotionally crawled inside myself for a long, long time. I don't think I've ever been really great at relationships."

"I don't agree with that," he whispered and she smiled. "I didn't even ask, are you married?"

"No, never married, no kids. I own a small boutique advertising agency here in Manhattan. Been involved in a couple of semi-long-term relationships, but never got married."

"Well I guess that you figured out that I married CJ."

The silence was saturated with unspoken pain, before Mia was able to speak again.

"Why Schooner? Did you always love her?" Failing to keep the hurt out of her voice, she could hear it creeping in. Between nervous hands she twisted her blanket.

"Oh Mia. No, I didn't love her. This is just so fucked up. I loved you, but I didn't want to ever hurt again the way I did when I lost you. Best way to avoid hurt, don't put yourself in a situation that can hurt you. That's what I thought I was doing. I was in a situation I could control. What we had was out of control. I knew I would never be emotionally over my head like that with her."

How sad, Mia thought. She was sad for him. The thought of him hurting was gut wrenching, but on some level, she was so happy to hear him say he was with CJ because he didn't love her deeply. There was something very satisfying in that knowledge, especially after today's revelations. Satisfying, yet sad. For everyone.

"Are your kids wonderful?" she asked, needing to change the subject and get away from all the hurt they'd inflicted upon one another.

The smile in his voice was evident when he spoke of them and she listened intently, hearing the pride and love in his words and tone.

"Schooner, things played out the way they were supposed to so that you would have your kids."

"Maybe so. I definitely don't have any regrets there. Did you ever want children?"

"I kind of tried not to go there," she began. "The relationships I've been involved in weren't right to bring a child into, so it just never really worked out."

"But did you want them?" he persisted.

His personality was so much more forceful and no nonsense as an adult. *He's really tenacious*, Mia thought, "If the situation had been different, I might've let myself go there, but it wasn't, so I put it out of my reality."

"I'm sorry," he whispered.

"Don't be," she sighed, smushing deeper into her covers "It is what it is."

They were silent for a few minutes and he asked, "Did you miss me?"

She was silent, trying to pull her thoughts and composure together so that she'd have a fighting chance of controlling a threatening onslaught of tears.

"I guess that's my answer," he sadly assumed when she didn't respond.

Mia could hear the fresh hurt in his voice. "No. That is not your answer. I was just trying to make sure that I didn't start crying again." She took a deep breath. "Schooner, it felt like part of me died when I left. It was years before I was even semi-okay again. I just hid inside myself. I was angry and hurt and immature and losing the guy I loved felt like I'd had my heart cut out."

"You never lost me."

"I was a freaking emotional mess," she went on. The floodgates were now open. "So yes, the answer to your question is yes, I missed you. I was just empty. Broken. How do you even start with someone else after us? Nothing felt like that and it was my only point of reference—the way that we were together. It took me a long time to figure out that every relationship was different and that no two were alike. I wanted to feel again what I felt with us."

"Did you ever find it?"

She could hear the concern for her in his voice.

"I think at times I tried to convince myself that I did. But eventually I'd figure out that I was lying to myself. So, the answer to that question would be no."

They were silent for a while, but it wasn't uncomfortable. She could feel the intense emotion and energy across the telephone line. This was so much for each of them to process. Years of preconceived notions, dispelled. Truths that they had convinced themselves of, crumbled, turning out to be a house of cards, their house of lies.

"I'm really glad I found you again, Baby Girl."
She smiled. "You know what?"
"What?"
She could hear his smile.
"I'm really glad you found me, too."

Chapter Four

It was 4:45 A.M. when Mia texted Seth.

Mia: Are you awake?
Seth: I am now.
Mia: He moved out tonight. He's staying at The Ritz.
Seth: Holy shit, he didn't!
Mia: Holy shit, he did!
Seth: I love him.
Mia: LOL
Seth: So when's he coming to NYC?
Mia: Not soon enough!!!
Seth: There's hope for you yet, BBC. There's hope for you yet.

Chapter Five

It was Thursday morning at 6:45 A.M. and Mia's cell phone was ringing. It no longer displayed the 949 number. It now said *Schooner—mobile*.

"Hey," she answered. Already awake for about half an hour, Mia was too wired to sleep. She had woken up and looked at the time on her phone's clock every hour throughout the night.

"We're on the tarmac."

The PA announcements were blaring in the background of the call. "Welcome to New York!" Mia was beaming, ear-to-ear. *Oh my God, he is here*.

Holy smokes—in less than an hour he'll be at my apartment, she realized. He had flown in on the Wednesday night red-eye. What a crazy few days.

She had arranged for her favorite limo service to be there to meet him.

"I'll see you in a few."

She could hear the smile in his voice. "Oh my God, Schooner." Mia was already shaking with nerves. She had so much nervous energy that she felt like she was vibrating on another frequency.

"I know, Baby Girl. I'll see you soon."

Mia texted Seth.

Mia: He's landed and he's on his way!!!!
Seth: OMG
Mia: I'm a freaking wreck!
Seth: What are you wearing?
Mia: Since it's only 6 A.M., I don't want to overdo it. Jeans, black V-neck cashmere sweater.
Seth: V-neck is good. Show him that great boobage. Cashmere is touchable. Shoes?
Mia: Right now barefoot.
Seth: Stay that way. I know you just had a pedicure. Make-up?
Mia: Just a little blush.
Seth: Do a little brown liner at the outer corner of your eyes. Hair?
Mia: It's down and I'm having a good hair day.
Seth: Bangs in your eyes?

Mia: Yes.
Seth: Sexy. Love it. I am so nervous 4 u!
Mia: Ditto. I feel sick. Too bad it is 2 early in the morn to eat a Xanax!! Ok, will call you later. Wish me luck!
Seth: All will be great. He found out about u on Sat. night and Thurs morning he is here. I love this. So romantic. Don't fuck it up BBC!
Mia: LOL. Pray 4 me!

Mia tried staying busy to keep her nerves in check. She made a pot of coffee. Sliced bagels. Unloaded her dishwasher. Turned on the TV. Tried to watch CNN. Brushed her teeth for a second time. Dabbed her lips with just the slightest bit of gloss. Tried to do deep breathing exercises to stop from shaking. But she just could not stop trembling, no matter what she did.

The call came from the doorman in the lobby and she had them send him up. He was in her building. Getting into her elevator. It was all so surreal. In just moments, she would be face to face with Schooner Moore again. She remembered the last time she saw him as he walked down the steps from her dorm, not letting go of her hand until their fingertips no longer touched.

And there it was, the knock on the door. She whispered, "Showtime", as she went to open the door (not knowing that he whispered the very same word to himself on the other side of the door).

Holding her breath as she opened the door, she prayed that she didn't do something embarrassing like hyperventilate and pass out.

There he was.

She looked up into his handsome face and was sure her smile was as wide as his. She didn't think about it, her arms just went around his waist immediately, and she felt his arms tighten around her, crushing her to him. She felt his lips in her hair and heard an "mmm" come out of her.

She looked up at him and his beautiful smile eased away a good portion of her nerves (not all).

"Come on in," she finally said.

"I was so nervous on the ride here," he admitted.

She held out a hand to show him how she was shaking and they both laughed.

"I want another hug," she whispered and he complied, wrapping his arms around her again. She buried her face in his chest, deeply breathing in his clean scent, feeling the hardness of his stomach muscles and nuzzling her face into them. She looked up at him again and he gave her a small soft kiss on her forehead. She knew she could not wipe the silly smile off her face.

She led him over to the breakfast bar in her open kitchen. "Coffee?" she offered. "You hungry? Can I make you some breakfast?"

He sat on the bar stool, his long legs stretched out, just smiling at her.

"What?" she asked, smiling back at him.

No one should look that good in faded jeans, she thought. Faded jeans and a blue Henley sweatshirt—the man was a living Brooks Brothers ad. And there he was in her kitchen. Smiling at her. Schooner Moore was sitting at her breakfast bar, in her apartment, in Manhattan. Surreal didn't even begin to describe the situation.

He just shook his head. "Saturday night I was at my own birthday party in Newport Beach and I was miserable. Truly miserable. I was out on a deck alone, away from everyone at my party. Away from my party. And Beau Gordon shows up out on the deck with a joint—I haven't gotten high in like ten years—and we smoke this joint and start talking about that time we got high at the freshman retreat and he asks me who was the girl that was with us? I tell him it was you and he tells me that he had a fight with you on Facebook. That was Saturday night. It's 8 A.M. on Thursday morning. And I'm here with you. In your apartment. In New York."

Mia could not wipe the smile off her face. "Pretty fucking surreal, huh?"

He laughed, "Very fucking surreal."

Mia poured two glasses of orange juice and handed one to Schooner. She held hers up in a toast, "To Beau Gordon, you AK-47 toting son of a bitch. Thank you!"

"Here! Here!" Schooner clinked glasses with her and they laughed.

It's still easy, Mia thought. *It's still so easy with him.*

Grabbing the bagels that she'd cut apart earlier to help calm her nerves, she asked, "Hungry?"

He shook his head, yes. "Do you have whole wheat?"

Mia gave him a *what are you crazy* look. "Whole wheat? Did you just ask me for a whole wheat bagel? What's next, are you going to want to spread avocado on this?"

He laughed, "Bite me."

"So tempted," she volleyed back. "Okay, your choices are onion, everything and pumpernickel."

God, he was gorgeous and he was sitting at her breakfast bar. This man, whom she had loved more deeply than any other man in her life. This total stranger.

"Please tell me you know what pumpernickel is?" she teased.

"Well by process of elimination, it's that one." He pointed to the pumpernickel bagel.

She knew she'd been smiling ear to ear since he'd gotten there. "Did you sleep on the plane?"

"I can't sleep on planes." He shook his head.

"Oh no, not good. Well, after this adrenaline rush wears off, you're going to crash," Mia began. "I need to do a conference call, which I'll take from here at 9 A.M. It should last about an hour and a half. You should nap. Go crash out in the bedroom."

"Can I crash on the couch, so I can hang out with you? If that doesn't bother you."

"Whatever is comfortable for you," Mia offered.

"I'm a guy, just put me on a couch."

Mia laughed, "Okay, I'll stick the remote in your hand, that should put you right to sleep."

Reaching out, Schooner took Mia's hand in his and gave it a squeeze. "I need to get gloves later. It's really cold here and I didn't think about bringing any."

"We can go do that after my call."

Schooner had arrived with a blast of arctic air. The day's high was only going to be twenty-three degrees and down into the teens at night with below zero wind chills. But the day was bright and sunny and the sky was the color of his eyes. *Schooner Blue,* Mia mused.

After breakfast, Schooner got on the couch and Mia brought him a pillow from the bedroom. Within minutes, he was fast asleep. She brought a quilt in and covered him, then just sat there staring at him. *Un-fucking-believable*, she thought as she watched him sleep in her living room.

Should I? she wondered. And then took a picture with her cell phone of him sleeping peacefully on her couch. Mia couldn't take her eyes off him. This wasn't real. This just could not be real.

She texted the photo to Seth.

Seth: OMG, he's adorable.
Mia: I know. Can I keep him?
Seth: LOL
Mia: Please please please. Please let me keep him!
Seth: Are you ok?
Mia: Yeah, a little nervous. Not quite sure—Do I touch him? Not touch him?

Seth: Stop over thinking it, BBC.
Mia: Ok…. got to get ready for conf. call
Seth: Update me later.
Mia: Will do

Schooner didn't stir the entire time Mia was on her call. He looked so beautiful sleeping. There was a hint of the young Schooner that she used to watch across her pillow as he slept. She was having a hard time processing it all. What were they doing? What was this? They were two people who had once loved each other deeply and had it ripped away. But who were they now?

Their marathon phone calls over the past few days had been deep, cathartic, brutally honest and surprisingly easy. But what about being together? She was attracted to him, how could she not be… *but was it mutual?* she wondered. He had a room reserved uptown at The Stanhope—he didn't want her to feel pressured about staying in her apartment and now that was hanging over her—*where would he stay? Would he even want to stay with her? At the end of the weekend, what would it be? Nice to see you again?*

Seth's words starting ringing in her brain, "Don't over think it" and clearly she was.

Not having the heart to wake him, she wrote him a note—this time she wouldn't leave without a note. *Not making that mistake twice,* she mused.

S- Ran out to the store. Will be back soon. Make yourself at home. Extra towels are out in the bathroom, if you need. See you in a few.-M

An hour later, Mia reentered her apartment, to find Schooner no longer on her couch.

"Hey, I'm back," she yelled out.

"I'll be right out," he called out from the bathroom. Putting the bags down on the couch, Mia took off her coat, scarf and hat. Her teeth were chattering, she was still so cold. Today was the kind of cold that just got deep into your bones and hung on tight.

The bathroom door opened, a cloud of steamy air escaped and Schooner emerged behind it, a towel wrapped around his waist, as he dried his thick fair hair with another towel. He smiled at her, clearly enjoying her reaction to his near-nakedness.

"I own health clubs," he offered, a very self-satisfied smirk on his face.

"And I eat bagels. This is so not good." Mia shook her head and walked over to the kitchen, needing water for her suddenly very dry mouth.

Schooner emerged a few minutes later, hair still damp, in his faded jeans and a button-down Ralph Lauren, sleeves rolled at the cuffs—barefoot. Faded jeans and barefoot and 6' 2, Mia took another sip of water for that very dry mouth of hers.

"C'mere," Mia said, sitting down on the couch and grabbing the bags from Barney's New York/Co-op. "I went and got some stuff for you while you were sleeping."

A real smile took over his face and she handed him the first box. Inside were black leather cashmere lined gloves. "I hope they fit. I knew you needed them."

He took them out of the box and put them on. "Perfect," he declared and leaned forward and kissed her cheek.

Okay, cheek kiss, not good, she thought.

Mia planted a smile on her face and pulled another box out of the bag for him and handed it to him. "What did you do?" he asked and she just shrugged.

Inside the box was a Scottish cashmere scarf—a blue plaid in navy and sky blue—a perfect match for his eyes. He brought it up to his face to feel the soft, plush cashmere. "This is really gorgeous, Mia."

Mia took the scarf from Schooner's hands and wrapped it around his neck, holding a side in each hand. She ached to pull him forward and kiss him, but instead just smiled at him. "It's very you," she said. "It matches your eyes."

His arms went around her and he hugged her tight.

"You ready to go out and brave the cold, California Boy?"

"Show me your New York." He stood and grabbed his coat. "Hey Mia," he turned to her and smiled and out of the pocket of his black and royal blue Columbia ski jacket he pulled out a black knit cap and pulled it onto his head, down to his eyes.

Mia's heart melted and stung at the same time. *Do I smile or cry*? she asked herself. He had the hat. *He still had the hat.*

"Well, look at that, I'm good for gloves, scarf and a hat," she joked. When in doubt, make a joke.

The tears burned at the back of her throat.

Chapter Six

They hit the streets and headed south from Mia's apartment in Chelsea to the West Village.

"Okay, so you had New York bagels this morning, it's now time for part two of your Big Apple culinary tour." Mia bounced down the streets of New York City. She always tapped into the city's rhythm and never quite walked when she was in her hometown.

Within the first few blocks, Schooner was bouncing beside her as she played tour guide.

"Please tell me part two is pizza." He raised his brows questioningly and she enthusiastically nodded back. "You weren't kidding about the bagels." He smiled down at her.

"We'll have to send you home with a bag," she offered and then immediately saw a shadow cross his face. She grabbed his hand, her other hand going to his forearm, "I'm not looking to get rid of you."

He squeezed her hand and smiled at her, "You'd better not be."

He didn't take his hand away and they walked down Sixth Avenue holding hands.

I'm walking down Sixth Avenue with Schooner—holding hands, like a couple. This is truly mind numbing, she thought. And if it weren't for the cold, biting wind stinging her cheeks, she would've thought she was dreaming. Stealing a glance at his handsome profile and just the sight of him, with the black knit cap she'd placed on his head nearly a quarter of a century before, overwhelmed her. *Is this what truly happy feels like?* she wondered.

They stopped for lunch at John's Pizza on Bleecker Street and Schooner had his first taste of New York coal oven pizza, with its thin, almost slightly burned crust and fresh mozzarella gracing the top.

"I'm not allowing you to put pineapple on this," she teased. "That's considered heresy in these parts."

Their day was the perfect mix of sightseeing, fresh air, stopping into little places for something quintessentially New York or just to warm up. They walked across the Brooklyn Bridge and back through lower Manhattan along Battery City Park and ended the evening at one of Mia's favorite little hole in the wall restaurants on Cornelia Street in the West Village, before walking back up to her apartment building in Chelsea.

Running the last few blocks, laughing, they unsuccessfully tried to escape the below zero wind chill gusts as they reached the lobby of Mia's building. Mia was shivering when they got into the elevator.

"Are you sure you want to go out to the beach tomorrow?" she questioned Schooner.

"Yeah, it'll be fun in this cold," he nodded and looked at his watch. It was almost midnight. "What time is the ferry we have to catch?" he asked.

"There's a 10:10 A.M. out of Bay Shore. We'll be going against traffic, but I still think we should leave ourselves plenty of time. There's supposed to be snow flurries overnight and in the morning, but if we're on the road by 8:30, I think we'll be okay."

"So, should I be back here by about eight?" he asked.

Mia nodded, her heart sinking. He was going to his hotel. Keep smiling, she reminded herself. Don't tank out now. Don't ruin a perfect day. Perfect until now.

Schooner grabbed his soft black Tumi bag and slung it over his shoulder. He smiled down at Mia, "This was a great day. Really, really great."

Then why the fuck are you leaving? Mia wondered.

"It was," she concurred, smiling back at him.

He gently grasped her upper arm, bent down and kissed her cheek. "I'll see you in the morning."

She couldn't speak. The salt from the tears rising toward their release was already burning the back of her throat. *Is he just not into me*? Mia questioned herself.

She stood in the doorway as he walked down the hall toward the elevator.

There was no way she was going to spend the night wondering and torturing herself. "Schooner…" she called, as he pressed the elevator call button.

He looked at her.

"Schooner. I don't want you to leave." There. She had put it out there. It was all on the line. She had to know.

He stood looking at her, his face inscrutable. The elevator door opened.

Don't get in, she silently begged. *Don't. Get. In.*

He stood there for a second not moving and then started down the hall toward her. She couldn't read his expression. His eyes looked kind, but he wasn't smiling.

Reaching where she was standing, in the threshold of her apartment's doorway, he stood before her. Taking her face in both of his hands, his eyes locked on hers.

Here it comes, she thought, the friend speech. Her eyes filled with tears, the hope of the feelings she'd felt resurrected the last few days quickly being extinguished. Her heart burned. *Why did I allow myself to go there?* she chastised. Another dream dies. Please don't cry, she begged herself, don't cry. Don't make him feel even more uncomfortable.

He held her face, looking directly into her eyes, his face expressionless.

She wanted to look away, to cry, but he held her face and her gaze. If her eyes could speak, the words she was silently trying to tell him were, "I just want you to love me again and I don't think I can take this rejection from you."

He pushed her bangs out of her eyes and a smile slowly overtook his handsome face. He ran his thumb over her bottom lip and bent down and softly kissed her lips. Parting her lips for him, his tongue explored in a way that felt both familiar and new. Mia wrapped her arms around his neck and did not hold back. Kissing him passionately, she let him know how much she wanted him, how much she wanted them again. She felt her tears finally release from where she was holding them at bay and run from her eyes to her temples. This time she didn't try to stop them.

He pulled back and looked at her, still holding her face and gave her a rough kiss on her lips. "I was hoping you'd ask."

She could feel her brows knit together in a questioning look.

"This had to come from you. It's been really hard to be hands off with you—but it had to come from you."

"I was thinking you didn't want me." Just put it out there, Mia, she told herself. This time you need to be totally honest with him—all the time.

He caressed her cheek, "Crazy girl." He laughed. "Don't you know how I feel about you?"

She shook her head no. "I think you should show me," she smiled at him and thought to herself, *Seth would be screaming BBC at me right now.*

He pulled her tight against him and she could feel his erection through his jeans pressing against her stomach. He gave her the Schooner smile.

She smiled up at him, tears still streaming from her eyes.

Wiping her tears with his thumb, he leaned down and whispered in her ear, "It *is* real, Baby Girl," answering her unasked question.

Taking her by the hand, he led her back into her apartment.

Chapter Seven

Mia was curled up in Schooner's lap on her couch, arms around his neck, as they made out like teenagers. She felt sixteen again. All the anxiety from the day was gone, as they were now totally on the same page—they still wanted one another after all this time. His hotel reservations had been canceled and he was staying where he belonged, with her.

Brushing her bangs from her eyes, he smiled at her. "I have something for you."

She wriggled in his lap, "I know, I feel it." She raised her eyebrows at him.

Schooner laughed, "That too. But you're just going to have to wait on that."

Her eyes were wide and she faux pouted. He took her bottom lip in his teeth and growled at her. *How can it just be so easy with someone*? she wondered. So damn easy.

Moving her off his lap and onto the couch, he stood and stretched for a moment, then walked across the room over to where his luggage sat by the door. She watched him gracefully bend down and unzip the outer compartment of his bag and remove a flat package. As he walked back toward the couch, she could not help but admire his athletic grace. There was a fluidity to the way he moved and she could almost see him back on the courts covering the space with lithe ease.

Smiling, he sat down next to her, silently handing her the package. Cocking her head to the side, she looked at him and took it.

"Open it," he demanded and she did, pulling open a tabbed end of the cardboard.

Inside was a large envelope and she carefully slid it out from the cardboard sleeve. Mia looked up at him and he nodded, urging her to go on. Opening the envelope, inside was a stack of 8x10 B&W prints.

Removing the photos carefully, she studied the first image in the stack. It was of a small African boy holding a soccer ball that was half his size. He was smiling and there was a wide gap between his two front teeth. The child was stood on a rutted dirt road with thatched roof cottage-sized dwellings in the background.

Mia looked up at Schooner, quizzically. "Did you shoot this?"

He nodded, smiling.

"Where? When? This is really good, Schooner." She was looking at him for answers.

"That was shot in the village of Macha in Zambia. I went there the summer after freshman year."

Mia started looking through the stack of starkly beautiful landscapes Schooner had captured, impressed with his natural ability for strong composition that led the eye around the frame. His portraits of the children were raw, journalistic and pure.

She looked up at him. "You are so talented."

He smiled. "I've wanted to share these with you for a very long time. When I shot them, you were in my head the whole time, reminding me about all the things I listened to you say about composition and lighting. When I got back, I had these made for you."

"What were you doing in Africa?"

"Well, I was kind of heartbroken that summer and my plans to come to New York kind of blew up. A family friend, an orthopedic surgeon, my orthopedic surgeon, suggested I come to Zambia with him and a group of other specialists and help them in establishing a hospital. He thought the change of scenery would be good for me. And it was. I definitely found my calling over there. I helped the doctors get set up, and after a few days I realized that there were all these families traveling long distances to the hospital and the kids had to wait all day for their parents, so I started a sports camp for them."

Mia's eyes widened and a smile lit her face as she listened to Schooner. "Your first health club venture!"

He laughed, "Essentially, yes." And then, "Okay, look through the rest," he ordered.

She went back to the stack of photos, understanding the joy Schooner had brought to these beautiful children, and then she came upon a picture of a waterfall that made her gasp.

"You gave me a picture of Forest Falls as a gift and I wanted to return the favor with a picture of Victoria Falls," he whispered into her ear.

Mia was in awe of his romantic heart. He'd saved these pictures, he'd saved the black wool cap. She just stared at him.

"What?" he asked.

"You. You just blow my mind, Schooner. There is so much to you. Do people know who you are?"

"A few." He took her hand and kissed it. "There's one more photo."

She looked back at the stack and lifted the last photo. Underneath his beautiful B&W of the falls was the only color photo in the stack. Standing in front of Victoria Falls was a devastatingly handsome nineteen-year-old Schooner Moore, smiling at the camera, a real smile, and squinting in the bright sunlight.

Mia caught her breath staring at the photo she now held in both hands. Smiling back at her was her Schooner, the Schooner she had carried in her heart, buried, for twenty-four years. She looked up at the man sitting next to her on the couch, smiling. Her Schooner. He was just watching her intently. She looked back at the photo and that's when she saw his casted right hand.

"Your hand? What happened?" There was alarm in her eyes as she searched his handsome face.

"I got into a little fight with a wall in a dorm hallway."

It took her a moment to process that. "You punched a wall?"

He nodded, "Not the brightest thing I've ever done."

Mia took Schooner's right hand in both of hers. Gently running her fingers over his knuckles, she brought his hand to her lips, tenderly peppering it with kisses, as she took in the enormity of what had happened. His casted hand meant that he couldn't play tennis and if this happened in a dorm before summer break, it happened the day she left him. He punched a cement wall. Lost in thought, she rubbed his hand against her cheek.

He just watched her.

So much more had been lost than even she had initially thought. The heaviness in her heart felt unbearable as she processed the casted hand, the orthopedic surgeon, what he must've felt that day not finding her after their sweet goodnight the previous evening, the damage to both his hand and his tennis career.

Mia stood with Schooner's right hand in hers, and placed it against her heart. "We are done hurting each other," she declared and holding his hand in both of hers, led him into her bedroom.

Chapter Eight

"Damn, it's cold in here!" Schooner grabbed Mia and pulled her close.

"Will be much better under the down blanket—naked." Mia said into his chest.

The now gale force winds were slamming her bedroom windows, chilling them with each rattle, a fine snow had begun to fall and sounded like sand hitting the window with each gust.

She started to unbutton his shirt and he took her hands, "Baby Girl, I'm getting naked under the blanket. It's freaking freezing in here."

Pulling her toward the bed, he lifted the down comforter.

"Afraid of shrinkage?" she teased, getting under the blanket next to him and pulling off her clothes.

He pulled her underneath his now naked body. "This feel like shrinkage to you?" He pressed his hard cock against her.

She threaded her fingers through his hair and pulled his lips to hers. "It feels like Heaven to me."

"Feels like home to me," he smiled into her mouth, before kissing her deeply.

Mia wrapped her legs around Schooner, his warm body covering hers completely. With each kiss, she could feel herself becoming wetter and wetter, wanting him inside of her desperately. She ran her hands down his back, feeling the definition of his muscles, kneading them, trying to memorize what he felt like to her touch.

His teeth were at her neck, softly grazing one of her most sensitive areas. Moaning, she tilted her head, giving him access, wanting to feel his teeth. Pressing his head into her neck, she could feel the pressure of his teeth biting harder and she wrapped her legs around him tighter and pulled his hair.

He moaned and his lips went back to her mouth, his kiss savage and rough.

She could feel the head of his cock pressing against her, maybe an inch away from where she wanted him, needed him.

Pulling her mouth away left them both panting, blood rushing frantically. "Schooner, did you bring condoms?" Even in the dark, she could see the shocked look on his face.

"Fuck. No. You're not on anything?" He was searching her face, trying to get his bearings.

"Forty and not dating anyone." She shook her head. Schooner gave Mia an incredulous look saying how could you not be seeing anyone.

She loved him for the way he saw her.

"Okay, ummm" He looked at her wide-eyed. "What do you want to do?"

"Well, there's a 24-hour Korean grocer about two blocks from here." They both looked toward the window. A heavier snow had begun to fall, swirling and dancing in the street lamps below, then being whipped in sheets by the relentless wind gusts. "Okay, not a good idea."

Schooner went to move off Mia, but she held him tightly in place on top of her with her arms and legs. "You are not making this easier." He gave her a soft kiss on the lips.

"That's because it's my job to make it harder." She pulled his head back down to her for another kiss.

He brushed her bangs from her eyes. "What do you want to do here, Baby Girl?"

She took his face in her hands and kissed him deeply. "I know what I want, Schooner. To me, there's no downside to this." She searched his beautiful eyes.

He sighed and smiled, "Are you sure?"

She nodded, "Are you?"

"You don't even have to ask," his voice was rough.

She smiled and nodded.

Pushing her bangs from her face again, the love in his eyes was more intense than she'd ever seen. It made her breath hitch and he smiled at her reaction. "It's everything I ever wanted," he whispered in her ear.

Mia looked at the beautiful man staring down into her eyes. *How was this even possible*? she wondered. "Schooner." His gaze was riveting. She nodded her assent and he was inside of her. She heard a sound coming from her, a mewling.

"Oh God, Baby Girl," he growled into her ear, "you feel so fucking good. I've waited a lifetime. A lifetime." He drove into her hard. Harder. "You are mine. No one is ever going to take you from me again. No one is ever going to touch you again. No one. Ever."

"Come in me," she whispered in his ear.

He stopped moving and looked down at her.

"It's mine," she whispered. "All mine."

And he rammed into her hard.

She watched his face as he was coming undone and seeing his pleasure threw her over the edge and she squeezed his cock tight. His eyes flew open and she was smiling up at him. "Give it to me, Schooner. Give me what I want."

And that was all he needed to hear to unleash his seed deep into her.

When they were done, they lay side by side facing each other. "Are you ready for us? For the future?" he asked, stroking her cheek with his thumb.

She smiled, taking his hand and kissing his thumb. "It's everything I ever wanted," she repeated his words from earlier, making him smile.

He brushed her tousled bangs from her eyes with his fingertips and kissed the tip of her nose. "Your first and your last," he whispered.

She smiled at the realization and nodded. "My first and my last," as it sunk in, her smile grew wider. "My first and my last. I love that."

"Is that all you love?"

"I love bagels," she teased, smiling at him.

"Yeah, with avocado slices."

"Ewwww!"

He laughed at her. "You're not going to tell me what else you love, are you?" He tightened his arms around her.

"You just want to hear me say it, don't you?"

He nodded at her.

Mia looked into Schooner's eyes and smiled. She traced his cheek with her fingers. "Schooner James Moore," she began, "five days ago, I was having the worst morning imaginable. We had just lost a big account and I knew it could potentially have devastating effects on my company. I was wrung out just from the events of the morning. And then I saw an email. And your name was on it. And I stared at it in disbelief. Schooner Moore sent me a friend request. *Schooner Moore* sent *me* a friend request? And I didn't even have to think for a second before I hit confirm. I went with my gut, my heart. I just reacted. Five minutes later, I was listening to a voice I thought I would never hear again in my lifetime, and just the sound of your voice touched me in a way I didn't even know I missed. It made me yearn for more, made me want more. More of you. All week, every conversation, I just kept saying to myself, how can it be this easy? This right? How can I just click… fit with someone so easily? And then today, today was perfect and I felt right for the first time in… forever. I felt right because you were with me and you get me and I can be me and it's fun to be me with you and I love everything about you… your heart… your sweetness… the way you are with me, the way you make me feel."

Taking his hand, she placed it over her heart.

"Do you feel that? Because it feels like it's going to beat out of my chest. Over the past five days, I swear, it has gotten five times bigger. I feel like it's going to explode, it's so full. I look in your eyes and, well the first thing I think is, I can't believe I'm looking into your sweet, beautiful eyes. Your eyes." She smiled and pushed the hair from his forehead. "It's every dream I ever wanted come true. Dreams I would never even dare to let myself consider, places I wouldn't allow myself to go, are now not only possibilities, but may actually be my reality. My reality with you. With you, Schooner. And to say I am mind blown is the ultimate understatement. So, if you want me to tell you that I love you, I will do that—but I don't think those words even begin to describe what I feel for you, what I have always felt for you, and I don't know what the right words are."

"You just said them."

Chapter Nine

Mia stretched out in her bed. She could feel how cold the air was on her face, but her body under the down comforter was toasty warm. Outside the window, the snow still fell from a gray sky, making it difficult to tell what time it was. Mia grabbed her phone off her nightstand. It was 8:20 A.M. Wow, she had slept late. Schooner was nowhere in sight. She reached over to his side of the bed. The sheets were cool, so he must've been gone for a while.

Mia saw Schooner's shirt on the floor, laying in the heap it had fallen, when she peeled it off him. Grabbing the cold shirt, she put it on under the covers and stayed there until the icy cold cotton warmed up. Finally getting the nerve to brave it, she got out of bed and went to her closet for a pair of Mukluk boot slippers. Mia knew the secret—when feet were warm, all else was bearable.

Schooner was sitting at the breakfast bar, cell phone in one hand, coffee mug in the other. *He looks so damn good in my kitchen*, Mia thought. The man looked so at home and so natural—like he was in his own space.

Seeing her approach in his shirt, his face broke into a wide smile and he put the coffee mug down to draw her to him, so that he could plant a big kiss on her lips. He held her to him tightly as he continued his conversation.

"Yeah, well I'm not too worried about that because Yoli will always vote with me and maybe we can just buy her out. As far as the rest of it, let's just give her what she wants. She's going to get 50% of everything. I'm not going to contest it. Just give it to her, I want this to happen fast… and smooth." He was listening. "No, I haven't talked to them yet. I'm going to do that as soon as possible." Listening. "Aaron, I don't really care. None of that matters. So, when can we serve?" Listening. Big sigh. "Okay, do it." He hung up without saying goodbye.

Schooner pulled Mia against his chest and wrapped both arms around her tightly. He kissed the top of her head. A gesture that always made her smile. A gesture that was always theirs.

She pulled back to look at him. "You okay?" Her concern for him was evident.

He nodded, smiling at her. “Yeah. Not easy stuff. Just want it done, yesterday.”

She reached up to his cheek and he laid his face in her hand, smiling.

“We said a lot of things to each other last night, Mia. By the light of day…” his voice trailed off.

“I can only speak for myself, Schooner. By the light of day, nothing changes. I meant everything I said to you last night. I don’t ever think I’ve ever laid my heart on the line so openly.” She smiled, “It’s pretty scary.”

“C’mere.” He pulled her tightly into his arms and held her against him, “The next few months may get a little funky. I’d be naive to think CJ will just give me this divorce without a fight—especially with you in the picture. That’s going to go over like a lead balloon. I’m basically going to give her everything she wants, with exception of control of the business, everything else she can have. It doesn’t mean anything to me. I just want out.”

Mia pulled back to look at him, his face was so sincere. “The kids?”

Concern clouded his beautiful eyes. “I’m going to fly up to Providence in a few days and talk to Holly. I’m sure she’ll be upset, but something tells me she’ll get it. Holly and CJ are not close. She’s Daddy’s girl.” He smiled and Mia could feel his love for his daughter radiating from him. “And I know she’ll want me to be happy. I also think you two will end up having a very good relationship. She will get us, Mia—I know she will.”

“And Zac?”

“That’s going to be a tougher nut to crack. He looks like me, but he’s CJ through and through.”

“Oh shit.” Mia had a look of mock horror on her face.

“Oh shit is right,” Schooner laughed. “That boy is deadly. He’s doing a semester abroad in Spain right now and honestly, I hope this is a done deal by the time he steps foot on U.S. soil again.” He sighed, “Be prepared. He’s going to be a shit to both of us, but I will not put up with him disrespecting you, so he and I will get that clear right from the start.”

Mia just looked at him, her mind racing a million miles per hour. It seemed so much less complicated under the warmth of her down blanket and now by the light of day, reality had a lot of details.

Schooner stood and poured Mia a cup of coffee. “What do you take in your coffee? So much to learn.” He smiled.

“Just milk.” She watched him pull the carton from the refrigerator and pour it into her coffee.

As he handed her the steaming mug, she thought, *I can get used to this.*

"So, let me run something by you," he began.

She cocked her head, listening.

"I'm supposed to leave at the end of the weekend. I don't think in 48 hours I'm going to be ready to leave you."

Mia could feel the smile growing on her face. "Then don't. Schooner, you can stay here for as long as you'd like. Use the apartment as an east coast base."

He smiled at her across the breakfast bar and she reached out for his hand.

"I know it's not a lot of space. Us New Yorkers get used to living in small spaces, but I would love for you to be able to think of this as your home. Our home," she corrected.

He squeezed her hand. "Let me cancel my flight."

Mia stood over by the living room windows looking out at the snow piling up. A real New York snowstorm, the kind that brought the city to a standstill. It looked so beautiful while it was falling, smooth drifts blowing into high peaks. Schooner came up behind Mia and wrapped his arms around her.

"Well, the weathermen got this one wrong. Flurries. Ha. Definitely not a beach day," she observed.

He laughed. "I've never had a snow day."

Turning to him, she smiled. "We'll get out and play in it later. I've been thinking about where I want to take you in a snow storm."

"Where is that?" He nuzzled her neck.

"Well, the place I would love to hang out with you and watch the snow fall is The Oak Room in the Plaza Hotel, but it's closed for renovations. So, I'm thinking maybe The Champagne Bar at The Plaza instead. Sort of an old New York way to weather a snowstorm."

He tightened his arms around her. "I'm smiling into your neck right now."

She laughed. "In the meantime, we can play indoors." And she led him back into the bedroom.

"Damn woman, this room is freezing!" he griped, snuggling immediately under the covers.

"Western exposure. Winds out of the west." Mia climbed on top of Schooner. "I'll warm you up."

"I love New York," he smiled up at her.

"That's good, because you're about to become bi-coastal." She kissed him softly and then looked at him, her expression serious. "Have you ever thought about expanding to New York?" She rolled off him and they tangled arms and legs, holding one another tight.

"Actually a few months ago, Yoli and I had a serious conversation about putting a flagship facility in Manhattan. A lot of our clientele have places here too and we would launch with a big built-in celebrity clientele who are already members."

Mia's brain started spinning and Schooner broke into a huge smile.

"What?" she asked.

"I can see that brain of yours spinning. You're already marketing the property in your head."

She threw her head back laughing. "You know me! That is exactly what I'm doing. What an amazing opening event you could do. I'm also thinking about location. You're known for your celebrity clientele, so a location downtown, here in Chelsea, The Village, SoHo, Tribeca, I would think that would be where many of your 'stars' are."

"That's where I would definitely need your help. We'd really need to do some feasibility studies because I don't know the city at all. I don't know the personalities and demographics of each of the neighborhoods. And I'd really want to see what my new agency thought about expansion to the east coast."

"Oh, who are you working with? Are you one of Scott Morgan's clients?"

How fun was this, Mia thought, to be all tangled up with Schooner, feeling his hard cock pressing against her and brainstorming business. Mia was excited on so many levels.

"No. He's a dirt bag."

Mia laughed at Schooner's accurate assessment of Scott.

"No, we're going to be joining the client roster of a little boutique agency here in Manhattan. I have a personal relationship with the owner and I know we'll get the personal attention that I demand." He pressed against her, watching her eyes widen.

"Are you a demanding client?" she asked, throwing her leg over Schooner and pressing his ass with her foot, his cock sliding deep into her. She gasped, biting her lower lip, but maintained eye contact with him.

"I'm a very demanding client." He thrust into her hard and deep. "I expect 100% attention on me at all times. Can you accommodate that?" He grabbed her ass and rammed into her. "Do you think you can keep me satisfied?"

"Absolutely, because unlike the large conglomerate agencies, who will sell you a bill of goods and stick you with underlings, you will always get attention from the very top with us." She pushed him on his back, straddling him and smiling down at him.

He thrust up into her. “Will you commit to personally handling my business?”

She reached back and fondled his balls. “I think I can commit to that. I’m very hands on with my clients,” she managed as she squeezed his cock and balls at the same time. “I will commit all my resources to you.”

“How do I know you’re not just selling me a bill of goods?” He pressed up into her, causing her to gasp.

“What can I do to convince you?”

“I’ll require a contract.”

She looked into his clear eyes, silently asking with her eyes, *are you asking me what I think you’re asking me?* Before responding, “I’d be very happy to solidify this relationship with a contract,” ending her sentence with a tight squeeze of his cock.

“Good.” He grabbed her hips and thrust up into her. “Consider it a done deal.”

“I like the way you do business.” She smiled down at him.

“I like giving you the business.” He held her hips tight, grinding his cock into her.

“That’s good, because I want all of your business.”

“I’m willing to give you every last inch of it.”

“I can handle it.”

She laughed… Seth was going to tease her relentlessly about pimping herself out for business, but this new business was truly going to be a labor of love.

Chapter Ten

"Good morning, Sunshine," Mia sing-songed, as she breezed by Seth's desk, depositing his favorite Starbuck's latte in front of him.

Putting her latte on her desk, she hung up her coat behind her door and proceeded to unpack her laptop from her vintage leather Ghurka bag when Seth appeared in her doorway, latte in hand, and watched her every move. As if it were a game they regularly played, she pretended to ignore him as she plugged in and booted up her laptop, took her phone out and got settled at her desk.

It was only then that she looked up at him, smiled and said sweetly, "Is there something I can help you with?"

"Don't you hold out on me, BBC!"

She laughed and he continued, eyes narrowing, as he looked at her. "You seem to be a happy BBC this morning. One might even say a glowing BBC. Frankly, I was expecting a sad, pining BBC today."

She shook her head. "Nope. Happy BBC."

"Aren't you sad that he left?" Seth made a sad face.

"Who said anything about leaving?" Mia looked like a Cheshire cat.

With eyes widening almost comically, Seth gasped. "He's still here?"

Mia smiled and nodded.

"Oh my God!" Seth clapped his hands together. "Why aren't you home in bed, fucking his brains out?"

Mia laughed. "Because I don't want you eating cat food, Princess!" Seth looked at her with a *tell me more* look and Mia continued, "He's working out of the apartment this morning and he'll be here this afternoon. We'll be using the conference room. Is Kami in yet?"

"Yeah, she's in her office dialing for dollars trying to find new clients. He's going to be here today? How do I look?" Seth immediately began primping, pulling at his collar, straightening the neckline on his argyle cashmere sweater.

"Please let her know I'd like to see her."

Seth stood and pointed a finger at Mia. "You are holding out on me."

"All in due time, my little princess. Now go get Kami."

"Wicked Witch BBC," he called over his shoulder. Mia laughed.

Kami Townes knocked on Mia's open door and Mia signaled her in.

"Good morning. How were your days off last week?" Kami asked, all soft southern drawl.

Mia smiled. "Exceptional."

"I'll bet they were!" They heard Seth yell from the outer office.

Both women shook their heads and laughed.

Like Seth, Kami had been with Mia since before the agency. She was Mia's go-to person and the staff member to which Mia entrusted the most important business. Kami was brilliant, driven and approached business with both left and right brain sensibilities. She was also very loyal. Kami and Mia had seen each other through personal hardships and some very wild, very hazy memory times, including an impromptu trip to New Orleans that was never, ever discussed.

The two women balanced one another out well. While Mia was a what you see is what you get, balls to the wall New Yorker, Kami was the epitome of Southern Belle.

Raised in Birmingham, Alabama, Kami was the daughter of a prominent cardiologist and a member of local society. She was a southern debutante whose pearls never came off—ever. Like any accomplished, good southern girl, Kami could insult you right to your face with such smooth grace and finesse that you never really knew what hit you… until later.

"We've got a really exciting opportunity," Mia began, "and I want you to be the primary on it. I'm going to be totally hands on, beside you on this baby—but you are going to be breathing, sleeping and eating this."

"I'm excited, what is it? Can you talk about it yet?"

"Have you ever heard of a California outfit Level 9 Health Clubs?"

Kami's face lit up and Seth came running into the office, parking in the chair next to Kami.

"No, you didn't!" he screamed.

Mia laughed, "Oh, yes I did."

"My friend Shelby Lee, the lawyer for Universal, is a member at their Studio City property. I went there with her last time I was in LA. Amazing facility. We have nothing like it here." Kami was intrigued.

"The first thing we're going to work with them on is finding the space for their first New York City location and we will handle everything—the launch, marketing, advertising, PR. Everything—this baby is ours."

Kami sat there with her mouth open and Seth started to squeal. Mia sat back and smiled at them. It was so nice to deliver good news.

"Your main contact is going to be their CMO, Yolanda Perez. She goes by Yoli. We have a conference call with her this afternoon. Their owner, Schooner Moore, will be here with us on-site for the meeting."

"Oh my God, I'm so excited he's coming here," Seth swooned.

Mia nodded. "He's coming here. And we have lots to do this morning to get ready for that meeting. We need to start pulling competitive data, look at where competitors are located. Let's make a list for Yoli of things we'll need from her. I want to see what their West Coast agencies have been doing." Mia pulled up their website on her laptop. "Slick site. This is beautiful."

"How did this happen? If you don't mind my asking," Kami inquired.

Mia smiled and she could see that Seth was bursting at the seams. "You want to tell the story? I'm sure you'll tell it so much better than I will."

Seth turned to Kami. Mia knew this was going to be dramatic and sat back in her chair, smirking. He looked down at his iPad and typed something in, then sighed and turned his iPad toward Kami.

Her pretty blue eyes shot open wide. "Hottie Toddy!"

And Seth continued, "That is Schooner Moore. Schooner James Moore, our new client and owner of Level 9 Health Clubs. Isn't he beautiful?"

Kami nodded vigorously.

"Well, it appears our little Miss Mia has been holding out on us all these years. This gorgeous man, who let me state for the record, I am in love with, was Mia's first love. And the bitch broke his heart. Left him. Heartbroken." He turned to give Mia a mock glare. "Last week, Mr. Moore tracked down the evil tart who broke his heart and flew here to see her, hence, her time off from work last week. Clearly their reunion was a happy one because he is still here in New York and did not leave at the end of the weekend as was planned, and is now opening a New York facility and we are their new agency. And there you have it."

Mia clapped. "Very good. You did it justice. And succinct too, I might add."

Kami put both hands up to her forehead with her thumbs on her cheeks, a common gesture she made when thinking or processing information, then she looked up at Mia. "Did he just make that sound incredibly romantic or is this incredibly romantic?"

"Look at that shit-eating grin on her face." Seth hit Kami in the arm playfully.

"So, what happened, Mia? C'mon don't leave us with just Seth's synopsis," urged Kami.

"I don't even know where to begin." Mia put her palms up, "The man was the love of my life and turns out he is still the love of my life." She looked at Seth, "And you will love this... he's serving CJ with divorce papers today."

"Noooooooooooo!"

Mia nodded, "Yes!"

"Oh, karma is such a bitch." Seth was preening. He turned to Kami to fill her in. "CJ is like this *Real Housewife of Orange County* and she purposely sabotaged Mia and Schooner when they were in college and that is why BBC over here left this beautiful man. She's evil, pure evil. Tall, blonde and evil." He turned to Mia, "I can't believe he's divorcing her!"

"He's flying up to Providence tomorrow to talk to his daughter."

Mia reached inside her Ghurka bag and pulled out an envelope. "I have something to show you." She was smiling as she handed them the photo of Schooner at Victoria Falls.

"He was so beautiful, Mia." Kami actually gasped taking in the image of nineteen year- old Schooner smiling his real smile for Mia.

Mia just nodded, feeling suddenly overwhelmed and emotional.

Seth was staring at the picture and then looked up at Mia, serious for the first time. "You deserve this, you know that."

Mia nodded, her eyes filled with tears.

"It's your time, Mia." He stood, picture still in hand. "I'm going to go get a frame for this." He smiled at Mia and left.

Chapter Eleven

Mia was brimming with pride as she gave Schooner a tour of the agency. This was her baby, and the look on his face and in his eyes when he saw what she had built and met her staff, made her beam. The sleek, trendy space screamed New York cool with its warehouse look and exposed brick walls.

"Get that off your computer right now!" Mia hissed in a whispered tone into Seth's ear. His new screensaver was the picture of Schooner sleeping on Mia's couch. She backhanded him on the side of his head.

After a very productive hour and a half phone session with Yoli, where she and Kami seemed like they had worked together for years, Mia brought Schooner back into her office and closed the door.

He sat on the edge of her desk smiling, "Come over here." He held out his hand to her.

Taking his hand, she let him pull her between his long legs and couldn't resist running her fingers through his hair and just looking into his beautiful eyes. Leaning into him, she kissed him, softly.

They stood together like that for a moment before he took her face in his hands, "Do you know how much I love you?" he asked, searching her eyes.

She smiled and nodded. There was stress in his eyes. She could see it, feel it.

"I talked to CJ this morning," he began. "It didn't go well. She's not going to make it easy, Mia."

"Does it matter?"

He thought for a second, as if that question had not yet occurred to him. "No, actually it really doesn't. I was concerned that it might matter to you."

"Me? How so?" Mia played with the locks of hair falling on his forehead, making him look nineteen again.

"That I'm still going to be legally married to another woman. She's going to drag this out."

Mia smiled and leaned forward, kissing the tip of his nose. "So, let her. The only grief she is going to cause is to herself. I don't want you stressing over that, Schooner." Mia stopped and thought for a second and then looked at Schooner with her devilish grin. “I’m a concubine!” she announced and they both broke into much needed laughter.

“My concubine,” he staked claim, kissing her.

“Damn right.” She hugged him tightly and then pulled back to look at him, “Seriously, as long as we are together and things are good between us—that’s all I need. I’m good, really.”

“Yeah, but I want to give you more.” His eyes were serious again.

Taking his face in both her hands, Mia shook her head. “I have everything I want, Schooner. Everything. The rest doesn’t mean anything without this. And I have this. So seriously, I don’t want you stressing over it. The rest will be great when it happens. Trust me, if she sees she can stress you out, she’ll step up her game even more. If you don’t give a shit, then it’s no fun fighting with you and she’ll stop.”

“Yeah, but in the meantime, I want to protect you. I want to make sure you are protected, Mia. I spoke to my lawyer today about ways in which I can do that.”

“Schooner, look around.” Her hand swept around her office. “I’m fine.”

He shook his head no. “No Baby Girl, I need to do a better job protecting you and I need to make sure all the legal aspects are in place.” He put his hand on her stomach and she looked down at his hand, when she looked up, their eyes locked. “I need to protect what is mine. Do you understand what I am saying?”

She nodded.

“You’re mine now,” he whispered in her ear in a gruff, emotion-filled voice. She smiled and laid her head on his shoulder.

Chapter Twelve

Mia reached for her buzzing phone to read the incoming text.

Schooner: Damn I am missing you!
Mia: How's Rhode Island?
Schooner: Even colder than NY.
Mia: How is it going with Holly?
Schooner: She's taking it really well. I told her everything.
Mia: Everything?
Schooner: Yes
Mia: Holy crap. That's pretty heavy.
Schooner: She needed to understand.
Mia: Does she?
Schooner: Yes, she told me that growing up she knew that CJ and I didn't act like parents of her friends. I feel terrible that she wasn't shown a more loving relationship
Mia: :-(
Schooner: I know. I'm taking her and her boyfriend out to dinner
Mia: Have you met him before?
Schooner: No
Mia: Don't scare him!
Schooner: LOL. Call you from the hotel later
Mia: Have fun.
Schooner: Love u
Mia: It's smoochal
Schooner: :-) ear 2 ear
Mia: smoochal 2 :-)

Mia was sitting in bed, working when Schooner called.

"Did I wake you?"

"Nah, I've got this new client. Lots of work to do to onboard them. How's Holly?"

Schooner's voice sounded relaxed. "Today went surprisingly well. I laid a lot on her and I kind of feel bad. She wasn't surprised about me and

CJ, she was very surprised to learn about you."

Mia sighed, "I'll bet she was. That can't be easy."

"After she told me about how she grew up knowing that CJ and I didn't have the same kind of relationship that she saw in other families around her, I just had to have a really honest conversation with her. It was a good chance for me to talk to her about mistakes and doing things for the wrong reasons and hopefully impart good advice about being true to herself and not settling." He paused, "She wants to meet you."

Mia scooched under the covers. "That really makes me happy to hear that. I know it won't be easy, her loyalty is to her mother."

"I don't think she sees it that way. She wants me to be happy. She said the difference in me from ten days ago, at the party, to now was… how did she put it… a transmutational shift."

Mia laughed, "Wow! Transmutational shift, huh?" They both laughed. "What's her boyfriend like?"

"Really nice kid. His name is Jared Goldman. He's pre-med. Totally smitten with Holly and from what I can tell treats her really well. I'd say they are in love."

"Oh Schooner…" Mia was smiling.

"It's weird to see. But I'm glad I had a chance to meet him. That's who she was Facebooking and texting all last weekend. Hey, how do you feel about the two of them coming to spend the weekend with us?"

"I'd love it. When do they want to come?"

"Friday."

Mia laughed, "Sounds like we're going to have a fun weekend." Hearing an odd sound, she asked, "What is that?"

"I'm punching my pillows, trying to fluff them. Crappy pillows here in this hotel. Not like we have at home." Mia smiled at his home reference. "Are you in bed?"

"I am."

"Remind me not to sleep without you in the future," he sounded lost.

"It's so weird that you say that. How many years did I sleep in this bed without you and tonight it just feels empty and lonely and cold. And I hate it." She paused, "remind me not to sleep without you in the future."

Chapter Thirteen

Schooner paced the apartment like a caged animal on Friday afternoon awaiting Holly and Jared's arrival. He was wound tight when Mia came home from work, and the apartment felt smaller than usual as he stalked around with long-legged strides. She could feel the tension radiating off him and see the stress in his eyes.

"Hey." She wrapped her arms around his waist, trying to get him to stop moving. "I know this makes it real."

"Yeah," his voice sounded choked.

"Don't worry. We're going to have the best time. I have a couple of big surprises planned for you guys." She looked up at Schooner, her devilish smile at full luminosity, immediately brightening his mood and allaying the gnawing fears.

"What do you have up your sleeve, Baby Girl?" He took her face by the chin and kissed her.

"I'm only going to tell you part one, because you are going to be soooo excited. I'm so excited."

He searched her face and she went on.

"Okay, so, I was talking to a dear old friend of mine today. We've been good friends and business associates since the 90's. He owns an event security firm and is very familiar with a lot of spaces around the city—really, really cool properties, the kind that lend themselves to photo shoots and events. I told him that we were looking for a Level 9 Flagship location in New York, and he told me about a space that just became vacant that sounds like the perfect amount of square footage, great neighborhood, has mass amounts of charm, history and quirkiness to it. He got the keys from the owners and is going to meet us this evening, after the kids get in, to show it to us."

Mia's excitement was contagious. "Schooner," she went on, "if Charles says it's good, it's going to be good. He and I have done enough events together over the years that I totally trust his opinion and he is really, really high on this space."

Schooner pulled Mia in for a tight hug. "You're amazing."

"Here's what I was thinking," she began. "After they get here, let's go meet Charles and view the property first, before we even go out to dinner. I think it will be an amazing ice breaker, give us all a lot to talk about. And if it's amazing and you love it, then we'll all be pumped up out of our minds and there will be no awkwardness in the conversation."

As Schooner ran his thumb down Mia's cheek and bent down to kiss her, the doorman call button rang. Mia told the doorman to send Holly and Jared up.

Mia and Schooner walked to the apartment door and turned to one another and simultaneously said, 'Showtime'. When they opened the door, they were both laughing, evoking immediate smiles from both Holly and Jared.

"Hey there, beautiful." A happy and now relaxed Schooner wrapped his arms around his daughter.

Mia couldn't help but smile looking at the two of them, though in the very first moment, she had to consciously remind herself that this was Holly and not CJ. The resemblance was staggering.

Schooner let Holly go and she looked at Mia. Mia immediately embraced her warmly and enthusiastically greeted, "Hi Holly, I'm Mia," and then embraced Jared with the same warmth.

Any fear that had gripped Schooner immediately dissipated as Mia set the tone with her warmth, openness and positive energy.

"Come on in, guys, and drop your stuff. Oh, it is so good to meet you." Mia's smile could've melted an icecap.

"What a great apartment. Wow, you can see the river," Jared commented. "I love Manhattan. My dream is to do my internship and residency here after med school and live here." Holly joined Jared at the window, admiring the view of the Hudson River.

Mia looked up at Schooner and smiled; he held his arms out to her and enveloped her in a hug. Holly turned to her Dad who met her gaze, the happiness in his eyes vastly evident at the immediate harmony between the two women he loved.

"How would you guys like a glass of wine?" Mia offered, grabbing a bottle and a corkscrew. "We're going to head out in a little bit to do something that should be really fun."

"A friend of Mia's found a space that sounds amazing for L9 and we're going to go check it out."

The love in Holly's eyes was evident as she looked at her Dad.

Mia thought she saw something else there and wondered if this was the first time she had seen her father this happy and connected to someone.

Charles Sloan stood very tall and still in his dark wool overcoat and navy scarf, observing everything and everyone with barely a movement of his eyes. He always reminded Mia of Jason Statham in The Transporter movies. While he appeared detached, he was anything but.

Charles broke into a wide grin as Mia and her group came into view.

"Meezie!" He enveloped her in a big hug.

"Chazicle!" She returned affectionately, kissing his cheek.

"Only you can call me that and not get killed." They smiled at one another with the genuine affection of old friends.

"Charles Sloan, I'd like you to meet Schooner Moore, Holly Moore and Jared Goldman."

Ever the gentleman, Charles shook Holly's hand first, then Jared's and then turned to Schooner, and much to Mia's surprise, said, "Nice to see you again, we've met before."

Schooner smiled, taking his hand. "Yes, we have. It was the Studio City event, wasn't it?"

"Yes, it was," Charles concurred.

A surprised Mia looked at Schooner and said, "One degree of separation this whole time. Who knew?"

Charles began to work on a series of door locks and opened a massive door. They followed him in as he began to flip a bank of light switches that elicited a collective gasp from the group.

The entranceway they stood in opened to a massive rotunda whose ceiling was lit with cove lighting, spotlighting immense frescos of mythological creatures, gods and beasts. On one end was a sweeping marble staircase with an elaborate wrought iron railing that led to a mezzanine level and a third level mezzanine above that.

"This building has housed churches, private clubs, theatres and is a space most New Yorkers don't even know exists," Charles explained. "Meezie, do you remember that gang that had the club in the church? They even owned this place for a while. Rumor was they were supposed to fully renovate it, but never completed it."

Mia started to wander around the space. She felt Schooner's arm drape protectively over her shoulder. "Meezie?" he whispered in her ear.

"Stop that. We go back a long way." She backhanded him in the stomach.

"I know. It just reminds me that I missed a big portion of your life."

"Excuse me? Your daughter is here. Talk about feeling the gap."

He smiled down at her, a sad look in his eyes and bent down to kiss her.

Mia put her arm around Schooner's waist. "C'mon, let's check this place out. It's gorgeous and so interesting. Funky vibe, right?"

Holly and Jared caught up to them. "Dad, this place is amazing. That third floor could be a track. Imagine running under those frescos!"

"Schooner, let me show you the offices," Charles offered and Schooner left with Charles.

"So, what is it that you call him?" Holly asked.

Mia laughed, "Chazicle?" and Holly nodded. "Oh, that nickname goes way back. Charles hates to be called anything but Charles, and when he's working, he's like an ice man, he's so focused and unflappable. So, the Chaz was me just being obnoxious with him because he hates being called that and putting Chaz and icicle together and calling him Chazicle."

"Was he Secret Service?" Jared asked. "He looks like he was a Covert Ops guy."

Mia laughed. "If I told you, he'd probably have to kill me." Smiling at them, "Let's go check out upstairs."

The three wandered around upstairs, finding a variety of rooms off the second-floor mezzanine. The place was massive and many of the original details from intricate wainscoting to wood and stone carvings still existed.

Schooner and Charles caught up with them as they continued to explore the space, looking for practical things, like plumbing for bathrooms and showers.

"Do you think the renovation will make it cost prohibitive?" Mia asked Schooner.

"Hard to tell, but it actually appears to be in pretty good shape because previous owners have done a lot of renovations on it already."

"I can help hook you up with some inspectors to take a look at this, if you're interested," Charles offered. Schooner nodded. The two appeared to Mia to have bonded during their time alone.

"I'm definitely interested. It's worth at least an initial discussion with the principals. And if that progresses, I'd want to get Yoli in here and an architect. It's a really interesting space." He was looking around, taking it all in.

Mia turned to Charles. "Imagine an opening here. Could be spectacular."

"There would be nothing else like it in New York. Really be an amazing extension of what's already a unique concept in California, but housed in an amazing space."

"So exciting."

Schooner, Holly and Jared had wandered off. Mia watched Schooner looking around with a critical eye. She knew he was envisioning his unique concept.

"Oh, before I forget." Charles took an envelope out of his pocket and handed it to Mia. "All instructions are inside."

Mia gave Charles a hug. "You are the absolute best. Thank you so much. I cannot tell you how much I appreciate this." She kissed his cheek.

Schooner appeared out of nowhere and Mia felt his hand on her shoulder as he addressed Charles. "I'm definitely interested."

"Great. Would you like me to see if I can set something up for next week?"

"That would be excellent." Schooner pulled Mia into him.

"Oh Meezie, before I forget, Gaby wants to know if you two will be available for dinner one night next week."

Mia smiled up at Schooner and looked back at Charles. "We'd love to. Tell her to give me a ring."

As they parted at the entranceway, Mia gave Charles a big hug. "I can't thank you enough… for everything."

He smiled. "My pleasure, we'll see you next week. Schooner, I'll call you on Monday after I talk to these guys. Holly, Jared, great meeting you. Have a good weekend everyone."

He winked at Mia and was off.

Chapter Fourteen

"I love that space, Dad."

They sat in a corner table of an intimate, hole in the wall Italian restaurant with possibly the best Caesar salad in Manhattan.

"I like it, too," Schooner admitted.

"The location is good," Mia added. "It's central to a lot of the neighborhoods where celebrities keep their New York homes, it's easy to get to, multiple subway lines close by, very safe neighborhood with a great demographic for the concept." She smiled at Schooner. "This is really exciting."

"What's that look you're giving me?" Schooner asked Mia, "you've kind of got a shit-eating grin on your face."

She giggled. "You know me well." Mia looked at all of them and said, "I've got a really fun surprise." Then dug around in her purse. Finally, she found the envelope that Charles had given her, opened it and pulled out keys. "Charles and Gaby have been nice enough to let us use their beach house on Fire Island for the rest of the weekend."

"So that's what you were off talking to him about?" Schooner was all smiles.

"Yes, that's what I was talking to him about! And what was with you getting all possessive tonight? What was that shit all about?" She called him out on his behavior, giving him a playful little whack in the arm.

He smiled and leaned down and whispered in her ear, "Mine."

Mia snorted at him, shaking her head. "His wife is one of my best friends in the world."

Holly and Jared just watched them and Mia looked at Holly and rolled her eyes as if to say, "Men!"

Holly had that same look in her eyes that she had seen earlier, making Mia wonder if his daughter was seeing her father for the first time the way Mia had always seen him.

"After dinner, we should stop at Trader Joe's and pick up groceries to bring out to the beach. If we're lucky, one of the bars in town out there will be open, but I'm not really sure. Basically, the island is pretty much deserted in winter."

Schooner explained to them that they would have to take the ferry out and that there were no cars allowed out on the island. "Just miles of endless deserted beaches to walk."

Holly and Jared were in awe of the evening they had already had and now they were going out to a beach house on an island in the middle of the winter.

As they walked back to the apartment later in the evening, Holly and Mia were a few feet behind the guys when Holly said, "Mia, thanks for making us feel really comfortable."

Mia put an arm around Holly and gave her a little hug. "I know this isn't easy for you."

"It's different," Holly admitted. "But he's so happy and I just love seeing him this way. It makes it a lot easier. Clearly Mia, you make my dad very happy."

Mia smiled. "He and I have always had a knack for being able to truly be ourselves with one another, if that makes sense." She looked at Holly and Holly was nodding. "So, I think because of that, we really bring out the best in one another."

"I'm glad you guys found each other again."

Mia gazed into the face of this beautiful young woman, who looked unnervingly like her mother, but possessed her father's sweet soul. "You are very special."

"Well, I love him and I want him to be happy." Holly's eyes radiated the depth of emotion she felt for her father.

"We have that in common." Mia smiled at her.

Schooner and Jared had already reached the building and were waiting for them. Mia could see how happy Schooner was watching them together and her heart soared.

As the ferry crossed the choppy waters of the Great South Bay that Saturday morning, they stood on the top deck, windblown and shivering, in the freezing cold sunshine. Reaching the ferry terminal at the town of Ocean Beach, they departed the boat with runny noses and dripping eyes and red wind burned cheeks. Walking through town, they noticed that one pub, The Castaway, was indeed open. Following Charles' directions, the four headed down windswept boardwalks to their friend's home on Ocean Breeze Walk.

Weathered shingles on the outside, the inside of the house was light and airy in pale blues and whites with driftwood furniture. There was a large stone fireplace downstairs and three bedrooms upstairs, two of them with decks overlooking the ocean and miles of unspoiled beach.

Holly and Jared immediately took off for the beach, leaving Mia and Schooner to unpack groceries, get the heat in the house going and start a fire in the fireplace.

Mia poured glasses of icy cold white wine (it had been on the ferry with them) and handed one to Schooner. Taking him by the hand, she led him to the couch in front of the fire, not losing a moment to snuggle into him. *This just might be Heaven*, she thought.

Schooner kissed the top of Mia's head and played with her hair. "Today is really special, Baby Girl." She looked up at him and he kissed the tip of her nose, "Being here with you on Fire Island was a fantasy I played over and over in my mind for so many years, you can't even imagine."

Mia took his hand in hers and looked into the fire. "Well, now that fantasy is your reality."

"No, it's not," he countered.

Mia looked up at him, surprised.

"It's our reality."

She smiled. "Holy shit, you're right. It is."

And they both laughed.

Later that afternoon, Schooner and Mia walked the beach hand in hand, another fantasy that they'd waited a lifetime to fulfill.

"Do you remember how I once told you that since I was a Newport Beach guy, that it was going to be hard to impress me with your New York beaches?" He bent down and picked up a smooth piece of cobalt colored sea glass and turned it over a few times in his hand.

"I do remember that." She smiled up at him and body bumped him.

He bumped her back. "Well, this is really amazing and you know what?"

"What?" She bumped him.

"It's almost exactly as I imagined it would be. Actually, it's even better."

Mia threaded her arm through his and sighed. "I'm trying so hard to stay in the now and think about our future, but sometimes Schooner, I just start mourning the lost moments. Which is crazy because how can you mourn something that never was? Pull me back to now when you see me going there, okay?"

He put his arm around her, pulling her close and kissing the top of her head. "I can do that. I'll pull you back and no it's not crazy. But Baby Girl, the now is so good. So, so good. We've got a lot of memories to make, Mia. So, let's try and keep each other in the now." He stopped walking and faced her, putting his hands on her shoulders. "And this is just the start. You know that, don't you?"

Her arms went around his waist and she held him tight, reveling in the feeling of her face against his chest. And there they stood on a beach they had dreamed of so long ago, finally beginning the chapters of stories they had yet to write.

Later in the afternoon, while having drinks and laughing with Holly and Jared at The Castaway, Schooner flipped through a local newspaper. Ripping out a page, he folded it and put it in his jean's pocket.

Mia looked at him curiously.

"Do you remember your birthday wish?" he whispered in her ear. "Because I do." He pushed her bangs out of her eyes and kissed her lips softly, then kissed the tip of her nose.

"We could rent a place for the week of my birthday."

Schooner shook his head, no.

"No?" Mia was surprised and a little disappointed, especially since he had just taken a page from the paper.

"We need our own place here." With a smile, he pulled the folded paper out of his pocket and unfolded it, revealing an ad for a beautiful house for sale with a deck off the main living area and one off the master bedroom that went directly out to the beach. "This is going to be our family getaway. This is where we are going to spend summers or just come to chill out, hang out, dig our toes in the sand, build sandcastles and eat lobsters and steamers in our sweatshirts after a long day on the beach."

Holly's mouth was hanging open. "Dad, you're going to buy a house here?" Her excitement and surprise were evident.

"Mia and I are going to buy a house here." Schooner squeezed Mia's hand. He leaned forward and whispered in her ear, "Happy early birthday, Baby Girl," letting his lips graze her cheek.

Mia was stunned into uncharacteristic silence. The look in his eyes told her everything. This was part of Schooner's grand plan to protect her, to take care of her and to build their future together. He wasn't kidding when he said he took care of what was his. Mia had never felt so loved or so in love in her life. And it was with her Schooner.

Chapter Fifteen

Seth rapped lightly on Mia's door and stuck his head in.

"I've got CJ Moore on Line One," he announced, his eyebrows standing at full attention.

"Oh really…" Mia gave Seth a WTF look, took a deep breath and hit the speaker button on her desk phone.

"Mia Silver," she answered, professionally. Seth sat down in one of the desk chairs facing Mia, his eyes wide.

"Mia, this is CJ Moore, Schooner Moore's wife," her voice was cool.

Almost Ex-…Bitch

Mia scribbled on the yellow legal pad in front of her.

"What can I do for you, CJ?" Mia's voice was even, professional.

"What can you do for me?" her tone was tense and started to rise. "For starters, you can stay away from my husband."

Do not rise to the bait!!!

Her pen practically ripped the paper.

"CJ, why are you calling me?" Mia had a mildly annoyed attitude.

Seth nodded, smiling, proud Mia was staying cool.

"I told you, I want you to stay away from my husband," her voice was now icy and tight.

"That's what you want?" Mia paused. "CJ, what would ever possess you to think that I would care what you want?"

Do <u>not</u> rise to the bait!!!

Mia again reminded herself.

"He's my husband, Mia, and just like he's done to you before, he's going to come back to me. You are just a little mid-life fling. We've built a family together."

Mia sat back and chuckled. "CJ, tell yourself whatever you need to get by, but this is a conversation you should either be having with your lawyer or with Schooner. I still do not understand why you are calling me."

"I'm not just going to sit back and let you steal my husband."

Mia typed something into Google.

Shaking her head, she sighed. "Do not mistake your husband leaving you for someone stealing him." She paused and when she began to speak again, her tone was very matter of fact. "CJ, I just want to inform you, that starting right now, I am taping this conversation. Although here in New York, I legally do not have to advise you of that, it appears that under California law, I do."

Seth was doing a happy dance in his chair at Mia's bluff.

Bitch played me once … won't get fooled again!

"I thought we could have a civil conversation," CJ began, "but I can see that you are very defensive and hostile, when I am the victim here."

"Oh, *that* is rich!" Mia's voice dripped of sarcasm. "CJ, you have never been a victim in your life. But as someone who was once a victim of your selfish manipulation, you need to understand, it is impossible for me to feel any empathy for you. The collateral damage you have caused people you *supposedly* love has been extreme."

"I'm not letting him go," CJ snarled.

"He's already gone," Mia's voice was little more than a whisper.

"Don't count on it," CJ threatened.

Mia was done, her face masked in disgust. "Okay, at this point you are just embarrassing yourself, so I'm really not going to let you go on here. As I recommended at the beginning of this conversation, you probably want to broach these things with either your lawyer or Schooner."

"Well, I'm not done …"

Mia cut her off, "Actually you are. Goodbye, CJ." And Mia hit the speaker button on her phone and ended the call.

"Bitch!" Mia screamed at the phone on her desk.

"Oh my God, you were fabulous!" Seth was clapping his hands together.

Mia picked up the phone receiver and slammed it back in its cradle. "Cunt!"

And again, "Whore!"

She looked up at Seth and did a primal scream, laughing at the same time.

"BBC, I have known you for a million years and you cuss like a sailor. I know it's part of your charm, but I have never, ever heard you use the "C" word!"

"Cunt," Mia screamed again.

This time Kami poked her head into the office. A surprised and amused look on her face.

"I bet that felt great." Seth was clearly enjoying Mia's tirade after the tension of the call.

Mia held her hand out, it was still shaking. "Was my voice shaking on the call?"

"No. You sounded so in control. I think that is what totally unnerved her." He was clearly pleased.

Kami sat in the extra chair. "Is anyone going to tell me what I missed?"

Mia looked at Seth, giving him the go-ahead to start. "Schooner's wife just called Mia."

"Noko…" Kami's eyes were like saucers. Her mouth hanging open.

"Yesssss…" Was the stereo response she got in return.

"What did she want?"

"She wants Mia to stay away from Schooner," Seth hissed.

"What is this? High School?" Kami was clearly astounded.

"Guess she still thinks it's freshman year in college and that she can still intimidate me. The M.O. worked for her back then. Fucking deluded bitch."

"So, what did you say?"

Seth continued for Mia, "She was brilliant. Totally in control."

Mia handed Kami her legal pad so that she could see the notes she was writing herself during the call.

"She accused Mia of stealing Schooner and Mia told her not to mistake her husband leaving her for him being stolen away," Seth and Mia screamed and laughed.

"You didn't?"

Mia laughed, "If Seth says I did, then I did. I honestly don't even know what I said to her. I just went into auto-pilot. I was trying really hard not to get baited and at one point," Mia stopped to laugh, "I informed her that I was recording the call."

Kami clapped her hands together, "Brilliant and evil. I love it!"

"Oh, oh, oh…" Seth went on with a point he remembered. "She said she wasn't letting him go and Mia told her he was already gone."

"How did it end?" Kami asked.

"Mia told her she couldn't let her go on embarrassing herself and click, pressed the speakerphone button and the evil witch was gone."

"Holy crap. What possessed her? I can't imagine her lawyer would have advised it." Kami just shook her head. "Yoli hates her. She is so thrilled Schooner left her. From what I can gather, CJ doesn't give Yoli the time of day and looks down her nose at her."

"Sounds like typical CJ," Mia concurred. "She and her pageant-girl friends hated me and my friends at school because we were different."

"Are you going to tell Schooner about the call?" Seth's eyes were suddenly very serious again.

"No." Mia shook her head.

"Why not?" Kami was clearly surprised.

"Schooner is very protective. I think he'll have a kneejerk reaction and call her and go ape shit and that is just what she wants. She wants to get to him. She wants to get to us."

"BBC, do not keep things from him. Seriously, the last time you didn't tell him about a little visit from her, look what it cost the two of you. Please tell me you learned from that mistake."

Mia sat back and listened to Seth's words. He was right. She could not let CJ come between them again. "Okay, I'll tell him."

Kami chimed in, "Mia, seriously. If Schooner finds out from CJ that you two spoke and that you didn't tell him about it, it will be a huge breach of trust for the two of you. You can't give her that power."

Mia had not even considered that, "Thanks, guys. You are right. I'll tell Schooner about it tonight. I don't want to ruin his day and I don't want him going off on her," she laughed. "So, I'll tell him in bed or something… when he's, um, compromised." Mia smiled her devilish grin.

Chapter Sixteen

As they walked in the cold, brisk air down Sixth Avenue, taking in the sounds and smells and movement of Manhattan on a winter's night, Schooner commented to Mia how refreshing it was to be able to walk everywhere.

"I think we don't even realize how much fresh air and exercise we get here because we don't get in a car to go everywhere. It just becomes the norm and you don't think about it." Mia had her arm around Schooner's waist and was smushing into him for warmth.

"I really like just being able to walk outside and get everything I want." He laughed, "I can't believe I'm turning into a city boy."

"You've always had a city boy's soul," Mia commented and he pulled her closer to him. "So, I think you are going to love Charles and Gaby's place. They have the bottom two floors of a brownstone, with a little backyard. It's amazing to have outdoor space in the city."

"Am I going to want to buy one of these, too?" Schooner laughed.

"I don't know, Mr. Real Estate Mogul—opening a health club in New York City and buying a beach house on Fire Island, while going through a divorce would be pretty financially strapping, I would think." Mia looked up at Schooner. She could see he was doing some sort of inventory in his mind.

"What do brownstones sell for?"

"It depends on neighborhood, condition, size. Here in The West Village, where these guys are, I'd say anywhere from $5 million on the low end to probably about $25 million."

He laughed. "That's quite a range. Having a little outdoor space sounds amazing though. A hot tub and a grill—what else do you need?"

"Schooner?" They heard a woman calling and turned toward the voice.

The very recognizable, screen-star, Katie Chisholm and her mini-me daughter, Sari, were rapidly approaching. Katie was wearing a surprised smile.

"What are you doing in New York?" she asked, kissing him on both cheeks.

"Katie, how are you? I'm living here now, actually I'm kind of bi-coastal these days." He pulled Mia close, "Katie, I'd like to introduce my fiancé, Mia Silver."

"So nice to meet you, Mia. Congratulations, to you both. Any chance we'll get an L9 here in the city now that you've become one of us?" Katie was looking for the scoop.

Schooner gave her the All-American boy smile. "Well, I'm planning on spending the lion's share of my time here now, so..." his voice trailed off.

The pops and bright strobes of camera flashes ended their moment as the paparazzi descended on Katie and Sari, taking photos of the four of them.

Katie rolled her eyes and sighed. "It's a school night, we'd better get going." She gave Schooner a kiss on the cheek and Mia a hug. "I hope to see a lot more of you both now that you're here in New York! And congratulations," she called as they headed down the street.

Mia smiled up at Schooner with her devil grin and raised eyebrows. "Fiancée?"

He pulled her close to him. "Mmm-hmm."

"Did I miss the memo?" she laughed, as they turned onto West 11th Street.

"Wow, I love this block!" Schooner's eyes started searching the brownstone lined street. "I really love this."

"Well, maybe if Katie Chisholm invites all her New York friends to join L9 we can afford to live here. And... you changed the subject on me!"

He laughed and hugged her into him. "I actually wanted to tell her what I really feel."

"Oh, and what is that, Mr. Moore?"

"That you're my wife." He leaned down and kissed the top of her head. "But I unfortunately can't say that just yet."

Mia didn't look up at him, she looked straight ahead and kept walking. The morning's phone conversation with CJ was weighing heavily on her, as she knew that was a conversation they had to have... later.

"We're here," she said brightly, as they climbed the stone steps to the brownstone's main entrance and rang the bell.

Charles answered the door, holding in his arms a beautiful doe-eyed little girl with long silky dark brown hair and a cloud-chasing smile. She was already dressed for bed, wearing Little Mermaid footie pajamas.

"Auntie Meezie," she flew out of Charles' arms into Mia's.

Mia covered her face in kisses, as she giggled. "What are you doing still awake, my little angel-pie?"

"Papa said you could put me to bed."

"Oh, did he now?" Mia continued to kiss her. "You smell so good, I'm going to eat you."

Schooner and Charles shook hands and exchanged greetings as they entered the front hall vestibule.

"Paola, I want you to meet someone very special. This is Schooner."

She gave him a shy smile and Mia whispered in her ear, "Isn't he cute?" Eliciting a round of giggles.

Gaby appeared in the hallway behind them, flowing in gracefully, as only Gaby could.

Charles had met Gabriella Rossetti on a photo shoot in Positano, Italy when she was modeling for the Elite Modeling Agency out of her hometown of Milan. He was providing security for Gaby and four other models and was totally entranced the moment he laid eyes on her. Tall and willowy with a sheath of shiny dark hair, expressive luminous dark eyes and olive skin, Charles knew that he was not leaving Italy without her.

After the shoot had wrapped up, he didn't go back to the States with the rest of the security detail, but instead followed her back to Milan where she was still living in the family's ancestral home.

Her father was leery of the tall, quiet American who was coming around to see his daughter. Until one Friday night, when Charles was welcomed to join the older man for Friday night services at the local synagogue. As Charles recited all the prayers in Hebrew, Giancarlo Rossetti warmed to the young man, who was about to become a fixture in their home.

Three months later Charles and Gaby were married.

"Mia," she embraced Mia warmly, kissing her on both cheeks. "I have missed you."

"Gaby, this is Schooner."

Gaby smiled up at him and greeted him with a kiss to each cheek. "I am very pleased to meet you, Schooner. Charles has told me much about you." She turned to Mia and Paola, "I think it's bed time. Auntie Meezie and I will put you to bed now."

Charles held up a bottle of Johnny Walker Blue, "Schooner, will you join me?"

"I knew I liked you, man!" Schooner laughed, as he took in the charm of the brick walls and working fireplace and original ceiling medallions.

Mia could see the real estate lust in his eyes.

"We're going to need this," Charles informed him. "We're on grill duty out back." They clinked glasses and then shared the look men have on their faces when that first stream of single malt scotch begins its satisfying burn southward.

Gaby and Mia headed down the wide mahogany staircase with Paola. Her room was Classic Winnie the Pooh and stuffed animals lined the floor. They tucked her and a very bedraggled yellow stuffed rabbit into her youth bed with its white eyelet comforter. Then both sat down on her tiny bed.

"Your Schooner, he is so handsome, Mia."

Mia smiled and nodded. "Yes, he is."

"Charles tells me that you know him since you were young." She tossed her long sheath of hair over her shoulders.

"I was sixteen when we met."

Gaby's eyes widened, "He was your first love, Mia?"

Mia nodded at her friend.

"He looks at you with such love, this Schooner." Gaby was smiling at her friend.

"We ran into Katie Chisholm and Sari on our way over here. Katie knows Schooner from his health clubs in LA. He introduced me as his fiancé. I almost fell over."

Gaby grabbed Mia's hand and squeezed it. "He is the one, I know this."

"Gab, he's been the one since I was sixteen."

"This is so romantic."

Mia rolled her eyes. "More like tragic. We missed twenty-four years of each other's lives."

She shrugged as she stroked Paola's hair. The little girl was fighting to keep her eyes open and listen to the conversation. "That is the past. Now you have forever. This Schooner is very much in love with you, Mia. I can see that. And you, this is your love?"

Mia smiled at Gaby. "Yes, this is my love."

Mia and Schooner walked back up Sixth Avenue, arms around one another talking about their evening.

"I belong here," Schooner ventured. "People are real. It's not about the bullshit or show. This city and the people," he gave Mia a hug into him, "this is me."

She looked up at him, "You feel at home here, don't you?"

He nodded. "Just the way I have always felt right with you, I feel that way in this environment. I was more comfortable tonight hanging out with Charles and Gaby than I have been hanging with anyone I know in Newport Beach. Tonight felt like I'd been hanging out with everyone my whole life. I didn't feel like the 'new guy' in the bunch."

Mia smiled. "That makes me happy."

"Me too, Baby Girl." He kissed the top of her head.

They were holding hands and swinging arms, like kids, when they walked into the building. The doorman and the guard at the front desk smiled widely at them.

Mia leaned up against Schooner as they waited for the elevator, snuggling into his side.

As they got in and the doors closed, he backed her to the corner and tilted her chin up. "I could not wait to get you home tonight." He put a hand on her lower back and pulled her up against him, his erection pressing hard into her stomach.

Mia's arms went around Schooner's neck pulling his mouth down to hers, threading her fingers through his hair. The elevator doors opened and he grabbed her hand, pulling her down the hall, breathless, stumbling and laughing.

In his haste, Schooner fumbled with his keys, unsuccessfully trying to get them into the lock.

"Sticky fingers?" Mia teased.

He turned to her, hooded eyes and a sexy smile. "We'll see who's got sticky fingers soon."

They made it through the door, peeled off their jackets and gloves. Schooner had Mia backed up against the inside of the door. Pulling her hands above her head, his palms flat on her palms, he pressed the back of her hands against the hard, cold wood of the door. With his lips hovering near hers, he ground his hips into hers.

Mia lunged for his lips and he moved his head back, taunting her, just out of reach. She tried to pull her hands away so that she could grab his hair, but he held them immobile above her head. Panting and out of breath, she ached to kiss him, trying her hardest to reach his teasing mouth, feeling his rock-hard cock grinding into her and pinning her up against the door.

"I loved watching you with Paola tonight," he whispered, kissing her neck.

His teeth gently grazed her skin, eliciting the moan he knew it would. Knowing the spots to get her out of control, fast came as second nature to him.

He ground his cock into her harder. "I want you to have my baby." He let go of her hands and pulled her legs around his waist and carried her into the bedroom.

Falling onto the bed on top of her, she wrapped her legs back around him. "I'm not kidding, Mia. I want you to have my baby."

She stroked his cheek and smiled. "Aren't I supposed to be the one worrying about the biological clock?"

He sat up straddling her and unbuttoned his shirt, slowly, letting her enjoy his gorgeous muscles. His eyes were blazing as he stared down at her.

"What?" she asked.

He smiled. A slow, sexy smile. "I want to get you pregnant."

"We haven't been using anything."

"Would you consider IVF if we don't get pregnant on our own?" he asked.

Mia hesitated, "Honestly Schooner, I've never even thought about it." She saw the disappointment cross his face and grabbed his hand. "I'm not saying no."

"Do you want a baby?"

In that moment, she knew she would do anything to make him happy because it would bring her equal happiness to do so. "I want your baby. Yes." And she reached for the button on his jeans, unbuttoned it and unzipped his fly.

Rolling off her, he kicked off his jeans and boxers and helped her peel off her jeans and panties.

They lie facing one another, softly kissing. She turned over so that her back was toward him and pulled his leg over her as she slid down his body until she could feel the head of his cock ready to press into her from behind. He pulled her tight against him, face buried into her neck, teeth grazing her shoulder, as he rammed deep into her.

"Oh yeah," he whispered in her ear and she squeezed his cock tight. "Oh yeah, just like that." And she squeezed harder. "I'm going to fuck you so hard," he growled.

"Then do it," she taunted and he rammed into her with a force that made her gasp. "That's what I need, Schooner. Give it to me. Give. Me. What. I. Need." He slammed into her harder. "Just like that. Just like that." And she clenched her muscles tight around his cock.

"Yesssssssssss," he hissed in her ear. "That's it, Baby Girl. Milk it out of me." He put his hand on her stomach and pressed her back into him as he buried himself in her as deeply as he could. "Come for me. I want you to come for me".

Taking his hand from her stomach, she moved it down to her clit. And with his forefinger in hers, she pressed her clit hard and started moving in circles until their fingers found just the right spot that sent electric volts scattering through her. She started to quake under his finger, muscles convulsing around him, squeezing him hard.

"Oh fuck yeah," he hissed pulling her over the edge with him as he drove up into her, deep and rough.

She collapsed back against him, panting and quaking with aftershocks.

He kissed her shoulder. "I love you, Baby Girl."

Rolling over, she placed a hand on his cheek and kissed him softly. "I love you too, Schooner," she said, breathlessly.

As she stroked his cheek and looked directly into his beautiful clear eyes, she gathered the courage to say, "I have something I need to tell you."

He looked at her. "Okay…"

"I didn't tell you earlier, because I didn't want to ruin your day and because I didn't want you to get pissed off and go ape shit."

"What's going on?" Concern shadowed his eyes.

"CJ called me this morning."

He pushed back from her and screamed, "What? And you are just telling me this now? Why didn't you call me this morning? Immediately." His face hardened in anger, a total transformation from the man who had been lying next to her mere seconds before.

"I didn't tell you because I knew you'd be pissed off and call her, and I didn't want to give her the satisfaction that she was even important enough for me to go running to you about."

"What exactly happened?" He ran his hand through his hair, clearly exasperated.

Mia recounted the details of the phone call and Schooner listened silently. After she finished, it was a moment before he spoke.

"On one hand, I want to kiss you for handling her so brilliantly." He leveled Mia an angry glance. "But on the other hand, I cannot even begin to verbalize to you how pissed off I am that you did not call me about this immediately."

"I think you should just kiss me for being brilliant," Mia said, softly.

He shook his head no. "I'm really pissed at you, Mia."

"Schooner, she wanted a reaction and I didn't want to give it to her."

"That's all good and well, but that was a decision we should've made together. First, you need to tell me these things, so that I can contact my lawyer immediately, who will contact her lawyer, and have her stop her harassing you. More importantly, however, is you not keeping things from me—especially where CJ is concerned. Last time you did that it cost us twenty-four years of our lives, Mia."

She felt sick. To hear Schooner verbalize that her actions or inactions had cost them twenty-four years felt like a huge wet slap across her face. Rolling away from him, she went to get out of bed.

"Where are you going?"

She didn't answer, but instead continued to walk into the kitchen to get a glass of cold water. Leaning against the breakfast bar, she sipped the water.

Joining her in the kitchen, Schooner stood in front of her. "Are we going to finish this conversation?"

"I'm listening." She looked up at him, full blown New York attitude on her face.

"You can't hide stuff from me, Mia. Why is it that you feel you can't come to me?"

She shrugged. "Look, I once told you, I'm not very good at relationships."

"Bullshit," he screamed, startling her.

She put her glass down on the breakfast bar and crossed her arms over her chest. "Well, I've never had a successful one," she scoffed, maintaining her defensive pose.

He shook his head and rubbed his forehead. "Listen, I'm sorry I screamed at you, but here's the deal. I need you to be totally honest with me all the time, not hide *anything* from me—especially where CJ's concerned—and have enough faith in me that I will handle situations appropriately and always do what is best for us. Us, Mia."

"I'm sorry, Schooner. I understand why you are so upset, I really do. Especially with a situation where CJ pulls something and I don't tell you. I get it—it will always be a big gaping wound for us. My poor handling of it in the past fucked up both of our lives. I get that. I just didn't want her to win this time and by treating her like her call meant nothing helped me marginalize her. Does that make sense?"

"Yes, Baby Girl, it does." He walked the few steps toward her and she stood still, arms still crossed over her chest. "But you have to promise me that you will always come to me immediately with everything. Give us a chance to work it out together, Mia. You always want to take on everything alone. You are not in this alone anymore." He put his hands on her shoulders. "Look at me, Mia. I'm not going to always get it right. I'm going to fuck up. Sometimes royally. I'm going to react with anger or I'm going to want to protect you. And that is exactly why we need to do it together. No secrets. Let's learn from our past and then leave it there."

He was right. Seth and Kami were right. Holding back anything from Schooner had been and would continue to be their undoing if she didn't start thinking of them as a team in every aspect. This man, who willingly was giving up half his world, starting a new life 3,000 miles from the only home he had ever known, and told Katie Chisholm that she was his fiancé, was asking for a little faith, and she would be the biggest fool in the world not to give him all that he was asking of her. Losing him again was not an acceptable option.

She uncrossed her arms and wrapped them around his waist. "No more secrets." She looked up into his eyes, "I promise." And then whispered into his chest, "Ever."

Smiling, he whispered into her hair, "You really told her you were recording her?"

With an almost bashful smirk, she nodded and he tightened his hold.

He laughed. "You are so freaking awesome."

Chapter Seventeen

Mia sat at her desk, reviewing Excel spreadsheets of operating expenses when the text alert on her cell phone sounded. She looked at the display. Schooner, texting from LA. She smiled.

Schooner: Sitting across from her now.
Mia: You're at the lawyer's office?
Schooner: Yes
Mia: And you're sitting at the table texting?
Schooner: LOL—that I am!
Mia: You're so bad!!
Schooner: That I am!
Mia: It's part of your charm.
Schooner: So you tell me.
Mia: So … how is it going?
Schooner: She's going to drag her feet. Nothing we didn't anticipate.
Mia: :-(
Schooner: Don't be sad, Baby Girl
Mia: Sad for you. Hate anyone making you unhappy.
Schooner: LOL she's clearly pissed I'm texting
Mia: LOL… tell her I say hi.
Schooner: Not!
Mia: Still seeing your parents tonight?
Schooner: Yup
Mia: Please send my love.
Schooner: I want your love.
Mia: You have my love.
Schooner: I hate being out here. Can't wait to come home.
Mia: :-) love having you home.

It was close to 10 minutes before her cell text beeped again, surprising her as she was absorbing the spreadsheet's numbers.

Schooner: This whole thing is starting to piss me off.

Mia: Oh no :-(
Schooner: Tell me something good.
Mia: Ummm… I love you
Schooner: That is very good. And it's smoochal, Baby Girl.
Mia: :-) yes, it is.
Schooner: God, she's such a huge bitch.
Mia: No comment! Do you need me to come out there and scratch her eyeballs out (or just hang the phone up on her again)? LOL
Schooner: Lol. Oh, that embarrassed her good when she was told to stop harassing you (I think I was smiling).
Mia: God, I love you.
Schooner: Oh God, she is laying it on really thick now.
Mia: And you're texting.
Schooner: Yeah :-)
Mia: So, you know how you always want me to share things with you?
Schooner: Yeah…
Mia: It may be nothing, but…
Mia: I barfed my guts up this morning.
Schooner: Holy shit! Have you taken a test?
Mia: No, will wait until you get home to do that. Want to do it together.
Schooner: I have to leave this meeting now and come home
Mia: You'll be home in two days.
Schooner: I want to be home NOW!
Mia: Soon and forever…
Schooner: Soon and forever (never going to be able to concentrate now! If she ends up with the business it is your fault, Baby Girl)
Mia: Lol… go concentrate. Call my ass when you get out of there.
Schooner: Call your ass hot.
Mia: :-) Bye! Concentrate.
Schooner: Bye :-(Never going to be able to concentrate after the barfing bombshell.
Mia: Hmmm … Barfing Bombshell … I think you called me that after too much tequila in college.
Schooner: LOL… ok about to stick it to her and not in the way she wants. Bye.

Mia woke to his arms wrapping around her and his long leg slung over her, pulling her into him, as he planted a kiss beneath her ear.

"Mmmmm," and through her cobwebs, "you're back?" It was a question more than a statement.

"I couldn't stay away." He nuzzled into her neck, his fingers finding her nipples and pinching them.

She moaned and ground her ass into his hard cock.

Pulling her beneath him, his hands gently cupped the sides of her face. He could see she was half asleep and unsuccessfully fighting to keep her eyes open, as she dozed off. He spread her legs with his thighs and without any foreplay rammed into her hard. She gasped, her eyes opening and a smile overtaking her lips.

"Morning, Baby Girl," he growled and kissed her hard while fucking her at a punishing rate. He rammed into her relentlessly, taking what he wanted. This was going to be quick. When he was through, he curled up behind her and pulled her close. They were both asleep in a matter of seconds.

When Mia woke, she found a surprise on the bathroom counter. Inside a Duane Reade Drugstore bag was a package containing not one, but two pregnancy tests. She smiled and thought, how very Schooner. Unwrapping one of the sticks, she thought to herself as she was taking the test, that this was the first time ever in her life she was hoping for a positive result.

She watched as the pink line started to form and within a minute it turned into a cross. Clicking the cover back onto the test stick, she crawled back into bed next to a sleeping Schooner and bit him on the shoulder. *As good a way as any to wake him*, she thought.

He rolled over to look at her and with a shit-eating grin she waved the test stick in his face. Schooner's eyes shot wide open as he realized what she was doing and he grabbed her hand mid-wave.

"Very good hand-eye coordination, I'm impressed," she laughed.

He focused in on the stick and saw the plus sign and looked up at Mia, who was nodding her head and smiling.

The look in his eyes melted every inch of her. "Baby Girl," he whispered hoarsely, as she smiled at him. He pulled her head down to his chest and kissed her hair. She peeked up at him and could see his mega-watt gorgeous smile, but he was lost somewhere.

"Where are you, Schooner?"

He smiled at her, "Thinking. I want this divorce NOW."

"Don't worry about that," Mia reassured.

"But we have a baby coming," he was verbalizing it for the first time and she could see the enormity bursting in his every thought.

"I promise I'll put your name on the birth certificate." Mia gave him her devil grin.

"Bitch!" he laughed, grabbing her and tickling her until she yelped. He then smiled at her and took her face in his hands, becoming serious again. "Mia Alyse Silver, you are having my baby."

"Schooner James Moore, yes I am."

His smile was so beautiful that Mia thought if there is one moment she wanted to take with her into the next life, this was it, right now. The feeling in her heart and the look in his eyes and his smile, made her think, this is all I want from this lifetime. It doesn't get better than this.

"Hand me my pants. They're on the floor by your side of the bed," he asked. Mia rolled away from him, grabbed his jeans and flung them at him, whipping them into his face.

"Ouch." He pulled his jeans off his face and smiled at her. "You know," he began, "sometimes parents are very smart. Take my parents, for example, they are very smart people. They loved you the minute they met you. Me, well, I was not quite as smart. I was totally intrigued from the moment I met you, but I was also more than a little intimidated by you. You were different and cool and you totally embraced it and you clearly didn't give a shit. Me, I was afraid to be different, even though deep down, I knew I was. So, I did everything I possibly could to fit in. I didn't quite know what to make of you, Mia, and frankly, I didn't know how to act around you because I thought you'd see right through me and my bullshit. I was afraid you would know what a fraud I was and that you wouldn't like me. You were this total enigma, this cool New York girl and I already knew you were so much fun to be with, just from the time we'd spent together and from watching you around campus." He nodded his head with the admission. "Yes, I watched you—in the dining hall, on The Quad. And I envied the fun you and everyone around you were always having. But you, you were always at the center of it. So, on that first day of Interim, I was thrilled when I saw you sitting there, because I knew I was going to have a chance to get to know you and that was something I really wanted. And later that day, you called me out on my shit and I went back to my dorm that night and lay in my bed thinking about you, and how you made me feel. It was like the fairytale where the wooden boy comes to life," he laughed, "except I was a plastic boy and you made me feel real. That magic that I had watched all first semester, well now I had a front row seat in that magic circle. And I just wanted to be with you all the time. You were my high, Mia. You taught me how to let me be myself and to like that guy and that is probably the greatest gift anyone has ever given me. Ever. And you liked that guy too and that made my heart soar. I wanted you to like me, not Mr. Hotshot Tennis God. I wanted you to like me. And it was when we were on that mountaintop together, that I was actually able to put it all together. I was in love and it hit me like a brick or maybe a snowball. I had fallen in love with you."

Mia stroked his face and smiled at him, her eyes filled with tears.

"So, yesterday afternoon I sat down with my parents and told them everything for the first time. And they are thrilled that you are joining our family." He brushed away Mia's tears with his thumb and then reached into the pocket of his jeans. "Mia Alyse Silver, the minute, and I mean the minute, that my divorce is final, I want you to be my wife, forever." Out of the pocket he pulled a ring box. "This was my grandmother's. My mother wants you to have it and I want you to have it." He opened the box and removed a platinum and diamond art deco ring. "Marry me, Baby Girl." He slipped the ring on her finger and then held her hand tightly in his.

Momentarily lost in his eyes, the depth of the emotion she witnessed was mirroring everything her heart was feeling, everything her heart had always felt about this man.

She smiled and nodded, desperately willing her voice's hasty return, "Schooner James Moore, aka Baby Daddy," they laughed through their tears as Mia found her voice, "I guess we can just face the fact that I am smarter than you because I was totally smitten from the moment I first laid eyes on you. You were so damn pretty, your eyes and a smile that should be outlawed. And I was so shy meeting you, but I remember thinking that we could be really good friends and have the best time together, like crazy adventures good times. And although I was seriously crushing on you, I knew you were looking for a prom queen type, which yes, we can both admit, I was not," they laughed. "And I didn't quite know how to deal with you, so aloof was a very safe and easy way for me to relate to you. And, interestingly enough, I have been told by more than one man in my life that I am aloof. But I digress… so when I looked up in that lecture hall that first day of Interim and saw you, my heart skipped a beat. Then you came and sat down next to me and my heart was pounding in my chest. I was afraid you could hear it and I was also afraid you could read my mind, so cool girl came in and took over to protect me. I needed someplace to hide and she always provided the perfect ruse. And then Rick said that we had to break into groups and at that moment, I just took control because it meant I'd get to spend time with you and I might really get to know you. And what surprised me most of all was how you just fit in with us right away, you just came and took your place. And it was easy and I didn't need cool girl there, because I could be me with you and we were totally on the same wavelength. And that night after the mountains, you kissed me for the first time," she smiled at him, his eyes bright with tears, "and I slept in your arms and from that moment on, my life was never, ever the same. I remember thinking, '*The realization of a secret dream,*' which was this horoscope that came packed in some lip gloss I got when I was a really little girl, like five or six years old, and I hid it and held onto it for years and years. And that is what I was thinking that night as I dozed off with my head on your chest. The realization of a secret dream." They both had tears streaming down their cheeks. "I can't wait to be your wife, Schooner."

She held out her hand to look at the stunning ring, "Now this is the smartest thing you've ever done." They both laughed. "Are you sure this shouldn't go to Holly though?"

He shook his head, "This one is yours. I think my mother may have put it in safekeeping for you right after freshman orientation."

Mia laughed, "You were not kidding. She is a very smart woman. I knew I liked her."

Mia picked up her phone and took a photo of the ring on her finger. She looked at Schooner, devil smile at full tilt.

"Oh no, who are you texting that to?"

She just smiled, enigmatically.

"Your Mom?" he guessed.

"Nope."

"My Mom?"

"Nope."

"Seth."

"Nope, he'll be second."

"Kami."

"Nope."

"Gaby."

"Nope."

"CJ," he teased

"Ugh, nope," laughing, "I don't want to be responsible for an earthquake in LA."

He shrugged his shoulders, palms up. "I'm out of guesses.

"Katie Chisholm," smiled Mia and they both laughed.

Chapter Eighteen

Schooner's right leg bounced up and down at a frantic pace as he and Mia sat in Dr. Gary Cohen's waiting room. Dr. Cohen, one of the top-rated physician's in Manhattan for high-risk pregnancies, was known for his laid-back caring manner and was universally adored by his patients.

Mia had been one of Gary's first patients when he joined a prestigious gynecology and obstetrics practice—long before he was known as "The Man" for high risk pregnancies. A friend of Mia's, a nurse at Columbia Presbyterian Hospital, had recommended a doctor when Mia was suffering from irregular cycles and prolonged periods of bleeding. The senior doctor in the practice was no longer accepting new patients, so Mia was assigned to the new guy, who was just starting out and trying to build a patient roster. Nearly twenty years had passed since.

"You're making me nervous. Stop that." Mia placed a hand above his knee and gave him a pointed look.

"Sorry." He took her hand and squeezed it.

"So, when is Yoli flying in?" She needed to distract him or his nerves were going to start making her even more nervous than she already was.

"I think she lands about 11 P.M. tomorrow night." His eyes were darting everywhere.

"Schooner."

He looked at her.

"Stop," she implored.

"Sorry. I can't believe I'm this nervous." His eyes were wide and he looked like a lost boy to Mia.

Smiling at him, she thought, *God, he is sweet.*

Leaning over, she kissed him. "This is going to be a long freaking nine months. Keep it up and I'm sending you back to LA."

He smiled against her lips, "Bitch." And they both laughed.

"Mia Silver," a nurse was at the door.

Mia and Schooner stood and in sync looked at one another and said, "Showtime." They laughed as they headed back toward the exam room, hand in hand.

Dr. Gary Cohen entered the exam room, arms outstretched for a hug. "I hear my favorite patient is here."

Mia gave Gary a warm hug, "I'll bet you say that to all your patients."

"You and I were babies when we started," they both laughed.

"Gary, I'd like you to meet my fiancé, Schooner Moore."

Gary extended a hand and a warm smile to Schooner. "So, you're the guy responsible for knocking her up, huh?"

They all laughed.

"That would be me," Schooner confessed.

"Good job, man." Gary clapped Schooner on the shoulder.

"Alright, Miss Mia, I'm going to do a sonogram in a few minutes. We'll take a look and make sure this is a viable pregnancy, and then discuss some of the risks of being forty and pregnant, things we need to look out for, regimen, etc."

Gary turned to the sink and washed his hands. "Okay, let's get you up on this table, feet in the dreaded stirrups. I'm going to do a vaginal ultrasound on you. What we're looking for is fetal pole or possibly even a fetal heartbeat, depending on how far along you are." He squeezed gel onto the head of the ultrasound wand. "Are your periods still so irregular?"

"Yup." Mia nodded, bracing herself for what she knew was going to be a cold, goopy wand.

He laughed. "You've always been a mess. Ready?"

She nodded, holding her breath and biting her bottom lip. Schooner grabbed her hand and squeezed it. He smiled down at her, his eyes saying all she needed to hear. He was surprisingly calm after his mini-meltdown in the waiting room.

"Ahhhh!" Mia stiffened from the cold, wet feeling probe.

"Relax," Gary smiled up at her. He manipulated the wand, eyes intent on the screen.

Squeezing Schooner's hand tighter, she silently prayed, *please, please, please*. Gary kept making minor adjustments to the wand, moving it left, center, right.

And finally, a whoosh, whoosh, whoosh sound and Schooner let out a "Yes!"

Mia looked from Schooner's smile to Gary. He was nodding his head, "Good job, Mia," he was smiling. "We have a heartbeat."

She felt the familiar sting of tears in her eyes and turned to look at the monitor. The tech pointed out the baby's heartbeat and Gary told her to print it.

She looked up at Schooner who was watching the fetal heartbeat and mouthed the words, "Our baby." Lifting her hand to his lips, he kissed it.

Mia knew he was too overwhelmed with emotion to speak.

"Okay, let's get some measurements and we'll calculate a due date." They moved markers around on the screen and pressed buttons that sounded like snapshots to Mia. "Okay, we've got it," Gary informed his tech. "Mia, you can get dressed now and why don't you and Schooner come meet me in my office." He handed her a wad of tissues with a smile and she wondered if it was for her tears or to clean off the nasty goop.

Hand-in-hand, Schooner and Mia entered Gary's ultra-modern office and he motioned for them to have a seat.

"First, let me congratulate you. This is a very exciting day and I'm really thrilled for both of you. Schooner, I've known Mia for a long time and she is absolutely one of my very favorite people, so this pregnancy and her health are personally even more important to me than it typically is with a patient. I consider Mia a friend."

Schooner smiled at Mia, "She does have that effect on people, doesn't she?" He rubbed her hand in both of his, smiling ear-to-ear.

"Have you known one another long?" Gary asked.

"Twenty-four years," Mia offered.

Gary's eyes widened in surprise.

"We went out freshman year in college."

Gary was smiling. "How'd you guys get back together?

"Facebook," Schooner responded with a smile, as if that explained everything.

"Good for you." Gary looked at them, shaking his head. "Okay, let's get to the serious stuff. Here's the good news, Mia you conceived right away, with no problems. Considering your age, irregular periods and irregular ovulation pattern, that is great. The fact that the embryo implanted normally and we now have a heartbeat is also really good. The embryo has a CRL measurement of slightly over 5MM. Again, perfectly within the norm and very good news."

"What is a CRL measurement, Gary?"

"Crown to rump length."

"Cool." Mia was smiling, picturing a little head and bottom all curled up sleeping.

"Based on that measurement, we're looking at a fetal age of about 5 weeks and a gestational age of 6 1/2—7 weeks. If you go full-term, Mia, we're looking at a birth date right before Christmas."

She backhanded Schooner in the arm, smiling at him. "How's that for a gift from a Jewish girl!"

He grabbed her hand and brought it to his lips. Schooner was beaming.

"Now let's talk about the elephant in the room," Gary began. "Mia, you're forty. So, what does that really mean? It means we need to test for certain things, look for specific things, keep our eyes open and be prepared to make some decisions, should we need to."

Mia looked at Schooner, holding her breath. He rubbed her hand in his and the look in his eyes said, "No worries, Baby Girl."

Gary continued, "At age forty, the biggest risk is for Down's Syndrome. The statistics are 1 in 90 births, which is considerably higher than 1 in 1300 for a woman who is twenty-five."

Mia realized she wasn't breathing, she could feel the strength emanating from Schooner's hand to hers, that same strength he infused in her the night that she was raped.

"In about a month, we'll do some blood tests looking for some normal first trimester proteins, a few weeks after that we'll do Alpha-fetoprotein testing and at the same time we'll do an early Quad Marker Screen testing for four substances that come from the baby's blood, brain, spinal fluid and amniotic fluid. At that point, we'll also do an amniocentesis. We have a Geneticist here on staff and I'm going to have the two of you meet with him."

He stopped and looked from Mia to Schooner then back to Mia. "You are in good health, Mia, and we're going to watch you closely. If there are any issues, we're going to detect it early and act accordingly."

"Meaning?" Mia asked.

"Meaning a lot of different things—if we need to put you on bed rest, we'll put you on bed rest." He turned to Schooner and smiled, "Good luck with that one," and the two men laughed. "Like I said, you're in good health and your chances for a normal pregnancy are good. But you are high-risk and we'll watch you. For now, enjoy your life, eat healthy, don't drink, moderate exercise, take your prenatal vitamins and enjoy being pregnant."

As he saw them out, he gave Mia a huge hug, "I am so thrilled for you both." And to Schooner, "Take care of our girl."

Chapter Nineteen

Yoli stood in the middle of the rotunda looking up at the frescos. "Holy shit, Schooner, the pictures did not do this place justice. I cannot believe this. This space is not for real."

Schooner just smiled, looking up at the cove lit frescos. "Pretty amazing, huh. We're coming along on the build out faster than I thought."

"I can see. They really do things in a New York minute here, huh?" They were ascending the main marble staircase. "Amazing." Yoli was blown away looking at all the architectural details.

"Come, let me show you the offices." He ushered her into an area away from the rotunda. They entered a space with floor to ceiling windows. "Like my new office?" He flashed his catalogue smile, as he stood next to one of the windows.

"Are you ever coming home again?" she asked.

"I am home, Yoli." He gave her a real smile.

"I was afraid you were going to say that." She leaned up on the window frame facing him. "We need to talk about California."

"I want you to run it—all of it. It's about time I made you COO and let's backfill you in the CMO role. You've got some good people working under you. I don't think you'll need to go outside, unless there's someone you want to bring in."

"Did you just promote me?" She had a look on her face saying, *you didn't really just do that?*

He nodded and laughed. "*You* are the only thing I've missed about California." He opened his arms and she went to him for an embrace.

"Yeah well, I've missed your cranky ass, too." She gazed out the window, "What am I looking at?"

"Downtown. The financial district. That's the Freedom Tower."

She nodded and continued to look out the window before finally turning back to Schooner who was casually leaning against the opposite side of the carved window frame, watching her. "You're happy, Schooner." It was a statement. "I've never seen you so full of life as you are here. Mia is clearly really good for you."

He nodded. "She is really good for me. I did not think I'd ever be this happy again in my life, Yoli. It's a gift and I know it and trust me, I am treating it accordingly," Schooner admitted.

He put an arm around her shoulder and they started back toward the rotunda. "Let's head over to Mia's office, I know she and Kami were bringing lunch into the conference room and we're going to make it a working lunch." He shrugged, "Working lunch. Totally a New York thing. I'm really excited to have you finally meet Mia, but I also have to admit that I'm more than a little scared."

"Why is that?" The first hints of early spring were in the air when they stepped through the massive front entrance of the soon-to-be L9/NYC into the bright sunshine. Schooner stepped to the curb and hailed a cab, making Yoli think, he's really got this down.

"I really want you two to like each other."

"Well, I really like Kami a lot and she says wonderful things about Mia. And…" She looked at him out of the corner of her eye.

"…And what?" He shifted to face her, the black leather seat of the yellow cab creaking.

"I spoke to Holly." Yoli looked almost contrite. Almost, being the operative word.

"…And?" Schooner urged, surprised by Yoli's admission.

"She had great things to say about Mia, but more importantly, the thing that struck her the most, Schooner, was the change in you. You're happy."

Schooner nodded and looked out the window as the streets passed by.

They were laughing so hard, it didn't feel like they were working. Yoli was immediately blown away by the casual chic atmosphere of the agency that clearly came top down from their Levi's clad owner. Levi's, Yoli thought refreshingly, not 7 For All Mankind or Dolce & Gabana, but a well-worn, broken in pair of Levi's. And they weren't even camel-toe tight, they were more like boyfriend jeans.

"I think you'll be soft-opening in summer," Mia was saying. "Which is good, because a lot of people are out of town and it's just a great time to work out the kinks." They all agreed. "My recommendation is that we don't do the big event until after Labor Day when everyone is back in town. Here's what I'm thinking, Fashion Week is the week after Labor Day, make it part of the Fashion Week festivities. Means a lot of stars in town. Everyone is party hopping, throw a big opening gala in conjunction. Will give everyone something to look forward to in the fall social season."

"Do we run the risk of getting lost in the shuffle?" Kami threw out on the table.

"We do if we don't do it right. If we do it right, we can garner a lot of press out of it. If we launch prior, it's pre-Labor Day and no one is in town, and if we wait until later in September, we lose a lot of the star power that will be in town for Fashion Week—many of whom are already L9 members. I think we're locked into a box and we just need to manage it to our advantage."

Yoli made some notes on her laptop. "I'll pull a member roster so that we can start taking a look at who we think will be in town for Fashion Week. We have a lot of models."

"We've got enough time," Mia began, "to pull this together and really work on the details and make it a huge event. My concern is that it runs smoothly, and appears flawless to the attendees."

Grabbing a Black & White cookie from a tray at the center of the conference room table and looking at it like *I can't believe I'm going to eat this*, Schooner turned to Yoli and said, "Do we have our list together of staff that we want here for the opening and transition period?" Yoli pulled a sheet from a manila folder and slid it over to Schooner.

He looked over the list. "I wonder how they're going to feel about sleeping bags?" Schooner muttered. All eyes turned to him. He looked up stone-faced and looked around at all the sets of eyes on him, then broke into a huge smile, a real smile, "Scared you all, huh?"

"Asshole," muttered Yoli.

"Love her," Mia informed Schooner, pointing to Yoli.

"A woman to abuse me on each coast. Some guys just have it all," he quipped.

Mia looked at Yoli with her devil grin and lifted her hand for a high five, which Yoli was right there to meet.

Later in the afternoon in a small dark pub around the corner from the office, drink in hand, Yoli sat with Schooner watching Mia talk and laugh with Seth, Kami and other members of her staff.

"So, what do you think?" he asked.

"I think you got it right this time. She's so real. And you, you're a different person."

"I'm me," Schooner countered, lifting his Johnnie Walker Blue to his smiling lips.

"How bad is CJ going to make this?"

"She's going to drag her feet for as long as she can, but it's inevitable."

Schooner shrugged.

"And how is Mia with all of that?"

"Surprisingly unfazed." He turned to Yoli smiling and shaking his head. "She could care less. She's just worried about the aggravation it causes me."

Yoli tossed back the rest of her drink and motioned to the waitress for another. "Well excellent, that is one less thing you have to worry about."

Schooner turned to Yoli, a huge grin on his face. "Did you hear that CJ called Mia?"

Yoli's mouth momentarily hung open. "Are you serious?"

Schooner nodded, still laughing. "She accused Mia of stealing me."

"She didn't." Yoli laughed.

"And Mia told her," he was still laughing, "not to confuse me leaving her with being stolen away."

Yoli began to choke on her drink and Schooner patted her back. "And then she told her she was recording the call." They were both hysterical laughing.

"I knew I liked her!" Yoli confirmed.

Schooner went on, "I guess Mia said something to her about that she was just embarrassing herself and that she wasn't going to let her go on and CJ told her that she wasn't done yet and Mia said, 'Actually, you are,' and hit the click off on her speaker button and hung up on her ass."

They were both roaring with laughter. Mia smiled across the dark bar at them, clearly happy to see Schooner so at ease and laughing.

When Yoli could speak again, "That's it, it's official, I love her."

"Ditto. She is pretty damn adorable." Schooner beamed, looking at his love across the room.

Chapter Twenty

Heading home in a cab, Schooner sat staring blankly out the window.

"Hey, where are you?" Mia asked as they stopped at a red light.

"I'm here." He brought her hand to his mouth and kissed her knuckles.

Mia had noticed his preoccupation growing over the past few weeks. He had a lot on his plate; the divorce, building L9/NYC, still living two lives on two coasts while he transitioned California operations to Yoli.

"Let's not go right home," Mia suggested. "Let's go get some frozen yogurt and take a walk on The High Line and watch sunset."

As they walked The High Line, a linear elevated park built on an old railway spur on the West Side of Manhattan, Mia could feel the tension radiating off Schooner, even though they were in this peaceful environment surrounded by people leisurely strolling and enjoying the beautiful balmy evening air, an early precursor of the spring that was waiting right around the corner.

"What is bothering you, Schooner? Please talk to me." Mia looked up at his handsome profile, wondering how she could pull him back to her.

Mia spied an unoccupied bench and started steering them toward it. She sat down, tugging on Schooner's hand to sit with her.

"I'm lost." She looked at him. "Please talk to me. I've watched you going off into a space that doesn't seem like a happy space for a few weeks now, and I don't know what's going on."

A couple with a baby in a stroller and a toddler holding its mom's hand passed by and they watched them silently.

"I'm just concerned about the tests coming up," he finally admitted.

Mia took his face in her hands, so that she could look into his eyes, "Me too."

"I'm afraid you and I will have different answers if things don't turn out as well as we're hoping," his eyes looked sad.

Mia understood what he was saying and looked down for a moment to get her bearings. She sighed. "Schooner, can we cross that bridge when we come to it?"

"I've already been crossing it, Mia."

Mia nodded her head. She knew what he wanted to hear. He wanted to hear that whatever the news was that she would continue with the pregnancy.

She took his hand and rubbed it between hers and brought it to her face, rubbed her cheek on it and kissed it. "Okay, here's where you and I differ."

His beautiful eyes looked grave.

"I can't go there right now." Mia continued, "I can't go where you are going. I just can't do it. Just thinking that things are not going to be perfect upsets me. I can physically feel the anxiety and my blood pressure gets all crazy. So, I just can't go there. If I need to go there, because it's reality, then I will. But I refuse to go there when it's still speculative. I can't do that to myself or to the baby."

He nodded. "I just worry, Mia."

"Well stop, Schooner. Right now, you are worrying about a problem that doesn't exist and may never exist. If we find out differently, we're two intelligent people, we'll figure it out. Please just enjoy this time. It's my bliss time, Schooner. Please share it with me."

They sat in silence, watching people stroll by, skateboarders, dog walkers, and the sky turn from a blue the color of Schooner's eyes to opalescent pinks and oranges into rubies and then dusk.

On their walk back to the apartment, Schooner finally started to vocalize. "I just have this overwhelming need to protect you, Mia. I feel like I have failed to do a good job of it so many times in my life."

Mia sighed. "Schooner, Schooner, Schooner. There are some things we can't control."

"You'd be surprised." He was now smiling.

Mia laughed. "How do I get you to chill out?"

"Maybe sometime in late December, when we have a nice healthy baby." He hugged her to him as they waved hello to the doormen.

"Oh puhleeeze." She tightened her arm around him. "I think that's when your crazy neurosis is going to be in full bloom." They entered the elevator.

He laughed. "I swear I was much calmer about this in my twenties."

"Great, so what you're telling me is CJ got the good end of things here?" They both laughed. "That's just not fair," Mia muttered.

"I promise to try to chill." He kissed her as they entered the apartment.

"C'mon Baby Daddy, make it up to me." She pulled him into the bedroom.

Chapter Twenty-One

"You called Gary?" Mia was shocked.

"Mmm-hmm." Schooner nodded, long legs stretched out from where he sat at the breakfast bar, coffee in hand. "I had questions. I want to understand the whole procedure, the risks to you and the baby, when to expect results."

"And to make sure you could be in there with me?" He nodded.

Mia stood in front of him, between his legs. "Did you buy a lab to get immediate, priority results?"

"It occurred to me." He stared straight into her eyes.

"When did you become such a control freak, Schooner?" Mia cocked her head, looking into his calm blue eyes.

"You are seriously asking me that?" he asked, with a bemused look, putting his hands on Mia's shoulders.

She nodded.

"Mia, I always control everything. I always have. With the exception of you. You have always been the one out of control thing in my life. You. Everything that happens to you. What you do. How you react. Out of control."

Mia stood there thinking, while Schooner took one hand off her shoulder and grabbed his coffee cup. "People. Situations. Business. Emotions. I've always controlled them or was in control of them."

Mia's brows were knit, clearly doing a mental inventory of their past and their time together.

"But you, my Baby Girl, are like a vortex. I get sucked in and spun around and nothing is ever in control. And it's always certainly out of my control."

Mia smiled at him and pushed his hair from his forehead. "And does it surprise you how happy you are in my little out of control world?"

He nodded and she leaned forward and kissed him. "Exciting, huh?"

"To some extent," he admitted, taking a sip of his coffee. "But also very disconcerting. You've always controlled everything, Mia. Whether you realize it or not. I gave up control when I fell in love with you. You know why?"

She shook her head.

"Because I stopped putting me first."

"And this clearly gives you heartburn, Schooner?"

He nodded. "Mia, you have the power to pull the rug out from under me. I'm helpless. I'm just along for the ride."

She took his face in her hands. "Schooner, I probably shouldn't tell you this, but we are standing on that precipice together. You have a lot more power here than you give yourself credit for."

"I do what I can in little ways to try and gain some semblance of control over things." He stood to rinse his cup in the sink before putting it in the dishwasher.

"Like call Gary?" Mia realized she had her arms crossed in front of her and dropped them, consciously not trying to take on a defensive pose.

He nodded. Schooner's eyes were fixed on Mia's and very serious.

Mia gestured, palms up. "And? Do you feel better?"

"I do."

She rolled her eyes. "Don't make me drag this out of you."

"Gary and I both think that it's best that you don't do the tests as an outpatient. He's going to keep you overnight, in case there are any issues." Mia nodded and he continued, "And we can do something called FISH results and have answers the next day that Gary says are usually pretty accurate."

Mia nodded, turned on her heel and walked into the bedroom. Schooner walked in a few minutes later and Mia was sitting on the bed in running shorts and a sweatshirt, tying the laces on her sneakers.

He leaned in the doorway arms crossed, taking up most of the doorframe watching her. "Going for a run?"

"No. Probably more like a fast walk." She didn't look up at him.

"Are you angry?"

"No."

"Then why are you going out?"

She looked up at him for the first time. "I need space and I need to think."

"You need space from me?" he sounded annoyed.

She nodded. "I do. I need to think, Schooner. I'm really trying not to react."

"And you don't think walking out of here to think is not a reaction?"

Mia stood. "Yeah, it's a reaction, but it will give me time to process everything."

"Fine." And he turned and walked back into the living room.

Mia found him standing in front of the living room windows looking outside. Instead of grabbing her keys, she approached Schooner from behind and wrapped her arms around his waist, laying her cheek on his back.

"You overwhelm me, Schooner. I think when it comes to me you sometimes don't understand boundaries. I have to keep reminding myself it's because you love me and always want to protect me." She could feel his muscles begin to relax. His hands went to her hands, covering them. "Why didn't you talk to me before calling Gary?"

"Well, I knew he could answer my questions directly."

"I shouldn't be learning about it as an afterthought." She kissed his back.

"You would've stopped me." He turned in her arms to face her.

"Mmm-hmm," she acknowledged, "or I at least would've been part of the decision-making process, Schooner."

He nodded. "You're right."

"I'm not porcelain," she whispered.

"When you were sixteen, my dad told me to look out for you." He looked up at the ceiling, slowly letting out a lungful of air. "Do you know that I always felt that I let him down, that I let your dad down and most of all, that I let you down."

She grabbed him tighter, cheek against his chest. "Will I always wonder what our lives would've been like had I not left you? Yes, a little bit maybe. Okay, maybe more than a little, but Schooner, I've had a good life—so many of my dreams have come true. You've had an amazing life. And now, we have this chance. This chance to do it right. And we both have the life experience and the maturity to really appreciate and value it all. And we're having a baby. And the only thing either one of us should worry about controlling is our happiness. You have to lighten up."

He lifted her hand to his lips. "Not likely, Baby Girl."

Mia looked up with sad eyes into his beautiful clear blue eyes, turned and grabbed her keys off the breakfast bar and walked out of the apartment.

Chapter Twenty-Two

Mia had been walking for a while, zigzagging through the streets, not really paying attention to her surroundings, the dialogue in her head drowning out all else. Schooner was usually the calming factor to her over the top reactions, tethering her back to Earth, but now his desire to control and protect was oppressive. *Was it just driven by his fear that their baby wouldn't be okay or was this really just Schooner?* Mia wondered.

Really, who was he? Some guy she had known for a short while, a long time ago, who just came back into her life. A guy who had just left his wife for her (okay, the wife who stole him away with lies in the first place). And now she was pregnant with his baby. And at forty, this baby might not be healthy and could she deal with that? Did she want to deal with that? Could she even consider not dealing with it? She told him that she would cross that bridge when they came to it.

Reaching the corner of Greenwich and Gansevoort, she stopped. *What to do? What to do? Okay, one more block and I'll be at Christian Louboutin,* she thought. *I'll look at Louboutin shoes, that'll be a feel good.*

As Mia stood in front of what was considered the mother ship to many women, she realized that she didn't have her wallet or her cell phone with her. She couldn't buy shoes and she couldn't call Schooner and the thought upset her greatly.

And as she stood there looking at the beautiful red-soled skyscrapers, she realized that she couldn't buy Louboutin's anyway because every woman she knew that had a child said their feet grew as a result of their pregnancy. And just the thought of that was enough to push Mia Silver over the edge.

With her hands on her belly, Mia stood in front of Louboutin's window and sobbed. She sobbed for all the beautiful size 7 1/2's in her closet that she would never wear again. She sobbed for all the shoes she couldn't buy until her feet morphed into their new size. She sobbed for her favorite Old Gringo cowboy boots that she was not going to fit into as a cool new mother. She sobbed because her feet were soon going to be huge swollen platters that would only fit into Birkenstocks, and that alone, the thought of having to wear Birkenstocks, was reason enough to sob uncontrollably.

A gay man walking his Yorkie handed Mia a tissue. She thanked him and decided it was time to head home before the staff at Louboutin alerted the psych ward at Bellevue.

She tried making a mental list on the way home. Schooner was so good to her and so sweet to her and he was right, he always put her before himself. She thought back to what he was like even as a teen. He put his life on hold when she was attacked, taking over so that she could heal. He took over then, too. Why hadn't she seen that this was his way? She wondered if maybe she was the only thing he couldn't control because they were both alphas. Could two alphas live together and complement one another without smothering or killing the other?

It was dusk by the time she reached her building. She knew that whatever their issues were, they needed to figure them out because she was not going to live without him again.

Entering the apartment, she found Schooner was sitting on the couch with blueprints spread out on the coffee table. He looked up at Mia, his expression unreadable.

"Sorry I didn't call. I left my phone here," she began.

"I know. I was worried," his voice was terse.

Mia sat down next to him on the couch. "I should not have walked out. I'm sorry."

He sighed, head cocked to the side as he gazed at her. "We haven't really changed that much, have we? Our M.O.'s are pretty much the same."

Mia was shaking her head, no.

"How can you say no, Mia? You just walked out."

"I went out to think. You know that."

"And?" his voice was clipped.

"And I thought a lot. I thought how little we know one another. I thought about how we knew one another for a short time, a long time ago. I thought about, here we are involved in this big way and we're having a baby together. I thought about the fact that I can't buy Louboutin's because I don't know what size my feet will be after I have the baby. I cried in front of Christian Louboutin, Schooner!"

His eyes were wide, his look slightly scared. And as he pondered how to respond, he was very aware the slightest miscalculation could mean his head.

"That's right, you should be looking at me like I'm a crazy pregnant woman, because I *am* a crazy pregnant woman. And you are making me crazier. I think we're both alphas, Schooner, and we need to figure out a way to live with that, because I refuse to lose you again."

The imperturbable mask on his face cracked and the smile led all the way to his eyes. He opened his arms and Mia fell into them. Pulling her in tight, he kissed the top of her head.

"You need to learn to let me take care of you, Baby Girl. You don't have to be so tough all the time." He tightened his arms around her, lips still in her hair.

Chapter Twenty-Three

"Are you ready to take a look at your baby?" Gary asked an anxious Schooner and Mia.

They both nodded, smiling. Schooner held tightly onto Mia's hand.

"They need to come up with a warming version on that jelly," Mia complained.

Gary started moving the wand over Mia's now rounded belly. "I'm going to do a full ultrasound first, we're going to take a lot of measurements today, then we'll do the amnio and quad markers and then I'll do another ultrasound after the amnio. You ready?"

Mia nodded.

"Okay, here we go."

Within seconds, a 3-D image of a little head appeared on the screen. Mia heard a mewling sound come from her throat and felt the burning tears welling in her eyes. Schooner squeezed her hand tighter and she looked over at him. He was beaming at the screen. As Gary moved the wand down, they watched the tiny heart beating. He slowly moved down the length of the fetus, down long legs to the feet.

"The baby is looking good. We've got ten fingers and ten toes. Size and development look on target for this age." He smiled at Mia. "I'm going to do some measurements of the head and the brain, take multiple view shots of the heart, take full body measurements and long bone measurements. This is going to take a few minutes, so just enjoy your first home movie."

"Look at that little nose and mouth." Mia was bursting with joy. She felt Schooner's lips on the back of her hand and turned toward him.

His eyes were crinkled in the corners and tears streaked his face.

"I love you," Mia mouthed.

"Love you too, Baby Girl," he whispered in her ear and kissed her temple.

"Looks like you've got a little thumb sucker." Gary laughed as the baby moved its thumb to its mouth.

As the baby moved positions, Mia asked, "Ummm Gary, am I looking at some family jewels?"

He laughed. "You most certainly are."

Mia looked up at Schooner. "We have a little show off! I can already see my little lady killer preening on the courts."

Schooner just stared at the screen, too moved to speak.

"The measurements all look good. Everything is developing right on schedule. Okay, let's get ourselves ready here for the amnio. I'm going to put a little topical numbing cream on your stomach. What you're going to feel is basically the pinch of a shot and then some pressure. The whole thing won't take too long."

Schooner sat down so that his head was next to Mia's. "Look at me, Mia."

She looked at him, her head now turned away from the screen and from her stomach.

He squeezed her hand. "You are doing so great, Baby Girl. I'm so proud of you."

She winced as the needle inserted and he kept talking, "Just a few days and we close on the beach house." He brushed her bangs from her eyes. "I can't wait to wake up to the view off that deck. It's going to be so relaxing just to be out there. Walk miles of beaches." He leaned in and kissed her softly. "Barbeque at night. Get you to take it easy a little."

"You did great, Mia." Gary gave her other hand a squeeze.

"All done?" she asked.

"All done," Gary nodded. "I want to take a few more pictures of the baby and give you guys a gift for your refrigerator." They all laughed. "We're going to get you back to your room. I want you to relax tonight, let Schooner and the nurses pamper you. You might have some cramping and discomfort and, if that happens, I want you to let the nurses know immediately. We'll have the FISH results before you leave tomorrow and then full results in about 10 days."

Seth and Kami were waiting in the room for Mia and Schooner.

"BBC, I was so worried about you. How did it go?" Mia handed him the strip of photos.

"Oh my God, it's a baby," he exclaimed. "Well, it looks like it's got your big head, BBC. Oh, and what is this, Schooner's big head?" They laughed.

"Yes, meet our exhibitionist son. Handsome and well-endowed! Just the way I like my men," Mia joked.

"Was it scary?" Kami asked, as Seth plumped up Mia's pillows.

"No, Schooner distracted me, so I was just looking at him when they did it. It felt like a shot and some pressure, but I didn't see any of it, which is good."

"Did you look?" Seth asked Schooner.

He shook his head no. "I was too focused on my beautiful Baby Girl."

Bending down, Seth whispered into Mia's ear, "I love him."

"You have good taste, Princess." She squeezed Seth's hand.

Seth grabbed a bag off the couch and perched on the side of Mia's bed. "I have a treat for you, BBC." And slowly out of the bag he pulled a small Styrofoam container and a plastic fork. "Junior's Cheesecake."

Mia gasped in delight and Seth proceeded to feed her the creamy delicacy.

"Mmm mmm mmm." Mia finished the last bite. "A girl could get used to this spoiling."

Standing next to the bed, Schooner smiled down at her and brushed the bangs from her eyes. He leaned down and kissed her softly, "Get used to it, Baby Girl."

The next morning Dr. Gary Cohen delivered the news Mia and Schooner had been waiting for with bated breath, preliminary results showed a healthy baby boy.

They could now share this time of bliss fully, without the specter of additional issues hanging over them. It was finally time to enjoy the start of their new family.

Chapter Twenty-Four

"Call me or text me. I'm going to be worrying about you." Mia held onto Schooner's hand as she walked him to the front door.

"No worries from you, Baby Girl. It's all going to be fine." He bent down and placed a soft kiss on her lips. "I'll call you later."

And he was gone. Off to Kennedy Airport to meet up with CJ and Holly and await Zac's flight from Spain. They were meeting as a family to break the news to Zac.

The apartment felt empty without Schooner, and if Mia were to admit it, she felt empty without Schooner there. She didn't like being left out of his life, but she certainly did not belong with him or his family today. His family. A family she was not a part of. It was still hard for her to process that.

She was his family. She and their baby. And Holly. Mia loved her growing relationship with Holly. It was healthy and honest and this young woman, CJ and Schooner's daughter, had accepted her into her life as her father's partner and soon to be wife. It was so hard for Mia to conceive of the fact that there was another family, another life. Yet, she had lived an entire lifetime without Schooner.

Mia picked up her phone and texted Seth.

Mia: He's off to JFK to meet with CJ, Holly & Zac
Seth: Are you freaking?
Mia: Yes!
Seth: Why?
Mia: I'm just afraid it's going to be really ugly and I hate that for him.
Seth: If anyone can control the situation, it's Schooner.
Mia: Understatement! LOL
Seth: Want me to come over and help you pack for the beach house?
Mia: Hell yes!

Seth and Mia had suitcases, shopping bags and beach bags packed and lined up waiting by the door when Schooner and Holly arrived.

"Holly!" Mia greeted her with a hug. She had not been sure who, if anyone, would be accompanying Schooner.

"Mia, you look adorable. Wow, you really are pregnant!" Holly had not seen Mia and today Schooner broke the news to the family. Holly put her hand on Mia's belly and smiled. "I hear I'm going to have a baby brother."

Mia nodded. "So, how did it go with your other baby brother today?" She bit her bottom lip waiting for either Holly or Schooner to respond.

Schooner made his way to the refrigerator and took out the orange juice and was chugging it straight from the carton.

"Want some vodka with that?" Mia asked.

He shook his head. "I don't think that would've even helped. I am so glad that is over."

"That good, huh?" Seth interjected.

Holly and Schooner just looked at one another. "Let's just say, I don't think we're all going to be one big, happy blended family anytime soon."

Mia went to Schooner and put her arms around his waist. "I am so sorry." She could see the sadness and disappointment in his eyes.

He hugged her to him, kissing the top of her head.

"The good news is, they are on their way back to LA and we're on our way out to the beach. Seth, are you joining us this weekend?" Schooner asked.

"Well, it's your first weekend out there…"

"Please," Mia begged. "I could really use your help in setting up the house."

"Well, then let me run home and pack a bag. I can be back in an hour."

Mia sat down in the living room with Schooner and Holly. She looked from one to the other.

Schooner began, "Zac is very angry with me. He doesn't understand why we're getting divorced. He feels like I've betrayed everyone. He said some pretty ugly things. All I could do was let him know that I love him, that this wasn't about him and that I want him in my life. In our life."

Mia took Schooner's hand in hers. "It's a lot to process."

"And he's a shit," Holly piped in.

Schooner gave her a pointed look.

"Don't give me that look, Dad. He is, and you know it. He's a cocky, arrogant shit that only cares about himself. This was all about him today, not you, not Mom. Him."

"It wasn't the homecoming he expected, Holly."

She rolled her eyes. "I know that, Dad. But there's this little thing known as empathy, and he clearly was out partying with his friends the day that was handed out."

"I can't argue with you there." Schooner looked sad and resigned.

Mia rubbed Schooner's arm, "Give him a few days, call him and try talking again. Maybe he'll join us out on the beach at some point this summer."

"Don't ruin your summer, Mia." Holly got up and stalked off to the bathroom.

Mia turned to Schooner with a surprised look, this was so unlike Holly.

"Today got very ugly. She's very protective of me."

"I'm sorry." She laid her head on his chest and he began to play with her hair. "The beach will be good. For all of us."

As they walked through their small beach town later, little red wagons in tow, Schooner spied tennis courts, "We're joining whatever club this is, I'm ready to be out on the courts again."

"I'm going to sit in a beach chair and just grow bigger before everyone's eyes," Mia added.

"Maybe I can get a babysitting job and spend the whole summer out here," was Holly's contribution.

"And I'm just going to freeload off you people for as much and as long as you'll let me," Seth chimed in as they walked the boardwalk toward their house.

They reached the end of the boardwalk and in front of them was sand beach and the Atlantic Ocean, side lit by the late afternoon sun. They all just stood there for a moment, breathing in the salty, sea air and taking in the tranquility of the moment. The breeze off the ocean was still cold and Schooner reached down and scooped up a surprised Mia into his arms, hugging her to him. He tossed Holly the house keys and she walked the short path through the scrub pines and unlocked the front door.

"You're carrying me over the threshold?" Mia smiled at Schooner.

His eyes were locked on hers, crinkled at the edges. "Mmm-hmm." He nodded.

"I love you. I love you. I love you. I love you," she said against his mouth, kissing him.

Carrying Mia to the couch in the great room, Schooner gently put her down on the soft cushions. "Now you sit there and relax and we'll put everything away and set things up."

Mia began to protest and Schooner silenced her with a *Don't-Mess-*

With-Me glare, leaving her grumbling from her perch on the couch, while the others unpacked and set up the kitchen.

After dinner, Schooner joined Mia on the couch, a single-malt scotch in hand. "Rocky start to the day, but a perfect ending. We get to begin that summer we never had."

Mia curled up and put her head in his lap. "Do you think he'll come around?"

Schooner shook his head. "No. Or at least not for a long time."

Mia could see the tension in his strong jaw. He took a long sip of his scotch.

"Well, we'll just keep trying."

Schooner smiled down at Mia, brushing her bangs from her eyes, his look portraying his deep appreciation of everything she was doing to make his life happy.

"Maybe he'll come spend some time at the beach with us. The beach is like an elixir, cures a lot of ills," Mia tried to sound hopeful.

Seth and Holly came in from the deck. "Definitely need sweatshirts out there now," Seth informed Mia and Schooner. "Come on out, the stars are amazing."

The four grabbed sweatshirts and headed out onto the lower deck, sitting 100 feet away from the water lapping onto the sand. A jagged, iridescent strip of moon glow lit a path along the gentle surf. Mia went and stood at the wooden railing on the deck's edge, looking up at constellations hovering high above. Coming up behind her, Schooner wrapping his arms around Mia and she leaned back into him.

"This is my fantasy come true," she informed him.

"Mine too." He kissed the top of her head.

And finally, almost exactly twenty-four years after the fantasy had been conceived, the moment they dreamed of sharing together, at long last became their reality, and it was richer than they had envisioned so long ago, for now they shared it with two people they deeply loved and the baby that would soon join them.

Chapter Twenty-Five

Mia woke to an empty bed and staggered out to the deck off their bedroom. No Schooner, but she was immediately distracted by the ocean, the light on the waves and the smell of the sea breeze. Sitting down in one of the white Adirondack chairs and closing her eyes, there was nothing else she could do but enjoy the song of the gulls and the soft breeze lightly tickling her skin.

She heard the sliding glass door and felt his kiss before even opening her eyes.

Sitting down in the Adirondack chair next to her, they both remained silent. When she finally opened her eyes, it was to the surprise of Schooner dressed in tennis whites, a racquet casually laying across his lap. Mia's smile was automatic.

"First time I've held one of these in twenty-four years," he said quietly, fingering the racquet's grip.

Mia held out her hand and Schooner took it. They lapsed into silence again for a long time.

"I want you to spend the summer out here with Holly and Seth," Schooner began, breaking the silence.

Mia was glad, as his voice pulled her back from a *what-if* darkness she had become reacquainted with in the silence, remembering a bright tennis career, one with the words *potential top ranked NCAA player* attached to it, that she felt fully responsible for snuffing out.

She nodded. "I'll miss you."

He squeezed her hand. "I'll be back every Thursday evening. I'll try to schedule things so that I don't have to leave here until early on Monday mornings."

She looked at him and nodded.

He smiled, "What did you do with my Mia? You are clearly an alien imposter."

She laughed.

"What? No fight over this?" Schooner's face registered mock shock.

She shook her head, no. "No fight. Just a little sad that you'll have to be in the city part of the time, but you need to be there, especially now. And I can do everything I need to do via phone and laptop. And frankly, pregnant in the summer heat in Manhattan or pregnant in a beautiful beach house? I'm no dummy!"

They both laughed.

Mia looked at Schooner and shook her head. "I'm assuming you've already talked to both Seth and Holly about this."

He just smiled at her and she shook her head.

"You are going to get your way with me, aren't you?" she laughed.

He nodded. "I'm just glad you are taking this so well. This could have gone either way."

Mia squeezed Schooner's hand. "You are absolutely right, it could have. But you know what?" she paused. "I love that you've thought through all the details and are doing everything you can to make sure I have an easy summer—especially with the opening coming up."

Schooner moved his racquet to the floor and pulled Mia by her hand to him. She curled up on his lap. "Kami, Yoli and I can run point on everything in the city, you and Seth can Skype with your team from right here on the deck. Jared's going to come spend some time, so that makes me feel good that he'll be here with you, too. Gaby and Paola are two blocks over. I'll try and get Kami and Yoli, when she's in town, to come out with me on weekends." He laughed, "Charles and I are already figuring out our carpool schedule."

Mia buried her face in Schooner's neck. "You make me so happy."

He kissed the top of her head. "It's smoochal, Baby Girl."

"So, tell me about this new racquet." She looked up at him.

"I saw those courts when we were coming in yesterday and I just thought, *it's time*."

Mia nodded. "Was today the first time since…"

"It was," Schooner confirmed. "The last time I held a racquet was my last match freshman year, which I won." He smiled at the memory.

Mia buried her face back in his neck, she couldn't look at him. Couldn't let him see the guilt in her eyes.

"I know what you're doing," he said. "Mia, you did not make me punch a wall."

"What I did made you punch a wall, Schooner."

He gently stroked her hair, sighing. "It's not that simple, Mia. It was a whole cascade of circumstances, you know that. Stop taking that on and please let it go."

"You were really great…"

He laughed. "Yes, I was. But that wasn't the way my life was supposed to go." He felt her tears on his neck and pulled her head away so that he could look at her face. "We're here together. Now. We're having a baby. We're on Fire Island and we're going to spend the whole summer with the people we love. *Our* family. And by the end of the summer, I'm going to be kicking some butt on those courts, you watch." He wiped her tears away with his thumb and kissed her roughly on the lips.

Chapter Twenty-Six

"He is just beautiful to watch." Seth stopped just short of drooling.

Holly looked at Mia. "He must've been amazing when you two were in school."

"He was the rising superstar," Mia confirmed. "In his freshman year, the coaching staff was already talking to him about being team captain. He's just a natural athlete."

They watched him bouncing the ball with his racquet, getting ready for a serve. Just a few weeks of playing and Schooner was already formidable again on the courts.

"They used to clock his serves at over 110 MPH." Mia looked at him, still in awe.

"Holly, Holly!" Paola came running up to them and Holly scooped up her new little friend.

Gaby and Charles were several yards behind.

"Damn, you're getting bigger by the week," Charles greeted Mia.

"I'd say something nasty to you, except it's true," Mia laughed, hugging him and Gaby.

They all stood watching Schooner for a few minutes. "I am never getting on a court with him," Charles mumbled.

"He moves so gracefully," Gaby commented. "He is so tall, but he almost floats out there."

"Where did you tell Schooner to meet us?" Charles asked Mia.

She pointed. "Just right across the street at The Albatross."

They started toward The Albatross, but Mia hung back for a minute watching Schooner cover the courts with his lithe grace. His agility was truly a sight to behold as he slammed a return at his opponent.

She wondered if she'd ever get over the rush she felt at just the sight of him. It was the same heart stopping flash today as it had been walking up the path to Brewster Hall when he turned around and smiled at her coming toward him. He had looked at her, head slightly cocked to the side, with a look on his face of both bewilderment and excitement. Her heart had skipped a beat at just a glimpse of his oxygen-stealing smile. He was so beautiful, but it wasn't just that, there was something in his eyes that said he had the spirit to run with her.

Mia caught up to them on the small outside deck at the front of The Albatross, or the *Tross*, as it was known on the island.

"We ordered some Cajun Calamari," Seth informed her. "And I got you water."

"Not Iced Tea?" Mia pouted.

"No BBC, you should not be having caffeine." Mia made a face at Seth.

"You two are very funny." Gaby laughed.

"I'm surrounded by men who want to control me," Mia complained. "Including this little devil." She tickled her stomach, causing the baby to move and her stomach to do the wave.

They all laughed.

"Do that again," Charles requested.

Mia got Paola's attention, "Paola, do you want to see the baby dance?"

Paola nodded vigorously, pigtails bouncing. Mia tickled her belly and the baby scurried to the other side. They all laughed and Paola came over and started to tickle Mia's belly.

As Schooner came up to the table, he just stood there watching with a huge smile on his face as Paola tickled Mia. Mia looked up at his handsome smiling face with a beaming smile of her own.

Bending down, he gave her a big sweaty kiss and put his racquet down.

"Kick butt out there?" Charles asked.

"Oh yeah, annihilated him," they high fived. "I just signed up for a tournament." Schooner was back in his element and the happiness beamed off him like a solar flare.

Mia turned to Holly and winked. Mia knew she was wondering who this man was.

The waiter delivered the drinks to the table and Schooner immediately downed his water. "What time is everyone getting in today?" He grabbed a menu from the center of the table.

"Jared's going to be on the 2:30 Ferry." Holly was all smiles and anticipation.

Seth pulled out his iPad. "Yoli and Kami are hoping to make the 4:10, if not, they said they'd definitely be on the 5:10."

"Perfect timing for cocktails," Charles concurred.

This was it, finally the big beach bash for Mia's 41st birthday. Lobsters and steamers and corn on the cob on the beach. She looked for Schooner's hand under the table and squeezed it.

He looked at her with an "Are you okay look?" and she just nodded and smiled.

She was more than okay. She was experiencing the brimming heart syndrome that Schooner knew well from falling in love with Mia.

Stuffed with buttery lobster as the sun was setting, Yoli sat down next to Mia on the deck.

"You know our boy sold me a bill of goods," she confided in Mia.

"Rut-roh…" Mia was not quite sure with what Yoli was going to hit her.

Yoli smiled, running a hand through her bright red hair that was now standing straight up from the humid beach air. "The guy gives me all of California to run and this is how you people are living."

Mia laughed. "I know people think California is La-La Land! They clearly have not spent a summer here."

"This is amazing. It is like no place I have ever been before. I'm really glad you are getting to take care of yourself and the baby and spend the summer out here, Mia."

Mia looked into Yoli's big brown eyes and reached for her hand and squeezed it.

"As crazy as he makes me sometimes, that man is the most amazing gem in the world. I have never met anyone with such a deep sense of responsibility for those he loves." And Yoli clearly loved her best friend.

They were both looking at Schooner across the deck talking to Jared and Charles.

"He's the best friend I've ever had, Mia. And it's really refreshing that you don't have an issue with that."

Mia knew she was referring to CJ's disdain for their relationship. Mia gave her hand another squeeze and Yoli reciprocated.

"And what's so wonderful is," she continued, "I finally see him as one whole person. The way he's always been with me is the way he is 100% of the time now. He's not so conflicted anymore."

Schooner looked at them across the deck holding hands and talking and his heart was soaring in seeing the harmony amongst the people he loved the most in his life.

"I'm in so much trouble," he said to Charles and Jared, indicating the two women.

They laughed.

Across the deck, Yoli and Mia laughed.

"You've got that right," Mia yelled at him. "He's freaking out right now."

Evil laughter came from the two women, who just looked at each other smiling.

"So, tell me about Zac," Mia asked Yoli.

Yoli leveled a glance at Mia.

"That bad, huh?"

Yoli shook her head and exhaled. "You're going to want to like him because it's like looking at a young Schooner. So, for you, I can imagine it might be even more intense—because you have memories of Schooner at that age. But make no mistake, Zac is not a young Schooner."

Mia cocked her head, taking it in, as Yoli continued, "Schooner is intense, but if he loves you, he loves you. That's the way he's made. If you cross him, watch out, because he can be deadly."

Mia's eyes were wide, not blinking, as she listened to Yoli.

"I've seen people cross him in business, Mia, and I would not want to be on the other end of that wrath. But with Schooner, it has to be provoked for him to go there. He goes into protect mode. It's reactive, not proactive."

Mia nodded. "Schooner is very protective of what or who he feels is his."

Yoli agreed. "But it comes from a place of love with Schooner and you know that, so there's a way to wrap your head around it," she paused, thinking. "Zac doesn't have that inherent goodness that Schooner does. He's arrogant, entitled, calculating, manipulative, rude, dismissive…"

She paused and Mia couldn't pass up the opportunity. "And those are just his good qualities."

They both laughed.

"There's just something missing behind those beautiful blue eyes," Yoli finished.

"A heart?" Mia asked, seriously.

Yoli nodded, "And there's a very wide mean streak."

"I want to meet him, because I want things to be whole in Schooner's life again."

Yoli just shook her head. "Not going to happen, Mia. I mean, yes, at some point you will meet him. He'll be back east in the fall to go back to Exeter, but what you and Schooner have with Holly, you will never have with Zac. So, promise me this, you will not beat yourself up over it, because that leopard is never going to change his spots."

It was almost dusk as Charles carried a sleeping Paola in his arms and he and Gaby bid the rest of the party a goodnight.

Sitting out on the deck, under the stars, everyone in shorts and sweatshirts, Mia asked Seth, "Are you going to take everyone out to Cherry Grove dancing tonight?"

"But BBC, it's your birthday."

Mia smiled at him. "That is exactly why I think you, Kami, Yoli, Holly and Jared should go catch a water taxi to The Grove and dance until some ungodly hour. Just make sure you return Holly and Jared safely."

"Are you sure?" Seth triple checked.

"Don't make me hurt you," Mia threatened.

When the five finally left for a night of partying, Fire Island style, Mia turned to Schooner and wrapped her arms around his waist (they weren't wrapping around quite as far, now that her stomach was putting more distance between the two of them). He kissed the top of her head and they made their way out onto the deck off their bedroom and she curled up in his lap on an Adirondack chair, his long legs stretched out with his feet perched up on the deck rail.

"This is the first time we've been alone all summer." He played with her curls that refused to stay straight in the sea air.

Mia smiled. "This—right here, right now—is my birthday present. Me. You. The beach. The stars. Alone. It does not get more perfect than this, Schooner."

He tightened his arms around her. "You are correct, Baby Girl."

They stayed like that for a long while, listening to the waves lick the shore. This was their calm before the storm and they both recognized that. The fall would bring the opening of L9/NYC and the winter would bring the baby. Both would churn their lives in ways they could only imagine. For now, it was just the two of them celebrating Mia's birthday, savoring their happiness.

"I have something for you," Schooner whispered.

Mia got up off his lap and he went into the house, emerging a few minutes later, a large manila envelope in hand.

They sat down again and he handed it to her. "Happy Birthday, Baby Girl. I love you more than anything in this world."

Mia kissed him and opened the envelope. She pulled out a half inch of papers bound together with a large silver clip. Holding them up, she found a stream of light from the house that was flooding the deck, so that she could read what they said. It was the deed to the beach house. Schooner had put the entire house in her name.

He was smiling broadly when Mia looked up at him. Speechless, she leaned forward to kiss him softly. There was so much she wanted to say to him, this man who was so serious about taking care of what was his. This was his protection for her and their unborn baby. He was leaving nothing to chance this time.

She brought his hand to her mouth and kissed it, her eyes never leaving his. "I love you," she mouthed.

"Smoochal," he mouthed back.

Mia stood and extended a hand to Schooner, he took it and hand-in-hand they walked in from the deck to their bedroom.

Schooner took Mia's face in both his hands and kissed her passionately.

"Now can I have the rest of my birthday present?" Mia asked, devil grin on her face.

"Yeah, let's fuck like wild animals."

She laughed and grabbed his hand, pulling him to the bed, "Yeah, let's!"

Twenty-four years after she found it, on her forty-first birthday, Mia finally attained the full realization of her secret dream.

Chapter Twenty-Seven

Windows open and a breeze blowing the white sheer curtains, Mia and Seth sat at the kitchen table in the beach house. On the table, Mia's laptop was open and they were Skyping with the gang in the city—Schooner, Yoli and Kami.

"I'm floored at the response on the guest list. Have you guys fed Charles the most updated version? I know he's going to want to rendezvous with some of these stars' personal security to make sure everyone is in sync. I think we should be giving his people twice per week updates at this point, and if anything, or anyone, big pops up in between, just make sure we let him or his organization know."

"I'll up my contact with his people to twice per week formal reviews." Kami wrote down the task.

"Kami, do we only have Isabelle running PR at this point?"

"Yes. Do you want to step it up?"

Mia nodded. "I want you to put both Lisa and Denise on this. Have we been working the Los Angeles press in addition to New York, health and wellness and fashion press?"

"No. We haven't gone near Los Angeles."

"Let's do it. Schooner, are you okay with that?"

"Why wouldn't I be? I think it's a great idea."

"From a business standpoint, I totally agree. I just don't want to rock any boats, if you know what I mean." Mia's look conveyed her fear of causing more problems for Schooner with CJ and Zac.

"Mia, this is business and you're right, utilizing the LA press for even more buzz and possibly to alert members and press who will be in New York that week is just a good business idea, so I say we run with it."

"Okay, we're going to have three people on PR from now through the event. I told you I was willing to commit all my resources." She smiled her devilish grin at him.

"That is why I like giving you the business." He was giving her a pure sex look via Skype.

"Stop it you two, or I'm going to get hard!" Seth complained.

Schooner laughed. "Busted."

"Do you guys know when you'll be out yet?" Mia asked.

Being away from Schooner was becoming more and more difficult. She didn't sleep as well when he wasn't there. She found herself rolling over to his side of the bed, and burying her face in his pillow trying just to get the scent of him. She wondered if it was just a hormonal aspect of the pregnancy that was making her feel so needy.

"We should be on the 8:10 on Friday night. I'm meeting with the building inspectors at 4:00, so we're definitely going to be sitting in traffic out to Bay Shore."

"Yuck. We'll be thinking about you." Seth smiled.

"We can do better than that," she offered. "I'll have a Johnnie Walker Blue sitting on the table for you at Maguire's."

Schooner smiled. "Thanks, Baby Girl."

"You two are gross." Yoli rolled her eyes. "Are we done yet? I have work to do."

"Someone's going to need to dance off her nasty at-ee-tude in Cherry Grove this weekend," Seth snarked.

"Please get her laid while you're at it," Schooner begged.

"On that note, one that would send a Human Resources Director into a seizure, we'll sign off. Till tomorrow kiddie-winkles." And Mia hit end call on Skype.

"One big happy dysfunctional family," she laughed at Seth.

"They really fit in very well with us," Seth commented.

"Scary, but true," Mia agreed. "Beach time!" she announced with a big smile.

Saturday morning a sweaty Schooner, fresh off the courts and a walk back to the beach house, stripped off his tennis whites and crawled under the cool, crisp sheets next to his fiancé. Spooning up against Mia, he caressed her full breasts, "I love these," he whispered in her ear.

"They hurt," she complained.

"They were always gorgeous, but I really love them now. They are so round and your nipples are even more sensitive." He pinched and twisted the nipple on her right breast and she moaned.

He pulled her right leg back over his and positioned his hard cock at the entrance of her dripping pussy. "This is still a good position for us." He impaled her from behind with one hard stroke.

Mia gasped, "Very good position."

He held onto her leg and slowly drove into her. She squeezed his cock tight. "Oh yeah, you feel so damn good. I was slamming the ball on the court and thinking I couldn't wait to get home and be slamming into you."

Mia turned her head to look at him and grabbed his face down to her for a kiss. "Harder," she hissed into his mouth, as he drove up into her forcefully. "Oh God, your cock feels so fucking great." And she squeezed him tight. "I miss you so much during the week… oh yeah, just like that…" she gasped. "I love the way you fuck me."

He pulled out and dragged her to the edge of the bed and put her feet up on his shoulders and drove down into her. She gasped again and squeezed him tight.

"Mia, open your eyes. Look at me."

She smiled up at him.

Smiling back down at her, he rubbed her feet on his face, his teeth grazing her high arch. "Squeeze my cock, Baby Girl… oh yeah, just like that… oh God, that is good."

Mia's smile was huge.

"You are milking it out of me."

She tightened as hard as she could with each of his deep thrusts. "Pussy hug," she said, with a devil grin.

Schooner laughed and Mia bared down on him.

His eyes shot open wide. "What you do to me, Baby Girl."

He grabbed her feet tight to his face and she could tell that he was coming. His eyes were closed and he looked so young and sweet, his cheek pressed into the arch of her foot.

"Yes," he moaned, but Mia was already lost somewhere. The sweet look on his face with his cock driving deep into her had already thrown her over the edge and she was crashing and spinning like she'd caught a wave wrong.

Schooner fell on the bed next to her and looking across the pillow at his beautiful blue eyes, she reached out to stroke his face. Their sweet reverie was to be almost immediately cut short by the ringing of a cell phone.

Schooner growled and reached behind him and grabbed his phone off the night stand. "CJ," he mouthed, a look of faux horror on his face.

"Hello" … "Fabulous." He reached out to play with Mia's hair. "Well, when does his semester start?" … "Isn't most of his stuff still in storage up in New Hampshire? We put it in there before Spain." … "Well, he'll miss his first few days of classes, but I'm ok with that." … "Yeah, am sure he is, too. I'll take him up after the opening." … "You're right, I think it's best you're not there." … "No, I'm not trying to be mean. Pulling off an opening event is stressful as it is and yes, you being there is a stress I don't want to deal with. "…"You're right, I'm sure Mia doesn't want you there." … "She doesn't need to say it." … "CJ, I hate to break this to you, but you are not high on her radar screen and I suggest you keep it that way." … "New York is my home, CJ." … "Honestly, never again." … "Is he there? Yeah, let me talk to him." … "Hey Bud, I've missed you." … "Yeah, I'd love to have you here for the opening and then I'll take you up to school. If you want to come out a little early, come hang out on the beach. Holly is here with us." … "Yes, with me and Mia." … "Zac, I understand it's going to take some adjusting, but this situation is not going to change. Let me be really frank with you, I will be with Mia for the rest of my life and both of us want you in our lives." … "Why? Because you are my son and she knows how much I love you." … "I only ask that you keep an open mind and that you treat her respectfully, because I will tell you this, I will not tolerate you disrespecting me or Mia. Are we clear on that?" … "Look, I'm really happy we're going to get to spend some time together." … "Okay, well email me your flight info, when you've got it." … "Zac, I love you." … "Talk to you soon."

Mia stroked Schooner's cheek and smiled at him. "See, it's all going to work out. It will."

He pulled her head down to his chest and kissed the top of her head.

Chapter Twenty-Eight

Mia, Seth and Holly stood at the center of L9's rotunda looking around in awe. Huge concave custom projection screens lined the rounded walls of the first floor and technicians were testing them with a mixture of iconic urban and bucolic landscape images. Another team was testing the lighting, soft ethereal jewel-tone spots flickered on and off.

Mia began to survey the perimeter where the caterer had begun to set up royal blue skirted tables and stations. She felt an arm sling over her shoulder and the soft, slightly accented voice of Claret Events owner and brilliant conceptualist, Elan Gerstler, whispering in her ear, "I want you to know that I left the Hamptons for this. Only for you, Meezie," he joked.

Smiling, Mia looked up into Elan's big handsome brown eyes, "I understand, they made me leave Fire Island. I haven't worn shoes in two months."

Elan looked down at Mia's hot pink flip-flop clad feet and gasped.

Mia backhanded him in the arm. "Stop that. It's not like I'm wearing Birkenstocks."

Elan flagged down a worker nearby. "Let's see what that table looks like moved over there." And to Mia, "So, do you like?"

She nodded, smiling. "I love it. Clean, minimalist, chic."

Elan nodded, "Never more than three colors." Elan's designs were always steeped in classic with a modern edge that was so subtle it transported the attendee effortlessly to wherever Elan had chosen to send them.

"Meezie, thank you for this. I know you were wholly behind us getting to do this event for L9. We have been trying to work with them for years in LA and Brent Bolthouse has it totally locked up. This is our first time, so thank you."

"I told Schooner there is only one person I would let touch this opening." She rubbed his back.

"So, how do you know Schooner Moore?" Elan wanted the inside scoop.

Mia laughed and pointed to her belly. "Baby Daddy."

Elan's mouth and big brown eyes opened wide and Mia squeezed his arm, laughing.

"Isn't he married to a tall, blonde *shiksa* out in LA?"

Mia nodded, still smiling. "For the moment."

"You little tart, you." Elan stood back and looked at Mia. "He's very hot. How did you meet him?"

"He was my first boyfriend," Mia confided. "The evil *shiksa* broke us up. And it took a couple of decades, but karma is a bitch."

"Yeah, in the form of a short Jewish girl," they laughed. "I love this. I am definitely doing your wedding." Elan was looking intensely into Mia's eyes, clearly happy for Mia.

"Baby, you're doing the Bris, which might actually come before the wedding."

"My pleasure." he hugged Mia tightly (or as tightly as one could with her protruding stomach). "Now let me show you the rest of what we are doing here."

Elan walked Mia through the rest of the space, showing her the details that made the ethereal space magical. People were setting up banks of multiple sized white pillar candles along the railing edge of each of the mezzanines and on the marble staircase. Wide, white raw silk ribbon with a thick silk braided cord of royal blue wrapped the banister.

Mia spied Schooner and Charles talking over near the offices. "Have you met Schooner yet?" she asked Elan.

"Never formally. Just members of his staff."

"Come, let's change that. He's about to head to the airport to pick up his son."

Schooner was listening intently to something Charles was telling him as Elan and Mia approached. He was looking down and nodding his head. Mia couldn't help but feel pride as they approached this tan, impossibly beautiful man.

Schooner looked up at Mia, as if he could sense her approach, his eyes crinkling at the corners with his smile. "Hey, Baby Girl." It was evident to all, wherever they were, it was only the two of them in the room.

"Schooner, I want to introduce you to the brilliance behind all of this beauty," her arm swept the room. "This is Elan Gerstler, the President and Owner of Claret Designs."

Schooner put out his hand to Elan. "I've been wanting to meet you for a long time. This is beyond my expectations," he motioned to the rotunda.

"I'm thrilled to have been chosen for this project. Thank you very much."

"Mia and Charles both rave about you and I can understand why. I'm glad we have this opportunity to work together. Am sure it won't be the last time." Schooner flashed his All-American boy smile at Elan, who was clearly a new fan.

Schooner looked at his watch, "I'd better go get the car." His hand stroked Mia's hair and he bent down to kiss her. "I'll see you out at the beach tonight, Baby Girl."

Mia clasped his hand and he gave hers a tight squeeze and a long look in her eyes saying, *it's going to be okay*.

Chapter Twenty-Nine

Yoli and Seth were pounding down Bombay Sapphire and tonics while waiting with Mia at the beach house for Schooner and Holly to arrive with Zac.

"I wish you could drink, BBC." Seth gave Mia a sad face.

Mia was clearly nervous, pacing around the lower deck.

"Me too," she muttered, looking at the dusky sky over the ocean and tapping the deck railing with her foot.

"Me three, you're going to need it." Yoli was very tense.

"I'm glad you two are here. Hopefully that will alleviate some of the family dynamic thing."

Yoli shook her head. "Don't count on it. He's not going to give a shit who's here. Mia, I know this is going to be hard, but try to keep telling yourself that you're talking to CJ. You're going to think you're talking to a young Schooner, but you're really talking to CJ. Try not to forget that, please," Yoli was adamant.

"He really looks that much like him?" Seth asked Yoli.

"You know that waterfall picture in Mia's office? Haircut is different and Zac is not as tall as Schooner. I'd say he's maybe six feet tops and he's a slighter build than Schooner. But his face, it's that picture," she finished her drink, "with ice blue eyes."

She made an exaggerated shivering motion and Mia and Seth just looked at each other.

"Why am I so nervous about meeting a freaking teenager?" Mia looked at the two of them, palms in the air, shoulders shrugging.

"Because he's CJ's devil spawn." Yoli was on her next drink.

"You are not making me feel better." Mia laughed.

They heard the front door to the beach house and voices. Mia looked at Yoli and Seth, eyes wide, lips in a tight line and muttered, "Showtime" as they walked into the house.

He was exactly as Yoli had described and although she had been warned, Mia's face broke into a huge smile upon seeing Zac standing there.

In front of her was the boy on the path to Brewster Hall talking with her mom, the same one who knocked over a pitcher of water to save her from the evil sniffer, the guy who pulled her close to him on a mountaintop to warm her up after a snowball fight, and never left her side after her attack.

"Hi Zac," she greeted him with a bright smile and received an unreturned hug.

Stepping back, she looked at Schooner. "Wow, I know you said he looked like you, but wow. Flashback." Mia smiled brightly at Schooner, who bent down and gave her a quick kiss. Looking at Holly, it was clear she was not breathing, and Mia gave her a smile and wide eyes saying, *Rut roh!*

"Well, let's get you settled, get your stuff put away," and she turned to Schooner and Holly. "We've got reservations at Maguire's."

"Yes," Holly fist pumped. "Lobster." Getting a laugh out of everyone but Zac, who still had not uttered his first word to Mia, Yoli or Seth.

Mia turned to Holly. "Would you show Zac where his room is?"

"Follow me, Cretin."

When they were upstairs and out of earshot, Mia walked over to Schooner and put her arms around his waist, he hugged her and kissed the top of her head. She looked up at him, trying to keep the tears out of her eyes. His eyes were tense and sad.

"It'll get better," she whispered, trying her hardest to be positive for him, knowing he was in the middle of two people he loved.

He wrapped his arms around her tighter and gave her a hug, burying his face in her sea-air unruly curls. As soon as he heard Zac and Holly coming down the stairs, he let her go, and although she knew he didn't want to exacerbate what was already a tense situation, hurt and disappointment slammed through her.

Yoli caught her eye and Mia could sense Yoli's anger about ready to flare at Schooner. Knowing the Bombay and Tonics might make her already loose lips even looser, Mia asked, "Yoli, would you help me grab our stuff from earlier off the deck?"

The two women walked outside and away from the view of the sliding glass door.

"Holy shit!" Mia turned to Yoli, her mouth hanging open.

"Rude, entitled little piece of shit," she began, "and I'm going to rip his father a new one. What the fuck was that about?"

Mia grabbed her hand and squeezed it. "Trust me, I will take care of him… later. Sit next to me at dinner and we can kick each other under the table," Mia laughed at her own childish behavior.

"I need to be in kicking distance of Schooner."

Mia laughed. "Okay, that works for me, too."

They re-entered the house with empty glasses and half eaten bowls of munchies from earlier.

"Everyone ready to go?" Schooner asked, clearly forcing a happy mood.

Seth shot Mia a look silently begging her not to leave him alone with the Moores again. She rubbed his back and walked out of the house with him.

As they walked toward town, Mia said, "So Zac, what does your voice sound like? I haven't heard you speak yet."

Lines were being drawn and Mia was calling him out on his shit. Nice had not worked in the house.

He just looked at her, giving her an *are you kidding me look.*

Mia laughed. "Gonna be a fun week, huh?"

He shrugged.

"Stop being such an ass." Holly smacked him in the arm.

"Ouch, Bitch," he snarled at his sister.

"Zac!" Schooner finally came alive.

About fucking time, Mia thought to herself.

"I owe you a scotch," Maguire's manager Aiden McManus greeted Schooner as they walked into the packed, loud restaurant.

He leaned down and greeted Mia with a warm hug and a kiss, before turning back to Schooner. "You ripped it last weekend on the courts! What is it going to take to be your doubles partner next summer?"

"Free lobsters nightly!" Holly piped in.

"Totally doable." He smiled at her, clearly happy to see the beautiful young woman. "This has got to be your son." He turned to Zac.

Zac graced him with an All-American Boy smile (not as beautiful as Schooner's, Mia noted). "Yeah, hi, I'm Zac. Wow, great bar scene you've got here," reaching out to shake his hand, charm turned up on high.

You little shit, Mia thought.

"Come in on Thursday, karaoke night, you'll get to see your sister at her finest." Aiden laughed.

Mia looked at a blushing Holly. Without Jared there, Aiden was definitely making his interest known.

He showed them out to their table on the deck overlooking the bay. Mia and Yoli flanked Schooner on each side. The women smiled at one another as they sat.

Pots of steamers arrived at the table as an appetizer and everyone got busy dipping the sweet clams into broth to remove any excess sand and then into small ramekins of drawn butter.

"I used to clam on these beaches as a kid," Mia remarked. "We'd spend hours every day filling plastic buckets with clams."

"I can't wait to do that with the baby," Holly beamed at Mia.

"We are going to have such fun summers out here. I can't wait to teach him to body surf." Mia was smiling ear-to-ear. She reached for Schooner's hand under the table and gave it a squeeze. "So Zac, what was living in Zaragoza like?"

Zac shrugged, not looking up from cleaning his clam. "Like living anyplace else."

Yoli rolled her eyes at Mia. "C'mon Zac, you can do better than that," Yoli chided, sitting back and nursing her fresh gin and tonic.

"What do you want me to say about it?" He leveled her a cold glare.

"Did you get laid?" She didn't break her stare right back at him. Mia could feel Schooner tensing next to her.

Zac smiled at Yoli, a smile that did not come close to reaching his eyes. "As a matter of fact, I did. A lot."

"Anyone meaningful?" Mia asked.

His *are you kidding me* look returned as he didn't bother to answer Mia.

Ignoring him, she went on, "Actually Zaragoza is a place I would love to photograph." She looked at Yoli and Seth and said, "It was founded by Augustus Caesar and originally named Caesaraugusta. It had a huge thriving Jewish merchant and trade community from about 1000 AD into the 1400's."

"How do you know this?" Seth asked.

Mia laughed. "Okay, here's a random Mia fact that even you didn't know." She was smiling at him. "When I was a little girl, my mom used to take me all the time to The Met," she looked at Holly and Yoli and clarified, "The Metropolitan Museum of Art." Continuing, "We would enter through the Greek and Roman antiquities and I was obsessed with this marble bust of Augustus. I would just stand in front of it and look at him. And this started when I was really little. I would literally stand there, staring at him until my mother dragged me out."

Seth laughed. "BBC? Marble stalking BBC. That's a new one."

They all laughed, except for Zac who regarded the table with practiced disinterest throughout the rest of dinner.

Walking home, Mia reached for Schooner's hand and slowed her pace to ensure some distance from the rest of the group.

"You were right," she began, moving her arm around his waist.

His arm did not go over her shoulder, tucking her in to him in the way it always had since the first time he pulled her close walking along The Quad, after the incident with Beast in the Dining Hall.

"This is not going to be easy and you really need to nip this in the bud," she was adamant.

Mia looked up at Schooner and he was looking straight ahead. "Put your fucking arm around me, Schooner." There was anger and hurt in Mia's voice. She stopped walking. "I'm going to give you some time to be alone with your son and daughter tonight. You may not be able to fix the situation with him quickly, but I suggest you fix the situation with us immediately."

His face gave up nothing. He nodded and draped his arm over her shoulder, pulling her into him as they walked in silence the rest of the way home.

Mia was reclining on pillows propped up against the headboard on the bed, knees bent, another pillow on top of her swollen belly and her laptop perched on her belly/desk. She was still Skyping with Kami when Schooner walked into the bedroom. She gave him a big smile and went back to her conversation. He sat down in a chair facing the bed, kicked off his Sperry Made in Maine boat shoes and put his feet up on the bed.

"Well, what did Elan say about that?" Mia asked Kami, who was seriously going to need an amazing vacation after the event.

"He was not happy at all." Mia could tell by Kami's face that Elan was seriously displeased with one of his vendors.

"Don't sweat it," Mia advised. "If Elan was unhappy, it will be taken care of immediately. Were the membership brochures delivered to L9 today?"

"Yes, and they look good. I'll scan one and email it to you."

Mia nodded. "Yeah, I want to see one and I want to get it into Yoli's hands, so she can make sure the staff is properly trained." She turned to Schooner, "Membership desk at the event is going to be staffed with people from LA, right?"

He nodded and she turned her attention back to Kami. "It's all LA people staffing membership, so they'll be fine."

"Yeah, event night is not the night to make sure the NY team is properly trained on membership."

Mia made a face of fright. "Yeah, I agree. Okay, well get some sleep, you've been putting in sick hours. I think we should all come out here for a week after the opening and be beach bums. Oh wait, Seth and I have been beach bums all summer," they laughed and said goodnight.

Mia closed her laptop and put it on the night table. She smiled at Schooner, "It's all falling into place."

He just nodded.

She extended a hand for him to come on the bed with her.

He didn't move and she could feel panic beginning to rise and her throat close.

"Talk to me, Schooner."

"I'm so stressed over this."

"I know." Mia nodded and moved to the end of the bed so that she could sit facing Schooner. She reached for his hand and took it between hers. "But the answer is not pulling away from me."

He didn't respond.

"You know that, don't you?" her voice was tight with tension.

He removed his hand from hers, got up from the chair abruptly and walked over to the sliding glass doors, looking out into the black night.

Mia's panic was descending on her like a thick fog. *Oh my God, she said to me on the phone that he always goes back to her. She said that they were a family. He's going back to his family. He's going to leave me with a baby and a beach house. Oh God, the beach house was to assuage his guilt. He's going back to her. They are going to be a family again. He can't handle disappointing Zac.*

Mia could feel her dinner starting to come up and got off the bed as quickly as she could, running with her hand over her mouth. Making it as far as the bathroom, but not as far as the toilet before the heaving started, splashing around her feet all over the bathroom's beautiful terrazzo floor. She sunk to her knees, crying as the retching continued.

Schooner came flying into the bathroom, "Are you okay?"

She nodded, but really wanted to say, *What the fuck do you care?* But instead said, "Can you please close the door. I'll clean this up."

He looked down at her, clearly confused. "I'll help you clean up."

"Schooner, please leave and close the door."

Tenuously backing out of the bathroom, he closed the door. Mia reached up and locked it, the lock creating a deafeningly loud click. She then sat back down on the cold, terrazzo floor, put her head in her hands and cried.

CJ's words screamed in her head, "He's my husband, Mia and just like he's done to you before, he's going to come back to me. You are just a little mid-life fling. We've built a family together."

Zac would emotionally blackmail his father to ensure they remained a family.

Mia reached up on the wall behind her and pulled a towel from the towel rack on the wall and threw it down on the floor and started to clean. She unsuccessfully tried to stifle her sobs as she thought about the fact that she had not heard the words, "Baby Girl" since she was standing in L9, when he had no problem calling her that in front of business people. Yes, she told herself, I understand that we may need to dial it down a notch in front of Zac, but to act like there was no relationship at all, for Schooner not to show him how happy he was with her, Mia just did not understand that.

She wet a second towel and on her hands and knees washed the floor with hot water and hand soap. When she was done, she sat back and leaned against the wall and put her head in her arms. She was angry and disappointed in Schooner. Would this be another situation like after Interim, where he just couldn't do what he said he was going to do? That thought, hitting a raw nerve even after twenty-four years, set off a fresh round of body racking sobs.

He knocked softly on the door. "Come on, Mia. Unlock the door."

She didn't answer him. Instead she pulled a bunch of towels out of the linen closet, laid them down on the floor and took a stack of towels and linens for a makeshift pillow. Curling up on the towels, she cried herself to sleep.

It was only an hour later when she heard a scraping sound and the surprise of the light being flicked on woke her up. Schooner stood there with the door lock and a Phillips head screwdriver in hand. Squinting up at him, she covered her eyes to shield them from the light.

He came and sat down next to her. "What are you doing?" He was clearly annoyed.

"I was sleeping." She pulled a big beach towel tight around her shoulders.

"Why are you in here?"

She didn't answer him.

"Don't do this to me, Mia." Schooner was tired, stressed and his temper was quickly unraveling.

"I'm not doing anything to you, Schooner."

"You're acting like a brat."

Mia finally looked up at him. "I'm sorry that is how you see it."

"You're not sorry about anything." He sat back against the pale blue wall, sighing and shaking his head. "Please come to bed."

She noted that he still had not touched her.

Pushing herself into a sitting position, she asked, "Are you leaving me and Nathaniel?" A sob escaped.

Schooner looked like he had been hit in the solar plexus. "You think I'm leaving you?"

Mia nodded. "It's what CJ told me you would do. It's what Zac wants."

"And you think that is what I want?" He was clearly annoyed.

Mia nodded again. "It's why you gave me the house, right?"

Staring at Mia, his tone was distressed when he finally spoke, "Do you know how much that hurts?" He raked his hand through his hair and shook his head.

She nodded. "I do," her expression defiant.

"Where is this coming from, Mia?"

She picked at a thread on one of the beach towels, when she looked up at him, her cheeks were tear stained. "You're separating from me, Schooner." She looked back down and put her face in her hands, sobbing.

Schooner stood and walked out of the bathroom. Mia laid back down, curling as fetal as she possibly could with her pregnant stomach and continued to cry. *How could he be so cold?* she wondered and the sobs grew deeper.

Hearing his returning footsteps, she opened her eyes.

With a deep sigh, he sat down next to her. "I'm not even going to begin to attempt to understand what is going on here. Lift your head."

Sliding a pillow underneath her face, he sat down and placed his pillow next to hers on the bathroom floor. Lying down, he covered them both with a blanket.

When he didn't reach for her to pull her on to his chest, that made her heart break even more. "Please don't be so cold," she whispered and moved over to put her head on his chest and her arm around him.

He didn't move for a moment and then wrapped his arms around her and kissed the top of her head.

"Nathaniel, huh?" he finally said.

"Nathaniel James."

"Nathaniel James," he tried out the name. "Nathaniel James Moore. I actually really like that. A lot."

She looked up at him. "You do?"

He smiled. "Mmm-hmm. I do."

"It's just what I've been thinking of him as. We don't have to name him that." She got up on an elbow to look at him.

"Do you really think I would ever leave you and Nathaniel? I have waited half my life for this, Mia." His eyes looked wounded. "And this house? This is not a consolation prize. This is to always ensure stability for the two of you. God forbid something happened to me, Mia, before the divorce was finalized. I did this to protect the two of you."

Mia could feel his sincerity and her heart ached.

"Schooner, I know we are all walking on eggshells around Zac, but you can't treat me like I don't matter to you because you don't want to rock the boat with him."

He was silent for a moment, just staring at the bathroom ceiling. "I'm sorry. You're right. He needs to deal with reality the way it is, not us changing reality to accommodate him."

Mia was silent for a moment, running her hand over Schooner's bare chest, "I'm really sorry that I doubted your love and hurt you." Her face and eyes couldn't hide her overwhelming sadness.

Moving Mia off his chest, he placed her head back on her pillow and looked down at her, staring into her eyes, a sad small smile appearing on his face. "That was a very serious BBC moment there."

Gently, he pushed up her oversized tee-shirt, exposing her tan and shiny pregnant belly and lowered his lips to the rounded mound, planting a soft kiss. "Mommy got a little crazy tonight, Nathaniel, and Daddy definitely didn't help the situation, but do you think you can help me convince Mommy that sleeping in a bed would be a lot more comfortable than the bathroom floor." He put his ear to her belly and smiled. "Nathaniel's vote is for the bed."

He stood and then bent down to help Mia up off the floor. They grabbed the pillows and the blanket and went out to the bedroom and crawled into bed. This time Schooner reached for Mia, pulling her to his chest. "Do you remember me telling you that I never stopped loving you and that I never would?"

She nodded. "Yes."

"I know I was a jerk tonight and not handling things well, but you have got to believe that I will never, ever stop loving you, Baby Girl, not for a second. Don't ever doubt it, ever. Okay?"

"Okay." She looked up into his eyes and nodded.

He brought his lips to hers. "I love our son's name. It's perfect," and grazed her lips softly before they both closed their eyes and fell into an exhausted sleep.

Chapter Thirty

Mia, Seth and Yoli were spread out in the kitchen and great room, all on their laptops, Skyping, emailing and working on multiple details of the opening. Holly had gone to the ferry terminal to wait for Jared's arrival, Schooner was on the courts and Zac was laying out on the beach attracting the attention of a throng of teenage girls interested in the new handsome blonde boy from California.

"Oh yes! Just heard back from MJP, she and CB will be there," Seth announced.

"I knew she wouldn't let us down." Mia looked up from her laptop.

"MJP?" Yoli asked, draining her third cup of coffee.

"Mallory Jessie Prince. She and Chris Brody live right in the West Village, so we know them from a lot of events," Seth explained. "This is the most killer A list I have ever seen in my life. This event is going to rock Fashion Week and L9 is going to be the hottest ticket in all of Manhattan."

"Have we heard from Heidi Berg? She's been a member of our Brentwood facility for years and one of Schooner's favorite clients."

Seth checked the list. "Yes, Heidi plus one."

Yoli did a silent yes, with her fist pump.

A sweaty Schooner came through the front door, dripping from a workout on the courts. "Good to see you lazy people up and working."

Mia shot him the finger without looking up at him. "Oh, you'll pay for that, woman." He pulled off his L9 cap and bent down to rub his sweaty forehead all over her face.

She screeched, "Eww, you're gross!" pushing him away as he tried to pull her face under his sweaty arm pit.

"Actually, you're both gross." No one had noticed Zac come in from the deck. His face was screwed up with disdain.

Mia and Schooner were both laughing and said, "Yes we are!" in unison.

Mia looked up at Schooner smiling and he planted a loud wet kiss on her lips. She locked in on his eyes, silently telling him, "I love you."

"Zac, there are bagels and English muffins in the bread box, fruit, cheese and eggs in the fridge. Help yourself," Mia informed him, without taking her eyes off Schooner's face.

"Your girlfriend Heidi's coming," Yoli updated Schooner.

"I knew my girl wouldn't let me down." He was beaming, as he grabbed a cold bottle of Fuji water from the fridge.

"Heidi's your girl, huh?" Mia looked at Schooner with a questioning look and he nodded his head vigorously. "Seth, show Schooner the updated list."

Schooner walked over to where Seth sat on the pale blue and white striped couch and peered over his shoulder at the laptop screen.

"This is mind boggling. This list looks like the Red Carpet at the Oscars."

Even Zac's curiosity was piqued and he began to peer over Seth's shoulder. "This is the guest list?" he asked.

"This is actually the confirmed attendee list," Seth explained.

"Holy crap!" Even Zac was impressed.

"We take care of our clients." Mia was standing in front of the open SubZero refrigerator, staring at its contents, indecision marking her face.

"Glad I gave you the business." Schooner came up behind her, standing close.

She turned her head and smiled, "I'm glad you gave me the business, too." His proximity was making her horny.

He reached over her shoulder to grab a nectarine off the refrigerator shelf and whispered in her ear, "Come shower with me."

She leaned back against him. "I'll meet you in five." And he gave her neck a quick bite, then headed upstairs tossing his nectarine like he was getting ready for a serve.

"So, all the Fire Island girls wanted to know who the new guy on the beach was, huh?" Mia smiled at Zac. It was still hard for her not to look at him and just see Schooner.

"Apparently." He smiled and then caught himself, the cold veil sweeping over his eyes like a curtain.

"Did you bring clothes for the opening or are you going to need to shop when we get back to the city?" Mia asked.

"I'm from LA, this is no big deal to us."

Mia laughed. "Clearly you have never attended an event in New York." She smiled brightly at him, but anyone who knew Mia would have known there was nothing friendly in that smile. It was a rarity for Mia, but that was not a real smile.

And on that put-down note, Mia turned from Zac and headed upstairs to join his father in the shower.

Steam was coming out of the bathroom when Mia got up to the bedroom. She wanted so much to like Zac. He was Schooner's son and every time she looked at him, it was like looking at the beautiful boy who was the love of her life, but it was clear that forging a relationship with him was not going to be an easy path.

Schooner was standing under the streaming water of the rain head, his head tilted back, eyes closed. Mia just stood there staring at his long, muscular frame, his gorgeous chest that had always been the perfect home to her head, flat stomach, muscular thighs and his magnificent, thick cock. He was a sight to admire and she just stood there thinking about what she wanted to do to him.

Quietly, she slipped out of her sundress and into the shower through the open end of the glass enclosure. Her hands were on Schooner's balls before he opened his eyes, a rumbling growling sound coming from deep in his throat.

"Oh yeah." He looked down at her, smiling. "You are the cutest little pregnant thing."

"You think?" She smiled up at him and he just nodded his head.

"Oh, that feels so good." She was stroking the length of him with both hands, one after the other, getting him rock hard. "Now look what you've done."

"Handiwork." She smiled up at him and then dipped her head down to take the crown of his cock into her mouth while letting the warm water stream through her lips. She rolled her tongue around the rim, still holding him tight in her hands, squeezing and stroking. She straightened up, "Too hard for me to bend anymore," she pouted. "I think you should fuck me."

"I think that is an excellent idea." Pulling her hair to tilt her face up to him, his lips crushed down on hers in a deep rough kiss, as he backed her up to the wall, never breaking their kiss. "C'mere," he said, leading her to the corner of the shower and turning her around to face the wall. "This will give you *belly room*," he whispered in her ear, taking her hands and raising them above her head and placing one on each wall, palms flat on the tiles, his hands covering hers.

She moaned as his teeth grazed her shoulder.

"You like when I bite you," his voice was rough.

"I love when you bite me, especially my neck." She tilted her head to the right to give him access as he slowly bit his way from her shoulder to her neck, softly grazing his teeth and sucking.

"Spread your legs," he demanded and she did, sticking her ass out toward him so that he'd have total access. He ran his finger from her clit to her ass and back again sinking his thumb into her ass and his long forefinger and middle finger into her pussy.

Mia gasped and moaned.

"Feels damn good, doesn't it?" He worked his fingers in and out of each hole, bringing Mia to a frenzied point.

Muffling her sounds into the wall, she didn't want her guests downstairs to hear her on the edge of ecstasy from Schooner's fingers working both her pussy and her ass.

He reached over to the shelf and grabbed a bottle of mango moisturizing lotion and flipped open the top. "Just like butter," he read from the label and made a "Heh" sound.

Schooner pulled Mia's face around to him and kissed her forcefully. She felt his breath on her ear and his teeth pulling at her earlobe.

"We have a house full of people downstairs and I think this morning I want to fuck your ass. Do you want your ass fucked, Baby Girl?"

Nodding vigorously, she was way past the point of speaking, she needed him inside of her—anywhere.

"Say it, Mia. Tell me what you want. What you need."

She moaned.

"Come on, Baby Girl, tell me what you want me to do to you. Tell me," he hissed in her ear.

"I want you to fuck my ass," she whispered, harshly.

"I didn't hear you," he said into her neck, as he inserted two fingers covered with the buttery lotion into her tight, tight ass.

"I need you to fuck my ass," she gasped, as he worked his fingers in and out getting her ready to take him.

"Well that's a very good thing because I need to fuck your ass." He finished rubbing a thick layer of the mango cream on his rigid cock. "And that's what I'm going to do right now." He held her tight by her hipbones and pressed the head of his cock against her ass.

She moaned at the pressure.

"Feels good, huh? Well, it's about to feel a whole lot better," and he thrust deep into her ass.

Mia let out a loud moan.

"Fuck yeah, that feels good. You. Are. So. Damn. Tight." He thrust in and out of her unyielding ass.

Mia's head was back and she was whimpering sounds of pleasure. "Oh God, you feel so good," she panted. "I want it harder." And he complied.

"Play with your clit for me, Mia."

"No, this feels too good."

Schooner grabbed her by her hair, pulling her face back to him in the steam filled shower and kissed her roughly. "I said, play with yourself." And he gave her hair a tug.

She removed one hand from the wall and reached down between her legs to do what he said. After a moment she said, "It's too distracting. I just want to feel you," and put her hand back up on the wall to steady herself. She squeezed Schooner's cock tight with her ass muscles, knowing that would distract him and get his focus back 100% on his cock. Which is exactly where she wanted to focus.

"Oh God, what are you doing to me?" he moaned into her mouth as she continued squeezing and relaxing her muscles.

Wrapping both arms around her tightly, he laid his face in the crook of her neck as he thrust forcefully into her. The sounds coming out of him made her entire body quake with release.

"Oh, Baby Girl," she heard him whimper as his body shook, then finally stilled. They stood there both shaking, Mia with her hands bracing her against the wall and Schooner with both arms wrapped tightly around her, still inside of her, both being hit with muscle spasming aftershocks.

"Oh God," she whispered and he tightened his arms around her.

As he slowly pulled out of her, she gasped loudly and whimpered. Schooner turned her toward him pulling her to his chest as he led them back underneath the large rain head shower disc. They stood under the hot stream of water wrapped around each other for a long while until their bodies calmed from the rush.

A little while later, they descended the stairs hand-in-hand, both barefoot with wet hair, trying not to smile. Schooner gave Mia's hand a squeeze and she looked up at him, feeling like a shy sixteen-year-old with a secret crush. She hoped her tan hid the fact that she was blushing.

Chapter Thirty-One

They all stood in the center of the rotunda, L9's New York staff, L.A. staff working the opening and transition, Mia's entire team, Holly, Jared, Zac, and Yoli and her girlfriend, Debbie, who had flown in for the opening.

"As you all know, we've reserved several floors at The James Hotel in SoHo for tonight and also for tomorrow night after the opening. Tonight, we are taking over their rooftop pool and their roof bar, *Jimmy*, for a private party at 6:30," Schooner began.

A cheer went up from the staff, a crew that looked like a combination of models, movie stars and ultra-hip artists.

He continued, "I know this has been a long haul and tonight we just get to blow off a little steam—not too much though, because I need you all at 150% tomorrow. Tonight is our calm before the storm. When you check into the hotel, they'll give each of you your room assignments and a package with your itinerary and schedule. We're all meeting as a team for breakfast tomorrow morning and that meeting room will be noted in your itinerary. Also, in your packets will be your schedules and assignments for tomorrow and tomorrow night." He paused, "Tomorrow is a huge day—breakfast is at 9:30 and we are going to be balls to the wall for the next 18 hours. Tomorrow we take New York, folks. After tomorrow night, New York will not be the same. The biggest buzz in town will be L9/NYC. We've got an attendee list that rivals the Oscars and Mia and her team have the press in a frenzy over us."

Cheers and whistles went up from the team, who were getting pumped up.

"No man is an island, and what's been accomplished and what we are about to do, is because we have the best team on both coasts. The next twenty-four hours are going to be crazy, so let me take this opportunity now to say thank you to everyone. Trust me, everything you do does not go unnoticed nor unappreciated. What everyone has done this summer to get us ready for tomorrow night is nothing short of a miracle, and I know I'm also speaking for Mia when I tell you that we both sincerely thank each and every one of you." Schooner gestured to the rotunda, "This is all of ours." He shot them his best All-American boy smile. "I'll see you on the rooftop at 6:30. Now get out of here!"

The staff responded with clapping and whistles.

Seth tapped on his iPad. "I've got everyone's formalwear being delivered to the hotel and I'll take care of making sure they get to the correct rooms. You, Holly, Kami, Yoli and Debbie have hair, makeup and nails starting at 11:00 tomorrow morning at Enzo B's salon, which is only two blocks from the hotel."

"Is Enzo doing my hair?" Mia asked.

Seth rolled his eyes. "Yes, BBC. Enzo is doing your hair."

"Don't take that tone with me, Princess. Enzo has curls and he understands curls, not everyone does. After all, CurlBlaster is his straightener. Are you coming with us?"

"Can I?" He brightened up.

"Of course. It's always more fun if you're there. You should do highlights or that ombre thing with your hair."

"I think I will. I'm so excited."

Mia pulled Seth aside and whispered, "What about Zac and clothes for tomorrow night?"

"Oh, that one," he rolled his eyes. "Crisis averted with Devil Spawn. I've got him in an Armani Collezioni tux jacket, white Armani shirt, skinny silk tie the color of his cold blue eyes, he's going to wear his own pair of faded jeans and I got him those Armani jean sneakers, they're kind of like a blue jean suede."

"Oh my God, the kid is going to walk out of here with a modeling contract. The little shit's going to look gorgeous."

Schooner came up behind them. "You ready, Baby Girl?"

She nodded.

He took a moment to look around and take stock. "I can't believe this is the same space we walked into in February. Freaking amazing."

"It's really stunning," she agreed.

Even with Elan's staff and vendors still laboring throughout the club, and electricians and carpenters furiously working to ensure all the details were executed precisely to Elan's plans, the space had already taken on a breathtaking and unique aura.

Schooner draped his arm over Mia's shoulder and pulled her into him, kissing the top of her head. She peeked up at him and reveled in seeing his look of satisfaction and pride as he gazed around his latest concept club. His expression elicited an enormous smile of her own.

"What are you smiling at?" he asked.

"You look happy."

He hugged her tighter into him. "I am very, very happy, Baby Girl." Looking down at her, he added, "Truly happy." There was definite conviction in his words as he tilted her chin up to softly kiss her smiling lips.

Mia took one last look around, surveying the rotunda and side rooms. "You did it, Schooner."

He shook his head, "No, Baby Girl, we did it. Me and my team, you and your team. Our teams." His brows knit for a second and he corrected himself, "Our team."

Mia nodded, smiling to herself. He was right. What had begun in February as two separate people with two separate lives running two separate companies that were separated by the entire continental United States were now inseparable on every level, both personally and professionally. In six and a half months, Schooner and Mia had forged a union that encompassed all areas of their lives, allowing them to fully share and merge every aspect of their worlds. Together they had successfully built their tomorrow.

Mia felt her eyes begin to burn with tears. Every day had been focused on moving forward with their shared goal of the L9/NYC opening and making it the talk of the town, and now she was standing there watching Elan directing his team as they finalized the magnificent finishing touches. The enormity of what they had accomplished since she hit the "Friend Accept" button on that horrible Monday suddenly overwhelmed her.

"It's all real, isn't it?" she asked, unexpectedly astonished by the extent of all that had transpired since their reunion.

He hugged her to his chest and Nathaniel gave a hearty kick, sharply jabbing both Mia and Schooner. Mia looked up at Schooner, eyes wide from the jolt, and they both laughed, their eyes alight with the joy of feeling their son move and his timely surprise attack. "I guess that's my answer." Mia laughed.

"He's telling you, Mom, I'm very real and don't forget it or I'll kick you."

Mia tapped her belly, "Clearly a New Yorker in there."

Schooner laughed and tucked Mia under his arm as she snuggled into him. "Let's go check into the hotel and watch sunset from a rooftop."

As they left L9/NYC, Mia wondered how everything in her life had gotten so perfect and smiled to herself as she heard Seth yelling at her in her head, "Don't over think it, BBC!"

Chapter Thirty-Two

The sun was hanging low in the hazy sky to the west over Jersey City as Mia and Schooner exited the elevator onto the roof deck. A burly shaved-headed security guard, one of Charles' staff, greeted them with a head nod.

They stood there for a moment, taking in the view, a soft breeze blowing Mia's short pale pink silk caftan. "Okay, let's go greet our guests." Schooner bent down and gave Mia a quick kiss and they headed off in opposite directions to work the roof.

Mia held out her hand in front of her in a vertical fist, raising it in increments.

"What is that you're doing?" Kami walked up to her, nursing a gin and tonic.

"Oh, that's a photography thing to gauge how long you have until sunset. Each fist is about fifteen minutes and the sun is about three fists up right now. Comes in handy when you're standing on a mountaintop in twelve degrees waiting to shoot sunset," she laughed.

Yoli elbowed Debbie, a vivacious blonde with a deep, hearty laugh, "Just like CJ, huh," referring to Mia.

Debbie practically spit out her drink. "I cannot believe how opposite ends of the spectrum they are."

Mia laughed and walked over to their table. "I am choosing to take that as a compliment!" She gave Debbie's shoulder a squeeze.

Yoli smiled. "You know it's got to be killing her that she won't be there tomorrow night, but I'm sure spy boy will give her the blow by blow."

They all turned to look at Zac in the pool who had several female L9 staff vying to be on his shoulders in a raucous game of Chicken Fight.

"Looks like he'll be pretty involved in his own blow-by-blows," Mia snarked.

"Love her!" Debbie turned to Yoli.

"Our boy got it right this time," Yoli concurred.

"Awww, give Baby Daddy some credit. He actually had it right the first time. I was the dummy that got played and left him."

"Well, the dummy has got the last laugh." Debbie raised a glass to Mia.

"You can't laugh when the dummy's yours!" And they all laughed.

"I'm never leaving New York," Yoli announced, watching the sun on its descent. The breathtaking view from the roof of the James Hotel provided a nearly 360° vista and made Manhattan feel like it was their own personal little island. "I can't believe I'm saying this, but I really love it here."

"You need to move here." Kami looked sad. She and Yoli had grown to be close friends. "Can't someone else run the California facilities?"

"You need to talk to your business partner," Mia urged, as she got up to go talk to other guests.

Moving on to greet other guests, Mia made her way over to sit down at a table where Gaby, Holly and Jared were munching on Chef David Burke's Smoked Pastrami Salmon and Pretzel Crab Cakes.

"This could be my new addiction," Mia said to Holly, eating her third bite of the Pastrami Salmon.

Holly smiled. "This is so fabulous up here."

The sun was just beginning to kiss the Jersey City roof tops on the far side of the Hudson River.

"We're going to have a magnificent sunset once the sun drops below the horizon. That whole bank of clouds is going to light up." Mia pointed to clouds in the western and southern sky. "And we're going to get the whole show from the oranges into the pinks and reds tonight." She turned to Holly, "We had some great sunsets over the Great South Bay this summer, didn't we?"

"We had a great summer," Holly smiled at Mia. "This was one of my favorite summers ever."

"I really love that." Mia reached for Holly's hand and gave it a squeeze. "Lots more to come."

Holly leaned over and whispered in Mia's ear, "Dad told me the baby's name is Nathaniel James."

Mia gasped, "That man cannot keep a secret! Do you like it?"

"I love it. I just can't wait to see what he looks like. I still can't believe I'm going to have a baby brother."

They both looked over at the pool to see Zac making out with one of the LA staffers, a 20-something California blonde sporting brand new Double D's.

"I'm sorry he's such an ass to you, Mia." The pain and disappointment in her eyes was evident. More than anything she wanted her father to be happy and she knew Zac's behavior weighed heavily on Schooner.

"He's young. Hopefully it won't always be this way."

"Well, I'm happy you and my dad are together. It's very evident how much you love each other and you make him so happy."

Mia smiled. "Thank you for saying that, you can't even imagine what that means to me. I am thrilled that you are a part of my life, Holly. You are the bonus."

Holly smiled and then shook her head. "Mia, you would've been heartbroken if you had seen him at his birthday party. He was so out of sorts. There was a restaurant full of people and he clearly didn't want to be a part of it. He was hanging out on the deck all by himself, and it broke my heart and now, just look at him here. He is so at home and happy."

Sitting on the other side of the pool and laughing with Charles, Gaby and Seth, Schooner had his long legs stretched out, feet up on a chair, single malt scotch in one hand, cigar in the other. He was laughing heartily at something Seth had just said.

The sun had finally faded behind the buildings across the Hudson River and dipped below the horizon, so the sky show was about to begin.

Mia walked over to where Schooner was sitting, "Excuse me while I borrow him for a few minutes." She held out a hand to Schooner and he took it.

They walked along the western side of the roof deck to a spot where they were alone. Mia turned to face the sunset. Schooner stood behind her, his arms wrapped over her shoulders. She leaned back into him and he kissed the top of her head. Silently, they stood and watched the cloud deck, a sky carpet, turn from gold to orange to pink to ruby, before the colors faded to gray and the lights of the city began their show.

"I love you, Baby Girl," Schooner bent down and whispered in Mia's ear.

"It's smoochal." Turning her head back toward him, he bent down to complete the sunset with a kiss. "Okay, I am going to go check on where the next food course is, there should be rib eye sandwiches, grilled prawns and asparagus and a few other goodies coming."

He kissed her again. "I'm going to check on my scotch."

She laughed and walked off toward the bar.

"Hey Mia," she heard Zac call her from the pool. Mia walked over to where Zac and the California blonde were. He looked happy tonight, not surly Zac, allowing him to really look like a young version of Schooner. Mia walked over, smiling. As she got near the edge of the pool, Zac and the blonde scooped up as much water as they could, splashing Mia from head to toe with a torrential wave.

Mia immediately tried to wipe the water from her eyes, but her soaking wet bangs were matted down in them, as if she'd been swimming. Her short pale pink silk caftan was plastered to her body like a second skin, hugging her breasts and her belly, the fabric now translucent.

Zac and the blonde laughed viciously.

"Hey Zac," Mia said, returning his greeting, but with the added NY symbolism of rubbing her nose up and down with her middle finger.

"Classy bitch," Zac snarled at her.

The blonde laughed. "Real classy bitch."

Mia looked at the blonde with a *you didn't just say that* look. "What was the third word you just used?"

The blonde didn't speak, so Mia went on, "Let me refresh your fleeting brain cells. It was bitch. You just called me a bitch."

The girl just looked at Mia with an attitude.

"What is your name?" Mia asked. The girl remained silent. "Okay, let's try this one more time. What. Is. Your. Name?" Mia spoke in a slow cadence.

The girl answered Mia in the same cadence, thinking that she was amusing. "My. Name. Is. Mandy."

Mia smiled at Mandy, her eyes narrowed into slits. "Well, Mandy, unfortunately for you, cute *and* stupid does not have a long shelf life. You're fired."

"You can't fire me," Mandy retorted, breasts and chin thrust forward.

"I can and I did and it's in the past tense. You've been fired, Mandy. E.D. 'ed means past tense, à fait accompli. As you are no longer an employee of L9, you need to get out of the pool and leave this party, immediately. I'll have security accompany you to your room while you gather your belongings and leave the premises." Mia nodded her head at the big, bald security guy by the elevator who was watching a dripping wet Mia.

As he rapidly approached, Charles popped out of his chair at the far end of the deck and sprinted toward Mia. Schooner had his back to the situation and turned quickly to see what had gotten Charles to spring from his chair. He was immediately behind, racing up to a soaking wet, shivering Mia.

Mandy turned to Schooner enraged, breasts still thrust at full throttle. "She fired me. She can't fire me, can she?"

"Of course, she can. You're fired," Schooner said coldly, with narrowed eyes. "Get her out of here."

"But Dad…" Zac began.

"Get out of the pool and follow me," Schooner hissed at him. He turned to Mia, running his hand down her wet head, "You okay?"

She nodded and he kissed her forehead before turning and grabbing Zac by the arm and hauling him off toward the roof deck's indoor seating area.

Charles wrapped a towel around Mia. "You sure you're okay?"

"Yeah, just cold, wet and pissed."

Charles gave her a hug and whispered in her ear, "Fucking little dick."

"You pegged that one."

"Come Meezie, let's get you into dry clothes." Gaby was at Mia's side, leading her to the elevator.

Mia was in a quasi-half-sleep state when Schooner slipped into bed next to her and spooned her, kissing her shoulder. She turned over in his arms to face him and softly ran her hand down his cheek, smoothing her thumb over his cheekbone. "How is everything?"

Schooner sighed, "That is one very angry young man."

"Angry at me and you?" Even in the dark, she could see the sadness in his beautiful eyes.

He nodded, "And Holly, too."

"It won't always be this way, Schooner. He's a petulant, beautiful boy, but at some point, with life experience, he'll realize this isn't a war."

"Mia Silver, you are the one with the beautiful heart. I'm not so sure that my son has one or ever will. I will tell you this though, I was very clear with him on what is acceptable behavior where it comes to you. I will not tolerate blatant disrespect."

"C'mere you." Mia pulled Schooner's head to her chest, kissing the top of his head in a gesture which he had patently comforted and expressed his love for her. Schooner nestled into Mia's soft breasts, getting himself comfortable and let out a soft "mmm" sound. Mia wrapped her arms tightly around him and entwined her legs with his before drifting off into an uneasy sleep.

Chapter Thirty-Three

"We'll see you over at L9. It's 'Showtime' folks," was Schooner's last words to the team before dismissing everyone.

Everyone left the breakfast meeting pumped on adrenaline and excitement for the opening, clear on their assignments and ready to rock the New York social scene. The press for the event had already reached a frenzy and everyone was calling in favors trying to get an invite.

Charles was on hand to brief the staff on interacting with his team, as well as with celebrities and their private security. Mia and Kami gave precise instructions on dealing with the press and paparazzi. Yoli met with each of the teams and their team leaders to review roles and rotations throughout the night. There was some buzz about Mandy's departure, and if anyone was unsure of how Mia fit into the L9 organization, it was now clear that Schooner and Mia were partners in every sense of the word. Most of the staff were extremely savvy and professional and understood the ramifications of mouthing off to the boss. Calling your boss a bitch (unless you were Seth), was generally not a good career move.

"We're headed off to go beautify. I'll come over to the club when I'm done."

"Why don't you rest this afternoon, Baby Girl. You're going to be on your feet all night." Schooner reached down and brushed Mia's bangs from her eyes.

"I feel like there is some detail I'm going to miss if I don't do one last check." Mia looked up at Schooner, searching his face.

He shook his head. "Everything's under control. Between the two of us, Yoli, Seth, Kami, Elan and Charles, we've done as much as we can. I don't want you to push it."

"Are you trying to tell me I need to relax?"

Schooner laughed, "I would never…"

Mia swatted him in the arm, smiling up at him. "You know that is not in my DNA!"

"Baby Girl, do not make me sic Dr. Gary on you." His hands were in her hair, as he smiled down at her.

"Gary's coming tonight." She smiled back at him.

"Yes, I know, so don't make me rat you out to him." Schooner continued to play with her hair. “Go enjoy your girly stuff.” He bent down to softly kiss her lips.

“Schooner-,” she stopped.

“What, Baby Girl?”

“I love you.” Mia’s eyes were so earnest and every time she said the words to him, it was like she was saying it for the first time.

He leaned his forehead into hers and stayed like that for a moment before kissing her lips softly and saying, “It’s smoochal” into them.

Mia, Kami, Holly, Yoli, Debbie and Seth walked the two blocks down Grand Street through SoHo to the Enzo B’s Salon. Turning left on Wooster Street, the blue Enzo B Salon flag was gently blowing in the breeze.

“Oh my God, now it seems real, doesn’t it? We’re getting coiffed for tonight,” Mia commented, as they walked into the salon. The entourage was met warmly, with Enzo whisking Mia off immediately.

He started to play with her hair as they talked, “You’ve always had thick hair, but pregnancy has turned it into a mane.” He played some more. “I can see you have not been using the DualMint Scrub on your scalp.”

Mia looked guilty as she met Enzo’s eyes in the mirror, “Busted.”

“I’ll go easy on you because I know you’ve got a lot on your plate, but you are not leaving here without a DualMint Scrub Complete Pack. Now tell me about tonight, what you are wearing, your role, etc. This event is clearly the big ticket in town, everyone is talking about it.”

“They are? You’re hearing about it?”

Enzo nodded at Mia.

“Excellent, means we’re doing a good job. Okay, so obviously we are the agency of record and we are handling all aspects, advertising, marketing, PR, events—all the details for this event.”

“Have you worked with Level 9 on the West Coast? They are huge out there.”

“No. Frankly, I had no clue who they were until February,” Mia laughed. “Apparently, I was the only one.”

“So, how did you connect with them?” Enzo was trying out different parts on Mia’s hair, critically looking at her in the mirror as he pulled her hair up, put it back down, flared it on her shoulders, swept it to one side, then the other.

“Well, I have a relationship with the owner.”

Enzo stopped playing and leveled a glance at Mia in the mirror. “With Schooner Moore?”

Mia nodded.

"What kind of relationship?" Enzo was intrigued. Schooner was the new mystery man in town.

Mia laughed and rubbed her belly. "Knocked me up," she deadpanned.

Enzo let out a guffaw laugh. Laying his hand with the hairbrush on Mia's shoulder, "So, he is your significant other?"

Mia nodded.

"Mia, Mia, Mia. You have just made my day so much more interesting. Okay, so that makes you both the professional that has created the event as well as the hostess. Okay, let's get your hair washed and your scalp scrubbed."

Mia returned to Enzo's chair with her scalp feeling like it was glowing. "Tell me about your dress."

Looking at Enzo in the mirror, she rolled her eyes. "Maternity evening wear is penance for something I did wrong in a past life," she pouted.

Enzo laughed, "I'm sure you are wearing something very chic and flattering. Seth would not let you attend in something embarrassing."

"It's a midnight blue one-shouldered Grecian drape thing."

Listening, he combed through Mia's hair. "Length?"

"Short, above the knee."

Stopping what he was doing, he released a dramatic sigh. "Oh thank goodness, you are too small to carry long maternity."

Mia nodded, "That is what Seth said."

"Okay, so classic lines on your dress and since you are the hostess, I'm thinking old Hollywood for you tonight. Let's sweep these bangs over to the side. Think Rita Hayworth, Ava Gardner, Lauren Bacall. Soft waves for the rest. And I need to shape your hair, you are a mess from this summer."

"Do it!" Mia proclaimed with a smile. As she glanced to her left and her right, the rest of her party were in different phases of their makeovers.

When Enzo was done with Mia, she sat with her mouth open looking at her reflection. She checked out her left profile, then her right profile, tilted and cocked her head.

"You like?" Enzo looked very satisfied with his masterful handiwork.

"I love it."

As Mia headed toward make-up, she stopped behind Seth's chair. He spied her in his mirror and gasped, "It's movie star BBC. I likee!"

Chapter Thirty-Four

Mia stood in front of the bathroom mirror trying to maneuver her body into her dress properly. "This is some serious cleavage," she muttered at her changing body.

She heard the front door to the hotel penthouse loft slam.

"Hey, I'm back," Schooner yelled.

"I'll be out in a few." *Showtime*, Mia thought and wished she'd had her shoes and jewelry on, so that Schooner could get the full effect of the silver screen image that Enzo had created for her.

Schooner had his back to her when she emerged from the bathroom. He was already in the pants of his Fendi Steel Mélange black suit and white Armani Collezioni dress shirt and was fumbling as he attempted to insert black stingray leather and silver cufflinks.

"Need help with those?"

Schooner slowly turned around, his eyes widening and a real smile spreading across his handsome face at the sight of Mia. "Hey, Gorgeous," his voice was little more than a growl.

"Hey, Gorgeous yourself," she took the cufflinks from his hands and inserted them into his French cuffs.

When she looked up, he was smiling down at her, appreciatively.

"You look beautiful, Baby Girl."

"You think?" she asked over her shoulder with a devil smile as she headed to the closet. "Oh crap. Where are my shoes?" There was panic in Mia's voice.

"In the living room."

"In the living room, really?" Mia was confused and left the bedroom in search of her shoes. "What the…"

She turned around to see Schooner standing behind her with a shit-eating grin on his face. Mia cocked her head, questioningly. On the low coffee table in the living room were two matte black shoeboxes emblazoned with the silver *Jimmy Choo* logo.

Schooner took Mia by the hand and led her to the couch, where they sat down. She just smiled at him with a bemused look.

He took one of the boxes in his lap. "Christian Louboutin made you cry. So, I bought you Jimmy Choo's." His eyes never leaving hers, he removed the box top and watched her gasp as the recessed lighting in the hotel loft caught the glint off the shiny silver peep toe sling backs.

"Oh my God, Schooner." Mia was floored as Schooner took out the first of the *Clue* pumps.

"A sexy silver shoe. There just could not be a more perfect shoe for Mia Silver."

Mia lifted her foot for him and Schooner slipped the sexy and elegant silver shoe onto her left foot and then her right. She smiled at them in awe.

"They fit," Mia beamed at Schooner. "I love you so much." She leaned over and softly kissed his lips.

"Do you want to see what is in the other box?" He was the one giving her the devil smile now.

Mia nodded, but was clearly distracted by the beautiful sling backs gracing her shapely legs and high-arched, newly pedicured feet.

Schooner handed her the second box and she lifted the lid and gasped again.

"I figured your feet might not make it through the night in the first pair and you'll still need to look chic—or Seth will kill the both of us." He laughed.

In the second box, were a pair of Jimmy Choo flat silver thong sandals with a sexy ankle strap.

Mia wrapped her arms around Schooner's neck and pulled him in for a kiss. "You spoil me," she said against his lips.

He nodded, smiling. "And it's a rare treat when you actually let me."

She kissed his lips again softly and said, "Wait here."

Coming from the bedroom, she sat down and handed him a long thin burnt orange box with black piping. The box was sashed with a thin black satin ribbon emblazoned in white with *Hermès-Paris.*

"I needed to complete your New York transformation."

Schooner opened the box and smiled at Mia. Nestled in soft tissue was an Hermes Faconnee H jacquard silk twill tie that matched Mia's midnight blue dress.

"Now that's class," he whispered, as he removed the hand folded tie from the box. It was Schooner's first Hermès.

Handing the tie to Mia, she draped it slowly and sensually around his neck and under his shirt collar, smiling at him and making a slow meal of it, before tying a perfect double Windsor knot and pulling him in by his tie for a kiss.

"You're killing me here," he groaned.

"Good." She kissed him again, devil smile reaching her eyes this time.

They finished dressing and Mia was standing in front of the full-length mirror in the bedroom. Coming up behind her as he buttoned his suit jacket, Schooner looked at her petite and very feminine reflection, appreciatively. Silently, they both stood there drinking in the image in the mirror. Their image was not just one of beauty, but it also exuded happiness. Mia couldn't help but think there is nothing more than this.

Schooner and Mia did not just look like they belonged together. Schooner and Mia belonged together.

Chapter Thirty-Five

Schooner and Mia reached the Sky Lobby on the hotel's third floor where the rest of their party awaited. "Wait until you see your daughter." Mia squeezed Schooner's hand as they approached.

Dressed in an azalea red ruched Theia silk jacquard cocktail dress with her long blonde hair swept to one side, Holly looked as if she should be walking the runway. Schooner's face melted upon seeing his daughter and Mia gave his hand a final squeeze, before letting it go.

Schooner held Holly by her shoulders at arm's length looking at her. "You look…" he began to speak, but was overcome and shook his head, before pulling her in for a sweet hug.

Seth grabbed Mia's hand and gave it a squeeze as they smiled at the heartwarming scene unfolding in front of them.

It was then that Mia noticed Zac watching them from off to the side, where he stood leaning against a glass wall. Instinctively, she could not help herself from smiling at him standing there looking like a brooding Greek god. She knew who and what he was, yet could not control an underlying, and unwarranted, fondness—he was Schooner's.

"Zac, come over here. I want to take a picture of you, your dad and Holly." Mia motioned him over. It was the first interaction she'd had with him since the incident at the pool.

Zac stood there stone-faced, not moving.

Mia rolled her eyes at him and shook her head, "Just get your ass over there." Her tone was one that she would take with a friend, like Seth, saying "just cut the crap."

Not quite knowing how to take her, Zac complied and shuffled over. Refusing to smile for the picture, his scowl actually complemented both his looks and the eveningwear.

"Gorgeous," Mia said, showing Seth the picture. "You did an amazing job dressing him."

"I hate admitting how beautiful Devil Spawn is," he whispered at her through clenched teeth and Mia squeezed his arm.

Out of the corner of her eye, Mia saw Schooner nod his head at Zac and motion toward Mia. As Zac approached Mia, Seth gave her a look and backed away.

"Sorry about last night," he muttered, without conviction.

"Come walk with me." Mia took Zac by the upper arm.

They moved away from the rest of the party and rounded a corner before Mia stopped. She leveled a cold glance at him, her green eyes meeting his ice blue eyes head on. "Do you love your father?" she asked.

"Yes, I love my father." His eyes narrowed.

"Do you want him in your life?"

"What do you think?" Now out of sight of the rest of the party, he had no need for pretenses or civility.

"Trust me, you don't want to know what I think, and frankly, that is not the issue here. Do you want him in your life?" Mia asked for a second time.

"Yes, I want him in my life."

Mia said nothing more to him. She nodded her head, turned and walked away, leaving Zac standing there, confused.

"Mia?" He caught up with her at a quick pace and put a hand on her arm to stop her.

"Yes, Zac?"

"Was that it?" He wanted more, a conversation, a fight.

"Yes." Mia met him with indifference.

She could see his mind spinning with a million thoughts and before he went off in a direction she didn't want him to go, Mia decided to throw him off balance, "We have a really hot opening to get to and you look like a freaking model, so let's go." She slipped her arm through his and led him back to a surprised group and asked with the biggest, brightest smile she could paint on her face, "Everyone ready to hit the road?"

The limo pulled up in front of L9/NYC and there was already a crowd gathered out front comprised of guests arriving, security, paparazzi, and onlookers hoping to get a peek and photo of their favorite celebrity.

Mia saw Charles talking to seemingly no one, but knew he was giving staff orders through some type of hidden walkie-talkie device. A doorman opened the door to the limo and Yoli and Debbie exited first, followed by Kami and Seth, then Zac, who set off a flare of paparazzi flashes just by looking like a star or a model, the same with Holly and Jared.

Mia squeezed Schooner's hand.

"This is it, Baby Girl."

From a walkway in front of Brewster Hall to the sidewalk in front of L9/NYC with paparazzi and press awaiting their arrival, Mia and Schooner were entering a new world, together.

Schooner stepped out of the car and reached a hand down for Mia, escorting her from the limo. Putting an arm around her shoulder as they began to walk, she looked up at him and they both smiled and simultaneously uttered, "Showtime"—breaking into huge smiles at their trademark synchronicity.

It was at that moment that the surrounding cameras began to flash, and the image that was captured of handsome California turned New York entrepreneur Schooner Moore, and his beautiful and very pregnant New York love, Mia Silver, felt almost voyeuristic. Schooner and Mia were looking at one another with a love that made them oblivious to their surroundings, smiling as if they were clearly sharing a very private secret.

This picture would grace Women's Wear Daily, the social columns of the New York newspapers, fashion and fitness magazines, New York Magazine, The New Yorker, Paris Match and Vogue.

It would be this image that would forever remain in people's minds when they thought of Mia Silver and Schooner Moore.

Chapter Thirty-Six

The offices were set up for press interviews and a steady stream of journalists and photographers were booked for their one-on-ones with Schooner. Kami and Schooner had prepped extensively for the interviews, conducting due diligence on each of the reporters. As Schooner was both well-seasoned and a natural—especially with women reporters (it just took a flash of his All-American boy smile), they didn't anticipate any surprises or situations he couldn't handle.

Mia had come in and was standing in the threshold of the office as Schooner was finishing up his last scheduled interview of the evening. Sitting behind his desk, long legs crossed in his impeccable Fendi suit, he remained sharply focused on the interviewer.

The reporter, a small, serious woman dressed in vintage Chanel, had bird-like features and a champagne blonde French twist. She quickly looked through her notes before looking back up at Schooner, "I have one last question, Mr. Moore. What is the significance of the name Level 9?"

Schooner cocked his head to the side and looked at the diminutive reporter with a small, appreciative smile. "Do you know, that you are the first member of the press to *ever* have asked me that question?"

The reporter looked surprised and pleased with herself.

"What does L9 mean?" Schooner smiled, repeating the question, an introspective smile on his handsome face.

He was silent for a moment, clearly inside his head, remembering something and formulating his response. "L9 or what has morphed into Level 9, is my personal inspiration for not only attaining the best that I can be, but also the best that I can do for others. It's a philosophy that I not only try to apply on a personal level, but also apply to any impact that I may have in a broader sense." He paused, before looking directly into the reporter's eyes as he continued. "The summer after my freshman year in college," he began, his eyes flicked to Mia momentarily, and he gave her a small, sad smile, "I accompanied a group of doctors to the Southern Province of Zambia, to a village called Macha, where we helped set up a hospital. I went to lend an extra set of hands to the medical staff, or in my case, one hand, because my right hand was in a cast, at the time. Within the first few days after our arrival, I noticed that families were traveling long distances seeking medical attention and literally bringing their entire family on the journey. The children were waiting around all day with nothing to do while their parents were waiting to be seen by the doctors. So, after I had assisted with the initial set-up of the hospital, I asked myself, 'What can a one-handed jock do to really be useful to both the medical personnel and to the patients?' And there was only one answer to that. Start a sports and soccer camp for the kids," he laughed. "And with the help of nine very dedicated children from the local village, I set up an exercise, soccer and wellness camp for both local and visiting children." Schooner paused, smiling at a memory. "We did everything from basic exercise to soccer matches to learning lifesaving techniques such as CPR and oral-rehydration therapy. At the end of the summer, we held a soccer tournament that turned into a huge event, where everyone in the village came out." He laughed again. "Basically, a tailgate party, Zambian-style." Schooner was clearly enjoying the memory, "There was a village elder, named Levi Mambwe, who pulled me aside and had a very enlightening discussion with me on my last night there. He talked with me about gifts and passion and what I had done for the children of the village. His inspirational words touched me deeply, and I knew from that moment on, what my path in life would be. I also knew that the people of Macha had done much more for me than I had actually done for them. L9 is my way of paying homage to both Levi, and the nine children of Macha, who dedicated themselves to the sports camp. It has been my way of thanking them for what they taught me and the gift that they gave to me and that I have, in turn, been able to share with others. So, for me L9 is a level at which I aspire to live my life—a way of paying things both back and forward through inspiring people to maintain mind and body health. And that is the significance behind the name Level 9."

The reporter turned off her microphone and looked Schooner square in the eyes. "You are more than just a pretty face, Mr. Moore. I am honored that I will be the one to share that story. Welcome to New York."

Mia stood in the doorway smiling, as the reporter left. "Remember when I asked you if people knew who you really were?"

Schooner nodded.

"I think after this, everyone will have a really good idea."

With the interviews completed, Mia and Schooner went out to join the party. L9/NYC was packed, the champagne was flowing, waiters passed hors d'oeuvres on silver trays, live music pulsed from the center of the rotunda. Schooner grabbed a glass of champagne from a passing waiter.

They stood at the rail of the second-floor mezzanine surveying the ethereal club. Elan had created a scene from a dream.

"I want a sip." Mia reached out for Schooner's champagne.

"You do?" he was surprised, as she hadn't had a drink at all throughout the pregnancy.

"Mmm-hmm, just a sip. To celebrate." Schooner held the flute to Mia's lips and she took a small sip.

"Yum! I've missed that." She looked down at the throng of people in the rotunda below. "Look at this, Schooner."

She looked up at him and he was smiling, ear to ear. "Let's go work the room." She took his hand and they descended the marble stairs. At the bottom, she turned to him and gave him a quick kiss, "Go work your peeps and I'll go work mine." She gave his hand a squeeze, "till we meet again," and with a flash of her devil grin, they headed off in opposite directions.

Emma Stone, the Olsen Twins, Rachel Bilson, Bradley Cooper, Blake Lively & Ryan Reynolds, Kate Hudson, Liv Tyler, Selma Blair, Victoria & David Beckham, and of course, Katie Chisholm. Mia thought, okay those are the ones that I can name, as she stopped to say hello and greet guests. There were so many faces she knew that she should know who they were, but couldn't put a name to the face. *Okay, they are on that CW vampire show*, she thought, as she greeted a couple with a huge smile and a "Hi there, isn't this space fabulous, are you having a good time, great to see you…" *I'll remember their names tomorrow, when I'm standing in the shower*, she thought and laughed out loud.

After close to an hour of buzzing from conversation to conversation, Mia headed to the perimeter of the rotunda where there were a few tables set up. She had Elan keep the number of tables to a minimum, so that guests would have to mingle, but her feet were past the mingling point and her Jimmy Choo's were soon going to have a Christian Louboutin crying effect, if she didn't sit.

At a table situated near an alcove and slightly removed from the fray, Mia spotted Mallory Jessie Prince and Chris Brody sitting with a few people and there was an empty chair. Salvation, she thought, as she headed their way with a determined walk and a smile on her face. Her heart skipped a beat when she saw who was sitting next to the empty chair.

Coming up behind him, Mia placed her hands on his shoulders and whispered into his ear, "Just seeing you gives me a heart hard-on."

He turned to meet his whisperer, his huge trademark smile overtaking his face as well as a look of surprise, for he did not recognize the whisperer, who was quoting the words that he had tweeted out on Valentine's Day.

Mia met him with a huge devil grin and said, "I have the biggest crush on you! If I were a gay man, I'd stalk you."

His warm brown eyes widened at the bodacious introduction.

She went on, "Hi, I'm Mia Silver."

His mouth opened into a big surprised "O" before breaking into a smile, "*You're* Mia Silver? All night everyone has been saying to me, 'I can't believe you don't know, Mia' and 'You have to meet Mia'."

"Ta-Da." Mia put out her hands, "And now you have!" Before sitting down next to her secret crush, Internet TV sensation, Andy Epstein, Mia went around the table to greet Mallory Jessie and Chris.

"I can't believe you two have never met," MJP was surprised. "You look wonderful, Mia. How are you feeling?"

"Great, except for my feet tonight." She looked down at her beautiful shoes.

"Silver Jimmy Choo's—now that is perfect for you," Mallory Jessie laughed.

"I know! Schooner gave them to me. He thought the same thing."

"Schooner Moore?" Andy asked.

Mia nodded. "I had a meltdown in front of Christian Louboutin a few months ago thinking I was going to have big swollen platypus feet and that I was going to have to wear Birkenstock's, so Schooner thought that Jimmy Choo's would make me happy. And he was right." She laughed.

"I haven't met him yet," Andy began, taking a sip of his champagne, "which is amazing because he was quite the talk of all the *Real Housewives of Orange County* when I interviewed them."

"I'll bet he was," Mia rolled her eyes. "I'll introduce you." She scanned the room, "There he is." Mia pointed across the rotunda where Schooner was talking with Heidi Berg. "The Brooks Brothers model talking to Heidi Berg."

Andy looked at Mia and laughed, "No wonder he was the talk of the *Housewives*. He's gorgeous!" Andy grabbed Mia's forearm.

"Inside and out." Mia smiled.

"So, you're his ad agency?" Andy asked, leaning in close for the scoop on Mr. Hotness.

"Amongst other things." Mia smiled and ever the journalist, Andy cocked his head to the side in a 'tell me more' gesture. "Baby Mama," Mia added.

Mallory Jessie looked at Andy, "Get with the program, Epstein. That man is in New York because of Mia."

Andy leaned over and whispered in Mia's ear, "And the blonde OC *shiksa*?"

"A signature away from where she should have been twenty-four years ago when she hatched her evil plan to break us up. Gone. Goodbye."

Andy was staring into Mia's eyes shocked, when their attention was drawn away by a buxom bleached blonde shrieking his name, "Andy, it's been so long."

The smile was plastered on Andy's handsome face, but the look in his eyes said, "Who the fuck are you?"

Mia and Mallory Jessie exchanged smirks. She introduced herself and as fate would have it, she was a friend of a friend of one of the *Housewives* and had appeared briefly in the crowd at a party in one of the episodes, several years back.

"This is my cue to go upstairs and change into more comfortable shoes," Mia announced, standing to leave.

Before she could take a step, Mia heard her name being called as Katie Chisholm approached. "You look adorable! Schooner told me you two are expecting." Katie wrapped her in a warm hug, as if they were old friends.

"Katie," Mia smiled and hugged her back. "It's so good to see you. How do you like this space vs. the ones on the west coast?"

"This is amazing. I can't wait to start using the facilities. It is so unique. Just like Schooner though to create a fabulous concept."

Mia was smiling brightly at Katie's assessment.

Katie and Andy hugged and the *Housewife* wannabe was dying to get Katie's attention, but Katie and Mallory Jessie were already talking about school starting for their kids and Mia was left with Andy and the wannabe.

"Are you Mia Silver?" the wannabe asked.

Mia was concentrating hard on her face. It had no movement to it. Botox overload was Mia's assessment. "Yes, I am," Mia responded.

"I'm a friend of CJ Moore's. Schooner's wife." She leaned in toward Mia, with her tall, lean frame.

"Of course you are," Mia smiled. "Wonderful, then you'll be able to report back to her how fabulous *our* opening was. Now if you'll excuse me, Schooner had the foresight to buy me the cutest pair of silver Jimmy Choo flats to change into when these," she motioned to her gorgeous silver sling backs, "became too much."

She turned to Andy, "I'll introduce you and Schooner when I get back." And in a whisper, "Score one for the Jewish girl."

Andy's face broke into a huge smile, his eyes crinkling in the corners.

Mia made her way slowly through the crowd, stopping to say hello to guests as she migrated toward the main marble staircase. As she ascended the grand flight of stairs, she looked up and saw Zac standing at the top, a few feet from the steps.

He was leaning over the railing and looking at the crowd below. Mia couldn't help but smile at him, he looked so damn handsome. In his right hand was a champagne glass and Mia thought she was going to need to talk to the wait staff about cutting him off. Zac was still a minor.

She approached him with a smile. "Having fun?"

He shrugged his shoulders, "You know my mother should be the one here with him. Fifty percent of this *is* hers."

"Zac, I really do love how loyal you are to your mother." Mia was sincere as she looked into his glazed eyes. He'd clearly had quite a few glasses of champagne.

"Obviously not a trait I get from my father." He drained the remainder of his flute. "Since he's choosing a bitch and a bastard over me and my mother."

A waiter was passing by and he reached for a fresh glass of champagne.

"Zac, I think you've had enough to drink." Mia reached for his glass and he thrust his arm forward to push her hand away, knocking Mia backward, the champagne splashing down the front of her dress.

Mia felt the heels of her Jimmy Choo's slipping out from under her as she took a step backward to try and right her balance. The heel of her right shoe caught the edge of the top step, and as she began to fall backwards, she saw the complacent look on Zac's face.

The edge of the first step she hit slammed the lumbar section of her spine and she felt the pain searing through her body. "Protect Nathaniel" was the thought that flashed through her mind and she brought her flailing arms down to wrap around her stomach. She tumbled backwards over a few more steps feeling the stabbing pain in her shoulders as they slammed the cold marble, and then there was darkness, the pain gone as the back of Mia's head caught the very edge of a step and her limp body tumbled to the base of the stairs.

Chapter Thirty-Seven

Charles received the message in his ear that there had been an accident at the main staircase and that a woman was unconscious. Within seconds he arrived at the scene to see Mia splayed on the floor, blood already spreading from the back of her head. He gave orders to call 911 and have them arrive at the side entrance and have someone find both Schooner and Dr. Gary Cohen.

Kneeling next to her to take her pulse, Charles silently thanked God when he felt one.

"Meezie, we're getting you help. They're on their way. Just stay with us, Meezie."

Gary was now leaning on the other side of her, feeling the pulse at her neck. He had his cell phone to his ear making arrangements for what he needed in the emergency room.

Schooner arrived to see both Gary and Charles leaning over someone and as he got closer he saw Mia's shoes and pushed his way through the gathering crowd.

"Baby Girl," his choked voice barely audible as he dropped to his knees next to her. "Baby Girl," his panic was rising. Blood from Mia's head seeped into the pants legs of his suit.

"Is she going to be okay? What happened?" He looked from Gary to Charles and to the staircase Mia had just careened down. As his eyes traveled up the staircase, he saw Zac standing at the top, empty champagne glass in hand, a slightly amused, detached look on his face and in that moment Schooner knew all he needed to know.

Springing to his feet, his long legs taking the steps two at a time, Schooner charged up the staircase, a growl emanating from his chest. He rammed into his son head first, the force catapulting Zac fifteen feet backwards into the wall with the second sickening thud of the evening, knocking the wind out of him.

Schooner grabbed Zac by the neck and slammed him into the wall for a second time. "What did you do?" he hissed.

"I didn't do it on purpose. She was grabbing my drink. I was just trying to get her off me." Zac met his father's eyes with venom.

Schooner had Zac pinned to the wall. Although only two inches taller,

Schooner was dwarfing Zac with his aggressive stance. "If anything happens to her or the baby…"

Zac cut him off with an indignant, "Yeah, I know the bitch and the bastard are more important to you than me and mom, you've made that perfectly clear."

Schooner drew back his right arm, hand fisted, driving forcefully toward Zac's face. Inches before its intended target, Schooner's arm was jolted back, stopped in mid-air, and a very calm voice whispered in his ear, "Meezie needs you with her in the emergency room, not in a jail cell."

Schooner closed his eyes and let out a long slow breath. He nodded his head and in a low voice, "Get him out of here. I want him on a plane back to LA tonight. If you can't get him on a commercial flight, charter a plane. I'm not kidding. I want him out of here tonight."

"But Dad, Exeter…" Zac began.

"Exeter is done. I don't want to be within 3,000 miles of you. Get him out of here tonight," Schooner repeated.

Two of Charles' men were now flanking Zac.

Schooner raced down the stairs to where the EMT were arriving for Mia.

Charles put a hand on Schooner's back, "For what it's worth," Charles said to his friend, "I would've done the exact same thing."

Schooner knew he was referring to attacking Zac.

Mia was still not responding as the EMT's began to immobilize her, bracing her neck and head and gently log rolling her onto a stretcher.

Schooner stayed alongside of her, "It's okay, Baby Girl, they're going to get you to the hospital. Gary's already there, waiting for you. Everything's going to be okay. You're going to be okay. The baby's going to be okay."

The ambulance was waiting outside the side entrance of the club. Three EMT's slid Mia's gurney into the ambulance. Schooner began to climb into the ambulance when one of the EMT's put a hand on his shoulder, stopping him and said, "Sir, what is your relationship to the patient?"

Schooner looked at him with an incredulous look, "I'm… I'm her fiancé," he stuttered.

"I'm sorry, Sir. I can't let you ride with her. You're not family."

"Not family?" Schooner's voice was raised, "She's my fiancée. That's my baby." Schooner moved toward the ambulance.

"Sir, please stop." Two EMTs were now between him and Mia. "Sir, the longer you detain us, the more risk there is for the patient. Please let us leave."

They climbed into the back of the ambulance, the doors closing with a loud clank. Schooner winced at the sound.

Paralyzed, he stood there on the curb watching the vehicle recede into the night, the flashing red lights growing smaller as the ambulance moved farther away.

He heard a noise behind him and then Zac's voice, "Dad."

Schooner turned around as two of Charles' team were escorting Zac into an SUV. Their eyes met. Schooner felt nothing. Looking at Zac was no different than passing a stranger on the street. Schooner was numb.

He turned back around to see where Mia's ambulance was, but it was gone. No sign of the flashing red lights remained on the avenue. He heard the engine of the SUV as it pulled away, but it really didn't register.

Schooner stepped to the curb and raised his right arm to hail a cab. Within a few moments, a yellow cab pulled up in front of him. He reached for the door handle and as he went to pull it open, he realized that he had no idea where they had taken Mia. He did not know where Mia was or to what hospital to direct the cab driver. The realization slammed him with a wave of nausea.

He waved the cabbie on and stepped back from the curb.

As he stood staring up the avenue in the direction the ambulance had gone, Schooner had a sinking feeling in his stomach, a feeling of utter hopelessness that he had felt only once before, many years ago, in a dorm hallway. Mia's last words to him earlier in the evening were ricocheting around in his brain like an out of control pinball, "Till we meet again," she had said.

He closed his eyes and in a silent prayer begged, "Please don't leave me, Baby Girl. Please don't leave me again."

End of Book One

Bonus Chapter

The Night Before His Wedding
Hotel del Coronado
Coronado, California

They sat at the Sunset Bar, although it was long after sunset. Finally quiet, the evening had been a rip-roaring success, according to the best man, Beau Gordon, a guy who hadn't gotten laid in years, if ever. If you were the groom's only gay male friend, or the groom himself, for that matter, the assessment of the evening was not quite so glowing, and had taken a fast downhill slide the minute the four strippers were ushered into the steakhouse's private dining room.

"Did he really think I'd like that?" Schooner's words were slurred.

"I don't think he was thinking about you when he booked them," Henry laughed.

"They were pretty skanky, huh?" Schooner started to snicker at the absurdity of the evening.

"Drag queens would have been my preference."

The very drunk groom-to-be found the comment hilarious and let out a loud laugh, "Well, you know they would have been prettier."

"Is there something I should know about you?" It had been too long since just he and Schooner had hung out together. They'd gotten together a few times after college, but CJ insisted on being there and they never got to really talk, he never was able to get a true handle on his friend's happiness.

"I love this stuff," the bartender had poured Schooner another single malt scotch.

"I don't think it's going to be loving you too much tomorrow morning."

"You're probably right," Schooner lifted the glass. "I think this is going to become my drink."

"You may not be saying that tomorrow morning." Henry reiterated.

With his glass still raised, Schooner began a toast, "To a great buddy who has seen me through bad times and good times. May we always remain friends."

"Here, here." They clinked glasses.

"And the bad times were sure bad times," the alcohol was taking Schooner to a dark place.

"Do you ever think about her?" This was the talk they never could have with CJ around.

"I try not to, but she shows up at the craziest moments. And it feels like yesterday, both the pain and how much I loved her. I'd give my left arm to know what the hell happened between the time we said goodnight and the next morning."

Henry remained quiet and Schooner filled in the air left blank by Henry's unasked question, "I asked her and she swore up and down that she had no idea what happened and said that she had not spoken to Mia that night."

There it was, he had finally spoken her name. Mia. Henry didn't believe CJ for a second, but she had somehow convinced Schooner of her innocence. *Innocent, my ass,* thought Henry. Mia was head over heels in love with Schooner. What could CJ have said to make Mia run? Rosie always thought that maybe she'd told Mia she was pregnant with Schooner's baby and that he was going to do the right thing. Who knows? That was only Rosie's theory. But he and Rosie agreed, CJ MacAllister was at the bottom of running off Mia Silver. She had definitely done something.

"Why didn't you try to find her?" Henry was curious.

Schooner laughed, "Okay, this is sort of embarrassing. So, I went to the library once and got the New York City phonebook. There were over 120 R. and Robert Silvers. I went to the bank and got $50 worth of quarters and found a phone booth in the library. At about number forty-three, I stopped. She didn't want me to find her. Or she would've called me. Even just to tell me off. Which is something Mia would have done."

Agreeing, Henry took a sip of his drink. "You're right, Mia not calling you to rip you a new asshole is probably the most surprising thing of all."

Shaking his head, Schooner looked off into the distance. "God, did I love her."

Henry could feel the intensity of the heartfelt statement. The alcohol was letting Schooner's sadness bleed through. Everything his friend was trying to push under the surface and control was becoming dangerously close to being out of his control.

"Why are you doing this, Schooner?"

Taking a second to process that, "It's the night before. I can't very well cancel it."

"If this is not what you want, not what's going to make you happy, yes, you can cancel it." Henry put a hand on Schooner's shoulder. Maybe in this very drunk state he could get through to him.

"I'd upset too many people." Schooner was shaking his head, a lock from his thick blond hair falling on his forehead, clearly pained at the thought of disappointing others.

"No, you'd upset two people. CJ and her mother. They'd both hate you, but so what, it's not worth your happiness."

"I'm happy enough. I'll be okay."

"Not a good way to go into a marriage, my friend."

"Ah, that is where you are wrong," Schooner took another sip of the scotch, "it's the perfect way to go into a marriage. No illusions of everlasting love that in reality will smash your heart to smithereens."

"Don't you want to be in love?" Henry's ginger brows knit together, concerned.

"Fuck no." Schooner finished his scotch and the bartender brought another. "If you walked into a fire and got badly burned, would you walk into another fire?"

"If you could feel again what you felt with Mia, wouldn't you want that?" Henry countered.

"Yes and no." Schooner started on the next drink. "Yes, it would feel amazing to feel that again." He closed his eyes. "But no, I don't ever want to be that over my head again. I don't want to have such a lack of control in a situation that could be disastrous for me."

"And you don't see getting married to someone you don't love as disastrous?"

"No," Schooner shook his head, "I can control that situation. I won't get hurt."

Henry sat back on his bar stool, saddened. Why was Schooner giving up? Why wasn't he moving on?

"I can't imagine you don't want to feel with someone what you felt with Mia," pressing, he wondered how the hell was he going to get through to him?

Picking up his glass, Schooner took a long draw on the amber liquid. "I don't want to feel. That whole love stuff is not for me."

"Is that fair to CJ?" At that moment, Henry was forced to consider that he'd just entered an alcohol-fueled alternate universe. Sticking up for CJ? No one would believe that. He needed witnesses. Where were the witnesses?

"She knows what she's getting. I haven't been anything but honest with her."

"Wow," was all Henry could say.

Filled with overwhelming sadness for his friend, yet angry with him at the same time, Henry was frustrated that he couldn't figure out the right words, the right trigger to talk some sense into him and get him to pull the plug on this sham of a marriage before more damage was done. Schooner may have convinced himself that this was the smartest thing to do to never get hurt, but this self-inflicted penance was going to come at a huge price.

And then out of the blue, he slurred, "If I had her number, I'd drunk dial her right now."

"What would you say?"

"Why'd you leave me?" The pain in Schooner's voice was heartbreaking as he asked the unanswered question that had plagued him for years.

Henry remained quiet, hoping if he could get him to keep talking, that maybe he'd convince himself not to go through with the wedding.

"And I'd tell her I love her and no matter what had happened we could work it out if we were together, and you just don't find what we had every day and it was crazy to throw that away." His clear blue eyes began to focus as if an epiphany was upon him.

Keep going, Henry silently urged. The melting away of inhibitions was allowing Schooner to face what he'd buried for so long. Henry signaled the bartender for another scotch for his friend.

"And I'd tell her don't move, I'm coming to get you. And I'd get a freaking address this time," he laughed. Looking up at Henry, "I'm making a mistake, aren't I?"

It was the first time all night that he felt he was talking to Schooner. He could see it in his eyes. Schooner was there. He was back. Henry nodded, solemnly.

The two young men looked at each other for a long moment, then Schooner retreated into his head, a million emotions fleeting across his clear sapphire eyes.

"Yes!" thought Henry triumphantly, I found Schooner and I got through to him.

"There's my son-in-law-to-be," a loud booming voice was upon them, nearly knocking Schooner out of his chair with an overly hearty slap on the back.

CJ's father and three uncles descended rapidly, circling the almost groom. One of them stepped between Henry and Schooner's barstools, blocking Henry and essentially cutting him off from the conversation.

Henry could feel his panic rise. "No, no, no," the scream reverberated inside his head.

An overly gregarious Mr. MacAllister took over, extolling all the virtues of his new son-in-law to his brothers, bragging about how well his little princess had done finding this fine young man.

Henry stood, moving away from his barstool, to try to negotiate a position on the outside of the circle where he would still be able to be a part of the conversation, but the Brothers MacAllister had formed a tight perimeter. Between two of the men, he could finally see his friend's face.

The change had been sudden, swift and complete. The lucidity he had seen just moments before in Schooner's eyes was nowhere to be found, for Schooner Moore was nowhere to be found. Covering the clarity of his sapphire eyes was now a mask, propelling Henry into a moment of déjà vu as he watched the ghost of a boy he had once known who lived behind masks.

Moore To Lose

Julie A. Richman

Table of Contents

Part One Mia 281
Chapter One 283
Chapter Two 287
Chapter Three 289
Chapter Four 293
Chapter Five 295
Chapter Six 299
Chapter Seven 302
Chapter Eight 307
Chapter Nine 310
Chapter Ten 313
Chapter Eleven 316
Chapter Twelve 321
Chapter Thirteen 323
Chapter Fourteen 326
Chapter Fifteen 332
Chapter Sixteen 337
Chapter Seventeen 344
Chapter Eighteen 347
Chapter Nineteen 352
Chapter Twenty 355
Chapter Twenty-One 362
Chapter Twenty-Two 366
Chapter Twenty-Three 369
Chapter Twenty-Four 374
Chapter Twenty-Five 381
Chapter Twenty-Six 383
Chapter Twenty-Seven 391
Chapter Twenty-Eight 394
Chapter Twenty-Nine 403
Chapter Thirty 404
Chapter Thirty-One 406
Chapter Thirty-Two 410
Chapter Thirty-Three 414
Chapter Thirty-Four 421
Chapter Thirty-Five 425

Chapter Thirty-Six 427
Chapter Thirty-Seven 432
Chapter Thirty-Eight 434
Chapter Thirty-Nine 439
Chapter Forty 442
Chapter Forty-One 445
Chapter Forty-Two 448
Chapter Forty-Three 450
Chapter Forty-Four 458
Chapter Forty-Five 460
Part Two Schooner 465
Chapter One 467
Chapter Two 470
Chapter Three 476
Chapter Four 480
Chapter Five 484
Chapter Six 488
Chapter Seven 492
Chapter Eight 495
Part Three Schooner & Mia 499
Chapter One 501
Chapter Two 504
Chapter Three 506
Chapter Four 510
Bonus Chapter 512

Part One
Mia

Chapter One

Now …

Schooner Moore ran the towel over his right shoulder and down his rock-hard quadriceps, continuing along a well-defined forearm, up an equally impressive bicep and across his muscular chest. He then resumed the same process on the other side. As the owner of a formidable chain of health club/entertainment complexes, it was very clear that Schooner took impeccable care of his body and had been a lifelong athlete. The tall Californian looked more like an actor or a model than a businessman.

Continuing down to his superbly defined abs, Schooner had to laugh to himself that back in February he had wondered if forty-three was still hot. As he reached down to dry his thickening cock and thought of Mia sleeping in the bedroom down the hall, he ironically felt hotter and more powerful than he'd ever felt in his twenties or thirties, and more alive as one of eight million people in New York City, than he had as one of the most successful entrepreneurs in Orange County.

Grabbing another towel and running it through his thick, dirty blonde hair, it occurred to him that maybe he should start bringing a pair of gym shorts into the bathroom with him. Mia's assistant, Seth, had a key to their apartment and let himself in every morning. Not that Seth minded seeing Schooner in a towel.

As he exited the bathroom, the delicious smell of bacon cooking permeated the air. Schooner realized Seth must have already arrived and started breakfast for himself and Mia. Entering the bedroom, he hoped to get a few minutes of snuggling time with Mia before Seth brought breakfast into her. Standing in the doorway, he looked at the rumpled sheets. The empty bed. *I am going to kill her*, he thought.

With long legged strides, he was standing at the breakfast bar, arms crossed over his bare chest. Schooner was seething.

Mia looked up from the stove, giving him her devil grin. "I am so jonesing for bacon this morning."

"What do the words 'bed rest' mean to you, Mia?"

"Umm, that roughly translates to bored shitless." She was still smiling at him.

Schooner glared at her, his eyes, the ice blue of perfect sapphires, bored into her and she was getting turned on by his anger — giving Mia good enough reason to fuck with him a little more.

"Would you like one egg or two?" she asked, holding the spatula like a game show hostess from "The Price is Right."

With his hands now on the breakfast bar, he leaned his weight forward, his voice little more than a whisper. "I am not amused, Ms. Silver. Turn off that damn stove now."

Mia smiled, most amused by the fact that she was a horny pregnant woman.

They both turned their heads at the sound of keys in the door.

Seth Shapiro walked through the door, his expressive eyes delighted at seeing a towel wrapped, half-naked Schooner Moore. "Damn, what a fine sight," was written all over his face. It took Seth a moment to process that Mia was standing there — cooking breakfast — and Schooner was livid (and gorgeous).

"BBC, what are you doing out of bed?" Seth screamed at Mia, as he made his way toward her and plucked the spatula from her hand.

"It appears we have an NCBBC on our hands this morning."

Mia and Seth looked at Schooner for an explanation.

"A non-compliant BBC. Come on NCBBC, I'm taking you back to bed."

"Promises, promises," Mia muttered, as Schooner led her back to the bedroom, leaving Seth to make breakfast, muttering, "Bitch Be Crazy."

Putting pillows behind her back, Schooner shook his head. "What were you thinking? Gary made it very clear — total bed rest or he's putting you back in the hospital for the remainder of your pregnancy. Is that what you want?"

"Of course, that's not what I want, but come on, Schooner — it's me. Do I ever stop? I don't do well in the invalid role. I am going crazy."

Schooner ignored her. "So, what's your pain level today?"

Mia sighed deeply and looked Schooner in the eyes. He wasn't going to let her get away with anything. "About a six."

"How dizzy are you?" Gently rubbing her forearm, the ice blue of his sapphire eyes had melted forming clear blue pools into which Mia wanted to dive.

"Not much."

Schooner lay down next to Mia and pulled her head down on his chest. "I know this is hard for you, Baby Girl, I do. I really do. But we do not have all that long before Nathaniel is born to get you as healthy and as strong as we can get you. Best case scenario, Mia, is that we have eleven weeks to go. Once he gets here, you are not going to be wanting to deal with the headaches and the dizziness. You were a high-risk pregnancy prior to the accident."

Mia shuddered in Schooner's arms and he wrapped them around her tighter and kissed the top of her head. *No worries*, he thought, *she's lying in your arms*. Intellectually he knew that, but the lingering fear in his gut felt as real now as it had a month before when he didn't know what hospital she had been taken to or in what condition he would find her and their unborn son.

Standing curbside outside of his new Level 9 Health and Entertainment complex on its opening night and paralyzed with the fear that he would lose everything he loved most, Schooner admonished himself for once again failing at the promise he had made — the promise to take care of all those he loved, the promise he first made when he was eighteen years old, the promise to take care of Mia.

Not a person to remain incapacitated for long in any situation, Schooner gathered his thoughts and quickly found his friend and security expert, Charles Sloan, and the two men, along with Schooner's daughter, Holly, and Charles' wife, Gaby, headed to the hospital. Thank God, Charles and Gaby knew exactly where Mia had been taken.

Mia was conscious when he got there and being taken for a CT scan. Schooner was at her side as the gurney was being wheeled down the hall. "Baby Girl, I'm here. I'm with you. You're doing great." Mia didn't respond, her eyelids fluttering and closing.

"Mia, stay with us, I don't want you going to sleep. Do you understand what I'm saying?" Dr. Gary Cohen, usually very laid back in his approach with patients, was being very stern in his directives to Mia.

As they wheeled her into the CT Scan imaging room, Gary took Schooner aside. "Here's what we're doing. We need to take a look at Mia's brain and skull and assess what is going on there. That is of the utmost importance right now. The baby's well-being is contingent upon Mia's well-being. The fact that she is conscious is a great sign. Once we've determined what is going on with Mia, I'm going to do an ultrasound of the baby." He paused and Schooner nodded. "The good news is, the baby has a lot of cushioning. What we're going to be looking for is placental abruption or uterine rupture, but we need to check Mia head to toe first — and frankly it's her head that I'm most concerned about."

A month later and that was still the biggest concern. A fractured skull, moderate traumatic brain injury and ongoing headaches, dizziness and short-term memory issues.

All in all, Mia was one very lucky lady and Nathaniel appeared to have taken it all in stride. Gary and Schooner's major concern was Mia regaining her health prior to the baby's arrival, and with limited activity, lessening the chance of falling during a dizzy spell and causing harm to herself or the baby. Gary's goal was to get Mia as far along in her pregnancy as he could before having to deliver Nathaniel.

Mia looked up from Schooner's chest. "I have cabin fever, Schooner. I just want to run away."

Schooner stroked her hair and smiled down at her. "Try running away from me again and this time you won't get very far. I will track down your ass and hunt you down like a dog." He laughed, "It's not like the 80's anymore, Baby Girl, when if you wanted to disappear you could, and did, disappear. No internet, no cell phones. Those days are over."

Mia smiled. "I'd take you with me this time. I learned that lesson the hard way." And Schooner assumed she had.

"Now *you're* the Queen of Understatement, BBC." Seth commented on Mia's declaration about learning the hard way as he entered with her breakfast on a tray and sat down next to her on the bed.

Although Mia hadn't told Schooner many details of their years apart, he surmised that Seth Shapiro had always been there for Mia in both her brightest and darkest moments. Their love and bond was something to behold, and Schooner took comfort in knowing that in all the time he couldn't be there for her, the whole time she mistakenly thought he didn't love her, Mia had someone by her side who loved her deeply, understood her and knew when to reign her in when she was going off the rails. What Schooner didn't know was just how perceptive he was and that maybe *he* was the King of Understatement.

Chapter Two

Then ...

Tom Sheehan was loving life. Twenty-seven, MFA in creative writing completed, his Sci-Fi screenplay under consideration by two Hollywood studios, and an amazing teaching gig that had fortuitously landed in his lap. Most unfortunate for his old mentor, George Roy, who was convalescing from a massive heart attack and had to withdraw for both semesters from teaching his upper level year-long creative writing seminars – but very good luck for Tom Sheehan.

With his dark Irish good looks and the cultivated sensitivity of a poet, Tom's charm was working wonders on his students – 70% of whom were female. It was three weeks into the fall semester and he was already nailing two of them. At twenty-one, the two seniors, Sherri and Jacqueline, were old enough and certainly experienced enough to keep him very satisfied, but they were also young enough to look up to him like he was just short of a god. It was a heady feeling.

"We are almost done with the poetry unit." Almost all fifteen in his upper-level writing seminar cheered at the news. Students had submitted writing samples to Professor Roy, a particularly harsh critic, to gain entry to the coveted seminar, so Tom was working with a highly talented group comprised mostly of seniors, a few highly capable juniors and one sophomore transfer student. "Is everyone ready for short stories and screenplay adaptation?" Smiling out at the group, he could see that they were totally over and done with the poetry segment — never a favorite amongst students.

"I know poetry has not been everyone's favorite," he continued. "And I know you didn't appreciate some of the assignments." He smiled out at them as he effortlessly covered the front of the room in a slow, deliberate pace. "Especially the ones from the insect's and animal's point of view. But we have one more poetry assignment — the last poetry assignment, and it's due Monday. This will be the first assignment without character or theme constraints. This one is all you. And if you thought the others were difficult, they were nothing. For this assignment, you need to dig deep. Give me something so personal that you are embarrassed to look me in the face. If I get fluff, it *will* be reflected in your grade. I will pretty much be grading the poetry segment of the course on how you perform with this assignment."

He stopped his pacing and was looking down at the floor. Shoving his hands into his Docker's pockets, he slowly looked up and smiled at the fifteen. "Have a great weekend."

They started to shuffle out of the class, both Sherri and Jacqueline packing their backpacks slowly. His little transfer student made her way from the back of the classroom. This one was an enigma. She seemed to be hiding behind a mane of unruly curls and dark sunglasses that never came off.

"You going to give me something good with this assignment, Mia?"

She smiled. "I don't know about that. As I'm sure you've noticed, my poetry pretty much sucks. I promise my prose is significantly more adept."

"Poetry is a tough medium, even for a lot of very prolific writers." As he packed up his desk, he hoped Sherri and Jacqueline would leave. He continued talking to Mia, "Just try and be as raw as you can with this last assignment. There are no rules attached to this one." Her face belied little and he wondered what was going on behind those dark shades.

Mia snickered. It appeared to Tom that she wanted to say something, but checked herself and left him with, "Have a good one."

Tom was alone in the classroom – his stall tactic had yielded the results he wanted. As he turned off the light and locked the door, he wondered why Mia Silver was hiding behind dark sunglasses. Was it to appear cool and affected? Maybe, but he didn't think so. It felt like she was putting up her force field – something no human could penetrate.

He shrugged into his brown corduroy blazer as he exited the building. The crisp afternoon air cooled his cheeks as the late afternoon sun illuminated the campus, bathing it in a golden glow with its side lit beauty. There was nothing like fall in the northeast.

Chapter Three

That same side lit golden light was bathing the park early Saturday morning, and although the air still held the chill of the Indian summer night, Tom was bathed in sweat. Slowing down from his run, he began his cool down. It was the first time he really noticed the leaves and decided it was going to be a brilliant autumn. The yellow leaves popped against the flawless blue of the sky. Tom breathed the air in deeply and closed his eyes for a moment as he walked. Running allowed him to get lost in his own head, work out plot elements for his screenplays, visualize the nuances of his character's personalities and just dump all the shit that was bothering him.

He knew it was her by the unruly mane cascading over her shoulders. She was on her knees, bent over a camera on a low tripod with its legs splayed flat to the ground. Her camera lens hovered over a tangle of wildflowers – blooming goldenrod and purple asters, the last vestiges of fall flora. He quietly approached, not to disturb or alarm her. Tom found himself smiling as he noted the worn Levi's, hiking boots and open hoodie sweatshirt. It was quite the juxtaposition to her classmates and their designer everything, with labels prominently displayed.

It was interesting to watch her focus and intensity as she manipulated the lens, testing out different focal points. There seemed to be almost a surgical precision to the minute adjustments she made and her concentration was absolute.

Tom shifted his weight and some leaves crunched under his back foot. Mia shot up from her position in a single fluid motion, her eyes wide and flashing fear, her autonomic nervous system snapping into fight or flight mode.

"Whoa, sorry I scared you," Tom apologized. She looked like the proverbial deer caught in headlights. He could see the fear in her big green eyes and in the stiffness of her spine and shoulders. He felt terrible for scaring her.

It took Mia a minute to realize that she was not in danger, and he could see that as he watched her process the situation. He felt just awful for scaring her. He could see how visceral her response was – the rosiness from the cool morning air drained from her face.

"I'm really, really sorry, Mia," he apologized again. "I saw you here and wanted to say hi. I was trying not to disturb you while you were working."

Mia nodded and Tom could tell that she was not able to speak yet – or at least not without her voice cracking. He had an overwhelming urge to hug her and reassure her that she was safe, but his gut told him it was best not to make a move toward her.

"Hey, no sunglasses." He needed to get her to relax.

Mia smiled and nodded. "Would make it really hard to see through the viewfinder. I just got contacts," she explained, "and my eyes are really light sensitive. I'm really not trying to be a jerk in your class."

That admission elicited a smile. So that was the mystery behind those sunglasses and the reason for hiding those striking green eyes. "I didn't think you were being a jerk."

Mia nodded. "Want to see what I'm taking pictures of?"

Tom got to his knees in the dew damp grass and looked through the viewfinder of her camera. "Wow." He had not expected the amount and clarity of up-close detail or how large every minute element of the flowers appeared.

"I'm shooting with a macro lens and that allows me to get really close to the subject." Mia sat cross legged next to Tom while he continued to check out the colorful new world in the viewfinder. "On the end of the lens, I have two diopters stacked and they magnify everything, which is why you are able to see the amount of detail in the flowers. Pretty cool, huh?"

Tom looked up at Mia. "Very cool," and he was not just referring to the subject at the other end of her lens. He cocked his head to the side. "You're only a sophomore?"

Mia smiled and nodded. She looked up at the sky, squinting. "Looks like the good light is gone." She started to break down her equipment – removing the camera from the tripod, the glass diopters from the end of the lens – and loaded them into her backpack.

"There's a great little bakery on the edge of the park. Join me for coffee?" Tom didn't have anything (or anyone) to do until noon and Mia Silver seemed sweet, shy and intriguing.

Thirty minutes into their coffee, Tom changed his assessment – Mia Silver was not shy, she was very funny – bordering on bodacious, still sweet, but with a big bite of spice and very intriguing. And those eyes – damn. Three weeks in his class and this was the first time he was seeing those expressive green pools. And she was cool. He could definitely see being friends with her.

"So, you were in California last year? What was that like?"

"It was like being in a Heinlein novel." Mia played with her muffin.

"I don't know if I grok."

Mia looked up and smiled at Tom and their *Stranger in a Strange Land*[1] banter. "Okay well, it started at freshman orientation."

He saw a flash of something in her eyes. Pain, maybe?

But she continued, "I was the only freshman girl in jeans. Literally, the only one."

Tom looked at her, confused. "What was it, a nudist school?" he laughed. "What were they wearing?"

"Dresses," Mia whispered, as if it were a nasty word not to be mentioned in public, her eyes wide, and then a devilish grin overtook her face.

The sip of coffee that had just passed through his lips was spit onto the table in front of him as he began to laugh.

Mia laughed even harder at his reaction.

"Dresses? Seriously? I don't think I've ever seen a dress on this campus."

"I definitely don't own one."

"So, you didn't fit in? Certainly, you had some friends?" What was going on with this girl? He was interested to find out.

Mia smiled. "Yeah, I had some great friends. I didn't know I would miss them so much."

Definite pain in this one's eyes. Tom wondered why she had come back east. There was a story there. Part of him wanted to peel back the layers on this girl, find out what made her tick, but with Sherri and Jacqueline, he already had his hands full.

"I expect a great poem from you on Monday." He changed the subject on her.

"Don't hold your breath. My poetry sucks. You've seen it."

"Tell me, what makes writing great?" he challenged.

Without missing a beat, "It has to be honest."

Tom smiled. "Bingo!" Okay, even more impressed, he thought. He had asked that question a week ago in another senior level writing seminar and not one of the students knew that simple, yet essential answer. "Just be honest. Do whatever you need to do to get there. Smoke a joint, drink some beers, run, shoot photos – but get to an honest, raw place and give me one badass poem on Monday."

Mia was looking at him intently. Her eyes teared up. She grabbed a napkin and dabbed at them. "Freaking contacts," she muttered.

Contacts, my ass, thought Tom.

And with that she stood and grabbed her backpack. "Hey, thanks for the coffee and muffin."

"Anytime," he smiled.

And she was gone.

Tom sat back in his chair wondering what the hell was going on with that girl. She was witty and bright, but there was something going on there and he could not put his finger on it. Maybe it would come out in her writing during the semester, because if she was in pain, she needed to use that. She needed to take that pain and let it serve as the cornerstone of her creativity.

Tom Sheehan left the bakery at 9:30 A.M. on Saturday morning with the gut feeling that the girl in the back of his writing seminar with the dark sunglasses might just be the surprise talent of the semester.

[1] Robert A. Heinlein, Stranger in a Strange Land, (New York, NY, Putnam Publishing Group 1961)

Chapter Four

Tom sat down in the brown faux leather recliner in his furnished apartment. Coltrane filled in the silence and with an ice cold LaBatt Ale in one hand, he started to go through the class' last poetry assignment. There were definitely a few not making eye contact with him today, and he hoped that meant they had bared their souls in the assignment. Jacqueline, usually fairly brazen, seemed almost shy, while Sherri, on the other hand, spent the class looking at him like she was undressing him. Mia, as usual, took her seat at the back of the room, sunglasses back in place.

An hour later, Tom was mostly unimpressed. Why did they all feel the need to rhyme? Jacqueline's assignment was next in the stack and two stanzas into her three-typed page ode, Tom didn't know whether to blush or get a ticket for a Greyhound bus and high tail it out of town. Jacqueline had clearly taken their casual tryst as something more important than it was, and as was typical with an ode, elaborately glorified both the event and the person. And in this case, the person was Tom. "Oh crap," he thought, "I need to figure out a way out of this one." Jacqueline clearly did not understand casual.

Sherri's assignment, on the other hand, was so self-absorbed that Tom had to laugh. He opened another beer, and sat down with the assignment of one of the guys in the class. Finally, promise – a lot of self-loathing and angst – but at least promise. Tom finally gave out his first "A" to Rob Ryan.

Next up, Miss Mia Silver. Tom looked down at the page and groaned out loud. *Damn it, Mia,* he thought. He really had high hopes for her to turn in something substantive and there were like five lines on the page. He shook his head, feeling overwhelming disappointment and thinking, "C'mon Mia, I know you have more in you."

He started to read. Sky Diving Blues. Okay, good title. Sky, she starts high. Diving, she's descending. Blues, she's hit bottom. Okay, good start. C'mon Mia, surprise me.

Sky Diving Blues
Flying high
a flirtation with the sun

The slow descent
to a burned Rome
The neighborhood hasn't changed

Tom felt like he'd been punched in the gut. He put his beer down and read it again. Holy shit. She did it. Eighteen words in the body of the poem. Three words in the title. Twenty-one words. Twenty-one words and she gave it all. She put it all out there. He wasn't wrong. He knew she had it in her. He read it again. She understood raw. It was all there. It was succinct. It cut to the heart of it. No fluff. Mia Silver got to the net/net in twenty-one words.

Oddly proud of his youngest student, Tom wondered if the neighborhood that hadn't changed was her college campus in California. A burned Rome. Destruction. Devastation. Maybe a Nero fiddling – someone dancing over the ashes of her smoldering city, of her heartache. A flirtation with the sun. Someone who shone brightly for her, someone she held up in exalted esteem. Damn, she cut to the heart of it with a few words and the Rome burning imagery. Beautiful. Her cohorts were giving pages and pages of rhyming dreck – pure shit and in twenty-one words she nailed it.

When he finished the stack of papers he pulled out Rob Ryan's and Mia Silver's poems again and reread them. These were his two – the conflict was there within them. He could work with that. He'd teach them how to take that pain and use it as the fuel in creating. Two out of fifteen. Not bad. He couldn't wait to get his hands on Rob and Mia and mentor them the way George and others had mentored him.

Tom Sheehan was loving life.

Chapter Five

Mia took her seat at the back of the classroom. It gave her a great vantage point to observe her classmates and check them out. She loved observing people and listening and definitely knew more about them than they knew about her. Not that anybody in the writing seminar had made any real effort to get to know her, but she could tell a lot about them through her observations.

Tom Sheehan entered the classroom and put a stack of papers down on the desk at the front of the room. Mia was nervous about getting her poem back. She hoped he didn't hate it. Hanging out with him on Saturday had been really fun – he was very cool, although a little intimidating, and she felt like a kid around him. Mia wondered if she would ever feel as sophisticated as some of the other girls in the class. They seemed so sure of themselves around him. Mia felt self-conscious.

He started to walk around the room, returning the assignments by slapping them on people's desks, face down. *Uh-oh, he does not appear to be happy,* was her initial thought. When he got to her desk in the back, he smiled at her and gently laid the paper down. A look passed between them, but Mia wasn't quite sure what he was trying to relay. It made her uncomfortable and she was pissed that she hadn't worn sunglasses. She wanted to hide. And he was so damn cute. Not smart to have a prof crush on a twenty-seven-year-old single guy. Her prof crush on Rick Stevens was safe – he was older and married and definitely would not sleep with his students. Tom Sheehan, on the other hand, was a player. Smart, sexy, witty – but definitely a player.

Mia took a deep breath and turned over the paper. She let out a little surprised "Huh" sound. Tom had given her an A+ and written on the paper was, "I'm so proud of you." Mia looked up and Tom was looking at her, gauging her reaction. She beamed at him, surprised. His face remained neutral, but his eyes were sparkling. Mia smiled at him, a full devil grin and he returned her smile briefly. She looked back down at her paper, feeling very proud.

She read over her poem and could feel the sting at the back of her eyes. *Did you ever really love me, Schooner? Why the elaborate ruse? Flying high, a flirtation with the sun.* She was Icarus. He was the sun. And that brief flirtation melted her wings. Who was she kidding? Her wings were the least of the damage. He had her heart. And she didn't know if she'd ever get it back. She hated him for the betrayal and missed him and loved him and hated him. He and CJ probably had gotten a good laugh over it. Why had he betrayed her like that? She could feel her throat closing up.

Tom was at the front of the class talking and she had not heard a word he had said. She focused in. Holy shit, he was ripping the class a new one, embarrassed for them that they would turn in what they turned in. Wow – only two people got a passing grade on the assignment. Was he serious? She wondered who the other person was with the passing grade.

Tom sat on the edge of his desk. "What makes writing great?"

Mia smiled to herself, but did not raise her hand. Clearly, he was trying to see if anyone else in the class could answer.

Jacqueline's hand was the first up, "Strong subject matter."

Tom nodded his head, "Okay. What else?"

Chrissie raised her hand, "Descriptive writing. I mean, like heavy use of descriptions and imagery."

Tom nodded again and moved on. He pointed a finger at Matt, a thin, geeky kid. "Uh, the ability to get your point across clearly."

Tom didn't even acknowledge Matt. "Mia, what makes writing great?"

Mia locked eyes with Tom. "Honesty. Writing needs to be honest."

"Thank you. Writing needs to be honest to be great," he sighed, punctuating each word while pacing to the front of the room. "How many of you feel that your work, the assignment that you just turned in, came from a place of complete honesty?"

Hands shot up like flags in a stiff breeze. Mia gingerly raised hers to half-staff.

Tom shook his head. "Seriously? You really think your writing was honest? Was it gut wrenching to write those words? Was it hard to see the paper in front of you through your tears? Did you want to throw your guts up writing it?"

Mia could feel her eyes getting watery. Fuck, I wish I was wearing my sunglasses, she stressed. She couldn't see the paper in front of her while she was writing Sky Diving Blues. He was her sun, her light. And to betray her with that shallow, mean bitch? Expose her darkest secrets and pain. And to her? *Why, Schooner?* Actually, she didn't even want to know why. Just the fact that he did it – betrayed her, broke their trust, sent her hurtling from that exalted place he had taken her to depths so painful. Yes, writing that poem had made her sick to her stomach.

Mia looked down at her desk. *I hate you, Schooner Moore. I hate you so fucking much. If you were standing in front of me right now, I would pummel my fists into your chest. I would take my nails and scratch that pretty face of yours to ribbons. So why do I still just want you to hold me, you cruel mother fucking bastard? I want you to hold me and tell me it was all a mistake, Baby Girl. But it wasn't because you fucking betrayed me. How could you love me and betray me? You couldn't. So, you didn't love me. You never loved me. Was it all a big fucking joke to you and that witch?* I want you out of my head. I want you out of my heart. Why did I ever meet you?

Mia heard Tom saying her name. She and Rob Ryan were the only two that did not have to redo the assignment. She knew she needed to concentrate on what Tom was saying, stay there in the present, in the class, and not go to the place she had just disappeared to for the last few minutes. Mia groaned inwardly as Tom asked Rob to get up in front of the class to read his poem. Fuck that means I'm next, she cringed. Her stomach was already in knots from thinking about Schooner. Ick, I just want to go throw up, Mia could feel the bile rising. And Tom was calling her name. Thank God it's a short poem, this will be over quickly, was all she could think.

Mia shuffled to the front of the classroom, head down so that she could hide behind her veil of hair. Her eyes met Tom's as she reached a spot next to his desk. His dark eyes were reassuring and oddly comforting. With an almost imperceptible movement, he gave her a slight nod and her lips curled up in a brief semi-smile. "Showtime," she said in her head.

Sky Diving Blues
Flying high
a flirtation with the sun
The slow descent
to a burned Rome
The neighborhood hasn't changed

She started toward her seat.

"Mia, stay up here for a second."

Inward groan. Great. Tom's hand was on her shoulder. His touch felt good, oddly comforting.

"The body of that poem was eighteen words. Twenty-one with the title. Did it rhyme?" The class collectively shook their head no. "Right. It didn't rhyme. It didn't go on for pages. Twenty-one words that conveyed very clear emotion and strong imagery. The emotion was honest and raw. That is the level at which I expect everyone in this class to be operating." He tapped Mia's shoulder, indicating that she could return to her seat.

Heading to her seat at the back of the class, Mia longed to be sitting on the floor of her dorm room, her back leaning up against the bed, smoking her bong. Unfortunately, the dorm room she longed for was 3,000 miles away. She felt exiled from what she now understood was her home. Her true home. The place her heart resided. She missed them all so much – Rosie, Henry, Caroline, her dorm mates. She missed him. And she wanted him to miss her – but she knew that was unlikely, since he'd always been CJ's. *Miss me Schooner. Even just a little. Miss me. How could you not?*

Mia wondered when she was going to stop feeling like shit.

Chapter Six

When Tom found her in another section of the park the next Saturday, Mia was shooting long exposures of a stream. The photos would have a soft ethereal quality due to the length of the exposures, with soft white water flowing over the shiny rocks. Mia explained it to Tom, who was having a hard time visualizing it. "I'll bring prints to class, so that you can see what I'm talking about," she promised.

Entering the little coffee shop, Mia realized that Tom's attention made her feel good – feel special. She was also very aware that she was just using his attention as a way to allay some of the pain of losing Schooner. She needed to feel special. And in an odd way she was competing with the Jacqueline's and Sherri's of the class – the girls who turned heads and used their sexuality to get exactly what they wanted – all the time. On some level, Mia knew that she was making them her CJ's. And if Tom liked her because she was smart, funny, a talented writer – then that was her fuck you to all of them – fucking Schooner included. And Mia was itching to give them all the proverbial finger.

"So, I have something I want to talk to you about." Tom looked at Mia over his coffee, taking on a very serious, authoritative tone. "You and Rob Ryan are really at a different level than the rest of the class."

Mia smiled, she liked where this conversation was going.

"I'd really like to work with the two of you separately from the class. I'm going to leave the choice up to each of you as to whether you still want to attend the class for the rest of this semester, and next, in addition to working with you two separately or just work totally independently of the class."

Mia could feel the excitement welling up inside. "So, Rob and I will just work with you alone? Or individually? What are you thinking?"

"I'd like to work with the two of you together. We'll figure out a time that works with everyone's schedule. This way you two still have the benefit of bouncing off each other and doing critical reviews of one another's work. I'm probably also going to have you team up and write together – things like small screenplays."

Mia sat back, devil smile slowly commandeering her face. "Seriously?"

Tom laughed, his eyes coming alive at Mia's response. "Yeah, seriously. Some of my profs did this with me and some other students. It really accelerates your growth because it becomes an intensive workshop. If I keep the both of you just in the class, you won't get out of it what you could and I don't want to see that happen. I have a year to work with the two of you and I want to make the most of that year."

Mia ran her hand through her hair. "Wow. Thank you. Does Rob know?"

Tom shook his head, a shock of unruly black hair cascading down his forehead like some bad boy rocker. Don't do that, Mia thought to herself. You look like a hot bad boy. A year with this man ... holy crap. "He should be here in about twenty minutes. What are you smiling at?"

Probably would not be appropriate to say *your bad boy hotness* or *this is the first time I've been horny in like five months*, or *I'm just wondering if fucking you would help me forget him and make this pain go away*, so she just shook her head. "This is really cool."

Rob joined them and Tom outlined his plans. They would meet Tuesday and Thursday evenings from 7 P.M. – 9 P.M. It was Mia's first time talking with Rob, a scruffy senior from a small town in upstate New York. Social skills weren't his forte, and Mia wondered how this was going to work out with her and Rob working together. Knowing one of her strengths was drawing people out, and misfits had always been both her specialty and her comfort zone, Mia knew she'd figure out what made him tick. Maybe he was just shy, an affliction from which she rarely suffered.

By the time they'd finished their meeting, Rob and Mia had their first project from Tom. They had to take any short story and convert it into a screenplay. Their deadline was a week from Tuesday, and Rob and Mia had a date for Sunday afternoon to at least pick the story they would adapt.

The three left the coffee shop together. Rob heading downtown to his apartment and Mia heading back to campus and to the darkroom to develop the film she'd just shot.

Tom put a hand on Mia's shoulder, "You good with this?"

Good? More like thrilled, she thought. Scared. Scared of so many things – that maybe I'm not as good a writer as you think. That I'm afraid I'm going to develop a crazy-assed crush on you. That I want you to pay more attention to me than those other girls because I feel like such shit about myself after my last boyfriend – was he even a boyfriend? – after the last guy who fucked me over for sport, fucked with my head big time.

Mia gave Tom a bright smile, "Why wouldn't I be okay with it? It's a great opportunity. Working with Rob may take some doing – he's not exactly, umm, forthcoming."

Tom gave Mia's shoulder a squeeze. "Oh please, with your personality, you'll draw him out of his shell in no time. I think he's going to end up being pretty interesting."

This semester just got a whole lot more interesting, Mia smiled inwardly. She could smell trouble on the horizon and she was ready to wholeheartedly embrace it, immerse herself in it and just let the shit roll.

Chapter Seven

Mia met Rob at the pub on campus Sunday afternoon to discuss their joint writing assignment. Having never written in tandem before, she was not quite sure what to expect, and writing as a team with a total stranger was going to be an entirely new challenge. Rob Ryan had out of control light brown hair and a beard that was way overgrown. He needed to lose about 25 pounds and probably shower more than he typically did. The one feature that stood out was his deep blue eyes. They were the color of unwashed denim and very observant.

Rob ordered a pitcher of beer and Mia hoped that would loosen him up. She didn't want to have to work hard at making him talk. Rob poured Mia a glass from the sweaty pitcher.

Mia held up her glass. "To the writing team of Silver and Ryan." They clinked glasses.

"It's Ryan and Silver." His smile was kind of cute, what she could see of it underneath that beard. But, ugh, that beard – all Mia could think was, *he is never going to get a girlfriend with that thing all over his face.*

"Yeah, yeah, yeah." Mia retorted, tossing back a healthy swig of her beer, "We'll see about that."

"So, how many of the girls in the class do you think he's nailing?"

Mia practically spit out her beer, she certainly did not expect this from Rob. Laughing, she leaned in conspiratorially, "I'd bet Sherri and Jacqueline."

"No doubt, those two are like bitches in heat," Rob concurred. "That man gets a lot of pussy."

Rob Ryan just might be fun. "You think he's a player?"

"Oh definitely," Rob shook his head, "the man has great patented moves."

Mia leveled a devil smile at Rob. "You know, we should just go to class to see what happens and watch those bitches take each other down trying to get his attention."

Rob laughed, "I like you. You're kind of evil."

"Just part of my charm."

Rob poured them another round from the perspiring pitcher. Mia could feel the beer coursing through her veins, loosening her tension. "So, what's your story, Mia? You clearly got the shit slapped out of you, based on your poem."

Mia pulled over the empty chair next to her and put her hiking-boot clad feet up. Three beers in her almost empty stomach and she hadn't talked to anyone about it. Looking deep into Rob's eyes, Mia nodded. "I did. I got the shit kicked out of me."

"Bad break-up?" His gaze was intense.

Mia laughed, "I guess. We didn't ever actually break up. I just left."

Rob's brows knit together in confusion. "So, let me get this straight. You didn't break up with him. He didn't break up with you. You just left?"

"Pretty much." Mia poured herself a fourth beer and signaled to the waitress for another pitcher.

"Did he know why?"

"He's a bright boy. He'll figure it out." Mia started to play with her napkin. Talking about herself was uncomfortable.

"Oh man, that is harsh, girl." Rob sat back in his chair surveying Mia with an odd look.

"How so?" She wanted sympathy, not made out to be the evil bitch. CJ was the evil bitch. Not her.

"The poor bastard doesn't know why you left him."

"He and his girlfriend will figure it out." Mia stared defiantly into Rob's eyes, her tone dripping with rancor.

"I thought you were his girlfriend?" Rob was clearly puzzled and Mia wasn't doing much to help the pieces fit.

She looked down. "Yeah, so did I." Damn, it hurt to talk about this stuff. "So, where's all the angst in your writing coming from?"

"No. No. No. We'll get to me later. We're going to need another whole pitcher for that. Back to you."

"Rob, I'm really not that interesting." Mia was giving him her 'Don't fuck with me' face.

"Ha!" he laughed. "Au contraire, little girl – you are very interesting." He shook his head, still laughing. "How many girls would walk into a small writing seminar, sit in the back, wear dark sunglasses and quietly observe everyone."

"Sounds like you've been observing me." Mia was shocked and a little excited by his voyeuristic admission.

He nodded his head.

Why the hell was Rob Ryan been so interested in me? Mia wondered. Maybe he was like her in that he observed everyone in his classes and probably knew more about them from those observations than all of their other classmates combined. It was a writer thing, this observing.

"So, you bailed without talking to the guy?" Rob was clearly enjoying keeping Mia on the hot seat.

"There was nothing to say." Mia crossed her arms over her chest.

"How do you know if you didn't talk to him? You might not have had anything to say – but I'll bet he did. So how did you two leave it?"

Mia could feel his hand sliding down hers until it was only their fingertips touching as he descended the dorm's steps. She could feel the pressure from his touch even after their fingertips had broken contact. Her mind's eye held the image of Schooner turning around, that beautiful smile gracing his face as he yelled, "Hey, those pizzas and bagels better be as good as you've been bragging about" before disappearing into the dusk. How odd that those were his last words to her. And now they were 3,000 miles apart and no longer a part of one another's lives. The pain was searing.

Realizing that Rob was staring at her, as she tried to make the tears in her eyes evaporate, Mia grabbed for her beer.

Neither spoke for a long while and Rob's voice was very soft when he finally broke the silence. "I'm a few years older than you, so here's a piece of friendly advice. Call the guy. Get some closure. Because if you don't – it will fuck with you. It will fuck you up bad. If you really want to move past this, past him, get the closure you need."

Mia nodded at Rob as traitorous tears streamed from her eyes. She knew he was right, even if it was just to yell at Schooner and tell him what a dick she thought he was, while secretly praying he would somehow make it right.

As she wiped her eyes, she forced a smile. "Okay, now it's my turn to torture you."

"Hold that thought," he raised his hand to flag down the waitress for another pitcher.

Mia knew she was fucked up because her fingertips were numb. A physiological sign of her drunkenness and kind of an apropos thing she thought … numb fingertips – the last place on her body he had touched. Numb heart – the place in her body from which she wished she could extricate his touch. So, why was he holding on so steadfastly, she wondered. Why was she letting him?

Mia teetered off to the bathroom thinking about what Rob had said. Call him. Call Schooner. Get closure. As she washed her face and peered into the cracked and crackled mirror above the sink, she wondered if she could do it, if she could make that call now, after everything that had gone down with her leaving and not returning to school. She hadn't even considered picking up the phone to confront him – not until now.

Rob had refilled her glass and she sat down and lifted it for a long swig.

"You have really great eyes." Mia was more than a little drunk and now feeling confident because she knew she was going to call Schooner. She was going to get answers – get the truth from him – finally. And that truth would set her free to move on with her life.

"So I've been told."

"Okay, how about some friendly advice from a girl," she didn't wait for his response. "The hair has got to go. Seriously, you look like you've been living under a bridge. You're scary. The facial hair is totally out of control. I'm all for beards, I totally think Springsteen's circa '75 Born to Run bearded look was his best look, but no chick is going to kiss you with that thing all over your face. And forget going down on a chick and then trying to kiss her with that. Ugh. No!"

Rob's denim blue eyes flashed both shock and amusement at Mia's drunken diatribe.

"So, here's the scoop," she continued. "I want to cut your hair. Something cute and layered and a little longish. You can keep the beard if you must, but only about ten percent of it."

"You going to get on my weight while you're at it?" He was totally serious and Mia could not tell if he was amused or pissed off.

"Only if you want to. You've got that teddy bear thing going on and with your hair and beard cleaned up, girls won't mind it."

"You're not cutting my hair."

Mia's devil smile was at full-tilt. "Oh, yes I am."

"No fucking way, Mia, am I ever letting you near me with a pair of scissors."

"Afraid I'll carve my initials into your neck?"

Rob let out a huge belly laugh. "Oh man, you are a totally sick chick – I like it."

Later in the conversation, with continued prompting and probing by Mia, Rob finally confided his story. It wasn't pretty and the genesis of the angst in his writing immediately became very clear. Mia listened intently as Rob unburdened himself with details of his father's drunken abusiveness and the betrayal caused by his mother's departure when he was eleven, leaving Rob as the protector to his nine year-old sister as they dealt with and endured the aftermath.

Mia wanted to hug the scruffy teddy bear sitting across from her. When he was done, she wiped away the tears from her eyes. “Well, if that story doesn’t get you laid …” and they both sat back and laughed.

With the cathartic purging behind them and a new trust and respect built, Mia and Rob were now ready to move on with their writing partnership.

“Here’s what I think,” Mia began, “Tom is totally going to expect the two of us to give him something really heavy based on what we’ve already turned in. Let’s totally fuck with him and write the screenplay for a comedy – adapt a humorous short story.”

Mia could see Rob’s head already formulating ideas as his brain searched its mental files for a comedy to adapt. He was totally onboard with it.

When she left the campus pub to return to her dorm that evening, Mia felt happy. She had a new friend and a sneaking suspicion that they would become very good buds.

Fueled with the drunken confidence of more than a few beers, Mia Silver was going to take matters into her own hands and call Schooner Moore and confront him for telling CJ MacAllister of her attack and then she was going to rip him a new asshole.

Chapter Eight

Mia staggered back to her dorm room, totally obliterated and just hoping she'd make it back quickly enough to get to the bathroom to pee. "I'm shitfaced," she giggled aloud to no one. Although the cool fall air revived her and she breathed in deeply as she walked, there was no way she was going to be sober for hours.

I'm going to drunk dial Schooner. Find out why the fuck he told her everything. Find out why he felt I was an "obligation he had to fulfill." He could've just helped me out the first night at the hospital and then left me the fuck alone. I didn't need to be his little charity case (CJ told her those were his exact words). And to break my confidence with her. Fuck you, Schooner. She knew. She fucking knew. You promised me you wouldn't tell her. But then again you promised me a lot of things. Which mask were you wearing when you pretended to be in love with me? The let's fuck over Mia for sport mask? Tonight you're going to answer me so I don't have to keep carrying around all this pain. This pain and misery. Because yes, I am fucking miserable, Schooner. I'm heartbroken and I'm miserable. I believed you. I believed every word. I believed every time you stared into my eyes. I believed every time you called me Baby Girl that I was your Baby Girl. I believed I was your Baby Girl, Schooner, not an obligation to fulfill.

Mia practically ran through the lobby of her dorm, every step toward the bathroom felt like a million miles (and she didn't want anyone to see her tear stained face or ask her if she was okay, because no, she was not okay, and if she stopped to have to explain it, she would definitely pee in her pants). Reaching the bathroom and emitting a loud groan, she attempted to manipulate the button fly on her Levi 501's with her numb and fat-feeling drunk fingers. The price of having her ass look good was not worth it at the moment, she decided. And when she finally got them open and her jeans down, she had the confidence that she could now do anything – including calling Schooner.

Mia entered her room and closed the door behind her. She had a single room, for which she was very thankful. In her suite, there were three other girls and they shared a common area and a bathroom.

Sitting cross legged in the center of her bed, Mia looked at the phone in her lap. She could feel her stomach knotting and her confidence wavering. *No, no, no – don't be a wuss*, she told herself and started dialing the number to the campus' main switchboard. She asked for his dorm and they transferred her. She didn't even recognize her own voice when she asked for "Schooner Moore." She took a deep breath, the moment of truth was here, finally. "Showtime," she whispered.

One ring. Two rings. C'mon, Schooner, answer. Three rings.

"Hello." It was Beau.

"Hi, is Schooner there?" She wondered if he recognized her voice. Her accent was kind of a dead giveaway.

"No. He's not here."

Still the same jerk as ever, Mia thought. "Do you know when he'll be back?"

"Well, he and CJ just left, so he probably won't be back until morning."

Wham to the solar plexus. Why did it still hurt so badly? Feel so fresh. Breathe. Take in air. "Okay." Her voice was little more than a croak.

"Can I take a message?"

"No. No message. Thanks." And she hung up the phone.

Mia just stared at the phone in her lap. The pain searing though her heart was as profound as it had been on her last morning in California. Her emotions were at a pitch so severe as the walls inched toward her, their speed increasing, ready to cave in on her, as bile rose from the hurt in her gut, blistering her esophagus. She made it as far as the trash can under her desk before she was sick, and there she stayed, under her desk, knees drawn to her chest.

So, it was true. He was with CJ. He'd always been with CJ. The tears flowed as she relived the memories, combing through all their moments together, trying to figure out how she'd missed out on his deception. He had warned her he was good at acting. Why hadn't she seen that as a red flag? He seemed so sincere. And the way he took care of her and protected her – it wasn't real? Why the elaborate ruse?

Lying on the floor, Mia thought of the last time she'd slept on the floor and the memory elicited another round of body wracking sobs. The last time she'd slept on the floor it was with her head on his chest, wrapped up in his arms. The first time they'd kissed.

"Oh Baby Girl, you have no idea what you do to me."

"It's smoochal."

How could that have not *been real*? Mia wondered. How could she ever trust herself again if she couldn't have figured that one out? How could it have not been real, she asked herself over-and-over again, and it was that thought that plagued her as she fell asleep. *What did I miss and how could I have missed it?*

As Beau hung up the phone, the door to the dorm room opened, causing him to jump. A sweat-drenched Schooner entered, fresh from his nightly run on the track. With his uncasted left hand, he pulled off his black knit cap and Walkman earphones.

"Who was that?" he asked, since Beau never received phone calls.

"No one. Just a guy from my chem class." His lie was smooth.

Schooner nodded and grabbed a towel as he headed to the shower.

Chapter Nine

"You look like shit." Rob's smirk was annoying.

"How many pitchers did we drink?" Mia dramatically threw herself onto a couch in the Student Center.

"Too many for your lightweight ass." Rob was most amused. "So, did you call Romeo last night?"

Mia's eyes immediately filled with tears and she nodded. "He was off with the girlfriend."

"Are you just assuming that?" Rob's brows knit together skeptically as he dug through his blue nylon and suede JanSport backpack for his Marlboros.

"That's what his roommate told me."

"You need to hear it from him, Mia." He sat back on the couch and dragged deeply on his cigarette, watching the smoke curl in the air, before looking back at Mia. "I was thinking about you last night. You're a tough, pretty together chick, so why would this have you so shredded. There's something missing here."

Is this fucker psychic? Or attuned to me? Or does my story just not add up – because it doesn't add up to me either.

Mia took a deep breath, "Last year I was attacked and raped." She watched the shock and concern flash across Rob's denim eyes. "By two men who grabbed me when I left the darkroom on campus. It was a shitty night to start with – it was the night of the big spring formal and I was in the darkroom alone. And then that happened. I was trying to get back to my dorm and Schooner found me. He and I hadn't talked for months and he was back with her – or I assumed he was anyway, and when he saw what had happened to me, he made me go to the hospital. We walked there in the middle of the night and he stayed with me and then, after that, he just moved in with me – he just never left my side for the rest of the semester. He was very protective of me. He told me that he never stopped loving me," she had to stop to pull her shit together so that she wouldn't cry.

"And he went back to his old girlfriend?"

Mia looked up and nodded at Rob.

"Something's not adding up here. He's either the biggest motherfucker who has ever walked the face of the Earth, or there's been a colossal miscommunication, or you've been lied to. You need to talk to him, Mia."

She wiped at her traitorous tears. There was no way in hell she was calling again. She was not going to chase a guy who left her for another girl. Fuck that shit.

"Did you ever go for counseling or anything after the attack?" Mia shook her head, no. "You need to talk to somebody," his tenor was adamant.

"I'm handling it," eyes and tone defiant.

"Not! Seriously, Mia. Sounds like after you were raped, you just kind of let this guy take care of you, protect you. But did you ever really deal with what happened that night?"

Damn you, Rob Ryan for being so fucking smart. Mia had not even realized that she'd pushed the rape far down into the dark recesses of her psyche, behind a padlocked door, instead of acknowledging and confronting the pain and devastation of that evening. Falling asleep in the safety of Schooner's strong arms to the words, "I never stopped loving you, Baby Girl. Not for a minute" was what she had focused on to move forward. And from that day on, she had never looked back. But at what price, she just now realized. Those demons were going to escape at some point and wander through the labyrinth of her brain, wreaking havoc at every intersection.

Rob stubbed out his cigarette in an aluminum foil ashtray. "You're as fucked up as I am. Awesome. We're going to write great shit together." He pulled a copy of Woody Allen's *Without Feathers*[1] out of his backpack and tossed it at Mia.

Mia's devil smile spread rapidly. "Let's do "Match Wits With Inspector Ford." [2]She didn't miss a beat and hadn't even cracked the cover of the book to look at content.

"Impressed, Silver. Very impressed."

"As you should be, Ryan."

Mia and Rob spent the next three hours crafting the first of many pieces they would write as a team. Their odd senses of humor meshed seamlessly as they churned out page after page of humorous material. Their earlier heart wrenching conversation was now a million miles away on a distant horizon replaced with wry quips and side splitting laughter.

They were in the midst of a laughing jag, unaware of those around them, when Tom Sheehan approached.

"My two star students goofing off?" he reproached.

"Never," a ballsy Mia countered. "We're actually working on your assignment."

Tom picked up the copy of Woody Allen's book. "You guys are doing Woody Allen?" He leafed through the book, "Now that is something I never would've expected."

"Expect the unexpected from us." Mia looked from Rob to Tom. The look in Tom's eyes caught her by surprise. What was she seeing? She couldn't quite identify it, but it made her squirm and suddenly she felt very uncomfortable.

"Well, I'll leave you two to creating." He tossed the book back onto the couch. "Ryan," he nodded at Rob, addressing him for the very first time, "Mia." Another head nod and he was gone.

"What the fuck was that?" Mia made a face at Rob. "Was that as weird as I think it was?"

Rob grabbed for his pack of Marlboros. "I don't think he liked seeing us having fun together."

Mia looked at Rob quizzically. "What the fuck is that about?"

"I think our prof has got a crush on you, Silver." Rob looked very serious, as he dragged deeply on his cigarette.

"Oh please, he's fucking half the class." Mia sneered at Rob.

"But he ain't got you, Babe." She could see the wheels in Rob's head turning.

She placed her hand on his forearm and turned to face him full on. "He's not going to come between us, Rob. And I'm not going to let him fuck with you or your grade over some bullshit testosterone thing. I'll blow him if I have to so that he leaves you alone." A slow devil smile emerging, as she was clearly amused by her own joke.

"How magnanimous of you," he choked on the smoke he had inhaled, not expecting Mia's gracious offering.

"That's just the kind of chick I am," she laughed.

He reached over and ruffled her hair.

No one was going to get in the way of her new friendship with Rob and certainly not Tom Sheehan. As much as he excited her with his dangerous good looks and lofty intellect, that was a man who couldn't keep his dick in his pants. That would not be a good follow-up to the debacle with Schooner Moore. Other women would not be a good thing for Mia Silver's head and she knew it.

[1] Woody Allen, Without Feathers,(New York, NY, Ballantine Books (1972)

[2] Woody Allen, "Match Wits With Inspector Ford", Without Feathers, (New York, NY, Ballantine Books 1972) Pg. 115

Chapter Ten

"You sound like shit. Have you eaten anything today?" Mia asked Rob, as she hastily threw her books into her backpack. "Do you want me to bring you something after I meet with Tom?"

Rob coughed into the phone and Mia held it away from her ear. "No. I'm good."

"Damn, that sounds like a bark. I'll pick up soup and bring it to you."

"You don't have to."

Mia was rolling her eyes on the other end of the phone. "Keep up the martyr shit and I won't. I'll see you in a few hours. Keep your fingers crossed that he likes this piece better than last week's."

As Mia made her way across campus to the Student Center, she could feel the first hints of spring in the air. The air smelled different, it was heavier as the balmy evening approached. Winter would soon be a memory, she was smiling to herself as she watched the last vestiges of a pink sunset begin its ruby decline.

"I like seeing you smile." He surprised her as he fell into step next to her. "I have a habit of surprising and startling you, don't I?"

"I guess I just get lost in my head sometimes. It feels like spring tonight, doesn't it?"

Tom smiled at Mia, pleased with her simple observation. "Yes it does. So, where's your sidekick?"

Sidekick? What was his issue with Rob? He'd been snarky about him since the fall. "He's got a really nasty spring cold. I'm going to bring him some soup later."

"You are the dutiful little girlfriend," Tom's tone had a snide edge to it.

Mia stopped in her tracks. Tom followed suit and turned to her, surprised. I could be fucking up my grade, the thought flashed at the forefront of her consciousness, but oh well, it is what it is.

"I'm not a 'dutiful girlfriend'," her tone dripped with sarcasm. "I'm a good friend. And you know why, because that is just who I am and because he has been there for me this entire school year, and you putting us together was the best thing in the world that could've happened to me. So, thank you, Tom, because without Rob's friendship this year would've sucked."

Tom held his place, as Mia leaned toward him with an aggressive stance, hands on hips, eyes telegraphing nails. His smile was slow and his eyes narrowed. "Well it appears the correct response would be, you're welcome." And with that he put his hand on her lower back and ushered Mia into the Student Center.

"Let's work in the pub tonight," Tom suggested and started to descend the staircase. "I think we could both use a drink." He navigated through the crowded pub to a small table against the wall, put his leather Danish schoolbag down and headed to the bar, leaving Mia behind at the table.

Tom returned with two plastic cups of red wine. Mia had already laid out the current assignment for review. "I'm sorry, Tom, that was really rude and disrespectful of me before."

He leveled Mia a glance, a smoldering glance, she thought and the slow, bad boy smile. "Well, if I'm honest, it wasn't totally undeserved."

Mia looked down, feeling uncomfortable and suddenly shy, and picked at the napkin below her wine. She looked up to face him and plastered a smile on her face. "I hope you like this week's assignment better than last week's. I don't think I could handle another tongue lashing like last week."

Tom laughed and sat back in his chair. Taking a hearty sip of the bad college wine, he leveled another glance at Mia. "I think you'd do just fine handling another tongue lashing."

Is that a double entendre? she wondered. Mia held his gaze. "Oh, I think maybe you give me too much credit."

"I don't think so. I think there are a lot of ways you would surprise me and yourself."

"How so?" *Am I getting myself into dangerous territory? Do I care?*

Smiling at her again, he finally suggested that they take a look at the assignment. What was amazing was how quickly he could flip that switch, while Mia's insides were still quaking from whatever the hell that just was. And with the switch flipped, Tom Sheehan gave pointed, spot-on criticism of Mia and Rob's piece. His questions to her on character motive made her dig deep for her responses, having to delve deeply into the characters psyches and what motivated them.

Two hours later, the marked-up document was ready to be crafted into its final draft. "That all make sense?"

Mia nodded. "Yeah. Totally. It's so much tighter and stronger. It wasn't nearly as powerful before."

Tom got up and returned with more wine. *Well, I'm not getting out of here anytime soon. Sorry about the soup, Rob,* Mia thought to herself.

"You and Ryan really do write very well together," his tone was introspective. "I'm glad that's worked out well."

"I think we work because we bared some big demons to one another early on. We both realized we were seriously fucked up people and that could bode well for our writing."

Tom reached forward and pulled a white thread off the arm of Mia's crimson sweater and played with it. "I don't think you're nearly as fucked up as you think you are, Mia. You may have gotten into some fucked up situations or had some fucked-up things happen to you — but my gut tells me you're actually pretty damn stable and healthy."

"Maybe you shouldn't be trusting your gut, Teach." Devil smile.

Tom laughed, "Teach, huh? Well, only for a few more weeks anyway."

"This year has gone by so fast," Mia marveled as she gazed around the dark campus pub. It was almost a year since she'd seen him. How could that be? A year. Almost a year since she touched his fingertips. And yet she was still alive. She had some new friends. No boyfriends, but that was ok. That would have been incredibly hard to handle. He was probably totally immersed in tennis season by now. A vision appeared in her mind's eye of his tall body standing before her in white tennis shorts and his team shirt and cap, placing his racquets on her desk. Would the ache ever totally go away? It certainly wasn't as jagged as it had been. But it just never fully dissipated. Her chest still tightened and hurt.

"Where did you just go?" Tom's voice sliced into her reverie.

"Sorry, just spaced." Mia sipped her wine.

"But where did you go?" Those smoldering eyes were boring into her.

"There," her voice was little more than a whisper.

He nodded and let the silence between them reign.

After an uncomfortable moment, Mia grabbed the papers off the table without looking up at him and shoved them into her backpack. "Well, I need to go pick up that soup. We'll have the final draft ready for Thursday."

He was sitting back and gazing at her intently when she finally looked up. Mia sighed and stopped, returning his gaze.

"Mia …," but then he thought better of it. "I'll see you on Thursday. Tell Ryan I hope he feels better."

With a nod, she was off.

Mia Silver could not get out of there fast enough.

Chapter Eleven

"Okay, that's the last of the changes," Mia said into the phone.

"I'm really sorry I'm making you do this alone again." Rob had just recovered from a coughing fit. "I can still meet you there."

"Ugh, no. And get me sick? I don't want to be anywhere near all that nasty snot running out of you. Tonight will be easy. I'll turn this in and we'll go over what he wants for the next assignment. It'll be cake tonight, he's not critiquing anything new."

Mia took off for the Student Center feeling anxious about seeing Tom all alone again. *When had it all changed?* she wondered. All those great chats they had on Saturdays in the little bakery this past fall were never anxiety producing. And now, she was off to meet him for class and her stomach was all jumbled — a concoction of excitement and dread all rolled up.

He was standing outside the Student Center when she approached. "Ryan still sick?"

Mia nodded. "Yeah, he's got it bad."

Tom's hand was immediately on Mia's lower back turning her away from the building, "I just got out of a department meeting and haven't eaten yet. Have you eaten?"

She nodded again.

"So, have some dessert or something," he added, removing his hand.

Mia could still feel its warmth in her physical memory and it felt good. She wanted him to touch her again.

Looking up at him, she smiled. "What are you smiling at?" Tom was now smiling back at Mia.

"I'm imagining you being bored shitless listening to some of those old windbags in a department meeting."

Tom's laugh was hearty, "Were you a fly on the wall? Here, let's go here." Steering her into an Indian restaurant, his hand once again on the small of her back.

Mia was dying to let out an "mmmm" sound.

"Do you like Indian food?"

"I love it. I just wish I were hungrier."

"Just pick at mine." They sat down at a corner table. The heady, exotic smells of garam masala, curry and cardamom laying heavy in the air.

"Two Kingfishers," Tom told the waiter as he ordered too much food — Samosas, Rogan Josh, Sag Paneer, Chicken Korma and Naan.

The waiter returned with two ice cold bottles of beer. "Need a glass?" Tom gestured to Mia.

"Definitely not."

"That's my girl." His lips were smiling, but his eyes were smoldering.

My girl? Mia took a deep breath. She felt those two words deeply as they tingled through her body, and made her wish she wasn't so damn horny. She had not slept with anyone her entire sophomore year. She hadn't kissed anyone her entire sophomore year. "I add new meaning to the phrase 'Sophomore Slump'," she mused.

She could feel the icy cold beer cooling her throat and fueling her confidence. She sat back in her chair, beer in hand and just regarded him, wondering what it would be like with him.

"Do *not* look at me like that."

Mia giggled, nervously, "Like what?"

"Like that look you were just giving me, Mia."

The waiter brought the Samosas and Pappadam to the table along with several chutneys.

Mia reached for the Pappadam in the basket and broke off a piece of the crispy lentil cracker. She spooned some of the lush tamarind sauce onto her plate from the chutney tray and proceeded to break the cracker into little bits and drag it through the sauce, making ruby red patterns.

Looking up from her plate, she posed the question, "So, you're the only one allowed to dole out looks?"

"So, you've noticed?"

Mia practically spit out her Pappadam and started to cough.

She grabbed her beer to wash the cracker down. Tom was laughing.

"You are such a dog."

"I could fail you for comments like that, you know." He was nailing her with "the look."

"And I could bring you up to the Academic Review Board for sexual harassment."

"Have I harassed you?" He dipped his Samosa in mint chutney and took a bite, his eyes never leaving Mia's face.

"Not yet," she shot back.

"I would never harass you. I respect you too much."

"Yeah, yeah, yeah." Mia made a face at him.

He shook his head and laughed, "That is exactly what I like about you, Mia. You are so fucking real," and his tone became serious. "I need more real people in my life."

"So, the others aren't real with you?" Mia was leaning forward on the table — she wanted all the dirt.

"What others?" Tom finished his beer and signaled the waiter to bring them both another bottle.

"C'mon, you're like sleeping with half the class." There — it was out. She had just thrown it out — the big unspoken secret. If that didn't get her a failing grade, then she was home free.

Tom closed his eyes and shook his head. "Would you believe me if I told you that I have not had sex this semester?"

Mia shook her head. "Nope, would not believe you."

Tom laughed, "Sad, but true. I haven't slept with anyone in months."

"Then you must be incredibly horny." She slammed him with her devil smile.

"*That* … is a fucking understatement," and they both laughed as the food arrived.

Tom was ravenous, piling his plate high and voraciously attacking it.

"So, what happened to Sherri and Jacqueline?"

Choking on his food, Tom was momentarily stunned. "Was it that obvious?"

"Oh please." Mia rolled her eyes. "Talk about fucking understatements." She reached over with her fork and plucked a piece of chicken out of the Korma sauce on his plate.

"Ancient history. Jacqueline's not even in the class anymore."

"Wow. Ran the bitch off, eh?"

Tom couldn't help but smile at Mia's bodacious personality. "You know what I love about you? I can just hang with you. You're so damn amusing."

"When I so choose to be." Mia killed her second beer and Tom signaled the waiter for a third. She was picking off his plate again. This time lamb chunks out of the Rogan Josh.

"You can make yourself your own plate," he offered.

"Yeah, I know, but I don't want to." And she continued to pick at his dinner while he watched her with a most amused smile, loving the intimate act of sharing one meal.

It was after 10 P.M. when they got up to leave the restaurant. "Let me walk you back to your dorm. It's late."

Tom's hand was at her lower back as they exited the restaurant. She was more than a little buzzed from three Kingfishers and the cool night air on her face felt revitalizing. As they walked toward campus, his hand moved slowly up her back until it was around her shoulder. Mia momentarily closed her eyes. It felt so good. That human contact. It felt good. It wasn't until that moment, that she realized just how much she had missed it. How much she longed for it. She leaned into Tom and his arm tightened around her. The pressure of his arm around her back and his hand on her shoulder sent shock waves throughout her whole body. It felt so good, but evoked a sadness because she knew that in that one small act of leaning her body into Tom's, she was finally saying goodbye to Schooner, and those fingertips were moving farther away from her, disappearing into the dark night. "It's time for me to let you go," she told him in her head and silently prayed that Tom's kiss (which she knew was coming) would lighten the heaviness in her heart. And with a silent goodbye, Mia's right arm went around Tom's waist.

"So, there's something I need to tell you." She looked up at him.

"You're a lesbian?" His bad boy smile was disarming.

Mia laughed, "Not yet anyway. But it could happen."

"What do you need to tell me?"

With a deep breath came the admission, "I'm jailbait."

Their pace came to a screeching halt as he turned to her. "Ok, *that* I did not expect. But you're a sophomore." He was clearly thrown by her admission. "So, how old are you?"

"I'm seventeen."

"No way. You're just fucking with me," convinced Mia was kidding.

"I'll be eighteen in July."

Pushing his hair off his forehead, Tom was clearly agitated and thrown for a loop. Shaking his head, he looked at Mia and smiled. "You're serious. You're seventeen."

Mia nodded, devil smile at full tilt. She practically could see the thoughts racing through his head, as he tried to recover from the ramifications of this new tidbit of knowledge.

Tom shook his head at Mia. "You're amused, aren't you?"

"Very."

"You are trouble, you know that?" Tom was beginning to recover.

"Mmm-hmm, and now you know it, too."

"I knew you were trouble the minute I laid eyes on you, Mia. I just didn't know quite how much."

They started to walk again. Tom was shaking his head and laughing to himself. He looked down at Mia and she looked up at him, smiling. Grabbing her hand, he pulled her several yards to the side of a red brick building, pinning her up against it.

"Am I going to regret this?" His smoldering eyes made her catch her breath.

Mia nodded. "Absofuckinglutely."

And with that, his lips crushed down on hers and she hungrily opened her mouth to let him in, but that thought rapidly dissipated as her fingers burrowed into his unruly, dark hair and his hips pinned her against the wall. Letting her right-hand slide down his back, she pressed him into her so that she could feel him getting hard. Feel the power of what she was doing to him, how much he wanted her, ached to be inside of her. You want me. You want me. And surprisingly it didn't make the hurt go away, but the 'fuck you' felt good. And with both hands now on his ass, she could feel the outline of his entire cock. So hard. And she couldn't wait to have him.

Breathless and breaking their kiss, Tom pushed the hair from Mia's face. Laying his forehead against hers, he breathed deeply to refill his lungs. "You know you're going to drive me crazy for the rest of the semester."

"Mmm-hmm." Mia smiled up at him, her hands still holding him firmly against her, visions of him fucking her up against the brick wall, out in public, making her want him even more.

Running his thumb along her cheekbone, Tom planted a soft kiss on Mia's lips, "Okay, Jailbait, I need to get you back to your dorm, safely," he chuckled, "and then I need to go home and take a very cold shower."

Outside Mia's dorm people were milling about. With a smoldering look that said, "I want to fuck you every which way till Sunday," Tom squeezed Mia's shoulder and asked, "When did you say your birthday was again?"

Mia laughed, "Does tomorrow work?"

Laughing, Tom leaned down and put his lips to her ear, their softness sending an electric jolt through Mia's body, as they barely grazed her lobe. "Night, Jailbait," in the softest of whispers. And with a smile, he was gone.

Mia stood there watching as he disappeared into the night, thinking, *that man knows exactly what he's doing. Just what I need.*

Chapter Twelve

Mia and Rob were hanging out on the couch of the suite room in Mia's dorm. "He seriously didn't give you an assignment for us?"

"No, he was really hungry," understatement, Mia chuckled to herself, "and he'd just come from a department meeting. He just wanted to shoot the shit. So, when he didn't bring up an assignment, I certainly wasn't going to."

Rob leaned back on the worn couch. "It's like a freaking vacation. Sweet."

"Hey guys." Mia's suitemate, Joni, came in from class. Dropping her book laden backpack to the floor, she threw herself on the couch next to Rob. Rob turned to her with a smile. Mia could feel the tension building in the small room. It was becoming apparent that Rob's increasingly frequent suggestion that they work in Mia's suite had everything to do with Joni and not because it was a quiet place to work.

Mia could see them together. They were both from small, upstate towns, both bordered on brilliant, and were quirky as all get out. Mia looked at the two of them, smiling.

"What are you smiling at, Silver?" Rob was starting to blush.

"I have a brilliant, brilliant idea," she began, the devil grin escalating to full tilt. "I'm so fucking brilliant!" She popped up and bounded into her bedroom.

Emerging a few minutes later with a towel, scissors, comb and spray bottle filled with water, she stood before Rob. "Time for your makeover, Handsome."

Rob groaned and Joni clapped with excitement. She was on board to see what was under all the mountain man hair and scruff.

"You're not really doing this."

"Au contraire, my friend. We are really doing this. Go sit in that chair. Now."

"Bossy bitch," he grumbled, but moved off the couch to the chair.

Mia and Joni high-fived and began their handiwork. Mia sprayed Rob's hair with the water, then Joni combed it straight.

Mia turned to Joni. "Do you think we need to be high for this?"

"No, you crazy bitches," Rob bellowed, eliciting evil cackles.

Joni disappeared into her room and emerged, joint and lighter in hand. She handed them to Rob and patted him on the shoulder, "I think you're the one that needs this."

Rob snatched the joint from Joni and lit it. After his third hit he grumbled, "I can't believe I'm letting you do this."

"Shut up and stop Bogarting that joint." Mia combed his hair and grabbed the joint out of his hand with her free hand.

She passed the joint to Joni and picked up the scissors.

"I can't believe I'm letting you do this to me stoned."

"Trust me, whatever the outcome, it will be an improvement." And she whacked his shoulder before making the first cut.

Twenty minutes later, Rob's perfectly layered hair made him look like a different person. She then began on his beard, kneeling before him. When she was done, Mia looked at her best friend and was struck by a myriad of emotions. Under all that unkempt scruff, the guy with the denim blue eyes was surprisingly and incredibly handsome. A thought Mia never would have equated to Rob. Not only was he handsome, he was attractive. Attractive to Mia. Rob Ryan had been transformed into a head turning cutie.

"Why are you looking at me like that?" Mia's look was making him uncomfortable.

"You're gorgeous. How did I not know you were gorgeous? You are like a totally hot guy. Holy fucking shit."

Joni came around and gasped. Scruffy teddy bear Rob Ryan, who had dropped weight when he was sick with the flu, cleaned up beyond real nice. Rob Ryan now fell into the 'I'd fuck him' hot boy category.

Rob got up from the chair and headed to the bathroom to see what all the fuss was about. Mia and Joni stood in the suite room, mouths hanging open, muttering a steady string of, "Oh my God."

Rob emerged smiling. "I should've let you do this a long time ago."

"No shit." Mia smiled, but was feeling a tragic sense of loss. Her attraction to Rob had been to his personality, his intelligence, the way their wits meshed. But it had never been physical, which was why they were able to work together without conflict. And now, now she wanted to pull him into her room and fuck his brains out. But that window of opportunity was long gone. His interest was clearly in Joni, and all of the sudden Mia felt all alone again and like a third wheel. She felt like she was losing her best friend. Again. "You are so fucking handsome. Who knew?"

Chapter Thirteen

Tom was waiting at a table in the study area of the Student Center when Mia and Rob entered. A bemused and approving look on his handsome face acknowledged Rob's new appearance.

"Ryan, you look like a totally different person."

"Silver's good with a pair of scissors." He looked pleased.

"And it's best that you remember that." Mia smiled at Tom.

"I'll bear that in mind." He was giving nothing away.

At the end of their two-hour session, Tom gave Mia and Rob their final assignment of the semester, which they would have two weeks to work on before turning in what would be a simultaneous first and last draft.

He packed his papers into his leather Danish schoolbag and checked his watch. "So, you've got a break from me to work on this assignment, no class next week. I'll see you both in two weeks." And he was off.

Mia was breathless. What the fuck? Was this the same man who had her pinned up against a building, grinding his hard cock into her, nicknaming her "Jailbait," laughing with her over cold Indian beer as she ate from his plate? She could feel his tongue in her mouth, so greedy and possessive and she felt bereft. And foolish. And alone.

She and Rob walked together back to her dorm. And she felt alone. Joni was hanging out in her room with the door open when they arrived at the suite. Rob went in to go hang out with her and Mia went into her own room and closed the door.

Tom was fucking with her.

Her ambivalent feelings about Rob (and some level of jealousy over his growing relationship with Joni) were fucking with her. He was graduating and she was losing her best friend. Again. She was really starting to hate spring. It wasn't a rebirth for her. It was a season of loss. A season of goodbyes. Betrayals of the heart. Pain. Loneliness. Spring was overrated.

She tried hard to keep him out of her consciousness because she knew it did her no good. He was 3,000 miles away with a life of his own. She wondered if she would ever recognize something good again, or if she would let it slip away because it didn't feel like what they had. Would she recognize the real thing? And she silently prayed that one day she would feel again what she had felt with him. And if she didn't, she knew she would rather be alone.

Mia curled up in bed with her pillow next to her. It was becoming increasingly more difficult to remember what his chest felt like under her cheek. What his lips felt like in her hair when he would kiss the top of her head. *Why am I looking for that?* she wondered. *It wasn't real. So why is it what I want to feel?* And as she fell asleep, she still had no answers a year later, just memories that were quickly fading like photos that had not been properly put into a chemical bath of fixative.

It took a few minutes to realize the shrill ring of the phone was not part of her dream.

"Hello." Her alarm clock read 2:20 A.M.

"Jailbait."

"Hey." Mia took the phone in bed with her and curled up under the covers.

"I woke you." She could hear him moving around on his end.

"Well, yeah — it's like 2:30 in the morning. Are you drunk dialing me?" She was smiling.

He laughed, "No. I wish I was. I was grading assignments and I wanted to hear your voice."

Mia smiled and remained silent.

"You know you're fucking with my head, Jailbait."

"Ha. Didn't quite appear that way to me." He was so aloof earlier in the evening that she thought kissing him had been a huge, huge mistake. But now, hearing his voice in the middle of the night from the warmth of her bed, made her ache to be pressed against a brick wall with his hard cock grinding into her.

"Well, appearances can be deceiving. What did you want me to do? Pull you into my lap with Ryan sitting right there?"

"For starters," Mia whispered.

Tom groaned, "Jailbait, you are so dangerous. You know I can't touch you."

"But you already did."

"That, my little friend, was a huge lapse in judgment."

Mia could hear ice in a glass on the other end of the phone.

"You're just a big fucking tease." There was now annoyance in her voice. He gave her a taste of what it was like to feel good again and now he was telling her, sorry not happening. So, why the fuck was he calling her? Mia was tired, cranky, frustrated and starting to get pissed off.

"Is that what you think I'm doing?" There was surprise in Tom's tone.

"I don't have a fucking clue what you're doing." He had called her a lapse in judgment and she was starting to obsess and focus on that one statement.

Tom let out a long sigh. “I don’t either. I shouldn’t have called. I’m sorry.”

Mia remained silent. She didn’t want to say goodbye and she certainly didn’t want the conversation to take the turn it had taken.

After a few moments, he asked, “Are you still there?”

“I’m here,” her voice was soft.

“I’m sorry, Mia. I didn’t mean to upset you. Honestly, I’d been thinking about you all night and I just wanted to hear your voice,” he actually sounded contrite.

“I’m glad you called.” She could hear his smile on the other end of the phone.

“I wish you were here,” his voice was like silk in her ear.

“I want to kiss you again.”

He let out an “mmm” at her words. “Stopping at a kiss is the problem, Mia.”

“I know,” she giggled. “Do you know how wet I am right now?”

Tom let out a deep, sexy groan. “Who’s the tease now, Jailbait. Oh man. You are *killing* me.”

“Good.” She smiled. “You need to kiss me again.” She pictured him on the other end of the phone touching himself.

“You think so?”

“I know so.”

“You’re right. I do.”

“Think about me as you fall asleep.” Mia smiled into the phone.

“That’s a guarantee.”

“Night, Teach,” Mia whispered.

“Night, Jailbait,” his voice equally as soft.

Mia hugged her pillow next to her wondering what Tom’s chest would feel like under her cheek and hoping it wasn’t two weeks before she saw him again.

Chapter Fourteen

"Still awake, Jailbait?"

It was two nights later at 12:30 A.M. when she finally heard his voice again. Three little words made her melt into the phone. Forty-eight hours of his invasion into every conscious thought was killing her. Studying had been a joke, and if she masturbated one more time thinking about him she was going to end up with a raging infection. Damn you, Tom Sheehan. You're. Killing. *Me.*

"Yeah, just studying. What are you up to?" Mia invoked cool girl to come to her aid.

"Thinking about kissing you."

"Mmmm." The emphatic sound emerged before Mia could suppress it. *Cool girl, you suck!*

"That is exactly what I needed to hear."

She could picture his pure sex smile and his dark unruly locks cascading down his forehead. "Where are you?"

"I'm on campus. At my office," he paused. "I don't want you coming here. I don't want you walking across campus alone at night."

"Then come to me." *Is that my voice?* Mia wondered, who was this whispering seductress?

"That's probably not safe, Mia."

She hated listening to a voice of reason when all she wanted was to feel him, taste him, devour him. "Do you happen to have a baseball cap in your office?

Laughing, "As a matter of fact, I do."

"Put it on and come here. I'll wait in the hall so that you don't have to knock on my suite door. I'm 121 — it's a right turn through the front doors." She hung up before he could say no and quickly changed out of sweats into jeans, put on fresh underwear, brushed her teeth and fluffed out her curls.

Ten minutes later he was walking down the hall toward her. In jeans, a Cornell t-shirt (where he had earned his MFA in creative writing) and baseball cap, Tom looked like any other student on campus.

Mia couldn't help the smile on her face as he neared. He was so damn good looking in a bad boy, break your heart kind of way. There was only one way a relationship with this man would end … and happily ever after were not three of the words in the sentence.

His smile grew as he walked down the hall.

He's happy to see me, thought Mia. With a devil smile, she put her finger to her lips and said, "Shhh," as he approached. Silently, they entered her suite and he followed her into her room, where she quietly closed the door.

Tom took her face in both of his hands, "Is this what you wanted?" His eyes were smoldering as his lips softly grazed Mia's.

Smiling, she nodded yes, as he softly kissed her lips.

Pulling her head back by her hair, the look in his eyes was incendiary. He kissed her a little harder. "Is this want you wanted?"

Locked in on his dark eyes, she asked, "Is it what you wanted?"

"More than you can imagine, Jailbait." And his lips were on hers again, his tongue exploring, slowly, sensually, spontaneously. He pulled away and looked at her. "It is torture staying away from you and you don't make it easier — saying things to me like you're wet."

Mia smiled. "Your kiss does that to me. Thinking about your kiss does that to me. Right now, if you put your hand down my jeans …"

"No, no, no, Jailbait." He shook his head no, but his handsome bad boy smile looked like it was still a consideration.

Mia took Tom's hand and placed it between her legs on the outside of her jeans.

Without breaking eye contact, he started caressing her softly through her jeans. "I can feel the heat," he whispered.

Mia laid her head down on his shoulder, letting her lips gently graze his neck. She was so excited and she knew with a few more strokes she would explode. It had been so long (well, that someone else was actually in the room with her) and as much as she wanted to let go, that would be giving him too much control, too soon. And he was already ten leagues ahead of her in knowing how to play the game.

Taking his hand from between her legs, Mia led Tom over to her bed.

"You know we can't."

Mia nodded. "I won't make you do anything you don't want to do." *How odd that I'm the one saying that,* she mused.

Her words brought a bad boy smile to Tom's face and he tenderly ran a hand softly down her cheek. "Jailbait, that's the crux of the problem, there isn't anything I don't want to do to you. I want to fuck you in ways you never dreamed existed. I want to watch your face as you explode and lose control, knowing I'm doing that to you. I want to sit between your legs and watch you make yourself come for me. I want to push you up against that building where I kissed you and have you wear a dress," he paused and smiled remembering their first conversation about the California girls in dresses, "no underwear and fuck you up against that brick wall, pulling out of you just as campus security drives up. I want to fuck you in my office right before class and have you sitting in my class with my come dripping out of you and only you and I know that."

Mia couldn't breathe just listening to his words. *How fucking hot is that*? she thought. She was speechless. He was on a totally different level than she and Schooner had been. He was a sexy man. A twenty-seven-year old man. Worldly. Urbane. Sexy. And he was a player. Heartbreak on a stick, just waiting to happen. But right now, he wanted her. She was his obscure object of desire. His distraction. And for as long as it lasted, she was going to let him be her distraction. Being desired by this hot, sexy, smart man was a fucking godsend after the last year of her life. Schooner was fucking CJ, so why shouldn't she be happy? Why shouldn't she be fucking her writing professor? *Go away, Schooner,* she silently screamed. *Get the fuck out of my head. Get the fuck out of this room.*

Tom softly caressed her cheek. "Hey, where'd you go?"

Mia could feel her eyes fill with tears. "No place good."

"I upset you." Genuine concern clouded his handsome face. "I shouldn't have said those things to you."

Mia leaned her face into Tom's hand and shook her head, no. "I loved what you just said to me. Every fucking last word of it."

And then he did something she did not expect. Tom Sheehan enveloped Mia in his arms and pulled her in for a tight hug. "Someday maybe you'll tell me about it. And I know I don't act like it sometimes, but I'm glad you have Ryan to confide in. I'm glad he's there for you. I just want it to be me that you tell."

"I'm such a buzz kill. Do I know how to kill a mood or what?" Mia's smile was wry. Stay out of my head, Moore. Go back to Malibu Barbie where you belong and stay the fuck out of my head.

Tom threaded his fingers through Mia's curls and tipped her head back so that she had to look into his eyes.

What she saw was warm and caring.

"Jailbait, you are so different and so special and to tell you I want you does not remotely express what I have been feeling for a very long time — maybe even going as far back as being on my knees in the wet grass looking through your camera lens at wildflowers." His voice lowered to a whisper, "I don't want to scare you."

Mia shook her head. "You don't scare me, Teach. It's just," she paused to gather her thoughts. "It's just that I haven't been with anyone in a long time and I'm trying not to let the ghosts take control. I don't even want them here, near us. Does that make sense?"

Nodding, Tom smoothed back Mia's hair from her face. "Then don't let them." He was giving her that look, and she could hear the witch from The Wizard of Oz in her head saying, "I'm melting."

"You're making me melt, Teach."

He just continued to smooth back her hair and smile at her, the hotter than Miami on a summer's day look in his eyes, and then there were those greedy lips on hers again, soft and demanding, and Mia wanted to devour him but he was already devouring her.

"Jailbait."

Mia gazed up from Tom's fully clothed chest, where her head lay. They were both still fully clothed.

"Morning," he smiled, "it's still really early and I think I should get out of here now before people start milling about."

Mia moved from his chest, her head ached from lack of sleep. "Okay." She felt suddenly bereft, not wanting him to leave, to sneak off into the night.

"You okay?" His dark brows knit questioningly.

"Yeah, I just don't want you to leave."

"I like that, Jailbait." And he laid his head back down on the pillow next to hers.

"And just think, you are leaving here as pure as you arrived."

Tom threw his head back with laughter and Mia continued, "See, I told you I wouldn't make you do anything you didn't want to do."

"But I do want to." Tom pulled Mia against him. She dropped her hand down between them, grazing the front of his faded out, ass-hugging Levi's.

"Ohhh yeah, you do." Her eyes wide with excitement as she outlined the hardening bulge in his jeans with her fingernails. As he hardened beneath her fingers, Mia's devil smile grew wider and wider.

"You're incorrigible."

Mia looked at him with her 'You didn't just figure that out now, did you?' look and he laughed.

She could feel his erection straining against his jeans and she wanted to take it out probably as much as he did. With a quick kiss on the lips, she ducked her head down the bed. Tom started to protest and Mia looked up at him and put her finger to her lips, "Shhhh."

And then she did what he did not expect. She did not undo the top button of his jeans, she did not unzip his fly, she did not reach inside his jeans to pull him out and fondle him (even though she was dying to). With her teeth, Mia outlined Tom's cock through his jeans. As she moved from base to tip at an excruciatingly slow pace, she opened her mouth so that her top teeth were on one side, her bottom teeth on the other.

The sound of his moan and the feel of his fingers in her hair, made Mia ache to have him inside of her. She nibbled the soft head of his cock through the coarse fabric.

"Oh God, Mia." Tom reached down and pulled Mia on top of him so that they were lying face to face. Both panting, he took her face in his hands and pulled her lips down to his, kissing her roughly.

She could feel his cock between her legs and pressed down, "I want you," she said into his mouth, rubbing along the length of him, slowly clockwise and then lifting her mouth off his slightly to smile and changing her grinding to counterclockwise.

Grabbing her ass and pressing her tightly against him, Tom lifted his hips in sharp stabbing motions. Mia gasped into his mouth. "Yeah. That's what I want to do to you — make you gasp." He kept up the relentless stabbing while holding her firmly against him. The seam of her jeans was rubbing harshly against her clit, increasing sensitivity with each stab. Mia's eyes were wide, her breathing ragged. "Let go, Mia."

Mia shook her head no.

"Mia, let go," Tom demanded, pressing her into him with more force.

"No," she whimpered.

"I said let go," his voice was harsh, his eyes demanding. "Let go, Mia."

And then it was out of her control as she began to quake. Staring into his eyes and hearing her own sounds in her ears, feeling vulnerable and powerful, scared and excited, exhilarated and spent.

Tom pulled her face into his neck, hugging her to him tightly. "That was brilliant," he whispered in her ear, "That was by far the hottest thing I have ever done with my clothes on." Tom pulled her face close to his, looking into her eyes and smiling at her.

"What's that look?"

"I have a feeling you are going to be surprise after surprise, Jailbait.

Now, get some sleep." Tom got out of bed and grabbed his baseball cap, pulling it down low over his eyes. Taking Mia's chin in hand, he softly kissed her lips.

As he reached the door, Mia asked, "Hey, am I getting an A?"

"You're getting better than that. You're getting me." And with a sexy smile, he was gone.

Well, that makes it a "fuckin' A," Mia thought, amusing herself. As she dozed back off to sleep, the smile remained on her face as the fresh memory of what his chest (albeit clothed) felt like against her cheek.

Chapter Fifteen

Mia and Joni searched the sea of black caps and gowns unsuccessfully trying to identify Rob.

"I'm nervous about meeting his father and sister today," Joni confided. "I hope they like me. Rob said they won't be here for the ceremony. They are not coming until later."

"At least we're here for him. I'm nervous about meeting his father, too," Mia admitted. "I'm just afraid I'll go off on the man."

Mia scanned the stage for Tom. The last time she saw him was the night she and Rob turned in their final assignment and the three had quite the drunk fest. Tom convinced Rob to take grad level writing courses in the fall (even if it was at night) and to start applying to full time MFA programs. He then totally shocked Rob (and Mia) by offering to intervene at Cornell, if that was one of Rob's choices.

Sitting on an inside bench of a half-booth next to Tom, their thighs remained pressed against one another, the heat through their jeans overwhelmingly distracting. A few times, Tom's hand wandered off his thigh under the table to Mia's, gently stroking it. Just his slight touch was overwhelming — her satin bikini panties getting wetter and wetter with each caress.

As a semi-drunk Rob got up to hit the men's room, Tom waited for him to be out of sight of the table and grabbed Mia's chin and planted a hard kiss smack on her lips. Mia sat wide-eyed with a bemused expression at his public display of affection.

"I'm dying without you, Jailbait."

The smile that permeated Mia's eyes was immediately reflected in Tom's face. I'm dying without you. What amazing words to hear. I'm dying without you. This hot, dark, sexy man admitted, I'm dying without you. Four words that were music to Mia's heart and soul. I'm dying without you. Not "you're a charity case." Not "he feels sorry for you." Not "he can't wait for this semester to be over so he can stop pretending." Not "do you know how big a burden you are?" I'm dying without you. I'm dying without you. *He's dying without me — so go fuck yourself.*

Scanning the faculty up on the commencement stage, Mia found him on the far right. It looked like the hood on his gown was brown. That must be Cornell's color for MFA recipients, she ascertained. Picking up her camera, with its long lens, she focused on the stage. Yes, it certainly was Tom — unruly hair poking out from his cap, the sun playing on the planes of his sculptured handsome face, full lips in a half smile listening to something the faculty member next to him was saying in his ear. Damn, he's handsome. Just looking at him, Mia could feel the familiar tightening between her legs.

"There's Rob!" Joni interrupted Mia's reverie.

Mia trained the lens in the direction of Joni's outstretched pointing arm.

After a few minutes, Mia was able to pull him out of the crowd. Damn, he cleans up nice. Mia still marveled at her handiwork. She realized she was smiling at the sight of him — and not just because he looked adorable — but because of the love she felt deep in her heart for him. It was a brilliant stroke on Tom Sheehan's part to put these two broken souls together and have them work through their pain by utilizing their talent collaboratively to create works greater than each of them would have been able to produce individually. And on top of this inspired partnership, they had formed a deep, respectful love and friendship.

Mia pulled the camera strap over her head and handed her camera to Joni. After a few minutes, Joni exclaimed, "There he is. He looks so handsome."

An hour later, it was all done and Rob was bee-lining toward them. Joni was in his arms before he even reached them, locked in a passionate kiss, his cap and tassel somehow now on her head, as Mia stood by capturing the moment through her lens.

"So Silver, how do you feel about moving off campus and sharing an apartment with me in the fall?"

Mia screeched, "Are you serious? You've decided to stay here then?"

"Someone needs to watch over you two troublemakers." Rob beamed at Mia and Joni.

"I couldn't agree more," Tom's pronouncement took them all by surprise.

Nice stealth attack, thought Mia.

"Congratulations, Ryan." Tom actually hugged Rob, clapping him on the back.

Mia stood smiling at Tom, standing there in his robe with its brown hood, cap on head, sporting both a black tassel indicating a graduate degree and a red and white Cornell tassel. Devastatingly handsome were the two words running through Mia's head at the sight of him. Add his intellect on top of that and Tom Sheehan was dangerous and devastatingly handsome. A seriously fuckable combination.

Tom casually slung an arm over Mia's shoulder and gave her a squeeze. "I know I'll sleep better at night knowing you're watching out over this one."

Mia looked up at Tom, knowing the shocked look on her face was saying, "Ummm, what the fuck?"

"Mind if I steal her for a quick sec?" And without waiting for an answer, he steered Mia away from Rob and Joni.

"Hello? What is going on? Are we coming out?" Mia laughed.

Tom pulled her tighter into his side, "Yeah, why not? I'm not your professor anymore, grades have been turned in and with commencement complete, I'm not even on staff here anymore."

"So, what does that mean?" They stopped walking and Mia turned to him, searching his face.

"It means you have a new boyfriend, Jailbait."

She could feel the smile take over her face. He was so damn disarming. "Boyfriend?" her tone incredulous.

He nodded, sex smile beaming at her. "That is if you'll have me."

"I'd like to have you …"

He had both hands on her shoulders now, holding her at arm's length. "… And you will. What day of the week does your birthday fall on?"

"Ummm, I think it's on a Thursday this year."

"Take the day off from your summer job and take the next day off, too."

She could feel a bead of sweat running down her cleavage and wondered if it was from the noon sun directly overhead or the hotter than Miami look he was laser focusing on her. "Why? Do we have plans?" she challenged.

"We do." His smile was now blinding. "We're going to spend your birthday fucking like wild animals and the next day you are not going to be able to walk."

Mia pulled her hair up off her neck which was now drenched in sweat, wishing she'd remembered to bring a hair tie. She cocked her head to the side, slow devil smile taking up residence. "Promises, promises."

Tom tossed his head back in laughter and pulled Mia to him in an engulfing hug. "You are so damn good for me."

"You think?"

"Mmm-hmm, I do." And on a crowded football field, surrounded by graduates, fellow staff, students and families, Tom took Mia's face in both of his hands. Staring into her eyes, it felt like he was asking her permission to make their bold announcement. She nodded her head slightly and he did the same in acknowledgement. His kiss was soft at first, fingers threaded through her long curls. He pulled away and looked at her smiling. "You good?" She nodded again, returning his smile and this time their kiss was deep, passionate, ghost exorcising. They were all alone, together, on a crowded football field. As he drew her to him with his arm around her waist, Mia could feel how hard he was through his robe and her hands, which were resting on his biceps, went around his neck.

Feeling Tom placing his cap on her head, Mia began to laugh. She loved that she was wearing the cap he wore when he received his MFA. He beamed at her reaction and kissed her again, smiling down at her.

"Ready to go face the music?" His right eyebrow raised slightly.

"As ready as I'll ever be." Mia had a look of horror on her face.

Tom placed his arm around her shoulder again as they made their way toward where they had left Rob and Joni. This time Mia reciprocated by placing her arm around Tom's waist. Although a little afraid of Rob's reaction to their pairing, Mia felt good. Her heart felt good. Tom made her feel alive again. He was exciting. He was fun. He was interesting. He was sexy. He was handsome. He was real. He wasn't just a memory. And it was good to feel alive again. It was good to feel wanted.

Rob was not smiling, but Joni looked rather amused. "Surprise!" Mia announced, hoping to break the tension.

"How long has this been going on?" His eyes were trained on Tom.

"Well, nothing's really been going on." Mia tried to diffuse the tension resulting from Rob's intensity.

Tom stepped in. "It's been mostly a discussion up until now. But now with the school year officially over … " his voice trailed off.

"Mind if I steal her a sec?" Rob mirrored Tom's words from earlier.

As Mia walked off with Rob, she turned to Tom and Joni with a "rut-roh" look on her face and wide, expressive eyes.

When they were out of earshot, Rob stopped walking and looked at Mia. "You know what a player he is, Mia. This does not end well for you. That chapter's already been written."

"Rob, I have no illusions that this is anything but a fun time with a really hot, smart older man. I know his track record. I know he can't keep his dick in his pants. I know I'm not going to be the one to change him. I know men like him don't change. I know all that."

"Then why are you setting yourself up to be hurt?" Rob searched Mia's eyes.

"I like him. I enjoy spending time with him. I'm incredibly attracted to him. He makes me feel good," Mia listed her reasons. "And he makes you-know-who go away. I need him to go away, Rob. I need loving him so much to be a memory, not my reality." Mia could feel the sting of tears at just the mention of Schooner.

Rob wrapped Mia up in his arms, swaying with her. Pushing her hair behind her ear he whispered, "I want you to be happy, Silver. You deserve abundant happiness. If he hurts you, I will fuck up his pretty face."

Mia pulled her face away, smiling. "I'll give you the razor blade."

"Deal," they laughed.

"I love you, Rob Ryan. You made what I thought was going to be a shitty year a really good year. Thank you."

"You did the same and more for me, Silver." They started to walk back. "And I *will* fuck up his face if he messes with my best friend."

As they walked back toward Tom and Joni, Mia realized, on the last day of her sophomore year, that in the year that had passed since that devastating last day of her freshman year, she had successfully written a new chapter with a new cast of characters. And although she loved them, there was still a piece of her that yearned to turn the pages back to a previous chapter and feel his lips in her hair and hear him call her "Baby Girl."

Chapter Sixteen

It was 11:45 P.M. on the night of July 11th when the phone rang.

Mia sprung across the living room of her grandparent's apartment. "Hello."

"Jailbait."

Giggling, "You don't get to call me that for too much longer."

"No, I don't. I just got off the train. I'm in Grand Central. I'm going to catch a cab down to you."

"Okay, I'll see you in a few. It's apartment 22D." Mia hung up and danced around the apartment.

She hadn't seen Tom in over a month. He'd been in LA working on a pilot for a show about a Los Angeles law firm. With her grandparents off on back-to-back river cruises through Europe, she had taken over their apartment for the summer, with the promise of keeping Grandma's plants alive and her cat fed and loved. The sweeping three-bedroom apartment was located off Union Square on 16th Street and Fifth Avenue with a southern wall of windows prominently displaying the World Trade Centers.

The call came from the doorman in the lobby that Mia's visitor had arrived and she told him to send him up. The building's doormen had known Mia since she was a toddler and looked out for her whenever she stayed at her grandmother's.

Upon hearing the knock, Mia whispered, "Showtime" and opened the door to Tom's sexy smile and tousled hair. He was holding a bouquet of blood red roses surrounded by baby's breath.

"C'mere you," was all she needed to hear and she was in his arms. They backed up into the apartment, lips-locked. When their kiss ended, he held her face in his free hand, smiling at her. "Mmm, Happy Birthday, Baby. I have missed you."

"I somehow doubt that." Mia laughed, "Surrounded by all those Malibu Barbies."

"Mostly I saw the inside of a writer's room and a lot of very fake looking plastic surgery." It was then that the view outside the window caught his eye. "Oh my God, that is gorgeous." They walked over to the center of the windows to look at the Twin Towers all lit up at night. "What an incredible view."

Mia laughed, "I used to try and count all the floors when I was little."

Tom turned to her. "You are not little anymore." He thought for a second. "But I'm not going to stop calling you Jailbait."

"I'm glad. I kinda like it." She led him into the kitchen to put the roses in a vase which she handed back to him. Then she started rooting around in the refrigerator.

"What are you looking for?"

Mia poked her head out and with a devil grin announced, "Provisions. We may never pass this way again ..."

A few minutes later she was set with fruit, cheeses, nuts, cups, utensils and a pitcher of water. "Follow me," she called over her shoulder as she led him through the spacious apartment to the guest room where she always stayed. She put the provisions on a night table next to the bed and then took the vase from Tom and placed it at the center of the dresser directly across from the bed.

Mia then plopped herself down at the center of the queen-sized bed and reached out a hand to Tom. He took her hand and joined her on the bed.

Lying down with her head on a pillow, Tom followed suit, facing her. Mia reached out and smoothed his hair, fingering the individual irreverent locks.

I'm so toast, Mia thought. *This man is sex on a stick.* "I'm not going to lie to you, I'm scared, Tom. You're going to break my heart, aren't you?"

"Well, it's not my intent." His dark eyes flashing sincerity.

"But it is your M.O." She continued to play with his hair.

"I can't argue with you. But what I've done in the past doesn't minimize what I feel for you. What I have felt for you for a long, long time, Mia." He reached for her hand and pulled it from his hair to his lips, kissing the inside of her wrist.

"I don't have all that much experience and I'm afraid I'm going to be in over my head." And then there were the words she didn't say, and the myriad of emotions and thoughts flooding every cell in her body. Doing this tonight would be some kind of emotional end to Schooner — she knew that, and seeing the Twin Towers outside the window over Tom's shoulder brought back the dream she and Schooner shared of a special night up in Windows on the World, on the 106th floor. They had talked about celebrating her 18th birthday there and a wave of melancholy swept over her. Would it ever go away? Would she ever truly stop loving him? And she asked herself the question for which she did not have an answer — *why do I still love him?*

"Oddly enough, I feel like I am over my head with you." He was still holding her wrist, his lips pressed softly against the sensitive skin. The seductive sensation brought her back to the present.

Mia laughed, "No, you don't."

"I do, seriously. I care about you, I worry about you, I think about you. I see things and I want to share them with you. I want to hear about your day every day and I want you to know about mine. I want to know what you're seeing and how you'd photograph it or write about it. I see things in LA, and in my head, I can just hear you making a snarky comment, and I laugh out loud with no one there — or sometimes it's worse because someone is there and they have no idea of what I am laughing about and I can't tell them — they just wouldn't get it. I write a great line and I think, Mia's going to love this."

Mia was laughing at Tom's monologue.

"It's true. You laugh, but it's true. It is. The point of this, Mia, is you are with me in my head and my heart all the time. You have gotten under my skin because you are so real and you're real with me and I love that. I need that. I need you. I do." He was looking at her earnestly and shaking his head. "I need you and I want you and I have waited for tonight for what seems like an eternity. And everything about what I've just said is so unlike me. And I really kind of like it. And I feel like I'm eighteen again and I just want to be your boyfriend. And you're smiling at me. What's that smile about?"

Tom had just managed to pull Mia out of her melancholy and dissuade all her fears. He was so damn disarming. "I think I have a huge crush on my boyfriend."

"I know I've got a huge crush on my girlfriend." And then in a whisper, "Please don't be afraid."

"I think you should kiss me," she whispered back.

With his lips against hers, "I think I should ravage you."

"Yeah, that too."

In an unhurried dance, clothes slowly came off, piece by piece, until they were lying facing one another, both naked. Slim and muscular with a runner's body, Mia lightly ran her fingers from his shoulder down his biceps across his hairless chest. His skin was silken, baby soft and she rubbed it reverently.

"You feel so good." He watched her explore and become confident as she touched him, stopping every so often to find his lips. As she pulled away from his lips, she smiled, her hand dropping to his erection. She let her fingernails graze lightly from the back of his balls forward, up the shaft of his cock, to the soft head, which was already moist. She rubbed her thumb over the moistness and slowly brought her thumb to her mouth where she licked her finger clean, a smile on her face, her eyes trained on his.

"My new girlfriend is really hot." Tom's smile had a most amused tilt to it.

"Well, don't tell her, but I'm about to suck your cock."

"Oh really?"

"It's my birthday and I'm going to blow out your candle." Mia moved down between Tom's legs and took his thick and formidable cock in her hands. "Hello," she spoke directly to the one-eyed monster. "I've wanted to meet you for quite a while, but your owner wouldn't let us become acquainted. Not very nice of him. But you know what? Now you're mine and we are going to have so much fun together." And with that Mia's tongue slowly licked up the length of him as he throbbed to her touch. With the tip of her tongue, she rimmed the circumference of his cock's tip and used the tip of her tongue to lick the slit clean. She peered up at Tom and smiled, then used her teeth to lightly nibble the head of his cock.

"You exquisite tease," he laughed.

"Mmm-hmm," she agreed, smiling at him. And within a moment, he was down her throat and she took him as deep as she could take him, sucking him in past her lips with a tight suction. Hearing his sharp intake of breath, she moved her hands under him, an ass cheek in either hand, which she kneaded as she worked his cock in her mouth.

"Damn, you are good," he moaned. "I am the luckiest freaking man alive." After a few minutes, he reached down and pulled Mia up to him. "I don't want to come in your mouth, not this time."

"No?"

"No." He smiled. "I have waited so long to be inside of you, Jailbait, and I am done waiting." He pushed her wild mane out of her face and kissed her. "Are you on anything?"

Mia nodded, "Yes, I started the pill last month."

Tom reached between her legs. "I finally get to feel you without jeans on. Let's see if you're as wet as you always brag to me you are." He swiped two fingers between her pussy lips, stroking from back to front and settling on her clit, which made her gasp. With a self-satisfied smile, he moved his fingers back and inserted two into her, his eyes never leaving hers. "You didn't exaggerate, Jailbait. You get extraordinarily wet for me. That is hot. So fucking hot."

Mia returned the self-satisfied smile. "Told you."

"Yes, you did." Grabbing her by her long curls, Tom pulled her down for a deep kiss. "I have wanted to fuck you for so long," he growled into her ear. "By the time the sun comes up there will be no doubt in your mind who you belong to."

Gasping at his words, Mia grabbed a handful of his unruly hair and tugged on it hard, "That goes both ways, Teach."

A slow, sexy smile took over Tom's handsome face. "You are so fucking good for me." Tom Sheehan was reveling in the fact that he had finally met his match. Mia didn't just take it, she gave it right back, in spades. Flipping her on her back and getting on his knees he splayed her legs across his muscular thighs. Running his hand up the back of each thigh to her ass, he squeezed her butt cheeks, pulling them apart and watching her breath hitch.

"So, tell me what you want, Jailbait." His eyes were hooded and sexy.

"You know what I want."

Tom shook his head slowly, smiling down at her. "I want you to tell me exactly what you want me to do to you. You're good with words. I've read them. Now say them to me."

Mia cocked her head, devil smile just touching the corners of her lips. So, this is how he wanted to play it. If she wasn't so turned on by what he was asking her, she would've been too shy to comply. But he was challenging her, she could see it in his eyes and the smugness of his smile and challenging Mia Silver was like giving her a dare.

"I want you to rub the tip of your cock up and down my pussy, but I don't want you to go in."

Tom smiled down at Mia and hoisted her higher on his thighs so that she was spread wide open and he could rub himself on her. Holding his cock in his right hand, he slowly stroked its head along her moist slit, back and forth, the crown becoming lubricated with her juices. As he stroked for the third time, Mia could tell how turned on he was by his ragged breathing. As he reached her entrance, the head of his cock dipped in slightly,

"Uh, uh, uh — I didn't tell you that you could do that." Mia could tell that he was dying to plunge deeply into her.

Tom looked up from Mia's pussy to stare into her eyes. She smiled at the glazed over, heated look he was giving her. He was barely breathing.

"You are killing me. I have never wanted to fuck anyone as much as I want to fuck you. I need to fuck you."

She smiled and lunged at him, pushing him down on his back and straddling him. Before he could even speak, she began to do to him what he had been doing to her. Slowly rubbing herself along the head and shaft of his cock. But now she was controlling it — the speed, the pressure, the movement. When the head of his cock reached her opening, she let just the tip dip into her warmth and then pulled off him and she did it again and again and again.

Grabbing her by her hips, he looked into her eyes. "I can't wait any longer."

"Wuss," she smiled, teasing him.

And he gave her his dangerous smile back and rammed her down hard on his cock, penetrating her fully.

Mia gasped, her eyes widening at the infiltration.

Holding her down tight, he continued to drive up into her. "Feel like a wuss to you?"

Mia shook her head no and closed her eyes to concentrate on the exquisite feeling of being filled by this beautiful man.

She heard her own moaning and smiled. Opening her eyes, she looked down at Tom. "What are you doing to me?"

"Fucking the crap out of you."

They stared into one another's eyes as he relentlessly pounded up into her, filling her, stretching her, then lifting her and pulling out, making her yearn to fill the void, to feel him deep, buried. His gaze was so intense that just looking into his beautiful brown eyes was turning Mia on and she was falling past the veil.

"What? Say it," he demanded.

"Oh God, Tom. Oh God." Mia's head was back, she could no longer focus on anything but the exquisite feel of his cock pounding into her. "I'm going to come. I'm going to come." She was whimpering as she called out his name. "Oh God, Tom, oh God, Tom, Oh God, Tom."

"That's right, baby. Come on, you can take it. You can take it all."

And she wanted it all. With her feet underneath his ass, she pressed him as deeply into her pussy as she could get him, squeezing his cock tightly and making her own muscles quake around him. Mia's moans turned into a scream and the only sensation left in the world was the delicious friction of his cock sliding in and out of her pussy. Her pace was frenzied, riding him hard, caring about nothing but cresting the wave. She felt his hands at her waist driving her down on his cock, but she was lost and just wanted to make him come. She had waited so long to have him inside of her and now she wanted the control of making him lose control.

Tightly squeezing his cock and not letting up, she looked down at him, eyes locking on his, his gaze intense and she squeezed harder. Tom let out a loud moan and rammed her down hard on his cock. His eyes closed and Mia crested the wave, getting slammed. Collapsing on his chest, sweat drenching her skin and mingling with the moisture on his, she tried to steady her breath. He was still inside of her and she didn't want him to pull out, to leave a void.

Tom moved the hair away from Mia's face and taking her chin in his hand, he tipped her face up to his. With just a brush of his lips on hers, he whispered, "Happy Birthday, Baby. Was that ever worth the wait!"

Mia nuzzled her face into his chest. Tom Sheehan was the best birthday present in the world.

It was time to heal.

Sailing alone was the one thing that made him truly happy. He could think when he was out on the water. Put on music, watch a sunset, navigate by the stars. Being out on the water was the one place he could be honest with himself.

It was July 12th. He wondered if that day would always hold significance for him. Would there be years in the future where the day would pass and he wouldn't even think of her? Part of him hoped so. Part of him hoped that day would never come.

Tonight, as he looked at the stars shining against a black sky, they seemed to be mocking him. They had laid on a blanket on The Quad looking at these very same stars and they had talked about July 12th. Not last July 12th — this July 12th. This very night. She had described The Statue of Liberty Lounge in the Windows on the World Restaurant. It was on the 106th floor of One World Trade Center. He remembered all the details. She said that she had always dreamed that would be the place a special night in her life would take place. It was then he knew he would ask her to marry him, up there close to the stars, on her eighteenth birthday.

But he was already engaged and she was nowhere to be found, and the stars twinkling down on him on July 12th just felt like big, fat liars.

Chapter Seventeen

"Will your father let me pay for dinner?"

Mia looked up at Tom with an 'Are you joking' look.

"I'm still going to offer."

"He'll appreciate that. It will go a long way."

Tom and Mia walked up Second Avenue toward Murray Hill to meet Lois and Bob Silver for Mia's birthday dinner at The Palm. It was quite a surprise to Lois when her daughter announced that "her boyfriend" would be joining them for dinner.

"Is this someone you've met this summer at the internship?" Lois wanted details.

"No, I've known him since September. I know him from school." Mia hated inquisitions and she knew Lois would dig until she had every last detail. Mia also knew that the one thing her mother wanted to know more than anything else was, is this boyfriend marriage material?

"What's his name?" Lois had immediately started the twenty questions routine.

"Tom."

"Tom what?"

"Tom Sheehan."

"Oh, so he's not Jewish." She could hear "the tone" in her mother's voice and actually had to stifle a laugh because Tom not being Jewish was the least of the things her mother was going to hate about him. She was going to flip out when she found out that he was ten years older than she was and had been her professor. *Oh, this is going to be classic*, Mia thought.

Now walking toward the restaurant, hand in hand, with her hot as hell boyfriend, Mia contemplated that maybe this wasn't going to be so amusing and she was starting to pray for the best, hoping someone ordered a bottle of wine or champagne or something immediately upon being seated.

Luckily, that someone was her incredibly suave boyfriend who had a bottle of

Veuve Cliquot sent to the table to toast Mia's birthday. With a bottle of champagne in them, the conversation flowed nicely.

Mia sat back and watched Tom successfully work both of her parents. His intelligence and education were both formidable and impressed the Silvers, and they were very interested in the TV writing he was doing in Los Angeles.

"Do you plan on staying out there?" Lois asked the question that had been on Mia's mind.

"Not a moment longer than I have to," Tom laughed. "I am not a California guy. There's so much being produced out of New York these days, hopefully I'll be able to end up back here sooner rather than later. I'd actually like to end up teaching at NYU's film school."

Mia sat back and smiled. She liked the sound of that, although she knew chances were he'd be long gone from her life before ending up back at NYU. But you never know, she thought.

At the end of dinner, Tom tried to take the check and Bob would have none of it, insisting the champagne was enough of a contribution.

They walked for several blocks together and Lois slowed her pace. Mia knew exactly what her mother was doing. She wanted the men out of earshot to grill her daughter.

"He's very handsome, Mia."

Mia smirked. "Yeah, he's pretty hot."

"Were you in a relationship with him when he was your professor?" Here it comes …

"No, Mom. He was a perfect gentleman when he was my professor."

"He's very charming."

Mia laughed, "That, he is."

"So, what was it, you had a crush on him?"

"Believe it or not, he had a crush on me. I'm just that irresistible. Smart and irresistible," Mia kidded.

"He's very handsome," Lois repeated.

"Wanna tag team him, Mom?"

"Mia! You're terrible."

"It's part of my charm. You know that." Mia hugged her mother. She also knew Lois well enough to know that the Tom Sheehan discussion was far from over.

As they parted, Lois reminded Mia that they had the opening of the Hudson River School painters at the Metropolitan Museum on Wednesday night.

Tom shook Bob's hand and kissed Lois' cheek and they were off.

"How'd I do?" Tom smiled down at Mia as they walked downtown.

"Pretty good, I think. My mother wanted to know if I was seeing you when you were my prof. I told her you were the perfect gentleman." She smiled at Tom. "Which is mostly true, except for your slight lapse in judgment."

"I'll never live that down, will I?"

Mia shook her head. "So, were you serious about NYU?"

"Very. I'd love to teach screenwriting at their film school." Slinging his arm over her shoulder and pulling her close as they walked. "You're not going to get rid of me so easily, Jailbait, so Bob and Lois need to get used to me."

Looking up at him, Mia couldn't wipe the smile off her face.

"What're you thinking?" He kissed the tip of her nose.

"My boyfriend."

Letting out a hearty laugh, Tom looked pleased. "You've got that right. So, where should we go, Girlfriend?"

"Well, since it's my birthday weekend, I think it should be my choice."

"Whatever you want, Sweetheart."

"Let's go back to the apartment and fuck like wild animals."

Tom turned to an elderly man who was walking next to them on the sidewalk. "I have the best girlfriend in the whole world." And with that, he grabbed Mia's hand and started running toward the apartment on Sixteenth Street.

Tom's soft kiss on her lips woke Mia in the early hours on Monday morning. The room was dark and outside the Trade Centers were still lit up against the pre-dawn sky.

"I have to leave for the airport, Jailbait."

Mia just nodded. She knew if she spoke, her voice would crack.

"I had one of the best weekends of my life." He brushed her hair from her face. "And I wish I wasn't leaving you. I think this bi-coastal thing just became very hard."

Mia took his hand from her hair and brought it to her lips. "Thank you for the best birthday ever. You are the best gift in the world."

With those words, he took her face in his hands, his gaze serious and sincere. "I promise I will find a way back to you soon."

"Good, because I miss you already."

Tom Sheehan truly was an elixir.

Chapter Eighteen

Mia bounded up the stone steps of the Metropolitan Museum of Art. The Met was Mia's *happy place* in New York City and she could not wait to get through the doors. Not only did it hold some of the world's greatest antiquities and art, it also held a treasure trove of memories for Mia of many 'Girls' Day' outings with both her mother and grandmother.

Lois was waiting just inside the main entrance, impeccably dressed for the night's exhibit opening in a sleeveless peach shift dress and oversized white framed sunglasses.

"Oh, you are totally channeling Jackie O. tonight." Mia kissed her mother's cheek.

Lois laughed, "Except she's smarter than the rest of us. We're in the city on a hot night in July, and she's off in The Vineyard."

The former First Lady's apartment was located directly across the street from the north end of The Met at 1040 Fifth Avenue, and Mia thought that Mrs. Kennedy-Onassis was probably the only other person who found as much solace in the cavernous museum as she did. As with most New Yorkers who lived or spent time in the East 80's, Jackie was a fixture. You saw her walking down the street, sashaying about in top salons, squeezing fruit at Gristede's on Lexington Avenue and 89th Street, or as Mia did, wandering The Met and enjoying its treasures.

Over the years, they'd developed a smile and nod relationship. Mia remembered the first time she saw Jackie at The Met. Her face broke into a huge grin, because Jackie was someone she'd recognized and 'known her whole life.' It took Mia a moment to realize that Jackie didn't actually know her. Her first thought was, *wow, she's really thin*. They'd seen each other so many times over the years that Mia thought that Jackie had actually seen her grow up. There was a cardinal unspoken rule amongst New Yorkers and that was never to approach the former first lady and Mia respected that rule.

The first (and only) time they would ever interact was a week after Mia had returned from California. A devastated Mia stood before the bust of Augustus Caesar in the Roman Antiquities room. She had been drawn to this marble statue from the time she was a small child. Visiting Augustus had become a family joke. Mia never understood why she was always pulled to the bust, but she liked to think that maybe she had known Julius Caesar's nephew, Octavian, in another life.

Standing before the statue, she didn't even realize that she was quietly crying, although she was wiping tears away with the heels of her palms. She heard a click and saw a beautiful Mykonos Blue Hermès Kelly Bag being opened; the owner removed and handed her a white linen handkerchief trimmed with purple embroidery. Jackie was looking straight ahead at Augustus as she handed the delicate fabric to Mia.

Eyes trained on the handsome Roman, she observed, "I'll bet he was a heartbreaker." It was a voice she'd known her entire life.

Mia sighed, "I'll bet he was a tennis player."

Jackie nodded her head and smiled. "You're probably right." And she gracefully floated away, leaving a tear-stained Mia, linen handkerchief in hand, to her Augustus.

As Mia and Lois made their way through the museum toward the Hudson River School painters exhibit, Mia veered off to the left toward Augustus. Lois was used to indulging her daughter's obsession which had been on-going since the age of four.

"So, have you heard from Tom now that he's back in LA?" Lois was pretending to look through the new exhibit catalogue, but Mia knew better. The Inquisition was about to begin.

"Yeah, we talk a couple of times a day." They began to walk toward The Great Hall again to head upstairs to the opening.

"Is this serious?"

Mia could tell from her mother's tone that Lois was seriously worried.

"Define serious?"

"Do you see a future with him?" They entered the elevator with several other people, so Mia did not immediately answer.

As they exited onto the second floor, she answered her mother's question, "Short term, yes. Long term, no. I don't think he'll ever be your son-in-law, Mom, or that your grandchildren will bear the surname Sheehan."

Mia almost laughed aloud at the relief on her mother's face.

"So, what is it, just physical?"

"No, it's not *just* physical, but he is one damn fine specimen."

White-gloved waiters in short cut jackets were circulating about with trays filled with crystal champagne flutes. Mia grabbed two. She did not hand one to Lois. The first one was gone in two sips and she immediately began on the second. She could feel the alcohol hitting her bloodstream.

The last time she'd eaten was seven hours before and it had been a yogurt.

"I'm very concerned about the age difference."

Ta-da, there it was. The age difference. Mia knew this was coming.

Standing before Jasper Francis Cropsey's *Autumn on the Hudson River 1860*, Mia was astounded by the perfection of Cropsey's composition. Looking at it with her photographic-trained eye, she noted that the horizon was beautifully placed about one-third of the way up the canvas, a small pond on the lower left and a stream leading in from the right toward the center of the painting led one's eye around the canvas. Brilliant, Mia thought. Why had she never noticed before that the Hudson River School painters' compositions were like perfect photographs? She was having an epiphany moment, fueled by the champagne on an empty stomach.

"Look at this composition, it is perfection."

"Are you going to answer me?" Lois sounded annoyed.

"I'm sorry, Mom. What? What was the question?"

"There was no question, I said I'm concerned about your age difference. Tom is ten years older than you. He's a grown man and you are still a teenager."

"Mother, I'm a junior in college." Where are those champagne waiters? I could use one going by right about now, Mia thought.

"You're still a teen. And don't 'Mother' me."

"And your point is?" Mia grabbed a glass off a passing waiter's tray.

"My point is, how much do you really have in common with this man? At his age, men like to do different things than young girls your age."

"Really?" Mia squinted at her mom. "I hadn't noticed. Seriously." She pounded down the champagne. "Tom and I have a lot in common. We get along very well. And I know you noticed what an absolute fox he is."

Lois sighed. She clearly wasn't going to win this battle but the war was far from over. They stopped in front of Albert Bierstadt's *Lander's Peak.* Mia loved the jagged peaks of the mountains. They looked like the Rockies.

"I was really hoping that something would happen with you and that sweetheart."

Mia looked at her mom, a perplexed look on her face, wondering who the hell she was talking about.

"You know who I'm talking about." Lois continued, "That sweet, gorgeous boy in California. Schooner. Schooner Moore."

Mia could feel the muscles in both her face and stomach contract. "Schooner Moore? Yeah, he's a *real* sweetheart, Mom." And with that,

Mia turned on her heel and stalked away.

Lois didn't follow Mia, but watched her from across the gallery. The myriad of emotions flying across her daughter's face at lightning speed was both very telling and alarming to watch. Every muscle in Mia's being was bristling. Lois could actually see the tense twitches coursing through her daughter's body. She had clearly struck a chord just mentioning the young man's name.

For the first time in a year, Lois Silver finally had an indication of what had happened to her daughter.

Back in the Silver's apartment, Lois tore through papers she had stashed in the top drawer of the nightstand next to her side of the bed. Although nearly two years had passed, she was sure she still had Dee Moore's phone number somewhere.

The past summer, Mia had returned home from California sullen and withdrawn. She arrived on an earlier flight than scheduled and sat in the airport for five hours without contacting them to let them know she was there. Announcing that she would not be returning to school in California, Mia immediately inquired if either her mother or father had any connections associated with an east coast college, so that they could get her admitted, even though final admission deadlines had long passed for the fall semester. Lois and Bob were thrilled that Mia was not actually planning to drop out of school and began to call in favors. With Mia's strong academic record and high SAT scores (and the fact that the Silvers were actually paying for Mia's education in full versus her attending on a financial aid scholarship), it turned out to be surprisingly easy for them to get Mia placed at one of the most prestigious small Liberal Arts schools in New York state.

Barely emerging from her room for most of the summer, an unkempt Mia refused to confide in her parents the reason for fleeing California or for her uncharacteristically depressed behavior.

Her reaction this evening to Schooner's name and Lois' suggestion that she would've liked to have seen them together as a couple was extreme, to say the least, Lois thought. It was also very telling. Something had happened between Mia and Schooner that had left her young daughter devastated.

Lois wondered if Dee had seen any odd changes in her son's behavior the past summer. Did he come home from school sullen and miserable, too? Had Schooner and Mia experienced a tragic breakup? It was Lois' experience that when one party was so utterly devastated, the other party was suffering an equally miserable reaction — especially with a young love. Her daughter's response to whatever had happened between them had been alarming. Lois couldn't help but think that maybe the Moores had seen an equally disturbing behavioral change in their sweet (yes, he was sweet, very sweet, no matter what her daughter said) son.

After thirty minutes of unsuccessfully trying to locate a scrap of paper with a phone number scribbled on it, Lois gave up the search and reached for the telephone. She dialed directory assistance in the 714-area code and asked for the phone number of a Gavin Moore located in Newport Beach.

The directory assistance operator checked for the number and informed Lois that the Moores, in fact, had an unpublished number. An unlisted telephone number. She had struck out. Reached a dead end.

Lois hung up the phone and sighed. As a mother, she knew in her gut that her daughter had put 3,000 miles between herself and that beautiful blonde boy because he had shattered her heart. Her gut also told her that Mia had probably done the same to him.

Lois Silver's heart ached for the both of them.

Chapter Nineteen

"I see Rob with my parents over there." Joni was pointing into the large crowd.

"Where? Give me a landmark." Mia was scanning the field.

"Woman in hot pink, two rows up, a few people to the right." Joni was waving, but in the sea of black caps and gowns, it was unlikely they'd see her.

"Oh yeah. Yeah. I see them. Do you see my parents anywhere? Or Tom?" Mia continued to unsuccessfully scan the crowd.

"Looking." Joni joined the search.

Commencement day. A long way from walking The Quad in California during freshman orientation. That seemed like a million years ago. It was a million years ago. Mia pictured Henry and Rosie in their caps and gowns and smiled. She missed them and wished there were a way to share this day with them. But so much time had passed. She just hoped that their lives were happy and that they were moving on to exciting things in their post-collegiate worlds.

And then there was him. She'd successfully not thought about him in quite a while. But today, well today was graduation day, the last day of her college career and she had met him on the very first day of her college career. Long ago and far away. A lifetime ago. She tried to picture what he might look like, so tall and lean, in his cap and gown. So handsome. And she felt her eyes filling with tears. It had been three years. Three years this very week. She didn't hate him anymore. And that was a good thing. "I wish you happiness," she said silently, in her head, "I'm happy and I wish you happiness." And she was happy. She'd had three great years being in school back east, made wonderful friends, had Tom in her life and a job waiting for her in New York City at BBDO — one of the biggest ad agencies in the world, where she'd interned the past few summers. It had all worked out. Her whole world was before her, exciting and unknown. Mia was honest enough with herself though to admit to the slightest wonder, what would it all be like if she was sharing it with him? And then she told herself to let it go, because that was a dream that was never going to come true.

"I see them!" Mia tried to follow Joni's pointing finger.

"Landmark, please," Mia laughed.

"Right edge of the bleachers, like five rows up. There is a woman in turquoise directly behind Tom."

"I see him. I see him. I see him." Mia was jumping up and down and just the sight of him flung the thought of Schooner back 3,000 miles to his own graduation.

Mia hadn't seen Tom in two months — the longest she'd gone without him since they'd been together. Even from a distance he looked incredible. As if reading her mind, Joni pinched her arm. "He is so hot, Mia. The man is just sexy."

Mia laughed, "Too sexy for his own good. And for mine."

Ninety minutes later, Mia and Joni were college graduates and were milling their way through the crowd in search of finding their loved ones. Tom was walking towards her and all she could see was his smile. Breaking into a run, she flung herself into his arms and her feet were off the ground as he spun around with her in his arms.

"I'm so proud of you, Jailbait." Putting her down and taking her face in his hands, he kissed her deeply and she put her cap on his head, making them both laugh into each other's mouths.

Mia had not realized just how much she missed him until that moment. Turning to her parents for kisses and a group hug, she felt surrounded by so much love. After two years, Lois had finally accepted Tom as a part of their world and they actually got along well.

Later at dinner with Tom and her parents, Joni, Rob, and Joni's parents and younger sister, Mia felt like she had her own pack — Joni, Rob, Tom and her parents — they were the core of her world. She reveled in the moment because she was well aware that the very next moment would change everything. Rob and Joni were going to be living upstate in Ithaca where Rob would be working on his MFA (at Cornell!) and she was going to be moving down to the city. They would no longer be a part of one another's everyday world. Mia knew she would miss having them right outside her bedroom door, sharing the kitchen and the one bathroom in their tiny student ghetto apartment.

Tom was clinking on his wine glass. "To Mia and Joni, you now have a whole new world in front of you to explore. Be bold. Be adventurous. Take risks. Fail. Get up. Do it again. I'm really proud of you two and I can't wait to see you both conquer the world." He was met with a round of "here-here." He then reached inside the inner breast pocket of his blazer and pulled out an envelope. Handing the envelope to Mia, Tom smiled.

"This is the first part of your graduation gift."

"Shall I open it now?"

"Please do." Tom was beaming and looking at Mia like there was no one else in the restaurant, let alone at their table.

Mia opened the envelope and slipped out the sheet of paper and began to read. Her eyes grew wide and her mouth was agape. She looked at Tom and he nodded. "I accepted."

Mia screeched and threw her arms around him, planting a loud wet kiss on his lips and laughing.

"What is it?" Lois asked the question to which everyone wanted the answer.

"Can I tell them?" Mia asked Tom, clearly ecstatic.

He nodded again.

"You are all looking at the newest faculty member of NYU's Film School."

The news brought another round of toasts and cheers.

Mia had a million questions, "When are you moving back?"

"Baby, I am back," leveling an incendiary look that made Mia squirm. Tom leaned forward and whispered into her ear, "We need to find a place to live."

Mia leaned back, devil grin slowly taking up residence on her face. "Are you asking me to live with you?"

"Why do you think I wanted to come back to New York?" He was devouring her with his eyes.

"Because the pizza sucks in LA?"

Tom laughed, "That too, Jailbait." Slinging an arm around her shoulder, he pulled her close to him.

Across the table, smiles on their faces, Lois Silver and Rob Ryan were both writing the last chapter of this romance, and while their details differed ever so slightly, their ending was surprisingly similar. In neither tale did the final page bode well for this heroine.

Chapter Twenty

Mia was sitting in the employee cafeteria at BBDO eating tomato soup and a grilled cheese, totally engrossed in Stephen King's, *The Stand*[1], when she noticed feet standing right next to her. Looking up, she was surprised to see, peering down at her, one of the Assistant Account Executives. She'd seen him in the staff meetings and passed him in the hallways many times, but had never actually spoken to him.

Their eyes met, his brown eyes narrowing as if he were taking her all in and was slightly disgusted.

Mia glared back at him. "Can I help you?" her tone was less than pleasant.

"I doubt that."

Great, a dramatic queen, Mia thought, wondering what the hell he wanted.

He quickly went on, "But I can sure as hell help you. You are in need of some serious help."

On the verge of ripping him a new asshole and telling him to take a hike, he once again shocked Mia when he sat down next to her. She knew she was giving him her, *if looks could kill, we'd be burying you tomorrow* look, but he appeared completely undaunted.

"I've read the copy you are writing and you are really talented," he began. "And somewhere under that insane 'Bridge and Tunnel' hair, you are actually really cute, but concert tee-shirts and jeans are so 80's, and you could clearly spend more than a little time at a make-up counter. You really are a disaster. But I think I can work with you. I truly believe you are salvageable material."

Mia was actually shocked into silence. *Who the hell ...*

"If you don't already know it, I'm Seth Shapiro. I work on the Apple Computer account."

"Mia Silver, VISA."

"I know who you are, Little Miss Wunderkind Copywriter, you've created quite the buzz. Are you sleeping with one of the execs?"

"No. Do women have to be sleeping with someone to get recognition?" Mia was literally sneering at Seth, who was dressed like he was ready to walk the runway. He was groomed and coiffed impeccably. She wished her fingernails looked so good.

Picking at the crumbs on the table from Mia's grilled cheese, Seth again narrowed his eyes at Mia. "The pussy will get you far with these horndogs."

Mia leaned close to Seth. "I don't shit where I eat."

Eyes widening and handsome smile emerging for the first time, "I like you. You are a snarky little bitch."

Mia laughed at his assessment.

"But you have to let me take you shopping. I just can't look at you another day."

"Talk about snarky bitches."

He stood up. "I'll come by your desk at 5:30. Go look in the mirror and say goodbye to your hair because that is going to be the first thing that goes." And with that bombshell, he was off.

"Stefano, I know you love challenges." Seth was apologizing to the tall purple-haired Italian.

"Not so bad. I can work with." Stefano was lifting Mia's hair in sections and studying it. "You have nice high cheekbones. No more hiding. I want to side-part your hair and cut it into a bob just below your chin. We will have more than twelve inches. Would you like to donate it to the Locks of Love Organization?"

Mia smiled at Stefano in the mirror and nodded yes. Stefano proceeded to put her hair in a loose ponytail and cut off in excess of a foot of Mia's hair.

Mia gasped, "I love it already." And Stefano had not even begun to style it.

"Come, I wash you."

Mia followed Stefano through the funky East Village salon. The walls were painted black and the chandeliers looked like they'd been lifted out of a haunted house at the end of Halloween season. Mia laid her head back in the bowl and closed her eyes, enjoying Stefano's strong fingers scrubbing her scalp. She couldn't believe she agreed to let Seth have his way with her and thought maybe this was her karmic payback for her Rob Ryan makeover.

Forty-five minutes later, a chic Mia with a bouncy new 'do' was in a trendy boutique, buying a whole lot of new style. Seth had her in skirts with boots and wide belts and layers of southwestern jewelry. It was cool and it was funky and it was the new adult Mia.

"Oh my God, I want to wear this outfit home, my boyfriend is going to freak out." Mia was spinning in front of a three-way mirror, her skirt floating like an aura around her.

"So, you live with your boyfriend?" Seth was about to pounce for details.

"I do." Mia was handing the sales clerk a credit card as another associate was wrapping all her new clothes in tissue paper, tying the bundles in ribbon and bagging it.

"How long have you been together?" Seth was helping Mia carry all the bags.

"Like three years, but we've only been living together for a year." Mia was checking out her reflection in the windows of all the buildings they passed. "I don't even look like me. I love my hair short."

"Well, it's not exactly short, but it's stylish. Back to the boyfriend. What's his name?"

"His name is Tom."

"You met him in college, I'm assuming, if you've been together three years."

"Yes, I met him in college." Mia knew Seth was assuming Tom had been another student. Mia stopped under an awning, "This is my building, would you like to come up?"

"This is your building? You live in a doorman building?"

Mia laughed, "I do." She loved being able to shock Seth. Lois and Bob Silver were not happy when their daughter told them where she and Tom had begun to look for apartments. They were neighborhoods in transition, gentrification was taking place, but they were far from being considered good neighborhoods, and in some cases, were only marginally safe. And that is when Lois and Bob stepped in and gave Mia another graduation gift. They bought her an apartment.

As they rode the elevator to the sixteenth floor, Seth commented, "I never in a million years would have pictured you in a doorman building on the edge of The Village. I thought for sure you were living in Williamsburg or Boerum Hill or Astoria, but I did not expect a downtown Manhattan hi-rise."

Mia pulled her keys out of her beat-up leather satchel (the one thing that Seth did think was cool), and muttered, "Showtime," under her breath — she could not wait to see Tom's reaction to her transformation to adult, to cool New York City Ad Agency chic.

They walked into the foyer and stepped out into the open living room/

dining room. Tom was sitting at the dining room table grading papers. Contact lenses out for the night, Tom was wearing glasses, and looked even more handsome with them on. Dressed in a V-neck fitted black tee-shirt and faded jeans, the man could stop traffic.

Looking up from his work, Tom's face transformed from the seriousness of being focused on student screenplays to the delight of meeting his new leading lady. "Oh Jailbait, you are stunning." He got out of his chair and headed straight for Mia. Taking her face in both hands, his smile radiated both approval and lust. "Wow. You look amazing." And his lips came down for a crushing kiss that made Seth start shifting his weight from foot to foot. Seth never would have guessed in a million years that little hippie girl copywriter Mia lived in a doorman building with a sexy, I-want-to-fuck-you-right-now older boyfriend.

Tom broke their kiss and Mia smiled at him. "You like?"

"I love." His eyes already fucking her.

"Tom, I want you to meet Svengali, errr, I mean Seth."

Seth backhanded Mia in the upper arm, then extended his hand to Tom.

"Are you responsible for this transformation?" Tom was enjoying the view.

"Yes, Bride of Frankenstein here is my creation."

"You did good, Sven. I mean Seth."

Tom gave him one of his wicked smiles and Mia could swear she saw Seth's cock twitch in his pants.

Enjoying the same view as her grandparent's apartment of the World Trade Centers, Mia and Seth stood before the windows taking in the massive monoliths lit up against the night sky.

"This is amazing." Seth was mesmerized by the view.

Tom came up behind Mia and wrapped his arms around her neck. She could feel him grinding into her lower back and just the thought of being taken from behind in front of the windows made her wet. It was time to get rid of their guest — quickly.

Mia saw Seth out of the door and went and stood in front of the windows. She could see her own reflection in the glass as she looked out over the city. She was loving seeing her new bobbed mane and gorgeous clothes. Clothes that she couldn't wait for Tom to take off her.

Tom emerged from the kitchen with two glasses of crisp white wine. He handed one to Mia and stood directly behind her, so close that she could feel the heat from his body.

He sipped the cold wine and dipped his head to whisper in her ear, the chill of his lips sending a shiver through her. "You look so freaking hot. I can't wait to fuck you." He wrapped an arm around her and pulled her up against him. "Look what you've done to me. My cock has been aching since you walked in here." He splayed a hand over her lower abdomen and pressed her tightly against him. "Feel that? That's all for you."

Mia leaned her head back into him. Tom put his glass of wine down on the coffee table and with his right hand now free, found Mia's right nipple through her new blouse, pinching it hard and rolling it between his fingers until it was a tight knot.

"You are wearing way too much. I want to show this city how hot my girlfriend is. Lift your arms," he commanded and Mia complied. He lifted her blouse up off over her head and gently tossed it on the couch. Lowering his lips to her neck, Tom once again began to pinch Mia's nipple, this time through her cream lace bra. Mia moaned with pleasure and Tom ground his cock up against her ass. "I think this city needs to see how much you like to be fucked, don't you?"

Mia moaned again, already so turned on by what she knew was going to happen. Tom unhooked the back of Mia's bra and slowly pushed the straps down her arms. He was going to make a meal of this. As her bra dropped to the floor, Tom cupped her breasts in each hand, rolling her hardened nipples between his thumb and forefinger.

"Just think, in the building across the way or in the corner apartments that jut out, some guy is looking at your gorgeous tits and wishing he was sucking on them. He's watching me strip you and he's getting rock hard just watching you. Soon when I fuck you up against that window, he's going to have his cock in his hand and he's going to be jerking off watching me fuck you." Mia moaned loudly, turned on by Tom's words and the thought that someone (or several someones) was watching Tom playing with her body and getting ready to fuck her. "You like the thought of that, don't you, Jailbait? You like the thought of other men watching me fuck you." Mia moaned and Tom grabbed a handful of her curls. "Say it."

"Yes, I like the idea of some total stranger watching us. Getting off watching us." Mia spread her legs as his arm snaked around to the front of her. She leaned her weight back into him and his fingers started to stroke her very wet pussy.

"You are so turned on by this, my little exhibitionist. The idea of other men watching me fuck you has gotten you so hot." Tom had three fingers inside of her and her leg muscles were starting to quake. "I think I'm going to fuck you in front of the windows every night. They'll be waiting to see you come, cocks in their hands." Mia melted down and started coming at the thought of all the men watching her get fucked and Tom pressed the heel of his palm against her clit. "That's right, Jailbait. Come for them. Let them see your face when you're coming."

Mia's weight was against Tom as he undid his jeans and stepped out of them. Pressing her up against the window, foreplay was clearly done and he couldn't wait a second longer. Grabbing her hips, he positioned her perfectly and rammed into her. Mia gasped, her fingers clawing and sliding down the window, her cheek pressed against the cool glass. She could not believe how turned on she was at the thought that other men might be watching them and getting off watching her get fucked. Thinking about men sitting in their apartments, at their windows, seeing her naked and at Tom's mercy, started throwing her into her next orgasm.

"Oh God, Oh God, Oh God, Oh God." Her head was back and she could swear her eyes were rolling back into her head. As she pictured a man in the building across from her stroking his hard cock and coming, she took all of Tom's ramming.

"Grab the back of that chair," he ordered and Mia turned to her left, with Tom still inside of her and grabbed the high back of a plush chair. Her right side was now facing the window and with Tom right behind her, if anyone *was* watching, they could now see Tom's thick cock stroking in and out of her. Tom reached forward and grabbed a handful of Mia's hair, pulling her head back to him while he relentlessly drove into her. "I want them to see me fuck you. I want them to see you taking all of my cock." Mia moaned and whimpered at his words. "You like this, don't you?" She moaned again and he tugged hard on her hair. It hurt, but that turned her on even more. "I asked you a question."

"Yes, I like this."

"Why? Why do you like it, Mia?"

She was panting as he continued to tug on her hair. "It's hot."

With a sudden and painful sharp tug on her hair, he hissed, "You can do better than that. Tell me why you like it."

"I like the thought of people watching us. Getting off to us."

He pulled her head back by her hair so that his lips were brushing her ear, his cock buried deeply in her, "That's a good start, Jailbait. We'll get you there."

She wasn't quite sure where he wanted her to get to, but wherever she was, she was so far gone over the edge and was about to tumble for a third time. Mia heard Tom whispering in her ear, "You're my little whore, aren't you?"

"Yes," her cry sounded anguished, but she was tumbling down an abyss and wanted to take him with her. She squeezed his cock tight with her muscles and held it — she wanted to make him explode. She reached back and pulled his face into her neck by his hair, "Yes, I'm your little whore. All yours." And she heard him groan, his arm circling around her waist and pulling her down tight onto his cock.

"Oh God," he groaned into her neck. "Yes, all mine. My whore. You only come for me, Whore." And with one last deep drive, she felt his entire body shudder as he released into her.

Tangled, they didn't move, as they regained their breathing.

"Holy shit, Tom." Mia was the first to speak.

"Holy shit is right. Oh my God, was that hot." It was a statement.

Mia was nodding her head. "Very. I think we should make a nightly date of this."

Tom kissed her neck. "I really like this new you."

Mia turned to him — looking him in the eye for the first time and laughed. "I think you cheated on Mia tonight."

A slow smile took over his face and he shook his head no. "I think I may have met Mia for the first time tonight."

She laughed, "She's pretty hot, isn't she?" And she caught a glimpse of her reflection in the window — this new sophisticated look.

She was no longer a little girl hiding behind her mane of hair and after tonight she wondered how much this change had really exposed.

[1] Stephen King, The Stand, (New York, Doubleday 1978)

Chapter Twenty-One

Seth took full credit for Mia's rise at BBDO. "No one was really going to take you seriously with that hideous 'Bridge and Tunnel' hair."

"Yeah, yeah, yeah," she humored him. "There's something I want to talk to you about. Let's go get a latte."

Mia and Seth emerged out onto 6th Avenue, walked two blocks up to 54th Street and ducked into a new little San Francisco-style coffee house, complete with couches and big leather chairs.

"What couldn't you talk to me about in the office?"

Mia blew at the foam in her drink. "This goes nowhere." She leveled him a steely glance.

He met her steel with steel and upped the ante with attitude. Mia and Seth had become inseparable over the months, taking their breaks together at work, going to lunch daily and seeing each other socially on nights and weekends. Surprisingly, Tom and Seth got along quite well, a quality in Tom she really appreciated.

She leaned into him and in little more than a whisper confided, "I had drinks two nights ago with Brett Russell from VISA. He's leaving VISA and taking over all of print advertising for American Express. He hates Ogilvy, but can't pull it all from them, but wants to place the direct someplace else."

Seth gasped. "That is huge. Is he bringing it to BBDO?" The ramifications of BBDO taking any of Ogilvy & Mathers' AmEx business was enormous. David Ogilvy was the genius behind, 'Never Leave Home Without It' — one of the most iconographic taglines ever to come off Madison Avenue.

Mia just shook her head no. Seth's eyes were wide with confusion and that is when Mia hit him with a devil smile blast. "He's giving it to me."

"What do you mean he's giving it to you?" Seth slammed down his latte on the wooden table next to his chair, causing an arcing splash that hit the leg of his pants.

"I'm going to open an agency. American Express direct mail is going to be my first client."

The look on Seth's face was classic — the man who had a retort for everything was stunned into total silence. He picked up his latte and regarded Mia skeptically over the rim. “You lie, Bitch.”

“No lie, Princess. This is for real. I want you to come with me. Someone needs to manage things and you know I suck at that. I can do strategy, concept, write the creative, but I could not put a client schedule together if my life depended on it.”

“Are you offering me a job?” Now Seth was smiling.

“Well, in about 90 days. And the beauty is since AmEx is not a BBDO client they can’t come after me for poaching.” Mia looked pretty self-satisfied.

“Where are you getting the money for this, if you don’t mind my asking?”

Mia laughed, “I have a Ph.D.”

Seth now truly looked confused. Wunderkind BBC was still in her early 20’s, he knew she was smart, but a Ph.D? And what money would come from that? All that education would just rack up more debt.

Mia decided it was time to clear up Seth’s confusion. “Ph.D means Papa has Dough.” And she laughed.

“Bitch,” he bellowed.

“I met with my parents and grandparents last night and they are going to give me the seed money to get it off the ground.”

“You lucky little wench. This is so exciting. Our new offices are going to be so chic.” Seth was already envisioning the image he would create for the new agency. “So, what does dark, gorgeous, brooding poet think of all this?”

Mia shrugged. “He seems to be excited.”

“What are you naming it?”

“M. Silver & Associates. And I would like you to be my very first associate. We need to be on the lookout for more associates. We’ll need graphics, production, traffic, sales.” They got up and started to head back to the office. “Are you around this weekend to start looking at space?”

“Hell, yes.” He swatted her in the arm. “And I’m certainly not going to let you decorate.”

Three days later, Mia and Seth sat in BBDO’s auditorium watching a presentation from the sales team. Seth was critiquing all the presenters, starting with what they had chosen to wear for their big day on stage — and he wasn’t being kind.

The team of J.D. Barone and Kami Townes took the stage and Seth immediately dug his fingers into Mia’s knee. J.D. was part movie star handsome and part New York bad boy. With his thick, dark, slightly-too-long pushed back hair, olive skin and striking hazel eyes, it was evident that the man got more pussy than Purina.

"I want him," Seth whispered into Mia's ear.

"Ditto." Mia was mesmerized as he wowed the crowd with his very white smile.

"You have dark, gorgeous, brooding poet — don't be a pig." And he slapped her knee. "Check out the southern belle." Seth was giving Kami a quick once over. "Conservative, but smart clothes. The suit is Oleg Cassini and the shoes are Cole-Haan, but what's with that pearl necklace. I have never seen her without it."

"The only pearl necklace I ever wear…" Devil Mia was in the house.

"Do *not* finish that sentence." Seth shot her the evil eye.

J.D. and Kami began their presentation. J.D. was all fluff, smoke and mirrors, baffle 'em with bullshit, but Kami's comments were smart, insightful and backed up with a lot of data that she presented in an accessible and easily understandable manner. Within a few minutes, J.D. started speaking over Kami and cutting her off. In good southern girl style, she reacted to his behavior quite gracefully.

"He was really good looking until he opened his mouth," Mia whispered to Seth.

"What an ass."

J.D.'s boorish behavior continued to escalate, and what Mia originally viewed as a dazzling smile, was now an obnoxious obstruction that she wanted to slap off his smug face. Kami remained classy and cool, but Mia imagined her seething inside.

As they were all leaving the auditorium, Mia stepped out in the aisle next to Kami.

"You did a great job," Mia shared, motioning her head toward J.D., sneered and rolled her eyes. "Good looking until he opened his mouth."

Kami smiled, "Fucking dickwad."

Damn, that sounds so polite coming out of her mouth, Mia thought.

And in that moment, the conservative, ladylike southern belle was immediately someone Mia knew she could be friends with and possibly the newest member of M. Silver & Associates.

That Friday night, Mia, Seth and Kami went for drinks and with a few gin and tonics in her, Kami let loose about J.D. Barone and what hell it was to work with the misogynistic egomaniac. Stealing Kami's thunder onstage wasn't the first of her accomplishments for which he had taken credit. Kami was even talking about going back to Birmingham to go work for a local employer because she was so turned off by the cut-throat backstabbing environment amongst her sales colleagues.

"What if you could do what you are doing, but in an atmosphere where the ethos was more in line with your ethics?" Four drinks in, Mia was more convinced than ever that J.D.'s disrespectful display in front of the entire New York office was actually divine providence.

"Show me the place and sign me up." Kami slammed her gin and tonic down on the teak bar.

And that night, Mia's company went from M. Silver & Associate to M. Silver & Associates.

Chapter Twenty-Two

M. Silver & Associates had no problem assembling a dream staff and with American Express as an anchor client, Kami Townes' job of attracting and signing new business was surprisingly easier than they all had anticipated. There was a movement afoot within large corporations of bringing on boutique agencies for at least a portion of the business so that they would be able to truly maintain a hands-on partner relationship with their advertising agency. More often than not, it was new product launches where the corporations were feeling very protective over their new babies.

The new office of MS&A was a little off the beaten path — instead of being midtown with the Madison Avenue behemoths, MS&A took over some old warehouse space in the Meatpacking District on the west side. A large loft-like space with brick walls and wide planked wood floors, the building dated back to the 1890's and the funky ambience screamed Mia Silver. With the help of a young architect that Seth had met dancing one night at The Saint, they transformed the space to include private offices, conferences rooms outfitted for full-scale client presentations, a kitchen, bathrooms and a "living room" designed to become the central hangout and brainstorming space of the agency.

Mia stood alone in her new office, surrounded by cozy brick walls and southern facing floor to ceiling windows that showcased the same view as her apartment, the World Trade Center Towers. Appearing like sentinels in her life, these huge monoliths watched over her, even in this new space.

Walking over to the window, she just wanted to pinch herself. How many 20-somethings had pulled off something like this? Taking a deep breath, Mia realized she now had the responsibility for all the people that threw their lot in to take this leap of faith with her, and there was not a chance in hell that she would let them down. She would make this work somehow — if it took 100 hour weeks, Mia knew she would be the one there in the office with her sleeves rolled up burning the midnight oil. She would lead by example and she would set the example by being the example.

For Mia Silver, failure was not an option.

Everyone seemed to be moving on and settling in with their lives. Rob and Joni were getting married, and Rob was going to be teaching at Ithaca

College, Tom was a favorite prof at NYU and working on a new screenplay of his own, and Mia was now the owner of an ad agency. The owner of an ad agency. Surfuckingreal.

Smiling at the Twin Towers, Mia looked at the North Tower and thought maybe they should celebrate their opening at Windows on the World. Although she'd had dreams of another celebration there, that probably wasn't in the cards for her. She and Tom would never get married. He wasn't the marrying kind and their relationship was like good buddies who had great amazing sex (Mia laughed to herself, "Oh crap — he's going to want to fuck me in front of these windows, too." — an ongoing and regular favorite activity of theirs), but it wasn't love. Or at least not "in love" love.

Feeling the tears well in her eyes (it was rare, but it still happened at the oddest moments), she wondered where he was. Was he on the tennis circuit somewhere? Married? Still living in southern California? It was when she thought about what she didn't have with Tom that she missed Schooner most — or the memory of what she had felt for him. Yearning for that high, Mia wondered if she would only find it in other places. Places like work.

Mia knew that people thought she had it all or had gotten it too easily and too quickly, but what they didn't know was what she wanted more than anything seemed so elusive to her that she didn't even know where or how to begin to find it. The one thing that she would give up everything for was not a fantasy and she knew that. She had tasted it. She had savored it. She had consumed it. She had been consumed by it. And now, even if she had a treasure map leading her to it, she would still be at a loss as to how to find it. Or what to do with it, if she did find it.

Standing in her new office, in the shadow of the Twin Towers, Mia felt like she had it all and like she had nothing. She was bursting with pride and felt like an empty shell. And above all, even though she was in a relationship with a man she was living with and surrounded by a great staff who were more than just colleagues — Mia felt something to which she was no stranger — she felt alone. And she really would not have known that there was any other way to feel. This would not have been a bad thing. Had it not been for him. Damn you, Schooner — why did you show me what I was capable of feeling. She missed the blissful ignorance of not knowing feelings of that depth even existed. Not knowing that she could feel them. Not feeling alone.

"I didn't know I could feel so addicted to someone. I didn't know I'd

ever want to…" She had confessed to him.

And now she couldn't think of anything she wanted more.

Mia scrunched up her nose and made a face at the World Trade Center Towers. Then she stuck her tongue out at them.

Looking down the street, a road whose old cobblestones from a bygone era were exposed where asphalt had worn away, Mia decided that Artie's Warehouse, with their incredible Lamb Chops and Pasta Primavera, would be the perfect place to celebrate the opening of M. Silver & Associates.

Chapter Twenty-Three

The newborn leaves were that wonderful pale lime color that only lasts through the very first days of spring. Mia walked along 21st Street, the warmth of the noon sun beating down on her dark hair. The breeze still held a hint of a northeast winter that did not want to be totally forgotten. Smiling at a clear blue sky, *she thought, too bad I just can't play hooky the rest of this glorious Friday afternoon and just call it a weekend already.*

Mia was positive the Archetype Software folder must still be sitting on the dining room table as it was not stuffed into her Ghurka bag with the rest of the client folders. It was the last place she remembered seeing the file as she gave it a quick once over while eating her bagel that morning.

The thought of the leftover Eggplant Parmigiana from Stella's in the refrigerator made her begin to walk even faster. She'd been thinking about the delectable Italian food ever since she realized she would have to go home for the client file. Tom hated eggplant, so she knew he wouldn't have grabbed it for himself. Sometimes she'd have an urge for her leftover meals only to find his urge had won the footrace to the fridge.

Stopping at the mail slots in the lobby, Mia cleaned out the overstuffed mailbox. Mostly catalogues, a few bills, an invite to something. Emerging from the elevator, she juggled getting the key in the lock while she opened the invite. Tossing everything on the front hall table, her first thought was annoyance. Tom had left the TV on in the bedroom again. The man had to have some background noise all the time and was constantly forgetting to turn the TV off.

Walking down the hall to the bedroom, she felt her stomach begin to knot before her brain even began to process why. She stood at the threshold to her bedroom watching the back of a skinny blonde, with a raccoon stripe of dark roots, bouncing up and down on her boyfriend's cock. All she could see of Tom were his legs and his hands on the girl's hips forcefully bouncing her up and down.

"That's it. Come on, baby, give it to me. You know you want to. Just give it to me," his voice almost breathless.

The blonde moaned, her orgasm just beginning, and she tossed her head back, eyes opening to the sight of a blank-faced Mia Silver leaning in the doorway, arms crossed over her chest.

The girl screamed, disengaging painfully (based on his loud "oww") from Tom's cock and rolling to her left side, grabbing Mia's brand-new Ralph Lauren Egyptian cotton sheet to cover herself.

"What the fuck…" Tom had still not seen Mia standing there silently.

"Who are you?" the girl screamed at Mia.

"You are fucking my boyfriend, in my bed, in my brand new fucking sheets that I'm now going to have to burn because they are covered with your skanky body fluids and you are asking *me* who I am?" Mia's voice was reaching a dangerous pitch.

"Who is she, Tom?" With saucer blue eyes (also sporting a raccoon look to match her hair), she looked to a stunned Tom Sheehan for answers.

"Yeah Tom, who am I?"

Tom held up a hand. "Mia, I know this is upsetting."

"Upsetting? You think this is upsetting? What are you, a fucking rocket scientist?"

Mia walked to the closet and pulled out a large black nylon travel duffle and threw it at Tom, smacking him in the face.

"Pack your shit up and get the hell out of here," Mia hissed through clenched teeth.

"She can't throw you out of your own apartment." The skank had no clue as to the wrath she was summoning.

"His apartment? This isn't his apartment. It's my apartment. That's my bed." And she pivoted to point at Tom. "I have never said that to you." And she hadn't. She had always referred to everything as theirs, never hers. That courtesy had just ended.

The enormity of his upcoming life change was dawning on Tom and becoming visible on his face. He was clearly at a loss as to how to deal with a situation he had not anticipated.

"She's crazy. Can't you just throw her out of here?" The skank was clearly still not comprehending the dynamic.

"Crazy? Did you just call me crazy?" Mia bent down and picked up the pile of clothes off the floor. "I'd burn these, except I'd never get the smell of polyester out of my apartment." And in one swift move, Mia was at the window. She pushed it open from the wood frame and out went the girl's clothes, floating away like colorful kites on the spring breeze sixteen floors above Manhattan's street life.

The girl shrieked, threw off the gorgeous Egyptian cotton top sheet and started to lunge at Mia. Mia stood her ground (and the skank had a good four to five inches on Mia) and pointed a finger at her that said "back."

Stopping dead in her tracks, not quite sure what to do, the girl remained in her lunging position, naked and not moving.

"I'd kick you in the pussy, but I'm afraid I'd lose my shoe up there."[1]

Mia was on a tear. Something caught her eye and she bent down and scooped up a pair of Chukka boots. Holding them in front of her, Mia asked, "Are these yours?" She looked at them with disdain from multiple angles and then looked up at their owner. "They're ugly." And with a toss of her arm, the shoes sailed out the open window. "And now they are ugly road kill." Mia smiled, looking very self-satisfied, "The Shoe Gods are thanking me for that." Her attention now turned to Tom. "Start packing," her scream was shattering.

With her finger pointed back at the girl, she hissed, "Get out, skank." Mia picked up the top sheet and threw it at the shell-shocked girl. As the girl caught the sheet, Mia started pushing her out of the bedroom and down the hall toward the front door to the apartment.

"You are a crazy fucking bitch. No wonder why he cheats on you." Her twisted face revealing the hatred she spewed at Mia.

"Shut the fuck up, bitch." Mia pushed her out the door into the hallway.

Out in the hall were two men. Mia recognized one of them. He had moved in a few months back into the corner apartment two doors down. Mia had smiled and said hello and he had always returned her hello with a wide, friendly smile. His friend was a good-looking dark-haired gym rat with bulging biceps. The men were momentarily shocked by the naked girl in the hall holding the sheet.

"Crazy bitch," the girl turned back to scream at Mia as she wrapped herself in the sheet and feverishly hit the elevator call button. Mia was not leaving until the girl was in the elevator and gone.

"You're about to go out in the street naked and barefoot, wearing a sheet. Who do you think looks crazy in this scenario, bitch?" And the elevator door opened. Mia could hear her stabbing at the buttons and finally the door closed.

Mia turned to the two men and gave them a devil smile. "You got to love New York." Still shocked, they laughed at the levity Mia had brought to the moment. "Excuse me, gentlemen. One down and one to go."

Mia walked back in the apartment and Tom was standing before her, naked.

"Put something on. I don't want to see your skank diseased dick." Silently, he left and returned a few minutes later in jeans and a black tee shirt, looking every inch the bad boy brooding gorgeous poet.

Palms up with a shrug, “I’m sorry, Mia.”

“You’re sorry you got caught, Tom.”

Smiling, “That, too.”

“I’m not amused.” Mia’s anger was escalating to a dangerous threshold. She could feel her chest tightening and the bile rising in her throat. Do not cry, she commanded herself.

“I know.”

“In my bed, Tom?”

“Your bed?” his tone was ice.

“Yes, my bed. You don’t live here anymore.”

Running a hand through his unruly, just fucked hair, “So, that’s it? After all these years? Not even a discussion.”

Taking a deep breath to steady herself, “What’s to discuss? You can’t keep your dick in your pants. You brought someone into our home, Tom.” Mia screamed the last part.

“It was wrong. I’m sorry. Fucking her was wrong. Bringing her here to fuck her was just stupid.”

“Whatever. Just get your shit and get out of here.” Mia walked into the kitchen, grabbed a glass from the cabinet, she filled it with cold water from the refrigerator door. Leaning against the counter to steady herself, Mia slowly sipped the cold water as she gave herself a pep talk to hold it together just a little while longer.

Tom followed Mia into the kitchen and leaned up against the counter. She met his gaze with a cold glare. “It’s not like you’ve ever said you loved me, Mia.”

Mia’s cold glare turned to steel. “You are not turning this around on me, Tom. I didn’t come in here with another man and fuck him in your bed. And when was the last time you told me that you loved me. Ummm, let me think. That would be, ummm, never,” her tone dripped with sarcasm.

“Well, you never told me.”

“Told you what?” her tone was clipped.

He held her gaze and in a very soft voice, “Your secrets.”

Mia just shook her head. “I guess on some level I just didn’t trust you. How prophetic.” Mia looked down, as if contemplating, and then looked up at Tom. “Okay, you want my secrets, here you go. The first and second man I had sex with were two scumbags who grabbed me as I was leaving the darkroom on campus late one night at my college in California. They dragged me into the bushes in a park across from school and took turns using me as a punching bag and raping me." Mia could see the horror on Tom's face and in his eyes as if so many small pieces of the puzzle were snap clicking into place. Mia continued, "Guy number three who I slept with, was a guy I had been seeing, but was no longer seeing. He found me that night after the rapes. I loved him, I thought he loved me. But his girlfriend set me straight. I was a charity case he felt sorry for. He went back to her. And you were number four. Another one with other women."

"Mia." Tom started toward her.

She held up her hand, palm out to him. "Tom. Don't." Turning and putting her glass in the sink, Mia looked at the wall and said, "I'm going back to work now. I want you gone by the time I get home. Leave your keys on the dining room table. I'm going to have the locks changed tonight, and on my way out, I'll let the doormen know that you are no longer a resident of this building."

"Mia, I don't want to go. I don't want to leave you. I don't want us to end," his voice was pleading.

Mia sighed and turned to face him. "We've already ended."

"Don't you think there's something worth saving here? We could do couples therapy."

Mia just shook her head. "Tom, there's a reason why we've never said I love you to each other. I want to be in love. I want somebody who loves me. Somebody who would never dream of doing to me what you did to me today. I want that and I deserve that."

Mia brushed past Tom and grabbed the file off the dining room table. The file that had brought her home early on a Friday afternoon. "Let me know where to send your mail."

As she reached the front door, Tom called out, "Mia," and she turned. "Is that it?"

She nodded. "That's it," and left the apartment as she wrote the finale of another chapter of her life. A finale that both Rob Ryan and Lois Silver had penned with impeccable accuracy at her graduation dinner five years earlier.

It's shaping up to be another stellar spring, Mia thought wryly, as the elevator began its descent.

[1] Ellieism, Ellie LoveNBooks, 2013.

Chapter Twenty-Four

Mia bounced down St. Mark's Place in the East Village flanked by two handsome gay men. Seth linking arms with her on the left and his roommate, Rory, linking arms with her on the right.

"I would have killed to have been a fly on the wall watching you throw that bitch's clothes out the window." Rory had been marveling at Mia's story (which Seth told) for over an hour. "Well, don't you worry little BBC, tonight you will be surrounded by gorgeous, albeit gay, men who will treat you like the goddess that you are. Secretly Mia, we all want your tits."

As they rounded the corner to head down Second Avenue, they could already see the huge line blocking the sidewalk and waiting to get picked to get into The Saint to dance. Formerly the Fillmore East, and now renovated as the hottest gay club in New York City, The Saint's dance floor was legendary. Built under a huge dome that had been designed and constructed by a former NASA engineer, a planetarium quality star machine had been purchased by the club's land baron owner so that he would always have a place to 'dance under the stars whenever his heart desired'.

Nearing the crowd, Seth groaned as it stretched all the way down the block and around the corner. "We must know someone in this line." He scanned the crowd for a familiar party to join.

At the door, Mia checked out the security team. Three really big guys — all clearly straight — were deciding who was going to gain admittance for a night of dancing and possibly some hot balcony sex. Standing away from their view and watching them for a few minutes, it was clear that the tall handsome one in the suit and tie, at the back, was the head honcho.

Mia approached the red velvet ropes and caught the attention of one of the big goons. The man looked like a professional bodybuilder. Mia crooked her finger, indicating for him to come over. He approached her with an attitude. "Hey, can you go grab him. I need to talk to him." She pointed to the guy in the suit.

"What do you need to talk to him about?" The goon was all Brooklyn attitude.

Mia gave the goon an incredulous look. "C'mon, you work with him, so you *know* he doesn't like his personal stuff shared. I don't want him mad at either you or me."

The bluff was enough to send the goon over to the guy in the suit and deliver Mia's message. The guy glanced over at Mia and nodded at whatever was being whispered in his ear. He didn't take his eyes off her for a second.

He approached her slowly. Stone-faced. Mia made motion for him to bend down so that she could talk into his ear instead of trying to scream over the crowd. She put a hand on his shoulder and her lips close to his ear. "Today I left a file folder on my dining room table, so I had to go home at lunch to get it. Well, when I got to my apartment, I had quite the surprise. My boyfriend of seven years, who teaches at NYU, was fucking one of his students in our bed. After I threw the skank's clothes out the window, and I live on the sixteenth floor, I threw her out of my apartment, dressed in a brand, new Ralph Lauren Egyptian cotton sheet that I really loved. Then I threw the son of a bitch out. I'm here with my two gay friends because I really need to drink, and I need to be coddled tonight by gorgeous gay men who tell me how wonderful I am." Mia pulled away to look at the man's face.

"So?" His face did not betray a thing.

"So, can we go in?"

"What's your name?"

"Mia."

The guy gave Mia a hard look. "Do you think you're special, Mia?"

Mia stared into his eyes — they were a cool blue. "Tonight, not so much." She shook her head.

"You really threw her clothes out the window?" He almost smiled.

And Mia hit him with a full devil grin and nodded her head. "I did. I freaking did."

And they both laughed together.

"Go get your friends."

The look on Mia's face let him know he had made the right decision. She could see it in his eyes. "Thanks. Umm, what's your name?"

"Charles."

"Thanks, Chaz." Mia teased.

"Do you want to go to the end of the line?" He flipped to serious in a nanosecond, clearly not appreciating the nickname.

"Getting my friends." And she took off to grab Seth and Rory.

"How'd you do that, Line Cutting BBC?" Seth wanted to know. "Did you show that boy your tits?"

"Shut up." Mia backhanded him in the arm.

An hour and a half later, a dancing-sweat drenched Mia emerged through the front door and stepped out into the cool night air with two plastic drink cups in hand. Wordlessly, she handed one to Charles.

With a furrowed brow, he sniffed the contents of the cup, his facial expression immediately changing.

"How'd you know I was a scotch man?"

"Intuition. And when I saw a bottle of Glenlivet on the bar, I thought it would be a nice way to say thank you for ensuring I didn't go postal while waiting in line tonight."

Charles laughed, "Was that story you told me for real?"

Nodding. "Sad, but true."

"And this happened today?"

Mia continued to nod. "I was walking home from my office and thinking about this leftover Eggplant Parmigiana in my fridge that I was going to warm up and eat before I went back to the office."

"Bet you haven't eaten today." Charles finished his scotch.

Mia thought about that for a moment. "Wow, you're right. I haven't."

"The crowd's pretty thin here now. Have you ever eaten at Kiev?"

Mia smiled and just the thought made her stomach growl. "Best tuna in New York."

"Absolutely. Come on, let's go. Let's get some food in you."

"Just let me tell my friends and I'll be right back out. I don't want them to think I've jumped off the Brooklyn Bridge."

Mia and Charles headed one block up to Kiev. Out of date and seedy, Kiev was one of the best places in downtown Manhattan to people watch. East Village hipsters, punks after a CBGB's show on The Bowery, gays, straights, transgenders, the twenty-four-hour diner attracted all types. Renowned for their perogies and other eastern European delicacies (including their famed tuna, which was not Eastern European, but a delicacy just the same), Kiev was a New York staple for middle of the night munchies.

"So, you look like you're in pretty good shape considering your day." Charles sat back in his chair, regarding Mia.

"I feel pretty okay. My ego is severely bruised and battered, I'll tell you that. But I think I knew deep down that we probably had been at the end of the road for quite a while."

"It was comfortable?" Charles probed.

Mia nodded, her brows knit together.

Charles looked down at the table. "I recently got out of one of those."

The waitress, dressed in a 1950's style uniform, dropped off the tuna sandwiches. "Together long?" Mia picked up half of the overflowing rye bread.

"Four years."

"So, what happened?" Mia hoped Charles hadn't found her with another man.

"She wanted to get married."

"And you didn't?" It was interesting for Mia to hear the guy's point of view.

Charles shook his head.

They ate in silence for a few minutes, before Mia opened up. "What I am a little freaked out about is going home. I've never lived in my apartment alone. He was always there. I'm scared it's all going to hit me when I'm there all by myself."

Charles nodded and between bites. "It's weird. But after a few days, it's great."

Mia smiled. Her emotions were traveling at bullet train speed — angry at Tom for what he did, relieved that it was over, sad that it was over, scared to be on her own, excited to start a life that was just hers, missing him, despising him. She was starting to feel what she'd been too keyed up to feel all day.

"You'd be a terrible poker player," Charles laughed.

"It's starting to hit me, I think." Mia could feel tears welling.

"Let's go back. We'll do a few shots. I finish up in about an hour and I'll make sure you get home safely."

As they talked, it was clear they had a lot in common — both were young business owners feeling the weight of responsibility for those they employed, both had been involved in long term relationships with someone they had lived with, and both were dyed in the wool New York City kids. Their paths had just missed crossing many times at concerts and events they had both attended. By the time they had walked back to Mia's apartment she felt like Charles was a forever friend and they were discussing potentially working together on events for Mia's clients.

"Did you change your locks this afternoon?"

"No. I told him I was, but I haven't done it yet." And for the first time she started to feel nervous. It had not occurred to her before — what if Tom was up there?

As if sensing her agitation, Charles put a hand on Mia's shoulder. "I'd like to make sure your apartment is secure. I'll sleep better tonight knowing that you are not walking into any surprises."

Riding up in the elevator, Mia's nerves started to combust, her mouth began to feel like sandpaper and not taste much better. If Tom was in there, walking in with Charles at 4:30 A.M. was not going to be a pleasant scene.

Exiting on the sixteenth floor, Charles held out his hand for the keys and Mia handed them to him, her hands visibly shaking. "It's going to be fine," he reassured, as he opened the locks.

The apartment was dark and Mia flipped on the light. Nothing looked out of place. Charles walked through the living room into the dining room and then the kitchen. Mia thought it felt like a movie — checking to see if it was all clear. He pointed down the hallway and mouthed the word "bedroom?" Mia nodded and Charles headed down the hall. Please don't let him be in there, Mia prayed.

Charles returned. "All clear. One of your bedroom windows is open."

Mia rolled her eyes. "Yeah, well... Guess I forgot to close it after I threw her shoes out."

Charles let out a big, hearty laugh. "You threw her shoes out, too?"

"They were ugly." Mia was dead serious.

Charles shook his head, smiling. "You are very amusing. But I'm sure you already know that." And with that, he started checking the locks on the door and the window. "You know this place is not very secure. I'm going to have a couple of my guys come over first thing in the morning to make this a lot safer for you." Noticing the confused look on Mia's face, Charles explained, "Mia, I own a security company. It's not just goons deciding who gets into hot clubs. These guys are very well trained, people have specialties, and you would be surprised how many retired NYPD are on my payroll."

Mia noticed an envelope on the dining room table, behind Charles. It was at "his spot" at the table. The place he ate, graded papers, worked on screenplays. Mia walked over and picked it up. The word "Jailbait" was written across the front of the envelope in Tom's beautiful cursive. Reality was starting to grab at her throat and squeeze.

"Did he leave his keys?" Charles interrupted her thoughts.

"I don't see them." And she quickly went through the apartment. "No, he took them."

Charles just nodded his head. "How do you feel about an almost complete stranger sleeping on your couch?"

"I'll get you a pillow and a blanket." Mia felt relief in knowing she had protection staying in her living room. Not that she ever would expect Tom to do anything crazy or violent — that wasn't Tom — but a surprise scene would not be a good thing.

Before leaving this guardian angel, who with a large leap of faith she chose to trust, Mia sat down next to him on the couch, "Charles, thank you. Really." He nodded, but remained silent. "You'll now know when someone says they have something personal to tell you, you'll have your guys tell the person to take a hike."

He laughed and nodded, "No shit!"

Mia smiled and with a quick hug and a kiss on his cheek, she left him, letter in her hand.

Sitting down on the edge of the bed, she turned the envelope in her hands a few times, before taking a deep breath and gathering up the nerve to open it. She had the urge to say "Showtime," but didn't.

Jailbait,

I'm at such a loss for words. I want to make this right, yet I fear that is just no longer possible. I know you will never trust me again, and without that trust, we will never come close to being whole again.

First and foremost, my apology. I am sorry, Mia. I have hurt you, and until today, I had no understanding of quite how painful it is to know that you have hurt someone you love (yes, I just said the "L" word). I hurt for you and I would give up everything to change what I have done and what I have done to you.

I sit here writing this and I'm scared. I'll be honest with you, I am very scared. I don't know what life is like without you and I don't want to know what life is like without you. I have never had a relationship that has had the length or depth of what we have shared and I apologize for not treating it and you with the deserved love and respect.

You are my life, Mia. I know you don't believe that right now. I am an ass. I guess I wanted to feel like "I still had it," if that makes sense and the irony is, I now have nothing.

I am praying this is not the end of us. You have my commitment that I will do anything and everything to make this up to you, to make things right. Please don't close the door on us, Mia.

Today, I singlehandedly shot the sun out of the sky and I yearn to see it rise again, to see the glow of that beautiful golden side lit early morning light. Light that I long ago marveled at how it bathed a beautiful teenage girl and a tangle of wildflowers. But until then there is only darkness, for which I am responsible.

I love you, Mia. I really do. And I hope to not only tell you that, but prove it to you, every day of your life.

Forever, Tom

Mia stared at the page in her hands for a very long time. She felt nothing. Just numb. She couldn't even begin to process Tom's words or formulate what her reaction was supposed to be.

"I need sleep," she mumbled and fell back onto the bed. (She noted that Tom had actually had the decency to change the sheets). Curling up under the blanket, on her side of the bed, she grabbed her pillow and shoved her left arm under it. Something silky brushed against her wrist.

Mia rolled over and turned on the bedside light. Lifting her pillow, she gasped at what Tom had placed there. Underneath her pillow, Tom Sheehan had left her his MFA tassel from Cornell.

And there it was, a wave cresting and rushing to shore and Mia had caught the wave wrong and now she was being dragged under — her face scraping on the abrasive sand and broken shells lining the ocean floor. The sadness swept over her and finally the tears flowed freely. Once again, that feeling she had too often felt, a feeling she had been able to sweep to the darkest recesses of her mind for most of the past seven years, leapt out of the darkness like a stalker and began coursing through her veins. Subway cars speeding though darkened tunnels.

Although they were not strangers to one another, Mia Silver was not pleased to once again greet loneliness.

Chapter Twenty-Five

"Are you coming out with us?" Seth stuck his head into Mia's office.

Mia just shook her head, not looking up from her PC. "Too much to do."

"I would think you'd be more fun now that you're single, but you've turned into this huge BBC bore."

Mia smiled, still not looking up from her PC, "You certainly don't want a bore with you. Have fun."

Clearing off her desk for the weekend, Mia was feeling mighty proud of herself. Billings were higher than she had ever dreamed, they'd on boarded three new clients, and both she and the agency were up for CLIO and ADDY awards — an honor she could not believe had been bestowed on them.

Mia walked over to her window and looked out over lower Manhattan. The Trade Centers were just beginning to illuminate the night. Standing in the cocoon of her brick-walled office, Mia felt disconnected from the world outside, a world of people laughing together, dreaming together, growing together. Maybe it was just the long haired blonde girls who got what they wanted — the CJ's of the world, the blondes like Tom's skanky student. Maybe girls like her just got handsome gay friends and asshole rapists. And advertising awards.

With a sigh, she walked away from the window and started to pack up her laptop. There was a bar on the walk home that had great pub grub — wonderful greasy burgers and hand cut fries. Mia was in the mood to indulge in a little food therapy. Add a cold Pilsner Urquell on tap to that and all would be right in the world again.

Entering the pub, there was one seat at the bar next to two handsome guys, both dressed in suits. Sitting next to them, they did not notice her as their eyes were trained on two blondes at one of the tables. *Figures,* Mia thought, *blondes — the bane of my existence.*

Sipping on her beer, she quietly observed everyone, trying to figure out their stories. Her burger arrived and the suited guy next to her turned around. "That looks really good," he commented.

Mia had just cut the enormous burger in half and held up a half to him. "Want a bite?" And she gave him a devil grin.

"I can't eat your burger." He smiled back.

"You're saying no to eating my meat?" She raised an eyebrow, the smirk on her face hard to control. "I'd never say no to eating your meat."

He laughed and took the burger from her hands and took a big bite.

"You're very good with your mouth." She sipped her beer.

"And you are very funny."

"This is true." Mia acknowledged.

Thirty minutes and a shared piece of pecan pie later, Mia exited with the suited guy. On her way out, she smiled at the blondes. Score one for girls like her.

"So, what did you end up doing on Friday night?" Seth asked on Monday morning. "I called here, your cell and your apartment to see if you wanted to join us for dinner after we'd had a few drinks, but you didn't answer."

"I ended up stopping into a pub on my way home for a burger, a beer…," she paused and smiled, "and some dick."

"What? You got picked up by some guy and fucked him?"

"No." Mia was shaking her head. "I picked up the guy and fucked him."

Seth's eyes narrowed, "BBC, you've been blowing us off a lot lately. How often do you do this?"

Mia shrugged. "When I feel like it."

"Quantify, Bitch."

"I don't know. I don't keep count."

Eyes still narrowed, Seth leaned across the desk to Mia. "How many tables have we sponsored at AIDS benefits? How many benefits have we sat at and cried because the photos flashing on the screen were our friends — people we've hung out with, danced with, laughed with. I know gorgeous, brooding poet fucked with your head with what he did, but don't you dare put your life in jeopardy over an asshole who can't keep his dick in his pants. An asshole who I'm sure is miserable over losing what he had with you."

Mia rolled her eyes. "I've got this under control." *If I've got being raped by two assholes under control, then I've certainly got being cheated on by a total player under control,* she thought.

Standing to leave, Seth shook his head. "Sadly, you don't." And he turned on his heel and walked out of her office.

Chapter Twenty-Six

Mia was standing at the mailboxes in the lobby of her apartment building leafing through the contents of her overstuffed mailbox. She heard someone say, “Excuse me,” and looked up into the gray eyes of her neighbor two doors down.

Stepping aside so that he could have access to his mail slot, Mia smiled at him. She hadn’t seen either him or his friend since the day she shoved Tom’s naked skank out into the hall.

As she got into the elevator, he called out, “Please hold that,” and Mia pressed the doors open button and waited for him. He strode into the elevator with a confident gait. He was tall and wiry with short auburn hair.

“So, how have you been since … uh, that day?” He gave Mia a half uncomfortable, half amused smirk.

“That was quite a day, wasn’t it?” Mia smiled back. “I’ve been good.”

“The boyfriend is gone too?” He shifted nervously from foot to foot.

“Oh yeah. That very day.”

“Wow. That was really something.” He was now amused, seeing it wasn’t an off-limits conversation with Mia. They reached the sixteenth floor and the elevator doors opened. “Hey, I’m just about to sit down and smoke a joint. Do you want to join me?” he offered.

Mia thought to herself, why not? She hadn’t gotten high in the longest time and it was a Friday night, so she didn’t need to be sharp in the morning. Besides she had no other plans.

“Sure, let me just go change and I’ll be right over. My name is Mia, by the way.”

He turned around as he was heading down the hall. “Lyle.”

Mia knocked on his door about twenty minutes later, a bottle of red wine, a box of Carr’s water crackers, a hunk of cheddar cheese and one of triple crème bleu cheese, in hand.

“I didn’t know if you had food and I’m starved,” she explained. “And that’s pre-munchies.” Mia hit him with the devil smile.

She sat down on his chocolate brown leather couch. On the glass coffee table was quite the assortment of drugs. Multiple types of pot — large green buds, a stringy red variety, Thai sticks, chunks of dark hash, multiple joints already rolled. There were also single-edged razor blades on the table and little glass coke vials, letting Mia know that the glass top was not merely for decoration.

Lyle returned from the kitchen with a corkscrew, some wineglasses, plates and knives.

"Picnic." Mia smiled.

"Yeah. Kinda," he agreed. Lyle poured them both wine and they clinked glasses. "To getting rid of old baggage," he toasted.

"Here. Here," Mia agreed, wholeheartedly.

Lyle picked up one of the joints and handed it to Mia, flicking the lighter for her. Mia inhaled deeply and coughed out the smoke.

"When did I become such a lightweight?" She looked displeased with herself. Pointing to the table, "So, which varietal are we smoking?" She handed Lyle back the joint.

"This is a combination of Hawaiian," he pointed to some large bright green buds, "with a little bit of the Thai stick and some very finely chopped up hash."

One hit and Mia felt as if she were already trashed. This was good shit. "So, I'm thinking this is maybe more than a hobby?"

Lyle laughed, his fair, freckled skin turning red. "Yeah, it is. You're not going to narc me out or anything, are you?"

Mia dragged deeply on the joint and held it in her lungs for as long as she could before blowing out the smoke. Handing the joint to Lyle, she picked up her wine glass and laughed. "Narc you out? You just became my new favorite neighbor," and they laughed.

"Well, you've been my favorite for a long time." He smiled at her, handing her back the joint.

Lyle picked up one of the small brown glass vials and twisted off the black cap. With practiced expertise, he gently tapped on the tipped bottle, a small amount of cocaine flowing to the glass tabletop. With a single-edged razor blade, he began to chop the powder and in sweeping motions broke it up into lines. Picking up a cut-off straw from the table, he offered it to Mia.

She held up her hand. "No thanks, coke is not my thing. You have to scrape me off the walls, as it is." And she continued to smoke the joint she was holding.

Lyle shrugged and bent down, quickly inhaling four lines and wiping at his nose as he finished. He licked his finger and ran it over the spot on the table where the cocaine had been and then rubbed his finger on his gums above his front teeth.

Mia carefully handed what was left of the joint back to him and instead of putting it in a roach clip, Lyle stubbed it out and opened a small wooden box on the table and extracted a joint. Mia wondered what the difference was between the joints on the table and the ones in the box.

Observing Mia intently, Lyle lit the joint. “My special secret blend,” he offered.

Taking the joint from him, Mia took a hit and could feel the “special blend” lighting up every cell in her body. The effect was immediate. A buzzing clarity coursed through her veins, molecules on high alert. She felt caged. Her clothes were constraining. She wanted to pull them off and stalk naked through his apartment like a Mountain Lion seeking its prey. The brown drape valence hanging along the tops of the windows bothered her. She didn’t know why, but it just did. The curtains were brown. She didn’t like that they were brown. It annoyed her. She wanted to rip them down.

After a few hits, Mia waved him off when he went to hand it back to her. “I’m so trashed. I’m just going to focus on this wine for a little bit.” But figuring out how to pick up her wine glass correctly was a chore. *Come on, you can pull it together, keep talking*, she told herself. “So, tell me about your, umm, operation.” Mia motioned to the drugs on the table and hoped she could follow what he was saying.

“We deliver.” He grinned, looking like a bad red-headed teenager and making Mia think there was something cute about him in a non-traditional way.

“So, people call you. You tell them what is on the “menu” and then you deliver?” She wondered if what she was saying made sense. Lyle was nodding, so she guessed it did.

“I see you’ve done this,” Lyle laughed.

“Not in a while. But there used to be a place called The Church. Phone number was always changing. I remember them once delivering to me and my friends in a snowstorm.” *What the heck did I just say to him,* Mia wondered. *Maintain, Girl, maintain.*

“No place like New York.” Lyle helped himself to some cheddar.

Mia looked around, noticing things in her stoned state for the first time. “Your apartment has such a great layout. You have both southern and western exposures.” I think it’s southern and western, she questioned in her head, the word western sounding odd. *Western? Is that a word?*

She got up and the movement gave her a head rush. Everything spun for a moment and she waited for all parts of her body to catch up as she walked over to the dining alcove where Lyle's apartment jutted out. The windows faced west toward the Hudson River. "Wow, you have two great views," she observed. "The Trade Centers and the Hudson River. Oh God, look how filthy the windows are in my apartment." The thought amused her that she was listening to her mother coming out of her mouth. Dirty windows? What was she thinking? She giggled at the absurdity. Putting her hands up on the window, she leaned forward, placing her right cheek against the cool, smooth glass. Its chill was refreshing and she stayed like that for a few moments.

Lyle came into the alcove and was standing behind her. He was close enough that she could feel the heat from his body. The hairs on the back of her neck were standing up. "Your windows don't look so bad. I like your windows."

It was in that moment that Mia realized why she was Lyle's favorite neighbor. He reached around the front of her cupping both her breasts, his thumb and forefinger rubbing until her nipples hardened. "Oh crap," thought Mia, "I'm wasted and he's touching me from behind — the ultimate turn-on for me. I'm so fucked. Literally and figuratively." And she giggled again.

"I've loved watching you get fucked. You can't imagine how many nights I've gotten off watching you and your boyfriend. I've come with you so many times, Mia." He was whispering in her ear, and Mia couldn't decide whether this was creepy or hot and since she was so fucked up, and her inhibitions (and standards) significantly lower than usual, she went with hot.

Mia could feel Lyle's hard cock pressing into her and she rubbed her ass up and down on it getting him harder. "My business partner, Nick, and I jerk off to you all the time and here you are in my apartment and tonight I'm going to jerk off inside you."

Mia turned her head back to him and grabbed him by his hair, pulling his mouth to hers in a crushing kiss that she was controlling. "So, you want to fuck me, huh?"

"You know I do." He was panting.

"Well, if you want to fuck me, you need to make me come first." Mia broke from his arms and sat on the dining room table that was right behind him, the movement giving her another crazy head rush. "Take my pants off," she ordered and he unzipped her jeans and worked them down her legs, exposing pale pink satin bikini underwear. "Get them off, too," she demanded. She needed to control this situation with him and even in her dazed state, she knew that the most she could give him was the illusion of control — but never control itself.

Lyle looked down at Mia's glistening Brazilian waxed pussy. "Rub my clit and get me hot and then go down on me."

He stood looking at her.

"Do you want to fuck me?"

He nodded vigorously.

"Then do as I say."

He had manipulated the situation and now he was going to play by her rules.

Spreading the soft lips of her pussy, he ran two fingers up her slit, dipping them in and rubbing the wetness all over her clit. When she began to moan, he dipped his head down and spread her wide with both hands. Making the tip of his tongue pointy, he licked into her as deeply as he could go, pulling out to lick her clit and suck on it until it hardened in his mouth. Letting his teeth graze her firm clit, he sucked it into his mouth and swirled his tongue around it.

Mia threaded her fingers through his hair and pushed him in deeper into her pussy. "Suck me," she moaned, as she began to ride his face. Nothing else mattered but getting herself off on his face. Riding it furiously, she pressed it harder into her pussy. There was nothing in the entire universe but the nerve endings in her pussy and she had one single goal. One mind-blowing orgasm in this crazy, fucked up, drugged out state. Mia had been stoned many times in her life — but nothing felt like this. Whatever was in that second joint, the secret stash, was something she had never experienced before. This was the word euphoria personified. And right now, euphoria existed only one place in the universe — her pussy. "Lick me, I said. If you want to fuck me, you need to eat me until I come and then you can fuck me anyway you want to." She didn't care what he did to her at that point, as long as he gave her one mind-blowing, stoned orgasm. After that, she'd just ride the high and go with it because there was no option to get off the ride until she came down.

That was all Lyle needed to hear. He grabbed Mia by the ass, burying his face deep in her pussy and licking, sucking and nipping, spreading her wide open and sucking her clit until her legs clasped around his head and she started to quake.

"My turn now," he roared. "Now guys can jerk off to me fucking you." He pulled Mia off the table and led her back into the living room where he bent her over a chair in front of the window. Foreplay was over. He slapped her ass hard and she moaned. "Spread," he demanded and she complied. With one swift thrust, his unimpressive cock was buried deeply inside of her.

She'd been so lost in the sensation of Lyle eating her pussy on the table that neither one of them heard his business partner, Nick, enter the apartment. Bent over the chair, Mia was focused on Lyle's cock ramming into her from behind. Opening her eyes as she moaned, she felt her body jolt with surprise as she saw handsome gym rat, Nick just feet away from her, cock in hand, jerking off while he watched his partner fuck her.

Mia's eyes locked with Nick's. A slight smile tugged at the corners of his lips as she watched him. In his hands was by far the biggest cock Mia had ever seen in her life. No longer was she focused on Lyle pounding into her, now her eyes and thoughts were transfixed on Nick's huge cock as she wondered what it would feel like to fuck him. "I want to fuck you," she mouthed to him. "Tonight." His mouth opened, as if to say something, but only a moan emerged as he came. Mia endured the rest of Lyle's endless pounding.

At midnight, there was a knock at Mia's door. She had been stalking around her apartment like a caged animal. Grabbing her deep red satin robe, she wrapped it around herself, tying it loosely. Looking through the peephole, she immediately felt turned-on as she saw Nick standing there. She unlocked the door. He grabbed her by her hair and kissed her roughly, his tongue deep in her mouth. He lifted her so that her legs straddled him and walked down the hall toward her bedroom. Dropping her on the bed, she shrugged out of her robe and let it puddle on the bed. Stepping out of his jeans and boxers, he stood at the edge of the bed and Mia came over on her hands and knees and sucked the head of his cock into her mouth. The girth was so wide she was not able to get much more past the crown into her mouth. Licking and nibbling the head, she stroked him with both hands until he was rock hard.

Mia took Nick's hand and pulled him onto the bed, where she straddled and mounted him. Sinking as low onto his cock as she possibly could, she greedily took in inch after stretching inch, wanting to know what it felt like to have as much of this impossibly large cock inside of her. The pleasurable sensation bordered on pain that she wanted more of, and she began to ride him furiously, trying to get him deeper with each stroke. Nick reached up and grabbed Mia by the hips and rammed her down on him. She gasped loudly. And he did it again. And she screamed.

"Take it, Bitch," and at his words, Mia rammed herself down harder as if it were a challenge.

"Does he know you're here?"

Nick smiled and shook his head, "No."

"What would he think?"

"He'd be pissed. He told me that I wasn't allowed to touch you unless he was there, and only then for his pleasure, to watch us."

"So, he likes watching you fuck other women?" Mia was intrigued as she rode Nick. While she knew that she was still high as a kite, and all her sensations were magnified, her brain was starting to feel like it was attached to her body again.

"He does, but not usually his women."

Mia stopped moving and looked down at Nick laying beneath her, like a big gorgeous stallion. "I'm not his woman."

"You've been his fantasy for a long, long time. He's not going to want to give that up."

Mia looked down between her legs and wrapped her fingers around the portion of his cock that was not inside of her. "And I'm not going to want to give this up. Don't make me." And with that she squeezed him as tight as she could and began to ride him hard.

Waking up the next afternoon, Mia had never had a headache so blinding. She wondered with what the hell that second joint that Lyle lit up had been laced. Coke? Heroin? Had she really just fucked two men in one night? In all her pot smoking years, she had never been so uninhibited and out of control. What the hell was in that second joint? (And was Nick's cock really that big or was that a hallucination?)

She rolled over and grabbed her cell off her night table and dialed.

"Silver? Are you okay?"

"I don't know."

"What's going on? Talk to me."

Mia pushed her unruly curls from her face. "I think I'm really fucked up, Rob. On some level, I don't really care what happens to me."

"What's bringing this on, Mia?"

"I got high with my neighbor last night and I think he probably laced it with something. I ended up having sex with him. His business partner came in, watched us, and came over my apartment later and I fucked him, too." Mia was now sitting up in the middle of her bed. A frown on her face as she recounted the events of the evening.

"Shit, Mia. You are definitely acting out. Is it over Sheehan?"

"I'm sure that's a part of it on some level. I couldn't control him having sex with other women. And while I gave him the illusion of control sexually, I never actually handed the control over to him. But I like doing things that are bad for me, Rob. I get off on it and then I feel like shit and I just do some more."

"Are you going to forever punish yourself for being raped?" Rob sounded defeated.

"Is that what you think I'm doing?"

"There are healthier ways to know that you're alive and can still feel, Mia. You need to find them or you need to finally find a good therapist."

"But Rob, I want to do it again. Well, maybe not both of them in the same room again, but definitely one of them."

"Of course you do, Mia. The edge is the only place you currently feel alive." Rob Ryan was so fucking smart. What Mia didn't know was that Rob Ryan was scared for his friend. Very scared. He was afraid to think about what more she had to lose before she could start putting the shards of all that had been shattered back together again.

Hanging up the phone with Rob, Mia thought about her last conversation with Tom and what she told him she needed and wanted. Someone who would love her, treat her right. If she thought she was far from that goal with Tom, she had just self-piloted the Concord right off the flight path.

With a groan, Mia pulled the blankets over her aching head. The stark brightness of daylight was too painful.

Chapter Twenty-Seven

"BBC, are you still asleep?" Just listening to Seth's voice hurt and she groaned at him.

"It's 6 P.M. Are you sick or something?"

"I just had a really rough night" She pulled the cover over her head again.

"I'm afraid to ask."

"Suffice it to say it involved two men and a lot of drugs."

Seth gasped, "BBC, I am shocked."

"Yeah, well by the light of day, I'm kind of shocked, too."

"Don't leave me hanging, Bitch. Did you go to some neighborhood bar and pick up some more boys?" Seth would needle her until he got every last detail. Resistance was futile.

"No. It was the guys down the hall."

"The creepy one and the hot Mafia looking dude?"

Mia was picturing Seth's face, his eyes wide, perched on the edge of his chair. "The very same."

"And you fucked them both?" his voice went up an octave.

"Ugh. Yes."

"Together?"

"No." Mia sounded appalled and immediately she thought, *I am such a damn hypocrite*.

"One after the other?"

"Like hours later." Mia rolled her eyes at herself, as if waiting hours made it all right. Geesh, she was a mess.

"Seriously, Mia?" Even Seth was shocked and it took a lot to shock Seth Shapiro.

"We got high and I think there was more than just pot in the second joint. I'm pretty sure it must've been laced with coke, because to say I was wired and uninhibited does not even begin to describe what happened last night." Mia padded into the bathroom and under the harsh glow of the vanity light she groaned upon seeing the dark circles under her eyes.

"Well, are you up for coming to Limelight with me and Rory tonight?"

"I guess so." Mia continued to stare at her face in the mirror. Except for looking a little burned out, she still looked like the same person.

"Do you want to meet us there around eleven?"

"Yeah, okay. I'm going back to bed now." She was already under the covers.

She heard the knocking on the door and with a groan got out of bed again and made her way down the hall. Looking through the peephole, she could see Nick in the hall. "I'm not ready for this," she thought, but opened the door anyway.

He greeted her with a sexy smile. This man looked dangerous and even if he wasn't carrying a gun, she knew he was packing some serious heat. She'd met that pistol head on (or at least she thought she had — although she was seriously hoping it was just a drug induced hallucination).

Pizza box in hand, "Hey, Lyle and I were just about to have pizza. Want to join?"

Pizza? What the fuck, Mia thought. "Did I fuck you last night or did I hallucinate that?"

His smile was slow. "Did that feel like a hallucination to you?" It wasn't until that moment that Mia realized how sore she felt.

"Oh God." She covered her face with her hands.

"Are you embarrassed?" he laughed.

"More like mortified." Mia couldn't look him in the face. "Nick, what did I smoke last night? The joints in the box. What's in them?"

Nick stepped forward into Mia's apartment and put the pizza down on her dining room table. Mia sat down on the couch and he sat down next to her. Crossing her arms over her chest, her body language clearly showed her discomfort in having him so close.

"I'm not going to hurt you."

She was surprised that he was so perceptive in reading the situation. Or was she just that obvious?

"I know," but the anxiety in her voice was palpable.

"Then why won't you look at me?" He took her face by the chin and tilted it up. Mia was surprised to see concern in his eyes.

"I fucked your friend. You watched. Jerked off. And then I fucked you. That is so far past my normal boundaries and clearly you don't have any." She wanted him to let go of her chin, but he wasn't going to let her off so easy.

"And you didn't like that?" His proximity was disturbing. His full lips distracting.

"I did. At the time. But I was seriously wasted and you haven't answered my question, Nick. What drugs did I do last night?" Mia was becoming visibly upset.

Nick shook his head. "I don't know what was in what you smoked with Lyle. He rolled it. Based on what went down, it's pretty safe to assume you were smoking coke last night."

Mia pulled her face away from his grasp. "I told him I didn't want to do coke."

Nick reached over and smoothed down her hair. "He wanted you, Mia. Smoking coke is one of those things that makes people extremely sexually uninhibited. It was his best shot with you."

"Son of a bitch," Mia snarled. "Well, I can guarantee you that is never going to happen again."

"And what about us? Will we happen again?"

Mia cocked her head and narrowed her eyes. "Nick, you jerked off watching your friend fuck me." By the light of day, none of this seemed very hot anymore.

"Yeah and you looked at me and told me you wanted me to fuck you while he was fucking you." He had no trouble making eye contact.

"I was fucked up, thanks to your buddy."

"Mia, we were all fucked up."

Mia put her face in her hands and let out a primal scream.

Nick started to laugh.

"You think this is funny?" Mia stood abruptly. She could feel the heat rising in her face.

"I think it would be a lot easier if you just said to yourself, 'Damn, we were fucked up last night and that was one wild time,' and stop beating yourself up with guilt. C'mon, wasn't it a little bit fun?" His beautiful full lips broke into a smile and it was hard not to think about what they felt like crushed against hers.

"I don't want to fuck him again." Mia was not going to give Nick the satisfaction of knowing that part of her was very turned on by how "bad" she had been with them. Lyle grossed her out, but controlling him was a powerful feeling.

Nick stood up and reached a hand out to Mia. "C'mon, come eat pizza with us."

In her best sulky voice, she demanded, "Well, what kind is it?"

"Mushroom," Nick smirked.

"Figures," Mia laughed at the irony. "I need to change to go meet my friends, I'll be over in a little bit."

Chapter Twenty-Eight

Mia sat next to Nick on the couch as she finished her second slice of John's Pizza, washing it down with bottled water (that she brought with her and opened herself). She vaguely remembered Nick telling her something the night before about Lyle not wanting them together unless it was for his pleasure. So, while she felt more protected by sitting next to him, she was very conscious about not sitting too close. Trying to figure out the pecking order, if Nick worked for Lyle or if they were partners, she thought it best not to ask — the less she knew about their business — the better off she was.

Lyle picked up a joint that was sitting on the table and lit it. He held it out for Mia.

"I don't think so." Mia shook her head.

Lyle laughed and Mia noticed his uneven teeth for the first time. "It's just pot, Mia. You saw I just picked it up from the table."

Mia sighed and took the joint from Lyle and dragged on it. She could immediately feel the glow throughout her body. "Are you sure?"

"Yes, I'm sure. It's just really good shit from Hawaii so it gives you a different buzz than the Columbian that's out there."

Mia took another hit and it amplified the glow exponentially. She turned her body to Nick to hand him the joint, their fingers touched and she felt an instantaneous buzz in her nipples and pussy. She watched him inhale deeply, his full lips hugging the tip of the joint. After his third hit, he passed it back to Lyle, who took a couple of hits and handed it off to Mia. By this point, she didn't care if it was laced, and she was assuming, from the glowing feeling throughout her body, that Lyle had lied to her. She took a few more hits.

Having Nick sitting next to her and not touching him was killing her. Mia wanted to unzip his pants and see if the beast was as mythical as she remembered. She started to giggle thinking his cock is of mythical proportions. He turned to her and smiled.

"What are you laughing about?" He looked as high as she felt.

"A mythical beast." And she gave him a knowing devil grin.

"A mythical beast, eh?" And his smile was as devilish as hers.

"I gotta take a piss." Lyle staggered out of the room, heading down the hall toward the bathroom.

Nick's fingers were immediately threaded through Mia's curls, pulling her head toward him. He lightly brushed his full lips on hers. "Mythical beast," he said against her lips and she giggled. Her arms twined around his thick neck as he pulled her into his lap, straddling him. They kissed softly, rubbing noses and giggling, the sensation of their noses touching sent electric jolts through her body that coursed through her veins and dead-ended at her clit, which she was slowly rubbing on the extraordinarily large bulge in his pants.

Mia was fascinated by the sounds they were making — the mmmm's and the oooo's and ahhh's and grunts and she whispered in his ear, "I love the sounds we make together."

Nick pulled Mia's head back, pondering her words for a moment and wrapped his chiseled arms around her, tightly crushing her against his massive, bodybuilder chest, his tongue deeply exploring the caverns of her mouth, their noises continuing as they kissed.

With a sharp pain to the back of her head, her mouth was yanked away from Nick's, a clump of her hair feeling like it was being ripped from its follicles. Opening her mouth to scream, Lyle grabbed her head in a vice grip, ramming his cock down her throat. Still tightly surrounded by Nick's arms, the dark specter of being held in place by one man while another had his way with her rapidly descended, enveloping her in fear. Her autonomic nervous system overrode her drug-fueled libido and fight or flight instinct snapped into high gear.

Mia bared down hard with her teeth on Lyle's cock and instantaneously the metallic taste of blood washed over her taste buds. Lyle roared, smacking Mia's head back and she used the jolt to break free of Nick's hold. Lyle was bent over, bloody cock in hand and Mia jumped out of Nick's lap and grabbed her purse in one surprisingly smooth motion. She swung the heavy leather and brass outfitted Coach bag by its shoulder strap, smacking Lyle in the face, and ran for the door, pulling it open with a jolt and hearing it slam behind her, the sound reverberating as an echo down the hallway

Out in the hall, an elderly couple was entering the elevator. "Hold that please," Mia yelled and ran into the elevator. As the doors were closing, she heard Nick call her name. *Close, please close, please close, please close*, she silently begged but then realized it hadn't been silent based on the perplexed looks from her elderly neighbors.

Pacing around the elevator, it stopped at the fourteenth floor and four people got in. Mia moved to the back of the elevator feeling trapped behind the people. The car slowly descended, coming to a jolting halt on the ninth floor. Two more people got in and Mia's space continued to dwindle. She could feel her heart beating way too rapidly as the bodies were trapping her at the back of the elevator car. Please don't stop again, she silently begged. Fearful that Lyle and Nick had gotten into another elevator and would be waiting for her, Mia started to plan her escape. But first she had to escape from the claustrophobic elevator.

She tried to steady her breathing and calm herself down. The sensations were crazy, she wanted to claw at her own skin, she wanted to bust out of herself and out of the cramped, human filled box. The elevator was packed and it was taking forever and ever just to get to the lobby. When they finally got to the first floor, Mia pushed her way past the other residents without even an "excuse me," fleeing the elevator and running through the lobby, throwing open the glass door to the building, before the doorman could even get it for her, and fled at full speed out onto the sidewalk.

Out on the street, she continued to run. The night air felt invigorating against her skin. As she moved up Sixth Avenue toward Limelight, all the street lights and store lights blurred together like colorful neon waves, a school of phosphorescent fish moving in and out on the tide.

Crossing Twentieth Street, Mia could already see the crowd a block away gathered outside The Limelight, a nineteenth century stone church turned nightclub. Approaching the entrance with its red velvet ropes, Mia saw several of Charles' guys manning the door. Randy, the goon she had initially approached to get Charles' attention on the night they met, smiled and opened the rope when he saw her.

"Charles will be here later," Randy informed her.

"Cool. Please you let him know I'm here. My friends Seth and Rory will be here in a little while. Tell them I'm already inside, okay."

As Mia passed into the vestibule of the church, the pulsating rhythm of the music coursed through her stoned-out cells, making her feel like she was a part of the music. She began to move with the beat.

Brass plaques, with names and birth and death dates, lined the walls and Mia wondered if there were crypts in the walls. *Were people buried in there?* Passing into the main sanctuary, the dance floor was packed with wall-to-wall people; the strobe lights illuminated the stained-glass windows, reds and blues and greens glowed in the night. Mia had never before noticed how intricate and beautiful they were.

Making her way through the crowd, she bellied up to the ornate wooden bar. Looking at her watch, it would be another thirty minutes until Seth and Rory got there. She ordered a Sea Breeze and leaned back against the bar to people watch. The alcohol added another layer to the high she was already feeling.

Lyle and Nick. Just the thought made her feel queasy. Not so much Nick. But he was holding her when Lyle grabbed her head. She was restrained. She had no control. They had taken her control. Two of them. She felt the fright that she had felt that night in the park. They had taken her control. Two of them.

She finished her drink and ordered another. As she started to sip the fresh drink, she heard a voice in her ear, "I would have been very happy to have bought that for you."

He was seriously handsome — long and lean. Dimples when he smiled. The accent was classic New Jersey and he kind of had a Jon Bon Jovi thing going for him. *Very nice*, Mia thought.

"Well, then I'll let you buy me my next one." Mia hit him with a devil grin.

"I'm Paul." He bent down to talk into her ear over the blare of music.

"Mia," she yelled.

He put a hand on her shoulder as he spoke into her ear. His hand felt like it was melting into her. "Do you want to dance?"

Mia nodded and took his hand as he led her out onto the crowded dance floor. Her hand melted into his. She was loving this melting sensation. She felt like warm caramel.

Mia recognized the song, which was a rarity — since club music was not really her thing. But this was "*Smooth*" by Rob Thomas and Carlos Santana and Carlos' guitar playing was as unique as a thumbprint. Paul took her by the hands and twirled her around, causing all the lights to form celestial arcs before Mia's eyes. She staggered and bumped into the girl dancing next to her, a girl with big Staten Island hair like Melanie Griffith in "Working Girl." The girl sneered at Mia, giving her a dirty look.

"Sorry," Mia yelled into her ear and surprised her with a kiss on the cheek. Staten Island turned to Mia, shocked, and Mia hit her with a devil grin and all the girl could do was smile back.

Feeling every beat of the music throughout her being, Mia thought her body had never moved so smoothly. The music changed and "*Mambo #5*" started playing. *I know this one too*, Mia thought, feeling proud of her current musical knowledge and closed her eyes as she felt the music stream through her. Paul's arm wrapped around her waist and he drew her against him as they swayed together to the infectious tune. Mia could feel her pelvis melting against his and she wanted to sink further into him. With his leg between hers and his arm firmly around her waist, she bent the upper half of her body back, her curls whipping as he swayed her left to right and back again. With her eyes closed, tapping into the flowing sensation of the movement of their bodies, Mia pressed the lower half of her body against Paul. As she straightened up, his other arm came around her mid-back, pressing her full body to his.

Mia wrapped her hands around Paul's ass and pressed him into her, feeling how ready he was. She wondered how many people had actually successfully had vertical sex on a packed dance floor without people knowing. The thought made her pull him in even tighter to her as they swayed together. The song changed again and he was singing along to it. She took one hand off his ass and ran it up and down the front of his jeans.

"You are so hot," he moaned in her ear.

Smiling, she tugged the stiff zipper down past his even stiffer cock and inserted her hand into his jeans. With her body tight against his and blocking the view, she wrapped her hand around his hard cock and started squeezing it and stroking it to the beat of the music. His hand dropped from her waist to her ass and he started to knead her ass cheek, pulling at it, so it would spread her pussy.

With his lips next to her ear, he sang,

"They say you really like me
They say you really want me
That's what I want to know, babe"

Mia wondered if those were the words to the song or if that was what he was saying to her. With her head nestled against his chest, she continued to fondle him, wondering if she could make him come on the dance floor and knowing that if he kept pulling at her ass that way, she was going to come, leaning against him, in no time.

"Yeah, baby, I feel you taking me there
Don't stop, it feels good
Oh right there."

She started to moan against his chest, his cock totally lubricated with pre-cum as she squeezed and twisted him. His grip on her ass became tighter, pulling the cheek in the palm of his hand as he crushed her against him.

Swaying, he continued to sing into her ear, his teeth grazing her lobe,

"Yeah, baby girl
You got it right there
Oh baby girl"

Mia's eyes shot open wide as she pulled her head away from his chest in a swift and jerking motion. Her hand was out of his pants with equal speed and for the second time in one night, she wrenched herself out of a man's arms and fled. Pushing her way through the sardine-packed dance floor, much the way she had pushed her way out of the back of the elevator earlier in the evening, Mia got off the dance floor with lightning speed and frantically looked around for an escape.

Seeing a sign for the restrooms, she ran in that direction, pushing past people. The line for the ladies' room was long, snaking around the corner along a wall. Mia went flying past the impatient line of women ignoring the nasty comments of the other patrons. Once inside, she caught a glimpse of herself in the mirror, shocked to see the tears streaming down her face. She was crying. She didn't know that she'd been crying. And looking at her tear stained face in the mirror she wondered how she could not have known that — and the question that formed in her mind, in the clearest thought pattern she'd ever experienced, was 'Where is Mia?' followed by, 'You've lost Mia.' Looking at her eyes in the mirror, all she could think was, they look like a flag hanging outside a restaurant in Little Italy … red, white and green.

She was dressed all in black and her hair was pink and spiky. Mia knew that she worked at Limelight. Over the winter she was in coat check and Mia was pretty sure that it was Charles that had introduced them.

"It's Mia, right?"

Mia nodded. A new round of tears gushing down her face.

"Are you here with anyone?"

"I don't know if my friends are here yet," Mia choked out between sobs.

There was an attendant's chair in the corner of the bathroom and the pink haired girl led Mia to the chair.

Mia sat down and the wooden chair felt painful against her body. She couldn't melt into it and she just wanted to melt like caramel goo until she was nothing at all. But she couldn't melt and he'd called her *Baby Girl* and she just wanted to disappear.

The pink-haired girl's name was Nicole. And in her years working at clubs, Nicole had seen every kind of meltdown known to man (and woman). She'd seen Mia many times over the past five years and she never seemed to be drugged out at all. But tonight's Mia, that girl was seriously tripping out.

Walking outside the club, Nicole surveyed the situation and talking to two of the bouncers was Charles Sloan. Walking over, she touched him lightly on the arm to get his attention.

"Hey Nicki," Charles greeted her with a warm smile.

Nicole leaned into Charles and spoke softly in his ear. "Your friend Mia is in the first-floor ladies' room crying and I think she's really stoned out of her mind. I asked if she was here with anyone and she said she didn't know if her friends were here yet. She's in a pretty bad way, Charles."

Charles was on the move immediately. "I just spoke to Seth and Rory about a half an hour ago, so I know they are here."

Nicole nodded. "I know Seth and Rory." Immediately her eyes started to scan the crowded club for them. Pulling on Charles' suit jacket, she pointed over to the bar where Seth and Rory were drinking.

Seth smiled as they approached. "Hey there." But his smile faded when Charles' demeanor remained sober.

"Nicole's got Mia in the bathroom crying and thinks she looks pretty high."

"Oh shit." Seth closed his eyes shaking his head. "We saw her out on the dance floor before dirty dancing with some tall guy and we just joked 'Nobody puts Mia in the corner.'" Crap. Does she seem like she just smoked a joint high?" They all started moving toward the Ladies Room.

Nicole looked at him and shook her head. "This is way beyond a smoking a joint high."

Seth looked at Rory. "I'll bet it's those fucking neighbors."

All four entered the Ladies Room, to the surprise of some and no surprise to other patrons, and went over to where Mia was sitting. Huddled in a small mass, as if she were trying to make herself disappear, she was still crying inconsolably.

Charles squatted down in front of her. "Mia, what's going on?"

Mia looked up at Charles, fresh tears coursing down her cheeks.

"Tell me," he urged. "That guy that you were dancing with, did he hurt you, Mia?"

"He called me Baby Girl." A huge sob wracked her small frame.

"What?" Charles was not sure he correctly understood what she had said.

"He called me Baby Girl," and the sobs became uncontrollable.

Charles gently stroked Mia's hair and looked up at Seth questioningly.

Seth shrugged his shoulders and shook his head, his eyes wide with confusion. He called her Baby Girl? What the hell was she on?

Seth squatted down next to Charles. "BBC, Rory and I are going to take you home. Did you go to your neighbors' apartment before you came here tonight?"

Mia nodded, "We had pizza."

"I think you had a lot more than pizza, BBC."

Charles went to the sink and wet some paper towels with cold water. Squatting down in front of her again, he blotted her face. "Are you sure that guy didn't do anything to you. I will take care of him, if he did."

With a new stream of tears, Mia repeated, "He called me Baby Girl."

"I think her neighbor is more of the problem here than her Patrick Swayze partner was tonight."

Seth took Mia's hand and pulled her up. The effect of the motion clearly registering on Mia's face. Seth, Rory and Charles exchanged glances.

"I think we're going to get some nice fresh air and walk you home, BBC."

As they exited the bathroom, Seth gave Nicole a squeeze on the shoulder and mouthed, "Thank you."

Walking through the club toward the entrance, Charles whispered into Seth's ear, "What's the story on the neighbor?"

"Dealer. I think he laced a joint with coke and didn't tell her."

Charles just nodded his head. He didn't say a word.

"You don't need to come up with me. I promise I'll go right to bed." Standing under the awning in front of Mia's building, Seth was having none of Mia's shit.

"Sorry BBC, but when you are huddled in a public bathroom sobbing, you get escorted to your door." Taking her by the arm, he led her into the building, Rory trailing behind.

Mia could feel her insides tense up as they waited for the elevator. The ride down earlier in the evening had been the stuff that nightmares were made of and now Mia found herself praying the elevator car would be empty and that only the three of them would be in it. She got her wish.

As they ascended to the sixteenth floor, Mia paced the small space, glad that she could move around this time. She could feel her heart racing. Her apartment seemed like it was a million miles away.

The elevator doors opened and Mia stepped out, Seth and Rory right behind her. He was sitting outside her door, leaning against the wall. Knees up to his chest, arms crossed over his knees, with his head resting in his arms.

As he heard them approach, he lifted his head from his arms. Mia gasped and Seth put a hand on her arm to stop her.

She turned to Seth. "It's okay," and continued toward her apartment.

Nick's face was all bruised, his lip cut and swollen. His knuckles were swollen and bloody. Mia could only imagine what Lyle looked like.

"Mia," there was alarm in Seth's voice, but she extended a hand to Nick and he took it, stiffly rising to his feet.

Turning to Seth, "I'm okay. Really, it's okay." She unlocked her apartment door. Ushering Nick in, she turned back to Seth. "Don't worry. I'm okay," and she walked through the door closing it behind her.

There was no way Seth Shapiro was not going to worry and not for one minute did he believe Mia Silver was okay.

Chapter Twenty-Nine

In silence, Mia gently washed the cuts on Nick's face and hands. He winced from the pain, but she tried hard not to hurt him. When she completed the process, she again took him by the hand and led him down the hall to her bedroom.

In her bathroom, she washed her face and brushed her teeth before changing into an oversized tee-shirt. She emerged from the bathroom and handed him a washcloth and a toothbrush as she made her way to her bed. Nick went into the bathroom and Mia got under the covers and turned off the light.

He got into bed behind her and pulled her close to him. Within minutes they were both asleep. Not a single word had been exchanged between them.

Nick was gone when she woke up on Sunday afternoon, her head splitting from the drug hangover.

On Monday morning, Mia left a message for Seth saying she would be late to work. She called her gynecologist's office and told them that it was an emergency and that she needed to speak to the doctor directly. An hour later, a nurse was showing her back to an exam room.

Dr. Gary Cohen was someone that she could be totally honest with and Mia Silver needed two things from Gary Cohen that Monday morning — an exam that included STD testing and the name of a good therapist, preferably one that dealt with victims of sexual abuse.

It was time to get Mia back and it was also time to strip those two pieces of shit that had raped her freshman year of any, and all, control that they still wielded over her.

Mia wasn't willing to lose any more.

Chapter Thirty

Seth poked his head into Mia's office. "I've got Kami on line one, do you want to talk to her?"

Mia looked up from the campaign she was reviewing. "What is wrong with her? She's on vacation."

Grabbing the phone on her desk, "What does the word vacation mean to you?"

"It means I can't wait to come home," Kami sounded exasperated.

"Having trouble disconnecting?" Mia knew that Kami put in crazy hours and really needed to get away and enjoy herself.

"I think my problem is that I'm having a problem connecting. Coming out to LA to visit Shelby was probably not the wisest vacation choice. I just don't connect with this whole scene. I want to come home." Mia liked listening to Kami describe New York as home. When they met, five years earlier, Kami had one foot on a plane back to Birmingham, Alabama.

"I'm sure it's good to see Shelby though." Shelby Lee, a lawyer for Universal Studios, was one of Kami's Tri-Delta sorority sisters at Vanderbilt University. Shelby had been great about putting them in touch with the studio's marketing team for New York- premiere events and special projects.

"Please," she sighed. "I'm standing outside her gym right now waiting for her to finish up and she is taking forever. She's hoping some guy shows up that she has a huge crush on and I just want to go eat. But nobody eats in this city. And I'm the only chick without boobs." Kami was standing in front of the doorway dodging people who were going in and out of the busy health club.

"I'm not a big LA fan either. Come home. We'll eat," Mia laughed.

"Excuse me," Kami heard a man say, but didn't look up from the sidewalk and the overwhelming smelling eucalyptus plantings on which she was focused.

"Sorry," she apologized to the man, without a glance, and continued her conversation with Mia. "Do you want me to stop in and call on Scott Morgan while I'm here?" As Kami stepped out of the way for him to pass, he seemed to pause for a moment before resuming his long strides and heading through the door.

"No. You are on vacation. Scott Morgan is the last person you should be calling. Anyway, he's a douche. Don't fuck up your vacation anymore."

Kami laughed, "He is a douche. I can't believe you went to college with him."

"Did you see him? Did you see him?" Shelby was practically dancing in front of Kami.

"Shelby's done, so I'm going to head off. I'll see you and Seth on Monday."

"Travel safely and go eat something," Both women laughed.

Kami closed her Motorola flip phone. "What are you talking about?"

"You just spoke to him on his way in. Oh my God, isn't he the most perfect specimen you have ever seen?"

Kami shook her head. "Sorry, I was talking to Mia and I didn't notice."

"Oh my God, how could you *not* notice?" Shelby flung her long blonde hair over her shoulder, totally disgusted with her friend, but so happy she had gotten to say hello to him. He'd even greeted her by name.

The man had been mere inches from Kami. His only words to her had been, "excuse me." If she had handed him her cell phone and said the words, "Excuse me. It's for you," Schooner Moore and Mia Silver would have been reunited.

Chapter Thirty-One

Mia grabbed for the ringing cell phone on her desk and looked to see who was calling. With a smile, she hit the call accept button, "Chazicle."

"Meezie."

"How are you? That was a great event the other night."

"The Toy Story franchise is just golden."

"I loved that everyone brought their kids so it wasn't just the whole movie premiere deal that we usually see, but a fun family night. And the catering with all the kids' specialty food was a huge hit." Mia laughed, "Our biggest problem was keeping the adults away from the kids' food. I had to slap a lot of hands. It was kind of fun."

"Sounds kinky." Charles laughed.

"I said hands, not asses." Mia put her feet up on her bottom file drawer that was pulled out. Charles Sloan had turned into a great friend and business colleague. Mia secretly was thrilled that he hadn't been scared off by some of her off the rails behavior, but he stayed there by her side and was genuinely happy to see her happier and healthier than she'd been in a long time.

"So, I have an idea," he began.

"Hit me with it." Mia was intrigued.

"How about you and I throw a joint Millennium New Year's Eve Party at my brownstone. You invite all of your friends and colleagues and I'll do the same, and we'll just do a blow out New Year's."

"You don't have to work?" Mia was surprised. Charles' team was known to be involved in a lot of high profile New Year's events around town from Dick Clark's Rockin' New Year's Eve to posh private parties.

"My team's working and I'll check on everything earlier in the evening — but for the changing of a century, I'm enjoying this one."

"Excellent. Let's do it." Mia's mind was racing a million miles an hour. "I have a suggestion. Why don't we let Seth pull this together for us. You know he will create something magical."

Charles laughed. "I was hoping you'd offer him up."

"Set up like a bowling pin, wasn't I?"

"Absolutely, Meezie, and you just walked right into it."

Seth Shapiro, a millennium party and a large budget. Combinations like that only come along on rare occasions.

"What time do you want me over at Charles' to help you?" Walking around Jefferson Market, Mia continued to pick out an assortment of gourmet cheeses, pates, prosciutto, soppressata, olives, roasted peppers and other cold antipasti.

"If you're here by six to help, it'll be fine."

"Ok, just call me if you need me to pick up anything else on my way."

Mia emerged onto Sixth Avenue. The sky was overcast and it felt like snow. Everyone was buzzing with Y2K fever and that shift in energy was palpable. It was tangible. Everything about the day felt different. The air was crackling with all the energy people were giving off. The end of a century. The start of a new millennia.

Mia could feel the sense of melancholy as if it were seeping into her bones. Intellectually she knew there was so much to be thankful for — her business was successful, she was surrounded by friends and family who loved her, and with the help of her therapist, who specialized in PTSD related to rape and sexual assaults, Mia was making healthier choices and finally understanding what were her behavioral triggers. But on this day, December 31, 1999, Mia found herself talking aloud to the universe as she walked up Sixth Avenue toward her apartment.

"Where are you? Am I supposed to go through this lifetime without you? Were we just not meant to be together in this lifetime? Would I even recognize you if we were to meet?" As tears streamed down her cheeks, "Or did I already lose you?" You're my go-to, Schooner, she thought.

Wiping her tears, Mia decided it was just all the heightened energy around her that she was picking up on and that was what had brought on the melancholia. She ached for something. Someone. And it just seemed ever so slightly out of her reach. And that beautiful blonde boy was hanging around on the edge of her consciousness today and she couldn't shake him. There was a tugging at her heart and she had the sneaking suspicion it was him.

"You do show up at the oddest times, Mr. Moore." And another gush of unexpected tears stormed down her cheeks. "My therapist tells me I should forgive. I should forgive the creeps who attacked me. I should forgive you. I should forgive Tom and most of all, I should forgive myself. But I don't know how good I am at forgiveness. I don't think it's my strong suit. I don't hate you though. It's been so long that I just remember the fun

times." Mia continued up Sixth Avenue, talking to herself aloud with tears streaming down her face, but now she was smiling. "I remember the campus cops taking you away in cuffs when you tried to protect me during the mini-riot I started in the cafeteria, I remember dying for you to kiss me on a mountain top and laughing, I remember my face hurting from laughing so much with you. And now, you're probably some successful businessman or a tennis pro at some chic club in Palm Springs, with two perfect blonde children. And I don't hate you. I just want to find that person for me, that soul mate, that connection that I thought I had found with you. And I just fear that I am going to go through this lifetime and not find it."

Mia's phone was ringing as she entered her apartment. Putting the bags from Jefferson Market down on her dining room table, she grabbed the phone on its last ring before the answering machine picked up.

"Hello."

"Happy almost New Year, Gorgeous," said a voice she had not heard in a very long time, and she was actually surprised at not only the smile on her face, but the good feelings in her heart.

"Well, Happy almost New Year to you, too." Mia started to pull out the items that needed refrigeration and brought them into the kitchen.

"So, how have you been? I've seen you on Page Six at some of the events for your clients."

"I cannot complain about the business, it has been doing well. How are you doing?"

"I'm good. Happy to be on break."

There was an awkward silence.

"I miss you, Mia. I miss what we had."

"Am I correct in assuming there is no one in your life?" *What did he want?* she wondered. *A New Year's Eve date? Or had he too tapped into the odd melancholia that was buzzing on a new found clear channel frequency.*

"No one important," he laughed.

"I wasn't important." The melancholia was starting to seep back in.

"You were very important. I'm just an ass."

"So, did you call just to wish me a Happy New Year?" Mia sat down at the dining room table. She sat down in his chair.

"I did."

"I miss you too, Tom." Mia could picture his smile on the other end of the phone and she continued, "You were a really big part of my life and it's hard when a door shuts."

"More like slammed, Mia."

She laughed, "Well, yeah, and I was actually hoping it hit you on the way out."

It was good to hear his laugh, "Well at least I had clothes on when you threw my ass out."

"Consider yourself one lucky motherfucker."

"Oh I do, trust me, I do. So, can we be friends again?"

Mia sighed. The tears were starting to burn and she did not want to cry. "I think that would be really healthy."

"Me too. We're good as friends, you and I."

"Yeah, we are."

Hanging up the phone on the last day of the century, Mia wondered, maybe, just maybe she hadn't given herself enough credit for her capacity to forgive. Maybe therapy was actually working. It was a lot of work and maybe, just maybe, it really was paying off — and it would be very nice to have an old friend back in her world without any feelings of malice.

Wow, when did I become this mature? Mia wondered as the twentieth century rapidly drew to a close.

Chapter Thirty-Two

Mia gazed around Charles' brownstone in awe. Seth Shapiro had set a scene for the evening that was both magical and ethereal. Charles was still out, checking on his guys all over town and Mia thought, "He is going to flip when he sees this."

Long strips of sheer white fabric billowed from the ceiling in arcs and then draped majestically to the floor. Small tables covered in white starched linens dotted the rooms. Each table sported a brass candlestick lamp with a colorful beaded and silk rope shade. Potted palms and white pillar candles filled out the ambience.

Mia stood there speechless. "Casablanca," was all she could say.

"You are correct, BBC." Seth appeared out of nowhere. He was wearing a white dinner jacket with black tuxedo pants and a black silk bowtie.

"Hello, Rick."

"Ilsa," he returned, "Of all the New Year's Eve parties, in all the brownstones, in all of New York and she walks into mine."

Mia laughed, "I am impressed. You have created a magical place. It really feels like Rick's Café Americain." It was then that Mia noticed the 1940's Big Band music playing in the background. "This is really romantic, Seth."

The guests were a combination of Mia and Seth's friends and business associates and Charles' friends and associates.

Charles too was dressed in a dinner jacket as if he'd just stepped out of the Silver Screen.

"You look debonair," she greeted him.

"And you look gorgeous."

"It's just the atmosphere." Mia laughed, though she walked around greeting people and feeling like she was Ingrid Bergman playing Ilsa Lund for the night.

The crowds meshed beautifully and it was hard to tell whose friends were whose.

Working the room was exhausting as Mia spent time catching up with friends and colleagues and meeting Charles' friends. Stepping out into the small yard to get some fresh air and take a break from hostessing, Mia breathed in the cold winter air and took a sip from the old-fashioned Champagne Coupes that Seth had procured for the evening. The Coupes were broad bowled crystal glasses straight out of the thirties and forties and Mia wondered where Seth had found them. As she stepped further into the small, walled yard, her thought was that it still felt like it was going to snow.

Mia closed her eyes and breathed in deeply. Standing there with her eyes closed, she reveled in the relative silence and solitude. The day had been emotional, laden with ghosts, both real and perceived.

She didn't see him sitting on the bench against the concrete wall until she was just a few steps away. He was so still and quiet as he watched her.

Mia jumped, spilling her champagne.

"I'm so sorry. I didn't mean to scare you. Can I get you a napkin or a towel?"

"No. No. Stay there, I'm fine. I didn't mean to intrude on you. I didn't see you there."

"No intrusion. Would you like to sit?" And he moved down on the bench to make room for her.

Mia sat down next to the man, "I just needed some fresh air to re-energize."

"You were really working the room," he observed. He had a pleasant face. Nice looking actually, Mia thought. His light brown hair receding a little at the hairline. Even in the dark, Mia thought his light eyes looked kind.

"Don't kid yourself. Being a hostess is a tough job."

His smile was his best feature, Mia thought. It was genuine and sweet. "Sometimes being a guest is tough, too."

"I'm Mia Silver."

"Yes, I figured."

"You did?" Mia's nose scrunched up with surprise.

"Yes, Charles had mentioned he was co-hosting the party with his friend, Mia."

"And you are?" Mia was starting to get cold in the yard. The bench was freezing and it was going through the sheer fabric of her dress.

"Oh, I'm sorry. How rude of me. I'm Michael Portman." He extended a hand to Mia and offered a solid handshake.

"How do you know Charles?" Mia wrapped her arms around herself to keep warm.

Michael removed his jacket and gently draped it over Mia's small shoulders. Wow, a gentleman, Mia thought. Now *this* truly was a mythical beast.

"We were roommates in college and fraternity brothers."

Mia nodded. "You haven't been at any of the events."

"I just moved back to the states three months ago. I was overseas for the last three years."

"Really? How interesting. Where were you?"

"I was based in London."

Mia smiled at him. "I love London. It reminds me of Manhattan in the sense that it is like small villages strung together."

Michael regarded Mia for a moment and smiled, "Spot on observation. That is exactly how I would describe it."

"Let's go in. It's freezing out here." Mia stood and extended a hand to Michael. He took her hand and stood. Mia thought he must be close to six feet tall.

Before they reached the back door, Mia released his hand.

"BBC, it's almost midnight." Seth was on the other side of the door with Rory, Kami and her date.

"Hey guys, this is Michael. He's an old friend of Charles'."

"I see you've met." Charles had an uncanny ability to silently appear out of nowhere.

"Yeah, we were both ducking out of the party." Mia laughed.

"You two have a lot in common. You should talk," and he quickly moved away.

"Are we getting set up?" Michael had an amused look on his face. In the room's light, Mia could see that Michael did have nice eyes. Very nice eyes. They were grey-blue and large, rimmed with dark lashes. Mia could picture her mom saying, "He's got a sweet face, that one."

"I think we are." Mia concurred. "Charles Sloan, Matchmaker, whoever would have thought."

Mia and Michael were still talking as the new millennium approached. At the stroke of midnight, Mia felt awkward as everyone began to kiss. As if sensing her extreme discomfort, Michael smiled at her, a smile that reached his kind eyes. He gently took her chin in his hand and tipped her face up. His kiss was just a soft brush of his lips on hers. Looking into his big eyes, she could feel his need to connect as strongly as hers. As if he too had been adrift and in search of an elusive anchor for a very long time. Mia reached up and gently laid her hand on Michael's cheek. She smiled up at him. This was a nice guy. She could feel it. Michael Portman was a man worth knowing.

"Happy New Year, Mia."

She could hear the noisemakers and the fireworks but it all seemed far off in the distance. Michael and Mia were having a moment and as the new century began, so did the dream of hope. The music segued from "*Auld Lang Syne*" into "*As Time Goes By*", keeping with the party's Casablanca theme.

"Happy New Year, Michael," her hand was still on his cheek.

"Here's looking at you, Kid."

It had been a long time since Mia Silver had felt so special.

New Year's Day was nearing noon and Mia was still lounging in bed. She'd woken uncharacteristically early, but remained cocooned under her down blanket and kept dozing off to sleep.

The ringing of her cell startled her out of a half dream state. She looked at the name on the display and smiled.

"Good morning."

"Good morning," she could hear the surprising roughness of his morning voice. She liked the sound. "I have two questions for you."

"Shoot." Mia stacked the pillows behind her and settled in.

"Is it too early to call and is it too soon to call?"

Laughing, "Yes and no."

"Ok, two more questions. Shall I let you get back to sleep and would you like to have brunch with me today?"

"No and yes."

January 1, 2000 — what a difference a day makes, Mia mused as she got out of bed to start a new day, a new year, a new decade and a new century. Could there be a more optimal time for new beginnings she wondered. All the icky feelings and heightened energy of the day before had come and gone. It was as if it had been absorbed back into the universe, dissipated into the ether. Y2K had arrived, and as feared by techie geeks all over the globe, the electronic world had not come to a screeching halt. All was the same as yesterday, only better.

As Mia stood in her closet deciding what to wear for her first official date with Michael Portman, it occurred to her that Charles Sloan had this all plotted out when he asked her to co-host his party. Set-up like a bowling pin. Shaking her head, she had to admit, "Well played, Mr. Sloan. Well played."

Chapter Thirty-Three

Walking through the Peter Blum Gallery, Mia was just not connecting to the paintings on the wall.

"What do you think?" she asked Michael, who stood before a large canvas, his eyes roaming across the colors and images.

"I don't get it. Do you?" Turning to Mia as if he were hoping she'd have some concrete explanation.

Shaking her head, "This is all a bit esoteric for me," lowering her voice to a whisper, "and these people are really pretentious."

Michael laughed, "Can I twist your arm to blow this popsicle stand and head over to Balthazar?"

"Let's do it." Mia didn't need a second invitation to get the heck out of the art show opening and head to the brasserie for delicious French food. Balthazar was like being on a Paris cafe movie set.

Heading down Wooster Street toward Spring Street, Michael reached for Mia's hand. She looked up at him and smiled.

Seated at a little bistro table for two with a platter of cheese and pâté and two ruby ports, Michael looked a little nervous as he posed, "So, I have a question for you."

"I like your questions." Mia smiled at him and took a sip of her port.

He looked down for a second, "I'm not sure how much you are going to like this one."

Mia put her port down. She could feel her stomach knotting as she wondered where he was going to go with this. "Ask away." She attempted to be bold.

"So, it's been about a month. We see each other two to three times a week. Have I just been friend-zoned?"

Mia was caught by surprise. Answering this correctly was really important. She really liked Michael. Was she wildly attracted to him? No. And that was something with which she was grappling. Michael was so different — he was low-key, interesting, intelligent and nice. She enjoyed his company and really looked forward to their time together. Did she have an overwhelming desire to rip off his clothes and fuck him till he couldn't move? No.

"Maybe a little bit," she finally answered.

"I don't want to be in the friend-zone, Mia. I want to be lovers." His gaze was so intense with those big grey-blue eyes that Mia felt as if he'd nailed her to her chair. "Give me something back here."

"I liked hearing you say that. It's really pretty hot. I really have loved that we've gotten to know each other, Michael and now I'm a little fearful it will be weird after we have sex and then we won't have this. I would miss this."

"Would you miss me?"

"Oh God yes, of course I would."

"I want to be lovers, Mia."

Mia looked around the crowded bistro, as if searching for someone, leaving Michael with a perplexed look on his face. "Where the hell is that waiter, we need to get a check," and she turned back to meet Michael with her devil grin only to find his sweet smile ready to greet hers.

Michael was lounging across her couch, his suit jacket and tie finally off, when Mia returned with a bottle of Cabernet Sauvignon and two glasses. She poured Michael a glass and one for herself, and nestled in next to him with her legs tucked under her.

"To becoming lovers," she toasted.

"To falling in love," he toasted back.

This is a man worth knowing, she thought, just as she'd thought on New Year's Eve. This was a really good guy and this really good guy was seriously into her. She wondered if it was fear of getting hurt, fear of intimacy, fear of happiness or some other fucked up fear that was holding her back with him.

Michael took her wineglass and put it on the table next to his and then pulled her into his lap. Taking her face in both his hands and looking into her eyes, "I think you're going to find we're surprisingly good together." Mia smiled at his words, and didn't verbalize the ones going through her head, "I hope you're right." This was the most nervous she'd been in a long time.

With a smile that was captivating and eyes that sparkled with sincerity, Michael pushed the curls gently from Mia's face. "I really like you."

"I really like you, too," and she wasn't lying. This man was great, she enjoyed him so very much, so what was it that was holding her back?

Michael's thumb gently traced Mia's cheekbone and she closed her eyes, resting her face in the palm of his hand. With her eyes closed, she concentrated on the sensation his thumb left along her cheek as it trailed slowly down to her lips and softly across them.

Mia opened her eyes to look at him and his sweetness just made her smile. "He's too nice for me," she thought.

Cradling the back of her head in his palm with his fingers woven through her curls, Michael brought Mia's lips to his. He surprised her immediately when he took her lower lip in his teeth and tugged on it, causing a moan to involuntarily escape.

Damn, where did that come from, she wondered — both his painfully pleasurable move and her guttural reaction.

He drew back and looked at her, "You like that, huh?"

"I do. I like to bite and I like to be bitten." Mia ran her hands down his neck to his shoulders and down his arms. *He's pretty muscular for a stock broker*, she thought and that turned her on even more.

"Tell me where you like to be bitten." His teeth were grazing her jaw and his hands were softly on her neck.

Mia could hardly breathe, she was so turned on. He wasn't kidding when he said they were going to be surprisingly good together. Michael Portman, with his sweet, sensual style was rocking her world and they hadn't even done anything yet.

"I like to be bitten on my neck." Mia could barely get the words out.

Taking a handful of Mia's curls, Michael pulled Mia's head to the right, fully exposing the left side of her neck. He gently ran his nose and lips up the sensitive skin as if he were getting her feel and her scent. His teeth then lightly skimmed along the same sensitive path. She started to moan with pleasure and he tugged her hair a little harder, his teeth scraped her skin with more force as he bit her neck.

"Harder," she managed to whisper.

"I'll bruise you if I do it any harder."

She pulled away from him panting and repositioned herself in his lap so that she was straddling him. She wanted to feel him. Taking Michael's face in both hands, she looked deeply into his eyes, still panting, "I want you to do it a lot harder."

Michael smiled and yanked her hair, this time hard and the pain caused her to groan. His teeth sank into the nook between her shoulder and neck where he sucked and bit Mia's soft flesh.

The more she groaned, the harder she could feel his cock become. With her fingers in his soft, fine hair, Mia pressed him into her neck. "Oh God yes, just like that," and he sank his teeth into another spot on her neck.

When he pulled away, Mia looked at him, smiling, "Oh my God, Michael."

"Am I out of the friend-zone?" He kidded.

Mia nodded and leaned in for a kiss. "Permanently."

Shifting Mia off him, Michael stood up. He reached a hand out to her, "Let's become lovers."

"Let's." Mia took his hand and led him down the hall to her bedroom.

Feeling the ache through her entire body, she wanted to push him down on her bed and take what she needed, yet for some reason she felt shy and unsure — like there was a lot on the line and she didn't want to fuck it up.

They lay down on her bed, fully clothed, facing one another. Playing with her hair and pulling her in for panty wetting kisses, Michael Portman was taking his sweet time. His hands explored her face, her arms, the curve down to her waist and by the time he softly ran his hand over her ass, Mia was a four-alarm fire.

And then it occurred to her, as if an epiphany, that Michael's slow seduction was not just fucking, he was actually making love to her. She felt her eyes fill up before she could stop them.

Michael's look immediately changed to concern and his hand quickly moved off her ass and to her cheek. "What's going on?" His voice was husky.

"I'm sorry, I didn't mean to do that." Mia tried hard to make her eyes dry out.

"Please talk to me," he implored, gently stroking her hair.

She nodded and he wiped away her tears with his thumb, softly replacing each tear with a kiss. Who is this man? Mia thought.

"You were just being so sweet and tender and it's just been a very long time since I was in a relationship where someone has been like that with me," and she proceeded to tell Michael a part of her story, her ill-fated introduction to sex and recent work in therapy being the focus of what she imparted. If this relationship was going to go anywhere, he needed to know her secrets, know where the demons resided — a mistake she had made in her relationship with Tom by never telling him. Taking ownership of that was realization of how the hard work in therapy was truly paying off.

When she was done, he softly kissed her. "Thank you for feeling close enough to me to share that. I know it couldn't have been easy."

Mia just nodded. Please don't see me as damaged were the words she silently screamed in her head. She knew that was the chance she just took.

And in her ear, he whispered, "I like you even more now. If that's possible." Pulling her head to his chest, he wrapped her tightly in his arms. After a few moments, "We'll take this as slow as you want, ok."

Mia looked up at him, eyebrows drawn together.

"What's that face?" Michael laughed.

"That's a don't you dare get me all hot and horny and leave me hanging face."

Laughing, he pulled her on top of him. "Take me, I'm yours, baby."

Sitting up on him, Mia slowly unbuttoned Michael's shirt. His skin was smooth, hairless and he was surprisingly built. "I know the hours you work, when do you get a chance to work out?"

"Mostly during lunch. We have a gym at Cantor Fitzgerald and there's also a huge gym that we get membership to at Three World Trade Center. It's in the Marriott between the towers. Also, the New York Athletic Club has a Rowing Club, so I'll start that in the spring."

"Rowing Club?" Mia mouthed.

Michael laughed, "Yes. Rowing Club. I was Crew Team captain in college."

Mia tugged at Michael's shirt to get a look at his arms. "How have you been hiding these guns? Damn, you are just getting hotter by the minute."

Unassuming, easygoing stockbroker Michael Portman was quite the contradiction with his Brooks Brothers suit off. Mia had the upper half of his body bared. "Shall I even the playing field?" she asked, as she pulled her own sweater over her head, revealing a deep red lace bra.

"Leave that on. That's really pretty."

Mia leaned forward to kiss Michael and stretched her legs out so that she was lying on top of him. She slowly explored his mouth with her tongue, stroking his with a sensuously slow rhythm. His hands slid slowly down her back to her ass and he kneaded a cheek in each hand until he heard her moan into his mouth, and then he rolled her over onto her back. Softly kissing her neck, she felt the goose bumps rise as she shivered. Just as her shiver was reaching its pinnacle, Michael bit down into her flesh. Mia moaned, consumed by the exquisite pleasure of the searing pain.

She needed release and she needed it immediately and something inside of her told her that Michael was going to make a meal out of her before that was going to happen.

Rolling to her side, she pressed her lips to his collarbone and started kissing and nipping down his chest. She grazed her teeth along the side of one of his pecs and he shivered. "Ticklish spot?" She looked up at him with a devilish grin. He nodded and she continued down to his surprisingly defined abs. This man had a body she did not expect. She knew he was long and lean, but not tight and ripped. She softly ran her finger through the trail of light brown hair below his belly button and he jumped. "Are you ready for me?"

Pushing the upper half of his body up on his elbows, he volleyed back, "Are you ready for me?"

"I was ready twenty minutes ago." Mia laughed and undid the button and zipper of his suit pants. He became impatient as she worked them down his legs and kicked them off himself. "Oh, I like these." Mia stuck her fingers in the waistband of his black boxer briefs and let them snap back on him.

"Demon," he hissed at her, and they both laughed.

She looked at the sizable tent in his underwear and caressed him through the soft fabric. "Looks like you're ready, too."

"I've been ready since New Year's Eve."

"No. Not that long."

He nodded his head. "Yes, that long."

Mia cocked her head and looked at him, smiling.

"C'mere," he said and held out his arms to her.

Scrambling up the bed to him, she laid down next to him. He reached behind her and unclasped her bra. She pulled the straps down her arms and flung it to the floor.

"Now it's almost an even playing field," and smiling, she slipped her pants off. "Much better."

Both just down to their underwear, they tangled legs and tongues, touching everywhere. When Michael started to flick her nipples to hardness with his tongue, Mia grabbed him roughly by the hair.

"Enough," she announced, panting. "I am going to combust."

Michael shook his head, "I'm not done," and he pulled his head away and sucked her nipple roughly into his mouth. Wrapping her arms around his head, Mia began to whimper.

"Michael, if you don't start touching me, I'm going to start touching myself," and she took his hand and slipped it into her panties.

As his fingers slid through her wetness, "Wow. You weren't kidding." He stroked back and forth before starting to press on her clit. Mia buried her face in his chest, whimpering. It didn't take long before she began to quake around his fingers.

He was smiling at her when she pulled her face away from his chest.

"Are you ever going to fuck me?" she asked.

"No," he shook his head.

"Are you ever going to make love to me?"

"Every chance I get."

Mia took his face in her hands. "I need you to right now."

"What do you think we've been doing?"

"Torturing me."

Pulling her underwear off and then following with his own, "You are so impatient," he teased.

"Make me wait any longer and you are going back into the friend zone."

Grabbing her for a rough kiss, "I'm never going back into the friend zone."

"Probably not." Mia agreed.

He pulled Mia underneath him and smiled at her. "Say so long to the friend zone," and in one swift motion he was inside of her. Mia wrapped her legs around him as he drove into her slowly. With the same slow precision, he pulled out and then back in, as if acclimating himself to his new environment. "You feel really good," he whispered. "I knew you'd feel really good." And then he pulled all the way out of her. He was no longer inside of her. Mia looked at him, as if to say, "Come back," and he plunged forcefully back in, causing her to gasp.

"And you called me a demon?" And she pushed him, rolling him over on his back and straddling him. "Take my hands." She held onto him tightly as she rode the length of his cock. Taking him all the way in, she squeezed him tight. "You feel really good, too." He let go of her hands and grabbed her by the hips, controlling her speed and depth as his cock disappeared deep into her.

"I told you we'd be good together," he could hardly get the words out.

"Michael …" and she was gone. She heard him moan, but it was far away in the distance. Her ears felt like they were stuffed with cotton and although she had come, she didn't want to stop moving on him. It felt so good. Finally, she fell forward onto his chest and he wrapped his arms around her.

"I want to stay the night," he whispered in her ear.

"Did you think I would let you leave?" She smiled at him and kissed the tip of his nose.

As she fell asleep in Michael's arms, all Mia could think was, "This is a really decent man. Do not fuck this up."

Chapter Thirty-Four

Climbing the steps out of the Lexington Avenue Line subway station on 86th Street, the heavy balmy spring air made Mia smile. *Spring, you old foe*, she thought. But it was impossible not to smile. The air was warm, the days getting longer, leaves and flowers budding all over the city. It was a new century and this spring, Mia had hope that her season of bad luck was left behind in the last century.

Crossing Lexington and heading toward Madison Avenue, everyone and everything just seemed more alive, more vibrant. Wearing just a light sweater as opposed to the heavy weight of a wool or a down coat was reason enough to feel lighthearted.

The Met and the park were right in front of her now as she waited for the light to change and cross Fifth Avenue. The dappled greens of Central Park emulated the Monets inside the majestic Beaux-Arts style building. Bounding up the great stone steps to the entrance, Mia was excited to spend some time with her mother, who had just returned from wintering in Florida.

Lois looked chic in a navy and red St. Johns Knit with navy pumps and a Palm Beach tan.

"Mom, you look fabulous." Mia hugged her mother tight.

"So do you, darling. I love your hair this length." Mia's curls were layered to her jaw line with long curls hanging in her eyes.

Mia slipped her arm through her mother's and steered her toward Augustus. "Let's go see him. I haven't been here in so long." With a knowing smile, Lois indulged her daughter.

"Hey, handsome." Mia greeted the marble bust with a smile. It was impossible to not recall the Jackie moment when she visited him now, and through stream of consciousness association, Augustus Caesar had somehow become associated with Schooner Moore, although her infatuation with the ancient emperor long preceded her relationship with Schooner.

"He really was quite handsome, those lips and that strong chin, and straight nose. He was a hottie. Did you know that he and Bruce Springsteen share a birthday?"

Lois just shook her head at her daughter.

"What's that look?"

"My daughter, successful owner of a New York City advertising agency, thinks Augustus Caesar is a hottie and knows that he shares a birthday with Bruce Springsteen. How did I raise such an odd child?"

Mia laughed, "Ahhh, you didn't do so bad."

As they made their way toward the opening for *The Forgotten Friezes from the Castle of Vélez Blanco*, Lois asked, "So when are we going to get to meet Michael?"

Grabbing two glasses of champagne from a waiter's tray and handing one to her mother, Mia smiled, "You see I have this fear," she began, "if I introduce you to Michael, you are going to invite me out to dinner one night shortly after that, and when I walk into the place, I'm going to find that I've just walked into my own wedding."

"I'm going to like him that much?" Lois' eyebrows were raised.

"Oh please." Mia rolled her eyes, "You are going to love him." They stepped before the first twenty-foot carved pine frieze. Intricate Venetian woodcuts portrayed Julius Caesar in his chariot followed by citizens carrying victory branches. "Oh look, it's Uncle Jules." Mia laughed. "Look at all the work that went into these," and they both marveled at the detail and the craftsmanship that went into the narrative sculptures as they explored the rest of the exhibit.

Giovanni Venticinque was located only a half block away from The Met and was Mia and Lois' regular go-to spot to end their "Girls' Days" at The Met. Seated at a table for two in the corner of the cream and dark wood dining room, Mia quickly perused the wine list and ordered a bottle of Super Tuscan.

"Is it serious?"

Mia laughed and took a big gulp of wine. "I think this is called déjà vu."

Lois gave her daughter an annoyed look, "I have not asked that question in years," and then, "Well are you going to answer it?"

"Mom, we've only been dating a few months." The waiter arrived with appetizers and Mia dug into her Carpaccio, carving up the paper-thin meat with her fork and knife.

"At your age, I would think that would be enough time to know." Lois cut into her prosciutto and melon.

"At my age?" Mia shook her head, "I like him a lot. I enjoy being with him. He's a really special guy and he treats me like a princess."

Lois put her fork and knife down. "So, what have you found wrong with him?"

"Nothing." Mia shook her head. "He's a really good guy."

"Do you see it becoming serious?"

Mia picked up the wine bottle and refilled her mother's glass and then her own. They both took sips. "It's possible."

Lois put her glass down, "Ok, Mia, what am I missing here? There's something you're not telling me."

"Hmph." Mia scoffed. "That's probably an understatement. Right now I'm really working on me. And I need to get myself to a good healthy place before I even know that I can commit to someone else."

"What does that mean?" Mia couldn't tell if Lois was annoyed or concerned or a combination of the two.

Mia was silent for a moment as the busboy removed their plates. The waiter was right behind him ready to top off Mia and Lois' wineglasses. "Keep that vino coming." Mia thought to herself.

"It means that I am finally in therapy dealing with things that took a very long time for me to start facing."

"What kind of things?" Lois' voice was tight and Mia knew the next thing out of her mouth was going to be very painful for her mother.

"I'm ok now, Mom. I really am. But I wasn't for a long time," she paused and took a deep breath and blew it out. "I was raped spring semester of my freshman year in college."

The words hung between them as if suspended in ether. Mia watched the color drain from her mother's face, paling her beneath her tan. "Mom, take a sip of wine or water. I'm ok. I'm really okay. It was a long time ago."

"Was it that handsome boy?"

It took a moment for Mia to realize her mother was referring to Schooner.

"Schooner?" There was shock in her voice.

Lois nodded, "Yes."

"No. No. No, Mom. Oh my God, no. Schooner would never do anything like that. He was actually the one who took me to the hospital that night and took care of me afterwards."

"You had such a reaction the one time I brought him up."

Mia nodded. "Yeah well, Schooner and I didn't end too well. But he had nothing to do with me getting raped. I was just in the wrong place at the wrong time coming out of the darkroom late one night."

"Why didn't you tell me?" Lois' hand was visibly shaking as she lifted her water glass. "Why didn't you come to us?"

"It took me a really long time to deal with it, Mom. It was only when it got to the point where I was starting to destroy my life, where my behavior got really destructive, that I finally did something about it. I never even told Tom until he confronted me the day I threw him out. But all those years we were together I never confided in him."

"And therapy is working?"

"I'm telling you about it. That's a big step."

The conversation quieted as the waiter brought their entrees and Mia asked him to bring another bottle of wine. Thank goodness, she thought, in New York you can just cab it home. No worries about being the designated driver, because clearly she and Lois were going to be staggering out the door by the time they left the restaurant.

"Does Michael know?"

Mia nodded, "Yes. He does. And that was another big thing, being able to tell someone I'm in an intimate relationship with about my past."

It was clear neither of them were going to touch the food in front of them. Mia picked up the bottle and refilled their wine glasses.

"So, what kind of therapy are you in? Are you seeing a psychiatrist?"

"She's a psychologist."

Lois sat deep in thought for a moment. "So, is this why you left California?"

Mia shook her head no.

"No?" Lois was surprised. "Schooner?"

Mia nodded.

"What happened?" Lois was shocked, and yet she wasn't, as she remembered Mia's reaction years ago.

"He lied to me." Mia's answer was clipped.

"About what?"

"Loving me."

Lois wondered if all the alcohol they had consumed was bringing that old hurt close to the surface for her daughter. The pain in her eyes and in her face was still very much present.

"You were both very young, Mia."

"I know we were. But I have never felt so connected to another human being before or since. We were one, in two separate bodies, but we were one," and with a sad smile, "or at least I felt we were."

"Every love is different, Mia. Do not discount what you may have found now with Michael because it is not the same as what you once felt for Schooner."

"I'm trying not to, Mom. I really am."

As Mia lifted the wineglass to her lips, all she could think about was that amazing feeling of loving someone else so deeply, so fully and without reserve, and it seemed as elusive as being able to hold a ray of sunshine in one's hand.

Chapter Thirty-Five

Lois Silver was going to get her way, whether her secretive daughter was going to comply or not. On this warm Wednesday evening, they had just come from a pre-theatre dinner at longtime family favorite restaurant, Pierre Au Tunnel, and were making their way down Eighth Avenue to Forty-Fourth Street and the Shubert Theatre, where the musical *Chicago* was playing.

Lois walked slowly so that Bob and Michael would not be in earshot while she grilled Mia.

"He's got a sweet face," commented Lois.

Do I know my mother or do I know my mother? Mia thought. She had pegged that one way back on New Year's Eve, and here it was her birthday in July, and Lois commented verbatim. *Damn, I'm good.*

"He's a nice-looking guy." Mia agreed.

They stopped for the light at Forty-Sixth Street. The men had already crossed.

"I like this one. He's smart and personable. Obviously, he's crazy about you. Do you think this is the one?"

Mia threaded her arm through her mother's as the light changed and they stepped off the curb. Lois could cut to the chase with the best of them.

"Might be." Mia was going to make her work for it, just because she knew it would annoy the hell out of her, and if Lois was going to make her have this conversation, then she was going to enjoy torturing her.

"What do you mean might be. You've been dating him for over six months now. You know, the odds statistically drop like a bomb that you'll find a man after you're thirty."

Mia laughed, "So, are you telling me that if I do not marry Michael, I'm going to be an old maid?" Mia's smile was huge and she knew her mother did not appreciate it for one second.

"I'm just telling you the odds." They were silent for a half a block while Lois regained steam. "Well, how does he feel? Does he want to marry you?"

"Maybe someday, I guess. We're really happy right now. Why do we have to do anything?"

"Well, don't you want to have a family?"

"It's not high on my radar screen, Mom. The business takes up a lot of my time. I'm kind of married to that."

Lois just shook her head. "The business is not going to take care of you when you are old and sick."

Mia knew it was time to distract Lois a little without totally blowing her off. "So, I'm assuming you like him and you approve."

"Oh very much. He's quite an improvement. I like that you're closer in age and I think you have similar goals. And honestly, I don't think he would ever give you the heartache that Tom did."

"I agree." Mia nodded. "Michael is a really stand-up guy. And he does, he puts me first and he's very caring. He's a good egg, this one."

Lois brought them to a screeching halt before they met up with the men in front of the Shubert Theatre. "So, if he gives you a ring, don't be a fool. He's a catch."

All Mia could say was, "Oy."

As they entered the elegant theatre with its gilded graffito frescos, Michael draped an arm over Mia's shoulder, "So, does she approve?"

Mia rolled her eyes. "Pick a date," was all she said.

Michael threw his head back in laughter.

"And while you're at it, what do you want to name the first three kids? I told you they would love you."

"I was actually nervous." Michael confessed. "And I have a feeling if your mother doesn't like someone it is not an easy road."

"You are one smart man, Michael Portman, because you have that woman pegged."

As they made it to their seats before the curtain went up on *Chicago*, Mia noticed Lois' very satisfied look as she and Michael sat there holding hands, and when he leaned over to kiss her, she caught the small smirk on her mother's face.

If Lois had a mental checklist of what she wanted in a son-in-law, Michael Portman was scoring very high. Nice looking — check. Intelligent — check. Educated — check. Personable — check. Gainfully employed — check. Crazy about her daughter — check. Jewish — bonus check.

Michael Portman was Lois Silver's perfect ideal for a son-in-law. Now if there was only a way to ensure that her daughter did not screw it up, Lois would be able to rest easy.

Chapter Thirty-Six

"What are you doing, BBC?" Seth walked into Mia's office and over to the window where she stood.

"I'm waving at Michael," she laughed. "We said we'd go to our windows and wave at each other at exactly noon."

"You and White Bread are waving at each other? Well, that is truly nauseating." Seth's top lip was actually sneering at Mia.

"When he was here last week, we were trying to figure out exactly where his office is. So, look at the North Tower." Mia began.

"Which one is north?"

Pointing, "The one with all the TV and communications antennas on top. 110 is the top floor, go down six and that is the 105th floor, and just in from the northwest corner is Michael's office. He's literally right below Windows on the World." Mia stood pointing to a spot and Seth stood there looking at her as if she were insane.

"Ok, whatever," and he turned on his heel and walked away.

Mia's cell rang and she turned from her window to get the ringing phone off her desk. Looking at the display, she flipped it open. "Hi Mom. What's up?"

"Your father and I just booked flights to come up for Thanksgiving."

"You're coming up from Florida for Thanksgiving? Is everything ok?" Mia's parents left for Florida in October and returned in April every year, and if Mia wanted to see them in between, she had to fly down to Florida. Lois and Bob Silver swore never to step foot in New York City in cold weather again, so this was truly shocking news.

"Everything is fine. We just thought it would be nice to spend the holiday with you and Michael. You are spending it with him, aren't you?"

Sitting down at her desk and pulling up her email, "You know what, Mom, we haven't even discussed it. I'll send him an IM now."

"What's an IM?"

"Instant message. Hold on a second while I send it."

Mia: We haven't discussed Thanksgiving. What are your plans?
Michael: Well, what are your plans?

Mia: My mother just called. Am on the phone with her now. She and my dad are coming up. Maybe I'll cook. I hate going out on Thanksgiving.
Michael: Am I invited?
Mia: You're making the stuffing! :)
Michael: I know what I'd like to be stuffing.
Mia: Michael Portman! You pig! (translates to "don't get me horny during work with my mother hanging on the phone.)
Michael: LOL

"Ok, Mom. Michael is going to join us and we're going to cook Thanksgiving at my apartment."

"Maybe his parents would like to join us?"

"Mother …"

"Don't Mother me. I'd like to meet his parents. Have you met them?"

"Yes, I've met them. They are very nice."

"Invite them. I'd like to meet them." Lois demanded.

"You are an evil woman, Lois Silver." Mia just shook her head. That woman was bound and determined to marry her off.

Mia: Michael, please extend the invitation to your parents. And I apologize in advance for whatever nefarious plan that evil mother of mine is hatching."

Mia rolled over and bit Michael on the shoulder.

"Ouch, Demon."

"Wake up. The parade is on and we have to start cooking." Mia poked him in the ribs.

Michael rolled over and opened one eye. Mia put her nose against his, also opening one eye.

"We're going to have both sets of parents here today. Are you scared yet?" Michael kissed Mia's lips softly.

"I've been scared shitless since Lois told me she booked a flight."

"I'm glad I picked up all that wine last night." Michael's face was saying, "Yikes."

"Is it too early to start drinking?"

"Probably a little bit. But it's definitely not too early to start stuffing." Michael rolled on top of Mia and pulled her hands over her head. "Or trussing for that matter."

"Are you calling me a turkey?"

"Mmm-hmm," he started to softly nibble at her neck. "Do you know in my house, people fight over the neck."

"Well, in this house," and Mia could not help but moan as Michael's teeth grazed her neck, "you are the only one allowed to eat this turkey's neck."

"I'm the only one allowed to eat this turkey's breast," and he bent his head down and sucked a nipple into his mouth and bit down, the pleasurable pain causing Mia to writhe and moan and free a hand to pull his hair.

"Oh, we have a feisty turkey, I see." Michael smiled up at her with his sweet smile.

"Actually, you have a moist turkey." Mia couldn't wipe the smile off her face.

"That's a very good thing because no one likes a dry turkey."

"Well, there's always gravy." Mia added.

"I've got plenty of gravy for you, Babe, but still, no one likes a dry turkey."

"Poor dry turkeys. I feel for them."

Michael's lips trailed softly down Mia's stomach, causing her to writhe even more. "Now a lot of people like the thigh, 'cause it's meaty and juicy."

"I'd venture to say that I'm pretty juicy right now."

Licking a trail on the inside of Mia's thigh, along her bikini line, followed by his teeth grazing the same trail caused every muscle in Mia's pussy to contract.

"You're killing me."

Michael laughed, not removing his face from between her legs, "Well, that's good, no one likes to eat a live turkey," and with that he spread open the outer lips of her pussy and started to feast. First taking his tongue and licking out all the wetness, followed by spreading her open wider and sucking and licking and then focusing on sucking her clit into his mouth and then nibbling.

"Oh, God. Michael." Mia's crossed her legs in the air, clamping her thighs to the side of his head and using her feet to press him deeper into her slit. Bucking into his face, she could hear her own sounds through a cotton curtain, before it drew away and sight and sound returned.

With a satisfied smirk, he laid his chin on her lower belly looking up at her. "Did you say I was on stuffing?" he laughed. Getting up onto his knees, he pulled Mia up into a sitting position (which was no easy feat because after her orgasm she was like jelly), and positioned her over the tip of his cock.

With a smile he couldn't wipe off his face, "Ready to get stuffed, Turkey." And he rammed Mia down on his cock.

Mia gasped, still tender as Michael repeatedly rammed her down on his cock. She squeezed him tightly with her pussy muscles, loving the wince and groan she evoked from him with every squeeze.

"I have a feeling I'm about to be stuffed and basted." Mia leaned forward and kissed him, tasting herself on his lips.

"You've got that right," and he held her down tightly as he unleashed into her.

Mia eased off the bed a few minutes later and reached out a hand to Michael. "Ready to go cook?"

Smiling, he took her hand, "I thought we already had," and they headed toward the kitchen to cook their first holiday meal together.

Michael was bringing in the last of the dishes and stacking the dishwasher, as Mia hand washed the delicate wine glasses.

"I think that's the last of it," he announced. Going over to the big roasting pan, he picked up the turkey baster, "What would you like to do with this?" he asked, suggestively.

Putting a red wine goblet face down on a sheet of paper towel to dry, Mia reached into the sink and pulled out a metal object. "Well, then there is always this," she looked him square in the eye. "You know what to do with a meat thermometer, don't you?"

"Insert into meat," he pulled Mia into his arms. "They don't really need dessert, do they? Would it be rude to kick them out now?" He laughed. His mom and Lois were chatting at the dining room table and the men were on the couch, both snoring, while the Minnesota Vikings were trouncing the Dallas Cowboys on the TV. "I'm thinking Pumpkin Pie in bed."

"Have I ever told you that Thanksgiving is my favorite holiday."

Michael bent down for a kiss. "Have I ever told you that you are my favorite dish." With Mia's face in both hands, they got lost in their kiss.

Both mothers walked into the kitchen to see what was taking dessert so long to be served and looked at one another, both clearly pleased at seeing their children lost in a passionate kiss. The women left the kitchen, unnoticed.

"Okay, let's get that pot of coffee on. The quicker we serve dessert, the quicker they are all out and we get our couch back." Mia was already envisioning snuggling up with Michael to an old movie or a holiday classic.

"I'm on it." Michael smiled.

Chapter Thirty-Seven

New Year's Eve and the second annual party at Charles' brownstone. At 11:45 P.M., Michael pulled Mia out into the backyard. Wrapping his arms around her and pulling her to his chest, he whispered in her ear, "Happy Anniversary, Baby."

Smiling up at him, Mia realized how much more sane and stable her life was because of Michael. He was steady and calming and just there for her. Whether it was business or personal issues that she was bouncing off him, Michael's responses were intelligent and thoughtful. Her initial impression of him from one year before had not changed. The year 2000 had probably been the most stable year of her life and the happiest one in a very long time.

"It's cold out here. Brrrr." Mia was hopping up and down to keep warm.

"I just wanted to get you alone, away from everyone. And this is where it all started exactly a year ago." Bending down, Michael kissed Mia tenderly.

Mia wrapped her arms around Michael's waist. His body heat felt good in the frigid night air. "You are the best thing that has happened to me in a very long time, Michael."

"I love you, Mia."

She pulled away from his chest and looked up at him. Say it, she screamed at herself, say it. He is wonderful. Say it. The thought of not having him in her world was painful to just think about. So, it must be love, she thought. But it still didn't feel the same. It felt comfortable and it felt fulfilling. It just wasn't all-consuming. And maybe this is what healthy love feels like, Mia thought. It was hard to know. Just say it, an inner voice screamed. She could feel the smile on her face growing as she looked up at his sweet face.

"Hey, get in here, you're going to miss the ball drop." Seth screamed from the door.

Mia grabbed Michael's hand and headed toward the house. This year she didn't release his hand before entering. Pulling his hand and arm over her shoulder, she leaned back into him as they did the countdown in front of the TV. As it turned to 2001, Mia turned to Michael. This year there was not awkwardness between them as they shared the first kiss of the New Year.

Michael took Mia's face in his hands, "Here's looking at you, Kid."

Wrapping her arms around his waist, Mia smushed her face into his chest. What a sweetheart, she thought, and felt overwhelmed with guilt for not saying I love you back to him. The truth was she did love him. Very much. He had really grown on her and she felt very safe with him. Yet, it still wasn't that all-consuming, over-the-top, crazy OCD love that she wanted to be consumed by — that she knew existed. That she knew she was capable of feeling. But it was a comforting, secure love. Her mother's words, that no two loves were ever the same, seemed to be very astute.

Pulling away from his chest, Mia looked up at him.

"What?" He cocked his head to the side. "What's that look?"

Giving him a devil grin, she grabbed his hand and headed for the back door.

Michael looked surprised as Mia led him out into the cold night.

"What's up?"

"We didn't finish our conversation."

"You're right, we didn't." Mia's heart ached at the concern in his eyes as he was clearly not sure what would be coming at him next.

"So, I think we should finish it."

"Okay," trepidation had entered his voice.

"I love you, Michael."

The shock that registered on his face was classic. He appeared to have been stealing himself for not such a happy admission.

His smile was slow. But it was a sweet smile that immediately reached his eyes.

They both stood there, not moving in the cold night, frozen in a moment, each understanding that a chasm had been bridged.

Michael was the first one to speak. "C'mere, you." He pulled Mia snugly against him. "I didn't expect that. I honestly didn't know how you'd react," and in her ear, he whispered, "I'm so happy right now. You can't even imagine what hearing you say those words does to me."

And in her heart, Mia felt good. Knowing that she was making a sweetheart like Michael Portman happy, made her incredibly happy.

Maybe this is what love really is all about, she thought, laying her cheek against the warmth of Michael's chest. The new millennium was treating her just fine.

Chapter Thirty-Eight

Appearing like a beacon in the doorway of her office in his fire engine red cashmere sweater and pink scarf with funky red hearts, Seth announced, "BBC, you'd better get going. You don't want to keep White Bread waiting."

"Stop calling him that." Mia looked up from her computer, clearly annoyed.

Seth rolled his eyes and sat down across from her. "You know I like him. He's impossible not to like. I just like fucking with you because I know it irritates you."

"Hello Lois."

Seth threw his head back in laughter. "I'm channeling Lois. It's true. So, now put on a little lip gloss before you leave, and are you sure you don't want to take me to Chanterelle with you?"

"Don't you have a date tonight?"

"I do," Seth preened, "but I'd gladly blow him off for a dinner at Chanterelle."

"So, blow him and tell him to take you to Chanterelle." Mia smirked at Seth.

Standing up, he sneered at her, "Obnoxious BBC," and as he turned away, "now put on some lip gloss and get out of here or you will be late and White Bread might get stale."

"God, you're a bitch." Mia muttered under her breath.

"Yes, I am," he proudly retorted.

Packing up her desk, Mia leaned forward to smell the flower arrangement Michael had sent. Mia was never a huge fan of Valentine's Day, but the bright flowers on a dreary, grey winter's day had kind of an Oz in Kansas effect on her.

Heading out into the cold, wet dusk, Mia hailed a cab and told the driver Two Harrison Street. Chanterelle was one of the most feel good restaurants in New York City — airy, with ample space between the tables (a rarity in New York City), high ceilings and walls painted a soothing shade of pale yellow and, of course, Chef David Waltuck's divine tasting menu. Mia's mouth was starting to water at the thought as the cab driver turned south crawling through the rush hour traffic. Turning west onto

Washington Street for an easier run down through the West Village, the cab soared past some of Mia's favorite brownstone lined blocks. They were hitting the lights just right and the cabbie appeared to be proud of himself and his driving prowess.

Their traffic light good luck run ended two blocks before Harrison Street when they hit a red light at the corner of Washington and N. Moore Street. Mia looked at the sign and thought N. Moore, great — just what I need in my head on Valentine's Day — that ancient ghost to haunt my heart. She sat back on the squeaky black leather seat and closed her eyes and for the first time in a very long time, she could see him clearly, the way he looked on a mountaintop, the look in his eyes when he looked at her, and immediately she felt the pang in her heart. It wasn't that pang of pain, at least not at first. At first, it was that feeling in her heart — that feeling of overwhelming joy. The need to breathe every breath with and for this man. That elusive something that she yearned to feel again. Yearned to call her own. Yearned to share. Fuck, she thought, as she quickly wiped the tears from her cheek that had immediately made their escape. Just fuck. This haunted heart simply will not let me be.

Startled as the driver gunned the engine when the light turned green, Mia took a deep breath to gather herself and try to shake Schooner away before she entered Chanterelle. Here she was, in downtown Manhattan, meeting her boyfriend on Valentine's Day at an amazing restaurant in a funky, cool neighborhood. She never could have even envisioned her life today back when she was with Schooner. But that damn street sign. Her therapist would say, "Clearly, one of your triggers, Mia. So, what are your coping strategies here?"

I'm going to eat a five-course tasting menu, have some delicious wine, have Valentine's Day sex with my boyfriend — that is how I'm going to cope, Mia screamed at her therapist in her head. But still, as she got out of the cab and stood on the sidewalk in front of Chanterelle, she needed to take a moment to breathe and to shake off Schooner's ghost. But he wasn't leaving and she wondered where he was, what he was doing, what he looked like now and if he was happy. Standing on the sidewalk in the cold night air she spoke to him in her head.

You haven't been here in a while. A long while. You really show up at the craziest times. Yes, I know I saw that street sign. I'm never down in this neighborhood so I totally forgot about N. Moore Street. I'm sure it being Valentine's Day doesn't help. And that means two days ago was your birthday. I hope it was good. Okay, you have to go now. I can't take you into this restaurant with me. Go back to whatever box it is that I keep you in.

Shaking her shoulders as if to physically disengage from his touch, she closed her eyes again just for a second, overwhelmed by the memory of how much she had loved this man. *Have a great Valentine's Day, Schooner.* Keep forgiving, she told herself and reached for the door handle to Chanterelle.

Michael was already seated at the table, his smile immediate and contagious, catapulting her ghost from the physical plane. Ever the gentleman, Michael stood and kissed Mia, pulling out her chair for her.

"Have you been waiting long?"

He shook his head no. "You look beautiful tonight."

"Thank you." Mia smiled, "And no. Seth did not dress me."

Mia perused the handwritten menu, "What to do. What to do. Am between the Venison Carpaccio and the Foie Gras appetizer."

Michael smiled, "Me too. You get one and I'll get one and we'll share."

Mia looked at Michael with a big smile. "You make everything so easy." Taking her hand, he brought it to his lips. "You are so romantic tonight, Mr. Portman."

"You ain't seen nothing yet," he raised his eyebrows at Mia.

The waiter came over for a drink order. "Cocktail first?" Michael asked.

Mia nodded, "Yes, I'll have a French 75."

"Make that two, and if you can bring a bottle of Taittinger 'Comte de Champagnes' after our appetizers."

The waiter appeared a few minutes later with their drinks.

She held up her glass to Michael, "Happy Valentine's Day," and they clinked glasses. Mia could immediately feel the alcohol slam her bloodstream and the jolt felt good. She knew she needed food and soon.

As they finished their appetizers, Michael nodded to the waiter and he appeared tableside, linen napkin draped over his arm to uncork the bottle of Taittinger's. He popped the cork and handed it to Michael, who put it in his pocket. Filling the champagne flutes in front of Mia and Michael, he quickly receded from view.

Raising his glass to Mia, Michael smiled, "When I moved back to New York, I really felt adrift. I just didn't know where I belonged. Was it London? Was it New York? I really felt disenfranchised and when Charles invited me to his New Year's party, it was the last thing I wanted to do.

There was so much hoopla and hype around Y2K and I just wasn't feeling it. I walked into his brownstone that night and it was like stepping back in time, like I had entered the movie set of Casablanca. And you know what, I was Rick. I really was. This guy who seemingly was doing okay, but in reality, was totally detached from the world around him and from his own feelings. And when you walked out into the garden I thought, what is she doing here? I'd seen you throughout the evening working the room."

Mia nodded and laughed. She had been working the crowd hard that night and it was exhausting.

Michael continued, "You'd been at the center of everything all night and here you were and the look on your face said that you just wanted to escape, and I thought that maybe you wanted to escape from yourself."

With those last words, Mia could feel the tears welling up in her eyes and she nodded.

"And this woman who had appeared so happy floating around all evening was really but a finely crafted facade. You were not happy and I could feel that as I watched you standing there with your eyes closed, and you looked as if you were pleading to the night for something, anything. And Mia, it broke my heart. And in that moment, I didn't feel adrift any longer. All I wanted to do was see if there was something I could do to make it better for you. Make the happy person you were pretending to be a reality for you. Or at least I knew I wanted to try."

Listening to Michael's words, Mia was speechless. His vast capacity for loving and caring was overwhelming her.

"And I'm glad you've let me try, because the last year has been amazing. Every day, just knowing you're here, that you are a part of my life, that you are my life, has been that anchor and I'm not adrift anymore."

Mia realized the restaurant was quiet. Dead silence as Michael reached into his jacket pocket. For a moment, she thought he was going to pull out the cork from the champagne bottle, but as the adrenaline blasted through her veins, she could feel her face grow hot and it was suddenly hard to breathe. It was as if she were wearing a tight, wool turtleneck on a ninety-degree day. And the thought running through her head was, "The exit is behind me."

There was a box in Michael's hand and she never actually heard the words, "Will you marry me?" because she was so close to passing out that the sense of sound had already retreated. She could see the apprehensive look on everyone's face in the restaurant. They were all staring. Waiting. Eager. Breathe, just breathe, Mia reminded herself. Oh God, I want to run, she thought. I don't want this. Aren't we happy the way we are? Why does everyone think this is what is needed to be happy?

The thought of embarrassing this sweet man in front of a restaurant full of people made the tears start to stream. She couldn't humiliate him that way. The thought of hurting him, ever, was agonizing.

His smile had fully reached his eyes as he looked at her with so much love. Mia took a moment to just look into his eyes, calming herself with the anchor and tranquility residing deep within this special, special man. A moment in his eyes brought a true smile to her face and without saying a word, Michael slipped the ring onto Mia's finger.

Cheers went up throughout Chanterelle. Mia's hearing began to return as people began to congratulate them. The owners, David and Karen Waltuck, appeared tableside offering their best wishes and plates with a beautiful amuse bouche of prosciutto, foie gras and fig on brioche toast.

Michael pulled Mia to him and they kissed, the taste of champagne and salty tears mingling. And in that moment, the apprehension disappeared as he was saying, "I love you" into her mouth.

"Well, do you like the ring?" Michael was beaming.

Mia hadn't even looked down at it yet and as she held out her left hand, the diamonds sparkled like a prism through her tears. "It's beautiful. It's really beautiful." And it was. At the center sat a cushion cut diamond surrounded by small round diamonds in an antique platinum setting.

"Really? You like it?" Michael pushed her curls from her eyes.

Mia nodded. Reaching out, she put her hand on his cheek, brushing it with her thumb. "How long have you had this planned?"

"New Year's Eve 2000," his smile was contagious.

"No, seriously."

Michael laid his face in Mia's hand. "Seriously. New Year's Eve 2000. I knew when you walked out into the garden that I wanted to spend my life making you happy."

Tears fell freely down Mia's cheeks at those words. Michael Portman's sweet love and affection did make her happy. She knew on New Year's Eve 2000 that he was a special man, a very special man. And in the thirteen and a half months that had passed, Mia learned how very special he truly was.

Lifting his champagne glass in a toast to her, "Here's looking at you, Kid."

Mia smiled and hoped that her and Michael's story would have a happier ending than Rick and Ilsa's.

Chapter Thirty-Nine

Mia was on the phone when Michael let himself into her apartment. She waved and smiled as he put down his briefcase and took off his overcoat, scarf and suit jacket.

He was loosening his tie as Mia said, "Ok, I'll tell him. Love you too, Mom."

Smiling at her as she hung up the phone, "So, what did Lois have to say? Has she picked out a date for us yet?" Michael was chuckling at the thought.

Mia stood there with a tense expression on her face.

"Did you tell her we got engaged?"

"No." Mia closed her eyes.

"Wow. What's going on? Why haven't you told your parents yet?" Mia could see and feel the tension eclipse in Michael's eyes.

Walking over to the couch and sitting down, Mia reached out a hand to Michael to come sit next to her.

"What's going on, Mia?"

Looking down for a moment to collect her thoughts, Mia took a deep breath and slowly blew it out. "I am really happy with the way things have been between us — with the way things are. I love what we have, Michael. I do," looking earnestly into his eyes, "but I don't know that I want to be married."

"Are you afraid? Overwhelmed? Tell me what you're feeling."

"I feel like I'm choking."

Michael's eyebrows knit together, "You feel that I'm smothering you?"

"No. And that's kind of the whole point. I think what we have is perfect. I wouldn't change a thing about it." Seeing the hurt on his face as he was trying to understand her position was painful for Mia to watch. She was hurting him. And that was devastating and she knew in her gut that by the time this conversation was over, they would both be decimated. The train had left the station and there was no turning back now as it sped towards its wreckage.

"I thought we wanted the same things — to build a life together, a family. Did I dream this whole thing?"

"I do want a life together," Mia nervously played with the fringes on a burgundy throw pillow. "Honestly, I'm not ready to think about a family and I don't know how I'll feel in the future. I like kids and I think that someday I might like to have a family, but I think I'd also be ok if I never had kids."

Mia watched as Michael absorbed her words. He looked as if he'd been sucker punched. "So, are you telling me you don't want to be engaged?" and before she could answer, "Or are you telling me that you don't want to be engaged to me?"

Taking his hand in both of hers, "I don't want to promise you what I don't know if I'm capable of giving you."

Shaking his head in disbelief, "Capable or just don't want to?"

Mia looked down. She wished she had the answers to why just the thought of committing to this wonderful man, a man she loved and loved being with, caused her stomach to knot.

"Wow." Michael ran a hand through his hair. He'd just been blown out of the water. "Well Mia, I know what I want. I want to be married. I want a family. I want to coach our kids' sports teams. I want to take them on family vacations and make memories that we talk about for years. And I want to do that with you. But if you don't want to do that with me, there is no point in either of us wasting each other's time any longer."

Disengaging his hand from Mia's, he stood and walked out of the room. Mia sat there. Stunned. She had not been prepared for the course the conversation had taken. Both she and Michael had blindsided each other.

Coming back into the room with a packed duffle bag, Michael said, "I think I've got everything. If there's anything I've forgotten, just toss it." Picking up his suit jacket off the chair, he put it on.

"Michael," she could feel the panic beginning to rise. The anchor was being reeled in.

"What, Mia?" His tone was a clipped blend of hurt and anger.

"I don't want … "

"What don't you want? What do you want? Do you have any idea?" Anger springing from hurt was becoming the victorious emotion.

"I don't want this to be it. I don't want us to end." She could no longer hold back the tears.

"Well, this is it." Despite the anger in his words, she could see the pain in his eyes.

"Okay then," and she slipped the ring off her finger. Walking to him, she took his hand, placing the ring in his palm and closing his fingers over it.

"This is yours."

"Don't be gallant. If I can't keep up my end of the promise, it doesn't belong with me."

Nodding, he turned and walked out of her apartment without another word.

Mia stood for a long time staring at the door. Hoping to hear a knock, wanting desperately for him to come back through that door with a solution. But there was no solution. What he wanted she couldn't give him, and she knew that he was right to break it off and walk away. He needed to find someone who would give him everything he wanted. Everything he deserved. And she hated herself for not being the one.

Crawling into bed with her clothes on, Mia could not shake one thing that Michael had said to her. Was she not capable of successfully committing in a relationship or did she just not want to commit to him? And if it was the latter, what the hell was wrong with her?

Chapter Forty

Another shitty spring, Mia mused nightly, as she walked home from work at ungodly hours. The Trade Centers seemed to follow her like stalkers, always there, and she could not help but look at them and try to figure out if Michael's light was still on. Was he burying himself in work the way she was? Or had he found someone really great who could love him back the way he deserved to be loved?

In the mornings, the stalkers were still there and as she walked to work, she couldn't help but wonder if he was at his desk already wrapping up with the traders overseas or in the gym working out.

Telling Lois of their breakup had been painful, and Mia felt as if she'd dealt her mother the ultimate disappointing blow and yes, she was the ultimate in disappointing daughters.

Even Seth had expressed disappointment, "BBC, White Bread treats you like a queen. This past year is the happiest I've ever seen you since the day we met. He gives you a big, gorgeous rock and you dump him. Your mother is right, you know. You're going to be a Spinster BBC."

Mia's response, "Have I told you to go fuck yourself lately, Princess."

"I would if I could and then you'd never see my chic ass at work."

It had been over two months and there had been no contact between her and Michael. Charles had been in Spain for much of that time putting a security team together for a modeling agency out of Barcelona, which had limited most of their contact to emails. Although she missed him and their almost daily calls, Mia was glad that Charles was out of the country so that he didn't feel like he was in the middle of something between two close friends. Had he been in town, Mia feared she would have been pumping him for info about Michael and that would have put a strain on their friendship.

It was a Tuesday morning and Mia was reviewing campaigns prior to the weekly Tuesday afternoon staff meeting when she heard Seth talking a little too loudly, "Yeah, well good luck with that."

Mia looked up as Charles Sloan was entering her office. He closed the door behind him and came and sat down across from her.

Surprised, Mia greeted him. "Hey, you're back. How are you? Were you in the neighborhood?"

Shaking his head no, "You look like shit. I'm surprised Seth lets you get away with looking like that. When was the last time you ate or slept?"

"This morning and last night. And by the way, welcome home." Mia wondered why the hostile vibe.

"Mia, I have not seen you look this shitty since," he stopped to think, "years ago when that asshole drug dealer was living down the hall from you and you were going through a very messed up stage in your life."

"Thanks, Charles. It's great to see you too. Ok, so I'm sure you didn't come here to tell me what an abomination I am."

"I saw Michael last night, and with the exception that he is actually still combing his hair, he looked mighty similar to you. He's dropped weight, dark circles under his eyes. He's pretty fucking miserable, Mia."

Sitting back in her chair and crossing her arms over her chest, "I'm sorry to hear that, Charles. I really am. I don't like the thought of Michael hurting. I really don't."

"So, what's the story Mia? You just don't love him?"

"That's not true. I do love him, Charles. I do."

"Are you not in love with him?" Charles was in no nonsense mode and Mia was beginning to feel as if she was being cross-examined.

"I think if you're going to marry someone you ought to be crazy in love with them."

"And you weren't crazy in love with Michael?"

Mia shook her head. "Not as crazy as I should have been."

Charles shook his head, "Crazy is right," he muttered. Getting out of his chair, he came around to Mia's side of the desk, "Come with me." He took her by the arm.

"Where are we going?" Mia was about to protest.

Opening the door to her office and walking her out, Charles headed through the office and pulled Mia into the Ladies Room.

Turning her to face the mirror as he stood behind her. "Take a good look. Have you looked at yourself recently?"

Mia remained silent and Charles went on, "So, what is it you are looking for? Another guy to treat you like shit? Play on your vulnerabilities and take advantage of you? Cheat on you? Are those the kind of guys you fall crazy in love with Mia?"

"That's not fair, Charles." She shook her shoulders loose from his grasp and his hands were right back on them, holding her in place and not letting her turn away from the disturbing vision in the mirror.

"What's not fair is seeing two of my closest friends totally miserable apart when together they make one another very happy. What isn't fair is seeing the two of you with dark circles under your eyes, both looking like shit because neither of you eat or sleep and you are both burying yourselves in your work. What's not fair is seeing two people I love making the biggest fucking mistake of their lives."

"Are you done?" Mia was seething.

"No. As a matter of fact, I am not done. Can you tell me your life is better without him?" Charles looked into her eyes in the mirror. "And I'm not just picking on you, Mia. I asked him the same question. But here's the thing that is running through my head with you. Do you remember an old Supertramp song called "*Hide in Your Shell*" — because you really need to go home and listen to the lyrics. There's a line in the song and it is just so you, Mia."

"And what line is that, Charles? Please do go ahead and tell me, I'm just dying to know."

His eyes locked on hers in the mirror, "Go listen to it. I think maybe you're looking for a fantasy man and not a real man."

Mia stood silently. Her eyes remained engaged with his in the mirror. Charles Sloan had just sucker punched her.

Leaning forward, he whispered in her ear, "I really do want you to be happy, Meezie."

And with that, he released her shoulders and left the bathroom, leaving Mia to stand alone under the harsh florescent lights and observe her drawn reflection in the mirror as she let his words sink in.

Chapter Forty-One

Two nights later, curled up on her couch with a bag of pretzel sticks and the remote, Mia began to flip through stations. Partly heeding Charles' advice, it was only 8 P.M. and Mia was home and relaxing. Mia started to peruse the cable channels for an alternative. And there it was. She laughed out loud and said, "You just can't make this shit up."

The moment she heard the first strains of the Max Steiner score and saw the vintage map of Africa, she knew exactly how her next two hours would be spent, watching Casablanca. Tissues in hand, the story that always tore at her heart was now carving it up as if it had been their Thanksgiving turkey last year. As her resolve was diminishing and the volume of Charles' words escalated in her head, Ingrid Bergman's arm knocked over a champagne coupe, identical to the coupes Seth had procured for the Millennium Party. Bergman's Ilsa begged Humphrey Bogart's Rick to kiss her as if it were for the last time. The champagne spilling from the coupe and dripping to the floor was the lynchpin. Only in the garden on Millennium New Year's Eve, it had spilled all over her. "Do I need a bigger sign," thought Mia.

Reaching for her cell phone, she pressed send on a number she had never deleted.

"Hi."

"Hi."

"How are you?" The concern in his voice was genuine.

"I suck." Mia silently dabbed at the tears running from her eyes. Tears she was telling herself were being shed for Rick Blaine and Ilsa Lund.

"I suck, too," he laughed at her choice of words.

"Charles told me that you look like shit. He said I looked like shit, too."

"When did you see Charles?"

"He came to my office on Tuesday morning."

Michael laughed, "Well, he didn't waste much time. I saw him for dinner on Monday night."

Mia didn't want to make small talk. "Are we better apart, Michael?" He didn't answer, so Mia continued, "I don't want to be apart."

"I don't want to be apart either," his voice was little more than a whisper.

"Well then, why are we?" Mia was now mustering all her resolve to keep the tears out of her voice.

"Because we want different things, Mia."

The dam finally broke. "No Michael, we want the same thing. We don't want to be apart. That is the same thing." She was now screaming at him between sobs.

"I want to be married," he sounded resigned.

"And I want to be together. We will never have the chance of anything working out if we are not together. Why is this all or nothing? Why aren't we working this out? Why?"

And for the first time there was anger in his voice. Anger and hurt. "Why? You actually have the nerve to ask me why? Why? Because you don't love me enough."

His words hung in the air. Although stunned by both the intensity of his words and the elevated volume of his voice, Mia felt for the first time that there was a chance to work through this impasse.

"I love you enough that I don't want to be apart from you. I love you enough that I want to wake up tomorrow morning and smush up next to you and try and convince you to go in late to work. I love you enough that I want to snuggle on the couch with you tomorrow night, eat Chinese food from containers and watch TV. I love you enough that I want to stand in the rain and watch you teach kids from Harlem about rowing. I love you enough that I don't want to be wondering what it is you are doing because I know what you are doing. Why isn't that enough?"

He was silent and finally Mia asked, "Do you want to be apart?"

"No. Of course not." It was the sweet Michael voice again.

"Then come over here and let's work this out," and before he could respond Mia hit end on the call.

Thirty minutes later there was a knock on the door.

Opening the door, her first thought was, "Charles is right. He looks like hell."

"You look like I feel," she smiled up at him, "Come on in." Mia grabbed his hand as he walked through the door. "I'm not letting go of you," she shook her head.

They sat cross-legged facing one another on the couch.

"Do I make you happy?" she asked trying to read his big, sad eyes.

Michael nodded.

"You make me happy too, Michael. And we both said to each other on the phone before that we don't want to be apart. So, if we make each other happy and we don't want to be apart, let's figure this out. Together. Please," and then in a pleading whisper, "please."

The man who was always so good with words remained silent. Mia scrambled across the couch and into his lap. Twining her arms around his neck, she laid her head on his shoulder. It took a few moments, but his arms encircled her, cradling her as he buried his face into her shoulder.

"I want you to love me more," his voice was gruff.

Mia lifted her head from his shoulder, both hands sliding forward to his cheeks. "I'm loving you the best I can. I hope that's enough." Silently she willed him, please let that be enough. I wish I could give more. I don't know why I can't. I'd say I don't have the capacity. But I know I do. But that doesn't mean I don't love you, because I do.

Still holding his face in her hands, she brought her lips to his, "Please let it be enough. I want you in my world," and without letting him answer, she brushed her lips against his softly and then bit his lower lip, reprising his move from their first kiss.

"God, I've missed you." His eyes looked sad as he shared emotions he was finally permitting to bubble to the surface. "I feel like you are going to break my heart, Mia."

Shaking her head, no, "I promise I will not break your heart. I won't hurt you. I promise."

"Do you know how much I love you? Do you really know how deep my feelings are for you?"

"I do and you have to believe that I cherish your love. I adore you. You have made it impossible not to love you because you are so good. So, so good and so sweet. Your heart and your capacity to love me is astounding and I don't want you to take that away again. I am not letting you out of this apartment tonight," and for the first time all evening, a smile began to develop, first in the corners of her mouth and then traveling up her cheeks and soon spreading to her eyes, "I might not let you out of here … ever."

Michael sighed and shook his head, "You know I have a hard time saying no to you." He played with a curl hanging in her eyes.

"That's a good thing."

Laughing, he pulled her in for a kiss. "I suppose it is."

Chapter Forty-Two

Mia was stretched across the white quilted bedspread on the pine four poster bed, surrounded by classic Oriental blue and cream fabric throw pillows. A paperback copy of Nelson DeMille's *Plum Island*[1] was just inches from her fingertips.

Michael entered the villa and smiled, seeing Mia fast asleep. The French doors were open and a breeze off Easton Bay and the Atlantic Ocean cooled the room. Below their deck was a private patio and beyond that the beginning of Newport, Rhode Island's famed Cliff Walk with its spectacular ocean and mansion views.

Leaning his golf bag against the pine wainscoted wall, Michael lay down on the bed behind Mia and kissed her shoulder.

"Mmmm," she stirred and smiled, "I dozed off. How was the course?"

"Amazing," he nibbled on her bare shoulder, "What are you doing inside? I thought you'd be out in the courtyard."

"I was, but I got hot out in the sun and came in to read and I think the sea air and the breeze just knocked me out." It was the first weekend in September, the days were getting shorter and the nights had begun to cool down.

"Well, we have a few hours before dinner …," Michael's voice trailed off as he gently pulled at Mia's shoulder, flipping her onto her back, "and I know what I want to do."

"Me," she smiled.

"Exactly. I want to do you."

In the four months that they had been back together, Michael had steered clear of the marriage conversation and just let their relationship continue as it had prior to their time apart. But here in Newport, at the Chanler Inn, a popular destination spot for elegant weddings, Mia could sense that he was envisioning their wedding in a setting as glorious as Newport.

Stroking his cheek, the words running through her head, were spoken aloud, much to her surprise. "I want to make you happy, I do."

Pulling back a little to look at her, "You make me very happy." Assuming she was referring to having sex, he offered up, "Hot tub or Jacuzzi?"

"Hot tub in a private courtyard. I just can't resist that," and she pulled off her tank top and tossed it on his head.

Peeling it off his face, laughing, Michael grabbed Mia's hand and led her through the French doors onto the terrace and down the stairs to the walled private courtyard.

Climbing into the tepid water of the circular hot tub, Michael pulled Mia into his lap.

"We've never fucked in a hot tub," he observed, pushing the curls from her eyes.

"We've never made love in a hot tub, either," she teased, throwing back one of his lines at him.

Laughing, "Touché," and he pulled her in for a kiss.

Mia changed positions, straddling him and lowering herself slowly onto his already hard and waiting cock. "Damn, that feels good." With hands on either side of him holding his biceps as his arms were stretched along the edge of the tub, Mia slowly began to ride his cock, feeling the velvety warm water swirl away each time she took his cock deep.

"I think I've died and gone to heaven." Michael closed his eyes, leaning his head back as Mia picked up the pace and started to squeeze him.

This one was all for him. She was the giver this time and she let him be the taker — a role he rarely let her assume. As she slid up and down the length of his cock, she tipped her hips back so that his cock would graze the front wall of her pussy, making her gasp with each stroke as she forced herself down harder to take him deeper and deeper.

Watching his face, she could tell he was close to coming. Leaning forward, she whispered in his ear, "I love you," and he let out a guttural moan, his arms immediately coming off the back of the hot tub as he grabbed her hips and forced them down onto him. Mia wrapped her arms around his neck and nuzzled him. "That was so good," she whispered and stayed with him inside of her for a while before she shifted and snuggled into the warm water next to him.

They sat until twilight descended and a colossal full orange moon rose just above the horizon and hung there, stealing the show in the September evening sky.

"I don't want to go home tomorrow." Mia was starting to pout.

"Me neither." Michael sighed, "This is a moment I want to stay in forever."

Mia snuggled tighter into him, "Me too." She brought his arms that were around her to her lips and gently kissed them.

What she couldn't see behind her was the smile on Michael Portman's face and in his eyes. Mia Silver wanted to make him happy and she did. More than she would ever know.

[1] Nelson DeMille, Plum Island, (New York, NY, Grand Central Publishing, (1997)

Chapter Forty-Three

Seth sat across from Mia, laptop in front of him on her desk as they reviewed the agenda for the Tuesday afternoon weekly staff meeting, "Here's what I've got, he began, "start with campaign review by account management and production. Print is up first, direct mail next, media, events and then PR." Mia nodded her approval and he continued, "Dave's going to then give us a tech update and we'll finish up with sales."

"I looked through everyone's reports, I didn't see any red flags that need to be addressed first, did you?"

Seth shook his head no. "Summer vacations are over, so everyone appears to be really focused and there is that Q3 contest running through the end of the month and those bitches out there will plow each other down like linebackers to win it."

Mia looked up from her laptop and laughed at Seth's comment. He was now looking past Mia's shoulder out the window behind her. His face darkened, perplexed, brows knit together. Mia cocked her head, wondering what was bringing on this look.

Seth gasped, followed immediately by a blood curdling scream, "Oh my God, oh my God, oh my God." His hand flew to his mouth as all color drained from his face. He weakly pointed past Mia and scrambled up from his chair, nearly knocking it over.

Mia turned around to see what was causing the reaction. She heard a scream, not realizing at first that the sound was emanating from her. Rushing to the window, "Oh my God, it's One World Trade Center. What happened?"

"It was a plane, I saw a plane fly into it."

"Oh my God, it's below Michael's floor." Mia held onto the window frame as the realization made her knees start to buckle. The steps back to her desk to grab her cell phone seemed as if they were in slow motion, her legs heavy and not moving. Grabbing her phone, she hit Michael's speed dial number.

"Are you okay?" Relieved to hear his voice, the tears started to stream down her face.

"Yes. Do you know what happened?" Mia could hear chaotic noise in the background.

"A plane hit the building."

"I've got Mia on the phone," Michael was shouting out to colleagues, "she said we were hit by a plane," and then to Mia, "Was it some idiot in a Cessna?"

Mia turned to Seth, "Was it like a little Cessna or something?"

Shaking his head, arms wrapped tightly around his stomach, "It looked like a jet. It was flying low. It was huge."

"Michael, Seth saw it out my window, he thinks it was a jet. You've got to get out of there, Baby."

"I know, let me see what we've got to do to evacuate. I'll call you back in a few minutes." Michael hung up and Mia hugged her cell phone to her chest. Staff started to come into her office and they all stood looking at the burning sentinel to their south. Mia kept looking at her phone, willing it to ring.

At 9:02 A.M. Mia's phone rang. "Were you able to get out?" Her voice was panicked.

"We're trapped and it's filling up with black smoke."

"Michael, can you get to the roof?" Don't fall apart, she willed herself. They'll get them out of there. This is New York, they must have all kinds of emergency helicopters and equipment.

"Everything is blocked, Mia."

"Baby, I'm sure help is on the way. They will get you out of there." She turned to her staff, "Call 911 and let them know there are people trapped on the 105th floor."

Standing at the window, watching the plumes of smoke rise from the tower, she saw the plane coming in from the south. Her initial thought (which didn't make sense, but nothing made sense that morning), was that the plane was coming to help them. Here was the relief coming in to get Michael and the others out of there. The plane rammed into Two World Trade Center blasting the facade and plowing straight through the building, the jet's nose a fireball punching out the opposite side of the building.

Mia screamed. "What was that?" Michael's voice sounded panicked for the first time.

"Oh my God, Michael. Oh my God. Another plane just hit Two World Trade."

"Holy fuck, we're under attack."

Starting to sob, "There's got to be a way out. Michael, you have to get out."

"Hold on a sec, Mia. We're going to try and break a window. We need to get air in here."

Mia heard a crash in the background.

"Okay, we've got some air and it's letting the smoke out."

"Stay close to it, Michael."

Coughing, "I don't think I'm getting out of here, Mia."

"Yes, you are. Help is going to come. We just called. They're going to get you. They know where you are. We told them. You're going to be home with me tonight. You are."

"That's where I want to be. It's getting so hot in here."

"Hang tight, baby, they are coming for you. We're going to get you out of there."

"We are just filling with black smoke really fast."

"Stay close to the window, Michael. They'll be there soon to get you out and then you and I are getting the hell out of here and going right back to Newport or someplace quiet."

"Yeah. Let's get out of here," he managed between coughs, the irony slicing Mia to shreds.

"Or maybe we'll go to Scotland, you can golf at St. Andrews and I can take photos in the highlands. Michael, are you still with me?" Anything to keep him fighting, hanging on — until help arrived.

"I'm here," his voice was choked.

"Stay with me, Baby," she managed between sobs, "Stay with me, okay."

Mia heard his wheezing and gasping, her throat closing at the sound as if her own oxygen supply was being cut off with his.

"Get near the window, Michael. Try to get fresh air."

"I'm trying, Mia. I'm trying."

"Good. Stay with me. I'm here with you. I love you and you are coming home to me tonight. You got that, Buster!"

She could hear his smile, "Yeah, I got it. I love you, Mia. I love you so much."

Mia stood in front of the window rocking, as she watched the towers burn and tried to exorcise the image of Michael being trapped in there.

"Good, because you've got me for as long as you'll have me."

"The smoke is getting so thick. It's so hot in here. Mia, I don't want to say goodbye to you. Please tell my mother and father that I love them," his voice was getting weak.

"We're not saying goodbye, Michael. Not for a very, very long time. Help will be there soon, babe. Just hang on, ok. I need you to hang on.

Think about where we are going to go after this and the things we're going to do. We're just going to say fuck it, get out of this city, we'll travel, meet people, just go wherever the wind blows us. How does that sound?" She was covering her eyes with one hand, rocking at a harsh pace.

"Sounds great. Let's get married." His coughs were causing Mia's body to tense and twitch.

Mia laughed, "You are relentless, Mr. Portman. You know what I think? I think we should get married tonight."

"Yeah?"

"Yeah. Tonight." Mia was smiling through her tears.

"It's a date," he rasped, followed by racking coughs.

His breath was now coming fast and shallow. "C'mon, Michael, stay with me. Please. Please," she pleaded. "I love you so much. Stay with me." Salty tears ran into her mouth. "Stay with me," her pleas turning into sobs.

There was silence on the line, "Michael," she screamed, "Michael." Her wail had the guttural sound of a wounded animal — a sound that wasn't human. Looking at her phone, the call had disconnected.

Sinking to her knees, Mia tried punching in Michael's speed dial number, "Answer, Michael, answer. Please, please answer," she begged through her tears, but the calls repeatedly went through to his voice mail.

On his knees on the floor behind her, Seth wrapped his arms around an inconsolable Mia and rocked with her. Within minutes they were joined on the floor by Kami and other members of the MS&A family.

"We're going to get married when he gets out," Mia sobbed.

Continuing to dial his cell, she became more and more distraught, leaving voice mail message after voice mail message for him to call her. Someone brought her water and she drank it and then looked around at the staff on the floor of the office with her.

"Has everyone with kids gotten out of here? Is everyone's family okay? Do we know where everyone is? Is everyone accounted for?" And then looking at Seth, "Did we activate The Chain?"

Seth nodded, "Everyone who needed to leave, has. The Chain has been activated. Everyone knows how to get messages back." Mia nodded, satisfied that staff would be with their families.

"We need to call Charles."

"I'll take care of that," Kami offered, getting to her feet.

They heard the loud roar and the ground shook as if an earthquake had struck, but they were not prepared for what they saw as they all stumbled to their feet before the window. Tremendous gray-white clouds of pulverized concrete and gypsum rose high into the air and barreled up the streets like the special effects from a disaster ride at Universal Studios.

There was a collective gasp and deep groans from everyone in Mia's office. Then they stood silently in front of the window. Shell shocked and numb. Nauseous. Beyond the point of even comprehending or processing the levels of despair slamming into them in waves like electric shocks. When the dust cloud cleared, there was a hole in the sky where Two World Trade Center had once stood. Where it had stood that morning when everyone arrived at work. No one moved from the window.

Kami returned a few minutes later, "Charles went down as a first responder," she informed Mia.

"Stay safe and bring Michael back to me," she whispered.

Thirty minutes after the South Tower collapsed, the sickening roar and shaking began again and in a plume of gray-white dust, the North Tower sank to her knees and Mia Silver sank to hers with it.

Hours later, a white dust shrouded Charles Sloan entered Mia's office. He stood in the doorway, his usually handsome face a chalky grotesque mask of pain as he silently observed the group huddled before the window. They were very still as they sat silently watching the smoke and flames mar the otherwise perfect Indian summer sky. Mia extended a hand out to Charles and he took it, joining her and her team on the floor. No words were needed. Together they cried.

Michael Portman was not coming home that night.

Standing in front of the flat LCD screen TV mounted on the wall in front of his desk, Schooner Moore watched as the horror unfolded in New York, Washington, DC and Pennsylvania. Out on the gym floor, members congregated together, needing the solace of community, as they stood before the banks of TVs viewing images that were impossible to comprehend. Schooner preferred to attempt to process this alone.

Without knocking on his door, Yoli Perez, Schooner's business partner and confidante, silently entered his office and stood next to him.

After a few minutes she turned to him, "What did you say?"

"I didn't say anything."

"Yeah, you did," she gave him a look that he didn't see because his eyes were trained on the screen.

A few minutes later he again muttered under his breath, "Don't be in there, Baby Girl."

"What the hell are you saying?" On edge, Yoli's temper was shorter than usual.

Schooner looked at her with a blank stare, and she just shook her head and turned back to the burning towers, the pit of her stomach aching.

Neither spoke for a few minutes until Schooner broke the silence. "I smell smoke. Do you smell smoke?"

Yoli shook her head, "No. I don't smell smoke."

"You don't smell that?"

"No. I don't smell anything. I think you're imagining it watching this."

"No, I smell it," he was adamant, "It's making my throat burn. My throat feels like it's on fire from it."

"If it will make you feel better, I'll go check," and Yoli headed out of his office, closing the door behind her.

His eyes remained fixed on the burning towers, "Don't be in there, Baby Girl. Please be behind a picket fence up in Connecticut or something." The reporters were talking to someone on the 106th floor who had been attending a breakfast at Windows on the World. Their place.

The smoke was making his throat close and he could feel the beads of perspiration forming on his top lip and forehead. The a/c must've gone out, he thought.

As Yoli reentered Schooner's office, she heard a loud ripping sound. Schooner was pulling at the collar of his tee-shirt with both hands, ripping it from his muscular chest.

Yoli was shocked to see his chest was a deep crimson color as were his neck and face. He was panting, gasping for air.

"It's so hot. I can't breathe."

"Oh my God, Schooner." Yoli grabbed him by the hand, pulling him to the leather couch against the far wall. "Put your head between your legs." She rushed over to the small fridge at his wet bar and grabbed two large bottles of cold water. Opening one for him to drink and handing it to him, she sat down next to him on the couch and pressed the other bottle to his forehead and cheeks.

"Drink," she ordered. "There's no fire in here, Schooner. I think you are having some sort of anxiety attack." After a few minutes, she told him to wait there and rushed next door to her office and grabbed her purse.

Joining him again on the couch, she began to dig through her purse. Pulling out a pill bottle, she muttered, "I must really love you." Extracting two .5 mg. Xanax tabs (she had made the split-second decision that based on his size, he could tolerate two), she handed them to him.

"What is this?" He looked weary.

"Just trust me."

He nodded and swallowed the pills with water.

"It hurts to breathe, Yoli. It's burning."

Putting a hand on his forehead, his skin was burning hot.

"Schooner, you are having some kind of panic attack. Do you want me to get you another shirt?"

"No," he shook his head, looking panicked.

Going into his private bathroom, Yoli came out with cool, wet towels and laid one across his forehead and the other at the back of his neck. Sitting down next to him on the couch, she took his hand in both of hers. In all the years she'd known him, she'd never seen him have a panic attack of any kind.

Schooner's breathing started to settle down and the redness in his skin began to calm. Silently, they sat there and watched CNN. It was about a minute before 7 A.M. when they joined a shocked world watching a plume of white dust rise as the South Tower disintegrated before their eyes.

Yoli gasped and the sound out of Schooner was guttural and unnerving.

"Holy shit, are we really seeing this?" he asked. "Those were people who went to work this morning, people who were having breakfast at Windows on the World. People who were just sitting at their desk having coffee." He leaned forward, putting his face in his hands for a moment.

"Schooner, do you know anyone who works in the Twin Towers?"

Without looking away from the TV, "I hope not."

Thirty minutes later, the North Tower was gone.

Schooner curled up on his couch and Yoli brought him a pillow. The effect of the Xanax was hitting him full force. Thirty minutes after the North Tower collapsed, Schooner was passed out.

Yoli called her partner, Debbie. "Why don't you come here and bring some pillows and blankets. Schooner had a major anxiety attack and I gave him Xanax and he's passed out cold."

"Wow, I never knew he had problems with anxiety attacks."

"Neither did I." Yoli watched him sleep. As she sat there she wondered what it was he wasn't telling her. It had been a horrific day, but there was something else going on with Schooner Moore that she did not know about — she could feel it. Maybe someday he would confide in her.

In the days that followed, Schooner spent hours at his desk pouring over both the New York Times and the Los Angeles Times, devouring every detail being written about the attacks. He scoured the lists of victims. There were no Mia Silvers that perished on 9/11 in the Trade Centers. He just hoped that meant she was safe.

Chapter Forty-Four

September 11, 2002

Mr. and Mrs. Portman stood to her left. Charles, Seth and Kami to her right. The first moment of silence, observed at 8:40 A.M. was physically painful. What she heard in her head was heart stopping. And then the reading of the names. Both she and Mr. Portman held Mrs. Portman tight. This was her baby. He would always be her baby. It was just wrong.

The year had not dulled the pain at all. There was a hole in her heart, just as there had been a hole in the sky when the towers ceased to be.

As she listened to the names and the toll of the bells, she stood there fixated on watching seagulls soar through the air, trying to ascertain if there were any particular patterns to their flight paths.

She knew Michael would be proud of her. She didn't fly off the rails or fall apart or regress into any of her old destructive patterns. Instead she focused her energy on working with families of 9/11 victims, using her time, business and contacts for fundraising events, helping to raise money to ensure families had proper health care and children who lost parents had scholarship funds.

That would've made Michael happy.

September 11, 2006

More than anything else that morning, Mia was most saddened by the loss of Mr. Portman earlier in the year and how frail Mrs. Portman seemed in the wake of his passing. Holding her tightly, Mia tried to infuse her own strength into the aging woman.

Five years and it seemed like only five minutes had passed. Mia wondered if the day would ever come and go and not induce such sharp stabbing pain.

To her right stood Charles, with his new bride, Gaby. Mia observed Gaby's face throughout the ceremony and realized when devastation is so extreme, we are all just children of the Earth and no one gets by unscathed. Mia wanted to comfort Gaby who was clearly overwhelmed by the events of the day.

The moments of silence and hearing Michael's name in the roll call were as overwhelming on this day as they had been at the first memorial. Searing hot tears burned Mia's eyes.

Looking up at the sky to try and stop her tears from falling, Mia caught sight of a lone seagull soaring and diving. "That looks like fun," she mused.

September 11, 2011

Mia stood there, her arm around Michael's mother. The first moment of silence at 8:40 A.M. was deafening. Holding back tears was impossible. As impossible as it been for the last nine annual memorial services.

Recognizing some of the families, it was a joy to see how the children had grown. Toddlers were now teens and teens were now there with infants of their own. Life had gone on.

In their own group, the wonderful new addition that added joy to the somber day was Charles and Gaby's daughter, Paola. Mrs. Portman had assumed a grandmotherly role with the little girl and both Charles and Gaby were more than happy to indulge her. Even for their group, life had gone on.

After the service, they went to Katz's Deli on Houston Street (the deli made famous in the movie, "When Harry Met Sally" by Meg Ryan's famed "I'll have what she's having" fake orgasm scene). Shortly after they sat down, Mrs. Portman took Mia's hand, "It's been ten years, Mia. It's time."

Mia could feel her eyes fill with tears. "I've dated," she protested.

"Anyone serious?"

"Well, I did date an architect for about three months," defended Mia.

From down the table, Seth chimed in, "What a loser."

Laughing, Mia shook her head. "I can't argue with you there."

Mia knew the look on Mrs. Portman's face. She had seen it many times on Lois' face. It was the Jewish mother disappointed look. "It's time," she repeated, as if giving Mia her blessing and patted the younger woman's arm gently.

Walking home later that day, Mia wonder where the seagulls had been that morning. She had not seen any seagulls.

Chapter Forty-Five

Charles stood outside the venue with its owner and his Los Angeles contact from the Elite Modeling Agency. Today's event had been a huge success. The site lent itself perfectly to the fashion show and the after-party, to which Brent Bolthouse Productions had added an edgy touch, creating a trendy and dynamic ambience.

The venue's owner was engaging Charles in a conversation about event security and wondered if Charles was considering a west coast branch of his firm. They talked about both the opportunities and downside of bicoastal operations. Charles mentioned he had a toddler and was less inclined to spend time away until she was older. The venue's owner indicated that he too was a father and totally understood.

Charles looked at the display on his Smartphone, "Excuse me," he said to the two gentlemen and turned slightly away from them. "Meezie, what's up?"

"Chazicle, how's LaLa-land?"

"There's no place like home," he laughed.

"No shit. Hey," she continued, "are you aware that UNICEF changed the date of their event?"

"No, when did that happen?"

"I'm not sure, it appears I didn't get the memo either. I was totally blindsided by this today." An icky feeling was starting low in Mia's gut and moving rapidly throughout her body. WTF? This was a high alert, ill at ease. Anxiety, nausea, apprehension — this was a full blown physical freak out, coming out of nowhere and Mia was stumped by its genesis. *Where was the trigger?* she wondered. "What's that noise in the background?" Mia heard voices, it sounded like a TV show, something she should recognize, something she did recognize, but she just couldn't put her finger on it. What was it?

"Oh, I was just having a conversation with the venue owner and my Elite contact."

"Is there TV on or a movie? It sounds like something I know."

Charles laughed. "No, we're just standing outside talking. It's quiet out here. Brent Bolthouse has the place rocking inside."

"Okay, hey I'm going to call your office in the morning and make sure your staff has the correct info on this UNICEF deal." Mia started to shut down her laptop for the night. She had to get out of there, get some fresh air. Immediately. She kept hearing it in the background behind Charles' voice. It was so close, but just out of grasp.

"Thanks, Meezie. Let's get together this weekend." Hanging up, Charles rejoined the conversation with the other men.

Mia's subconscious had entered DEFCON 1, quickly surpassing levels 5,4,3 and 2. It was fully aware of what had just happened and was trying to quickly erect barricades to keep it from Mia's conscious brain. Mia's subconscious was in full blown protect mode. Protect the psyche at all costs. Yet, as hard as her subconscious was trying to scramble to get its shields up, the leakage had already busted through and was starting to affect her conscious thought — the physical discomfort, general ill at ease feelings.

That thing she was trying to grasp and couldn't quite reach, the familiar voice that sounded like it was coming from a TV show in the background of her call with Charles, was no TV show. It was reality. And she wasn't wrong. She did recognize the voice, on some level. As much as her subconscious would allow.

The last time she had heard that voice it had teased her that the bagels and pizza in New York had better be as good as she had been bragging they were.

It had been over twenty years, and unbeknownst to her, Mia Silver had just heard Schooner Moore's voice again for the first time since their fingertips had last touched.

Had Schooner known that Charles Sloan, a man he had just met that day, was standing next to him talking to Mia Silver, he would've rudely grabbed the phone right out of his hand. If he had known that this man was one of Mia's closest friends, and had been for many years, he would've invited him into his office, closed the door and pumped him for every last bit of information he could get out of him.

Mia left her office feeling very out of sorts. It was a little more than a spur of the moment decision to stop off at a neighborhood bar on her way home. Mia was on a mission and she didn't quite know who had given the orders.

Sitting at the polished oak bar, Mia was on her third gin and tonic when they entered. Three guys, mid-twenties, two dark haired and a tall blonde. Her eyes immediately went to the tall blonde. He had an athletic build, and although just moderately attractive, he was tall and blonde.

The bar had several circa 1980's pinball machines. Mia Silver was a pinball wizard. Joni and Rob used to tease her that she spent more time in the Student Center playing pinball than she did in any of her classes. Unfortunately, it was true.

Some people are pool sharks, Mia was a pinball shark and it was a skill she never lost. When you're good, you're good.

Choosing the most challenging machine, one that was multi- levels and shot multiple balls at once, Mia started in on her game, using her whole body to play (known as Body English). She knew it would be impossible for the boys not to notice her ass in her short, tight black pencil skirt as she swayed and lurched with her plays. It would also be impossible to ignore the lights and the bells, as well as the scoreboard racking up points in the millions.

It wasn't long before she had her own viewing gallery. Upon finishing a game, she noticed the guys were standing just a few feet away, watching her.

"Impressive score," one of the dark-haired ones commented.

Mia hit them with a full tilt devil smile, "Was my major in college." Feeding the machine again, she began her next game while the trio looked on. Her whole body moved with the machine as she concentrated on multiple balls careening down toward her flippers. With the precision of a maestro, she caught each ball with the flipper and flipped it back until she decided to let it slowly roll to the flipper's end and send it back up the fairway again.

In the background, because she was concentrating on the machine in front of her, she could hear their cheers as they were starting to get into her game. They were hooked and soon she would invite them to join her, to play with her. And they would drink together.

An hour later they were all old buddies tossing back pitchers and playing team-tournament pinball. She was teamed with one of the dark-haired guys and Blondie was teamed with the other. She flirted openly with all of them, giving the dark-haired guys more attention and long eye gazes to the blonde when no one was looking.

The dark-haired guys were up and Mia and the blonde were standing by watching. She excused herself to the Ladies Room and caught Blondie's eye, motioning for him to follow her. Knowing the other boys would not look up from the pinball machines, their escape was an easy one.

Walking past the bathrooms, Mia pushed open the back door to the bar. It led to an alleyway between old brick buildings and was empty save for a few green metal dumpsters. Emerging into the alley, with Blondie right behind her, Mia could feel the blood rushing through her veins, she was back on the edge — a place she hadn't played in a very long time. She imagined this is what it felt like to a recovering addict who just shot up.

Turning to the boy, her back to the brick wall, he put his hands on either side of her head and bent down to kiss her. This was going to be fast and furious and they both knew it. His tongue was down her throat and she reached around him, pulling him against her. Feeling how rigid he was through his jeans, she pressed him against her harder, before reaching between them to unbutton and unzip him.

Grabbing her by her ass, he pulled her up against him and Mia wrapped her legs around him, her skirt hiking up over her hips. She could hear the slit at the back of her skirt rip and she didn't care. She reached down and pushed the silky fabric of her bikini underwear to the side, giving him access to push up into her. They both grunted as he sunk deep into her wet pussy.

With his hands against the wall for leverage, the boy rammed up into Mia relentlessly. He started to walk with her, impaled on his cock and wrapped around him like a vine, until her back was up against one of the big green dumpsters, where he continued to drive into her. A metallic thud sounded with each thrust until he groaned and leaned into her, pinning her up against the cold metal.

"Wow. That was hot. You're amazing." The boy was panting.

"Glad you enjoyed it." Mia was straightening her skirt. "Say goodnight to your friends for me," she called over her shoulder as she began to walk down the alley.

Blondie stood there, shell shocked. "You're not coming back in?" He yelled down the alley.

"I think I've played enough pinball for one night." She didn't even turn around.

"So, we haven't had one of these visits in a very long time." Mia was sitting in Dr. Gary Cohen's office after an exam.

"I know. Gary, I don't know what set me off. I usually know my triggers. I've been able to identify the antecedents and put coping strategies in place before I do something risky or stupid, like I did the other night."

"So, nothing happened that you can identify?" Gary's concern was evident, both as a friend and a healthcare professional.

"No, I have no clue. I was talking to Charles Sloan on the phone and I could feel that crazy anxiety that I haven't felt in a long, long time. All we were talking about was a UNICEF event that we're both working on."

"Hmm." Gary shook his head. "I was really concerned you'd go to pieces after Michael's death and you didn't. You actually seemed stronger and more together than ever, so having an episode like this now, so many years later, really doesn't make sense."

"I know. Everyone was worried that I'd go a little bat shit crazy after Michael's death, but I kind of felt like I had Michael's strength to keep me moving forward. Like he wanted me to take the grief and the anger and use it for positive things and I did and it helped me heal. Helping others helped me heal. And since that time, the relationships I have had have been healthy. No great shakes, but healthy. And my behavior has not been destructive — I've felt really stable and whole for a long time now. I worked hard at facing some really ugly things and I really thought that I had come out the other end. So, what this was all about — I just don't know. It was like my subconscious had some big secret that it just didn't want to share with my conscious and my conscious said, "Screw you." I just wish I knew what it was that could have an impact on me like that. What could have that kind of effect on me?" Mia shook her head, wondering …

Part Two
Schooner

Chapter One

Recently …

The 2.64 miles between The Dock Restaurant and their home on Linda Isle was going to be one damn long drive, Schooner was sure of that. CJ was in a massive snit and if Holly wasn't sitting in the back seat of the Range Rover, he would just tell her to shut the heck up. Clearly, he didn't act the way she wanted him to act tonight, at his own birthday party, and he put at risk whatever she was trying to accomplish — obviously the real reason for his bogus forty-third birthday party.

"And you left me all alone to host. You could have at least pretended to be having a good time. I did this all for you and I have to continually put up with your selfish behavior and make excuses for you."

Schooner hit the satellite radio button on his steering wheel and selected XM20 — E Street Radio. Tonight, on his forty-third birthday, more than any other night in recent history, he wanted to blast Bruce's music and feel close to her again — so he hit the volume button to drown out CJ's bitching. And CJ hated Springsteen's music which made it all the more satisfying. Happy Birthday to me, he inwardly chuckled.

He wasn't familiar with the track playing, so he hit the LCD. *The Brokenhearted*. Hmm, he wasn't sure which album that appeared on.

The angst in Bruce's voice as he began to wail, wondering if this woman still loved and wanted him, was like a searing hot knife slicing into Schooner's chest. She was out there and now, finally, she was so close.

For so many years, there was no way to find someone who disappeared. If you wanted to be gone, you were gone. There was no internet. There were no search engines. People didn't have cell phones or smart phones. There were no apps to find people. Without hiring a private detective (which was more than a little out of his means as a college student), the tools available had been a phone book or directory assistance. Unfortunately, there were hundreds of Robert Silvers residing in New York City, and if you had an unlisted phone number, the trail ended there. By the time modern tools were available, he'd had fleeting thoughts (or fantasies, if he were honest with himself), of finding her again — but intruding on someone's life, someone who might have a family and children that could be affected, always held him back.

But she was on Facebook. She had put herself out there and Beau, of all people, had found her. Beau — who had never liked her, finds Mia. What a kick in the ass, Schooner thought as he pulled into their driveway.

"Do you want to go out for a sail?" He turned to Holly in the back seat.

"I do, but I think I need to sleep or I'll never get up for my flight in the morning." She looked beat.

"Sailing? You want to go sailing at this hour?" CJ's mood was getting fouler by the moment.

"It's my birthday and I'll sail if I want to," he laughed. Man, they were just toxic together.

Strolling into his home office, Schooner grabbed a bottle of Courvoisier 21-year-old XO cognac and a heavy Orrefors crystal snifter out of his bottom desk drawer, plucked a Cohiba from the custom teak and cedar humidor on the side table, grabbed his double guillotine cutter and a lighter. CJ was perched in the doorway watching him, but Schooner knew the Cohiba would keep her from following him and he was tempted to light it right then and there.

"I want to talk to you about tonight." Her arms were crossed over her chest.

"And I want to enjoy the rest of my birthday. Can't this wait until Holly leaves?"

"I'm *really* angry with you," her eyes flashed venom.

"I know and I just spent my birthday doing what you wanted me to do and now I just want to spend the rest of it doing what I want to do." I want to sail out in the middle of the harbor, sit on deck, look up at the stars and think about Mia. That is how I want to spend my birthday. As he brushed past her, he quickly kissed her cheek, "Thanks for the party," and he strolled out the sliding glass doors onto the deck and down to the floating wooden walkway leading to the dock.

Courvoisier in hand, surrounded by water and shrouded in the black night, Schooner was alone to get inside his head, and in there, the scenarios were running rampant. What was he going to find? He had successfully avoided getting sucked into social media until now and tonight he wished he'd paid more attention to it. Monday morning, he'd ask Yoli to help him get set up on Facebook. He could trust Yoli with this, but the thought of "coming clean" to his best friend and business partner, after twenty years, was daunting. She was going to be blown away that he'd never shared Mia with her. But there was nothing to share. Mia was gone. Until tonight. Talk about a birthday present. This was more than he'd wished for in over two decades.

"Mia Silver, little do you know, but you were my birthday present tonight," he toasted the night sky.

It was after 4 A.M., Yoli would be at work by 7 A.M. on Monday. I'm twenty-seven hours away from Mia, he thought. Twenty-seven hours away from possibly knowing. Finally. After all these years. No matter what the answer — he'd finally know what happened, what he had done to make her leave him, to make her run and never look back. Had her heart been broken like his? Had she ever missed him?

"Did you even love me, Mia? Did you ever think about me after you walked away?" Schooner couldn't believe he was verbalizing the specters that had haunted him long ago and in moments when he'd let them surface, for they never truly went away — ever. "Did you?"

He poured himself another cognac.

He just needed to make it through the next twenty-seven hours. He'd made it through twenty-four years, but these upcoming hours seemed a more impossible hurdle now that he knew he was so close to finding her. Finding her … a dream he had carried for a very long time, but was certainly *the* surprise of the evening.

Oh Baby Girl, what are you going to tell me? Are you going to break my heart again or help me finally bury this ghost? He knew, even as he verbalized it, that the ghost of Mia Silver was something he never, ever wanted to exorcise, for if he let it haunt him for the rest of his days, she would always be with him.

Chapter Two

"Anything yet?" Yoli poked her head into Schooner's office. It had been two hours since she'd set up his Facebook profile and he'd sent Mia a friend request.

He shook his head no. "But I've been checking out her Facebook page and pictures." The smile in his eyes was evident.

Yoli came around and stood behind him, looking at his computer screen. "There are a lot of pictures of her with this guy. Might be her husband." Schooner flipped through a few of the pictures to show Yoli.

Shaking her head, "Have I taught you nothing? That is not her husband."

"How do you know that?"

"Because he's gayer than I am. The man is a screaming queen. I like Mia already."

They continued to look through Mia's online photo album. There was one picture of Mia with a tall, slim man with light brown hair. Her hair was different and she looked a few years younger. They were standing outside an old mansion, maybe some type of an inn, he had his arm over her shoulder and hers was around his waist. "That one might be a husband or boyfriend."

Schooner nodded. From their body language, he had to agree. Mia looked happy, relaxed. He continued to flip through the pictures, but the guy wasn't in any other shots. His gut reaction was that he was glad, but immediately felt bad about it — he wanted Mia to be happy.

"No kids," Yoli noted. "I don't think she's married."

Heart racing, Schooner wondered if she might be right. There were no family photos, no kids celebrating milestones. No baby pictures, graduations, Halloween costumes. Could she be single? Breathing deeply to try and slow his heart beat, Schooner wondered if Mia was unattached and available and then immediately drew himself back from the thought. Don't go there, he admonished.

"Stop tapping your foot. It's annoying me." Yoli quickly brought him back and he had to consciously stop bouncing his right leg. "You are a mess, Schooner."

"I know," he laughed, "I really am. I am freaking out. I want to talk to her now. I want to hear her voice. I want to know what the fuck happened."

"Well, it's just about lunchtime now on the east coast, so she may not have even seen this."

"Maybe not," he continued to go through her pictures. "Why can't I get into these albums."

"They are not set to the public viewing setting. You can't see those unless you're friends. The other ones are set to the public setting."

"Maybe that's where the husband and kids are." See, he told himself, that's why you can't let yourself go there.

"Might be. You don't know, so don't speculate. Best case scenario she accepts your friend request. Have you thought about what you are going to do if she doesn't accept or you don't hear back?"

Schooner looked up and gave her his full blast smile. "I have thought about that. If she doesn't get back to me by midday tomorrow, I'm going to give Scott Morgan a call. Have lunch with him this week. You know he'd sell his mother for a piece of our business and I'll pick his brain about our old college classmate, Mia Silver.

Yoli smiled and shook her head. "You can't take your eyes off her, can you?"

He didn't look away from his computer screen, just smiled and shook his head.

Yoli left his office thinking what a shocking morning it had been and praying his heart would not be decimated by day's end.

It was a few minutes after ten when the email hit his inbox. Friendship request confirmed. She said yes. Wow. She said yes. She was ready to talk. She didn't hide. She didn't run. She didn't ignore him. She said yes. She wanted contact with him.

Logging on to Facebook, he saw her name in the right bottom corner of his screen with a green dot next to it. He grabbed the piece of paper with notes he took when Yoli explained it. Click on her name and a box will appear. Type private message.

Schooner: Mia are you there?

C'mon Baby Girl, answer me. The seconds that passed felt like millennium.

Mia: Yes

Okay, this is it. I've waited twenty-four fucking years for this.

Schooner: Mia, what's your phone number?

He waited. C'mon Mia, you did not accept my friend request without knowing we were going to have this conversation. You owe me this. And this conversation is going to happen now. Still no answer. Do not run. Do not run out on me again.

Schooner: Mia, what is your phone number?

And there it was and he was trying to dial and it was like being in one of those dreams where you keep trying to dial the numbers right and your fingers just will not cooperate. And then they finally did, the number was dialed and he hit the green call icon.

"Hi." God, I never thought I'd hear that sound again, he thought, closing his eyes. Just the word "hi" was the sweetest sound imaginable.

"Hi." He managed to get past the lump in his throat.

There was silence and he had to know. This had haunted him for twenty-four years, eaten at his heart, gnawed at his soul, scratched at his psyche. Forever changed who he was and the course of his life. She had that much control.

"Why did you leave me?" He hoped she didn't hear the tightness that was holding tears back — that was how emotional he was.

The silence on the line was deafening before, "You told her what happened to me." And there it was. He literally saw black and put his head down between his legs, taking his cell with him. You told her what happened to me. The ultimate betrayal of trust. Taking someone's most painful, darkest secret and sharing it with the enemy. Colluding with the enemy. Oh my God, he would never have breached his promise to her, but she'd just spent twenty-four years believing the guy she trusted and gave her heart to had betrayed every sacred thing that they had shared — making them all a pack of lies. Oh God. Oh God. Oh God. She was so fragile after the attack and she had trusted him to protect her, to become her lover and she spent her life believing she'd been betrayed. Oh God.

He sat up again slowly and began to shake his head, as if she could see him, "No. I never told her. Mia, I never told her anything. Did she tell you I told her?"

"Schooner," Oh God, just hearing her say his name made the lump in his throat expand, "it was a long time ago." It felt like she was already shutting down. He needed her to understand. She needed to know. She couldn't stop this conversation now. She needed to believe him. She had to believe him.

"Mia, I didn't tell her. I never would have betrayed you that way. All I ever wanted to do was protect you," he was fighting to keep his voice from cracking, "and I didn't know why you left me. I never knew why you left me." So much for keeping emotion out of my voice, he self-chastised, shaking his head. He knew he was beyond controlling it. "But I swear, I never, ever told her."

He tried to compose himself in the silence. What had she said to drive her away? Make her run. Mia had loved him. He knew that then and by her admission of the reason she had left, he knew that now. That was why she was so devastated, because she did love him so very much. *Oh Baby Girl, the whole time I was dying, so were you. We were both dying. This was so senseless. This never should have happened.*

"If she told you that she knew, then she was bluffing and she played you." The sob he heard come from Mia ripped at his heart. The realization was upon both of them. "Holy fuck," he groaned. Bad enough his marriage had always been a sham, that was the bed he made and he had to lie in it, but she had run off Mia, breaking the two of them — leaving them both with a lifetime of unanswered questions, heartbreak and shattered souls. And in the softest of voices, he begged, "Please believe me, Mia. You know all I wanted to do was protect you. And I thought I was doing such a good job, but I let you down again. I let her destroy you, destroy us."

He could hear her break, the sounds of her sobs ripping into him. He closed his eyes, wishing, just wishing that he could hold her, pull her head to his chest, kiss her hair. Tell her it was all going to be okay now. He'd found her. It was going to be okay.

And then she ripped him to shreds. "Oh my God, Schooner. I am so sorry. I am so, so sorry. Oh my God." It took him a moment to understand. Empathy. She was concerned about him. She was devastated over the hurt she had caused him and in that moment, his heart shattered. She was hurting for him.

"Do you believe me?" He needed her to believe him. He needed her to know he would never, ever have betrayed her. He was nineteen and trying so hard to be a man, to protect her, help her deal with her attack, heal her by giving his love. And he just needed her to believe him. Twenty-four years later and he needed her to believe him.

"Yes," her voice was soft, just slightly more than a whisper and he knew how overcome with emotion she was, "I do."

He sighed. And the nine-thousand-pound elephant sitting on his chest got up and sauntered across his office. Tail swishing. He took a deep breath. She finally knew. He would've never betrayed her. Ever.

"Schooner, how do I begin to apologize for being an immature sixteen year-old, for not trusting you, for believing what she said. I am so, so sorry I hurt you." There it was again. That empathy. Her concern over hurting him. It was just so foreign. Someone worried about him. Worried that he was hurt. It felt odd because he wasn't used to it and it took a moment to actually recognize it.

He wanted to soothe her. Take care of her. Soothe her heart. "Shhh, don't, Baby Girl," it was past his lips before he could think about it or catch it. Calling her Baby Girl just seemed so natural. No matter what happened after this phone call, she always was and always would be his Baby Girl. He'd carry that forever in his shattered heart. "You were a victim in this, too. What she did was malicious with the intent to hurt you and to put an end to us. And my whole freaking life has been based on a lie."

At that moment, he wanted to rip CJ's Barbie head off its Barbie body. Mia had clearly picked up on the nuance of his statement and her sobs were just painful to hear. That was the last piece of information he ever wanted her to learn. Letting her know that he had married CJ MacAllister was something he never thought he'd be sharing with Mia Silver.

This all still hurt so much — twenty-four years later and it still was clearly an open wound for both of them. The hurt had gone so deep that although the surface seemed to have healed, it was merely a protective mask over a wound that never seemed to fully mend. And the things that made the wound open over the years, it was hard to say what a trigger might be. Sometimes it was a full moon, or a date on a calendar, a song on the radio, or a national disaster. Sometimes it was a new member at the gym who had just relocated from the east coast or a curly haired girl with an attitude.

"Schooner, my assistant just came in and I've got to prep for a two o'clock meeting."

He wasn't ready to let her go yet. How could he let this end? Be bereft of her again. He just wanted to hold on and not let go. "What time are you up until at night?" He needed more.

"I'm kind of a night owl, usually between midnight and one."

Please don't let this be the end, Baby Girl. "Mia, are you going to answer the phone when you see my number come up?"

"Yeah."

"Say it, Mia." He needed to hear her commit. He could not handle her disappearing again.

"I will answer your calls, Schooner."

He let out his breath, nodding his head. "You promise?"

"Yes, I promise." He could hear the smile in her voice and involuntarily it brought a smile to his face. The first smile since the conversation began.

"Okay, I will call you later." He was already missing her. Ending this phone call was hell.

"Okay."

"Mia," he needed her to know, "it's really good hearing your voice."

And where he expected to hear the smile in her voice, he heard a sob escape and it felt like a punch in the chest. "It's really good to hear your voice too, Schooner."

"I'll talk to you later, Baby Girl." Just saying those two words was every wish he had ever made come true. They just flowed out from him so naturally because she was his Baby Girl.

Overwhelmed, he sat back in his chair. Today's events were extreme. He had just talked to Mia. Mia. His Mia. His Baby Girl. His love. He had just talked to Mia. A dream whose reality had been abandoned long ago so that he could save his sanity. Just processing that phone call was going to take some time. Talk about bombshells. And the bombshells had just begun to drop.

He picked up his phone and dialed Aaron Bender. "Hi, Leslie. It's Schooner Moore. Is Aaron available?"

A moment later his attorney was on the line, "I'm always available for you. What's going on?"

"I'm about to go home and end my marriage. I'm moving out today. I need a separation agreement immediately and I need you to start working on the divorce. I want to serve her so fast that her head spins off her body." It would be a tournament serve. It would be the championship ace his tennis racquet never had the opportunity to hit after she set into motion events that robbed him of all the things he loved most in life. And now this would be the ace she never saw coming. Game. Set. Match.

Chapter Three

Yoli rapped lightly on Schooner's closed office door while entering simultaneously, "You okay?" Her concern evident for her dear friend.

"I don't know." Schooner shook his head. Sitting at his desk, long legs stretched out in front of him crossed at the ankles.

"Did you talk to her?"

He nodded. A half-smile pulling at the corners of his mouth. "Yeah. We talked." And he just nodded his head, lost in thought.

Yoli was getting annoyed. She wanted to drag it out of him, but she knew him well enough. Give him a moment. Let him work through processing it and it will eventually come flowing out.

And just like that, he began. "So, poor Mia spent twenty-four years thinking I'd betrayed her," he shook his head., Yoli could almost feel the thoughts ricocheting around his brain as he tried to streamline and make sense of everything. "Did I tell you what happened to Mia?" Yoli shook her head no and he continued. "Mia and I had always talked about me being her first and then we broke up because I was stupid and too immature to even know how to communicate properly." He shook his head, clearly disgusted with a memory of himself.

"So, you weren't her first?"

A pained look shot across Schooner's face and Yoli assumed Mia had found another boyfriend.

"No. I wasn't. Mia's first and second were two animals who took turns beating the crap out of her and raping her."

Yoli literally gasped out loud, "Oh my God. That is horrible."

"It was. It was really horrible. But I thought if I loved her enough and protected her that I could help her heal," he looked Yoli in the eye, "and I think I did." Schooner paused again and took a deep breath.

Yoli watched the pain etched between his eyes. What the hell was going on, she wondered.

"There were only a few of us that knew what happened. Kind of the inner circle. Me, a couple of very close friends, her roommate — who essentially moved out of her own room so that I could move in and stay with Mia. Obviously, Mia didn't want anyone to know. And I'm sure you can imagine the one person above all else she didn't want knowing this."

He paused, looking Yoli in the eye, "She did not want CJ to have this information."

"Oh no." Yoli and Schooner locked eyes. She tried to read what was going on in his, but all she could detect was static, as if his mind were a radio caught between stations.

"So, when I asked her today, "Why did you leave me," his voice cracked, "She replied, 'You told her what happened to me'."

Yoli's eyes narrowed and she leaned forward, "You didn't tell her, did you?" Yoli ached for this woman she didn't even know.

"No!" Schooner erupted. "I never would have betrayed her. I loved her. All I wanted to do was protect her and I failed, Yoli."

"Stop that right there. Do not take that on." Yoli could get tough with this man who intimidated many. Schooner squinted at her, but quieted. She could tell he was seething. She let a moment pass before, "What did CJ say to her?"

"I don't know the specifics and she was way too upset to go into it. I just wanted her to know that I didn't betray her. I never would've betrayed her." Elbows bent on his desk, he put his head in his hands.

"Do you think she believed you?" Yoli's heart was breaking for him. The woman he loved believing he had betrayed her and finding out his wife was behind the betrayal. He didn't deserve this. He may not have always made the best decisions (marrying CJ being at the top of that list), but Schooner Moore was a good man. A very good man.

"Yeah, I think she did. I think she really did. She saw how shocked and upset I was and when she realized I never knew why she had left and hadn't been complicit, she literally went to pieces. Yoli, she shattered," he had to stop to gain his composure, and Yoli could feel her own eyes wet with the tears she was trying to hold back as her heart ached for him. Finally, "She was devastated that she hurt me. That I was innocent and she hurt me." It was finally too much and he turned his face away.

"What are you going to do, Schooner?" Yoli needed to ground him with action because he was too raw.

"I'm going to confront CJ. She's going to lie. And I'm going to move out. I've already talked to Aaron Bender." He nodded his head with resolve.

"Wow, you didn't waste any time," she observed.

"I wasted twenty-four fucking years." Schooner was starting to blow. And then, "I'm sorry, why am I yelling at you?" The question was rhetorical.

Yoli held up a hand, "I'd rather you yell now, get it out, work through it, so that you are totally together when you confront her."

Schooner nodded, "You're right. You are such a good friend to me." Yoli could see the love in his eyes and her heart melted, but there was no way to alleviate his pain except to be there for him, help talk him through the bombardment of emotions.

"This may not be the time, but can she do anything to us here?"

Schooner smiled for the first time and shook his head no. "Not unless you vote against me. You've got 20%. The most she can ever get, and she won't, would be 40%, so we're good."

Yoli closed her eyes, relieved. Clearly, nothing could be put past CJ. Yoli always suspected she was a dirty fighter, but now with Mia's revelation, they knew CJ would do whatever she had to do to win. Including destroy lives.

"So, how did you leave it with Mia?"

"I told her I'd call her tonight." There was something in his eyes that she'd never seen before.

"And she's okay with that?"

"She didn't tell me not to." And there it was, that gorgeous All-American Boy smile.

He's going to go after her, Yoli thought. "Be careful, Schooner."

"Don't worry, Yol. Mia's not like that."

"You're really vulnerable, Schooner. Neither of you is the same person that you were twenty something years ago." She felt very protective of this man who had taken such good care of her and always treated her with respect and deference. What he was about to go through with CJ was going to be explosive and she could tell in her gut that he was going to rapidly and relentlessly pursue Mia to put the pieces of his life back together the way he had once dreamed they would fit. Yoli feared that the reality would not be as pretty as his dreams.

"See, that is where you are wrong, Yoli. We may have just lived through a lifetime of experiences that were different and not shared, but we are the same people. It's my Mia. That's my Baby Girl."

Yoli sat there shocked, his 'Baby Girl'? WTF? This man who was so cool with women, detached, aloof, always staying one step removed, making him even more fascinating to them. He was the ultimate challenge to the women of Orange and Los Angeles Counties, an elusive prize. And that is what he stayed, elusive and untouchable, and they wanted him even more. And now he was talking about his 'Baby Girl'?

He went on, "And I will move Heaven and Earth to make sure that we finally have the chance that we were robbed of." He started to shut down his laptop and grabbed for his Floto Parma messenger bag. "I know what I heard today. We both went to hell and we each thought the other one didn't go there — and that made it even worse — and today we learned that we both went to hell — separately and alone. And now, I am going to fix this. I am going to make this right. We are going to have our happiness. I am putting this back on track — the way it was supposed to be."

Yoli sat there wide eyed and stunned, yet she had no doubt that he would do exactly what he was saying he would do. Schooner Moore was single-minded in his pursuits and in twenty years, she had never seen him fail.

He was packed up and ready to head home for the final showdown with CJ. "Do you have a Kevlar vest?" Yoli was only half kidding.

"No shit. This is not going to be pleasant."

"Good luck." She was more than a little scared for him.

"My luck changed today, Yoli. Mia Silver is back in my life. I never thought I'd have the opportunity to say those words again," he acknowledged with a sad smile. "The hell of not knowing is over. I now know why she left me. And now — Karma. Today the universe finally rights itself. Karma is truly going to be a bitch."

Chapter Four

Driving through Newport Beach toward their house on Linda Isle, Schooner almost felt a sense of relief that this would no longer be his home. He didn't know where his home would be or where he was going, but just knowing what he was about to do gave him a feeling of renewal.

"You told her what happened to me." That knocked him for a loop. Whatever was said to Mia must've been pretty on target and devastating for her to believe CJ, and not to have just told her to go fuck herself. For Mia to doubt what they had, what they shared and his love for her, CJ must've been very convincing. He wondered if she'd somehow caught wind of enough to be able to spin a tale close enough to reality. Maybe someday Mia would tell him, because he knew CJ sure as hell wasn't going to be spewing any truths today.

As he pulled into the driveway of his modern white and glass home, it struck him that this was the last time he'd be driving up as a resident. He wasn't sad about leaving it — it was just he and CJ living there now. No more nights of helping Holly with her homework or playing video games with Zac. He'd need to make arrangements to have his boat moved so that he could have access to it.

Walking into the foyer with its white terrazzo floors and sweeping rounded staircase with the wrought iron banister, he noted how cold an environment it was. It was a house, not a home. The views of the harbor were beautiful and the sunsets spectacular, but the house felt as much like a shell as he did.

Appearing at the top of the stairs, CJ stood and posed for a moment before she began her descent with perfect pageant girl poise, a talent she had never lost. "What are you doing home so early? Did you forget something?"

"No. I haven't forgotten a thing."

"Why are you home?" CJ reached her husband at the bottom of the stairs.

"Come," was all he said as he strode into the family room.

"Schooner, what is going on?"

He pointed to the couch for her to sit and she did. He stood before her, looming over her, 6'2" of solid built muscle, and in a deadly calm voice he asked, "What exactly did you say to Mia Silver that made her leave school and never come back?"

"What are you talking about?" She looked up at him, blue eyes wide.

"I want to know what you said to her." Schooners arms were crossed over his muscular chest.

"I don't know what you are talking about and you are asking me to remember something from over twenty years ago. What is going on?"

"I'm giving you the opportunity to come clean, CJ, before I leave you." Schooner felt no emotion and having this conversation was so much easier than he anticipated. He felt nothing.

"Leave me?" Her voice rose an octave. "What are you talking about?"

"We're done." The shock factor alone was worth the price of admission.

"I don't understand. What happened? Where is this coming from?"

"You know exactly where this is coming from. It took a while, but it did catch up to you."

"You've spoken to Mia?" Her voice was tight and she had visibly blanched beneath her spray tan.

His nod was almost imperceptible. "I have."

"What did she say?" CJ was fishing.

"She told me about your conversation with her and why she left. But now I would like to hear your side of it." He had not moved an inch, standing there formidably, his muscular forearms still crossed defensively over his chest.

CJ was silent. When she finally spoke, her tactic was diversionary. "Has it been horrible with me? Have we had a bad life?"

He was not going to be thrown off course. "I loved her, CJ."

"And I loved you, Schooner."

His voice was deadly soft. "No, you didn't. You loved the idea of me. You didn't care how much I hurt when you caused me to lose Mia. That's not love, CJ. That's manipulation. There is no coming back from what you did. It was malicious and done with the intent to destroy. Mission accomplished, Baby. And although I'd love to stand here and blame you for destroying my life, I can't do that. I take that responsibility. I did a great job of destroying my own life. Now it's time to rectify that."

Schooner turned and walked from the room, heading for the staircase.

"That's it?" she screamed after him.

"That's it." He didn't bother to turn around.

Rushing into the foyer, her anger finally starting to peak, "So, you're going back to Mia?"

Schooner looked down on her from the upper landing, "No, CJ, I'm leaving you."

CJ followed him up the stairs into the massive glass walled master bedroom. "You are going to believe some woman you haven't spoken to in over twenty years over your wife?"

"I'm listening," he didn't turn around to look at her as he wheeled an oversized suitcase duffle out of the closet. It still had tags on it from the last trip.

"Did it ever occur to you that she's after money?" Venom dripped from her words.

Schooner stacked trousers, jeans and shorts on the bed. "Nope. It never occurred to me."

"Well, maybe it should."

"Maybe you should start talking." He brushed passed her as he entered the closet and grabbed a week's worth of button down shirts.

"I can't believe you are doing this," her voice was shrill.

He finally stopped and looked at her. "Believe it, because it's a done deal, Babe." It occurred to him that they even fought like WASPS. He was ending a twenty-year marriage and there wasn't even passion in their fighting. Par for the course of a passionless marriage.

Next was socks, underwear, tee-shirts and polos. The duffle was now laying across their beautiful sleigh bed and he began to load the clothes in neatly. CJ stood there and silently watched. Schooner walked into the bathroom, grabbed his electric razor, toothbrush, hairbrush, travel toiletry case and sundry items.

CJ stood next to the bed, arms crossed. "Maybe she's the liar, Schooner, not me."

He looked at her and smiled and shook his head at the absurdity. That didn't even dignify a response.

CJ changed tact, "I don't want you to go. Let's work this out. Zac and Holly will be heartbroken. Don't break up this family, Schooner."

He moved back into the closet and emerged with several pairs of shoes and sneakers and then began to go through his nightstand — favorite watches, passport, a second wallet. He loaded the last of his belongings into his duffle and zipped it.

He stopped and looked at CJ, his voice even. "I will always be there for the kids, but I cannot live another day with you. There isn't enough counseling in the world that could ever make me want to be in the same room with you, CJ, let alone stay married to you."

"Why are you being so mean?" she yelled back.

"Mean? Oh, I could be really mean here after what you have done. This is not mean. I've been pretty straight with you today and you have chosen not to come clean. Not to be honest. I'm not surprised, but I did hope you would just own up to it." He moved passed her out of the bedroom and started toward the staircase.

"There is nothing to own up to. I haven't done anything wrong. You are making me out to be some kind of evil monster. Mia left you of her own free will and now she's making up some kind of lie about it. I had nothing to do with that girl transferring schools." CJ followed him down the stairs to the foyer.

Schooner opened a coat closet and grabbed a black and royal blue ski jacket. He unzipped the pocket and looked inside, smiled and zipped it back up. "You know, I actually think you might believe that."

"Of course, I believe it. It's the truth."

"Your relationship with truth has never been an intimate one, CJ." He slung the ski jacket over his shoulder and grabbed the handle on the wheeled duffle and headed toward the front door. He stopped and turned around. "My lawyer will be in touch."

And he walked out the door.

Exiting Linda Isle onto Bayside Drive and heading toward the Pacific Coast Highway, Schooner was astounded at how dispassionate that whole process had been. No screaming, no yelling, no tears. Very little emotion at all. He had expected somewhat of a scene, even anticipating his own anger being an issue. But it wasn't. Yes, he was disgusted with CJ and her actions, livid about what she had done to him and Mia, angry at her inability to tell the truth, but she wasn't worthy of any of his emotions, not even his anger — and he didn't give any of them to her. He was not going to give her that control. And the feeling was victorious.

Schooner Moore had only one thing on his mind that Monday afternoon as he drove away from his home on Linda Isle, and that was hearing Mia Silver's sweet voice again that night.

Chapter Five

He couldn't sleep. It felt like an endorphin high, as if the cells in his body were a multi-level pinball machine that released ten balls at one time, and he was working four flippers trying to save them from being lost down the dead center of the machine. They had talked until 1:45 A.M. his time and it was now a few minutes before 6 A.M. — almost 9:00 her time. She might already be at work — or maybe she slept in because he had kept her up until almost 5 A.M. eastern time. He had to know. Now that he found her, every second not in contact gnawed at him.

He grabbed his cell and hit her number.

"Hi," he could hear the sleep in her voice.

"I keep waking you," his morning voice was gravelly and sexy.

"Mmmm, you do," she didn't sound unhappy about it and he could picture her stretching under her blanket.

"Do you want to go back to sleep?" It was impossible to wipe the smile off his face. In the pre-dawn hour, he was in bed talking to his Baby Girl.

"Mmmm, let me think — talk to Schooner or sleep. Such a tough decision," she teased, "I wasn't sleeping very well anyway."

"No?" Tell me your thoughts, Mia.

"No. I was having weird stress dreams. You know when you really can't tell if you're awake or asleep."

"What were they about?"

"They were about you, Schooner. I couldn't get to you. I knew you were there, but I couldn't find you. People kept telling me to go places, that you were there. But you never were. So actually, I'm glad you called," she sounded distraught, as if the dreams were still holding onto the edges of her consciousness.

He could feel the small crack in his heart. He knew that nightmare all too well. That nightmare had been a long-seated reality. "You can get to me any day, any time, any hour and I mean that. If you wake up from a bad dream. you call me." *Though I'd rather be there next to you to hold you. I can almost remember what that felt like. Almost.*

"Call you. Wow. That's so weird. I'm so used to living without you."

He sighed, "I know. I was just thinking that I can almost remember what it felt like to have your head on my chest."

"Almost," she repeated and he could hear the sadness.

"Okay, I'm just going to say this and please just be honest with me about how you feel, okay? I've just gone for over twenty years without you and now that I know where you are and I know what happened to us, every second feels like hell. I want to be there with you. I want this exile to be over, Mia."

"Well, then you need to get your ass on a plane." Now *that* was *his* Mia Silver.

"I can do that." Damn, this woman knew how to make him smile.

"Then do it."

"You're a demanding little thing."

Mia laughed and he smiled just listening to that sweet sound. "It's part of my charm, Schooner. You know that."

"So, are you going to charm me?" He could feel himself growing stiff. Just hearing her voice and picturing her cute little devil grin.

"I thought I already had. Have I lost my touch?"

"Mmmm, I distinctly remember your touch." And he did, although it was his hand now doing the touching.

"And I distinctly remember touching you."

"You do?" Tell me more.

"Mmm-hmm, a girl never forgets her first."

Melt. Pure heart melt. *Her first, that's how she remembers me, as her first* — he was beyond elated. *Yes! Your first and your last, Baby Girl. Her first.* She had no clue the impact those words had just had on him.

It took him a few moments to speak again. "You'll always be my first."

She laughed, "Schooner, aka Mr. Stud Muffin Tennis Star, I was far from your first."

He was shaking his head no, "Quite the contrary, Baby Girl. I may have had sexual encounters before you, but you were very definitely my first."

Mia was giggling and he couldn't wipe the smile off his face, "Pretty boy, you just want to get laid."

"Well yeah, but you were still my first." *And I want you to be mine, Baby Girl.*

"I love that you think of me that way." *Oh Mia, Mia, Mia ...*

"You sound surprised."

"Schooner, I've spent most of my life thinking you never actually cared about me, that I was a charity case."

A sudden, surprising burn stung at the back of his throat as the air of the conversation changed abruptly. Charity case? What the hell had CJ said to her? "Mia …," and he had to stop to compose himself. Charity case. Holy crap. "It breaks my heart to think that you even went a single day thinking that what we shared was not real."

"I'm not going to lie. It's a big mind shift, Schooner," her voice a whisper.

"I was lost without you, Mia."

"But I didn't know that. I thought I meant nothing to you. I went over and over and over every minute we'd ever spent together and wondered how I missed it. How I'd misread the situation. Wondered if you were just wearing one of your masks with me because I was an obligation?"

"Oh Baby Girl, you were the one who taught me I didn't need any masks. You were the first person in my entire life that I felt comfortable enough to reveal myself to. And yes, I did have an obligation to you — and that was to protect you because I loved you. And I failed."

They were silent for a few minutes before Mia broke the silence.

"Schooner, I've lived my life thinking I had been hopelessly in love with a guy who didn't love me back. It took a long time to get you out of my head, and my heart too, and you crept back in at the most unexpected and inopportune moments. I wasn't one of those people who was like, "I was hurt and I'm going to build walls up," but I was cautious. And I wanted to be in love again. I wanted to feel what I knew I was capable of feeling. What I felt with you. I wanted that high again," she paused, "It's just so hard for me to process that reality, my reality for twenty-four years, feeling that I never meant anything to you, with what you have told me in the past twenty-four hours."

It would be so much easier if I were there with you and you were in my arms. He wanted to jump in and take over, but he was afraid the ice he was skating toward her on would crack. "I know, Baby Girl."

"Say that again."

"Say what again?"

"Baby Girl."

His real smile was out of control. "You like hearing me call you that?"

Mia just moaned.

"Don't do that," he admonished.

"Don't do what?"

"Don't moan, Baby Girl."

"Why not?"

"You make me want to touch myself."

"Mmmmmm," she moaned.

Sigh, "Baby Girl, do you have any idea what you do to me?" There were smiles at either end of the phone at the reprise of the words that started a lifelong love affair.

"Schooner …"

"Yeah, Baby Girl …?"

"It's smoochal."

And in that moment, he knew, twenty-four years of heartache were over. They had their demons to work through, but what he felt, what she felt, was real. It was real. It had always been real. They would work through the demons together. And he could not get her into his arms soon enough. She was his and no one was ever going to take her from him again.

Chapter Six

Schooner Moore strode into his office at an uncharacteristically late 9 A.M. on Tuesday morning. He was surprised that Yoli hadn't sent out a search party to see if he'd survived the showdown with CJ the prior afternoon. Passing Yoli's office, he poked his head in, but she wasn't there.

Setting his latte upon his desk, Schooner pulled out his laptop and started to boot up. It was time to find a flight to New York. Non-stop and first class were the criteria he punched in.

Smiling, he picked up his cell to call Mia. At least this time he wasn't going to wake her. It hadn't even been twenty-four hours yet since he'd first heard her voice again, yet his whole world had changed. What a difference a day makes, he mused.

"Hey you," she answered.

"Hey you," he smiled with a volley back. "Okay, I'm sitting here looking at flights." She didn't respond, so he continued, "You're being quiet. Are you okay with this?"

"I'm just too busy smiling."

"Me too. Okay, it looks like I can get a redeye out of here tomorrow night, be there early Thursday morning."

"Tomorrow night? That's really far away."

Schooner laughed. "I know, isn't it, but it will give me the chance though to get everything in place here to take off for a few days."

"Me too, I guess."

"You're pouting," he laughed.

"Yes, I am." Mia 'fessed up to it. "I want a Schooner fix *now!*"

Laughing, "You are very good for my ego, Woman."

"Schooner Moore, I've seen a picture of what you look like now and I am certain your ego is very well stroked by women."

Sitting back in his big leather desk chair, long legs stretched out, crossed at the ankles, Schooner could not keep the smile off his face. "That's probably true, but Mia Silver telling me she wants a Schooner fix is in a league all by itself, Baby Girl. So, I should book this flight?"

"You haven't already?"

"I just want to make sure you are okay with it."

"Schooner, I'm okay with it."

He closed his eyes and smiled. Mia wanted him there. Whoever in a million years would've thought this would happen? He certainly didn't.

"Okay, I'm booked."

"Yay! So, Thursday morning, huh?"

"Less than forty-eight hours and I'll be there." He picked up his latte and took a sip.

"I don't want to let myself get excited in case something happens or you get here and it's weird between us." He could hear the concern in Mia's voice.

"I don't think that is going to happen, Mia. But here's what I'll do. I'm going to make a reservation at The Stanhope."

"Schooner, you can stay here," she interrupted.

"Just hear me out. I don't want this to be weird. I don't want you to feel pressured. If you need your space from me. Or you're just not feeling it. Send me packing up to The Stanhope and we can just hang out during the day and you can show me New York. Does that sound okay?"

Mia was silent.

"Mia, talk to me. What are you thinking?"

"I'm thinking it's probably a smart idea. But I hate it. Does that make sense?"

Schooner laughed, "Oddly enough, yes. But it also gives us a chance to get to know one another again without the added pressure."

"Schooner Moore, you are such a gentleman."

He could just picture her sitting in her office, smiling. "My momma raised me right." The Stanhope was the last place he wanted to be sleeping, but Schooner knew that Mia had to want him there, she had to feel comfortable with him in her space.

He already knew that he would be devastated if she just wasn't feeling any more than seeing an old friend when they got together. But that was a distinct possibility. Spending a whole weekend with someone you'd just been back in touch with for seventy-two hours was weird to say the least. He felt so certain that he wanted her in his world, but there was a significant chance that once they were face-to-face, the old chemistry wouldn't be there.

As if sensing his energy, in a soft voice she reassured, "It is going to be amazing to see you, Schooner. I might not want to let you leave." *Good answer, Baby Girl.*

"I like hearing you tell me that, Baby Girl." He closed his eyes and sat back in his chair.

"Well, it's true. I can't think of anything but you."

He was smiling ear-to-ear, "It's smoochal, Baby Girl. It's smoochal."

Yoli entered Schooner's office and sat down across from him. She didn't say a word.

Schooner just looked at her and smiled.

"I don't see any visible wounds."

Schooner let out a hearty laugh. "No, of course you don't. We fight like WASPS. Considering, it was pretty civilized. I confronted her, she lied, I packed up and left."

"You know she's not going to go down without a fight." There was disgust on Yoli's face.

Nodding, "I know. This is going to get very ugly. And she knows I've spoken to Mia."

"She had to have been shocked, Schooner."

"Shocked that she was caught," he was smiling. "So, I'm taking a redeye to New York tomorrow night. I'll be gone through the weekend."

"I've got it covered," she assured him.

"I knew you would." He could count on Yoli for anything. She was so capable and knew the business inside out. She would make any absences easy for him.

"You excited?" She really wanted some details on this already.

Schooner sighed. Leaning back in his chair, hands behind his head, "I'm excited. I'm nervous. I'm scared. I feel naked, Yoli. Vulnerable. I feel very vulnerable. I'm not used to that. I hope I'm not setting myself up for a huge disappointment. But I don't think I am. You've seen her," he pointed to his PC, "she's adorable. And when we talk, it's there — that energy we had. The chemistry. It's still there. So yeah, I'm scared. I lost her once. I just hope that she feels for me what I still feel for her."

Yoli looked at Schooner with a furrowed brow. "I've never seen you not be confident, Schooner. Come on, you know how to turn on the charm better than anyone."

Schooner laughed. "You know what she would say about that?"

Yoli shook her head.

"She'd tell me, 'You'll have to do better than that, Pretty Boy.'"

Yoli burst out laughing, "She calls you on your shit?"

"Yeah, I think the two of you might be soul sisters."

"I love her already." As Yoli got up to leave Schooner's office, she turned to him. “Schooner.”

He looked up from his laptop screen.

“Take as long as you need in New York. If Mia has been in your heart all these years, go get her. Make sure she knows how deeply you feel about her and that you don’t want to lose her again. Don’t lose her again. You deserve happiness.”

“I won’t lose her again. She’s mine.” And the smile that overtook his face was his real smile.

Chapter Seven

It was almost midnight her time on Tuesday night when he grabbed his cell to call her again. They hadn't talked in nearly twelve hours and the need to hear her voice and make sure everything was still ok with them permeated his every thought. Consciously holding back all afternoon from dialing her, he feared his intensity might overwhelm her, scare her away. I'm beginning to feel like a Stage 5 Clinger wanting to spend every second talking to her, he self-chastised.

"Hi," she sounded sleepy.

"I woke you again, huh?" He stretched out on the hotel bed, stacking the pillows behind him.

"I must've dozed. I was reading some stuff for work."

"You still good with me coming?" Damn, I sound insecure, he thought.

"I'd be really upset if you cancelled."

Hearing her say that, he could feel the tension release from his shoulders.

"I missed talking to you this afternoon," she continued. *Good answer, Baby Girl.*

"I missed talking to you, too. I didn't want to monopolize your entire workday." *Actually, I did.*

Mia laughed.

"What's so funny?" He was smiling at the sound of her laughter.

"I have a secret to tell you, Schooner," she paused. "Whether you are on the phone with me or not, you monopolize my entire workday. My concentration has been shit since your friend request showed up. I can't think of anything but you. I am just a total spaced-out waste."

"Well, that's a good thing, because it's smoochal, Baby Girl."

"So, you really loved me freshman year?"

He could hear her ghosts filtering in like a fog. They both needed so much reassurance with one another. It was clear they were each waiting for — no, expecting — the rug to be pulled out from under them — again. It was like the internal alarms were sounding, "Don't get too happy, this all just might be a dream."

"Oh Baby Girl, it breaks my heart that you have spent most of your life thinking I didn't love you. I didn't stop loving you. But at some point, I finally had to let it go. You weren't coming back. And you never got in touch with me. I just had to finally let you go."

"I tried once," she whispered, "I tried to get in touch with you."

"You did? When?" When did she try to get in touch?

"It was a few weeks into sophomore year. I confided in a friend at my new school and he convinced me that I needed to talk to you and hear it all from you. So, I got up the nerve to call you one night and Beau answered. He said you weren't there. I asked him when you'd be back and he told me that you and CJ had just left and you wouldn't be back until the next day."

"What?" The scream was out of him before he could modulate it. Fucking motherfucker. There was no way a few weeks into sophomore year he was spending the night at CJ's. She lived in an all-girls dorm, so he never spent the night there, and early in the semester, he was still pining over Mia. "Motherfucker!"

Mia was silent in the wake of his volatile reaction.

"Sorry, Baby Girl, but there was no way I was spending the night with CJ. I wasn't even seeing her then. I was a fucking mess and if I was anywhere, I was off studying or running on the track. I never spent the night with her. Motherfucking liar. Why would he ..." as his thought trailed off, both Schooner and Mia knew the answer.

Schooner steadied his breath, calming himself down from the latest revelation. It just gets better and better, he thought. And then it occurred to him. She tried to find him. She tried to reach out to him. If he had just answered the phone that night. If Beau hadn't blatantly lied — corroborating CJ's claims that she and Schooner were a couple. They were so close to it being only four months instead of twenty-four years. So close.

"You called me?" He was stunned.

"Yeah."

"Shit."

"Yeah."

"Oh Baby Girl, we did not deserve this. Let me assure you, I loved you freshman year, I loved you long after freshman year. And if I'm being completely honest, I have never loved anyone else but you." There he said it. It was all out there now. His heart was out there. And it was the truth, finally expressed. He certainly didn't love CJ and he'd never again experienced what he had shared with Mia.

"I needed to hear that, Schooner. I needed to know we were real. That what I had thought you felt for me, well, that I wasn't wrong. I wasn't crazy. I didn't miss something."

"Mia, you didn't miss anything. And I didn't either. We got fucked. Royally. I thought by one person and now I'm thinking by two people. The bottom line is this — you loved me and I loved you — unfortunately, we both spent a really long time thinking that we'd been in love alone and that is why it hurt so bad. But the joke is on them now — because we know the truth."

"You know what?"

"Tell me." He needed to hear something good from her. This was like standing alone on the edge of a precipice with a strong wind at his back.

"If I'm completely honest, I never loved anyone else as deeply as I loved you, Schooner."

Damn, this woman could bring him to his knees. There they were — both standing there, naked. Vulnerable. The truth was finally out. And if he was standing there high on the edge of a cliff, he wasn't standing there alone anymore. Mia had joined him. She was as bold and fearless as she'd always been. This was the Mia Silver with whom he had fallen hopelessly in love.

"We're going to be ok, Mia," he reassured her. He wasn't going to allow himself to believe anything else. He could picture her shaking her head yes on the other end of the phone as he heard her trying to hide her tears. He pictured gently wiping them away with his thumb.

"You promise, Schooner?"

And as always with Mia, making a promise was so damn easy. "I promise, Baby Girl."

This time he knew better and God help the person who attempted to get in the way of him keeping his promise to her; he would make their life a living hell.

Chapter Eight

Schooner's seatmate on the redeye to New York was very pleased to see him. It wasn't often that the man sitting next to her was pure eye candy.

Putting his Tumi bag in the overhead bin, the smartly dressed businesswoman gladly moved her laptop case off the aisle seat — Schooner's seat.

As soon as he sat, she began talking, "I'm venturing a guess that New York is not home for you."

Schooner smiled politely, "No, it isn't."

The flight attendant interrupted, "What can I get you to drink, Mr. Moore?"

"What kind of scotch do you have?"

"We've got Dewar's White Label and Glenlivet Single Malt."

"I'll take a double Glenlivet on the rocks." He hit her with his All-American boy smile. Unfortunately, for his seatmate, the flight attendant totally ignored her and did not bother to remove her already empty glass, or ask her if she would like another drink.

Schooner dug out his phone, ready to call Mia while they loaded the rest of the plane, but was immediately interrupted by the woman next to him.

"Are you on business or pleasure?" She was crowding him, even though his first-class seat was quite spacious.

Schooner hit her with the full mega-watt smile, "Pure pleasure," he could hear her breath hitch, and now it was time to shut her flirting down with the killing blow, "The love of my life is a New Yorker and I cannot wait to have her back in my arms," and with another smile, "excuse me," he hit dial on his cell phone.

The woman put on a pair of Bose noise canceling headphones, plugged them into her phone and accessed her iTunes list. Hallelujah, Schooner thought, some quiet and privacy.

"Hey, Baby Girl," he was finally wearing his real smile.

"Are you on the plane?"

"I am. They're boarding now, so we have a few minutes," he paused. "Mia, Mia, Mia."

Mia laughed, "What?"

"You know what?"

"Yeah, I do."

"How the hell did this happen?" He laughed.

"Unbelievable, right?"

"I feel like I have a new lease on life," his voice just slightly more than a whisper. The flight attendant put down his scotch and he nodded and smiled at her.

"I can't believe that I am going to see you in a few hours."

"I know," he smiled, thinking about it.

"I never thought I'd see you again in my life," Mia was getting choked up just expressing that.

"Oh, Baby Girl, I know that feeling. When you didn't come back that fall, I knew I had to let my dream go."

"I wish I'd known you loved me, I would've been on the next plane," she sighed.

"Well, you know now and I'm not waiting for the next plane, I'm on this one."

They closed the cabin door and dimmed the lights for takeoff. As they lifted off the runway, Schooner reclined his seat and closed his eyes, knowing that sleep was not in the cards. On the other side of this flight, a car would be waiting to take him to Mia.

He couldn't get the picture out of his mind of rushing all over campus that first day back sophomore year, trying to find her. Her dorm, the dining hall. Everywhere he turned had been a dead end, and those first few weeks, letting it really sink in that the dream he held the entire time he was in Zambia, the dream that she would be back in his arms again, was not going to come true. Not that day. Not the next week Not the next semester.

The light had gone out in his world. A light he had not previously known existed, and when he was thrust back into darkness, it was actually a safe place for him. Schooner Moore knew how to operate in darkness. He knew how to shut everything down and how to protect himself. In doing so, he maintained absolute control. Control equaled protection. Protection meant he couldn't be gutted again. Slipping back into the pre-Mia world was easy, he knew the rules — it was a very comfortable playing field. And he knew how to keep himself safe.

Jolted awake when the 767 slammed down onto the runway, Schooner realized he must've dozed for a few minutes. His first thought upon the hard, abrupt landing was, "Navy Pilot." His second thought was, "Finally, our New York dream happens. Finally."

His seatmate had thankfully been asleep the entire flight, saving him from having to put up with twenty questions. She stretched and opened the window shade, letting in the bright morning sunlight.

The flight attendant announced that it was a "balmy 18 degrees" at New York's Kennedy International Airport. Just hearing that made Schooner smile as he gazed out the window. Eighteen degrees. He really was in New York. The thing that grabbed his attention immediately was the sky. It was so clear right down to the horizon, there was no smoggy brown haze hanging along the edge. And the color, it was mesmerizing. Just a clear, beautiful blue illuminated by bright sunshine on this cloudless day. It was picture perfect — a picture he had held in his mind's eye for over two decades.

Powering up his cell phone, he dialed Mia, "We're on the tarmac."

"Welcome to New York," she sounded exuberant.

He could not contain his smile. He was so close. So, so close. "I'll see you in few."

"Oh my God, Schooner." Her tone and sentiment exactly matched what he was feeling.

"I know, Baby Girl. I'll see you soon." As he hit end on the call, he realized two things; he was smiling ear-to-ear and his right leg was bouncing uncontrollably with nervous energy.

Schooner could feel his heart racing, exhilarated, as the plane continued to slowly taxi along the runway toward the terminal. He could not tear his focus away from the beautiful, sunlit winter sky. It was so blue. So clear. He wanted to get out of the plane and the terminal and feel the eighteen-degree air on his cheeks as he basked in the abundant sunshine.

After twenty-four years of being shrouded in darkness, Schooner Moore could not wait one more minute to meet the light again. He was fully ready to embrace the light and shed the comfort he had built in the darkness.

Part Three
Schooner & Mia

Chapter One

Now ...

Mia crawled back into bed next to Schooner, spooning up behind him.

"How does your head feel?" He rolled over and pulled her onto his chest.

"It hurts tonight. I just had to get some more Ibuprophen from the kitchen."

"I would've gotten it for you," he gently stroked her hair.

"I was trying not to wake you, Mr. Moore, but now that I have," she softly rubbed his chest, her hand moving in circles slowly down his flat stomach.

Schooner laughed and kissed her forehead, then grabbed her hand as it was rapidly heading south and brought it to his lips, where he kissed her palm.

"Ms. Silver, I give you my word that once we get the go-ahead after Nathaniel's birth, we will get your mom or my mom or both of them to come and watch him for a few days, and we are going to be holed up at either The Four Seasons or out at the beach house, and I promise to spend the entire time making you come and listening to you scream my name. But until that time, my sweet Baby Mama, no nookie."

"I hate you."

"Get over it," he wrapped his arms around her tighter and kissed the top of her head.

Mia was smiling in the dark. She had once told her mother that she thought that she and Schooner were one being, in two separate bodies. And here she was, years later, wrapped up in his big, protective arms, with their son growing stronger and bigger every day inside of her. Never, in her wildest dreams, through all the years that loneliness was her best friend and darkness her closest ally, did she ever think this could be a reality, much less her reality. She was resigned to thinking that this was a lifetime where she was meant to learn lessons (and she certainly had, the hard way), but she was certain that it was not a lifetime that she would share with another for more than a season.

"I need you to meet me when she takes her nap this afternoon. Text me when she falls asleep." Schooner said quietly to Seth.

"What's up?" Seth was surprised and intrigued. Schooner never asked him to meet up with him during the day, especially when he was staying with Mia.

Hitting him with his All-American Boy smile, Schooner cryptically called over his shoulder, "You'll see," as he headed out the door.

It was 2:30 P.M. when Mia was finally wiped out from hours of working from her bed. As she curled up to take an afternoon nap, Seth told her that he would be out running some errands while she slept, but that he would be back in a little while.

As he walked out of the bedroom, he texted Schooner.

Seth: BBC in dreamland
Schooner: Meet me at the corner of Mercer & Grand

As Seth headed down to SoHo in a cab, he could not fathom what Schooner had in store. Seth was amused as his cab pulled up and he saw women doing double-takes to stare at Schooner, who stood there oblivious, clad in jeans and a cream double cable knit sweater, looking every inch the male model. Seth just shook his head, what a waste — the man should never have given up that childhood modeling career.

"I'm tempted to throw my arms around you and kiss you just to keep the bitches away." Seth greeted him. "You know you're really too pretty to be straight."

Schooner just laughed, "C'mon, I want to show you something." Seth followed Schooner through the columned entrance of 100 Grand Street. Crossing the lobby to the elevator, Schooner pulled a key out of his wallet and inserted it into a slot on the elevator panel. The elevator car slowly ascended and opened.

Seth gasped and smacked Schooner on his muscular upper arm. "You didn't!"

Laughing, "Yeah, I did. Think she'll like it?"

Seth stood there, speechless, taking in the forty foot by forty foot living room set in an open loft space. Sun drenched by a wall of southern facing windows, the room retained all its original charm, a tin panel ceiling, ornate Corinthian columns separating spaces and polished hardwood floors.

"Is it the whole floor of the building?" Seth's mouth was hanging open.

"It is." Schooner was anxious to show him around.

Seth wandered through the spacious loft, marveling at the chef's kitchen, the three bedrooms (a true luxury in New York), a huge marble walk-in shower in the master bath, and a library with floor to ceiling bookcases.

"I think this should be the nursery." Schooner was saying as they walked into the second bedroom. "And I'd like to make the library into a guest room, a place for my parents or Mia's parents to stay."

Seth nodded. He still could not speak and then finally, "BBC is going to be so pissed that she didn't get to pick this out."

Schooner smiled, "Yeah, I know. But she was in no condition to and we really need the space before Nathaniel is born. Her apartment has been fine for the two of us, but it is not nearly big enough for the three of us, and I know both of our parents are going to want to come and spend time. Holly will also always have a place to stay."

"You are both such control freaks, how does it work?"

Schooner's eyes crinkled at the corners as he smiled, "We truly get each other. Honestly, Seth, I don't know where I end and she begins. I would do anything for that woman," he paused, "and what I need you to do for me is to decorate this nursery. Theme, furniture, walls, blankets, stuffed animals, whatever — just do it."

Seth's eyes were wide. "Heaven," he sang, "I'm in heaven."

Schooner stood in the doorway while Seth stalked around the room. He looked at the walls, inside the closet, up at the ceiling. "Jungle safari," he finally announced. "Palm trees, grass huts, giraffes, lions, monkeys hanging from the trees. Greens, yellows, blues and browns. I have a friend who can do the painting and I will find all the accessories. I'll probably have him do a hand painted crib, dresser and armoire. And maybe a rocker, too." Seth turned to Schooner, "Are you scared? You should be scared. I'm going to spend a lot of your money."

"Fine with me." Schooner shrugged his shoulders, "As long as Mia likes it. She's the one you've got to please."

"BBC will love whatever I do." Seth rolled his eyes, "After the makeover I had to do on her, this is a breeze."

Chapter Two

"Hello? Hello?" Mia repeated into her cell, but no one answered. "Who's there?" Somewhere in the distance she heard Schooner answering his phone and then his voice, loud and sharp, broke into her dream. It was his cell that had actually been ringing, not hers. Hers was only a dream.

Rolling over in the darkness of their room, she looked at the clock, 5:12 A.M. Something was wrong.

Schooner was sitting up in bed, "Is he alright? … Where did they take him? … Well, what are the doctors saying? … Do they know what he took? … Damn it, CJ, what was he doing out on a school night? … Do you even have any idea of what is going on in his life? … Yeah, yeah, yeah, I will … I'll get the first flight out … No, you don't need to come get me. I'll just rent a car and go straight to Hoag Hospital … Yes, I'll call you when I have my flight info."

Mia was sitting up next to Schooner with an arm around him. Kissing his shoulder softly, "Why don't you go shower and pack and I'll find you a flight and a rental car."

Schooner nodded.

"Is he okay? Do they know what he took?"

"They've pumped his stomach and he's stable." Schooner sighed deeply and rested his head on Mia's.

"I know what you're doing," she whispered.

"How can I not?"

The sadness in his voice tore at her heart. Nathaniel was up and kicking up a storm. Mia took Schooner's hand and placed it on her stomach, "Because Schooner Moore, you are a great father and Zac is very, very lucky to have someone who has been as dedicated as you have been."

"I haven't been there for him since the L9 opening. I've been so angry at him for what he did to you and Nathaniel." Schooner put his face in his hands, "Clearly, I have not handled this well."

"Stop that." Mia did not like where this was going. "You have spoken to CJ every few days. You always ask about Zac. About how he is adjusting to life back there, how he is adjusting to his new school. She has never once given you any indication that there was a problem. Actually, it's been just the opposite, that he has a new girlfriend and the first parent-teacher conferences went well."

Mia watched the myriad of emotions fly across Schooner's face at lightning speed. She ached for him as she watched him internalize what he was perceiving as failure, his failure.

"Schooner, look at me. Please. You are a good father. Such a good father. If this was his cry for help, get him help. But please don't blame yourself."

Putting his hand back on Mia's stomach, Nathaniel obliged with a hearty kick. "Ouch." Mia grimaced and Schooner smiled. "Now go shower and I'll get you on a plane."

An hour later, Schooner was leaving for the airport. "I feel like hell leaving you, Mia. Promise me you'll get Seth and Kami and Gaby here to help."

"I will," she nodded, distressed that he was leaving, yet trying not to let him have any indication of her real feelings.

"Please stay in bed. I'm going to worry about you," he cupped her check in his palm and she closed her eyes, focusing on the sensation of his hand on her cheek.

"No worries. You don't need any more worries."

Kissing her lightly on the lips, "I love you, Baby Girl."

"It's smoochal," she forced a smile and he was out the door.

Trying hard to control her tears and losing the battle, Mia felt guilty for not feeling more empathy for Zac and for CJ, but she just couldn't trust them.

Chapter Three

"So, have you seen him? What are the doctors saying? How did this happen?" Mia had a million questions for Schooner.

"It appears that he and some of his new buddies drank an enormous amount of alcohol, coupled with anti-anxiety meds taken from several parents' medicine cabinets." Schooner sounded tired.

"Okay, so it was stupid teenage behavior that went too far versus serious addiction stuff?" Mia was breathing a sigh of relief.

"It looks like it."

"Well, that's good news. That's a whole lot better than either rehab or suicidal behavior."

"I guess."

"Schooner, are you okay, Babe?"

"No," he was silent for a moment, "We're lucky we didn't lose him, Mia. Am glad one of these kids was responsible enough to actually call 911 and not just leave him."

"Me too," she said, softly. For as much pain and suffering as Zac had caused her, she did not wish the same for him. Seeing his father hurt, physically gouged her heart. "Was he glad to see you?"

"He's a very angry young man."

"God, I wish I could hug you right now. Oh Schooner, I feel so badly for you because I know you and you are beating yourself up right now. And you shouldn't be."

"Well, I don't know about that."

"I do." Mia was firm in her resolve. Changing the subject, "So, where will you be staying? We didn't make you hotel reservations."

"I'm going to stay here at the house," silence on both ends, "I'll stay in the guest room."

"Okay." Mia's stomach started to knot and Nathaniel began to squirm.

"How are you? Who helped you today?"

"Seth was here all day and he cooked dinner tonight. I'm covered. Don't worry about me."

"Okay."

And there was a pang of sadness, one she immediately felt guilty about. She wanted him to worry about her. And she hated herself for that.

She was a grown, self-sufficient woman and wanting him to take on any more worries was both selfish and childish. She needed to make things easier for him, not more difficult.

"It's been ten days, isn't devil spawn all better?" Seth had just finished the dinner dishes.

"He's 'coming along' is what I keep being told." Mia shrugged, looking even less happy about the situation than Seth.

"Yeah, well Nathaniel is coming along too, in how many weeks?"

"Eight." Mia was pulling at one of her curls and letting it spring back into place.

"Stop playing with that 'Bridge and Tunnel' hair. I wonder if I can get Sam to come to the apartment to cut off that hideous mop. With all those pregnancy hormones coursing through your veins you are hairier than a monkey."

"Are you done with those dishes yet?" Mia sneered at him.

"No." Seth sneered back.

"Well, then just throw them out."

"Fine," the man personified attitude. Lifting Mia's favorite Le Crueset pan into the air with a practiced flourish, Seth loudly dropped it into the garbage.

Grabbing his coat, he did not turn around as he announced, "I'll see you in the morning."

Mia winced as the door slammed. Schooner could not get home soon enough.

"Sorry I didn't call last night, we got home late from the Lakers' game."

Mia cringed at the word 'home'. There was so much wrong in what he had just said, but the word 'home' was what made her stomach knot the most.

"Do you think you'll be home this weekend?" Mia hated asking. She was beginning to feel like she was begging him to come back to her.

"I don't think so, Baby Girl. Zac is just beginning to open up to me. I really feel like we're starting to make progress."

Her anger was starting to surface as she fought hard to keep the tears at bay. "You've been gone for almost three weeks, Schooner."

"Do you think I want to be away from you?"

"I think at this point you don't really give a shit."

"Come on, Mia. That's not fair."

"Is it fair that I am alone, stuck in bed, with our son due to be born in seven weeks?"

She could hear an exaggerated sigh from him and her anger escalated. "Don't be dramatic. You are not alone. Seth and Kami and everyone have been there for you and I'm just a phone call away."

"Yeah, just a phone call away." Mia's voice dripped with sarcasm.

"You are really looking to pick a fight tonight, aren't you?" He was no longer trying to hide how annoyed he had become.

"Is that what you think is going on? Maybe you need to take a look around you and assess what is really going on. Why after three weeks they have guilted you into staying, keeping us apart."

"I cannot believe you just accused my son of faking things to keep us apart."

"Well, then let me clarify it for you." Mia could feel her blood pressure rising, "Your son and your wife will do whatever they need to do to keep you out there, Schooner."

"Mia, Zac has been going through a very rough time. Cut him a break."

Shaking with anger, Mia could not understand why she couldn't get through to him. "You did not just ask *me*, of all people, to cut Zac a break, did you?"

Schooner remained silent, angering Mia even more.

"You know what, Schooner, just stay out there. I did fine for twenty-four years without you. Nathaniel and I will do fine without you now." She hit end on the call.

He didn't try to call back.

Mia stewed for the next hour, her anger toward Schooner escalating as each minute passed.

Finally, she grabbed her cell phone and dialed.

"Are you okay?"

"No."

"What's the matter?"

"I have a question to ask you and I want you to answer me honestly, okay?" Mia needed to put it out there.

"Am I being a hormonal bitch or are CJ and Zac exploiting Schooner's Achilles Heel and his need to protect and to be a good dad? Are they just trying to keep us apart at this point?"

"Wow," Yoli slowly let out her breath, "Debbie and I just had this conversation about fifteen minutes ago."

"Did Schooner call you?"

"No, why?"

"Because we had a big blow out tonight about it, Yoli. I lost it on him when he told me to cut Zac a break."

"He didn't?" she erupted. Mia could hear Debbie in the background asking what was going on and Yoli relaying Mia's words. "I'm going to call him first thing in the morning and get him into the office with some problem, and then I am going to read him the riot act and open his eyes to what is going on. Zac's a big boy and CJ can certainly handle acting like a mother for once in her life. He needs to be home with you. I can just imagine the guilt they have laid on him."

"Guilt or no guilt, Yoli — he has chosen to live there with them — like they are a family — and leave me alone."

"Mia, if he thought, even for a minute, that you were not doing well …"

Mia interrupted, "I'm not doing well."

"I can hear that."

"He doesn't want to hear it, Yoli."

"Well, he's going to — loud and clear. Right now, Zac and CJ have him convinced that he is helping Zac recover. I'm sure the way they are playing this is that he is the key to Zac's recovery. That man will do anything for his family."

"Unfortunately, I'm not family." Mia wiped away her tears.

"Okay, now you're being hormonal, because no matter what, you are at the heart of his family, Mia. Always. You need to believe that."

"Unfortunately Yoli, right now I don't."

Turning off the lights to go to sleep, Mia wished she could be as certain as Yoli that she and Nathaniel were at the heart of his family, the heart of his world.

"You'll always be at the heart of mine, little boy." Mia wrapped her arms around her belly, hugging Nathaniel.

Schooner had still not tried to call her back.

Chapter Four

It was bad dream after bad dream, dreams that just led into one another, never ending, anxiety provoking. Schooner telling her that he was going back to CJ, trying to find Schooner at the beach house, but it was empty and filled with cobwebs, Zac sitting behind Schooner's desk at L9, his feet up on the desk, a smug look on his face, telling security to remove Mia from the premises.

Struggling up into a sitting position in bed, Mia put her face in her hands. Her subconscious was having a field day. It was better to be awake than to continue having nightmares, she thought. She looked at the clock. 4:27 A.M. Seth wouldn't be there for another four hours.

Grabbing her water bottle, Mia groaned. It was empty. Slowly swinging her legs out of bed, she made her way to the kitchen. As she approached the breakfast bar, she stopped at the sound of someone cracking their knuckles — except no one was cracking their knuckles and the sound was emanating from deep within her.

As she started again toward the refrigerator, there was no mistaking the immediate and considerable wetness in her underwear. They quickly felt soaked. With each step, a small gush seemed to release. "What the fuck?" Mia steadied herself with one hand on the breakfast bar and attempted to reach down with her other hand. Her fingertips were able to swipe at her inner thigh. Bringing her hand to her face, there was no odor to the wetness. "Holy fuck," she said to no one.

Heading back to the bedroom, Mia grabbed her cell. She hit dial.

"What's going on, Mia?"

"I think my water just broke. It sounded like when someone cracks a knuckle and then my underwear got all wet and it has no odor."

"Yeah, that's what it sounds like. How many weeks are you now?"

"Thirty-three."

"Okay, I want you to grab a cab to the hospital, that's going to be your quickest way to get there, and have the cab driver bring you right to the ER entrance. I'll be waiting there for you."

"Is he going to be okay, Gary? He's only thirty-three weeks."

"He's going to be little, Mia, but we have no indication at this point that he won't be healthy. And if he takes after his father, he won't be little for too long. Now get your stuff together and meet me." It sounded to Mia as if he were already on the move.

Mia quickly threw things into a small overnight bag. "Guess I should've had this packed," she thought. Slipping on a comfy maternity dress and flats, she grabbed a big colorful sweater and her cell and left the apartment.

The night doorman was surprised to see her when she reached the lobby.

"It's time," she announced.

"You're having the baby?"

"I am."

"Where is Mr. Schooner?"

"He's still in California." Mia's heart broke as she verbalized it.

"Well, I hope he gets home in time to see his boy born. It's all he's been talking about for months. Let me get you a cab, Miss Mia." The elderly gentleman went out to the curb.

Mia watched him standing at the curb with his hand raised in the dark night. She pulled out her cell and started to text.

> **Mia: Water broke. Heading to hospital. Gary's meeting me there.**

She sent the message to Seth Shapiro, Charles Sloan and Kami Townes.

The cab pulled up in front of the building's awning and Mia went out. Thanking the doorman, she slid into the back seat and gave the cab driver the hospital's address.

As he pulled away from the curb, she lovingly stroked her belly. "I will always be there for you, Nathaniel. Always. You can count on me. I won't let you down. You will always have me," she promised him, as the cab sped through Manhattan's empty pre-dawn streets and brought Mia Silver closer to meeting her son.

End of Book Two

Bonus Chapter

December 31, 1999
New York City

Michael Portman was in no mood to celebrate Y2K.

How the hell did I get conned into this? He wondered as he walked up Seventh Avenue, a bottle of chilled Perrier-Jouet champagne in hand. I just want to go to my apartment, sit around in sweats, read, watch an old movie and be left the fuck alone. I don't want to fake merriment, have forced conversations with strangers I don't know and will never see again.

As he continued to walk, his mood and motivation continued to sink lower.

Climbing the stone front steps to Charles Sloan's brownstone, he cursed his old college roommate for coercing him into coming to his Millennium New Year's Eve party.

"C'mon," Charles had said, "You've been back in the states for several months now, have you even had a single date?"

"You know what it's like when you're the new guy in the office," Michael defended himself. "I've got to work double time just to prove myself to the staff here."

"Seriously, man, have you had anyone in your life since Yvette?"

Michael remained silent.

"I thought so," Charles went on. "And that was what? Over three years ago?" Not waiting for a response, "You'll have a blast at the party. I'm co-hosting it with my friend, Mia, and we've given her very creative assistant, Seth, a healthy budget to design the party. I know him, he'll come up with something amazing."

Michael stood outside the front door, debating whether or not to ring the bell or make a quick escape, when another couple came up the stone stoop behind him. It was too late, he had to go in. Nodding to the couple, Michael pressed the bell.

A nice looking, overtly gay man in a white dinner jacket and black bowtie answered, "Come in, handsome." He kissed Michael on both cheeks and took the champagne bottle from him, "I'm Seth." Grabbing a champagne coupe from a passing waiter's tray, he handed it to Michael, "Enjoy the party."

Wandering the brownstone, Michael was very impressed with what

Seth had done with the budget Charles and Mia had given him. This was as close to the set of the movie "Casablanca" as he had ever seen. It felt romantic and he felt like a freedom fighter off in a deeply mystical and exotic locale. The tinkling of crystal champagne glasses, chatter and laughter, and Big Band music permeating the air, added to the atmosphere's authenticity.

Standing to the side, he observed the groups of people talking, but he was Rick Blaine, the Humphrey Bogart character; cool, detached, watching from the edges and staying just a centimeter above the fray, giving the impression he was a part of things when he knew clearly that he was not, nor did he wish to be. He had perfected the protection technique. Pleasant, but aloof.

A tiny brunette with big green eyes and a slightly turned-up nose was floating from group to group, introducing people and then making her way on, leaving her newly formed groups deep in conversation.

That must be Charles' friend, Mia, Michael thought and he watched her work the room, fascinated at how she could get people involved with one another with her bright smile. *That woman doesn't have a shy bone in her body,* he thought and began to look around the room trying to figure out which guy was her boyfriend. Whoever he is, Michael decided, that is one secure guy who doesn't mind standing in her diminutive but powerful shadow.

Michael looked at his watch. Eleven thirty-five. Well, he certainly couldn't leave before midnight, but by twelve twenty, twelve twenty-five, he could be grabbing his coat and leaving. After midnight wouldn't be considered rude to leave, he figured.

Snatching another glass of champagne off a passing tray, Michael tried to put a smile on his face and stood at the periphery of a group. After a few minutes, the overwhelming feeling of not belonging, of truly being an outsider, was becoming oppressive, stealing his air with reality, and all he wanted to do was loosen his tie and fill his lungs.

Making his way down the staircase to the lower level of the duplex, Michael walked to the back of the brownstone and slid open the door to the small walled garden. Being immediately hit in the face by the cold air was invigorating and he let it wash over him and claim him. After a moment, he took a deep breath and was thankful that it swept away the heaviness that had surrounded him all evening.

In the shadows of the garden, a stone bench faced the back of the brownstone. The cold from the stone immediately permeated his pants as he sat down. It felt good, but he knew it was too cold to stay out there for too long. Looking up, there were no stars. The night sky held a reddish-white cast and he just stared up at it, enjoying the solitude.

He heard the door open and out walked a woman. She was backlit from the windows in the house and he couldn't make out her features until she was fairly close.

She took a deep breath and let it out with a huge sigh. Watching her face crumble, her eyes squeeze shut with what appeared to be pain and her small shoulders droop with the exhale, it was clear the happy woman he had seen inside was anything but happy. What he had seen in the brownstone was all an act, and now outside, where she was unaware that anyone was watching her, she unmasked as she stood before him, her emotions unrobed, naked, and two words immediately flooded his mind – Haunted Heart. Without her seemingly brilliant disguise, Mia Silver was as lost and alone as he was, and it took every ounce of willpower he possessed not to leap up from his bench in the shadows and envelop her in his arms.

Feeling voyeuristic, he knew that he should make his presence known, but she had taken his breath away. In the party's light, he had thought she was cute, her energy invigorating, but by the muted glow of the moonless night, there was an ethereal beauty in her sadness. This was the real Mia and he wondered how many people had ever seen her. He surmised not many as her shell was perfectly crafted. He wanted to draw her into his chest, tell her it was all going to be ok now. He'd found her. She'd be ok. They'd be ok. And just those thoughts surprised him deeply. Seeing her cracked shell made him yearn to shed his own armor and stand there undisguised and vulnerable right alongside her.

With a profound sadness rimming her big green eyes, she took a few more steps toward the back of the garden and Michael held his breath, so as not to disturb her. At just a few feet away, their eyes met and she jumped with fright, spilling her champagne.

"I'm so sorry. I didn't mean to scare you. Can I get you a napkin or a towel?" He felt awful, he should have made his presence known the minute she walked outside. The look in her eyes when she jumped was true fear. Fight or flight. And he imagined she was feeling the effects of an adrenaline rush.

"No. No. Stay there, I'm fine. I didn't mean to intrude on you. I didn't see you there."

Ever the gracious hostess, Michael thought.

"No intrusion. Would you like to sit?" He made room for her.

They sat in comfortable silence for a moment breathing in the cold air. Surprised that the social butterfly he had witnessed earlier actually reveled in silence made him immediately like her. She wasn't one of those people who constantly needed to fill the silence with chatter. She respected it. Basked in it.

"I just needed some fresh air to re-energize," she finally broke the silence.

Michael smiled to himself. She was embarrassed by what she unknowingly revealed to him when she thought she was in the garden alone. Not wanting to further embarrass her, he went along with it, "You were really working the room."

And then her personality emerged again, "Don't kid yourself. Being a hostess is a tough job."

It was impossible to suppress a smile around her and he wondered how many times she'd been told that she was adorable. "Sometimes being a guest is tough, too," he shared his secret with a smile.

"I'm Mia Silver."

"Yes, I figured."

"You did?"

Suppressing a groan nearly killed him as her nose scrunched up. *Could she get any cuter?*

"Yes, Charles had mentioned he was co-hosting the party with his friend, Mia."

Looking at him out of the corner of her eyes, "And you are?"

Dumb ass, where are your manners? he self-chastised. *Great way to make a first impression.* "Oh, I'm sorry. How rude of me. I'm Michael Portman."

Extending his hand, Mia slipped her small hand into his and immediately he could see them slowly sauntering around The Village on a Saturday morning, hand in hand, wandering in and out of shops.

"How do you know Charles?" She shivered slightly and wrapped her arms around herself.

Without thinking, Michael removed his suit jacket, wrapped it around her small shoulders, and pulled it closed around her to ensure she stayed warm. Mia looked up at him, and in that instant, he wished he knew her better so that he could understand the look she was giving him. She looked shocked by his simple gesture. Smiling down at her, he could see she wanted to smile back, but was refraining and he wondered why.

They sat and talked in the garden until a few minutes before midnight. Both shivering, Mia stood and extended her hand to him. Taking it in his, Michael stood, towering over her. She looked up at him with a smile, as if she liked what she saw and his heart skipped a beat. This was so unexpected. She was so unexpected.

As one century passed into another they stood together talking. Feeling the discomfort and awkwardness radiate off her as couples around them began to kiss, he once again felt the need to comfort her, ease the anxiety that seemed to be rushing in at her in waves from all directions. Reaching down, he tipped her chin up with his thumb and forefinger. Looking into her eyes, he smiled down at her. Everything in his being wanted to tell her, "Don't worry, it's going to be ok," but instead he showed her. Being more forward than was generally his style, Michael bent down and kissed Mia softly, the feeling of her lips lingering on his long after the kiss ended.

"Happy New Year, Mia."

Unexpectedly, she reached up, laying her hand tenderly on his cheek, "Happy New Year, Michael."

She didn't remove her hand and he felt like he was her anchor. And he wanted to be her anchor. Not since Yvette had he been so drawn to a woman or felt the desire to come out of himself enough to really want to get to know someone else.

As he gazed into her eyes, the joy that he felt at this moment they were having, this connection, made him feel like a dark, scratchy blanket had been lifted off his shoulders. A blanket that had weighed him down, shrouding him like a relentless low deck of gray clouds. In Mia's eyes, he saw hope and possibility, endless hours of laughter and blue skies. In that moment, he finally felt at home again being back in New York. Maybe she was his anchor.

And then he saw the look he had seen in the garden when she didn't know he was there. She was letting him in. She was showing him. Fear of hurt? Is that what he was seeing? His heart soared that she felt connected enough to show him—especially since this time she knew he was looking.

It's okay. You're okay with me. I promise. It's going to be okay now. For both of us. This is why we're both here tonight. You are the reason why I'm not home in bed in my sweats eating Chinese food out of a take-out container. We're both supposed to be right here. Right now.

As *Auld Lang Syne* segued into Casablanca's penultimate love song *As Time Goes By*, he realized they'd been so caught up in their moment that they hadn't moved.

"Here's looking at you, Kid." He shared the film's classic line of affection with her.

Her smile was immediate and he knew she got the reference and its deeper meaning, making his heart overflow. She was totally in the moment with him. Totally in sync. And in that instant, it occurred to him that maybe the lyrics of the song were wrong. Maybe a kiss was not just a kiss. Maybe it was oh so much more.

Moore Than Forever

Julie A. Richman

Table of Contents

Schooner & Mia 525
Chapter One 527
Chapter Two 530
Chapter Three 534
Chapter Four 536
Chapter Five 538
Chapter Six 541
Chapter Seven 545
Chapter Eight 547
Chapter Nine 550
Chapter Ten 554
Chapter Eleven 558
Chapter Twelve 562
Chapter Thirteen 565
Chapter Fourteen 567
Chapter Fifteen 570
Chapter Sixteen 572
Chapter Seventeen 580
Chapter Eighteen 587
Chapter Nineteen 590
Chapter Twenty 592
Chapter Twenty-One 595
Chapter Twenty-Two 600
Chapter Twenty-Three 603
Chapter Twenty-Four 605
Chapter Twenty-Five 608
Chapter Twenty-Six 610
Chapter Twenty-Seven 614
Chapter Twenty-Eight 616
Chapter Twenty-Nine 620
Chapter Thirty 625
Chapter Thirty-One 628
Chapter Thirty-Two 631
Chapter Thirty-Three 634
Chapter Thirty-Four 638
Chapter Thirty-Five 640
Chapter Thirty-Six 647

Chapter Thirty-Seven 650
Chapter Thirty-Eight 654
Chapter Thirty-Nine 662
Chapter Forty 664
Chapter Forty-One 666
Chapter Forty-Two 668
Chapter Forty-Three 672
Chapter Forty-Four 674
Chapter Forty-Five 676
Chapter Forty-Six 678
Chapter Forty-Seven 682
Chapter Forty-Eight 685
Chapter Forty-Nine 689
Chapter Fifty 692
Chapter Fifty-One 698
Chapter Fifty-Two 701
Chapter Fifty-Three 703
Chapter Fifty-Four 705
Chapter Fifty-Five 708
Chapter Fifty-Six 710
Chapter Fifty-Seven 714
Chapter Fifty-eight 719
Chapter Fifty-Nine 722
Chapter Sixty 726
Chapter Sixty-One 730
Chapter Sixty-two 733
Bonus Chapters 736
Aiden & Holly 739

D.D.R.

3/9/26-2/15/13

The signposts were there. I just needed to follow them …

sign•post

[sahyn-pohst] *noun*

1. a post bearing a sign that gives information or guidance.

2. any immediately perceptible indication, obvious clue, etc.

Origin:

1610–20; sign + post1

Schooner & Mia

Chapter One

Now...

Kami and Seth were seated in a distant corner of the Maternity Waiting Room at NYU Langone Medical Center when Charles Sloan arrived.

"Any news?" He tossed his leather bomber jacket onto the chair next to Seth, too keyed up to take a seat himself.

"No, all we know is that she is in with Gary and we think he's going to do an emergency C-section on her." Kami took a sip of the lukewarm coffee she had picked up at an all-night grocer. Making a face, she wondered aloud, "Why am I still drinking this?"

Pacing the waiting room, Charles casually surveyed the other occupants, although there was actually nothing casual about what the trained security professional was doing. Circling back to Seth and Kami, he stopped to ask them, "Do you know what time Schooner's flight gets in?"

"No," they responded in unison.

"I'll bet he's beating himself up that he is not here with her," Charles was shaking his head. "Poor Meezie, how scary for her to be in there all alone after everything that has happened this fall. Thank God, Gary is her doctor. At least he's a familiar face."

Seth was biting his nails, "I've been such a bitch to her for the past week. I feel terrible."

"She'll love you again once she's seen that nursery." Kami patted his hand and Seth looked satisfied.

"Let me find out when Schooner's flight gets in. I'll either go or I'll send one of my guys to pick him up and bring him straight here." Charles pulled out his phone and began texting, as he resumed his pacing.

Charles: What time does your flight get in? I'll have someone pick you up.

Five minutes went by before a text came through to Charles' phone.

Schooner: I'm not on a flight. What are you talking about?

"What the fuck?" was Charles' kneejerk reaction. Looking at Kami and Seth, he was totally perplexed. "Would she not have told him? She told all of us."

"Maybe she didn't want to worry him?" Kami conjectured, but knew that didn't make sense the minute it was out of her mouth. "No, he would have been her first call," and with a weary look, she shook her head, "unless she was really pissed off about something."

Panic flashed across Seth's face as the other two looked to him for an answer. No one knew Mia Silver like Seth Shapiro. "Oh no," he began dramatically, "I have a feeling Vindictive BBC is in the house."

"Shit, I need to call Schooner." Turning, Charles walked out into the hall.

Schooner answered on the first ring, "Hey Bud, what's up?

"When was the last time you spoke to Mia?"

"About 9 P.M. your time. What's going on? Is she okay?" Immediate alarm was evident in Schooner's voice.

It took a moment for Charles to process that Mia had not called Schooner to let him know that their son was about to be born, seven weeks prematurely. *What the heck was going on?*

"I got a text from Mia a little before five this morning saying that her water had broken and she was on her way to the hospital."

"Oh my God. Is she okay? Is the baby okay?"

"She's in surgery with Gary right now. None of us have seen or talked to her, so we don't know what's going on."

"I have to get there. I'm going to drive up to LAX now and get on the first flight. Even then, I won't be there until late afternoon. Shit," he paused, "shit, shit, shit."

Charles could hear Schooner moving around on the other end as if he were quickly packing.

"You've got to keep me updated." Alarm had escalated to panic.

"You know I will," Charles reassured him.

"Crap Charles, I had a huge fight with her tonight. She wanted to know when I was coming home and I told her that I didn't know. She was really upset and hung up on me and I didn't call her back. Fuck, I could kick myself."

"Hey, no one knew this was going to happen," Charles was trying to calm his friend, knowing he was about to get behind the wheel of a car.

"Yeah, but she's going through it alone and I'm not there for her. I'm going to miss Nathaniel's birth. I'm not there for them. If something happens to either of them…"

Charles could hear a car door slamming and an engine starting. "Schooner, be careful driving. Call me when you have flight info and I'll keep you updated on events here."

"Hey Charles, if you see her, tell her I love her. And tell her that I'm on my way."

"I will. We'll see you this afternoon."

Walking back into the waiting room, Seth immediately jumped on him, "You have that 'Oh shit' look on your face."

Charles sat down next to Kami and faced the two of them. "He didn't know," shaking his head. "Meezie didn't call him."

"What?" Seth was shocked.

"It seems they had a huge fight earlier tonight. She wanted to know when he was coming home and he told her he didn't know. She hung up on him and he never called her back."

"Not a good move, Schooner." Kami was shaking her head.

"You know he's kicking himself. He's on his way to LAX right now."

"Yeah, but he wasn't here with her, he's not in there with her now and if anything happens to Nathaniel, he's not here for it." Kami put down the nasty coffee and stood up. She turned to Seth.

"Don't give me that look, Kami. I know how ugly this is going to be. She didn't let him know. That is the ultimate fuck you."

As they waited for news on Mia and Nathaniel, a dark pall settled over them. Mia had drawn a line in the sand, and by not letting Schooner know, she was clearly telling him that she was ready to go it alone.

"He was really just trying to do the right thing," Charles defended. "The guy is a really good father."

Seth looked distraught. "He is. He takes it very seriously, but right now he is missing the birth of his son and the circumstances here are not optimal."

Trying to lighten the air, Kami was resolute on remaining positive, "They'll work it out. They love each other."

Seth looked at her as if she were the ultimate BBC. "Oh please, have you ever met Vindictive BBC?" He shook his head. "My beautiful nursery may never get used."

Chapter Two

Night had fallen when he entered her hospital room. Lights from the city's buildings filtered in through the blinds' slats, casting patterned shadows across her bed.

Silently, Kami rose from a chair in the corner of the room when he entered. He went to her and gave her a hug.

"Have you seen him?" her voice a mere whisper.

He nodded. Even in the darkened room, the wet glint from his moist eyes was visible. "I held him. He's so tiny and so beautiful. How is she feeling?"

"She did well today. They've already had her up walking and she fed Nathaniel."

He nodded again and just watched her sleep.

Putting a hand on his arm, "Call me if you need anything."

Schooner silently pulled a chair over to Mia's bedside. He wanted to kiss her forehead, her hand, her lips, but he didn't, for fear of waking her.

It had taken forever to get to New York. As if the forces of nature had conspired against him, weather delays had backed up many major airports and planes had not been repositioned. Charles Sloan had given him the news that his son had been born. At four pounds-two ounces, Nathaniel was breathing on his own, being monitored closely in the NICU in an open crib with heat lamps.

Exhaustion and the come down from adrenaline were taking hold. Silently, he lowered the railing on her bedside and pulled his chair in close. Laying his head down on the bed next to her, he closed his heavy eyelids.

He had missed Nathaniel's birth and she hadn't answered his cell phone calls. His heart was heavy knowing the rift this was going to cause between them. Mourning a moment he had missed, a memory he had never created slashed at his heart - there was no way he was ever going to get it back - not through hoping or dreaming, his money couldn't buy it, this was not a situation he could wheel or deal or charm his way through. Never would he share the memory of his son's birth or be there to comfort Mia through the procedure. He would never be the first person to hold his son and he only had himself to blame for it.

As he lay there with his head on the hospital mattress next to her, he mourned the loss of a moment that would never be born for him, memories he would never possess. And he was so disappointed in himself for failing her, yet once again.

Feeling her stir, he realized that he'd been asleep. Her hand hit him in the forehead, and he took it in his and brought it to his lips, kissing her knuckles softly and holding it gently against his lips. Her grip momentarily tightened and her eyelids began to flutter, then open slightly.

"Hey, Baby Girl, how are you feeling?" He smiled up at her.

The corners of her lips began to curve up into a smile and then he watched as a veil descended over her eyes and her half smile rapidly receded. The blood in his veins chilled at her reception.

"I held him last night when I got in. He's so beautiful, Mia." His eyes filled with tears.

She did not respond and he went on. "I am so sorry I was not here for you, Baby Girl. I was trying so hard to balance everything and I clearly was not listening when you were reaching out to me. I feel like shit, Mia, and I'm devastated that I hurt you and that I wasn't here for you and that I wasn't here for Nathaniel. I missed possibly the greatest moment we could ever share."

Observing him with a detached glare, her voice was flat as she spoke her first words to him. "You chose to be with your family, Schooner." She pulled her hand out of his.

"You're my family, Mia. Nathaniel is my family."

"Nathaniel is a baby you fathered, Schooner."

Stricken by her words, he sat there in silence. "I know you don't mean that. You're mad at me and disappointed in me, but I know you don't mean that."

"You really don't know anything, do you?" her eyes were hard slits, her face an impervious mask.

"I know I didn't just father him. I'm his father. I do know that. We're a family, Mia. That I know, too." His exhaustion was starting to give way to defeat and he was trying to fight it. "Baby Girl…"

"Don't you call me that," she hissed. "Get out of here. I don't want you here. Go back to California. Go back to your family. Nathaniel and I don't need you. We'll be fine without you. Get out," she was screaming.

A nurse rushed into the room, alarmed.

"I'm just leaving," he snapped at the woman. As he stood, a paper on the night table caught his eye. It was the form to be filled out for Nathaniel's birth certificate. In Mia's neat print was the name, Nathaniel

James Silver.

Gutted, he turned to Mia and leaned down. Taking her chin in his hand, his face an inch away, he stared deep into her eyes. "You don't want to do this. You really don't want to do this."

Her eyes widened at his unveiled threat, momentarily taken aback at his forceful words and their meaning. "Get the fuck out of here," she spat.

"With ple…," he snarled, stopping himself mid-word, he checked his anger.

Releasing her chin, he straightened up, his eyes never leaving hers. With his eyes locked on hers, he stood there for a long moment, then shook his head.

"I am sorry." Turning, he walked out of her hospital room without a backwards glance.

Gary was standing at the nurse's station commenting on a chart when he saw Schooner coming toward him. With a smile and a handshake, "Congratulations, Schooner. That's quite a little warrior that you've got."

"A little warrior," Schooner scoffed, "maybe that is because his mother is the goddess of war."

Gary laughed, "I'm going to start calling her Athena. That'll really piss her off. What's going on? Did she give you a rough time?"

"She threw me out." Schooner leaned against the nurse's station, catching his breath. "She told me I wasn't Nathaniel's father, just someone who fathered him."

"Wow," Gary's brows knit together, "Athena was pulling no punches. Give her a day or two, Schooner. Her hormones are all over the place, she's trying to get her milk to come down, she just had major surgery. Her body really doesn't know if it's coming or going. Add that on top of the disappointment that you weren't here with her and the fear that something was going to go wrong, and that's why you're seeing this over the top response." He clapped Schooner on the shoulder. "I'll talk to her, but for now, let's go visit your boy."

Schooner nodded. Overwhelmed and exhausted and in love with this tiny little person, he knew one thing for sure, he, Mia and Nathaniel were a family and he was not going to lose them.

Gary walked into Mia's room to find her intently focused on the breast pump the lactation specialist had left behind. On her chest was a blanket that Nathaniel had been wrapped in, his scent being used as a stimulus to help bring her milk down.

"Frustrating, huh?" Gary smiled.

"Nothing's coming in yet." Mia looked stricken.

Gary sat down next to the bed and rubbed Mia's arm gently. "Give it time, your body has some catching up to do. In the meantime, he's doing very well with the donated breast milk."

Mia's eyes filled with tears. "I want it to be mine, Gary."

He smiled. "It will be, Mia. Who would have ever thought my little wild child patient would have such a strong maternal instinct?" He gave Mia's hand a squeeze and stood. The same piece of paper that had caught Schooner's attention earlier now caught his eye. He picked it up, read it, then folded it and put it into the pocket of his white doctor's coat.

Sitting back down, his demeanor serious, "Okay, now I'm your friend of nearly twenty years talking to you. I'm not letting you walk out of the hospital with this." He patted his pocket.

Mia's brows knit together and Gary could tell she was gearing up to argue. Athena was in the room.

"Mia, that man's biggest problem is that he loves his kids too much. When it comes to his children, he goes into protect and fix mode. Whether or not Zac's issues can be fixed is another whole story. But what does that mean for you? That means that little boy down the hall is the luckiest baby in that nursery. He has a father who would literally lay down his life for him. Unfortunately, in today's world, we don't see enough of that."

Mia remained silent and Gary got up to leave. As he reached the door, he turned, "You weren't happier without him. You've been happy for the first time in a long time. Work it out."

Chapter Three

"He's picking up my parents at the airport?" Ugh!" she groaned. "Whose brilliant idea was that?"

"His." Seth didn't look up from his iPhone.

"My mother is going to walk in here telling me how wonderful he is and what a bitch I'm being." Mia's face was screwed up in anger.

"God, you are a crazy hormonal bitch, BBC."

"Fuck you, Seth." Mia started to get out of the bed, her movements slow and limited by the C-section incision.

"Fuck you, too, BBC. Anybody who puts up with you is a saint."

"I'm going to see Nathaniel. Are you coming?" She put on her robe.

"Only if you lose that attitude. I don't want your negative energy around my nephew." Seth opened the door for Mia.

"You know I hate you for letting him go get my parents." She walked passed him.

"Yeah, well you need to get over that, you hormonal freak." Seth rolled his eyes and followed her down to the nursery.

Lois recognized him waiting at the bottom of the escalator. The minute he smiled, his real smile, this handsome man was the beautiful teen shaking her hand in front of Brewster Hall, a million lifetimes ago.

Only this time, he didn't take her hand, but instead enveloped her in a bear hug, pulling her tightly to his muscular chest. Yes, this was the sweet boy she remembered.

"Look at you." She smiled. "I would've recognized you anywhere."

Schooner shook Bob's hand and led them to the baggage carousel, his arm around Lois' shoulder.

"How are they?" She looked up into Schooner's clear eyes.

"Well, your daughter's not talking to me, but physically she seems to be doing well, and your grandson," he paused and took a deep breath, smiling, "he's amazing. He's doing beautifully. The neo-natal pediatrician said, besides being small, everything else is perfect." He dug out his phone and handed it to them, a picture of Nathaniel in his arms.

Lois looked at him. "He is beautiful. So tiny. I think he looks like you."

"Really?" Schooner looked at the picture, taking the phone back from Lois. "I think he looks like Mia."

"I think so, too," Bob agreed.

As they headed into the city, Schooner offered, "How about if I drop you off at the hospital and I'll take your bags down to Mia's apartment? You can stay there."

"Where are you staying?" Bob was concerned with the logistics of Mia's one-bedroom apartment.

"Well, I bought a loft downtown and I'm staying there." Schooner kept his eyes on the road, dodging crazy rogue cab drivers.

"A loft? Does Mia know?" Lois was starting her reconnaissance mission.

Schooner shook his head, no. "It was my surprise for her for when she got out of the hospital."

Lois could see the tension in his jaw. His thoughts were openly displayed on his face as he prayed it wasn't going to be the home he shared with his young son every other weekend. Reaching out, she took Schooner's hand in hers and gave it a squeeze. He was still that sweet boy she had met long ago.

"Lois, I stayed away too long. It led her to believe that I didn't love her. I wasn't here for her when she needed me most. I missed Nathaniel's birth," his voice cracked on the last statement. Looking over at Lois, his eyes exposed deep pain and the specter of something much more haunting.

"Give her a little time. She's angry and disappointed, but the two of you did not find one another again just to be apart. I'm sure of that. Have faith, Schooner, this too shall pass."

He nodded, but remained silent.

Lois Silver was a force to be reckoned with, and Schooner Moore prayed that she would get through to her very strong-willed daughter. Not that he planned on giving up. He had vowed he would never lose Mia again and now that vow became even more critical - he would never lose Mia or Nathaniel. He just wished he possessed Lois' faith, because losing Mia and Nathaniel was not an option.

Chapter Four

Sitting behind a privacy curtain in the NICU, Mia held the syringe of donated breast milk to Nathaniel's lips and pressed down, releasing a few drops.

She and Lois laughed aloud, startling him, as he greedily lapped up the milk.

"I hope you like my milk as much when it comes in, munchkin." Mia handed him off to her mother. "Here, you feed him, Mom."

Lois stared down into her tiny grandson's face. "Hello, beautiful boy." Smiling at him, she released a little more of the milk. "Look at the size of his feet. He's going to have Schooner's height."

"What did he say?" Mia pressed, as she gently ran a finger up the silky soft skin of Nathaniel's leg.

"What do you think he said?" Lois' voice had an edge. "He's heartbroken. He wants to be sharing this with you." Lois gave her daughter a hard look. "Why didn't you tell me you were alone, Mia, I would've come up and helped you."

Mia didn't look up from stroking Nathaniel's leg. "Because every day I thought he was going to tell me he was coming home, and I knew you and Dad were coming up when the baby was born. It's not so easy for you guys to travel anymore, especially with Dad having had pneumonia in September. I didn't want you leaving him." Looking up at the ceiling, Mia struggled to fight back tears. "I just kept thinking he was coming home to me, Mom, and he didn't."

"He's here now, Mia. Don't doubt that he loves you and don't for a minute think there was anything going on between him and CJ."

Mia's tears began to flow. Lois had touched a nerve that was so raw and exposed, years couldn't bury or dull the pain.

"We don't know that, Mom."

"Yes, Sweetie, we do." Lois released a little more milk onto Nathaniel's lips. "Things weren't good between them before, do you really think now that he knows what she did to the two of you, that she is suddenly going to become attractive to him? I think you are letting your imagination get the best of you."

The syringe was empty and Mia put a burp pad on her shoulder. Lois handed Nathaniel back and Mia gently patted his back until a large burp escaped.

They laughed. "That was a manly burp," Mia said to her son, kissing the tip of his nose.

"Look at those eyes," Lois commented, marveling at her beautiful grandson.

Mia smiled. "They're Schooner Blue." Looking up at her mom, she asked, "Is he staying with you at the apartment?"

Lois shook her head no and more tears rolled down Mia's cheeks.

"I see," she whispered. "I'm going to stay here after Gary releases me. They have rooms onsite for family. This way I'll be able to stay with him and feed him my milk once it comes in."

Lois ached to tell her about the loft Schooner had bought for them, but knew she needed to stay out of it, as difficult as that might be.

Chapter Five

On day four Mia's colostrum finally came in, and she cried as she fed Nathaniel the nutrient and antibody rich fluid from her body. The thick yellow liquid almost seemed symbolic to Mia, cementing the bond she was forming with her tiny son. She and Schooner had not crossed paths again, although she heard from everyone that he was constantly at the hospital. It made her wonder if he was purposely staying out of her path to avoid another confrontation.

It was on day five that Mia's breast milk had fully let down, and she headed to the NICU with a syringe filled with the warm milk.

Upon entering, she noticed Nathaniel's crib was empty and a Jamaican nurse pointed to one of the closed curtained areas. Quietly, Mia approached the curtain's opening and peeked in.

His back was to her and she could see Nathaniel resting in his large hands. Oblivious to her presence, he hadn't skipped a beat in his monologue.

"It's not a well-known fact, but I am a champion sandcastle builder. Yup. Bet you didn't know that. So, I am going to teach you all about the fine art of building sandcastles. I'm also going to teach you how to surf. Yeah, your old man's a California boy, so yes, I surf and we'll get you out on a board as soon as you know how to swim. Now your mommy is going to teach you all about body surfing. She is excellent at knowing how and when a wave is going to break and how to best ride it into shore. She has this sixth sense about the ocean, so I'm going to let her teach you that. She's also going to be the one to teach you about clamming. There's a whole science to that and I'm sure the minute you have your first pail and shovel, she's going to have you digging up clams." He paused and took one of Nathaniel's hands in his, placing a finger on his palm. "Look at that, your grip is getting stronger, even from yesterday. I can't wait to start coaching you in tennis. In a couple of years, you're going to be kicking my butt on the court."

Nathaniel gurgled and Schooner brought him up to his face and kissed his tiny son's cheek. "So, you do know your mommy and I both love you very much and we both will always be there for you. I don't know if it will be together. I hope it will be. But even if it isn't, I can guarantee you that both Mommy and I will always put you first. You know why? Because we love you that much. You will always be the number one priority in both of our lives. So, don't you worry, big guy, no matter what happens, Mommy and I will always be there for you."

Feeling a lump in her throat, Mia involuntarily sniffed before she could stop herself.

Schooner turned around, realizing for the first time that he and Nathaniel were not alone. At the sight of Mia, his face broke into a sad smile. "Mommy's here, Buddy."

Motioning for her to sit, Mia silently sat down on the chair next to him.

"Do you want me to go?" Concern for not wanting her to be uncomfortable was clear in his voice.

Shaking her head no, she smiled at Nathaniel nestled in Schooner's big hands. "Would you like to feed him?" she held up the syringe.

"Is that yours?"

Nodding, "It just came in today. The colostrum came down yesterday and I fed it to him last night." She placed it in his hand.

"So, this is the first of your milk."

Mia could see the mixture of sadness and awe in his eyes. "Yes, it is."

Schooner cradled Nathaniel in the crook of his right arm and put the syringe to his lips. He depressed the stopper a little and deposited the first drops of Mia's milk. A hungry Nathaniel's lips started to work immediately, lapping at the milk. The sound from deep in Schooner's throat was a combination of a laugh and a sob as he smiled through his tears. Intently, he fed Nathaniel the remainder of Mia's milk without looking up.

Mia placed a burp pad on Schooner's shoulder and Nathaniel looked like a toy against him. Gently, he patted and rubbed the baby's back until he let out a sizable burp.

"He must get that from your family," Schooner kidded.

Looking over at Mia, he smiled and leaned over to wipe a tear that was rolling down her cheek. Nathaniel was already fast asleep on his shoulder.

"He is amazing, Mia."

"He looks like you." It was difficult for her to choke out the sentence.

"I think he looks like you." Reaching over, Schooner gave her hand a squeeze.

"He has your eyes."

Schooner smiled. "Yeah, I noticed that."

Standing, he extended his free hand to Mia to help her up from the chair. Clearly stiff and still hurting from the surgery, she rose slowly, her movements deliberate to minimize the pain. Schooner and Nathaniel left the curtained area and Mia followed them.

With the baby back in his crib, they both stood there silently and watched his peaceful sleep, his little lips still moving as he made a bevy of funny faces.

"Where can we go to talk?" Schooner gently stroked Mia's hair, his eyes pleading.

"Nice assumptive close," she laughed.

Schooner gave her his real smile. "I was definitely not making that a yes/no question."

"Your daddy is a smart one, Nathaniel. Don't let those pretty boy looks fool you."

And together, for the first time, Schooner and Mia left the NICU nursery.

Chapter Six

They walked the hall in an uneasy silence to the on-site room where Mia was staying. Schooner entered the sparsely furnished quarters behind Mia. A bed, a night stand with three drawers, a straight-backed wooden chair and a recliner/rocker filled the cramped space.

Mia sat on the side of the bed facing the recliner and Schooner sat down across from her, perched on the seat's edge.

"I'm glad we're going to talk," he began. "Mia, I think you already know how sorry I am that I wasn't here for you, that I wasn't listening to you when you were trying to tell me you needed me, and that I wasn't here for you and Nathaniel when you went into labor." He paused, "I'm beyond sorry and I'll tell you that again and again and hopefully you'll see how sincere I am in my apology. My words can't even express my remorse."

Closing his eyes for a moment, Schooner attempted to gather his thoughts, "Where do I even begin with all this?"

"I'll start it for you," Mia began. "You moved back in with your wife and chose to keep the family you had. They are your priority. Beginning and end of story."

Opening his eyes, Schooner looked at Mia, shock registering on his face. Their gaze locked and they sat there, in silence, for what felt like an uncomfortable eternity. Remaining silent, he stood.

She looked up at him, defiance in her eyes.

Slowly, he crossed the space over to the bed where she sat. Sitting down next to her, he pulled her onto his lap and lay back against the pillows, pulling her along with him.

"What are you doing?" She was shocked by his move.

"I'm not sitting across from you having this conversation. I'm going to have it with you in my arms. I haven't held you for nearly a month." Wrapping his arms around her tightly and pulling her back up against his chest, Schooner buried his face in Mia's neck. "Are you ready to hear what I have to say?"

"Do I have a choice?"

"No."

"I didn't think so," Mia sighed. "Okay, I'm listening."

Schooner sighed back into Mia's neck. "There's so much I want to say to you. I think you got the wrong impression about me staying at the house. And I'm sorry, Mia, maybe I'm dense, or wasn't anticipating what you would feel, but I didn't think it would be an issue for you. You know how I feel about you, Baby Girl." When she didn't answer, he continued, "Clearly, I should have communicated everything a lot better than I did, but it was difficult because I was rarely alone, except for late at night, and with the three-hour time difference it was the middle of the night here and I never wanted to wake you. I wanted you to get your rest. And when we did talk, there was always someone within ear shot, so I was limited in how openly I could speak and what I could say to you."

"Why didn't you just stay at a hotel, Schooner?"

"Because I had to see what was really going on, Mia. If I'd stayed at a hotel, I would have had limited access to a lot of information and probably seen more of a staged show than the reality of the situation."

Mia turned her head to look at him, "What kind of information?"

With his chin resting on her shoulder, he began, "I wanted to get a good handle on the dynamic between CJ and Zac. Zac has been away at boarding school for the past few years and then he was overseas, so CJ has never had to be a full-time mother to a teenage boy. She literally has only seen him on vacations for the past few years. I was concerned that she was being neglectful, that she wasn't setting any boundaries for him and frankly, that she was an unfit mother, and that without me being there to balance things out, that maybe I had sent him into an unhealthy and somewhat dangerous situation."

"And did you come to a conclusion?"

"I did. I'm sending him back to Exeter right after Christmas break. It was the soonest I could get him back in. Mia…" he took her face by the chin and turned it toward him, "I'm sorry I was away for so long. I was walking a tightrope. I knew I needed to get back to you, and I really wanted to get him to a place where I wasn't dreading that the next phone call I got was from the police telling me that they'd found him dead in an alley. I was trying to get him to a point where I felt he wasn't a danger to himself and get back to you in plenty of time to be here to take care of you in the final weeks of your pregnancy. And then the tightrope snapped. I didn't say goodbye to him and I wasn't here for you and Nathaniel. I missed Nathaniel's birth. I can never get that back. I will mourn the loss of that moment for the rest of my life."

"But you were living with her, Schooner," Mia's voice exuded anguish, her eyes shrouded in pain.

Schooner let go of her chin and wrapped his arms tightly around her again. Putting his face up against hers, he kissed her temple. "You see, I didn't anticipate old ghosts creeping in, Mia. I know what you and I have. I'm secure in that. I know how I feel about you. I hate that the old ghosts got to you and made you lose faith. I hate that. And honestly, Baby Girl, that hadn't even crossed my mind. Not very empathetic of me. I see that now. But it was so far away from my reality and I just assumed you were right there on that same page with me."

With his cheek pressed against hers, he continued, "Before I even knew how to find you, things were bad with CJ and had been toxic for a very long time. The minute I found you, and found out what she had done to you, to us… well, being in the same room with her became unbearable. And then I came here, and you and I have this amazing relationship, and I'm happy and I now know what a great relationship is like, how it's supposed to feel. That actually made being out there with her 100,000 times worse. And I also realized something while I was out there, what you and I share now is an adult relationship, and I've never really been involved in an adult relationship. But now I know the difference, Mia. I know what it's supposed to be like. I finally know what being in a loving relationship with someone you love deeply is all about. And I couldn't help but to keep comparing 'us' to what it was like to be around her and to what I had shared with her. And it made me miss you more every second of every day. CJ and I formed some very unhealthy patterns as teens and that is how we interact and react to one another. It's not pleasant and it's not healthy. Does that make sense?"

When she didn't answer, he whispered, "Hey, look at me."

She didn't turn her head and he reached for her chin.

"Don't cry, Baby Girl, please don't cry." His eyes locked intently upon hers. "This should be the happiest time of our lives. I hate that there is even a single second that we are not sharing this together. I hate it, Mia. And I'm sorrier than you can imagine for everything I didn't do right here. And I didn't do a lot right. I know that. But you and the kids, all three of them, will always be my top priority to care for, provide for and protect. That is just me. That is who I am - for better or for worse, and I promise I will listen when you tell me you need me. I will be here. I will listen. I promise, Mia. And I will try and understand that you and I might not be perceiving things in exactly the same way. Please believe me."

"You told me you didn't know when you were coming back, Schooner. I was pregnant with our son and you told me you didn't know when you were coming back to me." Her eyes conveyed the deep wound of their last phone conversation.

"I just kept thinking, a few more days and I can fix this. Just a few more days, that's all I need. And I thought you and I still had about six weeks. Or I guess I was just hoping that, because it would buy me the time I needed to feel like I was leaving him in a better place, and getting home to you with plenty of time to spare." He paused and let out a deep sigh, "I am so sorry I was such an ass to you that night. I'm sorry I didn't call you right back when you hung up on me. You deserved an apology."

"I can't do this, Schooner." Mia put her hands-on Schooner's arms, the first time she had touched him in nearly a month. "I can't sit back and do nothing while I watch you being manipulated. CJ is the master of knowing how to manipulate you. She's been doing it all our lives. If she needs to do it through the kids, because that is the only way she can still get to you, she will. I just can't have you floating in and out of Nathaniel's and my life every time she pushes one of your buttons. I can't do it and I won't do it."

"And you won't need to do it. Will I do everything in my power to keep my three kids safe and healthy? The answer to that is yes. You're a mom now, so you get it. You would lay down your life for that little boy. You'd leave me, if you had to, to protect him. But you're never going to need to do that. I'm never going to float out of Nathaniel's life and I'm never going to float out of your life. I am in this for the long haul, Mia, and if there's one thing that you should know about me, it's that I take the responsibility of fatherhood very, very seriously. I was not a sperm donor here. That little boy is my son, and I will raise him and teach him and love him and be there for him. Always. And I'm never going to love anyone else but you, Mia. I didn't find you again to lose you. You can be damn sure of that. So, we need to work through this, because I am not letting you go. That is not an option, Baby Girl, and running is not an option. We need to work this out."

Mia closed her eyes as the tension from her body dissipated, collapsing against Schooner as if she were a deflated balloon.

"I thought you were already gone." Hot tears streaming down her cheeks fell onto his arms.

Burying his face in Mia's neck, Schooner finally let his own tears flow. "Never, Baby Girl. Never."

Chapter Seven

"Have you even left the hospital for a meal?" They had just fed Nathaniel again and stood at his crib in the NICU watching him sleep. He'd already gained close to two ounces, pleasing both the doctors and his parents.

Mia shook her head no. "Just the cafeteria."

"How about if I call your parents, Kami and Seth, and Charles and Gaby and see if everyone wants to meet for dinner? If you're up to it, we're just a short walk from Le Parisien or the Cask Bar + Kitchen."

"Filet Mignon Carpaccio. You are good." She looked up at him.

Pulling her close to him and kissing the top of her head, he laughed, "Yeah, I know the way to your heart. Le Parisien, it is then." Wrapping her tighter in his arms, he whispered into her hair, "You don't know how much I've missed you."

Returning to her cubby hole of a room, Mia asked, "What are you doing this afternoon?"

"After I call everyone and make dinner reservations, I was kind of thinking I'd love to curl up next to you in that uncomfortable looking little bed. If that's okay with you?"

Mia nodded. Speaking would have invited tears and she was fighting very hard to control her way-over-the-top emotions.

He spooned up behind her on the bed and pulled her snugly against his body.

She heard the "mmm" come from deep in his throat and was glad he couldn't see her face.

"I haven't even asked you how you're healing? Does it hurt a lot?"

Mia nodded. "Yeah, but it was worth it."

"I could look at him all day." Schooner kissed her neck.

Rolling over to face him, Mia smiled. "Me too. I just look at him and I can't believe he's my baby. He's our baby. We have a baby together, Schooner. How mind blowing is that?"

Brushing her hair from her face, he took a moment just to reflect on her words. "We have a baby together, Mia," and he pulled her tightly against his chest. "It's incredibly mind blowing and it's a gift. A gift that a year ago wasn't even a part of my wildest dreams. I never thought I'd see you again, speak to you again, hold you again. And now you are the mother of my child. How's that for dreams coming true."

"Schooner," she pulled her face away from his chest, "I love you."

His clear eyes immediately became moist. "That's a good thing," he whispered, "because you are my world, Mia."

Reaching up, Mia traced Schooner's face with her fingertips as if committing every line and every plane to memory. "I have loved you my whole life, Schooner. Promise me her words are not true."

Searching her eyes, he asked, "What words, Mia?"

"That you'll always go back to her. That you always have and you always will."

Taking her face in both his hands, "Boy, did she do a number on you. It's time for an exorcism, Baby Girl. We need to bury that ghost, because it doesn't deserve a place in our lives. I love you. I have always loved you. I have never stopped loving you. I will never stop loving you. You are the love of my life, you always have been, you always will be. So, don't let her get into your head, Mia. She has no power over me. Her desperate acts will yield nothing. She's been threatened by you her entire life. She's lived with the knowledge that she could never hold the place in my heart that has always been reserved for you alone. You. Only you. Always. I am yours for the rest of my life, Baby Girl."

"So, I'm stuck with you?" she deadpanned.

"Bitch," he threw his head back with laughter. "Now, *that* is *my* Mia."

And for the first time in way too long, Schooner watched the devil grin take over Mia's face.

"I've missed that smile." He brought his lips close to hers. "I've missed these lips." Softly, he brushed his lips against hers.

"Welcome home, Pretty Boy," and with fingers twined through his thick hair, Mia pulled him in for a deep, consuming, incredibly long overdue kiss.

Chapter Eight

Five tables for two were pushed together in the small French bistro. Lois and Seth sat next to each other on the banquette side of the table against the wall, giving them a clear view of who entered the restaurant. Schooner had invited them all out to dinner and said the reservation would be under his name.

"He was very cryptic," Lois spoke to Seth in barely over a whisper.

"Yes, same with me. I hope this is not bad news. Have you seen Mia today?" Seth looked stressed.

"No, Bob and I met up with some old friends today. She didn't answer her cell this afternoon."

"I called her, too. No answer. I hope Nathaniel is alright." Seth's eyes were wide as he started to work himself into a tizzy.

Lois put a well-manicured hand on his arm. "No, we would have heard if there was a problem with the baby."

The door to the restaurant opened and Lois dug her nails into Seth's arm. Schooner and Mia walked in together. He opened the door for her and his hand was at her lower back as they approached the table.

"Hi everyone." Mia smiled as if it were just another normal night out with her loved ones.

"Please tell me I'm not dreaming," Seth whispered under his breath to Lois.

Schooner pulled out a chair for Mia to sit, and she looked up at him with a smile, as she sat down gingerly, still stiff from the surgery. Sitting next to her, he moved his chair close and his left arm went around the back of Mia's chair. He winked at Lois.

"Sorry we're late, we stopped off at the nursery and just lost track of time," Mia apologized. "He is so cute. I swear he gets more beautiful every day. The neo-natal doctor was in there and we had the chance to talk to him. He thinks we'll be able to take him home in about two weeks if he keeps gaining weight at the rate he's been going and no other complications arise. His breathing has been solid. No signs of apnea. He's just doing great."

"That is excellent news. Do you feel up to doing some clothes shopping for him tomorrow?" Lois wanted to get her daughter alone and find out what the hell was going on. Just yesterday she wasn't speaking to Schooner and tonight they'd entered Le Parisien as a couple looking happier than clams.

"I'm coming with you," Seth announced. He too wanted every detail of this sudden, yet overdue, reconciliation as well as to ensure that Nathaniel was appropriately dressed as a 'City Kid'.

Schooner flagged down a waiter and whispered something in his ear. He quickly returned with two bottles of champagne and glasses for everyone. Uncorking the first bottle and pouring enough for a toast into everyone's glass, he receded from the table with the same haste, leaving the other bottle chilling in a silver bucket next to Schooner.

Holding up his glass, Schooner began his toast. "This toast is to my son, Nathaniel. He entered this world with a surprise appearance and I think that is the first of many surprises we can expect from him. His second surprise, and a wonderful one it was, is that he was blessed with good health. May he continue to grow healthy and strong and know a life where he is surrounded by love. Everyone at this table is, and will be, such an important part of his world, and he will grow up knowing that he is loved and supported. Thank you to all of you for being a part of his world and my world. You have all become my family this year and I've been so lucky to be embraced by you and accepted into your world. Seth and Kami, thank you for everything you do for Mia every single day. I am in awe of your friendship and sometimes a little jealous," Schooner chuckled along with everyone, "and the words thank you don't do justice to my sentiments for taking care of Mia and helping her while I was gone. Gaby and Charles, from the first night you had me over your house, you made me feel like I'd been part of the gang for a million years. Although we've been friends for less than a year, I feel like I've known you my whole life."

Schooner turned to face Lois and Bob. "Brewster Hall. It was divine providence that you and my parents met in that orientation session, started to talk and hit it off. Of all the parents of students in the freshman class, it was a pretty random thing that the four of you would meet, but that meeting changed my life. Lois, I think it was love at first sight for the two of us."

Smiling at him, she nodded.

"You and I just had an instant connection. You knocked me off my feet, right from the start. And then your daughter came bounding up the walkway and I should have known, in that moment, that she would turn my world upside down. Even at sixteen, she was a crazy vortex of energy.

What I didn't immediately realize was that I would get sucked into that vortex and never want to get out. Bob, I made a promise to you and my dad that I would look out for Mia. I knew, as I was making that vow, that it would not be an easy task, that looking out for Mia would be like flying into the eye of a category four hurricane. My assessment was correct. And as much as I have tried to look out for her, I've probably had as much failure as I have had success. But I promise you, I'll continue to try to take care of your little girl. At least as much as she'll let me."

Schooner turned to Mia, who looked up at him, eyes shining as if the tears were ready to flow. "You," he shook his head. "You. It's always been you. It will always be you. Always. Thank you for loving me. Thank you for letting me love you. Thank you for giving me the gift of that precious little boy. There is no need to ever question my love for you. You will have it always. That is something I can easily promise. I love you and I don't ever want to be without you. Not ever again."

Leaning toward her, Schooner gave Mia a brief, sweet kiss on the lips. With his hand on her cheek, his gaze clearly mirrored the words he had just spoken. When he looked away, the rest of the table was wiping their tears, even Charles and Bob.

Schooner lifted his glass again, "To Nathaniel."

"To Nathaniel," was the resounding chorus from the table.

Reaching for Schooner's hand under the table, Mia realized that he was right when he told her that they needed to exorcise CJ's ghost and the specter of destruction that she had cast upon Mia. Schooner Moore loved her as much as she loved him. Watching him tell his infant son of his dreams of all they would share was confirmation of his dedication to ensuring their son grew up loved and with a strong, present and committed father figure.

Learning how to fight, cope, share victory, tragedy, hope and disappointment was something they were going to need to learn to do together, without running or retreating. Schooner had made it clear that he had no plans to let her go. Ever. And for the first time since the phone call that had summoned him back to California without her, Mia felt that they had made it through a dark tunnel and were back in the light again. Together. And maybe even stronger than before. He was hers and she finally believed in them.

Chapter Nine

Sitting in the backseat of the Range Rover next to Nathaniel's brand-new car seat, Mia was thrilled to finally be leaving the hospital.

"Yes, you are going home, Little Man. All these new sounds you're hearing, I bet they sound funny to you, huh?" Rearranging his blanket to ensure he stayed warm in the early winter chill, "Are you warm enough?" she asked her infant son, who was bundled up like a snowman in his snowsuit. "Uncle Seth's snowsuit is nice and snuggly, isn't it?"

Looking up, she peered out the window. Feeling slightly disoriented, at first, after a month of living at the hospital, she finally got her bearings and something wasn't adding up. "Schooner, why are we still on Second Avenue? We're heading into the Lower East Side."

"Yeah." He stayed focused on the road in front of him. Cabs cutting in on all sides.

"But we should have turned. Second Avenue is about to turn into Chrystie Street."

"Yeah, I'm aware of that. Do you think it's too soon to introduce Nathaniel to E Street Radio?" he changed the subject.

"Where are we going?" Mia's sixth sense was kicking into gear. Something was not right.

"Home. Oh excellent, they're already playing Bruce's version of *Santa Claus is Coming to Town*. Nathaniel, this is The Boss." Schooner made a right turn onto Broome Street and started to head into Little Italy. "We've never eaten in Little Italy," he commented. "Why is that?"

"Because there are better Italian restaurants elsewhere in the city." They were approaching SoHo. "Schooner, where are we going? Are we picking something up?"

Making a left onto Mercer Street, he finally replied, "No, we're dropping something off."

"What are we dropping off?" Mia was perplexed.

Stopping in front of a white building with a Corinthian columned entrance, he turned around and hit her with his All-American boy smile. "You. You and Nathaniel," and he got out of the car.

Coming around to her side, Schooner opened the door and helped Mia out. Reaching across the seat, he unlatched the car seat from its base and lifted it out of the car.

"I don't understand." Mia searched his face.

Leading her into the building's lobby and over to the elevator, he smiled and said, "You don't need to."

They entered an old lift and Schooner inserted a key into a slot and the elevator started to ascend. With a shit-eating grin on his face, he leaned down and whispered in her ear, "Showtime."

The elevator door opened to a sun-drenched loft. Schooner could tell that Mia was still not processing what was happening. "Welcome home, Baby Girl." He stepped out of the elevator and onto the loft's gleaming hardwood floors.

Mia stood in the elevator, not moving.

Facing her and taking obvious delight in her confusion, he asked, "Are you going to join us?" Turning around, he walked past the couch and put Nathaniel's carrier in the middle of the coffee table.

"I don't understand." Mia finally stepped out of the elevator. "Where are we?"

"We're home."

He could see by her face that it was finally starting to click as she looked around and saw some familiar artwork from her apartment.

"This is ours?" The grandeur of the real estate was seeping in as she tentatively began to walk around, gently touching the beautiful columns, marveling at the wood burning fireplace and running her hand along the honed Calcutta marble countertop in the open chef's kitchen. She turned to him again. "This is ours? We live here?"

Taking Nathaniel out of his carrier, Schooner sat down on the couch with him to remove his snowsuit. Looking up, he nodded, "Yes. We live here."

"We moved to SoHo?"

"We moved to SoHo."

"When did this happen?" Mia sat down next to Schooner and Nathaniel.

"Before I went to California." He looked pleased with himself.

"You didn't tell me."

"It was a surprise." He handed Nathaniel to her.

"I hate surprises," Mia announced.

Shaking his head, "I know." Smiling, he stood up. "Come, there are more surprises."

"Do we have the whole floor of this building?"

Nodding, "We do. Follow me."

The first stop was Seth's masterpiece. Nathaniel's jungle room elicited a gasp from Mia.

"You can thank Uncle Seth for this, Big Guy," Schooner ran his thumb down the baby's soft cheek.

"Seth knew about this?" Mia's eyes were wide.

"Yeah. He designed this room."

"It's exquisite. The details." Mia walked around the room. "Look at the painting on this furniture and the walls and the ceiling."

"He had a friend come in to do it. I love the tree branches painted on the ceiling. It really feels like the canopy of a jungle."

"Schooner…" Mia was in awe.

"So, I'm dying here, Mia. Do you like the loft?"

"Like doesn't even begin to describe it. This is space you see in design magazines. I'm speechless."

Slinging an arm over her shoulder, he pulled her into him. "Come, there's more."

"Does it get better than this?"

Leading her into the spacious master bedroom, he said, "Let's focus on two main areas here - the bathroom and your closet."

"Oh, my God!" Mia exclaimed, as they entered the bathroom with its huge marble walk-in shower and separate garden tub. "It's heaven in New York City. Seriously, Schooner," looking up at him, her eyes filled with delight.

"A few more weeks and I have plans for that shower." He smiled down at her.

"Two more weeks and I'm yours." Walking around the spacious bathroom, she commented, "This is larger than studio apartments I've been in."

"Are you ready for your closet?"

"Am I going to want to come out of my closet?"

He shook his head no and led her in. Mia gasped again, shocked to see all her clothes and shoes neatly arranged in the massive space. One wall was all shoe racks, another contained built-in dressers, double and single rows of bars for hanging clothes and a huge full-length freestanding antique mirror.

"Oh my God," Mia repeated, "we live here."

"Welcome home, Baby Girl."

They walked out of the closet and back into the bedroom. An old-fashioned bassinet was set up for Nathaniel next to their California king sized bed. Running her hand along the bassinet's Scottish lace covered edge, Mia shook her head. "You really think of everything, don't you?"

"I try." He hit her with a real smile.

Mia got into the bed taking Nathaniel with her and Schooner joined them.

"So, you're not mad at me for keeping this from you?" He looked up at her with a well contrived sheepish grin.

Mia shook her head and smiled. "You are a control freak and I just need to get used to that. But no, I'm not mad. You done good, Pretty Boy. Real good. This place is exquisite and we're living in SoHo, which is uber-cool, and we have space for visitors and Nathaniel has his own room. And I have a huge bathtub. This is just amazing."

Nathaniel started to fuss and Mia propped up against the pillows and pulled off her shirt. "Someone's hungry."

Schooner lay back and watched them, a content smile on his face. "I think we're going to have a great life here. It really has a neighborhood feel to it, doesn't it?"

Mia nodded, "I'm just picturing all the shopkeepers knowing Nathaniel and watching him grow up."

"This is our life now.

"We took a circuitous route, but we got here," Mia mused, looking lovingly at Nathaniel and then at Schooner.

"One more hurdle, Baby Girl, and I'll have everything I want." He ran a finger softly up and down Nathaniel's arm.

"You're on a mission, huh?" she smiled, looking deep into his pale sapphire eyes.

"That, I am."

Mia nodded and looked back down at Nathaniel who had fallen asleep while nursing. Placing him gently on her shoulder, she rubbed and patted his back until he treated them to a raucous burp.

Laughing, Mia placed him in the bassinet and got back into bed facing Schooner.

Reaching out to play with her hair, he asked, "Two weeks more, huh?" and pulled her to his chest. "Oh Baby Girl, you have no idea what I want to do to you."

Looking up at him, she smiled, "It's smoochal."

With his arms tightly wrapped around her and their legs tangled together, it was only a few short minutes before they were both fast asleep, catching the first of many much needed, and often elusive naps in their new bed, while Nathaniel slept peacefully in his bassinet next to them.

Chapter Ten

As was becoming a morning custom, Schooner rolled over to look at the video baby monitor and watched Nathaniel sleeping peacefully in his nursery. Feeling his movement and sensing he was awake, Mia opened her eyes and watched their son along with him. The security system and cameras that Charles had installed throughout the loft provided not only a sense of security, but assurance that Nathaniel was safe and sound.

Kissing her shoulder and spooning up against her, Schooner began, "Remember when I promised that I would take you to The Four Seasons or to the beach house when the doctor gave us the go-ahead?"

Mia nodded.

"So, where do you want to go?" Schooner's chin rested on Mia's shoulder.

Turning to kiss him, she shook her head. "I don't want to go anywhere. I don't want to leave him."

Pulling her tightly against him, "I love that and I love you." He paused, "Do you feel ready? I'm afraid I'll hurt you."

Laughing, Mia rested her head back on his shoulder, "Oh, I can think of a few positions that probably won't stress my incision."

Letting his teeth graze her neck and enjoying listening to her moan, he asked, "Oh, what did you have in mind?"

"Well, in no particular order, I could push you onto your back and straddle you and sit on your cock and ride it."

"Yeah, that would work."

Feeling him grow stiffer against her lower back at just the suggestion, Mia laughed, "Hold your horses, Pretty Boy, I'm not done yet. Or we could stay in the same position we are in right now with you behind me. Or... I could get on all fours over at the edge of the bed and you could stand on the floor next to the bed right behind me and really ram it into me that way."

"Sold," he whispered in her ear. "But first, I need to spend some time kissing you. Roll over," he demanded.

Turning to face him, devil grin at full tilt, "Sex as a parent."

Tossing his head back with laughter, "Yeah, and this is the easiest we'll have it. When he starts walking, we're toast. You'll roll over and find him in bed."

"So, are you telling me we should have lots of sex now?"

With a real smile lighting up his face, he nodded vigorously, "Absolutely, and we have a lot to make up for. It's nearly Christmas and we haven't made love since the summer."

"Too long." Mia reached out to push a dark blonde lock from his forehead.

Grabbing her hand and kissing her palm and each of her fingers, he pulled her to him. Gently biting her lower lip, his hand slid down her back as she moaned. Pressing her tightly against him, he could feel her molded against his rock-hard cock.

"This is going to be fast," he laughed, "because I am not going to be able to control myself."

"Well, don't leave me high and dry." Her look was dead serious, but her eyes were dancing with delight.

Reaching between her legs, he pressed a finger into her. "That train has left the station, babe. You're dripping." Adding another finger, he gently massaged her clit and began to kiss her hard, her moans stifled into his mouth. As his tongue slowly explored her mouth, her thighs clenched his hand and he could feel her muscles begin to quake.

Pulling away from their kiss, he looked at a wild-eyed Mia and laughed, "I thought I was going to be quick."

Pressing her forehead into his chest, "Holy crap, I needed that. Have I ever come that quickly?"

Shaking his head no, "Think you can handle another?" he challenged, smile firmly in place.

"Fuck, yeah," Mia looked up into his eyes, meeting the challenge.

Rolling away, Schooner opened the drawer on the night table and pulled out a condom packet. "Remember these things?" he laughed.

Playfully pulling it out of his hand, "Vaguely," she laughed, "we haven't used these since we were teens."

Looking sheepish, "Yeah, well I knocked up my girlfriend, so I think we'd better use them."

"Would be a damn good idea, Pretty Boy, but today is your lucky day," Mia tossed the packet over her shoulder.

Schooner's eyes widened with surprise.

"Breast feeding is a great contraceptive." Shaking her head and laughing, "You knocked up your girlfriend, eh?"

"Yes, I did."

And they both laughed.

Getting off the bed and facing her, "Now get on all fours, woman, like you promised, so that I can fuck the living shit out of you."

Throwing off the blanket and grabbing a pillow, Mia complied. Backing up to the edge of the bed, her ass in the air, legs spread, she left herself open for him.

Spanking her hard on the right butt cheek, a surprised Mia yelped. Turning her face around to look at him, her eyes stinging with tears, "What was that for?"

Leveling her a steamy glance, "Where do I begin, my non-compliant BBC?" And with that he plunged into Mia's wet and very compliant pussy.

Gasping, tears ran down her cheeks, "Oh God, you feel good."

"That is smoochal, my Baby Girl. God, I have missed this. So. Much." Pulling all the way out of her, he rammed in hard again, Mia's muscles tightening around him.

Mia groaned, "It feels like you are going to come out my mouth. Did you grow while we were on hiatus?"

Grinding his cock into her deeply, Schooner held Mia's hips tight as he drove into her again and again, each time deeper and harder.

Mia was turned on by his sounds, each drive accompanied by the sound he made when he served a ball on the courts. Squeezing him as tightly as she could, his groans intensified.

"Keep that up and I will be coming very soon," he growled.

"It's our first time, how could I not give you a pussy hug. You know reunited and all that good stuff. And since I've already come, you get a free pass on this 'wham bam, thank you ma'am' fuck." She clenched around him as tightly as she could, squeezing, then letting her muscles relax, then squeezing again, slowly, then rapidly, then slowly again, before tightening around his cock as hard as she could and holding it.

"Oh God," he groaned, digging his fingers into her hips and burying himself as deeply as he could get. Pulling out, he fell onto the bed next to her, "My legs are jelly."

Mia rolled to her side to face him and immediately got lost in his pale sapphire eyes. "You're mine," she whispered.

Nodding, "Yes, I am. I always have been yours."

"I love you so much, Schooner."

Reaching out and brushing the bangs from her eyes, "I know you do, Baby Girl." Leaning forward, he grazed her lips lightly, "So many firsts this year. And soon our first holidays and New Year's together."

Something flashed in her eyes that he didn't quite recognize. A look of concern immediately clouding his own. Cocking his head to the side, silently imploring her, *"Talk to me."*

But Nathaniel was the first to speak and both their heads snapped toward the direction of the video monitor.

"Let me go get him. Somebody wants breakfast in bed." Schooner laughed, sitting up and swinging his long legs to the floor. As he walked out the door, he turned, "And I think somebody else deserves some breakfast in bed this morning, too."

Whatever he had seen in her eyes was now gone, replaced with happiness and contentment, sated from making love, as she snuggled back into the pillows to get ready for Nathaniel's morning feeding.

Chapter Eleven

"Is this your first Christmas tree, Mia?" Holly held Nathaniel close as she walked around the fragrant, live Fraser fir. Her baby brother had not left her arms since she'd arrived a few days earlier.

Mia nodded, smiling. "Yeah, it is."

Jared sat on the floor laying out the strings of lights as Seth unpacked the boxes of ornaments and ribbons he'd purchased. "Look, BBC, I found you these cool menorah and dreidel ornaments."

"I'm sure that would make my mother very happy." Mia rolled her eyes.

"When it's done, I'm going to take a picture and send it to her."

"You do that, Princess," Mia sneered at Seth.

"I will," he sneered back.

Joining Mia in the open chef's kitchen, Holly watched as Mia mixed the potato and onion Chanukah latke mixture. "You're going to have to teach me all this stuff so that I can impress Jared's mother."

Laughing, Mia looked at her conspiratorially, "I'll give you a crash course on making killer chicken soup. You'll blow her away."

"And I can tell her that my baby brother is Jewish." Holly kissed Nathaniel's cheek, which was getting chubbier by the day from his voracious eating. "I hate to say this to you, Mia, but he looks like Zac."

Looking up from the food processer, Mia nodded. "I know. I try to think of it as he looks like your dad." Walking to the refrigerator, she kissed him as she passed by. "Do you look like your daddy, my handsome baby boy?" And to Holly, "Have you spoken to Zac recently?"

"Yeah, a few days ago. He can't wait to get back to Exeter. He didn't sound very happy, but he wouldn't tell me why. I think he might be fighting with my mother."

Concerned, Mia asked, "Have you mentioned this to your father?"

Holly shook her head no.

Mia began to drop the potato mixture into an oversized skillet filled with hot oil. The first batch of latkes were cooking. Moving to another burner on the Viking stove, Mia stirred the homemade cinnamon apple sauce.

"You probably want to mention it to him so that he can see if there are any real issues and if he needs to send over your grandparents to check on things."

The elevator opened and in walked Schooner with Charles, Gaby and Paola. "Look who I found in the lobby," he announced.

"Auntie Meezie," Paola ran into the kitchen, "I have a present for Baby Nathaniel."

Mia bent down for a kiss, "I think he might have one for you too, sweetheart."

Kissing Mia's cheek, Charles reached for one of the cooling potato pancakes. Mia went to slap his hand, but the latke was in his mouth before she could stop him.

"You thief. Get out of my kitchen."

"You never made these for me before," Charles complained.

"It's very rare that I make them. But maybe this will be the start of a new tradition."

"Lots of new traditions this year," Charles commented, now that he and Mia were alone in the kitchen.

Turning to Charles, the look that passed between them was tinged with pain. "Are you okay with doing New Year's Eve here this year? It will be a lot easier with Nathaniel."

Rubbing Mia's arm, Charles reassured her, "I think that change in tradition is a good one. I know this is your first New Year's Eve with Schooner."

Mia nodded.

"Does he know?"

"No," her face still revealed the pain, "not that I'm hiding it, but it just never came up. It's probably a discussion that we would've had before 9/11, except I was in the hospital half unconscious at the time."

"I've never said anything, either. I didn't know how much he knew." Charles broke off a crispy edge on another latke.

"When the time is right, I'll tell him all about him. They both deserve that." Mia's eyes locked with Charles'.

"They would've liked each other," Charles smiled, breaking the tension.

Nodding, Mia returned his smile. "I think so, too. I'm really lucky that both of them have been a part of my life."

They were both silent, lost in their own thoughts.

"What's with you two, thick as thieves," Schooner interrupted, handing Charles a scotch.

As if programmed, Schooner's hand went right to the cooling potato pancakes and he snatched one. Popping it into his mouth, "Mmmm, these are delicious. How come you've never made these for me before?"

Turning to the two men, spatula pointed threateningly at them, "Both of you, out of my kitchen. Now. I'm on to you both. Pretending to talk to me and stealing latkes." Narrowing her eyes and pointing the spatula at Schooner, "You, tall one, make yourself useful and go put ribbons or something at the top of that tree."

Hearing the exchange from the open living room, Seth yelled, "You know you don't have to marry her. Get out now."

"You trying to steal my man, Princess?" Mia was smiling at Seth.

"You just keep on being you, BBC. It's like taking candy from a baby."

In front of a roaring fire after dinner, presents for Paola and Nathaniel were exchanged, while Holly, Jared, and Seth continued to work on the tree. Snuggled up against Schooner on the couch with a sleeping Nathaniel in her arms, Mia looked around at the people she loved, and the overwhelming thought that crossed her mind was that she was grateful. It had taken a long time to get to this place. Charles and Seth had been there through the good, the bad and the ugly. Mia inwardly laughed thinking that her escapades gave new meaning to the word ugly. But they had stayed there by her side, weathering it together with tears, laughter, support and some very tough love.

And then there was this beautiful man who she was snuggled against, holding his angelic child in her arms. This man who she held a connection with - a connection that defied time and distance. A connection that was never broken even when they were shattered into sharp, self-destructive fragments. A connection so powerful that she was certain that their souls were entwined in some dimension-defying realm.

Whatever the sources were in the universe that had conspired on the day they met, they were fully aware of the fate that lay before them. Led through a maze of mirrors and dead ends, false starts and photo finishes, punctuated by breathtaking highs and gut-wrenching lows, Schooner and Mia would eventually be led by those very same powers to this perfect moment. A moment for which Mia would be eternally grateful, as she basked in its simplicity, surrounded by the abundance of love that she gratefully accepted and wholeheartedly returned without reserve.

Smiling as she felt his lips in her hair, Mia looked up at Schooner, her eyes moist.

"You okay?" he mouthed.

Nodding, she smiled and then looked away, staring into the mesmerizing flames of the fire, in an attempt to compose herself.

"I love you, Baby Girl," he whispered into her ear.

Mia wanted to tell him it was smoochal, but getting words past the burning lump in her throat was not going to happen. Instead, she buried her face in their son's soft, sweet cheek and melted deeper into Schooner's side.

Chapter Twelve

The late March sun was streaming through the southern exposure windows of Mia's office, warming the room, as Nathaniel amused himself in his Exersaucer, cooing at the plastic jungle animals. Mia focused intently on the advertising copy on her laptop, trying to tighten a good concept into a snappy, succinct ad.

Picking up her ringing cell, Mia smiled at the picture of Schooner holding Nathaniel. "Hi Babe."

"Hey, Baby Girl."

She could hear it immediately in his voice. Something was very, very wrong. "Schooner, what's the matter?"

"My mom just called. My dad was out golfing today with Zac and some friends and he had a heart attack."

"Oh my God, is he okay?" Mia's sharp tone scared Nathaniel and she watched as his face crumbled, his lower lip starting to tremble. Putting Schooner on speaker, she laid her cell on her desk and went to Nathaniel, lifting him out of his seat.

"Yeah, I think so, it appears that it was mild and there was only a small amount of damage to the front of his heart, but they have him in CCU."

"Are there blockages?" Mia was gently swaying with Nathaniel, softly saying, "shhh" in his ear to calm him down. With his head on her shoulder, she could feel him relaxing and getting heavier with sleep.

"It doesn't appear that he's going to need a bypass. They are evaluating a stent in one artery."

"How is your mom doing? And Zac?" Mia's heart went out to them both. How scary for Dee, she thought, to see her husband of forty-five years, the patriarch of the family, the man whom she leaned on, downed without any warning. And what a difficult thing for an almost eighteen year-old to have to have witnessed.

"They are both very badly shaken up. Can you get away for a few days?"

His voice told her he needed her by his side. Her and Nathaniel.

"Of course. I just need to get with Kami and Seth and migrate some work over to the team and cancel my appointments for the rest of the week. Do you want me to get Seth to book us flights?"

"Yes. That would be great. It's kind of late in the day now, see what he can get us for first thing in the morning either into LAX or John Wayne. If we can get a flight into John Wayne, we'll only be about five or six miles from the hospital."

"Don't worry about it, we'll take care of everything. I'll meet you at home in a couple of hours." Nathaniel was now fast asleep on her shoulder.

"Mia, thank you," his voice was soft.

"Oh Baby, I just wish I could make it better and that I was there to hug you."

The weight on Schooner was evident in his voice. Control. Protect. Fix. That was his M.O. and things that were out of his realm of control disturbed him deeply. Especially when those he loved were at risk.

Mia wasn't sure if it was Schooner or Nathaniel or the irresistible combination of the two of them that was causing the bottleneck in the plane's aisle as passengers boarded the jet. Every woman that passed by had to stop to comment to Schooner about the beautiful bright-eyed baby in his lap. With his platinum ringlets that were just starting to come in and his father's smile, Nathaniel Moore was beginning his long journey of being adored by the female sex, and he was already loving it, as he quickly mastered the art of flirtation.

"You're like sex magnets," Mia elbowed him.

"He's a chick magnet," Schooner agreed. "If you ever throw my ass out, I'm just going to walk the streets with this one until some hot babe takes me in."

"Third one's a charm, she can be your trophy wife."

Leaning over, he kissed her softly, "Nope. No third for me. I've told you, you're stuck with me," he paused, as if thinking and then smiled a wry smile, "and unfortunately, I'm still stuck with CJ."

Mia rolled her eyes and looked out the window.

"Maybe we can kill two birds with one stone this trip and get things moving along."

"That would be good, but don't put that stress on yourself, Schooner. Your dad, mom and Zac are priorities for this trip. Fuck CJ. She's not worth any of your energy right now."

Taking her hand and bringing it to his lips, "You have been incredibly patient and good natured about this, Mia, and I really appreciate it."

"She won for a long time, Schooner. I'm done handing her wins. In another time and place I probably would have said that I'd kick her ass, but no more. She just doesn't deserve that energy from me. She's nothing. One of the most important things you've ever said to me was when you told me I needed to exorcise her ghost. I needed to hear that, because it just wasn't clicking, and when you said that to me and told me that she was always jealous of the place that I held in your heart, it was like I finally saw this picture that was right in front of my eyes that I could just never see." Smiling at him, "The only thing that annoys me is that she puts stress on you and that upsets me because I do want to kill anyone who hurts you."

Schooner remained silent with eyes trained on Mia's.

"What? What's that look?" Mia broke the silence.

"We're a team, Baby Girl. We're finally handling things as a team. Together."

Reaching out, she put a hand on his cheek and nodded, "And we'll just keep getting better and better at it." Then she chuckled and her devil grin took over, "Okay, so maybe I kind of do have a fantasy about a good old-fashioned bitch fight and taking her down."

Throwing his head back with laughter, "I'd pay good money to see that and my money would be on the scrappy babe from New York."

Chapter Thirteen

Exiting the elevator on the cardiac care unit at Hoag Memorial Hospital, Mia could see the deep concern and fear in Schooner's eyes.

"I'll meet you at your dad's room." Mia's nose was scrunched up. "I don't want your parents to meet their grandson smelling like this."

Ducking into a bathroom, Mia pulled out a changing pad and laid Nathaniel out on the plastic changing table. "So, Poopy Boy, you are going to get to meet your grandma and grandpa for the first time. You were too little to travel and we didn't want them to travel to New York in the dead of winter. And I'm going to tell you a secret, even though I talk to them on the phone all the time, I haven't seen them since I was a munchkin."

Tossing the offending diaper into the garbage, Mia dressed Nathaniel back up in his Baby Gap sweats.

"I'll bet just seeing you will make Grandpa feel so much better. I know when he sees Daddy, he's going to be very happy. And you are all smiles today, so we're all really lucky."

Picking him up and slinging the diaper bag onto her shoulder, Mia exited the bathroom, "Okay, let's go find Daddy."

As she stepped out into the corridor she nearly collided with a person walking down the hall.

"Mia?"

And they both stood there in shock, each as surprised as the other at their near collision. Mia's hold on Nathaniel became tighter, as she went into protection mode, and Nathaniel turned his face from Mia's shoulder to see why.

He gasped and choked out in a rough voice, "Oh my God, he looks like me." The look on his face was the same perplexed look she had seen on Schooner's face, so many years before, the first time he had laid eyes on her in front of Brewster Hall. And then she noticed the glaze as his eyes became wet.

"Yes. He does look like you. There's some strong genes in the family." Taking a deep breath, Mia attempted to outwardly regain her composure, before she went on. "Nathaniel, this is your big brother, Zac."

As if on cue, Nathaniel hit Zac with a classic Moore smile and Zac reacted without thinking, returning Nathaniel's smile with a real smile of his own.

Squirming in Mia's arms, Nathaniel was making it known that he wanted to go to Zac. This immediate innate trust of his older brother caused panic in Mia's gut. Would Zac hurt him? The incident at L9 could have been tragic for Nathaniel.

The tighter Mia held him, the more he squirmed, literally trying to throw his body at Zac as he began to fuss.

"He wants you to hold him." Mia locked eyes with Zac. The last thing she wanted to do was hand him her baby. Fear gripped her tighter than she was gripping Nathaniel, but somewhere deep down she knew she couldn't keep the brothers apart.

Zac searched her eyes, as confused by the moment as she was. "Is that okay?"

Nodding, Mia placed Nathaniel in his arms.

"You are so cute. Holly told me that you looked like me, but I did not expect you to be a mini-me," he laughed, his face a full-blown smile. "I have a mini-me," he said proudly.

Nathaniel rewarded him with a smile, cooing as if Zac were reading him an amusing story. Thrusting himself forward, he pressed his open mouth to Zac's cheek, leaving a big wet spot.

"What's he doing?" Zac's eyes were again wide with confusion.

Mia laughed, "He just kissed you. He doesn't know how to give real kisses yet, so that is how he kisses. He likes you, Zac."

"He's really cute."

Feeling the tears beginning to well in her eyes, Mia willed them to stop, but they weren't complying and she quickly brushed them away.

"Mia. I'm sorry about everything. I'm glad you're okay. Really, I am. And I'm really glad he is okay, too." He was transfixed on Nathaniel.

In his eyes, Mia saw contrition. Holding his sweet, innocent brother in his arms finally made the ramifications of what could have happened abundantly clear.

Not ready to verbalize anything to him, she nodded. Clearing her throat, "Let's go take Nathaniel to meet his grandparents."

As Zac led the way, his brother still in his arms, a shocked Mia walked alongside them wondering about the seemingly immediate bond that she had just witnessed between the two Moore brothers.

Chapter Fourteen

"The Brothers Moore have arrived," Zac announced upon entering Gavin Moore's hospital room.

Both Gavin and Dee's faces lit up at the sight of their two grandsons. Surprised to see his two sons together and his older son proudly walking in with a smiling Nathaniel in his arms, Schooner's face was a portrait in shock and astonishment.

"Oh, let's see this handsome boy." Gavin Moore was distinguished and handsome. His light hair now a thick shock of white, setting off his deep tan and pale sapphire Moore eyes.

Mia's smile matched the intensity of everyone's in the room. It had been nearly a quarter of a century since she had seen them, but the moment she was in their presence, she felt that same warmth they had shown her as a teen.

Giving Dee a welcoming hug, she could see the strain and fear in her lovely blue eyes. Mia gave the older woman's hand a reassuring squeeze, letting her know they were there now and she no longer had to shoulder the burden alone.

Going to Gavin's bedside, she bent down to give him a kiss. Pulling back to take in his handsome face, the look in his eyes told Mia they were happy about her place in their son's life.

"Look at you. As pretty as you were when you were a teen. And that's quite a good-looking boy you've got there."

Mia took his hand in hers and sat in the bedside chair that Schooner had brought over for her. "I'd say the Moore men are a good-looking crew."

"That's because we surround ourselves with beautiful women. You make us look better," Gavin laughed. "Look at the curls on this one," commenting on the first few curls of fair hair that were now just beginning to come in.

Zac handed Nathaniel to his grandfather.

"You are quite the handsome young man, Nathaniel Moore."

Smiling at his grandfather, baby Nathaniel was providing a cure that modern medicine could not rival. The dream for Gavin to be present and in good health for the milestones in this little boy's life dispensed the ultimate impetus to heal.

Schooner was standing behind Mia and she could feel his hands on her shoulders giving her a squeeze. Without even turning around, she instinctively knew the look on his face and in his eyes as he watched his father cuddling the newest member of the family. As Mia watched her small son flirting with his grandfather, she knew that she was not only Schooner's, but that she was a member of the Moore family, and while Zac might be the last hold out in his relationship to her, the bridge to détente would most definitely be Nathaniel.

Sitting back in her chair, she was hit by the enormity of the healing power this little boy brought. It appeared that he was much more than her miracle baby - defying the odds of conception after forty, good health, the auspicious circumstances of his birth - her little miracle had the power to bring hope and renewed resolve to his grandfather as well as to be the conduit to join together the disparate pieces of what had just recently appeared to be an irrevocably shattered family.

And in that moment, Mia too, had hope. Hope that Schooner's relationships with all his children would be in a place that brought him happiness again and hope that the three Moore children would have healthy, loving and supportive relationships.

Gavin handed Nathaniel back to her and she kissed her son's tiny nose. "Your Grandma has been very patient and I don't think we should make her wait another second before holding you. What do you think, Munchkin?"

Mia stood and walked over to a beaming Dee. Their eyes met as she handed Nathaniel over to her. The joy in holding her grandson for the first time swept away the storm clouds that Mia had seen hovering earlier in Dee's eyes.

"You look just like your daddy at this age," she kissed him on his almost chubby cheek.

With his head settled on her shoulder, Nathaniel was asleep within moments.

"You're staying with us," Dee announced.

"Mom, we thought we'd stay at the Ritz. We don't want to put you out or make any more work for you."

The look on Dee's face let Schooner know immediately that was not acceptable.

"You're staying with me."

Smiling at the dynamic between mother and son, there was no way

Schooner was going to disappoint his mother, and there was no way Dee was going to relinquish even a moment with her newest grandchild.

"What are you smiling at?" Schooner asked Mia.

"I've never seen where you grew up. You've seen so much of my world, but I haven't seen yours yet, so I'm really excited to see everything. And Dee, thank you for the invitation, we would love to stay with you."

"Wonderful, we'll have a nice full house. Zac has been staying with me."

Schooner looked to his older son and Zac just shrugged. "I didn't want Grandma to be alone and things at the house are really weird."

"What do you mean really weird?" Schooner's body language immediately tensed.

"Well, it's just uncomfortable there."

"In what way?" pressed a quickly agitated Schooner. It was clear that he was not going to let up until he got the answer to what was causing Zac's discomfort.

Taking a deep breath, Zac just looked at his feet.

"Zac, I asked you a question."

Getting her first glimpse of the tough, disciplinarian father, Mia could feel the tension in the room building to a fevered pitch.

And then, without any preamble, the bomb was dropped.

"Uncle Beau has moved in with Mom. He's moved into our house, Dad."

Chapter Fifteen

The air was sucked out of the room and all was still. Dead calm. All Mia could think of was the sky before a huge thunderstorm, where the air was heavy and dank, and the rolling gray clouds took on a tinge of green. Mia always described those few moments before the heavens let loose as feeling like she was in a fish tank, and she thought it was probably fair to say that at that moment, everyone (with the exception of Nathaniel) in Gavin Moore's hospital room probably felt as if they were drowning in the fish tank as they waited for the vessel to burst, propelling them, flip-flopping, through the rushing torrent of water onto the institutional tile floor.

"He's living there? Full-time or just staying over sometimes?" Schooner's cadence was clipped, his strong jaw tight and barely moving as he spoke.

"Well, when I got home for spring break, he was there. Every day. Every night." Zac appeared torn. On one hand, very uncomfortable having to break the news to his father and on the other hand, happy to be able to unburden himself and have someone to share it with that would be 'on his side'.

"I see," was all Schooner said.

Mia could see him processing it and wondered if he would blow or handle it with the cool precision of an assassin. There was so much she wanted to say, and with another crowd, she would have let her snark run wild. But it was Zac's mother and she knew she had to temper all responses. In her head, she and Seth were doing primal screams and happy dances - CJ and Beau - a match made in hell and they totally deserved one another.

"I don't think you'll find much of your scotch left, Dad. He's been hitting it pretty hard."

Is he trying to get a rise out of his father or covering up his own theft of the scotch, Mia wondered. With Zac, motive was not always pure, though she couldn't help but feel for him - everyone was seemingly moving on and finding new attachments.

It was Gavin who spoke up from his hospital bed, "Good, now maybe this ludicrous divorce can be finalized."

Schooner smiled at his dad, "Got to love a bargaining chip." A look of satisfaction passed between the two men.

So, it's the cool assassin, after all. Damn that's hot, Mia thought. Schooner was playing for the endgame. This was the hot, aloof man who built an empire in a competitive marketplace. If this was one of CJ's emotional ploys, it was already dead in the water. Those fish were no longer flip-flopping. Mia observed a marked difference between California Schooner and New York Schooner. California Schooner was a much colder, more dominant creature - which was an odd juxtaposition to California being a much more laid-back environment than New York City.

Turning to Zac, Schooner was very matter of fact, "You'll stay with Grandma and Grandpa until you go back to school."

Relieved, Zac looked from his grandmother to his grandfather to ensure that was alright and Mia could see that he really felt like an island, alone. There was no more running to mom because he didn't like that dad was in another relationship. And the man who had encroached on the relationship with his mother had not only made claim to person but also to property. Beau had moved into the only home Zac had ever known.

"You know there's always plenty of room for you out at the beach this summer," the words were out of Mia's mouth before she even comprehended what she was doing.

Surprised, Schooner turned to her and she smiled at him and nodded slightly. The opportunity to build the bridge was there and she had to at least attempt to seize the moment. She felt for Zac, but this was for Schooner.

"And I can already tell you that your baby brother would be thrilled," she continued.

"Thanks, Mia," thinking, he looked up and smiled at them, "that was a pretty great beach."

Saying goodbye to Gavin later in the afternoon, he squeezed Mia's hand. "You understand putting those you love first. My son is very lucky to have found you again. He hasn't had that."

Mia's eyes filled with tears and she nodded, "I'm pretty darn lucky, too. He is so special. Thank you for raising such a wonderful man."

As she leaned in to kiss his cheek he whispered in her ear, "Now let's finally make you a Moore."

Chapter Sixteen

Mia could not wipe the smile off her face as she walked through the bright sunlit living room to the wall of French doors.

Turning to Schooner, beaming, "So, this is where you grew up. I'm just envisioning you as a kid and even when I knew you in college."

Opening one of the doors for her, they stepped outside.

"Oh my God, you have your own pier." Mia was overwhelmed looking at the private pier, dock and boat slips and at the views across the Bay of Corona del Mar, China Cove, the coastline and out to the ocean.

Looking up at Schooner, his real smile was possibly the brightest she'd ever seen it, and she was captive in mirroring it back at him.

With shining eyes, he grabbed her hand and silently pulled her along down the pier at a hastened pace, his long legs on a mission. When they reached the dock, Schooner lifted Mia and placed her on the deck of a large sailboat that was moored.

"Baby Girl, meet your rival," smiling, he leaned forward and kissed her.

"This is your boat?" Mia's heart was singing at the joy in his eyes.

Nodding, he joined her on the deck. "Meet True Compass."

"True Compass? I like that. But did you name this after Ted Kennedy's book?" Mia began to explore the teak-decked Jeanneau Sun Odyssey 43DS, taking in all the details of its sleek and refined beauty.

"No, I had her long before Kennedy's book," Schooner laughed, "but I did love that it was the name of my boat and that I'd probably piss off more than a few not-so-liberal people in the OC."

"You're such a renegade California boy," Mia laughed. "True Compass - leading you to the inner place you needed to find?"

Cocking his head, "Do you know how amazing it is to have someone who understands you?"

"As a matter of fact, I do." And she could feel the familiar sting of tears at the back of her eyes.

"Wait here," and he hopped back onto the pier with ease, his long legs taking him quickly back to the house.

Mia descended into the deck salon, immediately taken with how light and open it was. Outfitted in woods and white leather, U-shaped seating surrounded a table. Across from that, a white leather couch. Exploring the kitchen area, she marveled at the space's efficiency. At the fore of the boat was a triangular shaped cabin with its own bathroom. Walking back through the salon, she was again struck by how light and airy it was with its plethora of side and ceiling windows.

At the stern of the salon was the pièce de resistance, a gorgeous aft cabin with a king-sized bed and a second bathroom. Mia immediately began to picture vacations, discovering small islands and spending time together as a family.

"Want to christen it?" Schooner came up behind Mia, a bottle of chardonnay and two glasses in hand.

Jumping and letting out a yelp of surprise, "Oh my God, I didn't hear you."

Putting his arm around her from behind, Schooner kissed the top of her head. Laughing, "Sorry, I didn't mean to scare you. I brought some cheese and crackers and fruit. Nathaniel is fast asleep. It was a big day for him and my mom and Zac are planted in front of a bunch of reality TV shows that they taped. I had no idea they were Survivor fanatics. My mother a Survivor fan. Whoever would have guessed it?"

"This boat is gorgeous, Schooner." Mia turned to him, awe written all over her face.

"Glad you like her. Let's get her out of here, sail out into the harbor, enjoy some wine and munchies and decompress from this long day."

"What about christening this cabin?" Mia's devil grin was beckoning.

"All in good time, Wench. First let's grab some plates and utensils and hit the deck. I need to get her out on the water."

Topside, Mia laid out the spread on the polished wood table at the center of the deck and sat on the teak bench as she watched Schooner in the cockpit, navigating the boat away from the dock and into the Bay of Corona del Mar.

"A cool thing about living in this house is that every yacht that enters or exits the harbor has to pass by here. So, I started coveting some very big boats as a really small child."

Mia just smiled. The man was in his element. Standing in the cockpit, behind the wheel, Schooner Moore was not only one with all he loved, but he was in command and commanding.

"This is where you came to think." It wasn't a question.

Smiling, he nodded slightly, "And dream and be honest with myself and work through shit and just relax," he paused, "and sometimes escape.

Okay, oftentimes escape."

"Well, what do you think about getting a slip at the Ocean Beach Marina? Having the beach house and the boat moored on Fire Island would be amazing." As she sliced up the cheese and fruit Schooner had brought aboard, Mia was picturing sunsets out on the Great South Bay and sailing up to Nantucket and Martha's Vineyard.

"When Nathaniel's older, I'd like to sail the intra-coastal waterway and then down to the Caribbean. Sail down to Virgin Gorda, dock at the Bitter End Yacht Club. Spend a vacation down there."

Sitting with her feet up on the teak bench, Mia hugged her knees to her chest. They were dreaming together again, just as they had done when they were teens. It was then that Mia realized they were back in California together, she and Schooner, and that it was her first time back in the Golden State since she'd fled so many years before.

Now in open water, Schooner cut the engines. Stepping out of the cockpit and onto the deck, he playfully gave Mia's legs a shove so that he could sit down next to her. Grabbing the cold bottle of Chardonnay off the table, he uncorked it and poured them both glasses.

Mia raised her glass, "To your father's good health."

Clinking glasses, Schooner agreed, "I'll second that. He looked good today. I feel better now that I've seen him. It sounds like they'll release him in a few days."

"I'm very glad we came. I know it puts your mind at ease and I'm sure both your mom and Zac are feeling so much less stressed out now that you are here." Mia tipped her head back, breathing in the ocean air deeply and holding it in her lungs.

Gently running his fingertips down her cheek, he smiled, "Thank you for inviting Zac to the beach house. You are an incredible woman, Mia Silver. You never cease to amaze me with your capacity for love and forgiveness." Plucking a piece of cheese and an apple slice off the plate, Schooner elbowed her, "So, what did my dad whisper in your ear right before we left?"

Turning to him, devil grin bright, "He said, it's about time you make me a Moore."

Slinging an arm over her shoulder and pulling her into him, "I'd say with today's bombshell that became significantly more imminent."

Without even looking up, Mia could hear the smile in his voice. "Holy shit, what a shocker, but not shocking at all." Looking up at Schooner, they both smiled at one another. "I didn't know if you were going to blow or go for the endgame."

With a hearty laugh, "CJ would love for me to care enough to blow, but she just handed me everything I needed to obtain everything I want. It's classic and I'm going to fuck them both to the wall with it, sooner rather than later."

Snuggling into him and watching the sun descend, a giant red ball partially obscured by hazy clouds over the Pacific, Mia noted, "You know, you are very different here. It's so interesting, you are actually more laid-back in New York than in California. There's something colder and much more calculated and dominant in you here. I can see why you have been such a successful businessman in this environment. And it's you, but you're not quite my Schooner here. Does that make sense?"

Pouring himself another glass of wine, "You're very astute, Ms. Silver. We may have the warmth of the sun, but LA is a cold, cold town. There's nothing real and no one you can trust and you have to fight steel with titanium in business. In personal relationships, there's nothing real here either. It's all 'how good do you make me look and can you help me get famous'. New York is tough and fast paced and everyone expects you to bring your A game, because they are on the top of their game, but it's all out there, you know what you're getting - in both business and personal relationships."

Turning around in his arms to look at him and noting his sapphire blue eyes had a glint of the titanium he spoke of, "Makes me understand your masks a little more."

He nodded, as he watched the sun begin to drop into the ocean. "For all that she's dragged her feet with this divorce, it's time to give her and Beau exactly what they deserve."

"Each other," Mia chimed in.

"Precisely, Baby Girl." He leaned forward to grab a bunch of grapes and went to pop one into Mia's mouth, then playfully pulled away making her lunge for it.

"Bastard," she elbowed him, "don't go all California boy on me here."

Laughing he gently placed the grape against her lips and she parted them, allowing both his fingers and the grape into her mouth.

"Aren't you curious how complicit he's been in all this?" Mia wondered.

"I think in college she flirted with him and he fed her the information she asked for. He definitely did her bidding." Schooner fed her another grape, enjoying the way she was slowly sucking his fingers.

"Do you think he might have sought me out on Facebook as a way to finally make his move after all this time?" Mia licked the squished grape juice from Schooner's finger.

"It worked," Schooner laughed. "From the minute he told me he'd had contact with you, I could not focus on anything else. I actually sat right here on this bench at 4 A.M. the night of my birthday party, drinking Courvoisier and counting the hours until Monday morning when I could get to the office and have Yoli help me set up a Facebook account."

"You seriously weren't on Facebook?"

Shaking his head, "I had successfully avoided social media until that night. I don't think Beau will ever tell me the truth, especially now that he's involved with CJ."

"I really felt for Zac today, Schooner. He was unhappy about our coupling, but he was able to run to CJ, and at least he had a situation with his mom that hadn't changed. But now, when he came home for spring break, she was gone, too."

Schooner nodded, "And to a family friend he's known his whole life. And the guy is now sleeping with his mother."

"And it's, Beau. Ick." Mia's face scrunched up as if she'd just eaten a lemon instead of a grape.

"Not to be rude and shallow, but what the hell," he laughed. "You actually knew him in his good-looking days."

"No," Mia bellowed.

"He's got the Barbie he's always wanted and she has a guy who is going to adore her and treat her like a goddess. She'll treat him like shit and he'll love it and feel like he's won the Super Bowl." He stroked Mia's hair.

"Karma," she said softly.

"Mmm-hmm and the two of them just gave me everything I needed to end this debacle of a marriage, which is perfect, because it was the two of them who forced us apart and kept us apart."

"Nice synergy, wouldn't you say."

Standing, Schooner reached out a hand to Mia. "Time to christen our boat."

It didn't escape Mia for a moment that his prized possession, his material soul mate, his 'True Compass' had already become 'our boat' and she could clearly see the family vacations that lie before them and the memories that they would make.

Pulling her to the aft cabin, "So, you seriously never had sex on this boat?"

He shook his head no.

"Oh Captain, you poor deprived man."

Schooner sat on the edge of the king-sized bed with Mia standing between his long legs, smiling. Slowly, she pulled the sweater off over her head.

"Mmmm," he moaned, "I think I'm going to like this. I would much rather be a depraved man."

With a slow precision, she began to unbutton her blouse, her eyes trained on his pale sapphire eyes. "I kind of like California Schooner, he's a little bit of a dick."

Laughing, his eyes never leaving hers, "Sweetheart, he's more than a little bit of a dick."

"But you're not that way with me." She cocked her head.

Shaking his head, "No. I'm not."

"Take your pants off, dick."

Lying back on the bed, he undid the button on his khakis and carefully negotiated the zipper over his hard cock. Wriggling out of his pants and boxers, he kicked them to the floor.

"Oh Captain," she smiled, "now that is one irresistible cock. What should I do to it? Do you have any suggestions?"

"I do," he smiled, his eyes burning into her, making her wet just from the look he was giving, "I want you to suck my cock."

"Aye-Aye, Sir." Getting to her knees on the floor between his legs, she urged him closer to the edge of the bed.

Gingerly, she softly licked the length of him from the base of his balls to the glistening crown.

Pulling her hair with a tug so that she was staring into his eyes, his voice gruff, "I told you to suck me, not lick me."

"God, you're a dick," her head was shoved down onto his cock before she could even finish the statement, and she moaned both from him plowing into the back of her throat and how turned on she was by him taking what he wanted. And he wanted her.

With his fingers threaded through her hair, he worked her head up and down, setting the pace and the depth. Controlling what he wanted and how he wanted it.

"You make me so fucking happy," he moaned.

He was dripping at a feverish clip and she knew he was close. Steeling herself to swallow everything he gave, she sucked harder, totally turned on by what she was able to do to him.

Abruptly, he pulled out of her mouth and she thought he was going to shoot all over her face. Panting, she just looked up at him. Grabbing her under her arms, he pulled her up and flipped her onto the bed.

"Get your pants off," he demanded and Mia immediately complied. "Spread your legs," and she did. Running his fingers up the insides of her thighs, she quivered. "You're glistening," his voice was gruff. Reaching down, he dipped a finger into her and ran it along her slit to her clit, rubbing her juices in circles on her clit.

Moaning, Mia closed her eyes, losing herself to the sensation. He had just the right spot with the perfect intensity and he was driving her to the edge at warp speed. Feeling a heated burning sensation on the soles of her feet, Mia knew she was close. As she opened her eyes to look at him, she was overwhelmed by the depth of the love she felt for this beautiful man standing over her. This man who made her feel safe and protected, who adored her and turned his whole world upside down to be with her. He literally had moved heaven and Earth to be with her and her heart overflowed just gazing up at him.

"I love you," and yet her words seemed inadequate even to her own ears.

"I love you, Baby Girl," and the steel in his eyes melted like glaciers. Dropping onto the bed next to her, he pulled her on top of him. Taking her face in both hands, he kissed her passionately and then flipped her onto her back. Smiling, he took her with a quick, deep thrust, a moan emanating from low in his throat as his lips sought hers again.

Slowly, he moved within her, his pace languorous and deliberate as if he were mimicking the gentle rocking of the boat. It took Mia a moment, but she realized he had tapped into the sea's motion. Pulling his lips away, he smiled down at her.

"This feels good," and he closed his eyes as he slowly plowed into her.

The friction and their motion and the gentle rocking of the boat felt exquisite. Focused in on where they coupled, feeling every luxurious inch of him sliding in and out, she was stripped of any and all control, and finally let go, "Oh God, Schooner," she called into his neck, "oh God." And to aid in the intensity of her release, her muscles spasmed around his cock, tightening as he took his last deep thrust.

Together they lay tangled on the sweat dampened sheets, skin glistening.

Rubbing the tip of his nose to hers, “You know what, Baby Girl…?”

“What?” she smiled at him.

“My True Compass led me back to you,” and he pulled her head down onto his chest, wrapped his arms around her tightly and kissed the top of her head.

Chapter Seventeen

Gavin was sitting up in his chair, reading glasses perched on the end of his nose, as he scanned the financial pages of the Los Angeles Times. Leading the way with Nathaniel in her arms, Dee entered the room, with Schooner and Mia following shortly behind.

"So nice to see you up in your robe and slippers," Dee greeted him with a kiss and handed him his grandson.

"Very good to be out of that bed," he responded. "Hello, handsome," he greeted Nathaniel. "Where's Zac this morning?"

"He went over to L9 for an early workout. He should be here soon." Schooner sat on the edge of the bed, "So do the doctors still feel they might be able to let you out in a few days?"

"The cardiologist was by this morning and I think another two days and then I'll get sprung. They want me to do cardiac rehab."

"I wonder if we can get them to let you do it at L9. Maybe we can have the rehab person meet you there. We've certainly got the equipment they need."

Taking advantage of Zac's absence, Gavin steered the subject away from himself, "Have you spoken to Aaron about that little bombshell Zac dropped yesterday?"

"I have a call into him. Leslie said he was in court, but she expected him back shortly."

"That gives you a lot of leverage to get this thing fast tracked, I would think."

"Absolutely," Schooner smiled.

"I never liked him," Dee voiced a sentiment that she had felt for years and kept to herself.

"Ditto," Mia added her two cents and a look passed between the two women.

"Do you think this has been going on for a while?" Gavin looked up from peering at Nathaniel.

"I think he's been in love with her right from the start, but I'd venture to say the physical relationship is fairly new." The wheels in Schooner's head were turning.

As if on cue, Schooner's phone rang. Looking at it, he smiled, "It's

Aaron," and he strolled out of the room into the hallway.

Before he could even greet his lawyer, he nearly ran into two nurses, both smiling at him as if they had already undressed him in that nanosecond. While flattered that he was still turning heads, he yearned for a ring telling the world what he'd known in his heart since he was eighteen years old: Taken. Heart Property of Mia Silver.

"Excuse me," he brushed past them. "Aaron, thanks for getting back to me so soon."

"How's your dad doing, Schooner? Leslie just updated me."

Strolling down the hall at a fast clip in search of an empty waiting area, Schooner was oddly comforted hearing Aaron's voice, knowing that his trusted attorney would bring him one step closer to finalizing a situation that had dragged on far too long.

"He's actually doing fairly well, considering. It was mild, and he's otherwise in good health, and meeting his newest grandson has gone a long way in keeping his spirits high."

"Am I going to get to meet the latest Moore and Mia this trip?"

"I think we can make that happen." Schooner poked his head into the waiting room to find it filled. He continued down another hallway in search of a quiet spot. Lowering his voice and speaking softly into his cell, "So, my son dropped a bombshell on us yesterday afternoon."

"Oh?"

"It appears my old college roommate, Beau Gordon, known to my kids as 'Uncle Beau', has taken up residence in my home with my to-be-ex-not-soon-enough wife and it's in more than the capacity of a roommate. Zac came home for spring break and felt so uncomfortable that he went and stayed with my parents." Giving up on finding a quiet spot, Schooner leaned his left shoulder against a wall to talk.

Aaron chuckled, "That's a beautiful thing."

Smiling, Schooner was nodding his head, "Game. Set. Match."

"Exactly. I'll get her lawyer on the horn today and tell him it's done."

With a sixth sense that emanates from somewhere deep within the gut, Schooner felt the summoning call to turn to his right. Following his instinct, he changed directions to face the other end of the corridor. As he began to process the scene down the hall that he was just beginning to witness, he could feel rising bile start to burn his esophagus.

Zac leaned casually with his back up against the wall. She stood before him, gently stroking his arm with the intimacy of a lover. It took Schooner a moment to place the last time he had seen her, and that memory disgusted him nearly as much as the scene he was currently witnessing.

Without another moment's hesitation, he started down the hall with his long-legged stride. He was in protect mode. Protect his young. A part of the animal kingdom, Schooner Moore was the king of his pride and it was his duty to take out this cougar. This was the very same cougar that had intimately stroked his arm at his forty-third birthday party moments before dropping her hand down to his crotch in search of his cock. And now she was standing too close to his son, touching him in a way that only lovers do.

Spying his father approaching, Zac extricated himself from the woman and headed toward Schooner. The woman disappeared into a patient's room.

"Hi Dad," Zac was trying to come off cool, but from his darting eyes, his rattled nerves were apparent.

"How long has that been going on? Don't lie to me, Zac." Schooner's demeanor was all business.

"It's not. I mean, there's nothing going on," Zac was clearly agitated. This was a conversation he did not want to be having with his father.

"But there was," Schooner was not letting him off the hook.

They stood in the middle of the busy hallway, hospital personnel and patients passed them on all sides but neither Moore saw another person nor heard another sound.

"Yes, there was," Zac looked down at his feet.

"When?" Schooner's tone was terse, his body language a warrior preparing for battle.

"When I was home fall semester. Before I went back to Exeter."

"How many of them were there?" the muscles in Schooner's jaw were now twitching.

"Three," Zac's voice was little more than a whisper.

"Three in addition to her?"

"No. Including her." Zac still had not looked up at his father.

"Did they know about one another?" Schooner's arms were now crossed over his chest and if Zac had looked up he would've noticed his father's mind racing a million miles per hour.

"Yeah. They did," Zac finally looked up.

"Go back to your grandfather's room. We'll talk later."

"Dad, are you mad at me?" Zac's eyes were pleading.

"I'm not happy with you, Zac, but you're the minor here. These women are adults who should know better. Go to your grandfather's room."

"Dad," Zac pleaded.

"Now, Zac," and Schooner turned on his heel and headed down the hall.

When he reached the room the woman had entered, he ducked his head in and beckoned for her to come out into the hallway.

As she emerged from the room, Schooner hit her with his All-American boy smile. "It's been a long time, hasn't it?"

"Yes, it has," she was caught off-guard and not quite sure how to react to his friendliness.

"It was my birthday party. That moment we shared," Schooner was summoning his acting skills.

He had her with her back to the wall and he was standing close, his arm outstretched, his hand flat on the wall over her head. He was smiling down at her, his eyes locked on hers, oozing sexuality. She was melting before his eyes. Schooner was taking all his natural attributes and harnessing them. Not saying a word, but just gazing down at her, smiling, as she was trapped between his body and the wall, he waited for her breathing to escalate, so that he knew he had her in just the condition he wanted her.

Anyone observing them would have seen a man and a woman having a quiet, very intimate conversation.

Leaning down, he whispered in her ear, "So, I know you like to fuck, huh?"

With glazed eyes, she smiled back.

Going along with it, he leveled a glance at her, knowing it would make her squirm. And it did.

"Is that your husband in there?" he gestured toward the room.

"Yes," her voice was breathy.

Leaning down to her ear so that his cheek grazed hers, he whispered, "So, how do you think he and the rest of Newport Beach are going to react when they find out that you're a registered sex offender?" Schooner leaned back, All-American boy smile plastered on his face, his pale blue eyes ice, as he watched her first shocked, then panicked, reaction.

"What are you talking about?" she choked.

"You've been fucking my son. He's under eighteen. Statutory rape is a felony. That makes you a sex offender."

She turned white under her spray tan, her eyes wide, her breathing shallow and barely perceptible.

"As a registered sex offender," he went on, "well, those databases are all over the internet and I will make sure that all of Newport Beach, heck, all of Orange County, knows about you and your friends," he let that sink in for a moment. "Yes, I know about all of you."

Her large blue eyes darted left and right, "He was willing. All too happy…"

Schooner cut her off, his voice soft, deadly calm, "He's a minor and you are an adult. Are you so depraved and bored that you have to prey on your friend's children to have someone fuck you? That's pathetic and sick," the disgust in his voice was evident, although from a physical posture it still appeared that they were having a pleasant, and possibly intimate, conversation. "You will lose everything, you know that. And you will be a social pariah in this town."

Closing her eyes, she exhaled all the air from her lungs, "What do you want me to do?"

With an arm now on either side of her head, hands flush against the wall, Schooner leaned into her, "Obviously, stay away from my son. And instead of spreading your legs, spread the word to your friends. If anyone of you even so much as says hello to him again, I will have you arrested on sexual assault charges," staring deeply into her eyes. "I will ruin you." And with his panty-wetting smile, one that did not even come close to reaching his eyes, he pushed away from the wall, turned and walked away.

Coming down the hall toward him was Mia, a perplexed look on her face. She had just seen him in what looked like a very intimate moment with a woman. His face was unreadable as he approached her.

"Is everything okay?" her voice was tentative.

"No," he shook his head and put his arm on her shoulder to indicate that she should turn around and walk with him.

"What's going on Schooner?" Mia's eyes searched his face for a clue. *Give me something here*, she silently screamed inside her head.

He saw a "Family Restroom" and tried the handle. It opened and he ushered Mia inside.

"Not the best place to talk, but it's private."

"Please tell me what's going on. Who was that woman you were talking to, Schooner?"

Walking to the sink, he turned on the cold-water faucet and began to splash water on his face. Looking in the mirror, he took a few deep breaths before turning to Mia.

"She is a friend of CJ's."

"Okay."

"And she and two of her other friends have been having sex with my son."

Mia's eyes widened, her hand flying to her mouth at the shocking disclosure. "Oh my God."

"What you just witnessed was me threatening to press charges if she, or the others, ever go near Zac again."

"Oh my God," Mia repeated. "Was this all going on under CJ's nose?"

"Apparently," he paused. "It seems this was all happening that semester he spent at home."

"That is disgusting. He's a child. What is wrong with these women? He's the son of one of their friends. Don't they have children of their own? What if it was one of their children?" Mia was ranting. Walking across the small bathroom to close the space between her and Schooner, she wrapped her arms around him tightly, "I know he's turning eighteen soon, but you need to seek full custody now. This happened under her watch along with that overdose. We need full custody, Schooner. He can't be left with her and Beau." Mia looked up at him, her own eyes filled with tears brought on by anger and frustration.

We need full custody, Schooner. We. She had said 'we'. In this dark moment, Schooner's heart soared. This woman was bringing so many firsts into his life. Having a partner to share the good, endure the bad and fight the ugly was new and amazing and Schooner could feel the brimming in his heart - the same brimming he'd felt right from the start with Mia, so many years before.

"Under that tough New York girl exterior is the biggest heart ever. For you to even accept Zac into our world after everything that happened," he just shook his head with disbelief. "You can't even imagine the burden you relieve from me, Mia."

Reaching up, Mia put a hand on his cheek, letting her thumb stroke gently, "We're in this together, Pretty Boy. He's your son. He's Nathaniel's brother. That means it's my family. She hasn't protected him, Schooner, and that makes me mad. Really, really mad."

He nodded, kissing her hand, "Me too, Baby Girl. It took everything I had not to choke that bitch. Instead I threatened to expose and ruin her if she so much as says hello to him." He ran a hand through his hair, eyebrows drawn together as he thought through his course of action, "I need to call Aaron. I want full custody until his eighteenth birthday and I want this divorce done yesterday. If she balks at all, the judge will be advised of everything."

"I'm so sorry, Schooner. I really am."

"We're going to fix this," his statement was absolute.

Pulling Mia close for a hug, as he kissed the top of her head, he realized that they shared a fundamental similarity in ensuring that they would do whatever was in their power to protect the ones that they loved, even if it meant putting their own prejudices aside for the greater good.

Schooner didn't think that he could love Mia any more than he already did; but in that moment, his love for this woman, his partner, his lover, the mother of his son, his one true love, reached a depth that he never even dreamed existed. And the thought crossed his mind that maybe they were one soul in two separate bodies.

Chapter Eighteen

The drive to Linda Isle was shrouded in a heavy silence. As they pulled through the gates, Schooner looked over at his son. "I'm not happy about your part in this, Zac. Did your mother and I not raise you with any understanding of right or wrong?"

Zac didn't answer, the muscles in his jaw twitching.

Turning into the white and gray paver driveway of his former residence, Schooner could feel his stomach knot and the bile begin to rise again from his gut, but overwhelming the physical sensations, was anger. Just being at the house set off a whole host of negative visceral reactions.

In the passenger seat, the tension continued to radiate off Zac like solar waves rippling through the highly charged air. "He's here," was all he said.

Beau's silver BMW sat in the driveway.

"I want you to go straight upstairs to your bedroom, pack your things and just bring them out to the car. No conversations with anyone. Is that understood?"

Zac nodded.

"Is. That. Understood?" Schooner was seething.

"Yes, sir," Zac's response was slightly more than a whisper.

Pulling out his keys at the front door, Zac looked at his father and knew they were entering a battlefield. Silently, he prayed he wouldn't have to face his mother.

Walking into the main foyer, Schooner noticed how sterile it all seemed compared to the loft in SoHo with Nathaniel's colorful toys and accessories strewn about. All was still, the air oppressive, and both Moores jumped slightly when they heard Beau's voice call out from Schooner's home office located just off the Great Room.

"You're back earlier than I expected."

Schooner nodded for Zac to go upstairs. Making it to the top of the staircase, Zac paused as Beau entered the Great Room and halted, clearly stunned at the site of Schooner Moore standing there.

Silently, Schooner stood there. Damned if he'd be the first to speak and relinquish power to Beau.

"Schooner," Beau stammered, noticeably shocked, "what are you doing here?"

Outwardly, Schooner appeared very calm. Cocking his head, he drew his brows together, giving Beau a look that said, 'What a strange question?' and nonchalantly, with an even, controlled tone, answered, "It's my house. I own it. I pay all the bills. What are you doing here?"

The level of awkward continued to escalate as Schooner strode into the room and stepped behind the bar. Pulling out a single rocks glass and placing it on the slate-topped bar, Schooner began to pull out bottles, one-by-one. First, a bottle of 21-year old Courvoisier, which he held up and examined before placing it on the bar. Bottles of Glenmorangie and Glenfiddich followed, with Schooner performing the same inspection prior to placing each bottle onto the bar with an unnerving thud. All three bottles had the same thing in common, only an inch of liquid remained covering the glass at the bottom.

Schooner looked up, "You still haven't answered me. What are you doing in my house?"

Beau had not moved from his spot. "CJ and I are together now."

Glaring, Schooner nodded slightly and reached down to pull out a bottle of Hennessy Paradis cognac. The deep amber liquid barely covered the bottom of its distinctive bell-shaped bottle.

"Bad enough I'm supporting you now too, and frankly I don't give a shit that you have access to my almost-ex-wife, but whatever gave you the impression," he lifted the bell-shaped bottle, "that you'd be permitted to touch an $800 bottle of my cognac? You will be replacing this, right?"

"Look Schooner, I know you are upset about me and CJ."

Schooner cut him off, "No Beau, I am definitely not upset about you and CJ. That was clearly a long time coming."

"What do you mean?" Beau looked like he'd just gotten caught with his pants down.

"Mia called me early in our sophomore year. You spoke to her. But you never told me she called. Now why would you not tell me that she called?" Schooner put the rocks glass back under the bar and pulled out a brandy snifter and poured himself the remainder of the Paradis and then let the bottle crash into the garbage with deliberate disregard.

Beau's eyes were darting around. "She said she didn't want to leave a message."

There it was, the admission that he knew it was Mia who had called, who had reached out to him. A phone call he had not forgotten after all these years. "And you didn't think it was important to tell me that she called? You knew the hell I was going through."

When Beau didn't respond, Schooner just shook his head, "You were her lap dog even back then."

"She was my friend. I was trying to protect her from getting hurt anymore by you and Mia."

"I was your friend, Beau, and it wasn't up to you to make those decisions for me." Schooner threw back the rest of the cognac. "So, did you seek out Mia on Facebook purposely knowing it might open the opportunity for you and CJ?"

"It wasn't planned, Schooner, but I certainly was going to fully support CJ in any way I could after you left her."

"She lied and deceived me. You lied and deceived me."

"You should be thanking me. First mention of that guttersnipe and you were on a plane to New York."

"What did you just call Mia?" Schooner was around from the back of the bar and inches from Beau in a quick fluid motion. "You did not just call Mia a guttersnipe."

Grabbing Beau by the collar of his polo shirt, Schooner backed him up against a wall. "Plotting with CJ so that she would notice you, lying to me to please her, here," he swept his arm around, gesturing at their grand surroundings, "to take on my discards as you live rent free in *my* house. You are pathetic."

"You just had it all so easy, didn't you? The looks, the business, the hot wife. Well, look who's got the last laugh now. I'm fucking your hot wife."

"I wouldn't fuck her with your dick," Schooner laughed in his face.

Struggling with anger to get out of Schooner's grasp, Beau's face contorted, "Yeah, well you're stuck with that pathetic chick who had to trap you with a bastard child."

Lifting him off the ground by the collar of his golf shirt, Schooner slammed him into the wall, the sheetrock crumbling behind Beau's head. "Don't you ever disrespect the woman I love or my son again." And with each word, "Do. You. Understand. Me?" Schooner slammed him into the broken wall again and again and again. Letting him drop, Beau slumped to a seated position on the floor.

"Oh, and fix the wall," Schooner gestured to the shattered sheetrock. "I want to sell the house."

Turning, he met Zac at the bottom of the stairs. Taking one of the large duffels from Zac, the Moores exited the house on Linda Isle, closing a chapter in each of their lives.

Chapter Nineteen

Pulling up in front of L9's flagship location and headquarters, Schooner was beaming with pride as he prepared to show Mia his other baby and introduce his staff to his love and his new son.

"Wow, it's huge," Mia was impressed with the glass and steel structure.

Schooner laughed, "I like big."

With a devil smile, "That's my line, isn't it?" Mia volleyed back.

Barely making it through the door, they were surrounded by staff and club members who hadn't seen Schooner in way too long. Mia was surprised at how many of the employees she knew from the L9/NYC opening. Welcoming her warmly, it was the flirtatious Nathaniel, who soon garnered all the attention.

"Come, let me show you around," Schooner took Mia by the arm.

Mia smiled, remembering the day, fourteen months earlier, when she proudly gave Schooner the tour of M. Silver & Associates, so excited to be sharing with him her finest accomplishment.

"There's my beautiful godson."

Mia spun around to see Yoli coming down the hall toward them.

"Nathaniel, this is your godmother," she kissed Yoli hello and handed the baby off to her.

"Schooner, he's you, but I see this hair is starting to form ringlets."

"He's been a little cue ball up until now, but it looks like Ms. Silver's curls have won out." He led them down the hall, opening the door to his unused office.

"Oh my God," Mia's hand flew to her mouth, "This is the size of a New York City apartment."

Standing there with a real smile, arms crossed over his muscular chest, he was clearly enjoying impressing 'his girl'.

"Schooner," she exclaimed, speechless. As she walked around, taking it all in, the massive glass desk, the bank of TVs, the personal gym, the bar, the couch and seating area, "so wait, are you that same jock I knew in college? You know, the guy that wanted me to read over his papers for him." The devil smile was glowing to her eyes.

His eyes and smile beamed back at her as he shared the magnitude of his accomplishments. Schooner and Mia were experiencing a Jay Gatsby-Daisy Buchanan, Heathcliff-Catherine Earnshaw moment. His heart was brimming with pride as the love of his life and small son took it all in.

"You will never cease to amaze me, Pretty Boy." Mia was fighting back tears. She was beyond proud of this man, she was in awe of him.

"As will you, Baby Girl."

"Your parents are gross," Yoli whispered into Nathaniel's ear.

He smiled and put his open mouth on her cheek.

"I don't do boys, but I have a feeling you are going to be the love of my life, little one." Turning to Schooner, she asked, "So what was it you had to tell me?"

"Well, my other son has been full of bombshells these past few days," and he brought Yoli up to speed on the situations with CJ and Beau, and Zac being the local boy toy of CJ's friends.

"Part of me wants to see you expose those bitches and part of me wants you to let it go," Yoli shook her head.

Looking at Schooner, Mia added, "If it were your friends and Holly?"

"I'd kill them," his answer was immediate and succinct, "and I feel incredibly hypocritical and sexist about my response to this situation. Am I doing the right thing?" he looked to the two women.

"What does Zac want to do?" Yoli already knew the answer before the question was fully out of her mouth.

"Do you think Zac sees anything wrong in the situation?" Schooner's question was rhetorical.

"You need to talk to CJ." Mia could see the ambivalence in his eyes.

"About quite a few things," he nodded.

Handing him Nathaniel and enjoying the way this big, powerful man looked with his tiny son, Yoli added, "Don't leave here without that divorce finalized."

Mia laughed, "We'll need a tiny Elvis suit for Nathaniel so that we can stop in Vegas."

Rolling her eyes, Yoli warned, "Don't even think about robbing Seth of the opportunity to plan your wedding."

"Or Lois," Schooner and Mia both said in unison, laughing.

Reaching over to squeeze Schooner's hand, Mia smiled. Silently she told him, "Let's go tackle the tough stuff, 'cause there's really great things waiting for us on the other side.'"

Smiling back, his silent message was, "My fearless Baby Girl. You make me a better man."

Chapter Twenty

Tossing a salad on the black granite topped island, Mia and Dee talked as if they'd been a part of one another's lives since first meeting so many years before. There was no doubt in Mia's mind that Gavin and Dee thought of her as family and she loved that these two wonderful people were her son's grandparents.

The doorbell rang and Zac yelled out, "I'll get it."

The bell had been ringing non-stop with deliveries from florists and neighbors dropping off food since Gavin had gotten home the day before.

Mia heard Zac talking to someone and Dee immediately tensed, her spine becoming very straight and stiff, her face taking on a hard mask. Mia could feel the change in the air and looked to Dee for an explanation.

"CJ is here," her tone was flat, her eyes devoid of emotion.

Mia's eyes grew wide, initially with fear, old ghosts flooding her space, rushing in from multiple planes and dimensions to choke her.

"When was the last time you saw her?" Dee looked alarmed at Mia's physical reaction.

Swallowing hard, "The night she told me that Schooner never loved me."

"I see," was all she said, then, "shall we?" and motioned toward the family room.

Schooner was on the couch, he had not even gotten up to greet them, his long legs stretched out in front of him, crossed at the ankles, feet bare. Nathaniel was fast asleep on his chest and his arms were wrapped around the baby. He smiled at Mia and his mother, his eyes crinkling at the corners. Schooner Moore was clearly going to enjoy this little visit.

Her back to Mia and Dee, CJ was still holding an over-the-top huge floral arrangement as she gushed over Gavin, "I have been so worried about you ever since I heard the news. Beau and I have been totally devastated."

Mia stood paralyzed as Schooner motioned her with his eyes to come sit next to him on the couch. Dee gave her the tiniest of nudges toward her son and Mia went to him.

As she sat, he put his head against hers and whispered, "Showtime," immediately eliciting a complicit smile from Mia. It was Schooner Moore hitting Mia Silver with the devil grin this time.

One look in his pale sapphire eyes and she knew she had the strength to face the ghosts and demons that she had let steal the light from her world and the confidence from her soul. She was Mia Silver. And anyone who knew Mia Silver knew that she was a formidable force. Not only would she slay the dragons, she was going to ride off with the knight in shining armor. It was time to relish her position.

Straightening up from placing the flowers on the table next to Gavin, CJ turned around to face Schooner and Mia.

"Mia," CJ attempted to smile through lips that wanted to pucker, "you've gotten contact lenses. I hardly would have recognized you without your glasses."

Smiling and nodding her head, "Is that so? Well then, maybe you need glasses."

"Well, I'm glad you stopped by," Schooner began, "because we actually have quite a bit to discuss." Turning his attention to Beau, "How are you feeling, Beau?" Schooner didn't wait for a response, "So, CJ, I assume you've spoken to your lawyer, because here is what is happening. There have been a few changes since we all last spoke. You'll have a new settlement tomorrow and based on everything that has come to light over the past few days, you will be signing that this week and it will be filed before the week's end. Aaron has assured me that it will be expedited before a judge."

Silently, CJ sat in a pale blue silk and dark cherry wood Bergere chair. Beau stood behind her and put his hands on her shoulders, obviously thinking his show of support was a good thing. Again, CJ puckered like a lemon.

Mia realized she had a smile on her face and thought about wiping it off, but decided against it.

Absentmindedly kissing Nathaniel's head, Schooner went on, "New terms are as follows, the house on Linda Isle is to be put on the market within thirty days."

CJ gasped and Beau momentarily tightened his grip on her shoulders.

"It's in perfect condition, so there really shouldn't be much that needs to be done to get it market-ready. A little drywall work in the Great Room," he smiled at Beau. "Whatever does need to be done, let me know and I will get contractors sent over immediately. Fifty percent of the profit after mortgage, taxes and broker fees will go to you. Obviously, that will be a rather significant sum. Now, I'm not going to be supporting this joker," he gestured toward Beau, "so if he plans on staying over more than one night a week, he will be paying rent. He will also be reimbursing for usage of things that are not his, such as eight hundred dollar bottles of cognac and use of office space."

Nathaniel started to move around and fuss on Schooner's chest, "Shhh, baby. Go back to sleep," he said softly near his son's ear and shifted him on his chest. Nathaniel stretched and quieted back into sleep.

"Now let's talk about the other elephant in the room here," Schooner continued, unequivocally commanding the situation. "Zac doesn't turn eighteen for another few months and I am suing for full custody until that time."

"That's not fair, Schooner." CJ was visibly agitated, her anger escalating.

"No, CJ, what isn't fair is that when he was home this past fall, you were clearly negligent in your responsibility as his mother. You were not there to watch over him and protect him. You didn't safeguard him from your abusive, so-called friends, since he was sleeping with three of them. He's a minor, CJ." Disgust was the prevalent emotion on Schooner's handsome face.

"Well, I didn't know it was happening," her voice was shrill, her eyes darting around the room.

"You might as well have been complicit."

Her eyes narrowed, CJ looked from Schooner to Mia and back to Schooner, "You're not taking my son away from me."

"I am until he is eighteen and then he can do whatever he wants. If he wants to come back and screw every one of your friends, I can't stop him. But as long as he is a minor, I will protect him from these pathetic pedophiles you call friends," and without missing a beat, "so, back to what I was saying at the beginning of the conversation, you'll have all the new papers tomorrow, you need to sign them immediately and this is a done deal."

"And if I don't," her chin was thrust high in the air.

Schooner shrugged, "I'll go to the judge about everything we just discussed and look at filing the appropriate charges against your friends. That should do wonders for your social standing in Newport Beach."

Glaring at Mia, "I hope you see what you're getting."

Schooner turned to Mia and their eyes met. Mia was in awe of this man, this good, good man.

"Very clearly," Mia answered CJ, without taking her eyes off Schooner, "very, very clearly."

Chapter Twenty-One

On the deck of the boat, alone again for sunset, Mia sat between Schooner's long legs on the teak bench, leaning back into his chest. "Is it possible to fall even more in love with you?" She turned to see his face.

Pulling her back tighter into his chest, "Mmm-hmm, very possible."

"I just have the best time sitting back and watching you do your thing."

"Mia Silver, you sitting back for anything is the only thing that is impossible here," he whispered into her ear.

Smiling, Mia silently watched the sun descending through a layer of Southern California smog, spraying the sky with an iridescent effusion of color. Smoothing her hair back from her forehead in gentle strokes, Schooner too remained silent as he focused on the grand show nature (and the spoils of mankind) were projecting onto the sky's canvas.

"I do sit back and let you take the lead, which is unlike me. Very unlike me," Mia broke the silence, as the sun was lost into the smog layer.

"I do the same, Baby Girl. Which is also very unlike me. Handing off control is not a comfortable space for me, you know that. But I trust you enough to sit back and let you go into action."

What Schooner couldn't see was the smile as it appeared on Mia's face after a moment of what looked similarly like shock. "Yes. It's trust," the epiphany apparent in her tone. "Trust," she repeated.

With the sun now below the horizon, the clouds scattered throughout the sky took over their portion of the show, with oranges transforming into pinks.

His cheek pressed to hers as he watched the sky, "You did very well being in a room with CJ and Beau, Baby Girl. I was very proud of you."

Turning in his arms, "I was in a room with CJ, Schooner." The look on her face imparted amazement.

Nodding, "Yes, you were. Though it probably wasn't anywhere near as scary as you had imagined."

Shaking her head and smiling, "No. It wasn't. Right before I entered the room, your mom asked me when was the last time I had seen her and I told her it was the night that CJ told me that you never loved me," Mia's eyes filled with tears just verbalizing it. "But today we sat, so many years later, me and you on one side of the room, them on the other, and there was nothing they could do to take us down. The truth, all the truths, were out there for everyone to plainly see and there is nothing they can ever do to us." Mia was smiling as the tears rolled down her cheeks, glistening in the fading light.

"Faith and trust."

She nodded, "Yes, faith and trust. We are unbreakable, Schooner. I know that now. I do. I really do. You are mine," nodding, the tears were flowing, "you are mine."

Taking her face in both his hands, "Baby Girl, I have been yours since you threw a snowball at my head."

"But I missed," she laughed through her tears.

"Yes, you missed my head, but you didn't miss my heart," pulling her face to his, he kissed her lips softly.

"Beau looks like Pee Wee Herman."

Mia's non-sequitur elicited a hearty laugh from Schooner, "Sad, but true."

"CJ looks good," Mia admitted.

"You handled her beautifully," his real smile was beaming with pride at how well Mia managed today's awkward and tense situation.

"I think it's time for me to handle you beautifully," Mia stood, taking Schooner's hand with the intent of taking him to a cabin below deck.

Shaking his head no, "Let's stay up here. There were so many nights I dreamed of you under these stars. Tonight, I will take you under these very same stars." Stars that once mocked me, he thought. Tonight, I'll show them who's got the last laugh.

"Then take me."

"That was my plan, Baby Girl. It's such a treat to get you alone. And in a few minutes, you're going to be standing naked before me on the deck of this boat."

Mia shivered at his words.

Standing before him between his legs, he reached forward and unbuttoned the top three buttons on her linen blouse. Inserting a hand, he gently ran his thumb over her lace bra, back and forth, until he was satisfied with the hardness of her nipple and her sharp intake of breath.

"Do you have any idea of what you do to me?" he moaned. "Just feeling your nipple harden beneath my touch and listening to you gasp has gotten me so hard," he pinched and rolled her nipple through the lace of her bra.

Standing very still, she waited for him to continue, the words faith and trust running around her brain. Unbuttoning the rest of her blouse, he pushed it down her arms and it silently fell to the deck.

"Take off your bra," his voice was gruff.

Reaching behind her, her trembling fingers fumbled with the hooks. He'd already gotten her worked up to such a feverish pitch that she was shaking and the cool breeze off the Pacific certainly wasn't helping. The bra joined her linen blouse on the deck.

Schooner sat back, smiling, arms crossed over his chest. "You really are so beautiful," he sat silently and she waited. "Take your pants off."

"Would you like to help?"

He just shook his head no.

Taking that in, she nodded and undid the top button on her pants and pulled down the zipper. Gently wriggling, they fell to the deck. Stepping out of them, she playfully kicked them out of the way.

Removing his crossed right arm from his chest, he pointed at her silk bikini underwear and made a slight downward movement with his index finger, clearly indicating he wanted them gone. Pulling down the soft fabric, she stepped out of them, too.

Leaning forward, Schooner picked up the soft silk panties from the deck and brought them to his face, his eyes closing as he took in her scent. Gently, he let them trail slowly down his cheek before discarding them on the bench next to him.

Opening his eyes, Mia stood before him, the last vestiges of a beautiful sunset painting the sky behind her, a perfect backdrop to his perfect vision. She shivered in the rapidly cooling sea air.

"Put your left foot up on this bench on the outside of my leg," he directed and she complied.

With one leg up, she was spread open before him.

"Very nice," he commented.

He was silent and she just stood there, waiting, wanting him to touch her, lick her or let her touch herself. Mia was getting more turned on with every second that passed. And he kept letting them pass.

"So many nights I dreamed of you, right here on this deck and on the deck of the boat before this one and the one before that. So many nights."

The cool breeze continued to swirl around her body, cooling it down, making her shiver. Or was she shivering in anticipation? She wasn't really sure. As the chilly air surged between her legs, she could feel how wet she had already become just waiting for his next directive.

"Touch yourself," his voice was rough.

Wanting to please him heightened her arousal, yet, at the same time, a wave of shyness was invading. *Shy around him,* she questioned, *how could that be? We've been intimate in every way possible*. Yet, standing naked on the deck of his boat, Mia felt more vulnerable and exposed than she'd ever felt in her life.

"Touch yourself," he commanded, with little more than a whisper.

Reaching between her legs, Mia was not surprised to find that she was wet. She was already aware of that. Finding that she was as wet as when she's had a tremendous orgasm, or two - now that was surprising. But that is exactly how wet she was already. Sensitive and slick, she gasped immediately and could see the flicker in his eyes. Dipping two fingers inside herself, she spread her juices forward to her clit and rubbed in a circular motion until she got the position and pressure just right, her shyness long gone, her focus split between two places, what she was feeling between her legs and what she was seeing in his beautiful sapphire eyes.

Involuntarily, she moaned, "Oh God, so good."

"Make yourself come for me," he was mere inches from her fingers, watching her work her magic on herself.

"I want you to touch me," she begged, gasping for air.

Shaking his head slightly, eyes never leaving hers, he made it clear that she would make herself come for him as he had asked.

Trying to make the wonderful sensation last and the exquisite build to release go on forever, Mia focused on Schooner's eyes. Silently, she tried to tell him everything with her eyes, everything she ever wanted him to know; the depth of her love, the all-consuming pain of loss without him, the incredible need to be his, for him to be hers, the dream of sharing every moment, good and bad, the solace and strength she felt when she was wrapped in his arms. She needed him to know all this. He had to know.

The screams in her ears were her own, yet they sounded miles away. It was Schooner's face and his own ragged breathing that let her know she was coming. He snaked an arm around her waist to hold her steady and worked his way out of his cargo pants with the other hand. Lowering her onto him, she moaned at the invasion as he filled her. Needing more, she quickly searched for her rhythm to regain the feverish pitch she had just tumbled from. Finding it, she rapidly ascended and then quickly began to fall behind the veil again.

"Mia," his voice, hoarse with desire, brought her back to a place where she was once again able to focus on his eyes. "Mine."

Vigorously nodding, "Yes. Yes," before she was gone again.

"Mine," he hissed into her ear with jagged breath, "Always. All ways."

He heard me, was her thought, he heard everything I silently told him.

Later, as she clung to him, wrapped tightly in his arms, her sweat quickly chilling in the night air, she lay her head on his shoulder. "I love your boat."

Pulling her away slightly so that he could look into her eyes, "Our boat. This is our boat, Mia."

Smiling, her eyes filled with tears and she nodded.

Pulling her back into him again so that her head could rest on his shoulder, he looked up into the night sky. Smiling at the stars, *"I got the girl,"* he silently told them.

Chapter Twenty-Two

Mia was in the kitchen feeding Nathaniel when she heard the doorbell ring.

"I'll get it," Schooner called out, as he was coming down the stairs.

She couldn't make out the conversation, but she could tell by the tone of Schooner's voice that he was very happy and excited to see whoever it was that was visiting. The voices moved into the family room and she could tell by Dee and Gavin's tones that they too were very pleased to see the latest visitor.

"Daddy is having the best time seeing everyone, isn't he?" Mia spooned the cereal and applesauce into Nathaniel's waiting mouth. "And I think you are having a good time too with everyone telling you what a beautiful boy you are." As if on cue, he smiled at Mia and made a sound, as if totally agreeing with her.

After a few more spoonfuls, she cleaned him up. "Are you ready to go meet the company?"

Talking with Gavin, Dee and Schooner was a distinguished looking man a few years younger than Gavin. He had thick salt and pepper hair and a golfer's tan. His hazel eyes were warm and inviting and his smile genuine when he saw Mia enter holding Nathaniel.

"Hello," the man stood.

"Hello," Mia extended a hand, "I'm Mia."

His grip was firm, "So nice to meet you, I'm Malcolm Faulkes and I'm guessing this handsome fellow here is Nathaniel."

Malcolm Faulkes. I know that name, thought Mia, why do I recognize that name?

Malcolm turned to Schooner with a quizzical look on his face, "Mia? Your Mia?"

Schooner's smile made his eyes crinkle as he nodded, "One and the same."

"I'll be darned," and he looked at Mia approvingly. "Well, this was most unexpected."

Mia looked from one man to the other, smiling, and waiting to get let in on this 'other' conversation that was clearly taking place. Handing the baby to Dee, she sat down next to Schooner.

"Is there something I should know about here?" Mia was beginning to feel self-conscious.

"Malcolm was responsible for both putting my hand back together when I smashed it and for taking me over to Africa."

Mia couldn't help but notice the joy in Schooner's eyes just at the mention of Africa.

"Coach Schooner here was quite the entrepreneur. Talk about a guy that knows how to play to his strengths. That village came alive with what you brought to it."

Smiling with pride, Mia watched the joyous look on Schooner's face as the memories started to flood back, "I brought soccer tournaments and tailgating to the village," he laughed.

"You brought a lot more than that, Schooner," Malcolm was not going to let him make light of his accomplishments. "You taught lifesaving techniques, the importance of exercise and diet, as well competitive team sports. Those kids had the summer of their lives with you. Every year when we went back, everyone always asked about you and if you were coming back."

Mia and Dee exchanged glances and all Mia could think of was a word she had learned from her grandparents, a word that had its roots in Middle High German, but was generally found in the Yiddish language. *Kvell*. To be extraordinarily proud.

Both Mia and Dee were *kvelling* from all they were learning from Malcolm about Schooner's accomplishments in Africa. A teenage American boy, from a privileged background, with his hand in a cast and his heart in a sling, took all he had learned and coupled that with ingenuity and humility to make a lasting difference on the children of a poor village in a developing nation. Mia could not wait until Nathaniel was old enough to understand his father's accomplishments and maybe someday follow in his footsteps.

Fascinated by the details of all she was learning, Mia asked, "Malcolm, have you been back recently?"

"Not in the last eighteen months or so. My associate, who is much younger, is making most of the trips these days. So much of the disease we're seeing over there is brought on by lack of sanitary conditions and the inaccessibility to clean water. So, there is still a lot of work to be done. One in five children don't make it to their fifth birthday."

All eyes in the room flashed to Nathaniel as the gravity of that statement hit everyone in the gut.

"Is HIV and AIDS still so prolific over there?" Mia was keenly interested and Malcolm was impassioned on the subject.

"Unfortunately, yes. The internists struggle with this terrible cycle that they can't break. Patients are sent home with anti-retroviral drugs and then take them with unclean water and end up with secondary infections that their immune systems are just too compromised to handle. You should join a trip. I think it would be meaningful to you," turning back to Schooner, "and you should visit Macha again. It was a transformative time in your life."

Looking at Mia to gauge her reaction, Schooner was somewhat surprised to see a look on her face saying, "We should do this."

"When is your team going back again?" Schooner had a light in his eye.

"Late spring, early summer," Malcolm had him hook, line and sinker. "I'll put you in touch with my associate Roberto Castillo. I'm sure you can take what you started and expand upon it."

Mia could see Schooner's mind racing a million miles per hour, "What are you thinking?"

"I'm thinking that orthopedic rehab is probably not as prevalent as it should be over there. I'm thinking the number one college physical therapy program in the United States is right here at USC, where I know you have excellent connections, Malcolm. I'm thinking that every health club in this country, L9 included, scraps perfectly good equipment when the new models come out and I'm thinking it's time to go back to Zambia."

Sitting there shaking his head as it all began to process and gel, Schooner was feeling a touch of déjà vu as the exact feeling he felt that day in Malcolm's wood and leather office resurfaced. That sense of purpose and the excitement of an unknown adventure lying before him once again snuck up out of nowhere and grabbed him.

But this time, there was no escape or heartache involved, only renewed purpose and the ability to share his expertise and good fortune with those in need. Now, Mia would be at his side and all the images he tried so hard to capture with his Nikon, everything he dreamed of sharing with her, would now be part of their shared memories.

"Baby Girl," that gorgeous All-American boy smile was beaming, "we're going to Zambia."

Chapter Twenty-Three

With her laptop propped on her knees and Nathaniel curled up on the bed next to her in the Moore's guest bedroom, Mia laughed at the shocked expression on Seth's face.

"I'm telling you, Seth, I'm not creative enough to make this shit up." Mia could see their office in the background of the Skype image and missed the crazy energy of her Manhattan agency.

"BBC, can't you send him to Africa on his own? This is not like a high-end safari tour you are going on."

"I think it will be exciting."

"You want excitement, we'll drop you off somewhere in Brooklyn or The Bronx with two dollars and let you panhandle your way home."

"Oh my God, I miss you," Mia couldn't help but laugh.

"Who's going to watch, Nathaniel?" His arms were now crossed, as he began to get worked up.

"Well, I can have Lois come up from Florida," Mia instinctively reached out and rubbed Nathaniel's back. When she looked back at the screen, it was clear that her last statement had not gone over well.

Tapping his fingers loudly on the desk, "I'm his Godfather, Mia. Do you not trust me?"

"It's a lot of work and it's exhausting. I don't want to saddle you with that, Princess."

"Fuck you, BBC. I'm watching Nathaniel when you go off on your Hemingway adventure."

"Okay, okay," Mia laughed. "Are you sure you don't want Lois up to help you?"

"That would be fine. You can call her. So, with all those little CJ/Zac shenanigans, what is going on with the divorce?"

Smiling, Mia scrunched back into the pillows, "Princess, Pretty Boy would've gotten you so hard…"

"He always gets me hard," Seth interrupted.

Mia laughed, "I don't think I want to know that. Well, he would've made you even harder than he usually makes you. He is really very different out here. I guess because he's in his own domain, his empire. He's really commanding," *and demanding too*, thought Mia, a visual of their latest tryst on deck causing a tingling between her legs.

"BBC, he's always commanding. If you'd just put that dick of yours away every so often, you might actually notice."

"Fuck you, Princess," but Mia knew he was right, "and you're right, he is always commanding, but it's like kicked up a notch out here. It's really kind of hot. Anyway, he just told CJ, this gets signed this week or I'm going to ruin your life."

"You're right, I would've come in my pants. So, what does that mean if she signs it this week?"

"It means as soon as it gets in front of the judge, he signs it. So, it could all be completed in a couple of days."

"Oh my God," Seth literally squealed, "so, Lois and I do need to get together. When do you want to do this?"

Amused at how he had already switched into wedding mode, Mia shrugged, "I don't know. Late summer out at the beach or maybe even late September/early October, when the leaves are changing, maybe somewhere up along the Hudson River."

Eyebrows drawn together, "BBC, you really have no idea what you want."

Laughing, Mia shook her head, "Not a clue."

"You are so useless. Little girls grow up dreaming of this. Us gay boys grow up dreaming of this. I've been planning your wedding since dark, brooding, can't-keep-his-dick in his pants poet."

"You and Lois will figure it out. Just don't start planning until the judge signs that divorce decree. I don't want to jinx anything."

"It's a deal. Just promise you won't go all Bridezilla on me."

"I miss you so much, Princess. I promise to be a good bride as long as you don't put me in a dress that makes me look fat. And I don't want to be fru-fru. No fru-fru. Got that?" pointing her finger at the computer screen.

Rolling his eyes, "You're so annoying. Give my baby a huge kiss from Uncle Seth and give Pretty Boy a blow job from me."

"With pleasure and with lots of pleasure," waving goodbye she hit end call.

Chapter Twenty-Four

Roberto Castillo was not a southern Californian. Hailing originally from City Island in The Bronx, his accent was heavier than Mia's, despite twenty years in California.

"Berto Castillo," he extended a hand to Schooner.

The smile was on Mia's face even before his hand grasped hers.

"I understand you're from my neck of the woods," his warm brown eyes were smiling.

"Grew up on West 85th," Mia felt immediately at home with him.

"Which High School?" New York City geography was a favorite game amongst native New Yorkers. It included schools, restaurants, clubs and more often than not, you knew someone who they knew, making the degrees of separation surprisingly small for a city so large.

"Fieldston," Mia said with pride.

"Whoa, nice. Great education," Berto was nodding, clearly impressed.

"You?"

"Bronx Science," Berto's pride equaled Mia's.

"Ah, a smart one here," Mia kidded.

His laugh was hearty, "That's what I try and convince my patients."

Sitting down across from him at his desk, Schooner began, "I understand you are going back to Zambia in a few months. I don't know how much Malcolm shared. I joined him on a trip twenty-five years ago."

"Coach Schooner, you are legendary."

"In my own mind, maybe," Schooner laughed.

"Seriously," Berto began, "you really had an impact on those kids. You were kind of a star athlete, coach, camp counselor and NGO worker all rolled into one. One of the doctors we work with, Dr. Banda, was in your soccer league. He's said on more than one occasion that it was the best summer of his life and that is when he decided he wanted to become a doctor. Apparently, you taught them CPR and Oral-Rehydration Therapy."

Glancing over at a smiling Schooner, his eyes crinkled in the corners. Mia reached for his hand, his right hand, the one that had been casted the last time he was in Africa. As if sensing her thoughts, he squeezed her hand.

"We're currently working in and around the capital, Lusaka," Berto continued, "so it's a much more urban environment than what you experienced last time. Malcolm mentioned that you were interested in outfitting a rehab facility."

"I've had the opportunity over the last few days to reach out to counterparts in the industry. There are multiple things we can do to help. The equipment piece of it is easy, we have a lot of buying leverage for new product and we all replace machines that are in perfect condition and there's no reason they can't be used in clinics. The other two parts that I'm really excited about are launching capital campaigns within our clubs. Maybe a portion of each membership is donated beyond what we fund directly and that would be used to build a state-of-the-art PT rehab facility. The third piece is setting up a scholarship fund through USC's PT program to work abroad."

With her own head spinning, smiling at her big-hearted love, Mia was thinking aloud, "My team can certainly put together all the collateral and point-of-sale materials for the membership/capital campaign drive. Brochures, posters. We should shoot video while we're over there."

"Excellent idea, especially for major donor appeals for the capital campaign. Get your Nikon out, Ms. Silver, I'm envisioning very large photos hanging in the clubs." They were in their own space, brains tag-teaming, the electricity crackling like a hot wire hitting a puddle.

Sitting back in his worn leather chair, Berto watched the creative volley and found himself getting caught up in their palpable excitement. Medical missions dreamed of partnering with wealthy scions of industry and Schooner Moore had a personal stake in this venture. He was coming full circle back to where it all began. This was his opportunity to pay back the land and the people that gave him the inspiration that became his life's blood.

"We'll be spending time at several medical facilities and also working with a few of the local orphanages," Berto explained. "We're trying to put in place a network of facilities and a group of medical personnel to rotate through them."

By the time they walked out of his office, Mia was tossing ideas at Schooner as fast as he could serve a tennis ball and he was volleying them right back at her. This intellectual collaboration charged every cell in their bodies. For Mia and Schooner, this was foreplay at its best. As they arrived back at his parent's house, they snuck through the yard like teens, and made their way onto the boat without being spotted. Staying moored at the backyard dock, they raced below deck, and into the aft cabin.

Tackling Mia on the bed, Schooner grabbed Mia's hands over her head and buried his face in her neck.

"Schooner."

Pulling away to look at her, he tilted his head to the side.

Mia's devil grin had reached her eyes and they smoldered like emeralds in the cabin's dim light. "Schooner, we're going to Zambia."

Her words were a portal to every emotion he felt that day he sat in Malcolm's office, his devastation rapidly receding, as the unknown adventure loomed before him and the realization hit, "I'm going to Zambia."

Nodding, he could feel his heart bursting as his unanswered dreams finally were becoming his reality. This time it wasn't 'I'm' going. This time it was 'we're' going. Feeling the old ache find a crevice to steal its way into his heart, it was the ache that accompanied him to sleep every night and greeted him at the dawn's light. The longing to be sharing the wonder of the adventure with her. And now he was staring down at her smile. Her wanting body beneath him.

"Yes, Baby Girl, we are. We're going to Zambia." And in that moment, he didn't want to make love. He wanted to fuck her hard. He wanted to fuck away all the heart-splitting memories of longing for her with every breath he took that summer. He wanted to fuck them away and leave an open path for them to walk together as he showed her everything he ever dreamed of showing her and discovering things he never dreamed he'd be experiencing.

Silently, he made a vow to himself. This time there would be a picture of them together in front of Victoria Falls.

Chapter Twenty-Five

The Moore men sat in the Family Room, patriarch Gavin, Schooner, Zac and Nathaniel.

"I hate leaving you," the worry was evident in Schooner's eyes.

"We'll be fine, Dad," it was Zac that was doing the reassuring. "I'll still be around for a little bit before I have to go back. Or I could stay."

"No," was the stereo response from both his father and grandfather.

"You need to finish school," Schooner was adamant, "or you won't be starting college next year."

Zac had applied to several small private colleges in the northeast and Schooner knew that paying full tuition without any financial aid would help Zac's chances considerably. Having him on the east coast would ensure that he could keep a closer eye on his unstable son.

"I will miss you," Gavin smiled at his older grandson, "it's been great having you here and I owe you my life." Zac's quick reaction on the golf course to his grandfather's collapse significantly impacted the outcome.

Giving him a squeeze on the shoulder, Schooner was proud of his son. How to channel more of the "good Zac" was the big question at hand. Nathaniel seemed to have a very positive impact and Schooner wondered how he might be able to leverage that.

"There's something I want you to have," Gavin reached into his pants' pocket. Seeing the glint, both Schooner and Zac realized the importance of the moment.

In Gavin's hand was an eighteen-karat gold money clip. Centered on the front was a one carat investment grade diamond, catching the light in the room and sending out rainbow prisms of color. On the back of the money clip was a deep engraved letter 'M' in a Victorian script. The money clip had been given to Gavin by his grandfather, James Moore.

Looking to his father for approval to accept the gift, Zac waited for Schooner's nod indicating that he was okay with it skipping a generation.

"Thank you, Grandpa. Wow."

"Now don't go and pawn it or anything," Gavin clearly knew his grandson, "that stays in the family and gets passed down."

"I'm not going to pawn it," Zac looked from his grandfather to his father, only to be met by a look from Schooner telling him pawning the money clip would ensure certain death.

"Zac, I know this has been a tough year for you, everything in your life has changed," Schooner began, "and we've had some really extreme moments, you and I."

Zac nodded and Schooner went on.

"Your grandfather and I are still very concerned."

"I'm okay, Dad. Getting back to Exeter was good for me. I was a fish out of water here and I did a lot of stupid things. I'm really sorry I've worried everybody."

Gavin took over, "When you are in California, your grandmother and I really want you to stay with us. We'd like you to split your time between us and with your dad and Mia."

As if a shill in the audience, Nathaniel started to fuss in Schooner's arms, making it known he wanted to be held by his brother. Handing him off to Zac, Nathaniel planted a gooey kiss on his cheek.

"I'm going to miss you, Mini-Me," Zac's eyes were telling the truth.

A look passed between Gavin and Schooner. This one little boy had the power to heal so much, but if they could only figure out how to harness this elixir and keep Zac on the right path.

Chapter Twenty-Six

Schooner Moore could rock a suit like he was walking the runway at an Armani preview. As he strode confidently into his lawyer's office, tall and sleek in a custom gray suit and a tie that set off his eyes, he was feeling as good as he looked. Today he and CJ would finally sign the divorce papers.

Aaron Bender's P.A., Leslie, led Schooner down the hall into a conference room where everyone was already waiting for him. He didn't apologize for making them wait.

"Let's do this," he reached inside his breast pocket for his favorite pen, a Montblanc rollerball, that today he was thinking of as his lucky pen.

CJ sat across the table looking cool and coiffed. Noting her hair was significantly thicker and longer than it had been just days before, Schooner wondered if this was part of her transformation to single womanhood - trying to look twenty-something and not forty-something. *How unnecessary*, he thought.

"May I have a few minutes alone with my husband," CJ was staring Schooner down.

My husband? Schooner's immediate thought was, "What the heck is she up to?

When all the other parties left the room, she began, "I really hated seeing you with Mia."

Schooner remained silent, not sure where she was going.

"I just don't get it, Schooner. What are you doing with her? The two of you look ridiculous."

Feeling the muscles in his brows tightening and knowing they were knitting together, he fought to keep his face a placid mask. *"Pretend you're in front of a camera and the photographer just gave you the direction to look pensive with a faraway look in your eyes,"* he told himself, immediately feeling his muscles ease. Years of training in front of a camera often paid off.

With his silence, CJ continued, "Are you sure you really want to do this? Seriously, Schooner, she is so plain and I know people must look at the two of you and wonder what you are doing with her. You two are just so mismatched. It's going to be very difficult for you to be judged by everyone."

Years of bad patterns and knowing how to push buttons should have equated to Schooner's anger surfacing and flaring. It should have. That was their pattern. But today, Mia was with him, inside his head. And she brought Seth along for the show. Hearing them, loud and clear, he wanted to laugh along with them at the absurdity of CJ's words.

Sitting back and crossing his long legs, Schooner observed CJ for a moment before speaking, "You know, you are still very beautiful and I'm leaving you quite well off. We're still young, CJ, and we both have the opportunity to enjoy relationships with people who love us and make us happy. I'm happy. I know nothing would please the kids more than seeing you happy, too."

It was CJ's turn for her brows to knit. Schooner had singlehandedly destroyed her poker face with his atypical response.

"What does she have that I don't?" CJ could be like a terrier until she got what she wanted.

Sighing, "She has my heart and soul, CJ."

"Why?" her pitch becoming shrill, "Please explain to me why?"

"Are you sure you want me to? I really don't think you want me to do this."

"Oh, that is where you are wrong."

Remaining silent, it took him a moment to formulate the right words to finally make her understand what for a quarter-century she could not understand. Not wanting to be cruel, but at the same time wanting to be blunt enough for her to understand once and for all who he was, what he felt and what she had done to him - to them. To all of them.

"You and I, CJ, we were two sides of the same gold coin. By the time we were eighteen, we had our acts so tightly nailed down that there was nothing, or no one, that we couldn't have. We were the quintessential, beautiful California kids and we both knew just how far our looks could take us and exactly how to manipulate our plastic, shallow environment to get even more. Think about it, we were both totally jaded by the time we stepped foot on that college campus for the first time and we were only eighteen. I knew you wanted me that first day. And the feeling was mutual. We both knew that we'd be that couple that everyone treated like a king and queen. That shit was important to us because that's southern California. That's what we grew up with, that's what we knew," pausing, he didn't wait too long. "It was through my friendship with Mia, and Henry and Rosie, that I was shown something else, and it was basically a really different set of priorities. Different parameters of happiness. And CJ, for the first time in my life, I felt I could stop acting. And it was okay not to be big man on campus, okay not to be a cool asshole. Caring about the things that really touched me was okay, it wasn't something I needed to hide because people might not like me. And not giving a shit what other people thought about it was not only okay, it was liberating."

"You're so full of shit, Schooner," CJ was shaking her head. "All the years we were together you were the epitome of California cool asshole dick."

He laughed, and the confusion on her face was evident. Where was his famed anger?

"Yeah, I totally was. CJ, I'll be the first to admit, I operated very well in this environment. I've been manipulating it since I was a little boy. It's a dark place for me and I unfortunately do excessively well in the darkness. It doesn't mean I'm happy there, it just means I know how to make it work for me."

Flinging her newly found tresses back, Schooner laughed at the absurdity of her new mane. Wasn't there a doll when they were kids where you pressed a button in its stomach and its hair would grow? He remembered that commercial.

"We were never a team, CJ. We co-existed. We each did our own thing and showed up for one another on a scheduled appearance basis."

"And you and Mia are a team?" she actually snickered.

Smiling, he nodded, "Yes, we are. And learning how to be, more so, every day."

Again, another snicker, "Well, here's a piece of advice for you, don't bother to move your boat, you'll be back here in a year. This is who you really are. This is where you belong. Your little Mia New York adventure is a role you're playing that will soon tire and bore you. This is the real you, Schooner. I know the real you."

With cool sapphire eyes boring into her, he shook his head, "You never knew me. You saw what you wanted me to be. What you wanted from me."

"What I wanted from you? I remember a time when you wanted it," her eyes hardened into slits.

"And you were all too happy to give it," they were now descending rapidly into Schooner and CJ mode.

"And you were all too happy to take it."

"Until I didn't want it anymore," he was done.

"You're cruel."

"You always knew what it was. You got what you wanted from me."

"No, I never did. But I'm getting all I want and need from Beau."

Smiling, Schooner shook his head at her pathetic attempt to evoke jealousy, "Tell him even leftovers aren't free."

"You bastard," she screamed, scrambling to her feet as if she were going to round the table to slap him.

Slowly getting to his feet, she stopped in her tracks.

"He's always loved me," she hissed, a little girl trying to inflict hurt.

"Well then, you're batting 500," his demeanor remained calm, as he turned to the door and opened it. "We're ready to sign now," he advised the parties waiting in the hall.

Twenty minutes later, with papers signed, the process was officially underway. Once signed by a judge, he was free to finally marry Mia. Aaron had already secured a spot on the judge's docket.

With his dad recuperating nicely at home, Zac soon heading back to Exeter, and the divorce papers finally signed by both him and CJ, Schooner was more than ready to head home to New York, get back to work and start focusing on making the Zambian rehabilitation project a reality for their trip overseas.

Getting in the car, he texted Mia.

Schooner: Done deal. On my way home, Baby Girl.
Mia: Love you.
Schooner: It's smoochal.

On his drive back to his parent's house, Schooner Moore did four things: he made two phone calls, first, to the marina in Ocean Beach on Fire Island, where he secured a boat slip for True Compass, then he called a local transport company he'd dealt with in Newport Beach and made arrangements for them to transport the boat. Driving into Costa Mesa, he stopped at South Coast Plaza, to pick up something he had ordered when they first arrived in California. The instructions had been to hold it until he was ready to pick it up. The last thing he did was stop into his favorite wine store and grab a chilled bottle of Cristal.

Getting back into the car, Schooner felt like the universe was finally starting to right itself and that his life in the light was drawing closer and closer.

Chapter Twenty-Seven

Dee was the only one downstairs when Schooner returned to the house.

"Where is everyone?" he picked at the grapes on the fruit platter she was cutting up.

"Zac is at L9 working out, your father and Nathaniel are napping and Mia is showering." She stopped cutting the fruit and put the knife down, "How did it go?

"It went. It's done," he smiled. "CJ and I had a very bizarre private conversation. I really tried to keep it positive and not fall into the old traps. But she kept baiting me and it got a little nasty." Picking up the bottle of Cristal, he walked over to the refrigerator and put it in.

"Are we celebrating?" Dee was trying not to smile.

Breaking into his irresistible All-American Boy smile, Schooner nodded, "Yes, we are." Reaching into the pocket of his suit jacket, Schooner pulled out a Tiffany's box.

Gasping, "You bought a ring?"

His smile continued to brighten his face, "I did."

"Mia is going to be so surprised," Dee enjoyed being complicit in Schooner's surprise.

"I know," his smiled took on a devilish lilt, "and Mia hates surprises."

They both laughed.

"I know she has grandma's ring, but I really wanted her to have something of her own, from me."

"I'm sure she'll love it," Dee was dying to see the ring in the box, "but you know, she adores my mother's ring, it makes her feel a part of the family, in a bigger sense, and that is important to Mia."

"Did she tell you that?" Schooner grabbed an apple slice off the tray.

"She did. She was really honored to be part of a family tradition."

Tossing the pale blue Tiffany's box in the air, "Hmm, maybe I should return this?" he joked.

"I wouldn't go that far," Dee laughed. "No woman doesn't love a gift in a Tiffany's box."

"I should mess with her and put something else in the box."

"Schooner!" Dee reproached her son, but the look in her eyes dared him.

"Oh come on, it would be the perfect thing to do to Mia." He started looking around the kitchen for small objects. "Let me think, let me think," and then his face lit up, "perfect."

Grabbing the Tiffany's box off the center island, Schooner headed to the counter stacked with pouches of Nathaniel's food and picked up a box of Animal Crackers, opening it. His delight was evident as he ruffled through the box looking for something specific. Finally finding what he was looking for, he slowly eased the white bow off the Tiffany's box. Opening the box, he removed the ring and slipped it into his pocket, replacing it with a cookie. He then eased the bow back on the outer box until it looked perfect again.

Grabbing a plate from the cabinet, he began to disassemble Dee's perfect fruit plate.

"What are you doing?" she feigned irritation.

"Just borrowing a few things." From the refrigerator, he took two blocks of cheese and the Cristal he had just put in there, and then some table water crackers from the cabinet.

Artfully arranging his cheese and fruit platter in an impressive manner, he looked up at his mother, who was watching intently. Smiling at her with pure joy, "Hey, I learned from the master."

He left the room and quickly returned with two champagne flutes. Arranging the platter and glasses, Cristal and ring box, he stepped back and held up his phone, focusing the camera on his still life masterpiece. Snapping a photo, he looked at the result, moved the position of the glasses and reshot the photo.

"Yes," he was rather pleased with himself. "I'm going to text Mia to meet me on the boat. Will you watch Nathaniel?"

"Of course," Dee laughed at her son's playfulness. It was nice to see Schooner not being serious.

Schooner: Meet me on the boat. (picture attached)

Quickly grabbing all the elements of his still life, Schooner gave Dee one last huge smile and was out the French doors, heading down the dock.

A few minutes later, Mia entered the kitchen, a most bemused look on her face, her hair still wet from the shower. Holding up her phone to Dee, she pointed to the Tiffany's box, shock registering on her face.

Dee laughed and pointed to the French doors, "I'll watch the baby."

Chapter Twenty-Eight

By the time Mia boarded True Compass, Schooner had the still life perfectly laid out on the teak deck table to mirror the picture he had sent.

"Q'est-ce que c'est, my friend?" she pointed to the Tiffany's box in the picture on her phone.

Making a grand sweeping gesture, Schooner indicated to Mia to take a seat.

"So, I'm assuming today went well?" it was a question.

"If by 'went well' you mean all the papers are signed, then yes, it went exceedingly well." Schooner had a smug smile on his face.

Clapping, Mia was getting anxious, "Tell me everything. I want details."

Schooner knew CJ's vitriolic comments were not worth repeating, so he opted for the abridged version, "She told me she hated seeing us together and asked me what you had that she didn't."

Mia's eyes were wide with surprise, "What did you tell her?"

Smiling, his real smile, "I told her you had my heart and soul."

Mia's face crumbled from the emotion and her eyes filled with tears, "Mmm, did you really say that?"

"I did," he shook his head.

"I love you, Schooner Moore."

"I love you, too, Mia Silver," and grabbing the Tiffany's box from the table, he handed it to Mia, "Open it."

"Oh my God," Mia's eyes were bright with tears.

Schooner nodded for her to open the box. With trembling hands, she slipped off the white satin ribbon and opened the robin's egg blue signature Tiffany box. Taking out the Tiffany blue ring box, she placed the outer box and ribbon on the table. Schooner held out his hand, indicating that Mia should hand the ring box back to him.

Dropping to one knee and kneeling before her, pale sapphire eyes twinkled as he took a deep breath, "Mia Silver, would you do me the honor of," and he paused, his All-American boy smile hijacking his face as he snapped open the ring box, "coming with me to Zambia?"

It took Mia a moment to process what she was seeing. Reaching into the ring box, she removed its contents, quickly bit the head off an elephant cookie and sat chewing it very slowly, never breaking eye contact with Schooner. Handing the uneaten body to Schooner, "Yes, Schooner, I will go to Zambia with you," and with that, she threw her head back with laughter. "You shit!"

Laughing so hard that tears were streaming down his cheeks, "You should have seen the look on your face."

"Oh man, you suck."

Schooner picked up the chilled bottle of Cristal and removed the foil around the cage. Still laughing, he began to twist the tab and eased the wire cage from the cork.

"That was so great," he chuckled.

"Payback is going to be a bitch, you know that." Mia fluffed her semi-wet curls.

"I would expect nothing less from you, Ms. Silver." Pointing the bottle away from Mia, Schooner held the cork tight and twisted the bottle, the champagne opening with a perfect pop. Putting the cork down on the table next to the open Tiffany's box, he picked up a flute, filled it and handed it to Mia and then filled one for himself.

Schooner loved toasts, "Well, it took over a year, but today all the papers are finally signed. Aaron's going to have them in front of the judge next week and then I am finally free to marry you."

"Yay. It feels like it's been five years since the process began, doesn't it?"

"Living out here was a lifetime ago to me," he looked around, "because I have a whole new life now and you and Nathaniel are at the center of it."

Holding up his glass, "Mia, Mia, Mia. Finally, to us. To getting married. To raising our beautiful son together. To waking up every day of my life next to you and to holding you in my arms every night as I fall asleep. To doing great and meaningful things together and to enjoying the love that we have always had for one another. I feel like in the months since Nathaniel's birth that we have figured out how to be a team. A family. You are just there for me in ways I never knew someone could be there to support me and cheer for me and make sure I stay on track and am ok. Does that make sense?"

Mia nodded. Smiling.

"You know I have waited for this moment since I'm eighteen years old," his eyes started to glisten.

"I know," Mia's voice barely more than a whisper, "it was all I ever wanted."

"Well, now you have it and I hope it's as good as you dreamed," his eyes searched her face.

"My dreams never even came close to the reality you have given me, Schooner. I thought you were wonderful when I met you, but I had no idea of the man you would become. Nathaniel and I are so incredibly lucky to be sharing our lives with you."

"Yeah, well that is smoochal, Baby Girl. I know I gave you the ring from my grandmother and I understand it means a lot to you, but I want you to have something that is just ours. Just me and you. From me."

He put his champagne glass on the table and reached over and took Mia's glass from her and placed it on the table next to his. Getting down on one knee again, he took her left hand and slipped off his grandmother's ring. Taking her right hand, he slipped the heirloom ring on her right ring finger.

"Looks good there," he mused, taking her left hand in both of his. "Baby Girl, I know I've asked you this before, but now I'm finally free to ask you again and this time set a date. It's a little bit past your eighteenth birthday."

"Just a little," she laughed.

"And about three thousand miles away from where I'd planned to ask you."

A dark cloud passed over her eyes and he could see the tears gather. Realizing the specter of the World Trade Centers must've crossed her mind, he squeezed her hand supportively.

"But here we are, finally. And it's our time. I love you more than I dreamed I ever could, Mia. Every day I love you more and more. You make me a better man. You make me want to be a better man. You see what I'm like out here in this environment. I'm existing. But with you, in our world, I'm finally living. And it's really good to be alive."

"Yes, it is," she whispered, locked in on his eyes and holding on tight.

"So, tell me that you will spend the rest of your life with me, as my wife. I promise every inch of my heart will always be yours. Always. Marry me, Baby Girl. Marry me."

Mia sighed, "I don't know, Schooner. You know, I kind of think that maybe I'm not the marrying kind."

Flashing shock, his eyes widened and his jaw went slack, her words had rendered him speechless. Still on one knee, dressed in his impeccable gray suit, Schooner searched Mia's eyes, his grip tightening around her hands, he couldn't let go. He wouldn't let go.

And then there it was, slowly tugging at the far corners of her lips until it consumed her entire face and her eyes - the devil smile.

"Oh, you bitch," he shook his head. Pulling her by her hands off the bench and onto his bent knee, "You know you should be face down on my knee and not sitting on it."

"You handed me a Tiffany's ring box and it had an animal cracker in it," putting her forehead to his and her lips against his, "son of a bitch. That is just cruel," she was laughing.

"Yeah, I know," he looked rather proud of himself, "so now give me my answer," his tone was demanding, but his eyes danced with delight.

With her right hand, she pushed his hair from his forehead, "I don't have a very good track record of saying no to you, do I?" Her eyes became serious as she intently studied his clear blue eyes, "Do you know, I once told my mom that I thought we were the same soul in two separate bodies and when I look back on that, I really had no idea at the time just how true that was. Me and you, Schooner. It has always been me and you."

"It's always been only you and me, Mia. Pretty much our entire lives."

"And now for the rest of our lives," Mia kissed the tip of his nose.

Smiling, "So, is that a yes?"

"Pretty Boy, there had better be a freaking ring to go with that box."

Laughing, he shifted her on his knee and reached into the pocket of his suit pants. Taking her left hand, "Baby Girl, will you marry me?"

Nodding, "Schooner Moore, I have dreamed of being your wife since I was sixteen years old. So, hell yes!"

Sliding a simple round brilliant diamond in a classic platinum Tiffany setting onto her left ring finger with his right hand, he weaved the fingers of his left hand through her still slightly damp, wild mane. Pulling her into him for a kiss, and then another one, and then another. Mia finally drew away. Breathless.

He held her left hand out before her.

Picking up the sun's rays and color from all angles, Mia gasped at the beauty of the solitaire ring. It was simple. It was elegant. It was timeless. And it was huge.

"Schooner," she looked up at him, "it's gorgeous, but it's huge."

With a real smile and a look of pride, "Yes, it is and no one will ever doubt that you, Mia Silver, are mine."

Chapter Twenty-Nine

It was already dark as he walked the last few blocks from Kee's Chocolates to their loft. There was a heavy balminess to the air that said spring and all its possibilities were on the horizon, looming just up ahead and around the corner. Turning south on Mercer Street, Schooner Moore had never felt more at home anywhere in his life. Their SoHo neighborhood was really a neighborhood, and he knew more about these people and their lives in the few short months that they had lived there than he had ever known about his Linda Isle neighbors. The thing he loved most here in SoHo was the quirky sense of camaraderie amongst neighbors and shopkeepers and how they all looked out for one another. Nathaniel would grow up with a community that was looking out for him and that brought Schooner both a sense of well-being and belonging.

The apartment was quiet, it was past Nathaniel's bedtime and Schooner could hear the shower running. He took off his jacket and went into the kitchen to grab two champagne glasses. Uncorking the bottle of chilled Cristal, he carried the champagne, glasses and the box from Kee's into the bedroom.

"Hey Baby Girl, I'm home," he yelled out, not wanting to scare her by just appearing in the bathroom.

"Hi babe. I'll be out in a few minutes."

"Take your time," he yelled back, kicking off his shoes.

With the champagne glasses filled, he entered the steam obliterated bathroom. The glass on the shower was so fogged up, he could barely make out Mia. Opening the foggy glass door, he stuck his arm in with a glass of cold champagne.

Mia squealed, "Are we celebrating?"

"We are celebrating. Down that baby so I can refill your glass."

With a devil smile, Mia tossed back the fine champagne, stuck her arm out the shower door and held her glass out for a refill.

"Open your mouth," he was going to have some fun with her.

"Why?"

"Open. Your. Mouth," his sapphire eyes bore into her.

"Shall I close my eyes, too?" she challenged.

"God, you are a mouthy little thing. But yes, close your eyes, too."

Giving him a devilish grin, she slowly took a sip of champagne and then closed her eyes and opened her mouth.

Weaving his fingers through her wet hair, he pulled her head to him, softly brushing her lips with his.

Her moan was almost immediate and his kiss became more urgent, his tongue sensuously stroking hers. Pulling away, he took a sip of the cold champagne and pulled her head back as he let it slowly dribble from his mouth to hers, until she was sucking it out of his mouth.

With his free hand, Schooner hastily unbuttoned his shirt, shrugging it to the floor. Reaching into the front pocket of his faded jeans, he pulled something out of his pocket and slipped it in his mouth. Using both hands, he pulled Mia's face in for another kiss and with his tongue deposited what was in his mouth into hers.

Opening her eyes, surprised, she looked at him questioningly. He stood there looking very satisfied.

"Bite down," he ordered.

Complying, the look on her face turned from surprise to pure pleasure as the dark chocolate crushed in her mouth, gushing blood orange infused cream and Grand Marnier.

"Mmmm-mmmm. Oh my God."

Taking her champagne glass from her, he set it on the marble ledge outside the shower and picked up the bottle of Cristal. Lifting it to his lips, he decadently drank the expensive wine straight from the bottle.

Handing her the bottle just inside the shower door, where she still stood, "You are a man of surprises," she noted, lifting the bottle to her lips, devil grin glowing.

Pulling down the zipper on his faded jeans, freeing his pent-up erection, "You ain't seen nothing yet." Stepping out of his jeans, he took the bottle from her as he joined her in the shower.

"I take it we're celebrating?" Mia pushed her wet bangs from her eyes.

"Baby Girl, you haven't even begun to take it yet," his smile was mesmerizing as he turned her around and pulled her back snugly against his stomach. Reaching for the shower gel, he squeezed a healthy amount into his palm before replacing the tube and then rubbing his hands together, lathering and warming the cool gel. Slowly, he rubbed his hands down the sides of her neck down to her shoulders.

"Why are you assuming I'm a dirty girl?" her voice already breathy from his stroking hands.

"Even though you've been in this shower long enough to turn you into a prune, I know my little wild girl likes it hot, rough and dirty." His hands continued to slide down her arms to her hands, fingers interlocking with hers. He brought her hands up to her breasts and hand over hand had her start pinching her own nipple as he controlled her fingers like a puppet. "Feels good, doesn't it," he whispered hoarsely in her ear.

"Yes, it feels really good," her sentence ending in a moan.

"I love watching you do yourself," he pinched her fingers tighter to hear her whimper. "I love making you do yourself for me."

"Yeah, I've noticed. And it's a good thing because I like doing myself for you."

"Don't stop playing with your nipples," he removed his hands from hers and reached for a washcloth and the gel. As he squirted the gel onto the washcloth, he kissed the length of her neck, "Do you know how much I love you, Mia?"

Nodding, "I think so, but you might want to remind me."

Pulling her hips tight against him so that she could feel how hard she had made him, "Does that refresh your memory, Baby Girl?"

"I think I get your point," she ground her ass into his hard cock.

"I plan on making my point over and over again," with his face buried in her neck, his right hand slid the washcloth between her legs. "But first I want to hear you come for me." Slowly he pulled the washcloth from front to back, making her moan from the rough sensation. Sinking his teeth into her neck, he felt her weight shift to him as she began to whimper. Tossing the washcloth to the floor, he pressed her clit with his index finger and inserted the next two fingers into her. With his left arm across her chest he held her to him.

"You know what I want to do to you, don't you?" his lips grazed her ear as his fingers skillfully moved in and out in a "come here" motion that made her quiver.

"Yes," her voice was trembling, "it's been too long."

Laughing, "You're right. It has been too long." Grabbing another tube off the shelf, "Is this the same stuff we have out at the beach?"

"Yes, the mango butter lotion," she nodded. "Give it to me."

"You want it?" his expression was most amused.

"Give it to me, Pretty Boy," she held out her hand over her shoulder.

"All yours, Baby Girl," he handed it to her.

Turning around to face him, she flipped open the top of the tube and brought it up to her nose, inhaling deeply, the aroma inducing a smile at the memory it evoked. Holding it up to Schooner's nose, he too took a deep whiff of the scent.

"Reminds me of summer," Mia's eyes were smiling.

"I can't wait to get out there."

"Me too," she squirted a healthy amount onto her palm and put it back on the shelf, "I can't wait to see how Nathaniel reacts to the sand and ocean," looking up at him with a devil smile, "but for right now, I just want to see how you react to this." Taking his cock in both hands, she slathered him in the rich lotion.

"I think you got the reaction you were going for."

"You know how I hate to fail," she slowly slid her tightened hands up the length of him, one after the other, feeling him grow harder and harder.

"Failure is not an option here, Baby Girl," his voice was choked as he reached for the mango butter tube, "turn around."

Complying, she placed her hands on the wall for leverage. Hearing the top flip open on the lotion's tube made her shiver. Not warming the lotion in his hands, he pulled her butt cheeks apart and swiped the lotion up her crack.

"Ahhh," she jumped at the contact with the cold cream, "you bastard."

Schooner laughed and reached around her pinching her nipples, "Make that cruel bastard."

"Mmm, you'd never be cruel to me, would you?"

Pinching harder, "We'll have to see about that. Now give me that ass. Grabbing the mango butter tube, he quickly covered two fingers, inserting a long index finger slowly and easing it out before pressing two fingers back, "God, you're tight. I can't wait to be in there," and he slowly pulled them out.Pressing the head of his rock-hard cock at the opening of her ass, his teeth grazed her neck, as he pushed in, he pulled her head to the side and bit down.

"Oh, fuck," she moaned.

"Are you ready to take it?"

"As much as you can give me," she challenged, bracing herself against the marble wall.

"That's my girl," and he pulled out, till just the tip of his cock rested against her and without warning, rammed all the way back in until he was completely buried inside of her.

Her moan resonated in his ears, propelling him into a rhythm where he got lost in the tight, gripping sensation of her ass, "Oh God, I love you," he growled in a deep whisper. "Your ass is so damn tight around my cock." He wasn't sure if the sounds he was hearing were his or hers, a primal symphony of lust, want and satisfaction taking him to a space far away as he pounded as hard as he could into her. "I own your ass, you know that don't you, I own it."

"Yes," was all she could manage, lost to the overwhelming sensations, "so good," her voice an actual whimper, "so good."

Grinding into her, he stilled, totally embedded within her, his arms wrapped around her tightly. "I have something to tell you," and with his right arm he reached out and grabbed the bottle of Cristal off the shelf. Holding it to her lips, he tipped it back, cold champagne going into her mouth and dribbling down her chin before dripping onto her shower-warmed breasts. "God, you're so hot." Lifting the bottle to his own lips, he took a healthy swig and placed it back on the shelf. Wrapping both arms around her again, he began to drive into her relentlessly, at a fast pace, the friction making his balls tighten as the pressure climbed and expanded inside his cock.

She reached a fevered pitch, her moans testifying that she had gone someplace else, somewhere deep inside herself, lost to the sensations of the heightened nerve endings he was voraciously stroking deep inside of her.

Ramming as hard as he could, all control gone, he shot deep into her. It was at that moment, he chose to share more than just his seed, "I'm all yours, Baby Girl. I'm divorced."

Chapter Thirty

Repeatedly kissing Nathaniel's cheek, "I am going to miss you so much, my sweet boy."

"He'll be fine," Lois reassured her. "Seth and I have it covered."

"Will you be a good boy for Nana and Uncle Seth?" Mia could feel the aching tug in her heart, a combination of both longing and the guilt of leaving Nathaniel for the first time. "I love you so much, sweet boy."

"So why are you going again?" Seth's idea of adventure was taking a subway to Brooklyn to shop for ethnic foods. "I can't believe he's turning you into a do-gooder."

Laughing, "You just want to go with him. Admit it."

"BBC, there isn't anything I don't want to do with that man," Seth licked his lips.

"He is rather nice looking," Lois added.

"Rather nice looking?" Seth raised his eyebrows.

"Okay, okay, he's hot and if I were thirty years younger."

"Ewww, Mom, stop that. He's going to be your son-in-law. He's the father of your grandchild." The look on Mia's face was of pure disgust.

"Oh, wipe that look off your face. I'm not dead and the man is hot. And just remember, I saw him first."

"Nathaniel, I cannot believe we are having this conversation," Mia said seriously to her smiling son.

As if on cue, the elevator to the loft opened and in walked Schooner, faded jeans, pink Ralph Lauren button down rolled at the cuffs, exposing muscular forearms and a pair of beat up Gold Cup Topsiders. In his right hand, he carried a long cardboard tube.

"All my favorite people in one place," he hit them with the smile.

"He's talking about me," Seth whispered to Lois.

Bending down to kiss Mia, he took Nathaniel from her arms. "Want to see something cool?" he asked the infant.

Nathaniel responded with an open goopy kiss to Schooner's nose.

"Are you trying to eat my face?" Schooner responded with a raspberry to his son's neck, eliciting a giggle from the baby.

"Do not even say it," Lois warned Seth.

"You were thinking it, too, BBC Mom."

Sitting down on the couch, he handed Mia the tube. She popped off the plastic end and reached for the documents inside. Sitting down next to Schooner and Nathaniel, she unrolled a set of blueprints on the table and smoothed down the paper.

Looking at Schooner with a huge smile, "Coach Schooner, you are truly going to be a legend there."

Motioning for Seth and Lois to come over to their side of the table, he walked everyone through the plans.

"My architect has got contractors from Germany that are very familiar with working in Lusaka and they are going to oversee the construction. You enter here into a reception area with intake offices and that leads into the main physical therapy area. We'll have most of the exercise equipment here and this will be the main hub. Over here to the left will be hydrotherapy and these rooms here are private treatment rooms. We're actually going to add this small wing as a workshop lab area for making and fitting prosthetics. Across from that is the children's therapy area. Oh, and over here, will be a waiting area outfitted with toys and games for children and siblings who have to wait. I remember that was a huge issue when I was in Macha and it was why I started the soccer camp."

Mia poured over the blueprints looking at the flow and traffic patterns. "Where are bathrooms and kitchen? Staff break area? Will there be separate employee bathrooms?"

"Good catch, that was not put in. Public bathrooms are here," he pointed to a spot, "but you're right, we really need a bathroom and a shower over here with some employee lockers." Slinging an arm over her shoulder and pulling her to him, he kissed the top of her head. Picking up his phone, he quickly texted his architect. "Now is the time to catch this stuff."

"Why don't you two look," Mia said to Lois and Seth, "you both have good eyes for this."

Taking over the couch, Lois and Seth poured over the blueprints and began to discuss it in fine detail.

"Are you going to be okay leaving him?" Schooner asked Mia as Nathaniel babbled at the two of them.

"No. I can't even imagine what a day is going to be like without him. Are the copies of our wills back yet? I want to make sure everything is in place before we go."

"We should actually have them by the end of the day today, so don't worry about that."

Indicating that he should follow her down the hall away from Seth and Lois, Schooner followed Mia into Nathaniel's jungle room.

"What's up?" he cocked his head.

"I was thinking. Do you want to just go down to City Hall and get married before we go?"

"Are you kidding?"

"No. I'm not. This way with us being married, if something should happen," she didn't finish her sentence.

Shaking his head no, "Mia, from a legal standpoint should something happen to either or both of us, we have everything locked down, married or not. It's all taken care of. I'm all for getting married sooner rather than later, but you know what, you deserve a wedding. We deserve to celebrate with everyone we love."

"But I don't need," she began her protest.

"No, you don't need. But what I would like for you to have, what I'd like for us to be able to share together, are wonderful memories of a day we've waited for since we were kids. This was our dream, Mia. Me and you. Married. That was our dream."

Nodding, "You're right. You're absolutely right."

Taking a sleepy Nathaniel from him, she laid him down in his crib. Standing beside her, Schooner pulled her close to him. "And this is the other part of our dream, Baby Girl," they stood and watched him as he fell asleep, this beautiful little angel who brought light to everyone's life.

"Here's what I think," he began, "let's go to Zambia and make some dreams come true for other people, and then we'll come home and make the rest of our dream come true. How does that sound?"

Mia smiled and nodded. She couldn't speak for fear her voice would crack. Here was this man, this beautiful man, who told her that she made him a better man. That she made him want to be a better man. How could that be? It was he that made her a far better person. Didn't he see that?

As she stood looking at Nathaniel's sweet face, she wondered what Schooner would think if he knew all her secrets. Would he still look at her the same way? Would he still feel that she made him a better man?

Chapter Thirty-One

Driving down the Jacaranda lined streets of Lusaka, Mia was amazed at how the city was so cosmopolitan, its vitality exuding a different and unique beat than she was used to hearing.

"I don't know what I expected. I knew it was the capital, but somehow the wilds of Africa were in my head."

Joined by Berto, his wife Marit and their daughter, Liliana, who had just completed her freshman year at Yale, they were doing a mini-tour prior to heading over to the first hospital facility.

Turning around in his seat, Berto explained, "You are going to see a huge divergence in lifestyles here, from walled suburban communities to shantytowns. There's been a huge influx of residents from rural areas into the city. Unfortunately, it hasn't been a boomtown and unemployment is at about sixty percent."

"Sixty percent? Holy smokes. That is beyond significantly high," Mia frowned, as she watched the scenery pass outside the van's window.

"This afternoon, we will visit Kabwata Village and that'll give you an opportunity to really get a flavor for the people and the culture," Berto explained.

"And to shop," Marit added.

"You just said the magic words," Schooner smiled at Mia.

Pulling up to the first facility, Berto explained a lot of what they could expect. "This is a newer facility and you'll find from a technology standpoint they are pretty well equipped. This is one of the facilities where I think we can help fill in the gaps in their PT Rehab area with equipment, but in general, this facility is offering premiere level service in Lusaka. Unfortunately, they can only see so many patients. So not everyone is getting this level of treatment."

After touring the PT Rehab center, Schooner, Mia and Berto sat down with the department director and Marit and Lily went to go tour the pediatrics' floor.

"I'm very impressed with what you've got in place. What's visibly missing are the multi-stack/multi-station gyms, and I would venture to guess you could probably use a few more leg extension/leg curl stations."

The director, a distinguished grey-haired gentleman who appeared to be in his mid-50's, laughed, "Have you been reading my memos to administration?"

"If we can put in just two of the multi-stacks, you'll be able to see so many more patients a day," Schooner continued to survey the facility.

"With just those pieces of equipment, we should be able to accommodate at least a fifteen percent increase in patients. And that's a conservative estimate."

Nodding, Schooner tapped his finger against his lips, "I don't see any issues with us being able to provide that." He walked over to where a therapist was working with a patient who had sustained a leg injury and watched them work through a series of exercises.

"I understand we're going to have PT's here on loan as part of a scholarship program you're setting up," the director mentioned as they were departing the facility.

"What we're envisioning is to bring them over to work at the facilities here in Lusaka first as they acclimate to being in country and then cycle them through some of the more rural facilities. We're going to try and assess some equipment and training needs for those areas, as well."

"Let me know how I can be of help in all this, Coach Schooner," the director's smile glinted in his eyes.

The surprise on Schooner's face at being addressed as 'Coach Schooner' was evident. In his eyes flashed a deep emotional response that wouldn't have been detected by anyone but Mia. On his face was his All-American boy smile. But it wasn't his real smile.

Schooner Moore was wearing a mask and Mia Silver was wondering why.

The next stop brought them to a hospital that wasn't nearly as financially endowed. Walking the old tile hallway, Mia's heart felt heavy. There didn't seem to be the hope in these corridors as there had been in the first hospital.

"Adjacent to this, on the property is where we will be breaking ground later this week for the new rehab facility," Berto explained. "There's also a small orphanage that is part of the facility."

Looking at the expressions fleeting across Liliana Castillo's face, Mia instinctively knew that they were both feeling a sense of uneasiness and frustration. There was so much that could be done to help, and so many superfluous things in their everyday lives, things that they would never miss, that could make a significant difference in the lives of these people. Walking over to her, Mia could feel the protective force field she had erected around herself. Mia knew it well. Lily might be protected by Human Shield v.2, a wall impenetrable by other human beings, but it didn't put Mia off, after all she had been the inventor of the original Human Shield v.1.

Casually slinging an arm over the teen's shoulder, "I am feeling positively disgusted at the decadence that I call my life."

Lily looked at Mia, her almond-shaped golden-brown eyes, widening and tearing up slightly. Nodding, she didn't speak, but also did not move away from Mia's embrace.

A handsome young doctor approached, coming down the hall toward them. In light blue scrubs, a surgical mask still hanging around his neck, he appeared to have been coming straight from the operating room. And then it happened, for the second time that morning.

"Coach Schooner," he exclaimed, loudly.

Mia watched as Schooner visibly stiffened at the moniker, until the young doctor smiled, and in that split second, Schooner Moore's face emoted pure joy as the two men came together in the hearty, warm embrace of brothers who had been separated for a lifetime.

From the moment she spied the young doctor's smile, Mia could feel the tears spurt forth from her eyes and begin their lazy trail down her cheeks. She would've recognized that smile anywhere.

The two men still held each other tight, swaying slightly. Where they had gone in their lives, who they had become and why they were once again together were inextricably tied together and always would be. This was fate at its best, taking paths and intertwining them, twisting them, turning them and then bringing them back together in a sublime homecoming that neither of them could have ever imagined. Such sweetness of fate was the ultimate gift.

"I want you to meet Mia," Schooner was wiping tears from his face with the back of his hand.

Wiping his own tears, "You got the girl!"

"Yeah, it took me awhile, but I got the girl," Schooner clapped him on the back.

And turning to Mia with his brilliant smile, the gap between his front teeth making her think, "the only thing he's missing is the soccer ball," was Dr. Sonkwe Banda, Schooner's eight year-old star goalie from the Macha Soccer Camp.

Chapter Thirty-Two

A man of great cheer and boundless energy, Sonkwe Banda proudly led the tour through the facility. It was apparent that he wanted one member of that tour group to be proud of him and his achievements.

Born of the heartache of that summer, Schooner was seeing firsthand the results of selfless behavior and of playing to his strengths. The nine children of Macha that became his "assistants" were as affected by the magic of that summer as he had been. They were his anchor, his reason to get up every day and drive himself as hard as he could. His commitment to them had kept him from falling into a deep depression - Mia was gone and his bright tennis career shattered.

And now, a quarter of a century later, he was building a physical therapy rehabilitation center at a facility where his goalie led the pediatrics' department.

"How does Schooner know Dr. Banda?" Lily asked Mia, as they trailed behind the rest checking out the different wards.

"After our freshman year in college, Schooner came over here with Dr. Faulkes to set up a facility in Macha. His hand was in a cast, so he couldn't do too much, but he realized that all these families were traveling long distances for medical attention and they would bring their children, who would end up sitting around waiting all day. So, with the help of nine kids from the village, Schooner set up a soccer and fitness camp for the kids. They played soccer and had tournaments and he taught them about exercise and nutrition and how to do CPR and other lifesaving techniques. Dr. Banda was his goalie."

"Is this the first time they've seen each other since that summer?" Lily's smile was bright.

"Yes, it is. Schooner has a picture of him holding a soccer ball. I recognized him immediately when he smiled."

Mia was taken by Lily's awe. It was the first time she'd seen the girl really smile since they had met.

"And now he's building this facility here and they are together again, that is incredible. What are the chances?"

"I know, right?" Mia laughed.

"I really feel like I should be doing something over here, Mia, not sitting in a classroom in New Haven with a bunch of pompous, over-educated professors and rich, erudite kids. I know I can do so much more here, like Schooner did."

They stopped to watch a blonde man working alone at his desk. He didn't have an office, his desk resided against a wall at the end of a hallway. In front of him, spread out was a variety of white plastic triangles in different sizes, a palette of paints and brushes. With a fine-tipped brush in hand, he meticulously painted the minute details of a pupil and an iris onto one of the white plastic shells.

Sensing he was being watched, he looked up, his warm blue eyes welcoming Mia and Lily.

"Hello," he spoke in a soft, German-accented voice.

"Hi, I hope we are not bothering you." Mia was fascinated by what he was doing.

"Not at all," he assured them.

"Are those prosthetic eyes?" Lily was in awe.

"Yes, these are the shells and after I paint them, they get cooked," he explained.

"For some reason, I always envisioned they'd be like plastic balls. Do you mind if I photograph you?" Mia asked.

"Not at all," his smile was as warm as his eyes. "They used to be more like plastic balls in the past, but the body continually tried to reject that. In recent years, doctors have begun to use implants that the body will accept and will actually become vascularized. These prosthetics that I make then sit on top of the implant."

"Like a big contact lens almost?" Lily was trying to envision it.

"Yes, exactly like that."

"Why do most people lose eyes?" She watched him closely putting in the fine lines of brown iris.

"A variety of reasons, accidents, disease, infection."

Pointing to several small shells, "Are those for children?" she asked, alarm in her own eyes.

He nodded, "Yes. I am just making a pair for a child who had cancer."

"In their eyes," both Mia and Lily said in unison, shocked.

"Yes, it is called retinoblastoma and it affects infants and toddlers, often before the age of two."

Mia put her camera aside, suddenly unable to breathe. Those were babies Nathaniel's age. Parents just like her and Schooner. *How could that be? How did they deal with that?*

"Is it deadly?" Lily was the first to speak.

"If not treated in time, like any other cancer," the sadness in his kind eyes surfaced. He had seen too many children whose diagnosis had not been made in time. "Unfortunately, if the diagnosis is delayed or if the tumors don't respond to other therapies, the eye must be removed to save the child's life. The goal is to stop the cancer before it metastasizes, even if that means losing one or both eyes."

How could this be? The ocularist's words surfaced one of the darkest nightmares a parent could ever face. What if Nathaniel were to be diagnosed with a life threatening or life-\altering disease? What if one day he was no longer be able to see her smiling at him? Would she have the strength to live through it?

"Will you be with the prosthetics staff in the new rehab center?" Mia finally was able to push past the burning lump in her throat.

"Yes, I will be. Are you here with the group that is responsible for it?"

"We are," Lily announced, proudly.

"Well thank you. I will finally get out of the hall and have an actual lab to work in. I am so appreciative."

"Well, we don't want to keep you from your work any longer. It was very nice to meet you. I'm Mia and this is Lily."

"I am Johan Baer. Very nice to meet you and thank you."

Walking off to find the others, Mia and Lily were quiet for a few moments. Mia couldn't shake the thought of babies losing their eyes to cancer. Her heart was shattering for the children and for their families.

"I have a feeling we are going to have a lot of very profound moments this trip, Lily."

"I don't think we're ever going to be the same, Mia."

Truer words may never have been spoken, Mia thought to herself. Schooner was Lily's age the summer he came over and Mia was finally getting a glimpse of the experience that transformed him into the man he would become and provide clear direction for his life's path.

Mia couldn't help but wonder how this chapter would rewrite all their lives.

Chapter Thirty-Three

"Where have you been?" Schooner casually slung an arm over Mia's shoulder as she and Lily joined the group.

"Lily and I just met the gentleman who makes prosthetic eyes. I was able to get some pictures of him creating an eye."

"Ah, you met Johan," Sonkwe seemed pleased. "He will be housed in the new facility when it opens. I know he will be pleased to be vacating his desk in the middle of a hallway."

Following along, they came to a door. "First I will show you the grounds for the new facility and then I will introduce you to my wife. She is the director over at the orphanage."

The construction site had already been surveyed and colored flags dotted the property. Mia looked up at Schooner, he was beaming, his sapphire eyes glowing. The look on his face was the same one she had seen the night Charles first showed them the L9/NYC property. Watching his head nod slightly as he examined each inch of the property, from left to right, like a panoramic photo he was envisioning.

Mia began to take pictures. These would be the baseline shots to show progress as the facility was built. Training her camera on Berto and Schooner, deep in conversation and pointing to things only they could see in their heads, Mia was envisioning something very different - the promotional materials she would produce to help fund ongoing projects and programs.

"I think he is happiest over here," Marit observed, watching the two men. "This is how he was about medicine twenty years ago. Now, it's the work he does over here."

"This is where Schooner got the inspiration for L9. And I know that look on his face. This is where he is truly a visionary," her words resonated with awe and respect. "My pretty boy jock," she shook her head.

Waving for the women to follow them, they crossed the field to a small white, wooden house.

"We currently have nine children and they range in age from eight months to eleven years old."

Entering the house, they could hear different sounds coming from all corners, the soft speaking voice of a teacher, a baby crying, the springs of a rocking horse pinging, a microwave dinging.

The first room was lined with freestanding chalkboards and bookshelves, four children sat with a teacher, going over their lessons, using old style notebooks with hard cardboard black and white covers. They all looked up, smiling in unison.

"Say hello to our guests," Sonkwe told the children, who then greeted in unison. Three boys and a girl made up this group; Francis, Theone, Ezekiel and Trina.

Next was the nursery, bathed in bright yellow walls with white trim and sunshine pouring through the windows. It was impossible not to smile walking into the room. Three cribs were set up, but only two had babies, Thomas and Sena, who were just going down for their naps.

The remainder of the children, two boys, Kelvan and Chibesa and one little girl, Msikana, were playing in the pre-school room. Again, the visitors were greeted by a chorus of hello.

"Hello," Mia crouched down next to the kids, "my name is Mia. What are you playing?"

"Star Wars," Kelvan picked up a Darth Vader figurine. His British accent making him sound so formal.

Mia laughed, thinking about how truly global some of the elements of pop culture had become. Kelvan and his figurine could've been part of little boys' play almost anywhere in the world.

Msikana came and sat down next to where Mia was crouched. Looking up at Mia, her big dark eyes excited to share her news with a stranger, "This is my doll, her name is Roberta. Today is her birthday." She handed the ragdoll to Mia.

"She's very pretty. How old is she?" Mia smoothed down the doll's messy hair.

"She's only two," Msikana was very serious.

"Maybe we should have a party for her," Mia suggested, pointing to a doll's tea set on one of the shelves lining the room.

Msikana ran across the room and gathered up as many teacups and plates as her little hands could carry and dropped them with a crash on a small round table. Immediately, she began to properly set the table. Running back to Mia, she grabbed Roberta and put her in one of the chairs.

Picking up her Nikon, Mia began to shoot frame after frame of the precious little girl. Checking her LCD screen, she couldn't help but smile. The lens loved this little girl.

"Lady, come have tea with us," was her invite to Mia.

With her British accent, Msikana could have been a little girl in London sitting with her dolly, as opposed to an orphan in Zambia. Mia felt the lump in her throat growing at the thought and quickly hid behind her camera lens.

"I need to visually document all of this," she reminded herself harshly, "there's going to be a lot of heartbreaking moments, stay neutral. Do your job."

"Mia."

Hearing Schooner's voice behind her, she gathered herself and quickly turned around, a smile painted on her face. With Schooner and Sonkwe was an attractive woman in a flowing brightly colored batik dress to her ankles. She was barefoot.

Extending a hand and a smile to Mia, "Hello, Mia. I am Sonkwe's wife, Bupe. We have been looking forward to this visit. Sonkwe's so excited about the new facility."

"We'll be back tomorrow afternoon," Schooner was telling Sonkwe. "I'm meeting onsite with the architect and construction foreman."

As she turned to say goodbye to the children, she felt a tiny hand slip into hers. Msikana was smiling up at her. "I'll see all of you again tomorrow," Mia promised.

As Sonkwe led them back to where their driver was waiting, he put a hand on Mia's arm, indicating she should fall behind with him at a slower pace.

"Thank you, Mia."

Cocking her head and smiling, "For what?"

"For Schooner. You brought him to us. Had fate not unraveled for you, he never would have come to us that summer. And now the fates have seen fit to bring us all together at last. There appears to be much work to be done."

Mia nodded, not sure she fully grasped all that he was trying to convey, but his words bounced throughout her brain, a pinball slamming into bumpers and ricocheting, leaving light trails in their wake.

Was it all unfolding the way it was supposed to? It had certainly shaped Schooner's life. While tennis had been taken from him, it had been replaced by something so much larger, something that touched and impacted so many more people. Had his hand not been broken, he probably would've had a career on the tour, at least for a few years. He would've played Australia, France, England, The Open and then he probably would've coached younger players on the tour.

But he never would have had the experience and inspiration that his summer in Macha gave him. Sonkwe would never have been taught CPR and Oral-Rehydration Therapy when he was eight years old by a motivational young American who brought soccer tournaments and tailgating to his little village.

"There appears to be much work to be done," Sonkwe had said to her. Mia couldn't help but feel that they were nowhere near the end of this journey.

Chapter Thirty-Four

As they strolled the crafts rondavels at Kabwata Cultural Village, alone for the first time all day, Schooner pulled Mia in close under his arm, kissing the top of her head and rubbing her arm tenderly.

"How are you holding up, Baby Girl?"

Looking up at him, she could see the compassion in his eyes, "It's a lot to process, Schooner."

He just nodded and they walked along in silence, stopping to look at the indigenous wood carvings of masks, figurines of people, birds and animals and beautiful hand-hewn bowls.

"That moment between you and Sonkwe today practically killed me. When he was coming down the hall toward us and he smiled, I immediately knew he was the little boy with the soccer ball in the picture you gave me," her eyes teared up just recounting it, "and my heart just wanted to burst out of my chest for the two of you." She was silent for a moment, "I'm so glad I'm experiencing this with you."

He pulled her tighter to him as they walked, but remained silent. Stealing a glance at his handsome face, Mia couldn't help but wonder what fate had in store for them.

As if reading her thoughts, he looked down at her and smiled, "I just keep thinking it's all unraveling as it should. Do you feel that, too?"

She nodded, but words wouldn't come. Today's reunion with Sonkwe was a sign. What exactly it was a sign of, she just wasn't quite sure. Things were starting to feel bigger than the two of them and control was no longer theirs, it somehow fell to the fates, and Mia silently prayed that the fates looked upon them kindly.

"I know he's a little young, but look at that little drum," he steered her over to one of the thatched roofed stands. "We have to get this for him."

Mia laughed, "Look at these beaded necklaces, they're gorgeous. I should pick some up for my mom, Kami, Gaby and Seth."

"Seth?"

"If everyone else gets beads and he doesn't, I'll never hear the end of it and can't you just see him wearing these out dancing on Fire Island?" Mia picked up a strand of brightly colored, chunky beads.

"Yeah," Schooner laughed, "I actually can."

After a lengthy conversation with the stall owner about where they were from and why they were there, they paid for their purchases.

Leaving the rondavel, "Are you ready?" he asked, eyebrows raised.

"Ready for what?"

"Lunch. I'm taking you out, Baby Girl," and he pointed to a shack down the dirt road and started dragging her along at his long-legged fast pace, "for the best nshima and ifisashi you will ever eat."

"Do they have beer?"

"Do they have beer, she asks. Do they have beer? I'm going to get you trashed on Mosi Lager and spend the rest of this afternoon fucking your brains out."

"Promises, promises," Mia snarked.

Stopping dead in his tracks, Mia crashed into him. "That you will pay for, Ms. Silver," and with a flash of his All-American boy smile, he dragged her into the shack for a traditional Zambian meal to later be followed by a very All-American dessert.

Chapter Thirty-Five

The first facility of the morning was located on the edge of the city in an economically depressed neighborhood. The halls were lined in institutional green tiles and the smell of disinfectant accosted the senses immediately upon entering the building. The impact on Mia's spirit was instantaneous as she intuitively felt the emotional ante upped significantly.

Specializing in prosthetic services for victims of disease, accidents and violence, the patients on this particular hall had lost various limbs and many had been waiting months to be fitted for their prosthetics. Others were in various stages of rehabilitation.

The hall was lined with at least sixty patients, patiently waiting for their turn to see the lone prosthetist. Sitting down to talk with them, learn their stories, hear of their attempts to assimilate back into their former lives and livelihoods was engrossing, fascinating and devastating all at the same time. With rapt attention, Lily, Marit and Mia listened, the Castillo women recording the stories as Mia visually documented the whole experience.

Prosthetist Mubita Lungu was a bear of a man, although Mia suspected that this imposingly large figure was in actuality more of a teddy bear than the tough grizzly he appeared to be. Watching him work with a patient to adjust the fittings for a new transtibial prosthetic leg, his precision, patience and expertise were a joy to observe. This was a man who took pride in making a difference in others' lives.

"So, I have to ask you this," Mia began. "Did you ever play professional football?"

"Your football or ours?" he was going to make Mia work for it.

Rolling her eyes at him, "You don't look like a soccer player."

With a hearty laugh, "I played for Tulane."

"That's a great school," based on his size and bulk, Mia was not surprised to learn that he'd played Division I football, but was a little surprised that he'd lived in the states and returned to Zambia.

"I'd kill for a good etouffé," he was serious.

Laughing, "Do you miss the states?"

"I like to visit, but I'm needed here," his dark eyes flashed sincerity.

"Yes, I can see that," Mia surveyed the long line waiting for him. "Well, I won't take up any more of your time. But I do have one last question. What do you need? What would help you do your job better?"

"Another set or two of hands," was his immediate response, "another prosthetist and an assistant would make this a lot more manageable. We'd be able to help many more patients in a timely manner and get them back to their lives and their jobs."

"And there's no budget for that?"

This time it was Mubita's turn to roll his eyes at Mia.

"'Nuff said," she gave his massive shoulder a friendly squeeze and left him to attend his patients.

"We need a scholarship program for prosthetists as well as bringing over more PT's," Mia advised Schooner, "and they need funding for assistants," as they settled into the van to head back to the construction site.

"What makes you say that?" He had not been with Mia in the prosthetics area that morning.

"Sixty people waiting in a hall to see one man," she was frustrated by the conditions she had just seen.

"Dad, I could do so much more here, even just helping out, expediting things. This is so much more important than anything I'm doing at Yale." Liliana was clearly questioning her pampered upbringing and feeling the call to make a difference. She was ready to throw caution to the wind and move to Zambia.

Berto gave Marit that wide-eyed look, perfected by every parent of a teen, that said, "Please deal with your daughter."

"Liliana, it is exactly what you learn at Yale that will make you more valuable in an environment like this once you have your degree," Marit espoused, knowing full well that reasoning with the passion of youth was a futile exercise.

"Bullshit," Lily rolled her eyes.

"Liliana!" Berto attempted the role of disciplinarian, something he clearly was not well practiced at with his daughter.

Biting her lip to stifle a smile, Mia knew better than to look up. She felt Schooner's elbow in her ribs and smacked his arm.

"Remind you of anyone?" he whispered in her ear.

"Moi?" she looked at him with wide, innocent eyes.

"The one and only," he laughed, giving her hand a loving squeeze.

Mia laughed internally at the thought that she had probably not been the easiest teen in the world and had given Lois and Bob a run for their money.

The architect and construction foreman were waiting in the empty field when they arrived.

"Are you ready for a groundbreaking?" the architect asked Schooner and Berto.

"We will be in two days," Schooner's excitement was palpable. A little boy getting to build something new. "We're just waiting for one more signoff and then we're green-lighted."

"Come, let me show you the final revisions to the facility." He motioned to a small trailer that was a new addition to the field since the day before.

Touching his arm, Mia advised Schooner that she was going over to the orphanage to shoot photos of the children.

Heading out the door as Mia was entering, the four school aged children tumbled out into the fresh air. She could feel the pent-up energy radiating off them. Recess, Mia mused, always the favorite part of the day for any student, anywhere on the planet.

Bupe was sitting at the table in the dining room spoon feeding one of the infants.

"May I join you?"

"Yes, please come sit."

Mia laughed as she watched Thomas spit out the green mush he was being fed. "How old is he?"

"He is currently our youngest, only eight months old." Bupe was persistent in getting the spoon into Thomas' mouth.

Feeling her heart pang, "I have an eight-month old at home. Nathaniel. Boy, do I miss him." Mia picked up her camera and shot a few frames of Thomas proudly wearing his lunch.

"Is this your first time away from him?"

Mia nodded and then consciously changed the subject to avoid becoming a blubbering mess. "Did Sonkwe know Schooner was coming?"

"Yes, he's known for about a month that Schooner was responsible for the new facility and the equipment for the other facilities. At first, he thought, can this be the same person?" Thomas was now on to a hard cracker and appeared much happier.

"There's probably not a lot of people named Schooner and he is truly one of a kind," Mia couldn't help but smile.

"He looks like a movie star."

"Please don't tell him that," both women laughed. "There's something that I want to send to you when I get home," Mia smiled at Bupe.

"Schooner took a picture that summer of Sonkwe holding a soccer ball. He has the hugest smile on his face. I will send you a copy of it."

"I would love a picture of Sonkwe as a little boy."

"So, what happened to Thomas' parents?" Mia watched as Bupe cleaned his face and then shot a few more frames of the fresh-faced baby.

"His mother was a young single mother, only a teen. She tried to deliver herself without going to a medical facility and hemorrhaged. By the time she was discovered and received medical attention, it was too late. We never knew who the father was and no one claimed the baby."

Trying to catch her breath, "Oh my God, that is heartbreaking."

"All of their stories will stir your soul. I just thank the Lord every day that they are all safe with us. If you want to read their stories, we keep a blue binder on a shelf in the classroom that documents their histories." Picking Thomas up, "Little one, you need a diaper change and a nap."

Following Bupe out of the dining room, Mia went down the hall to the toddler play room, noting, as she approached, how quiet it was.

Laying on brightly colored mats, it was rest time in the toddler room for the three children. Quietly, Mia stood in the doorway so as not to disturb them. She thought of shooting a few frames, but then thought better of it, not wanting the noise of the camera's shutter to intrude on their naps.

As if sensing Mia's energy, one of Msikana's eyes popped open and in an instant her face came to life. She was up and across the room in a nanosecond, arms wrapped around Mia's leg.

"Lady, you're here!"

Mia's heart fluttered at the warm and spontaneous reaction her mere presence evoked in the little girl. Smiling, Mia whispered, "How are you today, Msikana? You can call me Mia."

Msikana looked up, not letting go of Mia's thigh, "Mia," she tried out the word and smiled.

Reaching down, Mia picked her up and took her from the room so that they would not wake the boys. "You're supposed to be sleeping."

The little girl giggled and put her head down on Mia's shoulder.

Bupe was standing at a window looking out when she heard Mia coming down the hall. Motioning for her to come over, Mia could hear the noise before she could see what was going on outside.

Gasping with delight at the scene before her eyes, Mia felt her heart flip-flop for a myriad of reasons. Was it the joy and influence of the past? Or the past and the present coming together? Was it the energy that made time and experience simultaneous? Or was it merely the look of pure bliss on Schooner's face? Mia wasn't sure exactly what it was about the scene before her that was making her heart soar, but she knew one thing with absolute certainty, this time, she wanted to be part of it.

Heading to the door with Msikana still in her arms, Mia emerged into sunshine that was now punctuated with hooting and peals of laughter that floated on the breeze like church bells at noon. The construction site to-be was receiving its christening, as it had been converted into a makeshift soccer field populated by the school-aged orphans, hospital workers, the architect and his construction foreman, Dr. Roberto Castillo, the infamous "Coach Schooner" Moore and his star goalie, Dr. Sonkwe Banda.

Standing on the sidelines watching the joyous, raucous match, Mia wiped her tears with the back of her hand.

"Don't cry," the little girl looked stricken.

"These are happy tears, Msikana. See that man over there, the one in the blue shirt? We're going to cheer for him. We're going to yell 'Go Schooner', okay?"

The little girl nodded and yelled, "Go Schooner."

Shifting her onto one hip, Mia picked up her camera that was hanging around her neck. Realizing it would be impossible to shoot without putting the little girl down, Mia nudged a dial to shutter-priority to be able to capture the fast action and then pushed a small lever for continuous frame shooting and engaged her autofocus.

"I'm going to need your help here," she told the little girl, "when I say press, you're going to need to press the button at the top and when I say stop, you need to take your finger off it. Can you do that?"

The little girl nodded, excited to help.

"Okay, can you do that and still yell, 'Go Schooner'?"

Nodding again, she was up for the challenge.

"Let's do this," Mia told Msikana. "Go Schooner!" and she brought the camera up to her face. "Hold tight," she told the little girl as she momentarily removed the hand that was holding her to focus the camera and then brought it back around her, hoisting her back up.

"Okay, we are ready to take some pictures. Press."

The little girl giggled, pressed the button and screamed, "Go Schooner."

Watching him run the field, locks of thick dirty blonde hair cascading over his forehead, Sonkwe Banda as his goalie, Mia felt as if she were being given a second chance. Someone had turned back the hands of time for her and gifted her with a moment that she had missed. This time she was getting to live it with him, to share in the joy. As tears streamed uncontrollably down her cheeks, she directed Msikana when to depress her Nikon's shutter release. Not only would she have this moment etched into the memory plate of her mind's eye, but it would also be captured as a memento of a shared recollection.

The match ended with high fives and slaps on the back. Coach and his goalie sharing a victory. The Macha soccer league showing 'em how it's done. An elated Schooner and Sonkwe were creating a new memory born of a sacred time in their shared pasts. There was magic in this journey, and Mia had the sense that these two men were destined to accomplish great things as their paths intermittently crossed throughout their lives.

Seeing Mia on the sidelines, an out-of-breath Schooner made his way over to her, giving her a sweaty kiss. "That was awesome," he managed between pants.

Bupe had set-up a small table with cups and pitchers of water awaiting the players.

"Come let's get you water, old goat," Mia laughed.

"Go Schooner," Msikana looked up at him through her lashes, clearly flirting.

He laughed, "Now, who is this pretty lady?"

"I'm Msikana," she was very matter-of-fact with him.

Drinking his cup of water in one gulp and immediately refilling the cup, "Msikana, huh? That's a very pretty name."

Again, she dipped her head, looking up at him through long lashes, eliciting laughter from both Schooner and Mia. Letting go of Mia's neck, she reached out to Schooner.

"Well, I'm kind of sweaty, but okay." He took the little girl from Mia and she snuggled right into his broad shoulder.

"I see you have a new friend, Coach," a sweat drenched Sonkwe laughed.

"Yes, I've just met Msikana."

Her head popped up off his shoulder, "Go Schooner!"

The two men laughed at the precocious toddler.

"What does Msikana translate to?" Schooner asked Sonkwe.

"It means 'Baby Girl'."

Schooner shook his head, surprised. "Her name is 'Baby Girl'?"

Looking up from the LCD screen of her camera where she had been checking photos, Mia echoed Schooner's words, "Her name is 'Baby Girl'? She doesn't have a formal name?"

Schooner and Mia locked eyes for a brief moment. "Baby Girl," his lips silently mouthed.

Sonkwe shook his head, "A lot of orphans come through without names and they are known as boy or girl." He poured himself another cup of water.

Schooner looked at the little girl in his arms and then at Mia with a huge smile, "Be nice to me or I'll get a younger model," he teased.

"You do that, Pretty Boy," she couldn't help but laugh.

Snuggled back into Schooner's shoulder, Msikana was finally taking the nap she had missed earlier.

Chapter Thirty-Six

Three more facilities packed the next morning, the need for staff and equipment growing more obvious with every site visit as they ventured farther and farther from the center of the city.

"With all the visuals and stories, we should put together some kind of fundraiser when we go back home. Use L9/NYC as the host facility, do a fashion show and dinner or something," Schooner was thinking out loud as they drove over to the construction site.

"We would need to do it in conjunction with a non-profit organization that the funds raised would be going to. Do you have an organization in mind?" Mia turned in her seat to face him.

He was silent, but the look on his face said there was anything but silence inside that handsome head. His shoulders began to move as if he were dancing to a tune only he could hear, then his head began to bop, the All-American boy smile slashed across his face. Had he not been behind the wheel of their rented Jeep, Mia imagined he'd be cutting it up on his imaginary dance floor.

"I think we should start a non-profit." He was beaming as he looked into her shocked eyes.

"You want to establish a 501(c)3 organization?" Her tone more than implied, "Are you crazy?"

"Is that what it's called? I'm glad you know this stuff. Yeah, that's what I want to do. Start a 501 whatever," he was sporting a very self-satisfied look. "You've done work with non-profits, haven't you?"

"We've written fundraising campaigns and done special events, but that's pretty much it. It's a business, Schooner, you need a staff for it and you need to be very accountable that for every dollar raised the lion's share of it is going toward the programs and projects for which it's being raised and not being used for administration and overhead."

"So, good business skills are necessary and strong contacts to people with a lot of discretionary income." He pulled the Jeep into the parking area of the facility.

Laughing, "I don't think it's quite that easy, but those are two very important elements."

Nodding, he got out of the Jeep. The architect and foreman were ahead of them in the field speaking with three other gentlemen. The architect was pointing to something that was currently nonexistent.

Slinging an arm over Mia's shoulder, he pulled her close, and whispered, "Time for me to be charming and possibly generous."

"You wrote the book, Pretty Boy," she smiled up at him.

With raised eyebrows and their secret smile, he uttered their trademark phrase, "Showtime," giving her a chaste kiss as he headed toward the men and she made her way over to the orphanage.

The toddlers were just about to go down for their naps when Mia poked her head in the room, all three came running to her as she was now a familiar face.

"I was waiting for you, Mia," a very serious Msikana told her.

"Well today you are not getting out of a nap, young lady," Mia reprimanded her with a smile.

"I don't want to nap," Kelvan chimed in.

"Is it alright if I read them a story?" Mia asked Bupe.

Taking her phone from her purse, Mia pulled up her book app and chose the beloved classic, *Goodnight Moon.*

Settling into their mats, the three toddlers listened intently, before a strict Bupe insisted on lights out.

With the older students off doing laundry and household chores, Mia sat alone in their classroom sifting through the big blue binder that held the children's biographies. As she sipped black tea from the northern province of Luapula, she took notes on the records and life stories that had been entered for each of the orphans.

Grabbing her phone, she pulled up a favorite picture of Nathaniel, his bright blue eyes shining with her devilish demeanor and his smile oozing all of Schooner's charm. Feeling her throat immediately constrict and the empty pang in her heart, she put her phone back in her bag. It was impossible for her not to think of the love that surrounded him, the love he was learning to reciprocate as she turned each page in the binder.

As she transcribed facts about each of the children, facts that she knew would be the basis of stories used to engage club members and capital campaign donors, it was hard to assimilate that the horrors she was reading were about the sweet, happy, well-behaved children with whom she had spent the last few days.

Sitting back and taking a deep breath before moving on to the next biography, Mia was angry at the injustices suffered by these children. Reminding herself to stay detached, act like a journalist, she mustered up the resolve to move on to the next record.

Ezekial. Nine years old, birthday March 26th. That would make him an Aries, Mia mused. Chuckling out loud, he had been quite aggressive on the soccer field yesterday. Yeah, she could see him as an Aries. Her smile faded as she read on. A victim of sexual abuse before the age of five, he had undergone three surgeries before the age of seven to repair internal tears.

Again, Mia had to sit back to calm herself and consciously talk away the nausea. These were atrocities. Crimes against children. What greater offense could there be in the universe?

Trina and Theone were twins, born Christmas day. Both parents were lost to disease and their grandparents were too impoverished and sickly to care for them. Thomas' mother was a drug addict. Chibesa was abandoned on a road side.

Shell shocked. These weren't just stories. These weren't some mass-produced child-of-the-month club fundraising packages. These were toddlers to whom she had read. They were children who ran a soccer field with Schooner. It was a baby Nathaniel's age with green mush all over his face. They were real children. And in that moment, Mia fell deeply in love with Sonkwe and Bupe. They were angels on Earth. Heroes. Rockstars. And if her faith in humanity had been rocked by the stories in the binder, it was immediately replenished by the goodness in the souls of the Bandas'.

Mia held off on reading Msikana's profile. If that little girl has been sexually abused, I'm going to go postal on someone, Mia thought.

With a slow exhale, she gathered her resolve and turned the page.

Mia Silver never made it past the first line.

Chapter Thirty-Seven

Schooner watched Mia peering out the Jeep's window at the landscape as the urban streets of Lusaka rapidly receded in the rearview mirror. Had she not become so withdrawn and somber before they left the facility, he would have just assumed she was taking in the Zambian landscape and committing it to her mind's eye. The rapid change of facial expressions, unmistakably told him that something was just not right.

Reaching over, he took her hand and gave it a squeeze, "You okay?"

Nodding, she greeted him with a half-smile that didn't quite reach her eyes and immediately turned back to staring out the window.

"Do you want to skip the elephant orphanage today?" Their plan was to spend some time at the Lilayi Elephant Nursery that was adjacent to the grounds of their lodge. Mia had been looking forward to seeing the elephant calves and shooting pictures, and now Schooner was concerned that exhaustion was setting in and the emotional encounters that they had experienced at both the hospitals and orphanage were starting to take their toll on her.

"No. I don't want to miss it. I've been looking forward to it all trip."

"You sure?" he pressed. "A nap might be just what you need."

Without looking away from the window, "I don't need a nap."

Traversing the remaining thirty miles out to Lilayi in silence, Schooner tried to put together the pieces of the day. Something must've happened when he was meeting about shipping logistics for the equipment and she was shooting photos in the orphanage.

"Did something happen today?"

She shook her head, no. Still not turning to face him.

"Do you want to talk about it, Baby Girl?"

Again, her response was merely a shake of the head.

Entering the Lilayi Elephant Nursery, Mia's mood seemed to lift. Seeing the calves brought an immediate smile to both her eyes and her lips. Side-by-side, she and Schooner set their 24-70mm lenses onto their D800 camera bodies (holiday presents to one another). Nudging her with his shoulder, she looked up smiling. Photographing Zambia with Mia had been his dream, and he wished that she was feeling the same joy that he was.

"Okay, let's go check this out," and he slung an arm over her shoulder as they entered.

Leaning up on the railing of the viewing deck, the six calves came in for feeding. Handing them their bottles, filled with nutrient-enriched milk, they wrapped their trunks around the bottles, feeding themselves.

"That is so cute," Mia was focusing in on the smallest of the calves, Nkala, who had been orphaned at three months old and came to the nursery depressed and not wanting to socialize with the other orphans. Nkala was finally joining the other elephants in activities and mud baths and the personnel were very happy to see this breakthrough.

Listening to the stories of each of these creatures was heartbreaking. The staff began to tell the story of Suni, an eight-month-old orphan that had been dragging herself along a roadside when she was attacked by an axe to her back, damaging her spine. Schooner could see the tears streaming down Mia's face and pulled her close. Kissing the top of her head, he whispered, "Do you want to leave?"

She shook her head no, and continued to sniffle and wipe away her tears which only escalated with each of the calves' stories. Hiding her face behind her Nikon, Schooner knew she was trying to focus on her picture taking as a way to maintain what little control she had left.

Leaving the nursery, they made their way through the game farm to the Lilayi Lodge and on to their private, rounded chalet. Dominating the room was a beautiful, oversized four-poster bed with sheer white netting surrounds. Schooner took the backpack of Mia's camera equipment from her and placed it on the bed.

Walking into the large bathroom, he immediately began to run a bath in the limestone soaker tub. With a satisfied grin, he emerged a few minutes later and sat down on the bed next to Mia, who was scrolling through the pictures on her camera.

"I ran a bath for you, why don't you go soak in the tub and then come out and nap. I'm going to work for a little bit." He kissed the top of her head and got up to pull his laptop out of his bag. Sitting down at the desk and flipping open his computer, he looked over at her. She hadn't moved. "Tub now, Ms. Silver," his voice was stern.

Begrudgingly, she stood and made her way to the bathroom. As she passed Schooner, she gave him a half-smile and the finger.

Laughing, "Right backatcha, babe," and he swatted her ass as she passed.

Twenty minutes later she re-entered the room and headed straight for the bed, without uttering a word. Climbing into the center of the bed and getting under the covers, he let her be until he heard her breathing steady. Once certain she was asleep, he stripped off his clothes and curled up in bed next to her.

Whatever was troubling Mia concerned him. Was she just overwhelmed by the sad stories from the orphanage? Did the children just make her miss Nathaniel that much more? It wasn't like Mia to fall into despair and not be able to verbalize to him what was troubling her. A bath and a mid-afternoon nap were hopefully all she needed to shake the darkness.

The night's plans included dinner with the Castillos at the Lodge's famed restaurant. If Mia woke up and still wasn't feeling herself, he would call them and cancel and have dinner delivered to the chalet. The room had internet and satellite TV, they could relax, call home, watch TV from bed. The idea was starting to sound rather appealing.

Pulling her close up against him, he whispered, "I love you, Baby Girl," and kissed the top of her head before falling into a deep afternoon slumber.

Berto, Marit and Lily were seated at a round table in the center of the Lodge's thatched roof restaurant when Schooner and Mia arrived.

"Did you see the elephants today?" Lily's plan was to see them tomorrow.

Mia nodded, "Plan on falling in love. Each one has a story and it's heart wrenching," and then in a quiet tone, "much like the children at the orphanage."

A look passed between Lily and her father.

"There will always be time for this after college, Liliana." Berto was giving his daughter the *this is not negotiable* face.

Rolling her eyes at him made Schooner laugh.

"Lily, if I had a dollar for every time my kids gave me that exact same look, well, I'd be a much richer man." Taking a sip of his robust South African Cabernet Sauvignon, "I definitely need to introduce you to my daughter. Like you, she's also in New England, up at Brown."

"Yeah, that's not too far at all from New Haven." Although Lily had just completed her freshman year at Yale with excellent grades, the thought of going back was becoming less appealing by the day.

"I think you two would like each other. You were both brought up in

Orange County, yet are the antithesis of Orange County women," Schooner's pride when talking of Holly was very evident.

As the waiter delivered plates of smoked salmon ceviche resting in lemon, ginger and sweet chili, the conversation turned to the plans for the rehabilitation center.

"Don't you think I could make more of an impact here than back in New Haven, Dad?" Lily relentlessly continued to press her case.

"Lily, this is not the time or the place," Marit was clearly becoming annoyed with her tenacious daughter. Her steely-eyed look silenced Lily into a petulant silence.

Berto and Marit Castillo made a striking, if not odd, looking couple. Danish-born Marit towered six inches over her husband, her Nordic beauty an instant head-turner for both men and women. Liliana was an interesting combination of the two, with a long silky sheath of medium-brown hair cascading down her back and a creamy complexion that tanned instead of burned. Her light brown eyes, flecked with gold, flashed with the intensity of her very serious personality. Lily Castillo was not a fun, care-free teen and that was made even more evident by the fervor in which she embraced the emotional and physical intensity of the trip.

Mia remained conspicuously quiet throughout the meal with Schooner working double time to hold up the conversation for the two of them. Under the table, he reached for her hand to give it a squeeze. Her lack of response kicked up his alarms a notch further.

"You up for dessert," he asked softly, his face clearly conveying concern.

With a half-smile, she nodded and they stayed through the rest of the meal. After dessert, with kisses to each cheek, they bid the Castillos goodnight, with plans to meet early for breakfast and travel together back to the facility for the ground-breaking ceremony and press conference.

Under a black sky dotted with an impossible amount of twinkling stars that weren't obscured by ambient city light, they silently walked hand-in-hand back to their chalet. Letting go of Mia's hand, Schooner slung his arm over her shoulder, pulling her tightly into him.

"I'm worried about you, Baby Girl."

Without looking up at him, she uttered four words that chilled the blood in his veins, "We need to talk."

Schooner's alarms were now blaring. His gut told him, "This is not going to be good." And his gut was rarely wrong.

Chapter Thirty-Eight

Entering the chalet, Schooner went to the mini-bar and pulled out a bottle of Glenlivet. Holding it up, he silently asked Mia if she wanted a drink. She nodded yes and his anxiety ratcheted up yet another notch. He was dying. He just needed to know what was going on, so that he could fix it. Because whatever it was, he would fix it. Of that, he was sure. That is what he did best.

Handing her the glass of scotch, he put his forefinger and thumb on her chin and tipped her head up. "Talk to me, Baby Girl." The look in her eyes was something he could not discern and his throat closed a little more.

Mia nodded and walked over to the bed. Getting onto it, she sat in the middle cross-legged. Following, Schooner got on the bed, sitting up with his back against the pillows, facing Mia. He placed the bottle of Glenlivet on the night table next to him. They sat there for a few moments in uneasy silence.

After a long draw on her scotch, "I don't even know where to begin this, but there is a lot I need to tell you."

The thought that immediately flashed through Schooner's mind was that maybe after the orphanage the last few days, there was a baby in her past that she'd given up for adoption. Maybe that is what she wanted to share.

Mia let out a deep breath, "There's so much I've wanted to tell you for so long, but I just didn't know how and the timing was never quite right. And maybe part of me was afraid. I haven't really talked to you much about our years apart."

"No, you haven't. And you don't need to, Mia."

"I do, Schooner. I really, really do. And it needs to happen tonight."

He thought her last statement to be odd. Why tonight? What was going on that this conversation had to happen tonight?

"You know why I left and you know what kind of shape I was in when I left. I came home and my parents pulled some strings to get me into a good college upstate New York. I was able to get into a really coveted writing program because a student had dropped out, a slot had become available and my writing samples were strong enough. The instructor was George Roy, which was kind of a big deal, and looking forward to that program got me through that first summer. It was an anchor that I could hold onto, the thing that made me want to keep my head above water."

Feeling her pain was easy. He had spent his whole summer, right here in the country where they both now sat, trying to hold onto something, anything, to keep from feeling like he was going to drown. As she spoke, the excruciating desperation of that time in their lives grabbed onto his heart, wringing it harshly.

"When I got to school, I found out that Professor Roy had suffered a massive heart attack over the summer and had been replaced for the entire school year by his protégé, an MFA out of Cornell who was writing screenplays and TV scripts. A few weeks into the semester, he singled out me and Rob. You know, my friend Rob Ryan."

Schooner nodded. Although he had not yet met Rob, they had spoken over the phone on several occasions and he knew how close Mia still was to both him and his wife, Joni.

"Rob and I worked together, independently from the rest of the class and met with the professor two evenings a week. The guy was young, he was only twenty-seven, and good looking and was sleeping with a couple of the seniors in the class."

"That's not very professional," Schooner chimed in, his eyes narrowing.

Mia laughed and shrugged her shoulders, "It was the 80's. Life before sexual harassment," she took another sip of her scotch. "Anyway, I became pretty friendly with him, but it was nothing at first. Just kind of a harmless flirtation, until the end of the school year, when it became something more."

"Mia, you were a minor," there was alarm in Schooner's tone.

"No, we waited until my eighteenth birthday before anything happened."

Stomach knotting, Schooner remembered her eighteenth birthday vividly, and how despondent he was that night, sailing alone, thinking that was the night he was supposed to get engaged. That was the night it was supposed to happen. And now years and years later, just hearing this, he wanted to be sick. Shocked at how much this was already affecting him, he refilled his glass and took a healthy swig.

"Go on," he urged.

"Well, Tom, his name was Tom, and I ended up staying together for seven years."

"Seven years?" Not expecting any of this, the thought that Mia had been in a relationship for that length of time, meant it was a real relationship, and he was becoming uncomfortable with the jealous feelings it was evoking. *Had this guy come back?*

Nodding, "Yeah, seven years. And it worked because both of us were really limited in what we could give to one another emotionally. We got along great, enjoyed each other's company, had a fun time together, but Schooner, never once in seven years did I tell him that I loved him. And he never said it to me, either."

Taking a breath, he was pleased with her last statement. *Why am I so jealous*, he wondered, *this was ancient history and she didn't love him*? But he also knew, that sometime before this conversation was over, the other shoe would drop.

"So, what happened?" he could hear how tight with stress his voice was and wondered if she picked up on it.

As if reading his thoughts, she reached out and took his left hand. Smiling, "You're going to love this."

"Well I don't know about that."

Insisting, "No, trust me, you will love this. I had left a client file on the dining room table that I needed for a meeting, so I went home to grab it and have some lunch. When I got into the apartment, I thought he had left the TV on in the bedroom, so I went to turn it off."

Schooner's mouth opened, "It wasn't the TV, was it?"

Shaking her head, "Nope. He was fucking one of his students in our bed."

"And you walked in?"

Mia was smiling, the memory not at all painful, "I did and quite the scene ensued. I threw the girl's clothes and shoes out the window, which was on the sixteenth floor, and pushed her out of my apartment wearing a bed sheet."

Letting out a laugh, "Only you."

"I know. So me, right?" She released his hand.

"Well, what about him?" Schooner wanted this guy gone.

"I threw his ass out, too." She was proud of the memory.

"Good girl," equally as proud of her. "Did you ever hear from him again?"

"Not for a long time," Mia swirled the amber liquid in her glass, "and then I got a call from him on December 31st, 1999. It was a surprise call, but it was a nice call. A lot of time had passed and I'm guessing he was just a little melancholy," Mia smiled at Schooner, "and probably all of his students were home for the holidays and he had no one to fuck."

"Where does he teach?"

"He's at NYU."

Schooner was shocked. This guy was downtown, not all that far from where they were living. "And you've never run into him?"

"Surprisingly no. Which is pretty amazing," she took a deep breath, as if gearing up for something. "Well, after it ended with him, I went a little wild for a while. My behavior became more than a little destructive and risky. Rob had been bugging me since sophomore year to get into therapy and work with a professional to deal with what happened freshman year, and I just kept thinking it wasn't an issue and I could handle it. But it was an issue and I couldn't handle it. Right after I was raped, I had you there and you were so protective and I was so happy that you really loved me, that I could just push it away from reality. Just lock it away. I think by the time I left at the end of freshman year, I had somehow convinced myself that it never really happened. I just wrapped all my self-worth into my relationships with men, and after Tom, when I wasn't in a relationship, everything I'd locked away started to bubble up. I couldn't feel. I couldn't feel anything and I wanted to feel. And the more out of control I got, the more I thought, let me just go a little farther, a little closer to the edge, and I'll feel something, I will. But I never did. And I kept getting closer and closer to that edge. And I didn't care. I didn't love me. I knew Tom never loved me and I just didn't feel like I was lovable. I was the girl that got used and raped and thrown away and cheated on and left. That's who I was, that's how I saw myself. And I guess that is who I had become."

Schooner could not breathe. Mia Silver was probably the strongest, most resilient, self-sufficient woman he had ever known and hearing her verbalize the struggle, knowing that he had added to it - whether it was his fault or not - was shredding his heart. *How could this amazing woman think she was anything but wonderful?*

"Mia," he reached out his arms for her and she held up her hand, shaking her head no. A wave of devastation enveloped him. *What the hell was going on?*

Continuing, "I got really bad. I was a mess and I kind of had to hit rock bottom and get to a place where I didn't even recognize myself anymore before I finally took the advice that both Rob and Seth had been giving me for years, and that was to get into therapy, find someone who specialized in working with victims of sexual assault." Mia sat quietly for a few moments, "I worked really hard in therapy," their eyes met, "it was really hard and really, really painful, but it got me to a healthier place." Again she paused, looked down, brows knitting as she worked through her thoughts. It was a moment before she looked up at him again, "And it was only then, when I'd faced some painful truths and learned to identify and control my triggers, that I could get into a healthy relationship."

Oh God, here it comes, thought Schooner, feeling impending doom. Remaining silent, he was afraid his voice would crack if he spoke and asked her to go on.

"That same New Year's Eve when Tom called me, the millennium, I met someone really special," she paused, smiling, the look in her eyes beaming pure love. "His name was Michael Portman."

Wanting to know everything, yet not wanting to hear another word, "How did you meet?"

"Charles and I threw a joint New Year's Eve party and he was there. He had been Charles' roommate and frat brother in college."

Nodding, "You met through Charles," he repeated the fact that she had just disclosed. Charles, who had become his best friend in the past sixteen months. They all knew. They all knew everything. Only he didn't know and now for the first time, he felt like he'd inserted himself into their group - a group with a bevy of secrets - and he was the outsider. The only one that didn't know. *Was he ever really one of them?*

As if not taking note of Schooner's clearly disturbed reaction to her admission, Mia continued, "Michael was an amazing man. He was so good to me, Schooner. You would have liked him."

Schooner remained silent. Where the hell was this going?

"For the first time in a long time someone made me feel special and loved and worthy. Although I don't know that I was ever worthy of someone as wonderful as him. He was so good to me and he was so good for me."

"When I told you that I'd never loved anyone but you, you told me that you never loved anyone as much as me. That told me that there was someone you had loved. Was it this guy?" he needed to know. He needed to know everything Mia and all their friends knew and he didn't.

Mia nodded.

"And your Facebook picture, the one in front of the mansion. Was that him?"

Mia's face showed surprise that Schooner even knew about that picture. "Yes, that was him. That was Labor Day Weekend in 2001. We were up in Newport."

Starting to fidget, she played with the glass in her hands and he could see that she was on the verge of tears.

"Well, what happened with you two?" he had to know - this was becoming painful. The anticipation. Would it all crumble? Was it all that fragile? These thoughts had never even crossed his mind before and yet now, he was filled with dread.

Reaching for a box of tissues on the nightstand, Mia dabbed her eyes and took a deep breath, but didn't speak.

Wanting to reach out and pull her to him, hold her tight so that she knew she was his, Schooner just sat there, not moving. Everything about Mia's body language was saying, "Don't touch me" and he was paralyzed by it.

Glancing up, she looked Schooner in the eyes, her bottom lip trembling, "Michael worked on the 105th floor in the North Tower of the World Trade Centers."

There was no air in the room. Someone had stolen his air, forced it out of him with a sucker punch. The ultimate blindside. There was no way to have anticipated this. His ears were ringing. *Where was the air?*

Feeling the sting of tears as they filled his eyes, he heard his voice saying, "Oh my God," but didn't remember saying it, "oh my God."

Tears steamed in a torrential river down Mia's face and Schooner no longer cared whether she wanted to be touched or not. Closing the space between them, he pulled her to his chest, holding her tightly, rocking her, kissing the top of her head.

"Your office, your windows face the Trade Centers. You saw it, didn't you?"

Looking up at him, she nodded. "We just watched it. We couldn't do anything, we just watched it. We watched them burn and fall and Michael was in there," she sobbed into Schooner's chest.

Remembering his anxiety attack that day, he wondered if in some cosmic way if he was feeling her pain, if he was somehow with them on that day.

"I talked to him after the first plane struck and they were trapped, he couldn't get out. We stayed on the phone, I stayed with him, until the call cut off and he was gone. He was just gone."

The pain in her eyes was so overwhelmingly profound at the memory that Schooner could not control his own tears. The thought of Mia's pain watching it all unfold and being totally helpless, the thought of Charles losing an old and dear friend, ripped into him deeply, but more than anything else, the thought of this man, not just a name on a list in the Los Angeles Times, but an actual person that the people he loved, had lost, and what he must've gone through on that day, as he awaited certain death, crushed Schooner so completely that his chest physically hurt. It wasn't an event on TV for these people. It was their reality, it was their friends and loved ones and they were as helpless as the people trapped inside the burning buildings. Schooner's heart broke for Mia and her friends. And his heart broke for Michael Portman.

"I'm so sorry, Mia. I am really so sorry," and he was.

Wiping her eyes and nose, "You would have really liked him, Schooner. He was just a really good person and you would've been really happy with the way he treated me and cared for me. He was just a good, good man."

In that moment, Schooner knew she was right. In his absence, he would've welcomed someone who took good care of her, loved her and made her feel loved. Silently, he thanked Michael Portman for taking care of their Baby Girl.

Pulling away from him so that she could face him again, "I wanted you to know all this because," looking for words, "do you believe in signs?"

"I'd like to, but I think I'd need to be hit over the head pretty hard to believe it. What signs have you been getting?"

"That little girl, the one they call, Baby Girl, I took to her before I even knew about the name. And then we learned about her name, and yes, it was a cute coincidence. Every day she comes running to me and doesn't leave my side and she's like a ray of sunshine. She just makes my heart sing," Mia paused. "Well today, I took a look through her paperwork as to why she was orphaned," again pausing, this time she took a deep breath, her bottom lip trembling again with emotion, "and Schooner, her birthday is September 11th. She was born on September 11th."

Silent for a moment, he stroked her hair, "You have a really big heart, Mia Silver."

"I feel like she is a gift from Michael, that she is supposed to be ours and a way for me to honor his memory. Does that make sense?"

Nodding, Schooner could feel the smile rising on his face, but he was too moved for words.

"I want to name her after him. All day today, I was thinking Portia and that we could keep Msikana as her middle name."

"A little girl," Schooner was smiling, as he rocked Mia in his arms. Several minutes passed before he spoke again, "Well, tomorrow we'll find out what adoption laws and procedures are and figure out how to get this done. How does that sound?" Being a businessman he knew this was going to take contacts and filling some people's needs and wants to pull this off. It was not going to be easy, but it was a negotiation he knew he would win. For Mia. For Michael. And for that sweet little girl.

"You're okay with this? You're okay with adopting her?" Mia looked up, searching his eyes.

"Mia, I think it's wonderful on so many levels. We get to make a significant difference in this little girl's life, we give Nathaniel a sister close in age and they can grow up together, and you get to honor Michael in a really profound and meaningful way. And through this, I get to thank him for taking such good care of you when I wasn't here."

Their eyes locked, then he bowed his head to softly kiss her lips.

"You are such a good man, Schooner Moore. Such a good, good man," smiling, her thoughts taking her back to the soulful-eyed little girl. "She just really got into my heart and then when I saw her birthday, it just felt like it was meant to be."

Placing his hand on her cheek and nodding, "It was meant to be, Baby Girl. Portia was meant to be our daughter." Pulling her to his chest and kissing the top of her head, Schooner felt a thousand pounds, that he didn't even know were there, lift.

Tonight's conversation was not going to break them up - it wasn't going to test their fragility. Just the opposite. Tonight's conversation forged their strength. He chastised himself for his lack of faith, for allowing old fears to invade this house they had built. This little girl was the catalyst in bringing about a very special moment, a moment that would strengthen everything he and Mia shared. The secrets were no longer secrets.

One little girl, looking to be loved, held the key to finally bridging the past and the present. One little girl, who would now be a part of their future.

Chapter Thirty-Nine

Holding her until she fell asleep, Schooner covered Mia and drew the sheer mosquito netting around the bed. Standing outside the drape for a moment, he watched her sleep and tried to process everything that had just happened and all that he had learned.

Refreshing his glass with ice and scotch, Schooner stepped out onto their private verandah, letting the cool night air rush over his face. He felt flushed and keyed-up, yet drained. Sitting in one of the high-backed wicker chairs, he stretched out his long legs and hoisted his feet onto a matching ottoman.

Silently, he sat and reviewed all she had told him. A seven-year relationship with a dirt bag who couldn't keep his dick in his pants. Schooner hated insecure men like that, hated guys who had to prove their manhood in sheer numbers. He had a woman like Mia and was fucking students in her bed. Only a fucking moron would do that.

Feeling a testosterone fueled fantasy coming on, Schooner hoped that they ran into this Tom someday so he could show him how a woman like Mia, the mother of his children, should be respected and to let him know that she was with a real man now. A man who only needed one woman to be happy. A man who could make and keep one woman happy.

Staring at the star-studded black sky, Schooner began to verbalize what had been an internal monologue, talking to the stars, as he often did.

"Well, I knew there had been someone and I knew she loved you. And yeah, I was jealous. But realistically, I certainly didn't expect or want her to live her life without love. I knew the first time I saw that picture of the two of you together, that she loved you. She looked so happy. Really happy. And at peace, if that makes sense. So, thank you for taking care of her and making her happy. And thank you for making her believe she's as wonderful as we both know she is. It sounds like she had some really rough times, really lost her way there for a while before she met you." Taking a sip of his scotch, he collected his thoughts.

"When she started to talk about you tonight, my heart was in my throat. You're the other guy she loved and she was so despondent all day, I just really didn't know where she was going with it. I had no clue. I didn't know if you had come back into the picture or what. I never in a million years expected to hear what she told me." Shaking his head and slowly exhaling a lungful of air, "I can't even imagine how horrible that was. For you, for her, for your family. I remember watching it and falling to pieces. But you and Mia, you were living it. That was your freaking goodbye. That was the end. That is how you said goodbye to one another. Holy shit," he wiped a tear away with the back of his hand and took a healthy slug from his glass, "I don't even know how to process what the two of you went through that day. I can't imagine the hell you endured being trapped in there. How do you come to terms with that in the time frame you had?" Schooner sat silently staring at the stars.

"I'm glad she was there with you at the end and that you got to be together in those last minutes. I am just devastated for you both and it hurts knowing that she's been carrying this pain around inside of her this whole time. I'm glad she finally told me. You shouldn't be an off-limits topic for us. You won't be an off-limits topic for us, I promise you that. She should be able to honor you as much and as often as she needs and wants. I promise you that I will spend the rest of my life taking care of her, just the way you would have. She'll know that she is loved and cherished every single day. I will take care of that for the two of us. You can count on it. Mia will always know that she's our Baby Girl."

Standing, he raised his glass to the night sky as if in a toast, "To you, Michael. Thank you for entrusting me with our daughter."

Chapter Forty

"What time is it?" Mia was startled and slightly disoriented. "Aren't we supposed to meet the Castillo's for breakfast?" Her eyes were still swollen from crying the night before.

Schooner reached for her and pulled her to his chest, "No, I cancelled. I'm having breakfast brought to the room." He kissed the top of her head and tightened his arms around her. "You know you can tell me anything, Mia. There is nothing that is ever going to make me stop loving you. I hope you know that." He tipped up her chin, so that he could look into her eyes.

"I think I didn't tell you about Michael because we were so new last year and then we got caught up in the L9/NYC opening. In the back of my mind, it was a conversation I thought we'd have right after the opening. 9/11 was the following week, it was your first 9/11 living in New York and when it came around, I was in the hospital barely conscious, so we never talked about it. 9/11 had passed before I was even aware of what day it was. The rest of that stuff isn't good stuff for me, Schooner," her eyes reflected pain.

Smoothing down her hair, "I know that, Baby Girl, but those experiences are what make you so incredibly strong and wonderful. I can't even express to you how proud I am of you for seeking help and working on getting healthy. I know that had to have been both painful and difficult. And I have to be honest, for me, it makes our time apart feel even more distressing, because you know how I am about wanting to fix things."

She nodded, her eyes ready to spill tears.

"That takes guts, Mia, something you are not short of," his eyes crinkled with his smile. "I don't know if you realize how much I admire you and your strength. You make me stronger."

"I don't think so," she shook her head.

"Yeah, you do. I have to be formidable just to keep up with you. You challenge and push me. I feel like I can do anything with you at my side."

Shimmying up the cool sheet so that she was facing him across the pillow, Mia just stared into Schooner's clear blue eyes, a smile brightening her face. "I feel like I can do anything with you at my side. I love the way you step in and create and build and take charge. You are this huge presence and sometimes I am just in awe of you."

"You're stealing my lines," he laughed, leaning forward, he brushed her lips softly with his. "Last night you let me into a very painful and dark place and I thank you for letting me through that door. I know it wasn't easy. But I'm really glad it's not a locked door between us anymore." Gently stroking her cheek with the back of his hand, "I don't want you to ever feel that Michael is an off-limits topic with me, honor him the way you want and need to, okay. I will always be okay with that."

Burning tears spilled in hot splashes onto her cheeks. "Thank you," she whispered.

Kissing her forehead softly, "No more secrets, Baby Girl." He closed his eyes, momentarily overcome by grief. Secrets had caused him to doubt everything he knew to be true, everything that gave him life. Secrets were the only thing that could drive a wedge between them and destroy them.

"Schooner, there isn't anything or any part of my life that I don't want to share with you." Pulling him on top of her, she smiled up into his handsome face, "and right now, I just want you to kiss me."

Chapter Forty-One

With her camera trained on the smiling faces of Schooner, Berto and Sonkwe, Mia watched with pride as she shot frame after frame of handshake after handshake with officials, the cutting of the ceremonial ribbon and the groundbreaking first shovels full of dirt. Wearing a construction hardhat, Schooner Moore was in his element and Mia could not help but wonder if one of the people he was schmoozing would ultimately be the person responsible for allowing them to adopt Portia.

Earlier that afternoon, when Sonkwe apprised them of the dismally low number of children that the government had allowed foreign families to adopt, Mia's spirit took a nose dive. She hadn't even considered that the government wouldn't permit them to adopt a child in need of a loving family. To hear that in a country with 1.3 million orphans that the government had permitted under twenty children to be internationally adopted, was deflating.

Although Los Angeles was ten hours behind, Schooner called Aaron Bender, waking him, "I know this might be a long shot, but who do we know with high level contacts at the State Department?" explaining the circumstances to his lawyer.

"Probably two ways to go at it," Aaron's voice was rough from sleep, "I know a lawyer in DC that works with USAID, his contacts report directly to the Secretary of State and I've got a client who is a retired Admiral in the Navy. He's very connected throughout Washington. They can at least help us get to the right people and my buddy in DC owes me one, so let's see what he can come up with."

Taking her face in both hands, Schooner shook his head, "Do not lose hope. Don't even go there, okay. We are in a very different position than most people. Very different. I'm not leaving here without her, don't you worry." He was so confident in his conviction that Mia clung to those words and his positive attitude.

"Okay?" he reiterated.

Mia nodded, forcing a smile.

"Say it, Mia," he demanded.

"We will get Portia. We will bring her home."

Smiling, he gave her a quick swat on her bottom, "Damn right we will.

I have a lot of leverage. People want things from me and there's only one way they'll get what they want."

"But Schooner, there's a three month in-country foster period."

"Yeah, well that's nice. Give me three weeks," and with his confident All-American boy smile, Schooner Moore strode out onto the field to break ground for the new L9 Physical Rehabilitation and Prosthetic facility and to broker the deal of his lifetime.

Chapter Forty-Two

The lines in Customs at JFK International Airport were insane. Knowing that Nathaniel was outside a door at the end of the line made the wait interminable. Closing her eyes, Mia pictured his reaction upon seeing her. His beautiful smile and bright eyes both beaming, his face becoming totally animated. Every minute without him in her arms became more painful. Mia Silver needed to hold her son.

Searching the crowd as she exited Customs, she saw Seth's arms waving. Standing next to him was her mother holding Nathaniel. Trapped behind slow moving tourists, Mia attempted to negotiate through the crowd without being rude and was finding that to be impossible as she started to weave through people, bumping them.

"Nathaniel," she yelled out, trying to get his attention over the noise.

Turning at the sound of his mother's voice, his arms reaching up in the air in her direction as he tried to wriggle out of Lois' arms, his need to get to Mia as strong as hers to hold him.

And then he was in her arms and for every kiss she planted on his chubby cheeks, he mirrored it back with his open-mouthed goopy kiss, until mother and son were in their own world of laughter, neither hearing or seeing anyone around them in the crowded airline terminal.

"I missed you so much." Tears streamed down her face.

"Ma-ma," he nestled his head into her neck.

"Did he just say Mama?" Mia looked at Seth and her mother with total surprise.

"He's been saying it non-stop for the last four days." Lois leaned over and gave her daughter a kiss.

"Did you miss Mama, sweet boy?" As Mia held him tighter, Nathaniel becoming more content. He had been saying Da-da for a while, and like most new mothers, although knowing that the "m" sound comes later to speech, she longed to hear her son call her Mama. "Well, that was the best homecoming present a mommy could ever ask for." Wiping her tears, "I missed him so much."

"So, what did they detain Schooner in Customs for being gorgeous or something?" Seth was looking over the crowd for a tall blonde coming at them.

"Schooner didn't come home," Mia surprised them both.

"Is the project delayed?" Lois asked.

"Let's get out of the fray here and get over to baggage claim and I will tell you all about it."

As they coursed through the crowd, "Please don't tell me you ran him off, BBC." Seth was starting to go into panic mode.

"I did and now he's all yours. But you're going to have to go to Africa for him," Mia laughed at the horrified look on Seth's face. "Was Poopy Boy here good for you?"

"Don't change the subject. Where is Schooner and why isn't he here?" Seth was getting annoyed.

They reached the baggage claim, which was surrounded by passengers, but no luggage.

"Let's go grab some seats." Mia headed for a bank of chairs. Lois sat down next to her, while Seth remained standing, hands on his hips, now glaring at Mia.

"I've got some news," Mia looked at Lois and Seth, a bemused grin on her face, "Breathe, you two. This isn't bad news." Pausing, just to torture them a little more, "Nathaniel is soon going to have a sister."

"You're pregnant?" Lois' face was a portrait in shock.

"No. Oh God, no," Mia laughed.

Seth's hand flew to his mouth with a gasp, his eyes wide.

"One Angelina Jolie comment out of you," Mia was pointing at him, "and I will fuck you up."

"Mia, watch your language around Nathaniel," Lois admonished.

Mia turned to her mother with a look saying, "That's what you took from this?"

Lois smiled, "Well, I was thinking more Mia Farrow."

"Eww," Seth looked at Lois, "Schooner is so Brad Pitt and thank God not Woody Allen."

Mia sat silently in disbelief that this was the conversation after she had just dropped a bombshell. And then it hit them both.

"A sister?" Lois' eyes filled with tears.

"Oh my God, oh my God." Seth sat down on the other side of Mia, "I'm going to be an uncle again. Don't just sit there BBC, tell us what is going on."

"She's three years old, almost four. She's absolutely precious, personality to burn. She's like a little ray of sunshine. I miss her already," Mia's smile was that of a mother talking about her child. "Oh, there's my bag," pointing to the carousel.

Seth jumped up and grabbed it, wheeling it back to them and sitting down, "What is her name?"

"Well, they call her Msikana."

"What does that mean?" It was all beginning to sink in for Lois that she was about to have a granddaughter.

Mia's eyes burned with tears, "It means 'Baby Girl'."

Both Lois and Seth gasped and Mia could feel Seth's fingers digging into her upper arm.

"It's a sign," they said in stereo.

Mia nodded, "That was the first sign."

"There's more?" Lois was on the edge of her seat.

"Her birthday is September 11th."

"Michael," Lois took a sharp intake of breath, her hand reflexively flying to her mouth.

"Oh my God," was all Seth could repeat, his grasp on Mia's arm becoming tighter.

"We're going to call her Portia. Portia Msikana," Mia kissed Nathaniel's head as tears started to flow.

"Portia. After Michael Portman. It's his initials reversed." Seth tightened his jaw, trying to control the onslaught of emotion that was surfacing. "Does Schooner know?"

She nodded, "Schooner knows. He knows everything."

"Everything?" Seth's voice rose an octave.

"What is everything?" Lois asked.

"Trust me, Mom, you don't need to know everything. Schooner, on the other hand, needed to know everything."

"And he was okay? He still wants to marry you?" Seth broke the tension with a snark.

"Fuck you, Princess, of course he still wants to marry me."

"God Angelina, you are such a touchy BBC."

Mia sat back in the chair, Nathaniel now fast asleep on her shoulder, laughing, "I really missed you guys."

"Back to Portia…" Lois was not going to let them get sidetracked.

"So, from the minute I met her, we just had this bond and then there was the 'Baby Girl' thing and when I found out that she was born on 9/11, it just felt like Michael was giving me signs. Signs that she should be mine. Mine and Schooner's. And that it would be a way of honoring and memorializing him. If that makes sense." Mia noticed that all the people from her flight were gone and passengers from the next flight to claim their luggage were arriving.

"When will Schooner be back with her?" Seth had finally let go of Mia's arm.

"Hopefully in a few weeks. Zambia is non-Hague Agreement country and it's very difficult to do international adoptions from there. Aaron Bender has legal contacts that work for USAID, which is part of the State Department, so we're hoping between them and the contacts that Schooner has in Lusaka that we won't have the typical red tape."

Shaking her head, Lois looked at her daughter with deep pride, "The two of you go off to help build a physical therapy center and come home with a daughter. You two really are perfect for one another."

"More than anyone can ever imagine." Smiling, clearly reminiscing, "This one is definitely going to be daddy's girl. You should see her with him. When he's holding her in his arms, she dips her head down and looks up at him through her eyelashes." Mia pulled out her phone, finally remembering she had photos and there it was, the scene she had just described.

"She's adorable," Lois was beaming. Handing the phone to Seth, "We are going to have so much fun shopping for this one."

Scrolling through Mia's pictures, Seth could not contain his smile, "Oh, she is precious. She has no clue what is about to happen to her life," looking up at Lois and Mia, unable to contain his excitement, "and I finally get to shop for pink."

Chapter Forty-Three

Departing the plane with Portia in his arms, "Do you want to practice again?" He kissed her cheek.

She nodded, smiling.

"Okay, what's my new name?"

"Daddy," she squealed with delight.

"What's Mia's new name?"

"Mommy," she was clearly very proud of herself.

"What's your name?" his smile was contagious.

"Portia," she grew more excited with each name.

"What's your baby brother's name?"

"Nathaniel," she was all giggles.

"Do you have any more brothers and sisters?"

Nodding and ready to show her new daddy how smart she was, "Zac and Holly."

"Very good. You are so smart," they stood on a Customs line, "So what are you going to say when you see Mommy?"

"Mommy," she screamed, the people in line turning around and laughing.

The long, exhausting journey had not dampened the sunshine of her mood or her hungry curiosity as she took in all the new sights and sounds. She was a brave little one, Schooner mused, definitely destined to be Mia's mini-me. The only telltale sign of her anxiety had been her continued tight clutch on her ragdoll.

Exiting Customs, Schooner surveyed the crowd, his heart melting at the sight of Mia and Nathaniel.

"Da-da, Da-da," Nathaniel was screeching like a pterodactyl, pointing at Schooner and trying to throw himself out of Mia's arms to get to his father.

Coming together, they did an immediate child-swap, smothering each little one in kisses.

"Mommy," Portia was elated to see Mia, clinging to her neck as Mia continued to cover her in kisses, tears streaming down her face.

With his free arm, Schooner pulled Mia close. When she gazed up at him, the look in her eyes matched the euphoria in his heart. They did it!

And it had been just as he expected it would be. No surprises as to what it would take for him to make this happen. Yet still, it wasn't until the plane's wheels lifted off the runway in Lusaka that he allowed himself to feel both satisfied in what he was able to pull off and happiness that his family had just expanded. He would do anything for Mia. But this time it was even bigger than that, and he was fully aware that this accomplishment cemented together his family and confirmed his own unequivocal berth.

Bending down, he planted a sweet kiss on her lips, "I have missed you, Baby Girl."

"It's smoochal, Pretty Boy. You are a sight for sore eyes." Looking back at the toddler in her arms, "Portia, this is your brother Nathaniel."

"Hi Nathaniel," Portia reached out, touching his arm.

Looking at her very seriously, he surveyed the new little girl smiling at him from his mother's arms. Reaching out, he touched her arm, rubbing it with his finger, then poked her. Looking up to take her all in, he remained very serious until his new sister shrieked, "Nathaniel," and he immediately broke into his classic Moore smile and the two started to giggle.

Schooner and Mia looked at one another and broke into laughter at the first interaction between their two children.

"Portia, I see you've brought Roberta with you," Mia was smiling at the little girl.

Portia suddenly looked stricken, "Mommy, Roberta is the only one who didn't get a new name."

Again, Mia looked up at Schooner, her look saying, "Isn't she adorable," and at the same time understanding the deeper significance.

"Do you want her to have a new name, too?"

Nodding her head vigorously, "Yes, she needs one too."

"What would you like to name her?"

Holding out the ragdoll and looking at her, Portia thought for a long moment, "Bupe. I want to name her Bupe."

"I think that's a wonderful name for her." Mia kissed the little girl's cheek, "And you know what, I think she's going to really like her new name. It fits her perfectly."

Pulling Mia under his arm and kissing the top of her head, Schooner didn't need to see Mia's face to know that there were tears streaming down her cheeks.

"Let's go home," he said to his family.

Chapter Forty-Four

The loft was empty when they arrived home. The plan was to let Portia settle in and get rested before meeting her very colorful extended family. Lois and Seth had insured that the loft was filled with things to make Portia feel right at home from the minute she walked in. Dolls, stuffed animals, a tea set, little ponies in a multitude of colors and a fantasy wardrobe that could only be purchased by a doting grandmother and a fashion plate gay uncle.

So fascinated by the sights and sounds of the city, she stared out the window on the drive back from Kennedy Airport. Knowing that Portia had never slept alone before, Mia made the decision to add a toddler bed into Nathaniel's nursery and of course, Lois and Seth rose to the task by finding a bed with a pink and white dollhouse headboard and painted picket fence sideboards.

Taking her by the hand, Mia showed Portia her new home.

"This is where Mommy and Daddy sleep." And taking her down the hall, "Here is your bathroom." Mia loved the look of awe on the little girl's face. Just the grand scale of things was a lot to take in. "Are you ready to see where you and Nathaniel sleep?"

Walking her into the jungle room, Mia knew it would be like walking the little girl into a fantasy.

Portia looked up at Mia, her excitement barely contained, but questioning, if it was okay.

Mia nodded, "Yes, sweetie, that is your bed."

With a gasp of delight, Portia ran to her bed, Bupe still in her tight grasp.

"Look there's a spot here for Bupe, too. Are you tired?"

The little girl nodded and placed the ragdoll in one of the empty cubbies in the dollhouse headboard, letting go of her for the first time since her journey began. Mia felt the sting of tears. One small action spoke volumes.

"Would you like me to read you and Bupe a book?"

Knowing exactly what she was going to choose off the bookshelf, Mia came and sat on the floor next to the bed. "I think you already know this one," and Mia held up the vividly colored book.

Gasping, “It’s the moon.”As Mia started to read her the book they shared daily together in Zambia, Portia sank deeper into her pillow, curling up into a ball under pink and white eyelet covers. She was asleep long before the end of the book.

Quietly carrying a sleeping Nathaniel to his crib, Schooner stood watching as Mia tucked in Portia.

Getting up from the floor, she went to him, arms wrapping around his waist, face buried in his chest. They stood there, silently, for the longest time before leaving their children to their naps.

Chapter Forty-Five

"You must be exhausted," they closed the door to the kids' room.

"I could use a nap and some Mia time." He kissed the top of her head as they walked down the hallway to their bedroom. "Hello bed, I have missed you." Schooner sat on the edge and pulled off his shoes. "I have been in these clothes for far too long." He stripped down to his boxers.

"Do you want to take a shower?"

Shaking his head, no, "I'm too tired to shower."

"Poor baby," Mia lied down next to him, pulling his head to her chest, gently brushing his hair back from his forehead.

"Mmm, that feels good. You feel good," he looked up at her, "I missed you, Baby Girl." And then the smile, "When did I become such a wuss, I hate being without you."

Laughing, she dipped her head to kiss his forehead, "Not a wuss, you're a family man. You just love being with your family."

"Mmm, I like that answer." He nuzzled his face into her soft breasts, "I spent the last three and a half weeks dreaming of making love to you."

"And you're too tired," she finished his sentence.

Looking up at her, his tired sapphire eyes twinkling, "Still love me?"

"More than ever, Pretty Boy," she continued to gently stroke his hair. "So, let me ask you a question."

"Shoot," he began to rub his thumb over her nipple, clearly enjoying making it hard.

"Did you have to sell your soul for this?"

Focusing on taking her breast out of her shirt and bra and getting her nipple into his mouth, he didn't look up, "Nah, not my soul. Just some stock and that's pretty soulless stuff anyway."

Running his tongue around it until it contracted into a hard little knot, he drew it past his teeth, sucking hard until Mia began to moan. Tangling his legs with hers, he pressed his throbbing cock against her thigh.

"Are we going to be okay?" she wanted to finish the conversation.

He stopped sucking and gave her nipple a hard lick before looking up at her, "Yeah, we're fine and even if we weren't, I still would have done it. She belongs with us."

"I love you."

"It's smoochal, Baby Girl." He sucked her nipple back into his mouth and ran a hand up her thigh, excited to see how wet his sucking had gotten her. Releasing her nipple, he looked up at her with his All-American boy smile. "Sleep is overrated. I'll sleep later," and plunged two fingers into her warm, awaiting wetness, totally turned on that he did not find the usual silk bikini under her sundress.

Pulling her underneath him, he pushed her thighs apart with his, "I need a welcome home pussy hug," and he was not going to wait another second to take what he needed as he drove deep into her with a low guttural moan.

Chapter Forty-Six

Dressed in a bright colored Mini Boden 'Vintage' dress, courtesy of Nana Lois and Uncle Seth, Portia Moore was enjoying being the center of attention at her "Welcome Home" party.

Practicing all the new names; Nana (Lois), Poppy (Bob), Uncle Seth, Aunt Kami, Uncle Charles, Aunt Gaby, Paola, Aunt Yoli and Aunt Debbie, Portia was not at all overwhelmed in meeting her new family. She had met Grandma Dee and Grandpa Gavin and her other brother and sister, Zac and Holly, via Skype earlier in the morning where Holly had asked, "Dad, can I call you later?" Both she and Zac were staying with their grandparents.

"Is everything okay?" Schooner was concerned.

"Yeah, fine. There's just something I want to talk to you about."

"Wonder what that is about?" Mia and Schooner were both perplexed at the end of the call.

"We'll find out tonight," and he and Mia continued to prepare for Portia's party.

With the homecoming celebration in full swing, Schooner grabbed Yoli and headed down the hall to the study. Yoli had come in to mind L9/NYC during Schooner's prolonged absence.

"It's good to see you. She is really adorable, Schooner."

With a proud smile he nodded, "She is something special, isn't she?" Sitting down at the desk, "It's really good to be home." He stretched out his long legs, leaning back in the chair, knitting his fingers behind his head. Schooner was happy and relaxed.

"I'll bet. Mia and Nathaniel have missed you. And I think so has the staff."

Laughing, "Ah, so you've been going all Dragon Lady on them?"

Yoli rolled her eyes, "Believe it or not, no. I love this staff, that have so much more on the ball than most of our west coasters. Everything is just done immediately here, without having to ask even a first time. They anticipate and I like that."

"So, do you like New York?" He opened the bottom desk drawer and pulled out a bell-shaped bottle and two heavy crystal, ultra-modern glasses. Pouring two fingers of the amber liquid into each snifter, he slid one across the desk to her. "Do you like it enough to live here?"

Yoli choked on her first sip, "Come again?"

"As soon as I can get my hands on Mia," he loved making her grimace. "Seriously though, how would you and Debbie feel about moving east."

"We'd love it, but what's going on? Please don't tell me you're retiring or doing a John Lennon stay home with the kids and bake bread thing."

Laughing, "Damn, I miss you." Schooner took a sip of his cognac, "I want to continue the work I've started overseas. Expand it and formalize it, too. I want to establish a foundation to begin funding physical rehabilitation sites in developing nations."

"Would it be the L9 Foundation?"

"That's what I'm thinking. Expand on a respected brand."

"Wow Schooner, that's exciting."

"I'd like to officially move L9 headquarters to New York, Yoli. I want you to step into the President's role and oversee all U.S. operations." As he said it, he could feel his excitement growing. His whole life was beginning to truly take shape on the East Coast. With Zac starting college in the fall at a small private school outside of Boston, he would have his whole family, except for his parents, on the Eastern Seaboard.

"You know what my concern is, don't you?" Yoli looked him square in the eye.

"Not having a strong enough operations person to run multiple sites on the west coast."

She nodded and took another sip, "I don't have backfill strong enough there yet, Schooner. Lucas is good, but I think he'd be in over his head and we really need someone we can trust. Someone who will be in it for the long haul."

"The trust piece of it is the most important aspect. There is someone I'm thinking of who I would totally trust, he's run multi-facility organizations, just not in this industry. Smart guy, likable, and between us we can teach him what he needs to know. Let me reach out to him and see if he'd even be interested in making a move. If he's interested, I'll put you two together."

Out of the corner of his eye he saw her standing in the doorway looking up at him through her eyelashes.

"Hi, Daddy," she twirled slightly from side to side, her dress and its bright yellow underskirt swishing with her.

"Hi, Sweetheart," and the minute he held out his arms she came bounding into the room and up into his lap.

"Are you having a good time at the party?" Yoli asked.

The little girl nodded vigorously and settled herself against Schooner's chest.

"She is precious, Schooner. It's very clear who's going to be Daddy's girl."

Nodding, he laughed. The extra time he had with her in Zambia created a bond that he never saw coming. Just as she had found her way into Mia's heart, Portia stole his, and every morning he rushed from his hotel over to the site to spend time with his soon-to-be daughter. It wasn't long before he found himself taking her everywhere, and as the days turned into weeks, there was not a shot in hell that Schooner Moore was leaving the country without his daughter, Portia Msikana Moore, in his arms.

"You're so Brad Pitt," Yoli teased.

Hugging his young daughter to his chest, he let out a guffaw, "Do not call Mia Angelina or she will go absolutely postal on you."

Portia's eyes were getting heavy as she tried her hardest not to fall asleep, but the excitement of the day (and probably a little too much sugar) had worn the little girl out.

"Was it hard to get her out?" Yoli whispered.

He just nodded, his somber eyes locked in on his friend's.

"Harder than Mia knows?"

He nodded again.

"Are you okay?" her brows drawn together, there was concern in Yoli's deep brown eyes.

"Oh, yeah, we're fine. The business is fine. Don't worry about anything. Let's just put it this way, the sale of the house on Linda Isle was very timely."

"Wow," Yoli knew the house had sold for a staggering amount of money and even with giving half of it to CJ and paying broker's fees, Schooner's share was high seven figures, "you are such a good guy. You really are."

"She makes me better," he nodded his head toward the living room where Mia was entertaining everyone.

"She does. She makes you better," Yoli agreed, "but I have a feeling you make her better, too."

With his real smile shining all the way to his eyes, he appeared reflective, as if he were smiling internally, "We are a pretty formidable team, she and I," and then his smile became external. "Did I ever tell you about the conversation CJ and I had the day we signed the divorce papers?"

"Pour me some more of that, I have a feeling I'm going to need it," and she slid her glass back across the desk to him.

Picking up the bottle of Hennessy Paradis, "Do you believe that scumwad, Beau, drank a whole bottle of this at my house. Eight hundred bucks a bottle and he just helped himself," Schooner just shook his head, poured Yoli a stiff drink and slid the glass back across the table. He started to laugh again, his eyes dancing, "So, she told me not to move my boat back east, because Mia and I didn't look good together and I wasn't going to be able to handle that," he could hardly finish his sentence he was laughing so hard, nearly waking Portia.

Yoli's mouth hung open, "I'm speechless. Has she totally lost touch with reality? It's amazing how little she understands, even after all these years, just what makes you tick. So, what did you do?"

"The only thing I could do. Left the meeting and made two phone calls. One to the transporter guy in Newport Beach and the other to the marina in Ocean Beach to rent a slip."

"True Compass is here?"

Schooner nodded, "I haven't seen her yet. We're planning on going out next weekend. Charles has seen her, said she looks fine. Arrived without a scratch on her."

"Aunt Yoli's present, let me buy the kids little life vests."

"That's a great gift, Yol. You are an amazing Aunt." Yoli Perez was the sister Schooner Moore never had and he couldn't have been happier that she wanted to be a part of his children's lives.

"So, when are you getting married?" she sipped the smooth cognac.

"Good question," Schooner shrugged his shoulders, "I just got home, so I don't know. Ask Mia," and with a smile and sparkling eyes, "or better yet, ask Seth and Lois."

Together they laughed at what they knew was the absolute truth.

Chapter Forty-Seven

With the last guests gone and the kids asleep, Schooner and Mia finished cleaning the kitchen. Out of the corner of his eye, he caught Mia smiling at him.

"What are you smiling at, Baby Girl?" his panty wetting smile was at full wattage.

"Us. Look at us." She leaned against the marble counter.

Coming to stand in front of her, Schooner lifted Mia and sat her on the counter. Smoothing her hair, that was curling in the summer humidity, he smiled down at her.

"It's pretty nice, isn't it?" continuing to smooth her curls with his fingers.

"It's so," Mia paused to think, "normal," and she hit him with a devil grin.

And they both laughed.

"Don't you just love it?" Schooner was relaxed and calm, rested from his long journey with Portia.

"I do. I'm just thinking how wonderful the rest of this summer is going to be. I can't believe it's July and we haven't been out to the beach house yet."

"Next weekend."

"I can't wait to see how the two of them respond to sand and the ocean. Don't forget to bring the video camera, I have a feeling our kids will put on a good show for us."

Schooner laughed, "Why do I have this suspicion that Nathaniel is going to be a sand eater?"

Smiling up at him, "Because he is going to be a sand eater. Everything goes in that mouth."

Taking his finger and running it gently along her lower lip, he watched her intently, a small smirk on his face. Mia opened her lips slightly, the tip of her tongue coming out to meet the tip of his finger, swirling around it slowly.

"Nice tongue action, Baby Girl. Is that a preview of coming attractions?"

"Help me clean this kitchen and it's a promise."

"You know what, I forgot to call Holly back." Schooner grabbed his phone off the counter.

"Anything to get out of cleaning this kitchen. I know your tricks, Pretty Boy." She pointed a serving spoon at him.

Laughing, he dialed Holly's cell, "Hi, Sweetheart, I wanted to get back to you … oh yeah, it was great, she did really well meeting a lot of people … I know, isn't she adorable. She's such a good girl, too. Sonkwe and Bupe have done such a nice job raising her … So, what's going on." Schooner's eyes widened and the look on his face was pure amusement. "Really? She wanted you to personally tell me that? Well, I'm sorry she saw fit to make you the messenger, Sweetheart … Seriously? She wants my reaction? … Okay, well tell her I laughed and said, "He'll never marry her." … Yes, exactly like that… How are Grandma and Grandpa feeling? … good, good … So, are you going to spend some time with us on the beach? … Sweetheart, don't ever feel like you need to be asked … we want you there always … Mia's nodding her head … Zac wants to know if it's okay if he comes, too? … Tell him of course," laughing … "Yes, Mia is still nodding her head. But that might be a headache … we're going out next weekend and I'm sure Mia will be there with the kids through Labor Day … I know, he misses you, too … you're not going to believe how big he's gotten … okay, Sweetheart," laughing, "yes, that is my message … I love you, too. Get some plane tickets. Goodnight."

"What was that all about?" Mia looked truly perplexed.

"CJ and Beau are engaged," Schooner's smile told a tale of happiness.

Mia screeched, hands flying to her mouth, "Oh no, I hope I didn't wake the kids," but there was no sound from their bedroom. "Wait, she wanted Holly to tell you that? That's so fucked up."

"That's so CJ," he laughed.

"And your response was, 'He'll never marry her?' I don't understand," Mia's brows were knit together.

Nodding his head, his sapphire eyes were truly alight.

"I don't understand your response," Mia was still perplexed.

"There is a method to my madness, Baby Girl." This time he jumped up and sat on the kitchen counter, long legs dangling.

Going over to stand between his legs, "Okay, 'splain it to me, Lucy."

He laughed, "Well, if I tell CJ, he's never going to marry you, she is going to be hell bent on proving me wrong and she will get that fucker to marry her yesterday."

"And that means no alimony."

"You are right, Baby Girl. It's not that I have an issue paying CJ alimony, because I don't. I was married to her for a long time and I get that. It's supporting that fucker that really chafes my ass. He actually sold his condo and moved into my house. I was paying that fucking freeloader's rent. So yes, I want her to marry him, because it is my alimony check that he is living on."

Rubbing her hands up and down the front of his thighs, Mia thought reflectively, before speaking. "Do you think he'll marry her?"

"Fifty-fifty shot. I'm sure he likes the current financial arrangement and marrying her means she becomes his expense and CJ is not a cheap expense. He's also forty-four years old and has never been married. So those are the cons. On the pro side, he's wanted her his whole life and he's thrilled to have her as arm candy."

"And he's getting laid," Mia couldn't hide her devil grin.

"Yeah and not paying for it," Schooner cracked himself up. "Well, he is paying for it. He just doesn't have to call and schedule it through an 800 number."

"So, shall we take bets? Will they or won't they? And if they do, the date."

"You're on, Baby Girl. I say they do. If he balks, she'll seal it with a blowjob," picking up his phone and hitting the calendar app, he scrolled, "Sunday, August 25th."

"Let me see that," Mia reached for his phone. "I agree, she will get him to marry her. It might take some coercing, but she will get her way." She looked up at Schooner, "we know that first hand. But I don't think they will stay married for too long. I give it twelve to sixteen months. Hmm, let's see, Friday, August 15th is my guess. If she gets married before that I win and get the prize of my choice. If it's after the 25th, you win and choose your prize. I think she'll want to do it before Holly and Zac are back east in school, but she'll want to mess up their time on the beach with us."

"Oh you know she's going to want to do that. Now, why don't you think they'll stay married."

"He's not rich enough or good looking enough. He's just a fuck you to you and me. That's all he is to her," was Mia's assessment.

"Well, the big fuck you is that neither you nor I care. And speaking of fucking, is the kitchen clean enough for a blow job yet?"

"I'd tell you to lose the cargo shorts, Pretty Boy," the devil was in the kitchen, "it's known as counter service. Jumping down from the counter, he grabbed her hand and started to pull her toward their bedroom with long-legged strides. Looking back, "We really did become normal," and the smile on his face said he loved everything about it.

Chapter Forty-Eight

Toes dug in the sand, Nathaniel asleep in his Pack 'n Play under the umbrella, Mia and Gaby sat on their beach chairs watching Portia and Paola looking for holes to appear in the sand each time the ocean receded after a crashing wave. They'd see a bubble and start digging, knowing that under the gritty muck was a clam waiting to be put into their buckets. Each clam discovered brought elated squeals and a shout of, "Look Mommy," before finding its way into a brightly colored pail.

"I have missed being here," Mia Silver looked more relaxed and content than she'd possibly ever looked in her life.

"I've missed having you. It's lonely here without you during the week."

"I assure you that I am not stepping foot off this island until after Labor Day," Mia promised, unconsciously digging her toes deeper into the sun-warmed sand.

"Mommy," Portia was jumping up and down, her thin limbs flailing. As she held up the clam for Mia to see, a stream of salt water shot from the clam's foot. Laughing, squealing and jumping simultaneously, Portia cried out, "Ahhhh, clammies' making a pee-pee," causing both little girls to shriek and jump around.

"Well, you just saved Paola's summer, she was moping after the fun she had last year. I had her in the little camp they have, but she wasn't happy."

"Holly is coming next week, so we've got our babysitter back."

"Holly and Portia. Paola's summer just got a lot better."

The two women spoke without looking at one another, both sets of eyes trained on the little girls at the shoreline, playing as if they'd been lifelong friends.

"So Mia, you know I must ask you, when are you and Schooner finally getting married?"

Mia laughed, "You do know the correct answer to that question is, ask Seth." Picking up her water bottle she took a long swig, "I really want Portia to settle in this summer without a lot of craziness. The minute we go into wedding mode there will be no way to avoid the tension that comes with it. Know what I mean?"

Gaby nodded, "You're right. I hadn't even thought about that. You are such a good mom, Mia."

Laughing, Mia gave Gaby a look, "Tell me that again when she is sixteen." They sat in silence for a few minutes, "So, what I've been thinking is, taking the rest of the summer just to relax and bond as a family, really have Portia settle into the groove of life with us. I can put in a few hours a day of work from out here, especially once Holly and Zac arrive."

"Zac?" Gaby's voice rose an octave. "Are you serious?"

The girls now sat in the wet sand digging holes and putting the clams back into the holes.

"Mommy, Mia, look the clammies are going home," yelled Paola.

"They are so cute together," Mia put down her water bottle and grabbed a bright pink chiffon scarf to pull her wild hair off her face and neck. "Yes, Zac is coming. Hopefully, he'll be on better behavior than last summer and I think he will. He was okay this spring in California and actually pleasant at his graduation. What's going to shock you the most is how amazing he is with Nathaniel."

"Are you serious?"

"I know, right?" Mia smiled, "He's amazing with the baby and Nathaniel loves him like crazy. It will be interesting to see how he is with Portia."

"I'm just in shock, Mia. What a difference a year makes. Will Holly want to babysit again this year?"

"She's counting on it," Mia smiled devilishly at her friend. "Yes, we get free time."

"Hallelujah! Holly cannot get here fast enough." Looking at her watch, "Speaking of time, how long should it have taken them to check out Schooner's boat?"

"My guess is that those two are somewhere on the Great South Bay halfway to Block Island by now."

"Or still in the marina, half trashed. And you still haven't answered my question, when are you getting married?"

"Oh yeah, that," Mia laughed. "Okay, so if we're here through Labor Day, that brings us to the beginning of September. Luckily, I have another year before I have to worry about Portia starting school the Wednesday after Labor Day, but still it will be the change of moving from the beach back to the city and a week and a half later is 9/11 and her birthday."

Gabby winced, "Are you going to go this year?"

Mia nodded, "Michael's mom is flying up from Florida and she's really looking forward to meeting Portia and Schooner."

Biting her lower lip, the ghosts of those ceremonies were clearly swirling around Gaby, "Schooner has no clue what he's in for."

Mia nodded, "I know. But he really wants to go. And then we'll leave there and do something really fun to celebrate Portia." Glancing at Portia and Paola, "Girls, come closer to us," Mia yelled, and the little ones moved away from the ocean's edge. "I really want her to have a special birthday and then I can go all bridezilla."

"I thought you'd get married out here, but there will be few services on Fire Island available late in September."

"I know, I really thought we'd do it here, too, but Seth and Elan are looking into places out in Montauk. I have a feeling we'll end up at Gurney's Inn. It's beautiful, located right on the beach and they have facilities for catering and weddings."

Mia couldn't help but remember the idyllic mansion in Newport, Rhode Island where she and Michael had spent their final Labor Day weekend together. The Chanler Inn at Cliff Walk was truly the most romantic location for a wedding she had ever seen. Lifting her sunglasses, she wiped away the salty tears that were escaping her eyes. Even after all this time, memories of sitting under a full Harvest moon that weekend made her heart hurt. And Michael had been right, it was the absolute perfect place to be married. Mia sighed. That was a fact she would keep to herself, saved as a special Michael memory.

"Daddy," Portia yelled, all smiles and fluttering limbs as she ran up the sand past Mia and Gaby.

Scooped up in Schooner's arms, he and Charles joined them on the sand chairs.

"So, did you take her out?" Mia knew the answer before she asked the question.

Schooner's smile confirmed it and Charles' exuberant gushing helped fill in the blanks, "Oh my God, that is one gorgeous boat. Sunset cocktail sails need to become part of our repertoire."

"I'm down with that," Mia agreed. "We should seriously do that, bring a picnic dinner, if the kids get tired, we put them in one of the cabins."

"When am I going to see this famous boat?" Gaby was feeling left out.

Schooner looked at his watch and hit her with the smile, "First family sunset sailing in about five hours."

Standing up and pulling a sundress over her bathing suit, Mia turned to Schooner and Charles, "Okay Daddies, you are now officially on munchkin duty. Gabs and I need to go plan and shop for our first family sunset dinner."

Joining her, with a swish of her long hair, Gaby and Mia set off to arrange the perfect inaugural sail menu.

Chapter Forty-Nine

The monitor in baggage claim indicated that Holly and Zac's plane had landed. Schooner paced the terminal, his long-legged strides rapidly covering the space. He hadn't seen his two oldest in a few months and was anxious to get out to the beach with them and have them meet their newest sibling. Mia had told him that she had let the kids take extra long afternoon naps so that they'd be awake and in good moods when he arrived from the airport.

Waving as the escalator brought them down to him, he didn't realize how much he missed his two older children until he had his arms wrapped around them forming a huddle.

"It's so good to see you two," kissing both of them on the temple, Schooner was clearly not shy about showing his children affection.

"Do you think Mini-Me will remember me?" Zac wondered aloud as they loaded duffel bag after duffel bag into the Range Rover.

"If not immediately, he'll warm up pretty quickly."

"I think he'll remember me," Zac did not like Schooner's answer.

"Holly, how much stuff did you bring?" Schooner was arranging the bags so that they would all fit.

"Dad, I'm going straight from here back to Brown," rolling her eyes at him, "I need my stuff."

Having all four of his children with him for the remainder of the summer was the key to Schooner's happiness. As he pulled out of the parking lot at Kennedy Airport he realized this summer was without the trepidation of the year before. Even Zac wanted to spend the summer with them on Fire Island.

"Wait until you meet Portia," Schooner was beaming with pride, "she is so sweet and smart."

"Mom almost shit when she heard you were adopting a kid from Africa," Zac laughed.

"Yeah, well your mother's idea of diversity is changing hair salons." Schooner noticed a look pass between his children, "Okay, one of you spit it out. What's going on?"

"You tell him," an agitated Zac said to his older sister.

"Mom got married two days ago," Holly genuinely looked scared delivering the news.

"No shit?" Schooner was smiling, "Damn, I lost a bet. I hate losing bets. So, she convinced Beau to marry her, huh?"

"He's a douche monkey," Zac piped in from the back seat.

Instead of admonishing his son for inappropriate language, Schooner stretched his hand back for a high five, "He is a douche monkey and will from this point forward be referred to as your mother's douche monkey."

Grabbing his phone, he quickly texted Aaron at the first red light.

Schooner: CJ married Beau 2 days ago
Aaron: No shit?!

Laughing, Schooner pointed the phone at his kids, "Check out Aaron's response."

Aaron: I'll get the paperwork into the courts
Schooner: TY

"So, you're not upset, Dad," Holly seemed surprised.

"Not at all, sweetheart. I'm glad your mother is moving on with her life. Do I think Beau is the right person for her? No. But who am I to say what makes another person happy," he smiled at Holly, hoping that would put her at ease.

Getting off the ferry in Ocean Beach, they loaded red wagons with the duffels and headed toward the beach house.

"Oh man, did I miss this place. I am so ready for a lobster at Maguire's."

Schooner smiled, wondering if she was also looking forward to seeing the restaurant's manager, Aiden, to continue their harmless flirtation that had begun the summer before.

"Mia made reservations to go there tomorrow night."

They approached the house and Schooner turned to his kids, "Let's make this a good summer, okay? It's really different having two small children in the house, so just make sure you keep that in mind."

Walking through the door, the first thing they heard was an ecstatic little voice, with a British accent, screaming, "Daddy," as a pink blur came running and ended up in Schooner's arms.

"How's my sweet girl?" he kissed her cheek and was rewarded with giggles. "Are you ready to meet your big brother and sister?"

Portia nodded, all smiles, "Hi Holly, Hi Zac."

Schooner knew Mia had been practicing with her. Mia came down the stairs with Nathaniel in her arms.

"Look who's here, Nathaniel. Hi guys! How was your trip?" Nathaniel's face lit up and he pointed to Zac and began his pterodactyl screech. "Okay, okay, you can go to your brother."

Mia placed Nathaniel in his older brother's arms and Zac surprised Mia with a kiss on the cheek.

"Mini-Me, you remember me." Zac was elated at Nathaniel's reaction.

Giving Holly a big hug, Mia couldn't help but compare the energy in the room this summer to the prior summer's and marvel at what a difference a year had made.

Portia already had Holly by the hand and was taking her to meet her dolls.

Feeling his arms wrap around her from behind, Mia and Schooner watched as the two sets of children became one. She didn't have to turn around to know the exact look in his sapphire eyes. All his dreams were coming true right in that room.

"Are you ever going to marry me?" he whispered in her ear, rubbing his cheek along her neck.

"Yeah, I'm sure at some point. Ask Seth. He's got all the answers."

"Oh, by the way, you won the CJ/Beau wedding bet. They got married two days ago," he gently bit her neck.

Turning her head to look at him, she remained silent, her mouth hanging open, before she finally regained her voice, "No shit?"

Laughing, "That seems to be the general consensus. We were wrong about one thing, at least she won't be interrupting the kids' time on the beach with us."

"So, I know exactly what I want for winning the bet."

"Oh yeah, what's that?" he smiled down at her.

"Let's just put it this way, I'm really glad that I just bought a new tube of Mango Butter lotion for the shower."

Tightening his arms around her, he laughed, "Damn, Baby Girl, do you have any idea of what you do to me?"

"It's smoochal," and she melted just a little further into his arms.

Chapter Fifty

"I don't hate him as much this year," from the deck, Seth was watching Zac on the beach surrounded by three girls ready to claw each other's eyes out for his attention.

Mia laughed, "He's just wishing he had three dicks right now. He's definitely a much less douchey version of himself this summer. And I have to admit, he is really great with the kids, he's like the Pied Piper."

Seth continued to watch him, eagle-eyed, "He must get so much pussy."

"Old and young," Mia was shaking her head. "If he flunks out of school, he definitely has a career as a gigolo."

It was another picture perfect cloudless day on Fire Island, Holly had the two girls, Paola and Portia, and Nathaniel was quietly playing in his Pack 'n Play, while Mia and Seth worked on the deck.

"Kami sent the final comps on the point of sale pieces for the Africa/ Health Club Membership campaign," Mia opened the document. She regarded it for a long moment, "You know, I have not been able to figure out what it is about this piece that is just not sitting right with me… until now. It's the font. What is this, an AR Christy font?" She looked up at Seth, "It's too frivolous and this is not a frivolous piece."

Immediately, she messaged Kami, telling her to have the Art Department change out the font.

"Speaking of fonts," Seth grabbed his laptop bag and gave Mia a coy look, "I have something else that needs your approval."

Mia looked lost. Reaching into the bag, he slowly pulled out a large thick padded envelope and placed it on the table, sliding it over to her.

"What is this?"

"Just fucking open it, BBC."

Unfastening the clasp, Mia reached into the envelope and gasped as she pulled out the surprise contents. "Oh my God, wedding invitations."

"Your wedding invitations."

"Oh my God," there were tears in Mia's eyes as she leaned over to kiss Seth.

"Well, look at them already. I'm dying," Seth grabbed the contents from Mia's hands, laying out three very different prototypes, a black linen envelope fastened with a cream satin ribbon, a six-inch long thin white box bound with a two-inch white and gold paper sheath, and a flat square black raw silk box.

Mia started with the black linen envelope. Inside was a simple and elegant black and cream wedding invitation, timeless in its elegance.

"This is beautiful. It is classy and classic," smiling at Seth, "much like the man I'm marrying."

Seth nodded, "That's a good way to describe him. He is classy and classic. I like that."

Already removing the gold and white paper sheath from the thin white box, Mia was clearly going to power through this, hoping to make a decision and get it out of the way. Loving the details of putting together an elegant affair, Seth would have loved for her to savor this part of the process, but Mia was going to have no part in that.

Opening the box, "Ahh, a scroll. Very cute," she unraveled the parchment and picked up the two elaborate gold rods that inserted at the top and bottom of the scroll. "It's cute but it requires assembly, so this one is out."

Reaching for the black satin box, she opened it and quickly rifled through all the black and white components inside. "This is very elegant, too, but maybe a little showy and I think way too formal for a beach wedding."

"So, if you had to rank them, the black satin envelope with the cream sash would be your first choice?"

Mia looked at them all a second time, then nodded. "Yes, it's beautiful, but again, is it too formal for what we're doing?"

Seth shook his head, "Yes and no. There's no right or wrong in a situation like this. It just comes down to personal preference. Yes, you are getting married on the beach, but this is not some hippie wedding out of the '70's. You're getting married at one of the most prestigious resorts on the east coast."

"You shit," Mia punched Seth in the arm, "did you forget to tell me something, Princess?"

"Oh yeah, I guess I should have mentioned this. You're getting married September 27th at Gurney's."

"Ahhhhhhhhhhhhhhhhhh," Mia's scream scared Nathaniel, his lower lip immediately starting to tremble as his little face collapsed.

"Oh my sweet boy," Seth went to him immediately, scooping him out of his Pack 'N Play. "Did your crazy BBC mommy scare you. She scares me too sometimes."

"How am I going to be ready for a wedding at the end of September," Mia's green eyes were wide with fear, "there's so much to do."

"BBC, you need to stay out of this," Nathaniel had his head on Seth's shoulder, while Seth gently rubbed his back, calming him down. "Elan and I have this under control. We'll let you and gorgeous know when we need you to step in." Sensing a combination of panic and Bridezilla behavior coming on, "Breathe, BBC. We're not continuing until you get hold of yourself."

"Bitchy queen," she muttered under her breath.

"I heard that," he continued to rub a now sleepy Nathaniel's back. "Okay," he continued, "because I know you as well as I do, there's one more invitation I'd like to show you."

Reaching back into his laptop bag, Seth extracted a square tan kraft box embossed in gold "Join Us" with a fancy gold scroll design above and below the letters. He slid it across the table to Mia.

The simple box was significantly more casual than the first three options Seth had presented. Mia lifted the cover from the box. Inside was gold pearlized tissue paper. She could see something dimensional beneath the paper and was eager to find out what was below. Flipping the tissue paper back made Mia gasp. Looking up at Seth, her mouth hung open.

"I love it," she exclaimed. "You knew I'd love it."

"Mais oui," he looked very satisfied as he confirmed in French.

Underneath the tissue paper was a beautiful, white starfish - a real starfish, lying on heavy ocean blue and sand-colored damask cardstock, secured with a double gold rope tied in a nautical knot.

"It's creative, it's different, it's whimsical, it's beautiful and it totally fits a beach wedding."

Inside the box was a host of components; a sand dollar shaped invitation that opened like a bloom, a reply card and matching envelope, an additional information card and a gold paperclip with a seashell topper holding the whole thing together.

"So, do we have an invite?" He got up to put Nathaniel down in his playpen to sleep.

"As far as I'm concerned, yes. But I guess I should run this by Schooner."

Waving his hand at her, Seth dismissed her comment, "Trust me, he doesn't care as long as you, BBC, are happy. Okay, well I need to get firm invite counts from the two of you because these are handmade and assembled by a woman out of Newport, Rhode Island."

Mia felt her stomach knot at the mention of Newport. "When do you need the counts?"

"Yesterday." Going back into his laptop bag, he pulled out several pieces of paper, "On to the next item we need to take care of." He paused, "you."

"Moi?" Mia reached for a bottle of water.

"So, I've been scouting dresses…"

"Oh God, I love you. If you could try them on for me, life would be perfect."

"I may borrow your dress for Halloween. Get a big gold necklace that says BBC. Go as you."

"Anything for tits, huh?" Mia laughed.

"You know it. Anyway, here is what I was thinking. Obviously not some big, garish, overwhelming dress."

"Right, I was thinking tea or cocktail length. I think long and sand is a mistake."

"I totally agree and we have to make sure it's mature enough without being dowdy," he added, rifling through the papers.

"Totally agree," Mia reached for the papers he had cinched in his hands. He quickly pulled them out of her reach.

"Not so quickly, BBC. I looked at the designers you'd expect first. Didn't find anything with the right length that wasn't poufy. And I know you don't want poufy. It would be hideous and you'd look fat."

"Thank you," she fake smiled.

"Well, you know it's true. So, I did find some possibilities, first is this champagne lace sheath from Monique Lhullier," he passed the first sheet of paper to her.

"That's very pretty. Very elegant. I need to start dieting now." Mia studied the dress closely.

"Then I thought, what about vintage?"

Their eyes met, Mia had her hand out for the second sheet of paper, but Seth was not handing it over.

"I like vintage. A lot. Just as long as it's not a big skirted thing."

"Unfortunately, that was most of it, but I did find this edge-of-the-shoulder Ian Stuart at Kleinfeld's." He finally handed the page to Mia.

"Oh, that is very pretty. I love the lines and the lace. But it's total bride. I think I'm going to look ridiculous in a real wedding dress at my age, don't you?" Seth nodded, "It's a risk. And it's not Schooner's first wedding and he's got two grown kids."

Mia started to pout, "Why am I even doing this Seth? We should just go down to City Hall and be done with it."

"Not an option, BBC," he snarled at her, pissed off that she would even suggest such a thing and rob everyone around her of the enjoyment. "You are so selfish."

"Show me that last piece of paper, Princess."

Without saying a word, he handed it over to her. Mia's face immediately lit with delight.

"I like this. I like this a lot. It's dressy, but casual, age appropriate, it's understated, you know" she continued to study the BCBG/MaxAzria white lace high-low dress, "and it's got a great line to it, so I think it will fit me fine."

"You do realize that your shoes will be more expensive than this dress?"

Looking over at him, Mia laughed, "That's actually really funny. But you're right." She looked back at the paper, "I should order one and have it shipped out here to see if it fits."

"No need," Seth walked in the house and came out a few minutes later with the dress in her size, "I've been dressing you for how many years now," was all he said.

Grabbing the dress, she ran passed him into the house. Seth picked up Nathaniel and brought him in, laying him down at the center of Mia and Schooner's bed.

A few minutes later, Mia emerged from the bathroom.

Seth's eyes immediately teared up, "So, what do you think?" he asked, no snark at all in his voice.

Mia just nodded her head. She couldn't speak, overwhelmed by a myriad of emotions, as she stood before her best friend, wearing her wedding dress.

"You look beautiful, Mia."

Again, she nodded, her lips forming a silent thank you as tears began to roll down her cheeks.

"We have been through so much, but we came through it. And here you are, about to marry your true love, a guy who came back for you because he was as broken without you as you were without him. He stayed married to someone he didn't love because he didn't want to feel, and you almost drove yourself over the edge trying to feel, something, anything. But I have to tell you, you two are not broken when you are together. You complement each other's strengths and fill in the gaps of each other's weaknesses. You guys dream together and then turn it into reality. I know what I want now, Mia. I want to find the other half of me. My Schooner."

Crossing the room to the bed where he was sitting, Mia sat down next to him and put her arms around him. The tears burned at the back of her throat and nose too much to speak at first, "He's out there, Seth and he's thinking the same thing you are, 'Where is he?' And he's dreaming about Sunday Brunch and the New York Times and art openings, and traveling together. Think about it, before that day that Schooner's friend request showed up, none of this was even remotely on the horizon. I wasn't even dating anyone. And now I've got two kids and on September 27th I am marrying the love of my life." She looked up at him, "It can happen. It will happen. And we will laugh about this moment because it will feel like a million light years away from your new reality."

"You'd better be right, BBC."

Mia stood up and put her hands on her hips, "Haven't you figured out by now that I'm always right," the devil grin was shoving the tears away.

Rolling his eyes and snorting, "Just get the dress off before you ruin it."

Chapter Fifty-One

"Is it Friday yet?" Snuggled in their bed at the beach house, Mia was under the covers propped up against a wall of pillows.

"Two more days, Baby Girl and I'll be out for a long weekend." Schooner was in the same position as Mia, but in their loft's bedroom.

"So, I have a lot of news for you," she was smiling and twirling a curl.

"Okay, lay it on me," he laughed, stretching out and getting comfortable.

"We're getting married on September 27th."

"Wow. That is huge news. Where?" Schooner found it amusing that he and Mia were just being told where and when to show up. The two of them were alpha, control freaks and here they were both riding shotgun on the biggest day of their lives.

"Gurney's Inn in Montauk."

"Are you happy with that?" Schooner wanted this to be the best day of her life.

"I'm not unhappy with it."

"Mia, that's not what I asked you. If you are not ecstatic then they need to scrap the plans and start again."

"No, no, no. I'm fine with it. It's a beach wedding, it's perfect for us. It'll be elegant and casual at the same time. I think that fits us."

"Baby Girl, I want you to be ecstatically thrilled about our wedding. If you want to do an elegant Manhattan space, we can do something like 583 Park Avenue."

"Schooner, 583 Park is stunning and I'll bet if I had gotten married in my twenties, that is exactly the kind of cool and elegant space I would have wanted. But it's us and the babies, and Holly and Zac, and I want it to be lovely, but still have a laid-back vibe and I think we'll get that at Gurney's." Mia shifted the phone and grabbed one of his pillows. It still had his scent. Breathing it in deeply, she could feel tingling between her legs and smiled.

"Then why does it sound like you feel you're settling?"

"I don't know, maybe because I'm not doing the bridey kind of stuff. But with Seth and Elan and my mother working on the details, you know it's going to be mind-blowing. I did pick out invitations and a wedding dress today," smiling, she knew he'd be shocked at the news.

"What?"

His response didn't disappoint.

"Yup, our invitations are awesome. It's a box and there's an actual starfish in the box, but it's not tacky or kitschy, it's actually done in a really elegant way with gold rope tied in a nautical knot."

"Rope?" the smile in his voice was evident over the cellular waves.

"Yes, rope," Mia laughed, "maybe we should do a BDSM theme wedding. That might make Seth and Elan happy, my mother not so much."

"Tell me about your dress. Am I going to want to rip it off you and fuck you?"

"Schooner Moore, where is your right hand?"

"You know where my right hand is, Baby Girl."

"Mmm, tell me what you're doing." Mia reached under the summer quilt and pulled off her silk bikini underwear.

"I'm just very slowly stroking myself and thinking about you in that wedding dress with the tip of your tongue running up between my balls and around the base of my cock," his breathing deepened, "slowly up the shaft, just like I'm doing with my hand and now I'm rubbing my thumb hard over the head of my cock, thinking about your teeth scraping my skin and the tip of your tongue in my slit."

"You already have me so wet. I love running the head of your cock along my slit when I'm this wet. Oh my God, the way it feels when it slides up to my clit and then you move it back down and push just the head into me. Oh baby, I just love the way that feels."

"Take your clit between your thumb and forefinger and rub it in that up and down motion, the way I do it," he could hear her breath hitch, followed by a mewling sound. "Oh Baby Girl, I love your sounds. Put the phone next to your ear and with your left-hand twist your left nipple really hard for me." Her breath was catching faster, "That's it, roll it hard and think about me sucking it and pinching the other one with you pinned down underneath me." She was losing control, he could hear it in her moaning. "Can you hear how hard I'm stroking myself. I can't wait to have my cock pumping inside you this weekend. We're going to go out on the boat alone and fuck up on the deck at sunset right out there in front of all the other boats on the bay." Hearing her go over the edge, he could feel his balls tighten and the pressure rise the length of him. Grabbing a tee-shirt, he heard his own moans as he came right after her into the shirt.

Listening to Mia regain her breath, he closed his eyes, picturing he was in their bed at the beach house, instead of being all alone in the loft.

"Will you marry me?" she asked, a devil smile in her voice.

"Yeah, why not. I've got nothing else going on September 27th." His real smile was out of control.

Chapter Fifty-Two

Lois had learned how to Skype. Her standing date every morning with Seth included coffee and an update on wedding details, her grandchildren and any gossip that was worth knowing.

There was a morning calm before the residents of the beach house came alive and Seth Shapiro used that time to have his undisturbed morning tête-à-tête with Lois. The sun over the ocean cast a long golden trail, like a yellow brick road leading to the horizon and the only sounds beside their computer chat were the gulls and the ocean lapping against the shore.

"She really looked beautiful. I was in tears," Seth was speaking with his hands. Very dramatic.

"I'm looking at it on my computer. Do you think it's too plain?" Lois' brows were knit together and she had 'that look' on her face that said she was not totally pleased.

"It's a very simple line, but it looked stunning and elegant. She's little so we don't want the dress to overpower her, and honestly Lois, I think she'd be uncomfortable in anything more fapitzed." Seth lapsed into Yiddish, using the word for 'all dolled up'. After all, this was the woman he once had to drag out of Levi's and tee-shirts.

"I trust you on this," Lois was sipping coffee out of a soup bowl sized cup. "I know you wouldn't let her be underdressed for her own wedding."

"If she looks like shit, it's a reflection on me and that is not happening. She will be simple, understated elegance, even if it kills me. You know my motto - 'WWJD - what would Jackie do?' Did you get the link for the invitations?"

"Yes, they look adorable and I love how you're able to keep the theme flowing to all the elements."

Seth held up the box and started opening it for Lois. "They are even cuter in real life. The artist has done such a nice job on them and the materials are really high quality. I'm very impressed."

"Okay, I've been looking over the menu," Lois began, "and I think the choices for the sit-down dinner should be a choice of Chicken Francaise, Pan-Seared Salmon and the Sage-Crusted Veal Chop."

"Ugh," the sound came from behind Seth, "no sit-down dinner. Can't we just do heavy hors d'oeuvres?" Mia emerged from the house, Nathaniel in her arms and Portia trailing behind, sipping from a juice box.

"Nana," Portia climbed into Seth's lap to see the screen, "Mommy taught me how to ride waves."

"Good morning, sweet girl," Lois smiled at her latest grandchild. "Your mommy is an expert wave rider. Poppy and I used to call her a water rat when she was little because she never wanted to come out of the ocean. Are you having fun out at the beach?"

Portia nodded vigorously and climbed off Seth's lap.

"She can't expect people to drive hours out to Montauk and not feed them a full meal," Lois was not going to let this go.

"I can hear you," Mia said loudly from the other side of the table where she was looking at the back of Seth's laptop.

"Good, because you are not feeding people just hors d'oeuvres."

Rolling her eyes, "We are not doing pre-arranged seating."

In Florida, Lois sat at her table, rolling her eyes. Seth looked back and forth between mother and daughter hoping this didn't get ugly, but was fully prepared to enjoy it, if it did.

"Okay BBC and BBC-Mama, compromise here. Sit down dinner after the cocktail hour, open seating. Does that work for you two?"

Both mother and daughter nodded their heads. Neither looked happy.

"I want Surf 'n Turf," Mia chimed in, determined to get the last word. "Do they have a filet mignon and lobster tail option?"

Seth scrolled the online menu, "Yes, they do."

"Well, that's what I want. We can get them to make you a veal chop if you want, Mom. Oh, and the other thing I want, I want baby lamb chops served butler style during the cocktail hour."

"Anything else you want, BBC?" Seth was actually sneering.

Mia got up with Nathaniel and started to walk into the house, "Nope. That's all. Bridezilla out."

Chapter Fifty-Three

"I knew you'd like him," Schooner sat at his desk at L9/NYC Skyping with Yoli.

"He seems like a real stand-up guy, very easy going and personable."

"He's smart as all hell, too. He'll be a real steal. How long do you think you'd need to stay out there after he comes on board? If he comes on board."

"A month, six weeks. I mean we'll only be a phone call away and he'll have Lucas here backing him up."

Schooner picked up his phone to look at the calendar, as he scrolled. "So, will Lucas be okay not being your backfill?"

Yoli laughed, "He will be relieved. Dealing with stress is not his strong suit."

Looking up from his phone, "So basically I can have you here full time before the wedding."

Registering shock, "You've set a wedding date and you didn't tell me?"

Laughing, "I just found out myself. It seems Seth just advised Mia of the details. We're getting married at a resort on the beach on September 27th out in Montauk, which is on the eastern tip of Long Island."

"Well, then I need to get to New York before that to find a place to live." Yoli started scrolling through her calendar.

"Why don't you and Debbie use Mia's old apartment when you first get here and look for a place to live once you're here? It will be much easier and you can get a feel for neighborhoods and what you want."

"Well thank you. I think we will take you up on that." Putting her phone down, "I have to tell you, this whole wedding thing is so odd. You and Mia relinquishing control, it's kind of unbelievable considering both of your personalities."

Laughing, "I know. I was thinking the very same thing last night, but we've got the dream team on this, two gay men and a Jewish mother, I cannot even imagine how beautiful this is going to be."

"Well, we can't wait."

"And I can't wait to get you here full time."

Ending the Skype call, Schooner picked up his cell, "Hey there."

"I was just thinking about you."

Schooner laughed, "Yeah, well, I was just talking about you."

"I had a great meeting with Yoli. I really like her. Smart, straight shooter."

"Think you could work with her?

"Yeah, actually I do. I think we'd make a good team."

Sitting back in his chair, Schooner stretched out his long legs, "Excellent."

Chapter Fifty-Four

Although Schooner was angry at his older son for not returning home until sunrise, without so much as a phone call as to his whereabouts and for not answering repeated calls to his cell phone (the battery died excuse), their end of the summer dinner at Maguire's had none of the tension as the meal they'd shared there the summer before, on the night that Zac had arrived.

Waiting up and worried that morning, Schooner railed on his college-bound son about respecting the people around him and hoped he'd gotten through to him at least a little bit. On the second to last night of the best summer of his life, Zac had been out enjoying the spoils of being eighteen, rich and exceedingly handsome, in one of New York's most coveted summer playgrounds.

Crawling into bed as the sun came up, Zac was in that half sleep state when he instinctively felt like someone was staring at him. Opening his eyes, he was face to face with a smiling set of large, near black eyes.

"Daddy's mad at you," Portia laid down next to him, her head on his pillow, "he's very, very mad." It was the first time Portia had seen Schooner angry and she was clearly upset by it.

"Dad's often mad at me, Po." Not being able to say Portia, Nathaniel referred to his new sister as Po, and now both of her brothers were calling her that.

Her face took on a very serious cast, "I still love you, Zac."

And he knew she did and always would. This sweet and well behaved little girl, who was now his sister, loved him and looked up to him. The way her face and Nathaniel's face lit up every time he entered a room, continued to blow his mind and make his heart feel things it had never felt before. And what blew him away even more, was just how much he loved his new little brother and sister. That was a twist Zac Moore did not see coming.

"C'mere you," he pulled her to him, "can you go back to sleep or are you going to keep me awake?"

"I'll sleep," and she cuddled up next to him.

Now sitting on the deck at Maguire's, Mia, Schooner, the kids, Seth, Charles, Gaby and Paola enjoyed a relatively drama free dinner.

"Holly, I'm sure you are excited about seeing Jared again," Gaby passed her the pot of steamers.

Pulling out a clam and dipping it in broth, then drawn butter, Holly nodded, "I can't believe he spent the entire summer in Michigan."

Zac snickered, "A certain manager of this very establishment didn't seem too sad that he wasn't here this summer."

"Shut up, Cretin," Holly snapped.

"No name calling around the kids," Schooner was playing the disciplinarian.

Smiling at him, Mia could see that he was loving every minute of this, including the normal teenage banter of his older two.

"This was a really good summer," Mia noted and everyone at the table agreed as they worked on the pots of steamers. "I wish it wasn't ending."

The next day Schooner would be driving Holly and Zac up to Providence and Boston, getting them settled into their dorms, and Mia would be heading back into the city with the two little ones.

"Oh don't get all maudlin, BBC, we'll all be together again at the end of September." Seth turned to Holly and Zac, "I'm having your clothes for the wedding shipped to me, so all you two need to do is show up."

They both knew better than to argue with him, especially when it came to the wedding.

"Daddy, how long will you be away?"

Schooner had just spent the last ten days out at the beach with them and Portia had been at his side the whole time. This was her first sign of separation anxiety.

"Only two days, sweetheart and then I'll be back in the city with you, Mommy and Nathaniel." His response seemed to allay Portia's concern.

"So, what are the honeymoon plans?" Gaby asked, raising her eyebrows suggestively.

"We're not…" Mia began.

"I've got that taken care of," Schooner cut her off.

"You do?" Mia's face was a picture in shock. "We're going on a honeymoon?"

"I've got it taken care of," he repeated and focused on cracking a lobster claw.

Mia turned to Seth. He shrugged his shoulders and shook his head, clearly clueless. Next, she turned to Charles with a questioning look, and he too, shook his head.

"Ooooo Kayyyyyy," Mia picked up the cracker for her lobster. Again, she looked at Seth and Charles, hoping to pick up a sign. Either they both had great poker faces or Schooner Moore was keeping one hell of a secret.

Mia Silver was finally excited about her own wedding.

Chapter Fifty-Five

They all disembarked the ferry the next morning on the mainland. Schooner and Zac reloaded the Range Rover with all the college bound duffels, while Charles loaded Mia and the kid's stuff into his Yukon.

"We'll come out next weekend and get the rest of the stuff out of the beach house," Schooner promised Mia.

Sensing the change, Nathaniel started fussing in his stroller and holding his arms out to be picked up, "Zaaaaaa Zaaaaa," fat tears rolled down his cheeks as he called out to his brother.

Squatting down next to the stroller, Zac tried to comfort him, "You're going to see me in less than four weeks, buddy."

"Zaaaa," he continued to cry.

"You can take him out of the stroller, Zac. I need to get him in the car seat," Mia was getting choked up watching the scene.

As soon as Zac picked him up, Nathaniel quieted down. Walking away from them, he took his brother across the parking lot for a private conversation with the infant. When they returned, Zac's eyes were red. Handing the baby to Mia, he walked over to the Range Rover and got into the front seat without a word to anyone.

Mia and Schooner exchanged a glance. Was this the same angry teen that had nearly ripped their lives apart last summer?

Portia banged on the car door with an open hand, "You forgot to say goodbye to me, Zac."

Opening the door, he reached down and pulled her up onto his lap. "How about if we say, 'I'll see you in four weekends'?"

Smiling, "Okay, I'll see you in four weekends," and with a quick kiss on the cheek, she climbed out of the car, turned to Holly and with a smile as bright as the noon sun reflecting on the ocean, "I'll see you in four weekends, Holly."

As they drove off in the Range Rover, Charles slung an arm over Mia's shoulder, "Had I not seen that with my own eyes, Meezie, I'd never believe that actually just happened."

"Do you think he's salvageable material?" Mia looked up at Charles, her face still registering shock.

Laughing, "I think the jury is still out on that one, but I think for the first time we just got a glimpse that he is actually Schooner's son, not just some surly teen wearing a Schooner mask."

"Well, he's certainly got a fan club in his little brother and sister."

Leaning down, Charles whispered in Mia's ear, "I still wouldn't stand next to him at the top of a staircase if I were you."

Laughing so hard, that tears were running down their cheeks, Mia playfully punched Charles in the arm, "Now *that* might just be the best piece of advice you have *ever* given me."

Chapter Fifty-Six

September 11th

Nathaniel was fast asleep in his stroller when they reached the memorial site. Scooping Portia up into his arms to ease negotiating through the crowd, Schooner followed closely behind Mia and Nathaniel. Dressed in her pink party dress, Schooner could feel her trepidation being around so many people, many of whom were sad and crying, and he knew his daughter was picking up on his own anxiety.

Mia looked back to make sure they were close behind. She tried to smile, but her face was having no part of it. Today was a big day, and even if it wasn't, she didn't think it would ever get easier. The plan was to meet everyone over at the section of the fountain where Michael's name was engraved. Being here with Schooner, Nathaniel and Portia changed the equation and her normal level of 9/11 discomfort was greatly amplified.

Seeing Charles, she waved to catch his attention. With a smile, he returned the wave and Evelyn Portman turned around. Their eyes met as Mia approached, and the floodgates released, tears openly spilling down Mia's face. This deep-seated feeling of betrayal kept bubbling up and she knew that it was ridiculous, but she dreaded today's memorial more than any since its inception.

Evelyn greeted Mia with a sincere, warm smile and embrace. Looking down at the sleeping baby, "Mia, he's beautiful and you look wonderful, sweetheart."

Rubbing her arm lovingly, "You do, too. That is Nathaniel and I have two more very special people to introduce to you."

Schooner had just caught up and Portia was hiding her face in his neck.

"Schooner, this is Michael's mom, Evelyn Portman. Evelyn, this is my fiancé, Schooner Moore."

With his real smile, Schooner bent down and kissed Evelyn's cheek, "I am so happy to meet you, Evelyn. Mia has told me so much about you and Michael."

"Portia, I want you to meet somebody really special."

The little girl turned around with a shy smile.

"Portia, this is your Grandma Evelyn and she's been really looking forward to meeting you."

Evelyn's eyes filled with tears, "Hello, Portia."

And with a shy smile, "Today is my birthday, Grandma Evelyn. I'm four," and she held up four fingers.

The surprise and delight on Evelyn's face at Portia's British accent was evident. Turning to Mia, "She is precious," she leaned into Mia and whispered in her ear, "and he looks like a movie star."

Laughing, "Don't tell him that," Mia whispered back and both women laughed.

Looking up at Schooner, she could sense his discomfort. It was the expectation of the unknown and she remembered Gaby's first memorial service and how profoundly affected she had been.

"Daddy, I want to go down," Portia squirmed in his arms.

As soon as he put her on the ground, the little girl positioned herself in between Mia and Evelyn. A look passed between the two women.

Looking at her watch, it was 8:35. With a hand on Schooner's arm, she felt a need to warn him, so that he could prepare himself. "The first moment of silence is in five minutes."

He nodded and she could see the tension in his jaw and knew he couldn't speak. Letting her hand slide down his arm until they were hand in hand, she realized how pivotal today was in all their lives. Today was the day it all came together, past, present and future to form the complete tapestry.

It was 8:40 and the silence was as deafening as it had always been. Mia wondered if everyone else heard the same screams and cries inside themselves that she heard, felt the same clawing and anguish. As her eyes blurred with tears, she looked to her left and Portia had taken Evelyn's hand. Mia could feel her knees almost buckling at the knowing and enormity of that gesture. Looking to her right, a distraught Schooner stood staring straight ahead, his spine stiff and his shoulders squared, tears staining his cheeks as he was somewhere far away, off in his own head. Mia squeezed his hand. He needed to know he was connected. He needed to know he was a part of all of them. As were Gaby, Paola, Nathaniel and Portia. They were now all forever woven into this tapestry, each with their own place. Mia saw them in her head like ribbon dancers, each with a unique color, weaving inextricably through the tapestry as they all became one.

Squeezing her hand back, he looked down at her, searching her eyes for answers. But she had none. She knew Schooner well enough to know that had he been there that day, he would've been right there, by Charles' side, digging through hot ash in search of their friend and others' loved ones.

Nathaniel was now awake and wanted out of his stroller. Mia picked him up and handed him to Schooner, sensing he needed to hold him, that he needed an anchor. Portia was now holding onto Evelyn's leg and her new grandmother lovingly had an arm around the little girl's shoulder.

Mia stood there alone. An island. Trying so hard to breathe. Today felt different than all the other memorials. Portia was there. Her tribute to Michael. Nathaniel was there. The light that she created in her new relationship. And Schooner was there.

Schooner Moore, who on some level, had stood between her and Michael. *Was bringing him here a betrayal*, she asked herself. The conflict was raging so deeply, ripping new jagged edges of guilt to the pain.

I did love you, Michael, the monologue in her head pulled her away from her physical surroundings, I really did love you. Probably more than you even realized. So much of who I am today is because of you. You gave me so much strength and you made me see that I am worth loving. You were just a gift. A very precious gift, for which I will always be grateful. I carry you with me everywhere and I always will. And now with Portia, I feel like there is a living piece of you that I will always get to celebrate. And Schooner wants me to honor you - he doesn't ever want me to hide that or feel like I can't. So, I will always honor you. I will forever honor you through Portia.

They were in the P's on the reading of the names, getting close to Michael's. Mia looked up to the sky to try and stave off the flood of tears she felt rising to their release. A flock of seagulls circled overhead. *They're back*, she thought, w*hy are they back?* Swooping, the birds circled around and back, forming a perfectly straight line. Five seagulls flew overhead keeping flawless pace with one another, their precision a sight to behold. Mia watched the five seagulls as they maintained their undeviating line and then, without warning, the gull at the center, shot up from its flock, disappearing into the vast blue sky, leaving the remaining four birds continuing together on their path.

Hearing herself gasp, and the cry from deep in her throat, Mia felt her face crumble. What was that? She couldn't put her finger on it. But it was something deep, deep in her soul and it was shattering, and yet, she just couldn't figure it out. But she knew that she should know.

And then there it was, the memory became crystal clear. It had been a cold January day, the year before she left for college. Home sick with the flu, Mia watched from her bed the TV coverage of the memorial service for the Space Shuttle Challenger. At the end of the ceremony, the Air Force performed an aerial salute, the Missing Man Formation, where one jet shot away from the formation signifying the fallens departure to the heavens. That simple tribute had rocked Mia to the core as she lay in her bed sobbing for those lost in the tragic accident.

And now today, she had witnessed it again. Five birds. One ascending to heaven. And four were left behind. Mia. Schooner. Nathaniel. And Portia.

With tears flowing, she nodded her head. He had been giving her signs. Msikana. Portia's Birthday. And now the gulls. The gulls who had been bearing messages all along, how apt that they would deliver this final message, their symbolism as clear as the sky.

Michael's ascension to the heavens, leaving her and Schooner behind with the kids was the sign Mia needed. She could feel complete again and it was okay. He was okay with it. She was in the place he wanted her to be.

In that moment, Mia knew that she was free to marry Schooner and that it was Michael Portman who would be giving her away.

Chapter Fifty-Seven

The traditional rehearsal dinner on Friday night became an open friends/family/guest affair for all out-of-town guests and those who had ventured the three hours out to Montauk from the city the day before the wedding. Held on a terrace outside at 6 P.M., the guests would get to enjoy sunset on this balmy fall evening.

With sitters in tow to watch the kids, in addition to Holly and Zac, Schooner and Mia were actually enjoying the rare leisurely process of getting dressed in their private cottage. The team that Seth had hired had come by earlier to do Mia's hair and make-up and now all she had to do was slip into her dress, a simple Michael Kors black drop-waist lace sheath, and shoes.

Emerging from the bathroom freshly shaved and smelling overwhelmingly fuckable, Schooner came up behind Mia and wrapped his arms around her.

With his teeth gently skimming her earlobe, he whispered, "I'd better not find anything on under that dress."

Feeling rather proud, her devil grin at full tilt, Mia took Schooner's right hand and placed it down near the hem of her dress. Reaching down a little farther, he found the hemline and slipped his hand underneath, moving it up the back of her thigh at a languid pace. Reaching her bare ass, he moaned in her ear as he kneaded it roughly and pulled her tight against his hardening cock.

"Good girl," he whispered, his other hand finding a nipple through the lace dress and pinching it.

Reaching behind her, she let her fingernails gently graze his cock through his khaki dress pants. By the end of her stroke, he was rock hard and she was feeling very powerful.

"Shall we go greet our guests?" Mia was enjoying the torture.

"I can't wait to fuck you." He softly kissed her neck and felt her shiver.

Turning to him, she looked up into his clear smiling eyes, "I am so wet right now." And with a coy smile, "let's go greet our guests."

Laughing and grabbing her hand to head out of the cottage, "You are such a tease, Silver."

As they walked down the path toward the main hotel, the resonant sounds from the party on the terrace intensified. Entering hand-in-hand, about fifty guests milled about, enjoying drinks as white-gloved servers threaded through the crowd with silver trays of hors d'oeuvres.

Looking at one another with bright smiles, the realization was upon them - it was really real. Without a word, they both began to laugh and simultaneously uttered, "Showtime," their smiles becoming wider. And then the guests descended upon them.

Working the crowd, still hand-in-hand, Mia spied a couple standing near the bar. Excusing themselves from the people to whom they were talking, she led Schooner toward the bar.

"There's someone I'm dying to have you meet," as they got closer, Mia yelled out, "Rob, Joni," and a couple at the bar turned around.

Hugs, kisses and handshakes, Schooner had spoken to Rob Ryan on the phone several times, but this was his first opportunity to meet Mia's old friend.

As Mia and Joni caught up on news of the children, Schooner had the opportunity to say something he'd waited over a year to say, "Thanks for being a really good friend to her during some really hard times."

"We both needed each other," Rob confessed. "Sheehan was a pig, but I do have to thank him for Mia and that ultimately led me to Joni."

"Sheehan was the teacher? The one Mia ended up with?"

"She told you about him?" Rob could barely contain his sneer.

"Yeah and she told me how it ended, too. What an ass." Schooner had a natural distaste for the man, but was glad that Mia didn't end up with him permanently.

"The guy was just a player. He was a good teacher though, and Mia and I learned a lot and became much better writers."

Schooner clapped him on the shoulder, "Well, I can't thank you enough for always being there for her."

"No problem, man. I love her. I'm just thrilled she's happy and in a good place and that you two ended up back together."

"Thank you. That means a lot to me. Excuse me a sec, I need to go greet someone who just came in from out of town," and Schooner took off across the deck in long-legged strides.

Seth approached Mia and did a once-over on her, "You look good, the make-up people did a nice job."

"Thank you. Wow, an actual compliment," Mia teased.

"Well, I did choose the make-up artist."

"Who's got the kids?" Mia asked, starting to look around.

"Last I saw," Seth was surveying the crowd too, "both of them were with your parents and Schooner's parents."

"Okay, good," Mia felt relieved. She saw Schooner over the crowd in an animated conversation. He was surrounded by Yoli, Debbie and a man whose back was to her.

Feeling her stomach jolt, it was something in his lean stature, the angle at which he held his head, that triggered a barrage of tears to flow unchecked from her eyes.

Looking at her and seeing the tears, "Oh no you don't," Seth chastised, "you're ruining your make-up. I could kill you, BBC."

Mia appeared not to hear him and the tears continued in rivulets down her cheeks forming light colored riverbeds in the make-up that had been applied to her face. Seth turned to follow Mia's line of sight and identify what had set off the tears.

Gasping, he grabbed her bare upper arm, digging his fingers in, "Oh my God, who is he?"

It was as if Mia didn't hear him.

"BBC," he snapped, "who is that man? And why have you kept him from me?"

Wordlessly, she grabbed Seth's hand and began to drag him across the expansive deck. Coming up behind the man, Mia let go of Seth's hand and wrapped her arms around the stranger hugging his back.

"I'm so sorry, I'm so sorry," she repeated through her tears.

Twisting around, he negotiated her to the front of his body, pulling her into a tight embrace. "It's okay," he whispered into her hair.

"It's not okay. I'm so sorry," Mia continued to cry into his sport coat, "I was a terrible friend."

Seth stepped in, "Why don't you two come with me, we need to do a little make-up repair," and he led Mia and the stranger toward the main building.

Mia finally looked up at the handsome ginger and grey-haired man to find him smiling down at her, "I have missed you so much and I was always too embarrassed to try and find you after what I had done."

"Shhh," he calmed her. "Rosie and I always knew exactly why you did what you did."

Mia smiled, "Is Rosie here?"

"No, she couldn't make it but she sends her love and the message, 'It's about fucking time'."

Mia laughed through her tears.

Finding a bride's powder room, Seth led the three of them in there.

"Sit BBC," he ordered and then turned to the man and with his most charming air, introduced himself. "Hello, I'm Seth Shapiro, BFF of the crazy one here."

Reaching out a hand, "Hello, I'm Henry Clark, an old lost friend of the crazy one."

"Have you and Schooner been in touch this whole time?"

Henry nodded, "Pretty much."

"He never told me," Mia shook her head not understanding why.

"Keep still," Seth was blotting her makeup with little sponges that were kept in crystal bowls on the marble counter. "Good, now look up. Raccoon does not suit you."

Henry smiled at Seth and Mia's rapport. "I think he stayed mum about it so that he could surprise you."

"Well, this was a huge surprise. I am so happy you are here and having you be here to see me and Schooner get married, it's just so, well, it's so right."

"Yes, it is," nodded Henry, smiling. "I'm just so glad he found you again. Rosie and I knew she did something. She played it so cool, she didn't even go after him right away, just acted like a concerned friend, dated a football player a few times and just pretended that she was 'there for him' when you broke his heart."

"Bitch," snarled Seth, finishing off the repairs on Mia's face.

"She married Beau," Mia was smiling at Henry.

"Think about it, Mia," he laughed, "in your most vindictive moment you never could have come up with anything as awful as those two together. That is totally karma at its best."

There was a knock on the door of the powder room and Henry got up to unlock the door.

"Everything okay?" It was Schooner.

"Yeah, come on in, we're just catching up."

Coming through the door, he locked eyes with Mia, "You okay? I probably should have told you. I just wanted it to be a surprise," he smiled sweetly at her, his eyes conveying concern.

"That it was, Pretty Boy."

"Does she know the other half of the surprise?" Schooner asked Henry.

"Not yet," Henry's handsome face radiated pure joy.

Both Seth and Mia stared at Schooner with a look saying, "Spit it out."

Putting a hand on Henry's shoulder, "I'd like you to meet the new

Executive Vice President of West Coast Operations for L9."

"Oh my God," Mia jumped up and hugged Henry. "Congratulations. You're taking Yoli's role?"

"Well, I don't know that anyone could actually take Yoli's place, but I will be heading up the west coast."

"We'll all be working together," Seth interjected.

Henry smiled at him, "It appears we will be."

Seth grabbed Mia by the arm, holding her back as Schooner and Henry exited the powder room, "Why did you keep him from me, BBC?"

"I wasn't intentionally keeping him from you. I haven't seen him since I was sixteen."

"He is really handsome," Seth was gushing. "Do you think he thought I was good looking?"

"How could he not, Princess," Mia laughed.

"He doesn't seem to be here with a significant other. You know I can help him get up to speed on all the west coast promotions," Seth's intensity was starting to hit a fevered pitch.

"I'm sure he'd appreciate it. Come, let's go back outside and enjoy my rehearsal dinner," Mia took one last look in the mirror to make sure she looked okay.

"Don't worry, no one missed you, BBC." Seth linked arms with her.

Mia laughed, "Thanks for making me feel so special, Princess."

Chapter Fifty-Eight

Everywhere he turned all night, she was there. Who was she? The word that came to mind when he looked at her was exotic. Rare, exotic and beautiful. He shook his head at the odd thought.

And now she was standing on the far end of the deck, talking to his sister. Every time she moved, her long silky mane swayed with her. She was shapely, not like the girls he'd been with on the beach all summer who'd starved themselves to bicycle rail thin. This girl was soft and curvy and had an ass that was making him hard just looking at it. He couldn't get the vision out of his head of what she would look like riding him, her long silky hair brushing his chest, full breasts bouncing and more than anything, the thing that was making his cock twitch was the thought of his hands on her gorgeous ass as she took him in deep.

Who was she? And why was she here at his dad's wedding? Surmising that she was from Mia's side, he assumed she wasn't a relative based on her mixed ethnic look.

With plates in hand, she and Holly headed to a table where Jared was already seated. Zac headed over to one of the food stations where prime rib was being carved and got a plate.

"Zac," Portia came running across the deck, all smiles.

"Hey Po, are you hungry?"

The little girl nodded, "I want shrimp."

"Oh, you do, huh? Well, you've got expensive taste for a four year-old. Let's put some on my plate and then we'll go sit down to eat."

Loading his plate with shrimp, he picked up Portia with his free arm and made his way to the table where his sister was sitting.

"Hey Cretin," Holly greeted him as he sat down with Portia in his lap.

Looking around the table, Portia's eyes grew wide with delight and she flung herself out of Zac's lap and ran around the table straight to Zac's object of desire.

"Lily," she shrieked, hugging the girl tightly.

Lily pulled Portia into her lap, hugging and kissing the toddler, "It's so good to see you."

"How do you know my sister?" Zac asked, totally surprised by what was unfolding before him.

"I was with your dad and Mia in Africa. I'm Liliana Castillo."

"Zac Moore." *How fortuitous*, Zac thought, *my little sister is going to get me an in with this hot, golden-eyed girl.*

As the evening wore on, a frustrated Zac was shocked that Lily Castillo paid no more attention to him than she did to the busboys filling her water glass. She wasn't particularly interested in anything he had to say. When she mentioned to Holly that she was attending Yale in New Haven, he chimed in that he'd be just two hours up the road in Boston. She didn't bother responding.

Zac hated the way this girl was treating him. Who did she think she was? And that air of dismissive superiority. Chicks didn't dismiss him. He dismissed them when he was done. From sixteen year-olds on the beach to forty year-olds in a pool cabana, no female had ever cast him off without so much as a second glance.

Zac Moore had never been so intrigued by a girl in his life.

Mia joined them at the table and immediately fell into a deep conversation with Lily about their experience in Zambia and future work that needed to be done. They discussed the new foundation that Schooner was forming and how all their lives had been irrevocably altered by the trip. Sitting there quietly listening, Zac learned that Lily didn't want to go back to Yale, but wanted to return overseas to assist in the work that was being done.

"I understand both sides of it," Mia was nodding her head. "Your parents want you to have the choices that a degree from Yale will afford you. It doesn't mean that you can't go back or that you shouldn't go back, they'd just like to see you do it with a degree under your belt."

"I'm so much happier there. I feel like what I'm doing means something. I have an immediate impact."

"That's not going to go away, Lil. And think of the stronger impact you can have with your degree. I can absolutely see you with USAID helping to change policy. This is not a choice of one or the other. You can have both."

She listened to Mia intently, hanging on her every word, and Zac could tell she saw Mia as some sort of mentor, but he could also tell that her heart was not set on staying in college. Whatever they had all experienced together over in Zambia had touched her very deeply. This girl was very intense and serious, so different from anyone he'd ever met.

Sitting back in his chair with a look of practiced interest, he was transfixed on the luminescence of her creamy skin, fantasizing about putting his mouth all over her and trailing his tongue up her arm to her neck. He wanted to hear her giggle with delight and realized he'd never heard anything remotely approaching a giggle or a laugh out of her all evening.

When the party broke up, she went off in search of her parents without so much as a backwards glance at Zac. He felt empty at the lack of her presence and wanted to run after her. But he didn't, knowing he would try again tomorrow.

"She's pretty intense," Mia said to him with a laugh.

"Very serious," he agreed.

Mia nodded, "She's too young to be that serious. I'd love to see her loosen up and have some fun."

I'd like to be the one to show it to her, thought Zac, and surprisingly, his thoughts were not all sexual.

Chapter Fifty-Nine

Schooner and Mia bid the last of the guests' goodnight, as people headed back to their rooms. Left outside, filling one table, was their core inner circle, Seth, Kami, Gaby, Charles, Yoli, Debbie and now much to Seth's delight, Henry, who Mia could not stop touching as if he were a ghost that had materialized.

"What are you smiling at?" Mia asked Schooner.

"This group."

Smiling, she nodded slightly, knowing exactly what he was saying. "This was quite a surprise," she squeezed Henry's shoulder.

"The first of many, my love," he teased.

"Do tell," Mia wanted to wrangle it out of him.

Raising his scotch glass to his lips, he looked at her over the rim, eyes smiling playfully, "Not a chance."

"You know I hate surprises."

"Tough darts," he laughed.

"So where are you going on your honeymoon?" Debbie joined in, the perfect shill.

"That's a great question," Mia gave Debbie props.

Schooner remained silent, a shit-eating grin plastered on his face.

Turning to Charles, Mia pointed a finger at him, "You know. I know you know."

He nodded, "You're right, Meezie. I do know. Doesn't mean I'm telling you."

"You suck. You all suck," Mia looked around the table. "Just promise me this, someone is packing the right things for me." Turning to Seth, "Do not let them forget my tweezers."

All the women at the table laughed and the men looked at one other totally baffled.

"Okay, whoever is on packing duty and I know it's one of you," she pointed to all the men at the table. "Tweezers. Seriously. Or my wrath will be legendary."

Heading down the dimly lit path to their cottage, “This was a really nice night,” Schooner remarked, his arm dropping from Mia’s shoulder to her ass as he started inching up the lace fabric and sliding his hand underneath, “and it’s about to get nicer.”

Moonlighting placed in the taller trees provided a soft glow to an already ethereal setting.

“C’mere you,” Schooner pulled Mia slightly off the path, backing her up to the rough, gray trunk of a Wild Black Cherry tree, a scattering of freshly turned yellow leaves underfoot. Taking her face in both of his hands, he smiled down on her, “It’s your last night as a single woman. Any regrets?”

Mia shook her head, “Only that the internet didn’t happen sooner, so we would’ve been able to find one another before any significant amount of time had passed.”

Pushing her hair from her face, he bent down, his lips gently grazing hers, his kiss soft and sweet. Just the tickle of his lips made the familiar ache between her legs intensify. She wanted to feel his body cover and claim hers.

“Hey, why don’t we go grab one of those mattress cabana things on the beach,” he pulled her away from the tree.

Taking off their shoes, they headed out on the sand toward the shoreline. Stopping at one of the tan colored portable cabanas that dotted the beach, Schooner and Mia undid the ties letting the curtains surround the mattress on all sides, except the one facing the ocean. As they climbed into the queen mattress sized enclosure, Schooner immediately slid Mia underneath him, his hand pushing her black lace dress up to her waist.

“The only thing I could think about all evening was your wet pussy underneath this dress and I how I couldn’t wait to get my mouth on it.”

“Please don’t let me stop you,” Mia teasingly pushed his head.

Running his hands from the insides of her knees slowly up her thighs and pressing outward, he spread her wide, letting the cool night air lick her wetness. Slowly, he ran his hands back down the insides of her thighs until he felt goose bumps rise on her skin. The late September night air was chilly and he wanted her hot, wet pussy to cool down.

Taking a finger, he ran it up her wet slit, dipping it into her, before pulling it out and slowly licking his finger.

“Mmm,” was all he said, and he pushed her legs further apart, burying his face in her.

“I love when you go down on me,” her fingers were combing through his thick hair as she pressed herself harder against his face.

Pulling away slightly, the tip of his pointed tongue gently traveled up her pussy until he reached her clit, licking all around it in a slow, sweeping motion.

"Oh God, that feels so good. More."

His tongue moved back, lapping up the wetness and with both hands, he spread her wide, and began to suck.

"Fuck," she screamed, "oh fuck, Schooner." Pressing his head into her harder, she thrust into his face and tongue, desperately trying to get herself off. Tightly wrapping her legs around his head, she began to quake around his face.

When her tremors subsided, he looked up at her, shit eating grin on his face and sang, "Baby Girl, I want to marry you," as he undid his pants and kicked them off.

"I think the song is little girl not baby girl."

Climbing up her body and pinning her beneath him, a hand trapped on either side of her head, "Excuse me, who's The Boss?"

Her lips started forming a Br sound.

"Who's The Boss?" he repeated, spreading her legs with his and pushing deep into her.

"You," she croaked.

"That's right and I say the song is Baby Girl, I want to marry you," he sang again.

"Whatever you say, Boss," she smiled and wrapped her legs around him, pressing his ass with her feet to get him deeper into her.

"So, this may be your last time having sex as a single woman, unless I decide to fuck you in the morning," he smiled down at her.

"What if I have a headache?" she hit him with a devil grin.

"Then I'll let you blow me."

"You'll let me, huh?"

He nodded, smiling, a lock of dirty blonde hair falling down on his forehead.

"I'm just that kind of guy," he laughed.

Smiling at each other in the dark night, just the glow of the moon illuminating a path along the ocean, they rocked together with a slow, easy rhythm feeling every luxurious inch of one another.

"You feel so good inside of me." She sought his lips, tasting herself on them and licking them with the tip of her tongue. "Harder," she urged him on.

"Like this?" and he rammed into her repeatedly.

"Yes," her voice quivered as her muscles clamped down hard on his cock, milking everything out of him.

Moving his cheek against hers, he took a few deep breaths filling his lungs up with the cool night air and whispered, "I promise I'll love you forever."

"That's not long enough," she whispered back, holding his head against her tight.

"God, you're a greedy little thing," he was smiling into her ear.

"Yes, I am. And I want you to love me for more than forever."

"It's a deal, Baby Girl."

Chapter Sixty

"The kids are taken care of?" it was a question. "Who's watching the kids?" Mia was stressing as the stylist coiled her curls into an up do, pinning each one with a tiny white rose and seed pearl bobby pin.

"The kids are fine," Lois reassured her, "and your father and I will be staying with them while you are gone."

"How long will you be there?" Mia pressed.

"Do you think I'm going to fall for that? Let your husband tell you when he's ready." Her mother was not going to be the one to share Schooner's secret plans.

"I don't have a husband," Mia sulked.

"Keep that up and you won't, BBC," Seth's nerves were starting to get the best of him.

"Can I open this?" Joni picked up a bottle of champagne. "I think we all need this."

"Please do," was the resounding chorus from those in the suite having hair and makeup done.

Pouring glasses for Mia, Lois, Seth, Kami, Dee and herself, Joni raised a glass, "To marrying the love of your life. He was always in your heart and now he'll always be in your arms."

Mia's eyes filled with tears and Seth pointed a finger at her. "Don't," was his single word command.

There was a knock at the door and Kami got up to open it. Holly was there with Nathaniel and Portia.

"Mommy, you look so pretty," Portia came running in.

"Dad said he'll meet you back at the cottage when you're ready," Holly delivered Schooner's message and poured herself a glass of champagne. "Ah, so this is where the fun is."

"Big fun. Now drink up," Seth said to Holly, "you're next," pointing to the stylist's chair. "Come here, Portia, I'll put some make-up on you." The little girl ran to Seth.

"I miss them already," Mia mumbled.

"You will be taking vacations with them for the next twenty years. Trust me, enjoy this one. You deserve a honeymoon," Joni spoke from experience.

"So where is your dad taking me?" Mia asked Holly in the mirror.

Laughing, "I've only had one glass of champagne, Mia. I'm not falling for that."

"You will all pay for this, I promise you." Mia glared at them in the mirror.

Refilling her champagne glass, Seth leveled her a glance, "Drink up, Bridezilla, before we all drag you out to the ocean and drown you."

"Hey Gorgeous," he greeted her with his real smile when she entered the cottage.

"Hey Handsome." She went to him for a kiss.

Laughing, "You look stressed, Baby Girl."

"You have everything covered with the kids while we're gone?"

"Mia," he looked into her eyes with an 'Are you serious?' look.

"Of course, you do. I'm just stressing." She threw herself down on the couch, dramatically.

Picking up a bottle of champagne, "Everything is taken care of, now just enjoy yourself. This is our party, there's nothing for us to do besides have a good time."

Handing her the champagne, he smiled, "I have something for you."

"Funny, because I have something for you, too." She put down the champagne and went into the bedroom emerging with a box wrapped in silver foil paper topped with a sapphire blue ribbon.

"You go first," he urged and she handed him the box.

Carefully, he removed the paper and opened the rectangular box, his eyes crinkling with his smile. Removing the object, he held it up to his nose, breathing in the heady aroma of hand-hewn leather. Turning it over in his hands, running his thumbs over the vintage distressed leather, Schooner marveled at the craftsmanship of the leather-bound travel journal, but what amazed him most, was the silver clasp with the leather ties wrapped around it. Anchoring the book to keep it closed was a sterling silver replica of True Compass.

"Wow," looking up at her, speechless. Unwinding the straps, he opened the journal. In neat handwriting were pages that had been filled in with a fountain pen.

"It's some poems and things that I've written over the years. Things about you and my journey back to you. The rest is blank. It's for the journey we haven't written yet."

Schooner nodded. He couldn't speak. Looking back at the book to avoid tears, he read the first entry.

<u>Sky Diving Blues</u>
Flying high
a flirtation with the sun
The slow descent
to a burned Rome
The neighborhood hasn't changed

"When did you write that?" his voice was choked.

"The beginning of sophomore year."

He nodded without looking up and continued to leaf through the journal until he reached the last entry.

September 27th
My wishes on a million twinkling stars come true today.

Sitting very still, he closed his eyes, breathing in deeply. "The best gift ever," his voice was hoarse with emotion, "and I promise we will fill the rest of these pages with incredible memories."

Reaching behind a pillow on the couch, Schooner pulled out a flat rectangular Tiffany's box.

With a devil grin, "What's in it this time? Potato chips?"

His smile matched hers and he nodded, "Pringles," knowing how much she hated the 'fake' chips as she often referred to real potato chips and French fries as the perfect food.

Handing her the box, she worked off the ribbon and opened the outer box. Removing a flat Tiffany blue velvet box, she gazed up at Schooner.

"Open it," he silently mouthed.

Now it was Mia's turn to try and fight tears. Lying on a blanket of silk was a white gold chain. Dangling on the end were three keys, a pink rose gold key with a heart at the top containing three small diamonds, a silver key with its heart embossed in Tiffany baby blue enamel, and in the center, was a larger key encrusted in diamonds and sapphires the color of Schooner's eyes.

There they were, the three keys to her heart; Portia, Nathaniel and Schooner.

"It's my family," she looked up at him, her voice now choked and tight.

Reaching into the box, Schooner removed the necklace. “Turn around.”

And she did.

Fastening the symbolic necklace, he leaned forward, giving her neck the softest of kisses. Mia shivered.

Standing, he helped her up from the couch. “I’ll leave you to get dressed now.”

She held onto his hand until the contact of their fingertips broke, the feeling of his touch lingering long after their separation.

“Schooner,” she called out to him as he was through the door.

Stopping, he turned back.

“I love you.”

Cocking his head to the side and regarding her, he smiled brightly, “It’s smoochal, Baby Girl,” and closed the door behind him.

Chapter Sixty-One

Photographers refer to it as 'The Golden Hour'. It happens early in the morning shortly after sunrise and again in the late afternoon just prior to the sky's spectacular sunset light show. With the sun low in the sky, warm golden rays bathe everything in a soft honeyed side-light.

Rows of white chairs lined the beach. Down a center aisle ran a runner of white raw silk that Elan Gerstler had his team attach to wood. At the end of the runner was a white silk organza canopy, the traditional wedding chuppah, its flowing fabric tied back by arrangements of roses in white and pale pink. The sun's warm rays illuminated the sheer fabric setting off an exquisite, diffused glow.

At the chuppah, waiting for his bride, stood Schooner Moore. Looking as one with his surroundings, he was dressed in a beige Bianco Brioni linen suit the color of the sand, his linen shirt, a pale blue that matched his eyes with thin white stripes, open at the collar. He wore no tie.

If someone had wandered onto the beach, they might have thought this to be a photo shoot for a men's suit company, the handsome model playing the groom. Everything about the setting evoked a magical, ethereal air.

Dressed in a simple sheath dress, the color of Schooner's shirt, Yoli came and stood next to him. His arm immediately went around her shoulder as he pulled her into him for a side hug and smile.

Strains of music began and Schooner listened closely. *What is this?* he asked himself. He knew that he knew it, but it wasn't expected and therefore he couldn't quite place it. As it continued to play, he started singing in his head and when he realized what it was, he actually laughed out loud. *His Mia,* he mused, as he continued to sing to himself Bruce Springsteen's *If I Should Fall Behind.*

There was a round of laughter as Portia stepped onto the white silk runner dressed in a pale pink taffeta dress. She carefully plucked pink rose petals from a white wicker basket and placed them gently on the runner. As she slowly walked down the aisle, stopping along the way to smile at people, she evoked more laughter from the crowd.

Nearing the front, she yelled out "Hi Daddy," and Schooner beamed, waving back and laughing with everyone else.

At the sound of her voice, Nathaniel came alive in Holly's lap, pointing and screaming, "Po, Po, Po," to get his sister's attention. Raucous laughter erupted from the crowd. Jumping up from his seat, a laughing Zac scooped up Portia when she reached the front of the runner and brought her back to an empty seat next to him.

With her children stealing the show, no one noticed that Mia and her parents had arrived and were standing at the far end of the runner. Laughing at her baby's antics, Mia nerves floated out with the tide.

"So much for a classy affair," she whispered, laughing.

Looking up at the chuppah, her eyes met Schooner's for the first time and she could feel her smile matching his in magnitude and luminosity. His real smile had never looked so beautiful and the fifty feet she was away from him felt like miles. She couldn't get to him soon enough.

Lois and Bob walked her halfway up the aisle and kissed her goodbye and then Schooner began his journey to meet her halfway, the strains of *If I Should Fall Behind,* still playing.

Their eyes locked upon each other, he took her arm in his and looked down at her.

Simultaneously they whispered, "Showtime," and broke into laughter, as they continued on their journey.

Passing the front row, "Mommy, you look beautiful," Portia was waving and again, all the guests roared with laughter. Mia blew her little girl a kiss and she blew one back.

Standing, Seth joined Mia under the chuppah. In a charcoal grey suit and a tie the color of Schooner's shirt and Yoli's dress, he had pulled off elegant in outfitting this very untraditional wedding party.

Mia squeezed his hand and leaned over to kiss him, "I love you, Princess," she whispered.

He squeezed her hand back tightly. Seth Shapiro could not speak.

As the judge commenced his oration, the clouds over the ocean began their spectacular light show, beginning with a golden glow that quickly migrated to a soft orange hue, casting like colored light onto the waves.

Finishing his part, he asked Schooner and Mia if they wanted to speak.

Schooner looked to Mia, who slightly shook her head no.

"You don't want to cry?" he whispered.

And she affirmed with a smile and a slight shake of her head.

"I'd like to say a few words," Schooner began in a strong voice. "Mia has chosen not to speak because she doesn't want to cry. If she cries, her makeup will get ruined and Seth will kill both of us."

The crowd laughed and Seth turned to them, "It's true. Smart move."

Taking both of Mia's hands in his, he smiled down at her. "Bet you didn't know I speak Italian," he began and looked out at the guests. "This woman here is my love, mi amour," he paused. "Mi amour, Italian for my love and maybe just divine providence, because it also happens to be my wife's name, Mia Moore." Looking back at Mia, "Or maybe it was just always meant to be, because you have always been my love. My one true love. You know I take my promises to you very seriously, and here's one that will be very easy for me to keep, I will spend every day of the rest of my life loving you."

"It's smoochal," she whispered for only him to hear.

Looking at the judge, he asked, "Are we married? Because I really need to kiss her."

Laughing, the judge hastened his speech, "By the power vested in me by the State of New York, I now pronounce you husband and wife. You may kiss your bride."

"Forever mine," he whispered against her lips, before claiming their long awaited first kiss as Mr. and Mrs. Schooner James Moore.

Chapter Sixty-Two

Kissing a sleeping Portia and Nathaniel goodbye in Lois and Bob's hotel suite, Schooner and Mia took one last long look at their beautiful babies before making their way back to the terrace.

Starting to make the rounds of bidding guests goodnight, it appeared the party was going to continue long after they were gone.

"Come," Schooner pulled Mia by the hand after hugging their parents and closest friends. Leading her through the hotel's main lobby, they exited the front door.

"Check that out. How cool," Mia pointed to a vintage yellow checker cab circa 1950-something.

Smiling, Schooner pulled her in the cab's direction.

"Is that for us?" there was excitement in her voice.

"Yes, we're actually going to get into a cab together tonight."

"Oh wow, married life is different," Mia joked, as Schooner opened the cab door for her.

"Good evening, Mr. and Mrs. Moore," the driver greeted them.

"Please say that again," Mia's delight was contagious and the driver obliged.

Pulling out of Gurney's Inn, the cab made a right turn onto Old Montauk Highway, heading east.

"Schooner, where are we going? We're heading east toward Montauk Point." Mia was confused as they headed for the very eastern tip of Long Island's famed south fork.

"You always did have a good sense of direction," he teased.

"You're not going to tell me, are you?" She punched him playfully in his solid upper arm.

After a few miles, the driver took a left turn onto West Shore Drive.

"Are we staying in one of the hotels in town?" Mia guessed, as they drove in the direction of the South Fork's north shore and Montauk's little downtown area.

"This is killing you," he smiled, clearly taking delight in his wife's discomfort at her lack of control.

"You suck, Schooner Moore," she feigned anger, but her ear-to-ear grin gave her away.

Nodding, he leaned over and kissed her, "Yeah, I do, Mia Moore."

Before town, the cab made a right turn onto Star Island Road, quickly passing over a thin causeway strip of land onto Star Island itself. One more right turn and the cab pulled up to the circle in front of the Lighthouse Building at the Montauk Yacht Club.

A bellman from the yacht club opened the cab door for Mia and Schooner. Smiling brightly, he greeted them, "Welcome Mr. and Mrs. Moore."

Schooner and Mia walked into the building hand-in-hand. Off to their right was guest check-in, but Schooner kept walking straight and led them to the dockside back door.

Out on the promenade they walked along a dock lined with boats and yachts of all sizes that gently swayed with the tide in their berths. When Schooner steered her right onto one of the walkways off the main dock, it finally hit her.

"True Compass is here?" It was as if she'd finally solved a game of Clue.

Smiling, he nodded, "She is."

"Where are we going?" They were at the very tip of Long Island, perched on the Atlantic Ocean, the possibilities were endless, north was Block Island, The Cape, Martha's Vineyard, Nantucket. South was Cape May, Delaware, the Chesapeake Bay, the Outer Banks.

"Yellow, orange, red and green."

"Is that a hint?" They continued down the walkway.

"It is," he smiled, knowingly.

They stopped as they reached the slip where their boat was moored.

"Yellow, orange and red. Fall foliage in New England?" she guessed.

"Very good. Now what about the green?"

Mia thought for a second, "Acadia National Park?"

"Ehhh," he made a buzzer sound, "good answer, but wrong. Here's a hint," and he pointed up.

"North of Maine?" she questioned. "Canada?" and then it dawned on her. The time of year was perfect, not just for foliage in New England, but if they were very lucky, "Northern lights in Nova Scotia," she blurted out.

Smiling, he nodded.

"Please tell me all my camera equipment is on that boat."

"You're in luck," he laughed.

"So, what are we waiting for," Mia began to move toward True Compass.

"Whoa, where are you going?"

Stopping, she turned around, her nose scrunching up with a questioning look. Scooping her up in his arms, Schooner Moore was not letting his bride walk across the threshold.

Mia laughed, "I forgot."

"There are some things I never forget."

The look in his eyes was melting her, "Oh really, what else haven't you forgotten?"

"A promise I made to myself when you were just sixteen."

Reaching out to lay a hand on his cheek, "And what was that promise?" she whispered.

With a look that summed up twenty-five years of love, heartbreak, loss and utter bliss, as he carried her over the threshold onto their boat, he whispered back, "Your first and your last, Baby Girl. Your first and your last."

Bonus Chapters

The Night Before Their Wedding
Gurney's Inn
Montauk, New York

The irony didn't escape him. One wedding on the Pacific Ocean, the other on the Atlantic Ocean. That was, however, the only similarity between the two occasions. A quarter of a century later and this time the groom was sober, jovial and deeply in love. There were no masks over his eyes and his heart was not shrouded, hiding beneath an impenetrable breast bone, daring anyone to approach.

It was a joy watching Schooner and Mia together finally. And even more exciting to know that he was going to be part of their lives again on a very regular basis.

"Look at how domesticated they are." Seth Shapiro walked up alongside Henry, watching Schooner and Mia interacting with their guests, each with a sleeping child perched on their shoulder.

Henry just nodded, he couldn't speak. Afraid his full heart would cause his voice to crack and he assumed Seth would fill in the quiet. From the little he had seen of Seth, there was not a shy bone in the man's body.

"She was such a mess when I met her," he began. "What I didn't realize was how shattered she was internally. She hid it so well. That bitch is lucky to be alive, she was so out of control."

Finally finding his voice, "That's so interesting because he was dead. Just dead. The only signs of life in the man were when it came to either his kids or business. That was it."

"I want this fairytale," Seth sighed.

Henry remained quiet, too guarded to admit to Seth that he too wanted what Schooner and Mia had.

"I want to sit in a café on Sunday mornings in the West Village, reading the New York Times for hours with my lover sitting across from me, spend hours planning vacations to places like Bali or the Seychelles, have Schooner and Mia over for a gourmet dinner that we've cooked for them." Seth turned to Henry, "That's what I want."

Before Henry could utter the words, "Me, too. That's what I want, too," Seth was gone, crossing the vast deck to go to the bar.

Wow, thought Henry, I really misjudged him. I just wrote him off as this over the top New York queen, a total party boy dancing the night away out in Cherry Grove.

As the evening progressed, he had gotten the impression that Seth had been Mia's rock all these years, her partner, her confidante. But he was such a big personality, that he discounted his depth. Now watching him across the deck, he could see that everyone was attracted to him, everyone adored him, that he actually was the glue.

Observing Mia approach him, Henry was once again surprised by this man, the first thing he did was relieve her of a sleeping Nathaniel. Absentmindedly kissing the toddler on the head, he crossed to the other end of the deck to retrieve the baby's stroller and lay him in it, tenderly covering him with his pale blue blanket and tucking him in. Schooner and Mia's mothers called him over to where they were sitting to leave Nathaniel with them. Watching the body language of the two women with him, again he could tell they adored him.

Henry made his way over to Schooner, "Well, I was quite the stealth surprise tonight."

Schooner's smile said it all, "I think you were my wedding gift to her." Fast asleep on his left shoulder was a serene looking Portia and in his right hand was a glass of scotch. Looking down at the glass, he commented, "I'm still drinking this stuff."

"Good to see you've been able to moderate the quantity this time around." Henry shook his head at the memory.

Laughing, "I don't want to miss a thing this time," and the two old friends smiled at all that meant.

Pulled away by other guests offering congratulations, again Henry found himself standing alone. Walking to the deck's edge, he watched the ocean rushing onto the shore and considered the turn his life had recently taken going to work for Schooner. Schooner and Mia were back in his life again in a big way. If he thought his life had taken a big turn, he just needed to take a look at them. They were together at last. If anyone had told him that he'd be standing on the Atlantic's edge celebrating their wedding, he would've told them that fantasies like that don't come true. As hard as one might dream.

But their fantasy did come true and now he had a dream job working for someone he respected. Looking up at the stars hanging out over the ocean like patrons in a balcony, he thought that maybe he needed to stop being such a cynic. Maybe he needed to believe.

His thought was cut short when he realized that he was no longer alone. Standing next to him, Seth took in a deep breath of the sea air, holding it deep in his lungs. Silently, he handed Henry a glass of champagne.

Clinking his glass against Henry's, "To love," was all he said.

"To love," Henry couldn't agree more.

Aiden & Holly

The Following Spring
Before Memorial Day
Ocean Beach, Fire Island

This last two weeks before the official start of summer was always a backbreaker. So much to get done before over 800,000 people descended the length of the island's beaches throughout the three-month season. Spring and fall were the best kept secrets on Fire Island and those who knew it were not sharing that info with anyone.

Walking out of Fire Island Liquors onto Bayview Way, Aiden McManus carried a bag containing two bottles of Chilean Chardonnay. He and the store's owner had just met with the wine's distributor and from his tasting, he was excited to be offering the vintage this summer to pair with lobster at Maguire's.

"Aiden."

His concentration on wine/food pairings was broken at the surprising call of his name and he was even more surprised when he turned to see who had called it.

Just leaving the ferry with a huge duffel bag slung over her shoulder was Holly Moore, waving at him, her smile bright.

As he started to walk toward her, he realized his smile matched hers. Holly Moore. That girl was always a sight for sore eyes. From her first summer in Ocean Beach, he had been drawn to her. A beautiful California blonde, who surprisingly didn't trade upon her looks, their relationship had always been flirtatious, there was something there, but they had stayed on the buddy level because she was involved in a long-term relationship with a good guy and man code dictated it would not be cool to pursue anything with her.

"Holly!" He was hugging her and gave her a swift kiss on the cheek. "Where's the rest of the crew?" The Moore's large oceanfront home was generally packed with family and friends, their extended dinner tables often took up a large section of the deck at Maguire's.

"Just me," she held her palms up. "Everyone else will be here in about ten days."

"Wow," Aiden was surprised that she was here alone before the start of season. "Do you need anything? Food, supplies?"

"I might have to hit you up for a few things."

"Anything," he couldn't wipe the smile off his face. Unexpectedly seeing her was a treat and he hadn't realized just how much he'd missed her beautiful smile over the off-season. "Hey," he began, "I just picked up these Chilean Chardonnays that we're going to be pairing with lobster this summer. Come over to the restaurant tonight and I'll cook you up a lobster and we'll uncork these."

"You'll cook for me?" Holly raised an eyebrow. As Maguire's manager, Aiden ran the front and back of the restaurant as well as the bar, and could sometimes be found pouring a cocktail, but never cooking.

With his Irish charm and dimpled smile unleashed, "Woman, you will taste the best lobster of your life tonight. Seven o'clock?"

"You're on."

As he walked back to Maguire's, he wondered what she was doing all alone on the island before season. Grad school would have probably just finished spring semester, so it wasn't to study. Maybe a little relaxation after a tough term? He'd find out in a few hours.

What an unexpected treat, he thought.

He was behind the bar when she entered the empty restaurant. "Looks different when it's not packed with people, doesn't it?"

"Amazing," Holly looked around. "It's weird being here and it's so quiet." She sat down on one of the barstools and smoothed out her flowered sundress. "I like it."

"Me too," he was smiling at her. Agitating an icy cocktail shaker with his right hand, he reached overhead with his left and slid two martini glasses out of the wood rack. Pouring two perfect cocktails, he slid one to her and raised his, "To the summer of our lives…"

Holly's smile was beatific, "To the summer of our lives. I like that."

They clinked glasses and each took a sip.

"Damn good," Aiden looked proud.

"Mmm, this is good. What is it?"

"It's called a Fleur de Lys. Let me mix up another shaker and we'll go out on the deck and watch the sunset over the bay."

Holly laughed, "We're going to be trashed."

Nodding, "The beauty of Fire Island, no cars, no designated drivers needed."

Sitting on the deck, they watched the sun begin its journey toward the horizon over the Great South Bay and the marshlands beyond.

"So, what are you doing out here?" He was dying to know.

"I needed some Me time." She suddenly looked very serious, brows knit tight over her clear blue eyes.

"Are you okay?" He wanted to reach out and squeeze her hand, but he wasn't sure that she would want him to do that.

Nodding, "Yeah, I am. I actually feel better than I have in a long time."

"Why is that?" He was squinting from the sun's descending side light.

"Jared and I broke up right after New Year's."

Shocked, he sat straight up. "Wow. I'm sorry. You guys were together a long time."

She nodded, "Yeah. We were. We were eighteen when we met. But it ran its course. He's a great guy, but it had been over for a while."

Aiden remained silent and Holly picked up the shaker and refilled her martini glass.

"Don't laugh at me," she looked almost scared, "but I just want to find my great love. I know that sounds silly to a guy like you."

"A guy like me?" Aiden's brows shrugged.

"You know what I mean." She cocked her head, her tone earnest.

"Actually, I don't." He was on the verge of becoming defensive.

"Handsome, charming, a little bit older than me, fun and funny, gorgeous women throwing themselves at you every night all summer long," she paused and smiled, "and you are a first-class flirt."

Laughing, he pushed his defensiveness to the other end of the deck. He had been expecting an insult, instead she poured a bunch of compliments on his head.

This time he reached out and squeezed her hand. "You are really sweet." Smiling, "I am a first-class flirt, aren't I." It was a statement, an admission.

She nodded over her martini glass and they both laughed.

"My first few summer's here, having my choice of women was a head trip. It got old really fast though. It's not who I am. I'm really kind of a monogamous creature." He stopped and smiled, "But I do like to flirt."

Holly laughed, "Yeah, I noticed."

"You had a boyfriend. A nice guy. I never quite knew how to balance it with you."

The four liquors in the Fleur de Lys were coursing through his veins, stripping all inhibitions and he knew it. This was getting scary and could either make for the greatest summer of his life or an extremely uncomfortable one if he kept going and got shot down. It was a crap shoot.

"I didn't go overboard, did I? Make you feel uncomfortable?"

She shook her head, "Never." On her face, he could see that she was grappling with a question, "Did I lead you on?"

Almost spitting out his drink, he shook his head. "Never."

They sat in silence as the sun sunk into the marshes, the last golden trail retreating with it.

"Do I have a chance with you?" Her question shocked him.

"Do you have a chance with me?" The shock in his tone was evident. "Do *you* have a chance with *me*?" he repeated her question. "Holly, are you joking?"

Although she tried to control her embarrassment and disappointment, her face crumbled slightly and he realized she misunderstood. Immediately, he was struck by the pain of hurting her.

"No. No. No. No. You misunderstood me. Come here." Grabbing her hand, he pulled her out of her chair and into his lap. Taking her face in both hands, he searched her eyes. "Holly Moore, you are my dream girl, but guys like me don't get girls like you."

With her face still in his hands, she began to shake her head up and down, "Yeah, you do."

And before he could explain to her Long Island's socio-economic geography, that he was a kid from the wrong side of the tracks who had worked really hard to put himself through school, she was kissing him and he was lost to the sweet taste of her mouth and the heat they were generating from all the summers of pent-up wanting of another guy's girl, a girl who was so far out of his league he could only hope to have someone as lovely as her someday. A girl he wanted to kiss like this from the first moment he'd laid eyes on her.

When their lips finally parted, "You're serious?" he asked.

Smiling, she nodded again.

Pulling her face back close to his, he leaned his forehead against hers, "You know this is going to be the best summer of our lives."

"I know," she whispered, smiling.

And Aiden McManus knew one thing for sure, he would do everything in his power to make it an endless summer.

Sneak Peek
at
Holly Moore's Story

Moore Than a Feeling

Julie A. Richman

Mid-Summer

Ocean Parkway was desolate as they drove the deserted stretch of beach road in the pre-midnight hour. Reaching across to the passenger seat in the darkened Range Rover, Schooner Moore gently pulled his wife Mia's thumb away from her mouth, as she unconsciously chewed the skin that surrounded the edges of her fingernail. Bringing her small hand into his lap, he lovingly stroked the area at which she had been gnawing.

Mia sighed, and in the shadows of streetlamps, perched like seagulls on weathered wooden polls that leaned away from the ocean, Schooner could see the tension that rolled through the muscles of his wife's face. Starting at her cheekbone and moving rapidly to her jaw, a wave of worry, inched toward Mia's mouth, making her lips twitch. Schooner's gut coiled as he watched and sensed her mounting tension and fear, with each mile they drove.

"She's going to be okay, Baby Girl," he attempted to reassure her, giving her hand a squeeze.

"What if we don't get there in time, Schooner?" The fear in Mia's voice was palpable and he ached knowing he was never going to be able to alleviate it. At least not until they were down there.

"We're on the earliest flight out in the morning. She'll still be in surgery when we get to the hospital." He brought her hand to his mouth, gently kissing the inside of her wrist. "Lois is not going anywhere, Mia. You know your mother is a force to be reckoned with." *The apple didn't fall far from that tree,* Schooner laughed to himself. "I'll bet you a Serendipity Frozen Hot Chocolate that she is well enough to fly up to New York for Po's birthday in September."

Mia smiled for the first time since they'd gotten in the car at the Fire Island Ferries parking lot, hastily leaving their beach house after a call from her father, and rushing their two small sleeping children, Nathaniel and Portia, to the nearby home of close friends, Charles and Gaby Sloan.

"Make that some hot shower sex and you've got a bet."

"Hmm," Schooner snickered. Giving her a side glance, "Is shower sex with me ever anything less than hot?"

"You've got a point, so to speak," Mia conceded, enjoying her own pun and giving her handsome husband's hand a squeeze as she smiled again, this time at a memory visible only in her head. "It's going to be good to be in the loft, even if it's only for a night."

Mia and Schooner had been out at their beach house with their kids, working from there for over a month and only Schooner's daughter, Holly, had been in Manhattan, living in their large sun-drenched SoHo loft.

"Yes, it will," Schooner agreed, already picturing melting into the cool, clean sheets, devoid of sand, on their king-sized bed. He hoped they'd be able to catch a few hours' sleep before an early morning Uber ride to LaGuardia Airport. With the travel gods on their side, they'd been able to secure seats on the earliest flight down to West Palm Beach, where Mia's mom, the incomparable force known as Lois Silver, would be undergoing emergency bypass surgery first thing in the morning.

"Did you hear back from Holly?"

Picking up his phone from the car's center console and glancing at the screen, Schooner shook his head, no. He had left her a voice message and a text to let her know what was going on and that he and Mia were on their way back into the city and would be staying at the loft for the night.

"No. She must be out or have her phone turned off. Maybe she's at the movies with some friends," he conjectured.

Heartbroken, Holly had decided not to spend the summer out on Fire Island with the family, knowing that seeing her ex-boyfriend, even for one more day, in the small beach enclave where they lived and worked, would be far too painful. Instead, she moved back into the city, where she was very fortunate, that late into spring, to be able to pick up a summer gig at NYU, teaching two classes of English as a Second Language.

Aiden McManus, the charismatic and handsome manager of Maguire's Restaurant on Fire Island had captured Holly's heart, lock, stock and barrel, several summers before. A Long Island boy, from a working-class family, Aiden helped pay for his community college education in Hotel and Hospitality Management through enlisting in the New York Guard.

Holly's previous love interests had all come from backgrounds similar to her own, well-educated at Ivy League schools with families of means. But Aiden was different, salt of the Earth and willing to get his hands dirty, Holly had never met anyone his age who was already a man. Aiden McManus wasn't a boy and that was the sexiest thing Holly Moore had ever encountered. There was no going back to boys after meeting Aiden McManus.

Prior to meeting, neither Aiden nor Holly would have ever seen themselves with the other, yet together they were a mutual adoration society. Holly enamored with this handsome, street smart man's man, and Aiden overwhelmed that this beautiful and brilliant California golden girl would even give him a second glance, nonetheless fall in love with him. And when she fell in love with the dark-haired, blue-eyed Irishman, Holly fell hard, with her entire heart, her feelings deeper and more complex than she'd ever known.

Their break-up blindsided and devastated Holly. Coming just a month before Aiden's reserve deployment to Afghanistan, his harsh words tattered her heart, literally slamming her to her knees.

"Don't bother waiting for me, Holly. This is the perfect natural ending point for us. We're just too different. When I come home, it won't be to you. So, please don't kid yourself and wait."

"You're just saying this in case something happens. You're trying to protect me, Aiden," countered Holly.

Shaking his head, his eyes never leaving hers as he delivered the killing blow, "I'm sure that makes it easier for you to handle, but the truth of the matter is, I've been wanting to end things for a while. We're really different. And I'm happier with a woman who's more like me. I've been thinking a lot about my old girlfriend, Katie, and I'd like to see if we can work things out."

Holly wasn't the only one shocked by Aiden's scathing declaration. Everyone who knew the couple couldn't believe not only that they had broken up, but how and why.

"I don't understand," she cried to her father and stepmother. "How could I be so blind to miss the signs?" She glanced from Schooner to Mia, her tear stained eyes positively devastated. But neither had an answer for her, because they were as shocked as she was at the sudden 180° turn in Aiden's feelings and intentions. It just didn't add up.

"It hasn't been the same without her on Fire Island this summer." Schooner missed his oldest child. Holly had been the light of his life through some very dark and lonely years and supported him and his happiness when he and Mia reunited after a twenty-four-year absence.

"I know," Mia agreed. Holly was such a delight to be around. She loved her relationship with her stepdaughter. They had bonded immediately over their deep love for her father. "I know Natie and Po miss her terribly. Maybe when the summer semester is done, she'll come back out to the beach. Aiden is already gone, so no worries about running into him."

Crossing the Williamsburg Bridge, both Schooner and Mia let out a huge sigh at exactly the same moment, turned to one another and laughed. The collective sigh had been brought on by the lights of the Manhattan skyline beckoning them home. There was relief in knowing soon they'd be in their own space to get some rest prior to leaving for Florida in the early morning's light and the unknown of what tomorrow would bring.

The old freight elevator opened directly into the loft and Schooner flicked on the Great Room's lights.

"It's good to be home." Mia looked relieved. "I'm glad we're staying here tonight." Home was a comfort to Mia. Whether in the city or out at the beach house, being in her space provided a level of solace well understood by Cancerians. Schooner always thought of it as her crab shell, a place she could retreat with just a moment's notice, an environment that was uniquely hers, with all the creature comforts necessary for her happiness and protection.

Coming out of the bedroom where he'd deposited their bags, Schooner picked up the remote and stood in front of the television laughing for a moment before settling into the plush couch.

"Baby Girl, *Animal House* is on," he called to Mia in the open kitchen. "Come watch it with me." If anything was going to calm her down and relax her so that she could get a few hours' sleep, it was a movie that they both could recite line for line.

"Do you want a bottle of water?" she called back to him.

"Yeah, thanks. Double-secret probation," he laughed, entranced by the show.

Sinking in beside him, Mia kicked off her espadrilles. With his arm around her shoulder, Schooner pulled Mia's head into his lap, feeling her tension immediately ease as he gently stroked her hair. Curled up with her feet on the couch, they laughed at the slapstick humor, momentarily trading in their reality for a much simpler one.

Half asleep, settled into the plush cushions, they were both roused and slightly surprised as the elevator opened to the apartment. They were more than slightly surprised when a couple kissing and laughing, wrapped in one another's arms, oblivious to the fact that they were being watched, tumbled out of the elevator and into the loft's Great Room.

Squinting, Mia immediately recognized Holly's long silky blonde hair. But the man, who was he? Tall, but not as tall as Schooner, he had thick silvery-white hair, wire-rimmed glasses and from what she could see of him, appeared quite handsome. Neither he nor Holly had yet to realize they were not alone, although the lights were on and the TV was playing.

Richard Gere. Why is Holly kissing Richard Gere? Mia wondered as she rubbed her eyes. Had she met him at some party? He was very handsome, but he was too old for her, were Mia's immediate thoughts. And what were they doing here?

Schooner cleared his throat and the surprised couple returned to reality, breaking apart to face Schooner and Mia.

The gasp that escaped from Mia's throat was involuntary and loud. It registered on the man's face as if she'd tossed him the full weight of a medicine ball, hard.

It wasn't Richard Gere that Holly had been kissing. It wasn't Richard Gere, at all.

"Mia?" There was surprise in the man's voice.

Holly looked at him, quizzically, clearly shocked that he knew her stepmother.

Mia breathed in deeply, rising to her feet and stood there for a moment, her eye contact with Holly's companion never wavering.

Finally, she acknowledged him, verbally. "Tom," she nodded, the single word, clipped. The loft took on a chill as there was not an ounce of warmth in her greeting.

Confused, Holly looked to Tom, then to Mia, and then back to Tom. "You two know each other?" She clearly was not processing how the pieces fit.

"Really, Tom?" Mia ignored her stepdaughter's question. She might not even have heard it. "You're older than her father."

"I didn't know." Tom Sheehan shook his head.

"Didn't know what? Didn't know her age? Didn't know that she was my stepdaughter? Didn't know that you were stepping too far over the line?" she screamed at the man.

"What is going on here?" Holly's face reddened, as she visibly became more upset.

"Will you tell her? Or shall I?" Mia's eyes never left his.

Tom turned to Holly, "Mia and I were involved," he stammered, "a long time ago."

"Get out of here, Tom, and stay away from my daughter." Mia took a step toward him, her tiny frame suddenly imposing.

Stepping forward, Holly blocked the path between Mia and Tom. "I'm not your daughter," she screamed at her stepmother. "And this is my home, you can't kick him out. My father bought this loft."

Mia felt a jagged tear in her heart as Holly drew the line. This beautiful young woman whom she loved as a daughter, just chose Tom Sheehan over family, letting Mia know that they would never be blood or share those ties.

Holly looked to her father, who had been standing there watching this drama unfold as if he were observing a bad Fellini film, her tone pleading, "Dad?"

Mia did not need to look at her husband to know the reaction his daughter was about to receive, she could feel his energy in every inch of her small frame and said a silent prayer that it didn't get physical. But one thing Schooner Moore had learned well over the years, was how deadly controlled rage could be.

Not even acknowledging Holly's plea, his pale blue eyes seared into Tom, a man he had forever longed to meet and one he had hoped never to cross paths with. While the loft had been filled with raised voices and emotion, Schooner Moore very quietly said two words in a tone that was both unimpeachable and deadly.

"Get out."

"You can't kick him out," Holly began to protest.

Schooner shifted his gaze from the man he perceived as his nemesis, to his beloved daughter, locking eyes with her and repeated what was not a request, but rather an order, that also applied to her.

"Get out."

End of Chapter One

Moore Than a Feeling

By

Julie A. Richman

Coming fall 2017

Final Thoughts

Thank you for purchasing the Needing Moore Series and joining Schooner and Mia on their journey. Along the way you met a lot of their friends and family and you'll be seeing some of them in future works.

If you'd like to know what's coming up next and want to receive an exclusive sneak preview, please sign up for my mailing list by clicking this link: eepurl.com/RYac1

I hope you've enjoyed reading about Schooner and Mia as much as I've enjoyed telling their story.

Till we meet again …

JAR

About the Author

Author Julie A. Richman is a native New Yorker living deep in the heart of Texas. A creative writing major in college, reading and writing fiction has always been a passion. Julie began her corporate career in publishing in NYC and writing played a major role throughout her career as she created and wrote marketing, advertising, direct mail and fundraising materials for Fortune 500 corporations, advertising agencies and non-profit organizations. She is an award-winning nature photographer plagued with insatiable wanderlust. Julie and her husband have one son and a white German Shepherd named Juneau.

Contact Julie

Twitter
@JulieARichman

Website
www.juliearichman.com

Facebook
www.facebook.com/AuthorJulieARichman

Instagram
www.instagram.com/authorjuliearichman

For the Reader

Thank you for purchasing and reading this eBook. If you enjoyed it please leave a short review on book-related sites such as Goodreads. Readers rely on reviews, as do authors.

Made in the USA
San Bernardino, CA
23 March 2018